EDWIN'S EXPLOITS

1st Edition

Published in 2016 by

Woodfield Publishing Ltd
www.woodfieldpublishing.co.uk

ISBN 978-1-84683-179-9

Printed in England

Typesetting & page design: Nic Pastorius
Cover design: Klaus Schaffer

Source document
Edwin's Exploits - Biddlecombe [final-5].ppp

A novel by

RICHARD BIDDLECOMBE

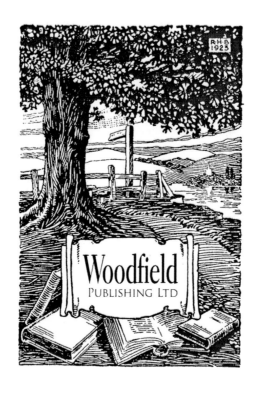

Woodfield Publishing Ltd

Bognor Regis ~ West Sussex ~ England ~ PO21 5EL
tel 01243 821234 ~ e/m info@woodfieldpublishing.co.uk

Interesting and informative books on a variety of subjects

For full details of all our published titles, visit our website at
www.woodfieldpublishing.co.uk

To Barry and Cheryle

I would like to thank Tasker and Kay Polk for their constant flow of encouragement whilst writing the story.

I would also like to thank Ann van Spall and my brother Bob for their invaluable feedback.

"The future has many names: For the weak, it means the unattainable. For the fearful, it means the unknown. For the courageous, it means opportunity."

Victor Hugo

CHAPTER ONE

EDWIN RAVENSDALE HAD FAILED his life. At least, that seemed to be the general opinion of just about everybody when the result of his Eleven Plus examination came through. It wasn't that he was dense. On the contrary, he was academically bright – and yet he had failed. The outcome didn't even have much to do with the pressure experienced as the exam dates had grown closer or of any expectation by others to perform well. It had far more to do with the fact that he happened to live within a geographical catchment area where a brand new secondary modern school had been built. And yet the stigma attached to failure at the tender young age of eleven was immense. If people were to be believed it meant that there could be no worthwhile future for Edwin at all.

The Art teacher tried to explain the situation to the class.

"Now listen, children. Those very few pupils who have managed to get through to the grammar school are the bright buttons. They are going to become the leaders of our society such as the managers, the lawyers, the politicians and the civil servants. And those who have made it to the technical school are the ones who will end up as the scientists and the engineers that make all the new discoveries and help industry develop to improve our living conditions. But you needn't worry because there'll still be plenty of jobs left for you – you're going to be the milkmen, the road diggers, the cleaners, the drivers and the factory workers."

If truth be known Edwin felt that he had been able to see right through this whole lousy educational system from the outset and had simply had no desire to comply with it. He had rebelled and even taken days off school when he was supposed to have been taking some of the tests. When the result came through, it was no great surprise to him. But it did mean that he was now destined to attend the newly built Ramsden Secondary School for Boys.

When he got there at least they had the common courtesy to place him in the top stream. But for whatever merits the kind of school might have had, one thing it did well was to expose everybody to an underclass of particularly unsavoury individuals, the likes of whom Edwin had never come across before. It had a large intake of kids from a massive council estate that seemed to specialise in the breeding of uncouth youth. Many had body odour and despite the smart blue school uniform they still managed to look as scruffy as possible. They had no respect for authority and were forever answering the teachers back with glib comments or holding up two fingers at them when their backs were turned. It was the first time that Edwin had seen a pupil spit on the floor in front of the teacher as an act of defiance.

Despite some degree of academic work being achieved it was essentially a school that was two-thirds full of rather dim-witted children and, despite having failed his Eleven Plus, Edwin knew instinctively that he didn't fit into that category and that he aspired to better things. If anything, he was over and above the entire education system.

Edwin had been raised in the Greater London suburb of Petts Wood in Kent. He was the eldest of three boys and it had been a happy childhood albeit in post-war austerity. His father commuted in and out of London by train each day to work at a branch of the Westminster Bank whilst his mother stayed at home and worked equally hard as a housewife.

The family lived in a semi-detached house in a pleasant cul-de-sac and the highlight of the week was the Saturday morning children's films shown at the Embassy cinema.

From certain parts of Petts Wood it was possible to catch a glimpse on the horizon of the iconic television transmission mast at Crystal Palace. One day Edwin determined to walk to it. He had no idea how long it would take but assuming it to be half an hour or so he took with him one of his younger brothers and one of their school friends, both aged about nine. After a four hour walk they successfully reached their destination of Crystal Palace and visited its adjacent park but when, with tired little legs they began making the return journey they ended up getting hopelessly lost. They found themselves in some back streets of Bromley involving a crescent that persisted in bringing them back to a point where they had been some twenty minutes earlier. Not only was it getting late but it was also getting dark and fears began to set in about whether or not they would ever find their way home. They banged on somebody's door to ask if they were even going in the right direction of Petts Wood and a sympathetic lady invited them all to hop into her car and drove them there. A welcoming committee awaited their arrival in the form of two sets of extremely worried parents both of whom were none too pleased to learn about such a jaunt. Later that night Edwin was severely reprimanded for having been so irresponsible. He realised that he fully deserved it.

Safer adventures became realised through his membership of the Boy Scouts. Edwin also acquired a full size bicycle which opened up a new world of possibilities. On one occasion the scouts had organised a cycle rally on a Friday evening which covered a fair bit of mileage out into the Kent countryside together with cryptic clues to be solved at checkpoints dotted along the route. Of the twenty-five participants, Edwin and another boy were in joint second place. They struck up a conversation together and, noticing an accent, it transpired that the other lad had recently arrived in Britain from South Africa. He introduced himself as Henry and, as he did so, his left pedal decided to drop off. Both cyclists braked, leaned their bikes against a hedge and walked back to retrieve it. Edwin had a spanner in his saddlebag and it wasn't long before they were back on the road again. However, they didn't get much further along the lane before the same thing occurred. The pedal fell to the ground.

"I reckon the thread's almost gone," said Edwin, trying not to tighten it too much for fear it would go completely.

"Thanks. Let's give it another try," replied Henry remounting his bike.

There was quite a lengthy downhill stretch which didn't require much in way of pedal power but as the lane twisted and started to become an uphill climb the same thing happened yet again. This time, as they were reconnecting the obstinate pedal, they were overtaken by five more scouts on bicycles thereby losing any likelihood of winning the contest.

"You can go on, if you like," volunteered Henry, "I'll be OK. I'm sorry for knocking you out of the rally."

"No it's alright," said Edwin. "It's beginning to get dark and at least I know the route. It wouldn't be fair to abandon you."

"That's very decent of you," he replied.

Four more members of the 2nd Petts Wood Boy Scouts came panting up the hill past them. One of them called out "What's up with you two? Do you need any help?"

"No. We're OK thanks," replied Edwin, "Just tell them at the final checkpoint that Edwin and Henry will be there as soon as we can."

"Will do," was the reply.

It was completely dark by the time they finally came in last at the end of the cycle rally which was at somewhere with the dubious sounding name of Pratts Bottom. The pedal had come off several more times but the situation had enabled Edwin and Henry to strike up a good friendship. Henry was a year older than Edwin and of rather hefty build. He too went to a secondary modern school although not the same one as Edwin. In addition to his strong South African accent he had a good sense of humour and a roaring laugh to go with it. Coincidentally his father also worked in the world of banking although in a somewhat higher realm. He was a Director of Barclays Bank International.

During the school holidays Edwin joined the Youth Hostel Association and encouraged Henry to do the same. Henry's bike had since been fully repaired and they decided to set off on a hostelling break that took in much of South-East England. There was something fulfilling about cycling all day long and reaching their destination by late afternoon. The hostels themselves with their bunk-bedded dormitories were affordable and welcoming and gave plenty of opportunity for meeting interesting people who were similarly exploring places. On one such trip Edwin and Henry made the eighty mile distance from Petts Wood to Dover in a single day. The early evening was then spent in preparation of a meal cooked over gas rings in a shared kitchen area. Invariably this was from a pack of Vesta dehydrated food from which a perfectly acceptable curry and rice could be conjured up within about twenty minutes. They would then unwind in the hostel's common room in the company of fellow hostellers and perhaps play a couple of games of table tennis before turning in for some well-earned sleep. The remainder of the trip was taken at a more leisurely pace of around twenty miles a day with overnight stops at a network of youth hostels throughout Kent, Sussex and Surrey. The locations of such places had enchanting place names such as Crockham Hill, Cudham, Goudhurst, Alfriston, Guestling and Ewhurst Green.

Probably the best single thing that Ramsden Secondary did for Edwin was a school trip to the Continent. In common with many of the other pupils it was the first time he had ever been abroad and the five-day trip included Belgium, Holland, Luxembourg and Germany. This first taste of foreign lands was an eye-opener to Edwin who became enchanted with everything he saw. He eagerly exchanged addresses with some girls from a German school party who were staying at the same hotel, one of whom became a pen-pal.

The Boy Scout Association also provided the perfect opportunity for many of its youths to learn how to smoke cigarettes. That came about when small groups of scouts would find themselves unsupervised and one of them would pull out a packet of filter-tipped Rothmans and offer them around. For the uninitiated it was something of a dare to take one and light up. To be able to inhale the smoke unfazed, without coughing or spluttering, was regarded as a sign of having mastered the art. In the company of others, Edwin tried it as did his friend Henry. Potential health hazards were not widely realised and although the legal age for smoking was sixteen it was thought to be a sign of maturity to have embarked on such a pastime at their respective ages of thirteen and fourteen. Of course, it was all done in secret and the last thing they wanted was for their parents to find out. A supply of cigarettes and matches would sometimes be hidden in a certain clump of bushes, having first been packed in a tin box and then tightly wrapped in a plastic bag to protect them from all weathers.

And then there was the experimentation with early-age drinking. Henry lived in a large house in one of the more affluent areas of Petts Wood from where his parents did the occasional spot of social entertaining and held dinner parties. In their front lounge was a massive, sturdy, cocktail cabinet made of ornately carved oak. Its large front door was always securely fastened by lock and a hidden key. What had been overlooked, however, was that immediately above the enclosed part of the cabinet was a hefty drawer containing corkscrews, coasters, serviettes and other related paraphernalia and that Henry had made an interesting discovery. If he were to remove that drawer he could put his arm through the resultant gap and reach down into the cabinet and lift out all manner of different bottles by their necks. One morning, when his parents had both gone out for the day, he demonstrated this feat to Edwin and lined up a variety of retrieved bottles of liquor with odd sounding names most of which neither of them had ever heard of.

"I'm pretty sure that's a brandy, oh yes, it even says on it that that's what it is," said Henry proudly, as he sported a bottle of Hine, "but Noilly Prat sounds pretty disgusting. I've no idea what that is."

"This one's called Chartreuse and looks like washing-up liquid," observed Edwin.

"Maybe that's what it is," replied Henry, "Shall we try a few samples?"

He fetched a couple of glasses from the kitchen into which a little dribble from each of the bottles was poured as they tasted and compared notes. After an hour or so they both decided that they hated the taste of gin and they couldn't understand how anybody in their right mind could ever wish to drink Pernod. They thought that Drambuie tasted foul whilst Dutch Advokaat, although partially acceptable, was reminiscent of the kind of suspension mixture used for medicine. They reached the conclusion that if they were ever intending to drink at all they'd probably be better off sticking to beer. They replaced the selection of bottles and put the drawer back in place.

Edwin was good at organising things. Whenever there was a school holiday and it came to planning the Youth Hostelling trips it was invariably he who worked out the route and made all the necessary bookings. A three week stay in North Wales was arranged as a walking tour rather than cycling and entailed a coach journey to get them there. Unfortunately it bucketed down with rain most of the time and Henry succeeded in rupturing himself when hoisting his rucksack up into the luggage rack of a local train compartment. However, they did manage to reach the summit of Mount Snowdon and to explore Capel Curig, Llangollen and Ffestiniog. There was even the opportunity to see the newly released Beatles film 'A Hard Day's Night' at the cinema in Caernarvon.

Several more bicycle tours were to follow that took in Winchester, Salisbury and the New Forest but they later graduated to hitch-hiking which enabled them to get still further afield and up to Bonny Scotland. On one particular trip via Dundee they were given a lift by a company representative from Dewar's Distillery who insisted on giving both of them a quarter bottle of whisky as a free sample.

The variety of people they met both en route and at the Youth Hostels was fascinating. Amongst them were nice looking young ladies from France, Holland,

Sweden and Newcastle-on-Tyne. Because most of them were a few years older than Edwin he began to make out that he was two years older than he actually was. The problem with that was that he still looked his thirteen years whilst Henry, by virtue of his large build, could just about pass as an eighteen-year-old.

Between such adventurous holidays, school was becoming increasingly monotonous. Some of the teachers couldn't discipline unruly class behaviour which had the detrimental effect of holding everyone back. Lessons given by the poor man who attempted to teach French to the class were spent in watching him yell his head off at certain unruly individuals until he was bright red in the face. Every now and then his patience snapped and he would hurl a blackboard rubber at one of them, earning him the nickname of Chalky. Such lessons became a predictable theatre performance from beginning to end. Although Edwin excelled at Maths, Physics and Technical Drawing he found subjects such as History, Geography and Religious Instruction to be dull and uninteresting largely because of the dreary way in which they were taught. He had a tendency to let his mind drift off elsewhere, occasionally getting caught out if the teacher suddenly threw a question at him and he hadn't got a clue what was being discussed, let alone the answer.

Every Monday evening there was a weekly meeting of the local Youth Hostel group held in a church hall in Orpington at which a guest speaker would deliver a slide show about their recent travels. Wednesday evenings entailed a bus journey to the regional branch of the Cyclists Touring Club held in Sidcup whilst Friday nights were earmarked for the Boy Scouts meeting held in a hut in Petts Wood. His South African friend Henry normally joined him for such events after which the general pattern was to dive into the nearest fish and chip shop for sixpenny bags of soggy chips to eat as they walked whilst listening to Radio Luxembourg on a transistor radio.

Yeah, you really got me now
You got me so I don't know what I'm doin', now
Oh yeah, you really got me now
You got me so I can't sleep at night
You really got me
You really got me
You really got me

Sometimes they would stop off in Chislehurst for half a pint of beer at some of the pubs. It surprised Edwin that no one ever questioned his age. Perhaps it was because Henry was the one who purchased the drinks from the bar whilst Edwin hovered somewhere in the background or sat down at a corner table. If they could afford it they'd each drink a half pint of best bitter at The Crown, The Bull, The Queen's Arms and The Tiger's Head.

Homework was never taken seriously and often consisted of a hurried last-minute attempt just before the time when it was due to be handed in and cribbed off somebody else if need be. Moreover there were several occasions in which Edwin and Henry played truant without anyone ever finding out. They would each set off for their respective schools with a change of outer clothing concealed in their duffel bags. At a predetermined place, normally in woodland, they would meet up and in the privacy of a rhododendron bush substitute their school blazers for jumpers and their trousers for jeans. They would then continue along pathways through the woods for a couple of miles before turning down a hill towards Chislehurst Railway Station where they would sit it a nearby transport café for several hours sipping from large mugs of tea to the strains of the BBC Light Programme on the radio in the background. They regarded the experience as a welcome break from the day-to-day monotony of school life. In the afternoon they would retrace their footsteps, get changed back into their school uniforms and return to their homes on time and just like returning from a normal school day. All that remained was to a write a short note offering some reason for the day's absence.

EDWIN'S MOTHER INHERITED SOME money that enabled several significant changes to take place. The family would be moving to Weybridge in Surrey and Edwin would be given the chance to go to a boarding school. For his part, Edwin was pretty neutral about both of those eventualities. The quest for change and new experiences seemed to be part of his makeup.

A public school called Lindisfarne College had been selected. Coincidentally it was located in North Wales which had a certain appeal about it based on the earlier youth hostelling trip in that region. Edwin's father drove him there for an interview with the headmaster. Set in the Denbighshire town of Ruabon the building and grounds looked impressive enough as did the long driveway that led up to it from the front gatehouse. The interview went remarkably well. Edwin rose to the occasion and seemed to strike a good rapport with the headmaster who, after asking him various questions concerning his favourite subjects of physics and mathematics, commented that he felt Edwin to be "of university material." Such praise seemed to finalise everything. Edwin would be joining the school at the start of the new term in September.

That day came around remarkably soon. He was suitably kitted out at the school's particularly expensive London-based supplier and now had two tweed jackets and trousers, school ties and shirts with collars that required studs. There was also a charcoal suit for Sundays. It all seemed a bit Billy Bunterish especially when a tuck box got included into the bargain.

The transition was weird. One minute he'd been part of a rough and tumble Secondary Modern experience and all of a sudden here he was amongst pupils from considerably more privileged backgrounds, all of whom spoke with a decidedly upper-crust accent. There was also a high percentage from overseas including Malays, Chinese, Indians, Persians, Venezuelans, Burmese and some Spaniards. The international mix was perhaps one of the school's main attributes and it was also the first time that Edwin had come into daily contact with people of a different skin colour.

The first term took a bit of getting used to. The iron beds in the cold dormitory on the top floor of one of the towers were reminiscent of his youth hostelling experience yet there was added discipline throughout the entire school. Heaven help anyone who walked past the slightest bit of litter lying on the floor. That crime was a punishable offence that normally resulted in an hour's worth of cleaning activity. Something else difficult for Edwin to get used to was the fact that there was no going out in the evenings. Instead everybody was expected to sit in little wooden cubicles doing a couple of hours of prep during which time there was strictly no talking. Such restrictions and the mandatory focus on one's studies to the exclusion of anything else seemed unjust and verging on imprisonment although he reasoned that it might ultimately prove beneficial if he could follow such rules for the time being. The class sizes were agreeably small compared to what he'd been used to. He soon found out that in some subjects such as Mathematics, Geography and French the standard of teaching was particularly high and yet in others, such as English, Biology and Physics, it was disappointingly low. A major blow was that whilst at his previous school he had excelled in Technical Drawing and in Metalwork yet neither subject was even taught at Lindisfarne where they seemed to have a preference for things such as Latin. But one particular area that Edwin was able to shine in was drama. In fact he took the whole school by surprise in playing the part of George Bernard Shaw in an end of term production of a play about the playwright and was subsequently given the part of Cardinal Wolsey in 'A Man for All Seasons' the following term. He knew that acting was in his blood and he had heard tales of one of his great-grandmothers who had trodden the boards.

Each morning would begin with the ringing of an electric bell at the crack of dawn at which time the whole school would quickly get dressed and, irrespective of whatever the weather happened to be doing, go out into the grounds for an early morning walk for about half an hour in groups during which a roll call would be taken. Then there was just sufficient time to take a quick shower and get properly dressed before going to the dining hall for breakfast after which there would be a morning assembly officiated by the headmaster before the start of the day's lessons.

After lunch everybody had to go and lie down of their beds for half an hour, normally accompanied by someone's transistor radio blaring forth with 'I'm her yesterday man' or 'Baby baby baby, you're out of time' or any other popular song of the time.

Sport took place every afternoon except on Sundays. Edwin opted for cross-country running and then hit upon an interesting idea for the following year. He asked whether it would be possible for him bring his bicycle to the school and go cycling each afternoon because, he reasoned, that was also a form of sport. To his pleasant surprise, permission was granted.

Edwin had the advantage of having entered such boarding school life at the age of fifteen and was able to draw comparisons with state education. The vast majority of the other pupils had been boarding throughout their entire academic life starting at prep school at the tender young age of four. He could think of nothing worse and it seemed as if some parents had deliberately shunned responsibility for their children's upbringing and had simply dumped them there. Although the school produced its share of perfect gentlemen who could loosely be considered as role models, there was also a percentage who were little more than jumped-up, conceited little prigs and, perhaps surprisingly within such a multi-cultural school, many of them were outright racists. The Jewish pupils were forever being bated and the word 'Chink' was in common parlance in reference to any of the Orientals. Then there was the question as to whether being cooped up in an all-male environment was a good thing or not. From what Edwin could see of it so far, it was pretty unnatural. His view had been especially reinforced one afternoon when an elderly member of the schools administrative staff about whom various rumours abounded approached him in a secluded corridor and suddenly threw his arms around Edwin's upper body, holding him in a particularly strong clasp. Edwin struggled to release himself and eventually managed to elbow the old pervert hard in the stomach leaving him bent double and gasping for breath. It was an encounter that Edwin would have preferred to have done without. After all his parents had paid good money for him to attend the school and one didn't expect any of that kind of unwelcome nonsense to be thrown into the deal.

The end of each term was always a joyous occasion. In the company of numerous other pupils who filled the carriages, the journey by steam train from Ruabon to London's Paddington station took several hours of gentle unwinding. On arrival Edwin headed for the Underground and took the Bakerloo Line across to Waterloo where he would then search for the platform number for the next train for his new hometown of Weybridge. There was a tremendous sense of freedom in such homecoming. Seemingly trivial things like purchasing a cheese and tomato roll from a kiosk on the station forecourt for one shilling and threepence were part of the liberation process, not to mention smoking a cigarette. During the school holidays he joined the local branch of the Young Conservatives and spent a fair bit of time with them frequenting the Hand and Spear pub. He decided that Weybridge was a place of character. The new family home was on the outskirts of an area called St George's Hill where some of the rich and famous lived, notably John Lennon and Ringo Starr – and comedians such as Eric Sykes and Charlie Drake also lived in the town. Through the Young Conservatives Edwin got invited to several lavish parties.

On 30th July 1966 Edwin went into London but not for the purpose of attending the infamous football match between England and West Germany at Wembley Stadium. Instead he would be meeting up with his South African friend, Henry, whose elder brother had invited the two of them along to a party near Marble Arch. None too familiar with the geographical layout of London, they had arranged to meet each other at Waterloo Station and make their way from there. Although they had written letters to each other they hadn't seen each other for over a year. Henry's first comment was that Edwin seemed to have acquired a plum in his mouth on account of his newly acquired public school accent. They stopped off at a Wimpy Bar in Villiers Street and reminisced about their former youth hostelling adventures whilst bemoaning the fact that they wouldn't be doing any in that particular holiday. Henry was at a catering college in Lewisham and had taken a summer job at the Savoy Hotel.

The party that evening was relatively low-key but pleasant enough. Edwin was by far the youngest person there but because he'd put on his suit for the occasion it made him appear to be a little older than he actually was. Three large wooden barrels of beer had been set up in the courtyard which ensured an adequate supply of liquid refreshment that would last throughout the entire night. Mick Jagger's brother was there and the newly released Rolling Stones album 'Aftermath' was being played repeatedly.

When you're three thousand miles away
I could never sleep the same
If I packed my things right now
I could be home in seven hours
I'm goin' home, I'm goin' home
I'm goin' home, I'm goin' home

As dawn was breaking two of the girls still present went out for a walk along

Oxford Street with Edwin and Henry where they took an early morning coffee at a branch of The Golden Egg.

TAKING HIS BICYCLE WITH him on the train for the new term made Edwin's boarding school life far more tolerable. Every afternoon, whilst everybody else was getting changed into their sports kit, he would put on his track suit then mount his trusty machine and pedal off at speed down the length of the school driveway and out through the front gate for two and a half hours' worth of freedom. He got to discover an entire network of back lanes and the surrounding area for miles around. One afternoon, as he rounded a corner he chanced upon a girl of about his age standing by the gate of a farmhouse. He pulled on his brakes and drew up beside her. Not knowing quite what to say he asked her for directions to the village of Penley. She smiled and told him that if he carried on along the lane, it was about two miles away, a fact that he already knew. However, he noticed that she had a slight accent that wasn't Welsh and he asked her about it.

"I'm Dutch," she said, "but my family has been living here for the past seven years."

"What, here on this farm?" asked Edwin.

"Yes, my father is the farmer," she replied, "What about you? You don't really sound Welsh either."

"Well no, I'm at the boarding school in Ruabon, Lindisfarne College, but I've just managed to escape the place for the afternoon," he said.

"Oh I see," she replied, "Well, would you like to come in? My mother's at home. I'm sure she'll make us a cup of tea."

The offer was irresistible. Before he knew it this young lady had introduced Edwin to her equally charming mother and the three of them were sat together in a tastefully decorated lounge with a pot of tea and a plateful of biscuits. Such an unexpected encounter and kind hospitality was a welcome break for Edwin. The Dutch girl's name was Klara and when Edwin asked if he might visit her again sometime she said she was always at home in the afternoon on Tuesdays and Thursdays. Throughout the remaining weeks of term Edwin arrived at the farm every Tuesday afternoon and every Thursday afternoon during which time they forged a close friendship with each other.

CHAPTER TWO

IT WAS CHRISTMAS IN Weybridge and Edwin had recently turned seventeen. He had precisely five GCE 'O' levels to his name and was beginning to wonder whether it was worth enduring much more of school life. One of the difficulties was that he had absolutely no idea what he would eventually like to do as a career. He discussed the matter with his parents who in their usual supportive way didn't necessarily think it a bad thing when he raised the possibility of leaving the school with its exorbitant fees and entering the world of work. Various suggestions for jobs were considered but none of them had any immediate appeal. Edwin went along to an interview at the locally based Ministry of Fisheries and Food but even though a place was offered him he was unable to generate sufficient enthusiasm to take it up. There was, however, an advertisement in the newspaper for an apprenticeship in an architect's office which Edwin thought might possibly be of some interest. Technical drawing had always been one of his favourite subjects from the Secondary Modern school even though he hadn't done it for a couple of years. By means of two bus rides via Esher he arrived for the interview at the practice which was located in the village of Claygate.

At around that same time, there had been talk of a family holiday in Spain. When the formal offer of the job at the architect's office eventually came through, that Spanish holiday had become more of a certainty and so Edwin accepted the job on condition that he could start at a slightly later date in order to accommodate the trip first, which was agreed.

So things were looking up. No more boarding school, a break on the Continent and a job lined up.

The Costa Blanca was one massive building site. Almost everything was dominated by construction work of one sort or another. New hotels were in various stages of being built and steel girder structures were already in place for multistory apartment blocks. It was evident that what had been little more than fishing villages were busily gearing themselves up to be able to cater for a massive influx of tourists that had already begun. It had even put a new expression into the Spanish language – El boom. The long sandy beaches, the guaranteed sunshine, the low cost of living and Alicante's newly built airport added up to the essential ingredients for an enjoyable holiday that rivalled anything back in Bexhill-on-Sea. And there was no great language problem because most of the waiters and shop assistants could speak a reasonable smattering of English – and many of the bar owners were British.

ON RETURNING TO ENGLAND Edwin commenced work at the architect's office. One of his main duties was to make blueprints from drawings that the five architects produced. That involved placing the drawings over a sheet of specially treated photosensitive paper and exposing them to a bright light box before taking it to a shed in the back yard which contained an ammonia bath. The yellowish paper had to be left above that for a while whilst a chemical reaction took place for it to turn blue. It was always advisable to take a deep breath before entering the hut and to remain inside it for as short a time as possible before the ammonia fumes penetrated too much into lungs, eyes and clothing.

He shared an area with a draughtsman from Durban in South Africa and in their spare moments they made jokes about the elderly authoritarian secretary who worked in the reception area downstairs and was generally regarded as being a right old battle axe. She had even been on the same single-decker bus as Edwin that morning and, on seeing him, had used the opportunity to call out to him down the length of the aisle with a reminder of the day's tasks that he was meant to do when they got to their workplace, thereby informing the rest of the passengers at the same time.

There were also opportunities for Edwin for creative work. Much of it involved retrieving specific architectural drawings from the many drawers of archive material and making minor modifications to them. Another assignment was to design the layout of a kitchen corner in such a way as to include a coffee area complete with table and a built-in bench. Because it was an apprenticeship there was not much pay involved and so to compensate for that he also took a part-time job washing up dishes in a French restaurant in Weybridge on Friday and Saturday evenings which paid more than the day job.

After some months Edwin began to wonder if he was that enthusiastic about a long term career in architecture. If he wanted to become qualified in the field it would entail studying at evening school for many years to come. The job in itself was alright but it just wasn't adventurous enough for him. There was something about getting stuck into the mould of a daily routine that seemed alien but he wracked his brain to think of a better alternative and found it difficult to come up with anything else.

One evening, whilst out for a drink in a rather unpretentious pub called the Prince of Wales in a side street in part of Weybridge called Oatlands Village he had a chance encounter with a comedian called Nat Jackley who happened to be there.

"I've just come back from a demonstration of colour television," exclaimed the comedian, "and it's absolutely fantastic, a complete revolution. And with the new BBC2 service about to start, there are going to be lots of new jobs worth looking at."

But Edwin had never been a television fan. "I just can't understand why people spend so much time staying at home watching other peoples' fantasy lives on a box whilst letting their own lives slip by when there's so much more that they could be doing in real life," he said.

"Oh, but television is here to stay as a fantastic source of entertainment to a great many people," he replied.

"Maybe that would explain why so many people seem to know more about the goings on in Coronation Street that about the goings on in their own street," suggested Edwin.

"I guess there might be some truth in that too," he admitted.

The comedian went on to tell a joke which although wasn't particularly funny in itself had the whole bar in stitches by the way in which he told it. "One morning a man went into a barber shop and asked for a short back and sides. As the haircut was about to commence the man noticed that the barber had dirty hands. "You're surely not going to cut my hair with your hands in that state," he said. "Oh, I'm sorry about that," responded the barber, "I haven't yet done any shampooing this morning."

Over another pint of ale some further discussion took place about the supposed future of television.

Weybridge had become full of au pair girls of varying nationalities most of whom attended English language lessons when off duty. Edwin had met a young lady from France and another from Germany both of whom lived with British families in houses nearby to where he lived. He wondered why there wasn't some equivalent male arrangement in which he could go abroad and work for a foreign family whilst learning a new language and absorbing a different culture. The problem was that there didn't seem to be any such thing as au pair boys. However, on carrying out a bit of research he found that although there might not be the same sort of possibilities as enjoyed by females there were numerous language courses available in most European capitals. The notion had a certain appeal despite the fact that it seemed to be something of a contradiction to the general direction in which he had been heading. After all, he had more of a leaning towards maths and science and the idea of suddenly racing off to learn a foreign language seemed rather out of keeping with that. Besides, wasn't there the great British expectation that the whole world should jolly well converse in English? But maybe the thought of spending time somewhere on the Continent was more of a cultural need.

The following weekend he discussed the situation with his parents.

"Let's face it, Edwin, you have a good opportunity to progress in what you're doing and an architect is a well-respected profession," said his father.

"I know that, Dad, but I also need to be realistic," said Edwin. "To become a fully qualified architect is going to involve evening classes and would also take around seven long years – I'm grateful to have had the initial taster but even at this early stage I can sense that my heart is not sufficiently in it."

"Well, it just seems such a shame to throw it in," he said, "What would you do instead?"

"I know it might sound strange but I'd like to go and work in France," he replied.

"But what kind of work do you think you could do there?" asked his mother.

"That's the problem. I don't really know. Just take any kind of work and learn the language, I guess," he said.

"That's all very well but don't you think you'd need to know the language first before you'd be offered any kind of work at all?" she asked.

"Yes, I know" he said, "I keep coming back to much the same sort of conclusion myself, whenever I try to think things through."

"Why France in particular?" asked his father.

"Oh, it needn't necessarily be France," replied Edwin. "It could be Spain, Holland or perhaps Italy. I just feel the need to broaden my horizons by having a change from England."

In the absence of a clear plan the subject was momentarily dropped for the next couple of months until one Sunday morning when Edwin who had been looking through the columns of the Sunday Times stumbled upon an advertisement for Spanish language courses of varying durations at the University of Madrid.

He showed it to his parents who were by no means dismissive of the idea. There was an address to write to for further details. There was a course that would begin in June and last for a full year.

CHAPTER THREE

THE FIRST PART OF the journey to Madrid involved taking the boat train from Victoria to Dover, a Cross-Channel ferry to Calais and then another train for the onward journey to Paris where Edwin would transfer to a different main line railway station. On arrival at the Gare du Nord in the late afternoon he was approached by a man with a strong Gaelic accent who asked if he could lend him ten francs until Thursday. In his naivety Edwin stopped and politely informed him that he would no longer be in Paris on that particular day.

"That's OK pal," said the man, "You can leave me your name and address and I'll send it on to you."

"I haven't even got an address yet," replied Edwin.

"Come on. I can see by your clothing that you're not exactly short of money," said the man, "Just ten francs is all that I'm asking."

"Sorry," replied Edwin.

"I can pay you back next week," continued the man.

"I can't spare any money," replied Edwin.

"Then piss off!" he retorted.

Charming, thought Edwin who continued on his way and took the Metro to the Paris railway terminus of Austerlitz. With four hours to spare before the evening departure of his train he made numerous walks around the perimeter of the station forecourt almost as if he was on an inspection of French railway architecture. With each lap he stopped to look up at the display board confirming that the remainder of his waiting time was slowly but surely diminishing. He purchased a baguette stuffed with Camembert cheese and a tiny cup of strong coffee from one of the station's kiosks. Afterwards he tried speaking in French to a young lady who was similarly looking up at the departures screen. She turned out to be a Spanish student who was studying in France but could also speak good English. She was from Madrid although was not travelling there on that particular day. Edwin explained that he was enrolled on a Spanish course at the University in Madrid. She gave him her family's address and said that she would be back there in two weeks' time.

Later that evening Edwin's train pulled in to Platform 4. He located his carriage and compartment and shortly after the train's departure tried to get some sleep in a couchette as it made its way to the town of Hendaye which was at France's frontier with Northern Spain.

IN THE MORNING EDWIN entered Spain. The blazing sunshine and scorching platforms of the Spanish border town of Irun virtually advertised the fact as did the railway tracks for Spanish trains which were of a wider gauge than their French counterparts. A small twig-like man with a dark and deeply wrinkled face was carrying a heavy bundle on his shoulder and aggressively addressing an equally tiny lady in a torrent of regional dialect. Why were these people so small? Edwin wondered. Could it be the effect of long-term exposure to the sun that had dried them out and made them shrivel up like that?

Having had his passport stamped at the counter Edwin had found the Spanish train awaiting him. Its line of carriages each had metal slot-in plates on their sides naming Madrid as the final destination. He hoisted himself up on board from the low level platform and made his way to an empty compartment where he sat down on a green vinyl seat. Little by little the train began to fill up with other passengers and it wasn't long before he had been joined by a man and woman who sat alongside him and an elderly lady who took a place opposite. A vendor who was wheeling a trolley along the platform stopped just below the open window. Locating his Spanish money, Edwin leant out and by pointing at things on display purchased a large bread roll containing several slices of a dark red spiced sausage and a litre bottle of cheap red wine. The couple in the compartment who had originally been conversing with each other in Spanish now switched into English. It transpired that they were husband and wife and that he was Spanish and she was English. They were on their way to Madrid to visit his family.

Edwin looked out of the window into one of the adjacent trains and saw that it had wooden strutted seats. Maybe in the heat that would have been more comfortable than green vinyl. There was still a wait of some forty minutes in the hot carriage before the scheduled time of the train's departure. Then, after a repetitive chiming of bells and the sound of a whistle being blown it slowly began to pull out of the station. The motion brought about a welcome breeze that travelled through the entire length of the carriage. Edwin decided it to be his cue for devouring his bread roll of Spanish chorizo sausage and also to peel off the foil top and remove the plastic cap from the wine bottle.

Life suddenly felt good and there was a sense of well-being. After the first hour or so of the journey the landscape changed from its largely green pastures of the northern part of the Basque Country to the light brown of the more arid hinterland, punctuated by dusty lanes and olive groves. By that time he had polished off the entire bottle of wine. As he hadn't slept particularly well on the couchette in the French train the night before, it wasn't long before he dropped off into a deep sleep. When he awoke the train had stopped at a station called Vitoria. The platform sign struck him as vaguely amusing after having departed from the not dissimilar name of Victoria the day before. An inspector entered the compartment and on scrutinising Edwin's ticket said something incomprehensible before giving a grunt of approval and continuing on his way. It was incredibly hot and an unsavoury smell from the lavatories was now drifting throughout the train.

Several hours later and after a couple of further mini-snoozes, they approached Madrid. As with many a European city the first impression was of drab-looking apartment blocks and lots of them. However the Anglo-Spanish couple were talking enthusiastically about the place. Edwin asked them if they knew whether there would be somewhere near to the train station that he could find a room for the night and they assured him that there were plenty of places, particularly around the centre of the city.

"Is it far to the centre of town from the station?" asked Edwin.

"No, not far," replied the Spaniard. "Maybe just five minutes by taxi."

But Edwin had no intention of taking a taxi. He was on a limited budget and knew that over the next days and weeks he would have to work out how to get by. Besides, if it was only a five minute drive it couldn't be that far to walk it – and his luggage wasn't that heavy. The train arrived at Madrid's northern railway station, appropriately called La Estación del Norte and which proved to be yet another museum piece of railway architecture. Edwin ventured out through the front of the station and realised that he was now in Spain's capital city, seventeen years of age, suitcase in hand and that he didn't know more than a couple of words of the Spanish language.

He asked people in English for directions to the centre of town, which seemed to work up to a point, give or take those who simply shrugged their shoulders to indicate that they didn't understand a word he was saying. It wasn't long before he had been pointed in a direction that followed a long avenue with a row of shops on one side and some kind of an enclosed building and gardens on the other. Several passers-by turned their heads and made comments about Edwin's locks of blond hair.

'Mira! Que rubio!' remarked a short, plump, elderly lady dressed entirely in black.

"Si! Pues, tal vez viene del norte," suggested another.

The temperature in Madrid was well into the nineties and, during the course of the uphill walk he soon found himself to be dripping with perspiration, Edwin broke his journey at a conveniently located bar. It was a rather run-down establishment with brown peeling paintwork on the outside and a plain white-tiled interior. Through the front window pane, the sight of a glass tankard being filled with ice-cold draught lager from a tap on a long stainless steel counter had looked so inviting. The barman plonked down a small oval shaped plate containing a thick triangular cut of potato and onion omelette with a cocktail stick pierced through its middle together with a morsel of bread. At first Edwin assumed it to be a mistake and that it was meant for somebody else but the barman insisted, "No, no, Señor. Es una tapa – es gratis!" It was Edwin's first introduction to such savoury snacks, collectively known as tapas, one of which was handed out for free every time a drink was purchased. The cold beer was most welcome – especially following the earlier wine consumption on the train that had left his throat feeling dried out. After draining the glass he ordered another and this time round the accompanying tapa was three cooked mussels in their opened shells served again with the mandatory morsel of bread. He was pleasantly surprised to find that such refreshment had cost him no more than ten pesetas in total.

The route into town became busier and there were several lanes of traffic in both directions. Although mid-evening, shops were still open and many people were out and about. The sun had dropped somewhere behind one of the many edifices that made up the city and street lights and neon signs were beginning to take over. Eventually he arrived at a bustling square called the Plaza de España. It had a park in its middle and pathways lined with trees and low-level white walls. There were various statues including one of Cervantes and centrally located fountains around which people were seated on stone benches. Again through asking people in English, he was directed to a nearby row of large terraced houses, one of which had a sign hanging from an overhead balcony which proudly displayed the word 'Hostal'. He entered through a huge doorway and climbed three flights of wooden stairs to a front door. The proprietor spoke no English but beckoned Edwin in through a dark hallway and showed him to a shared room containing four iron beds made up with grey blankets. Pointing to the one at the far end of the room, he then wrote 45 pesetas on a piece of paper. Edwin nodded his approval and breathed a sigh of relief that at least he'd have a roof over his head for his first night in Madrid. He managed to communicate that he would like to take the accommodation for three nights. He figured that by then he would have been able to find somewhere a bit more suitable – ideally a small room to himself.

Being then left him to his own devices; Edwin made good use of the shower to freshen-up but discovered the WC not only to be bereft of a toilet seat but also to have no toilet paper. However a generous supply of torn up newspaper pages had been considerately stuffed behind the down pipe of lavatory's cistern tank. Free from the burden of his suitcase, he then decided to go out and explore the immediate locality. When making his way back through the reception area, however, the language barrier became ever more apparent. The proprietor, who was watching a football match on a television set which apparently had no volume control, seemed to be indicating that the main door to the hostel would be locked at 10pm. He didn't give Edwin a key but instead jabbered away in Spanish about something, clapped his hand and mimed the opening of a door. Edwin couldn't understand what on earth he was on about but was left with the impression that for some inexplicable reason the hostel must have some kind of a ten o'clock curfew policy. That seemed unacceptably restrictive even if he did want to have an early night. It was already getting on for nine o'clock and meant that he would have little more than an hour before needing to return.

Descending the staircase, he stepped outside into what was one end of Madrid's main shopping street, the Gran Vía, whose wide pavements were positively bustling with people and stretches of which were lined with shiny metallic tables and chairs at which people sat outside with drinks and dishes of food served from adjacent cafeterias as they watched the crowds go by. Edwin walked ten minutes in each direction soaking up the atmosphere of neon signs, newspaper kiosks and cinemas, taxis and cars and the smell of freshly ground coffee beans, tobacco smoke, perfume and traffic fumes. Everything was well and truly alive. He entered an air-conditioned snack bar and ordered a toasted ham and cheese sandwich and a cup of tea. The tea consisted of a tall glass of frothy hot milk together with a separate tea bag to dangle into it. Spain was a coffee drinking nation.

The bartender could speak English and Edwin asked him about the hostel closing at ten o'clock just when everything else in Madrid seemed to be so full of life. But it turned out to have been a misunderstanding. Although its entrance door would be locked at that time, on-duty guards were allocated to the immediate area of each street and they had a massive bunch of keys for all of the doors on their particular watch. They stayed up right through the night and would happily open the door for a small tip of two pesetas. To summon the 'Soreno' there was a quaint custom of standing outside the street-level door and clapping your hands until he heard you from whichever part of his designated area that he happened to be in.

Grateful for the explanation Edwin paid his bill and noted that the establishment was considerably more expensive than the beer bar that he'd visited earlier, about four times as much. He made a mental note to avoid such places in the city centre in future. Returning to the guest house at a quarter to ten, he got undressed, climbed into bed and was out like a light.

The following morning he awoke shortly before seven and got up. The other three beds in the room were now occupied, as confirmed by the three mounds of grey blanket that covered three sleeping people and gentle rhythmic snoring. Edwin moved around quietly so as not to wake them. Moments later, equipped with his folder containing paperwork relating to the course at the university, he slipped down through the empty reception area, let himself out through the front door and descended the three floors. Turning the handle of the large main door he stepped outside into the glare of bright sunshine which hit his eyeballs causing momentary pain and a rapid adjustment of both retinas. The eight lanes of the wide Madrid thoroughfare were now a non-stop display of heavy traffic, many drivers of which were blowing their horns for the slightest of reasons thereby adding an additional chorus to the collective motor noise already created. Although hot, at least there was a fresh morning breeze.

The shops weren't yet open – it was still too early for that. However cafeterias were in action with machines hissing and blowing out small clouds of steam together with the clatter of cutlery and the chatter of people perched on lines of stools. Everybody had a cup of steaming liquid of one sort or another, mainly coffee but some took hot chocolate into which tubular strips of pancake were being dunked. Edwin decided that his own breakfast could wait. He needed to find his way to the university and had thought that he could best do that by means of the underground train network, which, as in Paris, was also known as the Metro. The previous evening he had seen that the place where he was staying was close to the Metro station at the Plaza de España and on his walk he'd also passed two more stations further along the main shopping street, one called Callao and the other Santo Domingo. He studied the large map on display at the top of the steps. It transpired that the university was situated near the northernmost station of Moncloa and only three stops away from Plaza de España.

The antiquated Madrid Metro had a flat rate fare of just two pesetas to go anywhere in its entire network which meant virtually anywhere in the whole of Madrid. Its logo and destination signs displayed along the platforms where similar to those of the London Underground except that instead of a blue bar across a red circle on a background of white it had a blue bar across a red diamond on a background of white. The dark red trains themselves looked as if they could have come out of a transport museum and Edwin felt that they had a certain degree of character about them. There were very few seats inside the carriages meaning that most passengers had to stand and cling on to one of the sweaty metal poles. Two long blasts sounded on a deeply-pitched on-board whistle signifying that the doors were about to close after which the train jerked into motion. It was hot and humid but some small vents were open to allow for a flow of air and a rather large lady standing opposite was supplementing her share of it by making vigorous hand movement with a fan. A green uniformed civil guard with the distinctively winged shiny black hat occupied a specially designated enclosure behind a tubular pipe construction. The policeman was deeply engrossed in reading a newspaper called ABC although Edwin assumed it not to be quite as elementary as its title suggested. The rest of the standing area was filled with Spanish commuters on their way to work chatting and laughing amongst themselves. Apart from the occasional affirmation expressed by the word 'si', Edwin couldn't understand anything that they were saying.

The first stop was called Ventura Rodriguez and the next was a seemingly unpronounceable place called Argüelles which was spelt with two little dots above the letter 'u' like a German umlaut – he hadn't known that such punctuation marks existed in Spanish. He had heard of a Spanish omelette but not of a Spanish umlaut. On arrival in Moncloa, Edwin emerged from the station back into bright sunshine. He removed a sheet of paper from his folder indicating the name of the university building he was supposed to be heading for and showed it to a young man.

'La Facultad de Filosofia y Letras?' the man read out loud. "Ah pues, si. No es bastante lejos de aquí. You espeak Inglees?'

'Yes, I espeak Inglees', said Edwin, unintentionally mimicking his pronunciation.

'You can go with tranvía', he said, pointing to the other side of the square where a tram was picking up passengers. "It goes there."

Some minutes later and aboard this particular mode of transport equipped with wooden seats, the old fashioned tram packed full of students trundled along its track. About ten minutes later Edwin arrived at the building and a receptionist directed him to Room 714B where a meeting was to be held for those arriving for the start of the course. He made his way along the first floor corridor and as he approached the classroom he could hear loud conversation from within and most of it with a tell-tale accent. He entered the room to find eighty or so fellow students already gathered there. With few exceptions everybody was from the other side of the Atlantic. Welcome to the United States of America.

At the appointed hour, a Spanish lecturer arrived with a list and proceeded to divide the assembled multitude into more manageable groups of around twenty a piece. They were then assigned to different classrooms to which they were ushered. Edwin found himself seated between a Mark from Massachusetts and a Sandra from Milwaukee. Behind him was a Tom from Maryland and in front of him were twins, Nancy and Beverly, from California. Another tutor arrived and spoke for one hour in Spanish, nothing of which Edwin could remotely understand. Occasionally questions were fired at the audience and various members of the class raised their hands and answered – in Spanish but with detectable American accents. Edwin patiently sat through it all and then suddenly everybody got up to leave and that was the end of the induction session. He spoke with Sandra from Milwaukee and gleaned that normal lessons would commence from ten o'clock tomorrow. She invited him to accompany her to the refectory in the building's basement to grab a coffee. Recalling that he still hadn't had breakfast, he was only too pleased to tag along.

The student cafeteria was hot, crowded, noisy and smoky. There was no orderly queuing system and people had to elbow their way through to the front and hope to catch the eye of one or other of the counter staff in order to get served at all. Edwin and Sandra eventually got there. She ordered a jumbo-sized cup of coffee with milk and he opted for the same. They then barged their way back through the crowd and succeeded in perching themselves on a stone ledge at the far end of the room.

Sandra was as fascinated with Edwin's English accent as he was with her American drawl. He hadn't met many Americans before, at least not at close range, and he thought that most of them sounded like something out of a cartoon film. She told him that apart from the American students already enrolled on the course, there were a whole lot more due to arrive the following week when Berkeley College would commence its exchange program. She herself had already had Spanish lessons for four years whilst at High School and knew the basics. Because she intended to work in the travel industry, she was in Spain for the year to become more fluent.

A bell rang and miraculously the cafeteria began to empty as almost everybody returned to class. Edwin and Sandra used the opportunity to reposition themselves on bar stalls adjacent to the counter where a vast array of dishes of different food was on display beneath a glass cover. The American girl ordered a coca cola which came in a tall glass, a generous number of ice cubes and a slice of lemon. The serving girl then looked quizzically at Edwin who by this time was developing pangs of hunger. He pointed to one of dishes on display.

"Ensaladilla Rusa? Si!" she said and she scooped a quantity of the cold potato salad mixed with tuna fish and diced red pepper onto a small elliptical saucer, which she then placed in front of him together with a tiny fork and three small chunks of bread. "Y para beber?" she asked quizzically.

"What's she on about?" he asked Sandra.

"She's asking if you'd like something to drink with it," she replied.

One of the first words that Edwin had succeeded in learning was the Spanish word for beer and it now seemed appropriate to put that piece of knowledge to good use.

"Cerveza, por favor," he said.

"Si, grande o pequeña?" asked the Señorita, using her hands to indicate large and small.

Edwin's command of the Spanish language was already showing signs of improvement.

"Grande of course," he responded.

Prices at the student cafeteria were subsidised to such an extent that it was one of the cheapest places to hang out in Madrid. The American girl duly departed saying something about having to go downtown to do something at American Express and, four glasses of cerveza later, Edwin thought that he too had better make a move. He'd also enjoyed a couple more tapas. One was sliced squid served in a pool of its own black ink and the other had been some kind of pork stew in a rich tomato sauce. As he went up the stairs he quietly belched his approval, lit a cigarette and stepped outside into the midday heat. Rather than take the tram again he decided to walk down to the Metro station in Moncloa. He knew more or less in which direction to go and there was a wide tree-lined walkway that seemed to lead in its general direction along which numerous other students were coming and going.

He passed the Science Faculty over to his right and finding himself to be walking alongside various groups of people he tried to tune in to stray bits of Spanish conversation but was unable to make out anything at all that they were saying. Some ten minutes later, the buildings of Moncloa were visible, his sense of direction having worked well. Down into the Metro station and onto a train again, he headed back to the hostel, dropped off his folder, had a quick freshen up and went back out into the city to explore.

It was his intention to try and line up somewhere more appropriate to live before his three night stay at the current hostel was up. If possible he wanted a room on his own. He walked south along the scorching stretch of the Gran Vía which, according to the map that he'd seen earlier, was also called Avenida del Generalissimo Francisco Franco at one end and Avenida de Jose Antonio at the other. He knew who Franco was but wondered who the Jose Antonio bloke could have been to have merited having such a main street named after him. Edwin knew nothing about Spanish history and so it was no wonder that the name of the founder of the fascist party, Spanish Phalanx, didn't mean anything to him. Nevertheless evidence of the Spanish Civil War was brought home to him by the numerous people with missing limbs who were sat outside on the Madrid streets either begging or selling lottery tickets. By mid-afternoon, apart from a small flow of traffic in both directions, the streets were almost deserted. The shops were all closed and it was the time of day in which most Madrileños took a break for their lunch followed by a nap, the traditional siesta. In view of the intense heat it was probably a wise thing to do even if it did have the effect of dividing the day into two separate parts. After such an interlude everything would come back to life at around five o'clock and go on until late into the evening.

In search of somewhere more suitable to live, Edwin worked his way down one side of the Gran Vía studying brass signs displayed at doorway entrances and looking up at balconies for any indication of available accommodation. Such places were plentiful enough and for the next couple of hours he found himself climbing staircases, getting in and out of a variety of lifts and standing at the front door of many such establishments. Invariably either a señor or a señora would answer the door, many of whom spoke a bit of English. However, either they were fully booked out or their prices were way above what Edwin could afford on his budget. He also discovered that single rooms were in short supply.

After scouring several blocks and receiving similar replies he reasoned that being slap-bang on the sought-after stretch of the Gran Vía was probably a contributing factor to high prices so he turned off into one of the side streets and had a go there. His search was partially rewarded at the Pension Mecca, a clean well-kept guesthouse one block behind the Gran Vía with rates that were reasonable enough – if he didn't mind sharing a room with one other person. Despite the fact that he was trying to find a single room of his own he allowed himself to be shown to the twin bedded room which was immaculately clean and had an en suite toilet and washbasin. It was available for the sum of sixty pesetas per night. He was introduced to the other occupant; a Cuban refugee called Pablo who spoke a bit of English and seemed pleasant enough. Edwin reckoned that, on balance, it was definitely a notch up on where he was currently staying and so, in the absence of anything else, he agreed to take it. The landlady gave him a printed card showing the name and address of the establishment and relieved him of eight hundred and forty pesetas as rent for the first two weeks. It was agreed that Edwin would move in on Friday. He returned to the street below, content at having accomplished what he'd set out to do. The name of the road was Calle de Caballero de Gracia and, pulling out his pocket dictionary and looking up such new words, he was amused to note that it meant something like street of gentleman of happiness, gentleman of amusement, gentleman of grace or gentleman of thanks. At the end of the road was the added convenience of another Metro station. It was also called Jose Antonio which, although on a different line from the one on which he'd travelled that morning, a glance at the map revealed that he'd be able to get to the university by changing trains at the centrally located Metro station of Puerta del Sol.

By this time the shops had re-opened and the wide pavements of the Gran Vía were once again crowded. Edwin continued to explore the area so as to take in the entire length of its shops, whilst mentally absorbing everything on the way. In addition to the large departmental stores of Corte Inglés, Galerías Preciadas and Sepu, there were also the smaller clothes shops, shoe shops, book shops, tobacco shops, hardware shops, millinery shops, a stationery shop and a wine and spirit merchant whose window display included bottles of white rum priced at forty pesetas. In some of the side streets he found grocery shops, a printer's shop, a tailor's shop, a bakery and an assortment of other commercial premises which he couldn't work out exactly what they were. At the far end the Gran Vía shops began to give way to large office buildings and banks. Architecturally pleasing, some of the tree-lined streets merged with each other at roundabouts sporting massive water fountains. Edwin crossed over the wide avenue and began to make his way back along its other side. On one of the corners was a palatial-looking cafeteria with a golden domelike roof. Despite misgivings about comparative prices of the previous evening he couldn't resist venturing inside. It was air-conditioned and every bit as refreshing as stepping into a refrigerator. The only problem was that all of its tables were already occupied. However, he saw that a Spanish girl was sitting alone at a small table near the door and he asked her if the other chair was free.

"Siéntase", smiled the girl, making a gesture to indicate that the chair was indeed available.

"Gracias", replied Edwin.

She said something else to him in Spanish which he didn't understand. She then said something to him in French which although he recognised it to be French, he didn't understand either.

"Inglés, Inglés," he said, pointing to himself.

Clearly amused by such an apparent display of patriotism, she chuckled and said something else in Spanish that was just as indiscernible to Edwin as everything else. A waitress came up the table and Edwin asked for a coffee and then tried to continue communicating with his table companion.

"Maybe you could teach me Spanish," he suggested.

She didn't understand but offered him a cigarette.

"Gracias," he said, again aware of severe vocabulary limitations

She started using French again "Comment tu t'appelle?" Even he could understand that.

"Je m'apelle Edwin," he answered.

She then introduced herself as Maria Luz, which she wrote out on a paper napkin with a bright orange coloured plastic ballpoint pen. Intrigued by such means of communication Edwin wrote his name on a different napkin and then fished out the card with the address of his new guest house and wrote out the details complete with telephone number – not that there'd be much likelihood of any phone conversation at this rate, he supposed. She took the paper and read it before folding it carefully and placing it in her handbag. The waitress arrived with Edwin's coffee. Maria Luz rose from her seat tapping her watch to indicate that she had to go and said, "Hasta la vista". He watched her leave; her petite figure in a short-sleeved floral blouse and a knee length green skirt. Through the glass door she turned, smiled and gave him a final wave before disappearing into the crowd.

IT HAD HARDLY BEEN a matter of any great linguistic skill for Edwin to have deduced that the Madrid Metro station called Banco de España was the equivalent of the London Underground station called Bank. Within its surrounding area lay a concentration of the headquarters of major financial institutions, both national and international, in the form of large grey stone buildings accompanied by massive doorways. He entered the Banco Hispano Americano and found himself in a large marble tiled, dimly lit, lobby area of dark stained panelling and shiny brass fittings with an overhead rotation of electric fans. Over to one side lines of people were queuing up to take their turn at cashiers' windows. Not exactly sure of the procedure, he joined one of the queues and double-checked that he'd brought along the paperwork and his passport.

It took nearly twenty minutes to reach the head of the queue but when he got there the lady looked at his documentation and then shook her head which rattled her large earrings in the process. She told him in broken English that he had to go to the Foreign Department which was upstairs on the first floor. There was an even longer queue up there and, as he waited, Edwin surveyed the open plan office and its array of conservatively dressed clerks and secretaries operating in the similar kind of quietness normally associated with a library. It struck him as being similar to a pregnant pause in a theatrical scene in which nothing much was happening. But it didn't look as if anything was suddenly about to spring into action.

It eventually came round to his turn and, on handing over his papers, the man behind the counter took them over to a desk and made a short phone call. He then returned to Edwin.

"Your money has not arrived," he said.

"That's odd. It should have done," replied Edwin, "It's supposed to be here by the fourteenth which is today."

"I am afraid that it has not arrived in our banking system," said the man.

"I was kind of depending on it being here," faltered Edwin.

"Sorry," said the man, "but maybe you can come again and check tomorrow."

"I suppose I'll have to," replied Edwin "but thanks, anyway."

He made his way back to the guesthouse, rather perturbed by the fact that the first of his regular weekly payments had failed to arrive. Although his rent was paid up he had intended making a further week's payment. He didn't have much left in the way of spending money either and could only hope that the payment would come through the next day. It also meant that he'd be tied up for another morning, meaning that he'd miss another day's Spanish class at the university.

A bar by the name of Dénia was situated in a side street called Calle de la Concepción off the main shopping street of the Gran Vía and Edwin drifted into it that afternoon, partly to escape the blazing sunshine and partly to unwind over a large cup of milky coffee that was dutifully brought to him by an elderly, doddery-looking waiter with a stubbed out, half-smoked, cigar hanging out of his mouth.

"You espeak i mingley?" the waiter asked.

"Yes, I speak English. I am English," replied Edwin.

"You want girl foki-foki?" continued the waiter, simultaneously banging his two forefingers together.

Edwin didn't know what the old bloke meant other than the fact that, if he'd heard what he thought he'd heard, it all sounded perfectly disgusting. A pale looking, bald-headed, Englishman who was playing chess at an adjacent table turned and addressed Edwin.

"Take no notice of him!" he said, "He's a senile bastard and they're about the only two English phrases that he knows." Then, turning to the waiter, he said, "Manolo! Un poco más respeto por favor – y me pone una copa de Chinchón con hielo cuando puedes."

"Si, Si, Charlie," responded the waiter who then toddled off in the direction of the bar.

Continuing the conversation the bald-headed man turned again to Edwin and asked him what he was doing in Madrid.

"I'm here on a Spanish language course at the university," he answered. "What about you?"

"I've been here for the past seven years," was his reply, "and, to be quite honest with you, there's nowhere else I'd rather be."

"What do you do here?" asked Edwin.

"Oh, I just tend to live life and enjoy myself," he said

"I meant what kind of work you do here in Madrid?" said Edwin.

"Work?" echoed the man, "Oh no, I'm afraid that life is far too short to keep having to work."

"Well, I guess that must be OK for some," replied Edwin.

"That's the great thing about Madrid," the man continued as the waiter returned with a glass of cloudy coloured liquid in a small goblet that clinked with ice cubes, "If you know the right places, it's easy to get by."

He turned back to his chess game which two moves later resulted in his opponent winning the game.

"There!" he exclaimed, turning again to Edwin, "That's your bloody fault for having been a distraction! That miserable-looking sod opposite has just checkmated me."

"I didn't mean to interrupt the game," began Edwin.

"That's alright, he normally beats me anyway," he said, with a sudden smile.

The man then turned his chair right around to face Edwin and introduced himself as Charles Tennyson, originally from London. Edwin saw that he was a relatively thin man with a surprisingly pale complexion for someone who had lived so long in Spain. He guessed his age to be somewhere in his late forties and despite his somewhat over-the-top manner he seemed to be quite knowledgeable and was obviously well-educated. During the course of further conversation it became obvious that some of the man's claims were exaggerations and yet, taken with a pinch of salt, they proved to be quite entertaining. It came as no great surprise to learn that he was an out of work actor and that he lived on a fixed income sent to him from an apparently wealthy sister back in the United Kingdom.

Although Edwin wasn't a particularly brilliant chess player he agreed to a game with Charlie and by a stroke of luck managed to trap him into a variation of fool's mate in relatively few moves.

"Let me buy you a drink!" suggested Charlie.

"OK," agreed Edwin, "what on earth is that stuff that you are drinking?"

"It's an aniseed liqueur," he said. "Try one if you like. It's quite refreshing when served on the rocks." He turned in the direction of the elderly waiter who was now slumped in a chair and half asleep.

"Oiga!" shouted Charlie, to which the old man sprang to his feet.

"Nos pone dos más, por favor."

"Oiga?" repeated Edwin. "Is that the old bloke's name?"

"No," replied Charlie, "It's what you say when you want to grab someone's attention and a bit like the "Oyez" that town criers used to call out in England. To get any kind of service at all out of this bugger you can either get his attention like that or else scream obscenities at him."

They chatted for an hour, interrupted every now and again, first by a lady selling cigarettes from a small display unit strung around her neck as if she were someone selling ice cream during the interval in a cinema, then by a one-legged man on crutches selling lottery tickets and finally by another poor soul who offered to polish their shoes. Two further glasses of the sickly sweet aniseed liqueur had the effect of blowing Edwin's brains out sufficiently to re-confirm his preference for beer.

"If that's what you'd prefer I'm afraid they only do bottled beers in here," said Charlie, "but right opposite there's an excellent cervecería which serves large glass tankards of cold draught Spanish lager at five pesetas a time and it also has the most amazing selection of tapas to choose from. We could go there for a while but I'm afraid I'm right out of money at present – unless perhaps you could lend me a bit" he said.

"I've not got much money myself," said Edwin, "There was supposed to have been some at the bank this morning but it hadn't yet come through. I've got to go down there again first thing tomorrow morning."

"Well, at least that's something to look forward to," said Charlie, "I'll tell you what though, why don't you let me settle the drinks bill here and then we could pop across the road and you could buy us a couple of beers over there."

It sounded reasonable enough. Edwin knew he still had a little over three hundred pesetas on him and, in any case, surely his money would be there at the bank in the morning. As they departed he noticed that Charlie hadn't settled the bill by paying cash but instead the bar's owner had written the amount owing into a notebook.

"It just makes things so much easier to periodically pay off the whole lot all in one go," his new acquaintance explained.

The beer bar called Peña El Aguila had a large glass frontage and was fully air-conditioned. It was brightly lit, had cream tiled flooring and the mirrors on all of its walls that made it look ten times bigger than it actually was. The entire length of its stainless steel bar surface had been laid out with a spread of ceramic dishes containing a vast assortment of tasty looking tapas. On small squares of toast, hard-boiled egg halves had anchovies placed across them held together by cocktail sticks. Others consisted of seafood coated with savoury sauce. There were portions of Spanish cheese in olive oil, cured hams, chorizo, prawns in their shells, meatballs in tomato sauce, thick triangles of Spanish omelette, mushrooms in garlic and parsley. Also in evidence were mussels, clams, crabs and oysters as well as kidneys, tripe, stewed pork, chicken drumsticks, and salads of every description. It was colourful, plentiful and impressive. Edwin tried to imagine what it would be like to eat his way from one end of the lengthy counter to the other, like a never-ending course of hors d'oeuvres.

The place was moderately busy. Some customers were seated at small square tables whilst others stood in groups at the bar. Most were drinking beer and many were eating tapas using tiny flimsy metal forks. The floor was covered with accumulated litter, bits of bread, prawn shells, cigarette butts, olive stones, paper serviettes and anything else that had simply been tossed aside.

Edwin and Charlie took their time over three large tankards of beer accompanied by several of the tapa snacks. When speaking, Charlie tended to adopt the Spanish way of using arm and hand gestures to further express whatever particular point he was making. Theatrical in his manner, he had a wealth of anecdotes about life in Madrid and was proving to be good company. Being slightly intoxicated made half of their conversation that much more amusing.

"One day, when we can get our hands on some money, we'll pick up a couple of women and go down to the old part of Madrid to visit some of the mesones to watch flamenco and drink sangria," announced Charlie, "but in the meantime we'll have to make do with the beer in here and maybe that wizened old whore standing behind you might be persuaded to jump up onto one of the tables and give us a dance."

Later that evening, and after Edwin had paid the bar tab of fifty-four pesetas, Charlie asked him whether he could possibly lend him a hundred pesetas for a couple of days.

"After all," reasoned Charlie, "your money is due at the bank tomorrow but mine is not due until Friday. And you can always find me over in that first bar, Dénia, every afternoon where I like to play chess with some of the Jordanian refugees who tend to congregate there."

"OK then, until Friday," said Edwin, handing over one of his two remaining hundred peseta notes.

They parted company on the Gran Vía. Edwin headed back to his hostal where his Cuban roommate, Pablo, gave him the news that the Spanish girl, Maria Luz, had phoned and that she would like to meet Edwin tomorrow afternoon at four o'clock in front of the main post office in Cibeles.

The following morning Edwin stepped outside into the blazing sunshine and made his way down the short hill to the Puerta del Sol which was generally considered to be the central hub or Piccadilly Circus of Madrid. He'd begun to realise that many of the Metro stations in the centre of town were only a hop, skip and a jump away from each other and that in some instances it was quicker to walk rather than descend into the depth of the earth and wait for a train to arrive and then climb up a lot of steps at the other end. All the more so from his local Metro station of Jose Antonio, which was entered by a slow running lift for which one was obliged to pay its operator ten centavos, a lightweight coin with the value of one tenth of a peseta that was more trouble than it was worth. Few people ever seemed to have such a coin handy and so after giving the man a one-peseta coin, they each ended up with a pocketful of ninety centavos worth of such toy-like money. Still, Edwin supposed that for those who used that station on a regular basis, the supply of such coins would be useful for the next time. He passed a bookshop with a row of volumes on a wooden stand outside and cast his eye along the titles. A grim reminder of the enormity of work he'd need to do even to get some basic grasp of the Spanish language. One book was entitled 'Bleak House' by Carlos Dickens. Carlos Dickens? he thought. That's a bit of a cheek isn't it? Surely they're not trying to kid everyone that he was a Spaniard.

The Puerta del Sol was a large oval shaped area of floral garden islands and fountains around which traffic slowly moved in an anticlockwise direction. As the city's central point, it was said that all major thoroughfares into Madrid eventually converged there. A government building lay along one of its sides whilst each of its numerous junctions were made up of a mixture of newsstands, metro station entrances, pedestrian crossings and cafeterias with tables and chairs outside at which people sat under sunshades with freshly squeezed orange juice, coffee and toast accompanied by their daily intake of carbon monoxide traffic fumes.

Towards one end of the curvature was a row of expensive shoe shops. Edwin mentally calculated the going rate for one pair to be the equivalent of four times his weekly allowance. It seemed to contradict the poverty stricken elderly men and women who stood nearby on the streets corners selling lottery tickets. Their hoarse voices giving out a haunting cry of "Para hoy! Para hoy!" could be heard repetitively from quite a distance – "Hay loteria para hoy!" Perhaps the real message was that you'd first need to win the lottery to be able to afford a pair of shoes. But it then occurred to Edwin that he'd need to win the lottery himself if his money didn't show up that day.

He arrived at the bank bright and early only to find that it was still shut and wouldn't be open for another half hour. To kill time he descended a flight of steps that led to an underpass of various boutiques alongside the entrance to yet another metro station called Sevilla and entered a glass-fronted cafeteria where a jukebox was playing the Beatles' latest release at full blast.

'I say high, you say low, you say why and I say I don't know. Oh, no.
You say goodbye and I say hello. Hello, hello,
I don't know why you say goodbye I say hello'

He unintentionally ordered a strong black coffee served in a tiny cup instead of a large milky version that he had originally intended but, perching himself on a stool, he managed to take twenty minutes over drinking it during which time he occasionally got a smile out of one of the waitresses.

Once the bank was open Edwin went straight up to the first floor's Foreign Department and joined the queue. An overhead sign said 'Extranjero' and he'd already learnt that the word could mean either foreigner or stranger. Evidently foreigners, of whom he was one, could also be regarded as strangers. How strange indeed, he thought. When he got to the head of the queue the same man from the previous day took his documents and gave him some recognition.

"Ah. Mr Ravensdale. Good morning. You wait one moment please. I again try for you."

The bank official went to his desk and made a phone call, speaking this time for considerably longer that the day before. But he then returned with a glum look on his face.

"I am sorry, the money has still not yet arrived," he said, handing back the papers.

Edwin didn't know how to react. He didn't want to have to carry out this charade on a daily basis and he was absolutely dependent upon the money coming through. The local branch of Lloyd's Bank back in England had carefully arranged it all and yet it seemed that something must have gone drastically wrong.

"But, I mean, these documents. Are they in order?" he asked, "They show that from yesterday onwards I'm supposed to be able to be receiving nine pounds a week, paid in pesetas, at this bank."

"The documentation is fine," said the man, "It is only that the funds have not yet arrived here."

"Is the delay in England or here in Spain?" asked Edwin, inadvertently pitching the two nations against each other.

"I do not know," replied the man, "All I can do is keep trying for you each day."

"Is there any chance that it might still arrive later today?" asked Edwin.

The man shook his head, "I'm afraid no. The transfers arrive one time each day. The best is we try again tomorrow."

Edwin thanked him and retreated back to the stairs. It was another bitter blow. He had a nagging feeling that he was beginning to understand the meaning of the Spanish 'mañana' although, at the same time he had to acknowledge that it might not have anything to do with any inefficiency at the Spanish end. After all, the man was obviously trying to help him even if, so far, nothing had worked out.

Edwin had one hundred and twenty-three pesetas left. On departing from the bank he lit a cigarette and contemplated what to do next. Unable to come up with any immediate solution, he spent the next three hours just meandering through the streets of Madrid deep in thought whilst inwardly digesting things that he encountered along the way. His route took the form of a big loop that passed by the south-serving mainline railway station of Atocha then on up through the Retiro Gardens with its boating lake before doubling back past the Prado Art Museum and on towards the more familiar territory of the Gran Vía. He continued towards Callao and, although in the heart of the tourist area, he then went into the large corner cafeteria called Manila, sat at a table and ordered a toasted sandwich and the inevitable large cup of coffee with milk. The toasted sandwich turned out to be a meal in itself, having four layers held together with tooth picks and stuffed full of chicken, cheese, ham, egg, lettuce, tomato and mayonnaise.

Later that afternoon he retraced some of his steps to the main post office building where the girl Maria Luz stood outside waiting for him as arranged. Communication was still a major problem when she asked him whether he'd ever been to the Casa de Campo. Not knowing what it was he shrugged his shoulders and let her lead the way which involved a metro journey to the Plaza de España followed by a more modern train that started off underground but eventually burst out into the open of an area of forest land. They alighted at a station called El Lago and strolled together through pine trees to a large natural lake around which families were eating picnics. Such surroundings were a complete contrast to the city centre and a welcome breath of fresh air in every sense. They spent an hour or so at the lakeside looking up words in Edwin's English-Spanish dictionary to amuse each other. As they made their way back towards the station, they passed through an isolated stretch and Maria Luz took Edwin's hand. A few yards further on, they stopped in their tracks, turned and embraced each other. The spontaneous mouth-to-mouth kiss might have had the potential to set new heights in Anglo-Hispanic relations were it not for the fact that Maria Luz's breath stank of stale garlic.

THE NEXT DAY'S VISIT to the Banco Hispano Americano brought exactly the same kind of non-result. However, on his way back towards the Gran Vía he got talking to an American girl who was also in Spain to learn Spanish although not at the university. She similarly lived in hostel-type accommodation and her command of the language was not much better than Edwin's. She had been sat outside a cafeteria whilst consulting a thick paperback book, which turned out to be a comprehensive guide to Madrid.

"I'm just looking for somewhere cheap to eat," she said, flipping over a page, "So far, I seem to end up in these darn tourist restaurants where I end up paying tourist prices all the time."

"I've taken to eating snacks rather than proper meals – or sometimes skipping them altogether," replied Edwin.

"Well, according to this guide, there are some real cheap restaurants a few blocks over from the other side of Puerta del Sol, which I might be tempted to check out this evening, if I'm not followed around by any more Spanish men," she said. She elaborated by saying that ever since her arrival in Madrid, being pursued by hot-blooded Latin males had been something of a problem.

"I've kind of worked it out that the difficulty here is that all of their women remain virgins until marriage and they wrongly assume that all foreign women are both available and willing," she said. 'Yet, if you look at me, I might be a bit on the tall side but I have long dark hair and an olive complexion and could almost look Spanish but I still get followed around. God help the blue-eyed blonde women who visit this place."

"If you like, I could come along with you this evening," volunteered Edwin, "Apart from anything else I'd be interested in finding out about one of those cheap restaurants myself."

"Gee, that's kind of you," she said. "Could you stop by for me at my hostel at seven? It's just across the street from here."

Locating the cheap restaurant street of Ventura de la Vega entailed weaving their way through a network of narrow back roads and passageways. Once there, however, the short cobble-stoned road was seen to have six or seven restaurants on either of its sides – and yet all of them were closed.

"Is Thursday their day off or something?" asked the American.

"Surely they wouldn't all decide to close on the same day," said Edwin, equally baffled by the two rows of lifeless interiors behind locked doors.

"The prices look cheap enough," she said, looking at a menu on display, "What a shame. I guess it's just not our day."

At that moment a man stopped alongside them, reached into his pocket for a key and unlocked the restaurant's door. Once he'd entered, however, he turned around and, reinserting the key, locked the door again from the inside. The American couldn't resist tapping on the window and attracting his attention.

"Are you going to open?" she yelled, through the glass pane.

The man retraced his steps and opened the door.

"Usted quiere algo?" he asked.

"We want to eat," she said, miming the suggestion by moving her hand up and down towards her mouth and smacking her lips. The man smiled.

"Abierto a las nueve," he said.

"What's he saying?" she asked Edwin.

"Dunno, something about a new opening, I think," he said, shrugging his shoulders.

She looked at the man again. "Que?" was the only Spanish word she could think of.

"Mire Usted," he said, pulling back his right sleeve to reveal a wristwatch, "Ahora son las ocho y media de la tarde. Estamos abierto aqui para cenar a las neuve!"

Edwin and the American girl looked at each other blankly and the man sensed that they were still none the wiser.

"Media hora!" he said.

"Hang on a minute. 'Media hora' – that means half an hour," she said, "Is the restaurant going to open in half an hour?"

"Si! En media hora!" repeated the man who, to emphasise the point, tapped his watch and then held up nine fingers, "A las nueve!"

"In half an hour at nine o'clock," said Edwin, as triumphant as if they'd just succeeded in cracking the enigma code. "Come to think of it, I'd heard that they normally dine late in Spain."

"At nine o'clock – A las nueve," echoed the American girl, "Gracias, Muchas gracias."

Edwin and the American walked around the next corner to a nearby bar in which they bided their time whilst awaiting the nine o'clock opening of the restaurant. He lit a cigarette. By now Edwin was getting used to Spanish brands which were available either with blonde or black tobacco. The cheapest pack of blonde cigarettes was called Bisonte as indicated by a picture of a bison on the front of its limp pack. They were without filter and were what Charlie normally smoked. The cheapest brand of the lot was called Celtas and had what looked like tiny bits of wood in its tobacco content that were somehow reminiscent of pencil shavings. If one was particularly skint it was possible to purchase cigarettes singly rather than an entire pack.

On their return to the street of Ventura de la Vega it had magically come to life. Its restaurants on either side were now open and filling up fast with people who had suddenly appeared out of nowhere. Out of loyalty they returned to the restaurant where the man had been so helpful only to find that all the tables were already occupied. Instead, they settled for another establishment on the other side of the road where they were soon sat down at a table and trying to decipher the Spanish menu. A waiter plonked down some drinking glasses and a jug of water together with two oversized bread rolls. The American asked if he spoke English.

"Inglés, no," he replied.

"I guess that we're just going to have to take pot luck on what we eat," she said to Edwin. "I can't make head or tail of what's actually on this menu other than the fact that the dishes are all at really cheap prices compared to anywhere else that I've seen."

"It'll probably work out OK if we just order something from the top of the menu then something from the middle and finally something from the last section," he said, "At least, I presume 'Postres' means desserts, judging by the number of times it's got the words 'Tarta' and 'Flan' in its list."

"Good idea. Shall we get a bottle of red wine?" she asked.

The meal was substantial and satisfying. They each had a bowl of thick pinto bean stew. Edwin was then served two large pork chops and fried eggs whilst the American had a veal escalope, both of which came with a mountain of oily chipped potatoes and a side salad. A desert of crème caramel rounded it off. But perhaps the most interesting thing for Edwin was the fact that the bill came to less than half what he had paid for his toasted sandwich on the Gran Vía the previous day. He'd have to make use of places such as this more often. Even though it was a bit of a walk and even if one couldn't eat until nine o'clock at night, it was still worth it.

THE FOLLOWING DAY WAS Friday. Edwin entered the bank once more but it was the same old story. The money had still not arrived. He had just fifty pesetas left. Although of course that bald-headed Englishman, Charlie, still owed him a hundred pesetas.

That evening, Edwin went to Bar Dénia and saw that Charlie was there but deeply engrossed in a conversation with a Spanish man. Eventually he looked up and noticed the presence of Edwin.

"Actually, I'm sorry to have to leave you but we are just on our way out to eat," said Charlie, "but if you're going to be around later we could have a drink together."

"That's OK. I'm a bit tired and might have an early night," said Edwin, in all honesty.

"Well, there's always the weekend," said Charlie, "Did your money arrive at the bank?"

"No such luck," replied Edwin, "I've got to wait until Monday until I can check again."

"Well, at least that's something to look forward to," replied Charlie.

"And in the meantime, I've been missing my Spanish classes," said Edwin.

"If you really want to learn Spanish, I suggest you find yourself a nice little Señorita," said Charlie.

"I already did that," replied Edwin, "but half the time she confuses me by speaking French."

"You don't want to let that bother you. It's when they start speaking to you in English that you never learn anything," he said.

Charlie and his Spanish companion then departed. Edwin ordered a glass of cheap red wine and crunched on the potato crisps that were placed next to him at the bar. It was the only thing that he had eaten that day.

A young Spanish man standing next to him then spoke with Edwin in English. He was a student and it turned out that he and group of five others would be escaping the heat of Madrid over the weekend by heading for the coolness of a mountain village where they would camp in a tent.

"If you like, and if you have the time, you could come with us," he said.

"That sounds like an interesting idea," said Edwin. "But I'm afraid that I haven't got any money just at the moment."

"You won't need any money," replied the man. "We drive there in my friend's car. We have a big tent and you can eat together with us. Then we come back to Madrid on Sunday. It was a kind gesture and the person seemed sincere enough. Apart from anything else such an excursion would take Edwin's mind off his financial worries over the weekend. They agreed to meet at midday.

In stark contrast to the heat of Madrid, the small mountain village where they pitched the tent that evening was decidedly cold. However, there was a warm bar within walking distance where the six of them spent Saturday evening drinking wine and eating grilled succulent pork steaks that had been marinated in paprika, olive oil, garlic and chopped parsley sandwiched between two halves of long bread rolls that had been split lengthwise.

It was almost pitch black as they made their way back to the tent. Edwin had been given a rather flimsy sleeping bag and spent most of the night wide awake and shivering. One of the others had decided to rest his head on a rock as a pillow. The warm sunshine of the following morning was the most welcome part of the overnight camping experience.

EDWIN'S FIRST PAYMENT EVENTUALLY came through although not until the following Wednesday. That was one day after the second payment was due which similarly had not yet arrived. In the meantime, he had gone for two full days with nothing to eat other than a chunk of bread purchased from the local bakery. He hadn't set eyes on Charlie any more even though he had peered into Bar Dénia several times in the hope that he might have been there with his hundred pesetas.

However, on Tuesday he had walked several miles across Madrid to the address given him by the Spanish student called Paloma that he had met at the Paris railway station on his journey down. Fortunately she was at home and interested in hearing about his first impressions of living in her city. She introduced him to a thirst quenching cold drink made from tiger nuts known as horchata and he was also invited to stay for a most welcome late lunch prepared by her mother.

Back at the hostal it had taken some effort to convince his Spanish landlady that money would soon be forthcoming to pay for his room. Now that it had finally arrived at least he was able to bung her a couple of weeks' worth of rent in advance which effectively shut her up for a while. She was a large lady who spent a lot of her time watching cartoon programmes on the television that were shown at odd times throughout the day.

Now that Edwin had money once again he resumed going in to classes at the university and hoped that he would be able to catch up on what had been missed. The main problem was that he could still sit through an entire lecture and not understand much of what was going on and then, in the break, revert back to conversing in English with the American students. He soon realised that he wasn't likely to learn much Spanish by such means.

Edwin's mailing address was the Lista de Correos at the main post office in Madrid and he periodically went there to check if there were letters for him. News came through that the son of a neighbour in Weybridge was contemplating joining the same language course in Madrid and was wondering if he might link up with Edwin when he got there. Edwin had mixed feelings about the idea not least because it would inevitably lead to still more English being spoken rather than making progress with Spanish. However, in the interests of diplomacy, he wrote back and said he'd be pleased to show him the ropes.

On Saturday evening as he walked through the city centre Edwin quite unexpectedly ran into Charlie again. He was sat at a table on the pavement outside a cafeteria on the Gran Vía together with a young married couple who were German and Spanish. He introduced them to Edwin.

"This is Herman the German," he said almost playfully, "and this is his highly pregnant Spanish wife, Marianna."

They shook hands and Edwin was invited to pull up a chair and join them. They were a pleasant enough couple and both fluent in English. Herman taught German at the Berlitz language school. He called the waiter over to order a further round of drinks. They chatted together for half an hour or so.

"Well, that was very nice," said Charlie to Edwin after the couple had departed. "It's not every day that one gets to sit out on the Gran Vía for drinks. That Herman is a generous guy. But do you fancy popping along to Bar Dénia? –it's a heck of a lot cheaper there."

"Could do, I suppose," replied Edwin. "Actually I've looked for you in there over several consecutive evenings."

"Oh, yes, sorry to have been so elusive," said Charlie, "but that doughnut-faced manager wouldn't let me have any more credit in there until I'd coughed up and settled my bill with him which I hadn't been able to do until this morning – but he's as right as rain with me now and I've already started a new slate. What about you? Has your money been coming through yet?"

Edwin explained about the further delays at the bank and how it had meant that he was living from hand to mouth because everything was running behind schedule.

"That's tough," said Charlie, sympathetically. "But listen, I'm going to a restaurant near here this evening with that same Spanish friend that I was with last time I saw you. If you want to find out where to get one of the most inexpensive meals in town you can come along with us."

"It depends how inexpensive is inexpensive,' said Edwin.

"It's as inexpensive as it ever gets. You'll see," replied Charlie.

In Bar Dénia they were joined by Charlie's Spanish friend, Umberto, who could also speak English reasonably well. Shortly before nine o'clock, the trio weaved their way through a couple of back streets and arrived at a corner building that contained a two storey establishment by the name of Copatisan. Stepping inside, Edwin could see that it looked run-down but nonetheless was fully functioning and popular. The three of them sat themselves down at one of the few vacant tables which had already been laid with some rather old-looking tarnished cutlery, a pitcher of water and drinking glasses as well as serviettes on a white tablecloth stained in various parts through continual use over the years and complete with several holes from cigarette burns. In the middle of the table a salt cellar with a rusting metallic top stood next to a small glass jar of toothpicks together with the inevitable ashtray.

A waitress plonked down a basket containing three large bread rolls and handed each of them a grubby, plastic-encased, hand-written menu. Even though Edwin didn't have a clue as to what the various dishes were, he noticed that the prices were expressed in single figure pesetas and were far cheaper than anything that he had come across elsewhere. His choice of starter and main course was helped by translation from the others. Everybody else dining at the restaurant was Spanish and almost all of them bowed their heads in prayer and crossed themselves prior to commencing with their meals. Neither Edwin nor Charlie was in the slightest bit religious but they respected this quaint custom of Catholic Spain and silently watched as Umberto observed the tradition.

A bowl of butter bean stew followed by a plate of pig's liver and chips went down well despite the fact that Edwin's pronunciation of the Spanish word 'patatas' had come out as 'putatas' much to the amusement of the waitress. Charlie had to explain that the way he had said it meant 'little prostitutes.' But half a litre of red wine later and Edwin was beginning to get the hang of things.

"That must be the cheapest meal I've ever had," he said, as they walked through the streets afterwards, feeling suitably sated.

"That's the great thing about Madrid," said Charlie, "Such places do exist. In fact there are quite a few other tucked away restaurants to get a meal at a similar price but you just have to know where they are. There's even somewhere behind the Telefónica building where you can get a large plateful of paella for five pesetas. But right now, there's a little bar around the corner called Casa Puri where we can go for a quick cup of coffee and then, if you like, I can take you to another of my special places. After all, this is Saturday night and so we are supposed to be out enjoying ourselves."

They each drank a small black coffee and then continued to another highlight of the evening.

The Calle de la Ballesta was notorious as being Madrid's red light street. Although located just one block away from the Gran Vía it was the first time Edwin had ever been there and that evening it was particularly busy. Charlie led the way passing various bar entrances outside of which stood a selection of Spanish ladies dolled up with heavy make-up. Halfway down the stretch, he turned off into a side street and entered a bar called Pigalle.

Two ladies behind the bar greeted them. "Hola, Muy buenas!" "Hola Charlie! Hola señores! Muy Buenos tardes! Que quieren tomar? Chinchón con hielo?" One of them began pouring Charlie's drink.

"This is the place where Charlie hangs out most nights," Umberto explained to Edwin.

"I see. What does he get up to here?" he asked, momentarily fearing that he might be being lured into some kind of a brothel.

"Oh, it's no harm," said Umberto. "He comes here to touch… cómo se dice tocar la máquina? To touch? No, to play. He comes here every evening to play the pinball machine in the room at the back."

Relieved by such an explanation the three of them then passed through a pair of louvred swing doors into a smaller back room in which there were three Formica-topped tables and chairs and entrances to the adjoining ladies' and gentlemen's toilets. The electric pinball machine cost five pesetas a game and although there were no prizes if one proved to be particularly good at it, it was possible to win additional games for free. As far as Charlie was concerned the object of the exercise was to play on the wretched thing for as long as possible and preferably throughout the entire evening for no more than the initial five peseta investment. Accompanied by a continual flow of drinks it represented a cheap evening's entertainment.

Bar Pigalle also acted as a hub for a circle of Charlie's friends, many of whom were intellectual, some who were quietly politically motivated and others who were artistic. Although there was the coming and going of ladies of the night often accompanied by their clients, there was little interaction between the two groups other than a kind of mutual respect of each other's right to be there. Besides which, the majority of Charlie's friends couldn't afford the services of the ladies – and the ladies knew it.

One of the regular visitors was an Egyptian diplomat called Nizam Massri. He enjoyed the buzz of English conversation that such evenings provided especially when Charlie was in one of his more entertaining modes. During such nocturnal events they all took turns in playing the pinball machine through to three thirty in the morning when the establishment would finally shut its doors. As usual Charlie ran up a bar tab although, in this particular bar, it was often the Egyptian diplomat, Nizam, who would step in and zero the account. His repeated generosity in that regard made it feel like a free pub.

Edwin stayed up with them through the night. He had several turns on the pinball machine and got quite apt at pressing the buttons of either side to activate flippers that knocked the ball-bearing back to the top again hitting various metallic springs in the process that clocked up additional points making electronic noises and bells sound each time.

It was still very hot outside. Edwin sat on a bench in the Gran Vía with Charlie, Umberto and Nizam until the break of dawn.

"Well, now that you know a bit about my routine I shall crawl back to where I'm staying and snatch a few hours' sleep until shortly before lunchtime," announced Charlie. "That's the good thing about Spain. There's no earthly need to get up until the afternoon."

They parted company and Edwin could now understand why Charlie's complexion was so pale. Anyone who slept during the day and stayed up through the night would end up much the same, irrespective of what the weather was like. But he also found it disturbing that the man had an obvious ability to run up bills everywhere and seemingly to scrounge off others whenever possible. Such a lifestyle was easy to get into, he supposed. Admittedly the evening had been entertaining and he now knew where he could find Charlie. But it wasn't what Edwin had come to Madrid for.

ON SUNDAY THE SHOPS were closed, the bank was closed and the university class was not being held. It was another roasting hot day and Edwin, who himself had slept in until ten got up and went out for a stroll down to the Puerta del Sol. He stopped off at a small coffee bar and bought a bread roll packed full of fried squid. Two Americans asked him the way to the Sunday flea market known as El Rastro and in the absence of anything much else to do he ended up accompanying them there. It was like an elongated outdoor jumble sale that stretched over several sun-drenched streets just south of the Plaza Mayor which attracted crowds of people. Almost anything second-hand, regardless of its condition, seemed to be available in this place. The selection ranged from antiques to worn-out looking household appliances and from used clothing, books, old shoes and gramophone records to curtain material and paintings, all being enthusiastically offered by loud and often scruffy-looking, vendors. Flamenco music blared forth from some of the stalls as people haggled over the price of watches, leather belts, carpets and miscellaneous items of jewellery. If nothing else, it certainly had atmosphere.

Edwin had found that it very easy to strike up conversations with tourists in Madrid and over the following weeks met a variety of them. However the fact that they were American, French or Australian was doing little to improve his Spanish. Although he made the effort to go into classes at the University more often than he got the feeling that he hadn't learned very much there at all. To help make up for that he purchased a set of study books entitled 'Spanish in Three Months' and began to work his way through them. It proved useful in understanding the basics and coupled with his day-to-day experience in Madrid enabled him to pick up several new phrases.

His money was now coming through but still in dribs and drabs. It was sometimes more than a fortnight overdue and he had written to the bank back in Weybridge informing them of the problem. On one occasion when his money still hadn't arrived he went out and purchased a fifty peseta lottery ticket with the last of his money. He had convinced himself that his number would win something and was rather indignant when it didn't.

Quite the reverse thing happened with horse racing. British newspapers were on sale at newsstands in the Gran Vía in the afternoons and whenever one of them could afford it they would buy a copy and take it in turns to digest its content. One day Charlie turned to the racing page and asked Edwin how people went about backing horses in England. Edwin was able to throw some light on the process and to elaborate about the odds involved. He also explained about accumulator bets in which the winnings from a horse in a first race would be placed on a horse in a second race and, if that came in the total winnings would then be placed on a third race and so on and so forth. To illustrate the point he took a ballpoint pen and encircled Happy Guy in the 2:50 at Exeter with odds of 22 to 1, Amber Light in the 3:40 at Warwick with odds of 33 to 1 and Whistling Cop in the 4:10 at Kempton Park with odds of 28 to 1.

"And in the unlikely event of all three horses coming first in each of their races – well, you can do the maths for yourself, but it's some astronomical figure" said Edwin, before going on to explain about each-way bets.

The following evening when Edwin was having a cold beer and a couple of tapas in the Peña El Aguila bar, Charlie arrived.

"I see you were right about the horses," he said.

"How do you mean?" asked Edwin.

"Well they all came in just like you suggested," said Charlie, unfolding that day's newspaper.

They scanned the racing results and to Edwin's astonishment Happy Guy, Amber Light and Whistling Cop had each come first in the horse races that he had singled out the day before. And they hadn't even been able to back them.

IN RESPONSE TO AN advertisement to teach conversational English, Edwin set off along the length of Calle Hortaleza in the heat of the day and eventually arrived at the Plaza Santa Bárbara. There he was shown into the third floor office of a company executive whose command of the English language was already quite good but just needed polishing. In the absence of any textbooks Edwin made use of a copy of the Daily Telegraph for exercises in reading and comprehension. The one hour class earned Edwin sufficient money for meals for a couple of days and it was agreed to give such tuition on a weekly basis.

In the evenings Edwin still met up with Charlie and they invariably went for a cheap meal together. A small restaurant called El Centro located opposite the far end of the red light street was a favourite. The combination of a large bread roll, a bowl of potage of lentils and a bottle of vino tinto had become a mainstay. Sometimes that was all that that Edwin could afford but on days when he was slightly more flush the meal would include a second course either of chicken or a meat and potato stew or perhaps some grilled fish. Sometimes ice cold gazpacho soup and paella were available. Desert was inevitably a crème caramel with a squirt of cream on top and it was then customary to go elsewhere for an after dinner coffee and goblet of coñac.

Charlie never seemed to have much money to his name and still hadn't offered to refund Edwin's hundred peseta loan. And Edwin hadn't yet asked.

In the unbearable August heat many inhabitants of Madrid closed down their businesses for the month and headed for the cooler climates of the coastal regions. However, there was still a steady flow of tourists from other countries. Charlie pointed out that even from a distance he could tell if a woman was American because she would be more sloppily dressed than Spanish ladies. Edwin put the theory to the test and discovered it to be true.

Edwin found it easy to get into conversation with them. On some occasions he even managed to bring a few of them over to Bar Pigalle for an evening of lively conversation that provided an alternative to the attraction of the pin ball machine. After a series of American females he brought a pair of French girls along one evening and then a couple of New Zealanders called Heather and Natasha. Because such girls were invariably in their twenties whereas Edwin was a mere seventeen-year-old, the noticeable age gap was a constant source of frustration to him – even if he did try to make out that he was nineteen.

The two young ladies from New Zealand were travelling around Europe. They had already been in Italy and France and were now passing through Spain and on their way to Portugal. Both were from farming families in New Zealand's South Island and Edwin and Charlie were fascinated by their broad accents and the various expressions that they came out with. They pronounced the word "yes" as "yis" and made frequent use of a term "skunjee" to describe anything that they found remotely distasteful. They didn't approve of the fact that Charlie didn't have a job and told him so to his face.

"You sound a bit like a wee bludge to me," said one, "doesn't it irk you jist to sit around doing nothing all day?'

"Yis, I reckon you'd do yersilf a favour if you got up bright and early tomorrow morning and hidded off to work," chimed in the other New Zealander.

Charlie attempted to defend his position and pointed out that with the best will in the world you couldn't just simply get up and go off to work in Spain as perhaps you could in New Zealand.

"So you're jist content with lolling about?" she persisted.

At that moment Nizam the Egyptian diplomat put in an appearance and bought everyone a round of drinks. The subject of the conversation changed and after a few facts and figures about their being ten sheep per head of population in New Zealand, Nizam became interested in the fact that the girls were going to go to Portugal. He said that he had some antique bronze medallions that needed delivering to a friend in Lisbon which he didn't trust sending by post.

"We'll be taking an overnight train from Madrid to Lisbon in two weeks' time and I dare say there'd be room in our luggage for them, if you like," volunteered Heather.

"Well, let's see," said the diplomat. "Maybe you'd all like to come back to my place when we've had enough of it here," he suggested.

At one o'clock in the morning, Edwin, Charlie and the two New Zealand ladies were led by Nizam the twenty minute walk to his attic apartment which lay in the neighbourhood of Tribunal. At the top of a flight of stairs everyone had to crawl through a tiny entranceway into a living area that resembled some kind of an Aladdin's cave. Surrounded by carpeted walls, the floor was covered with cushions to sit on amidst large ceramic vases. A hubble-bubble smoking device stood in one corner alongside several small cabinets displaying trinkets and knickknacks of one sort or another. There was also a cocktail cabinet and refrigerator. Nizam produced a bottle of Chinchón anis for Charlie whilst tall glasses of white rum and Coca-Cola were provided for everybody else. He then showed everyone the medallions that were destined for Lisbon.

THE FOLLOWING AFTERNOON THERE were three letters for Edwin at Madrid's main post office in Cibeles. The first was from his family saying that they would soon be taking a fortnight's holiday on the Costa Blanca and that, if he had the time, he would be most welcome to visit them there for a few days. The second letter was confirmation that the neighbour's son in Weybridge would be coming out to Madrid at the beginning of the following month. He would be joining the same Spanish course at the university and was grateful that Edwin had indicated his willingness to line up some affordable accommodation. The third letter was from the bank in Weybridge apologising for Edwin's irregular payments and saying that they would soon be issuing him with a chequebook with which he could withdraw his weekly amount in Madrid. That was good news apart from not knowing how soon the chequebook would arrive and whether or not it would be in time for any trip to the Costa Blanca.

In the meantime Edwin remained in touch with the two New Zealanders, Heather and Natasha, who continued to grace the back room of Bar Pigalle every evening throughout their fortnight in Madrid. When the day eventually arrived for their departure for Portugal, Edwin, Charlie and Nizam accompanied them to Madrid's Atocha railway station to see them off. There was a pang of sadness as the train pulled out of the station. The two girls had been such great company and had certainly succeeded in putting New Zealand on the map.

Nizam then let on that the antique medallions were in fact very rare pieces and that they were worth a small fortune. But he trusted both ladies to hand them over to his friend who would be meeting the train on its arrival in Lisbon. Edwin suspected that it amounted to some kind of cross-border smuggling but he didn't bother to ask.

As Charlie and Edwin made their way back to the city centre they happened to pass a short man smartly dressed in jacket and tie.

"Well, good evening to you Mr Dobson!" exclaimed Charlie.

"Oh it's you is it? You little shit," was the reply.

"There's no need to be offensive," said Charlie.

"Oh it's not offensive," cooed the man in a relatively sophisticated accent, "It's merely a statement of fact about exactly what you are."

"Come off it. That's a bit unfair," protested Charlie.

"I don't think it is," replied the man, "and what's more you know it yourself."

Once they were out of earshot Edwin asked who the man was.

"His name is Tommie Dobson," said Charlie. "He's been out here in Madrid for years and to be quite honest we've never got on. He keeps telling everybody some cock and bull story that he's an exiled prince from Montenegro but I doubt the whole thing. He's as English as you and me –or Welsh actually, I think."

CHAPTER FOUR

WITH STILL NO SIGN of a chequebook and with a continued delay with his money Edwin was fast reaching the conclusion that the visit to the Costa Blanca could only be achieved if he were to hitch-hike there. After all, he already had a fair bit of experience with that means of getting around in Britain although he hadn't yet tried it on the Continent.

On the eve of his departure, whilst sitting out in the Gran Vía in the warm night air, Edwin asked Charlie if he was in a position to refund him the hundred pesetas he had lent him when they had first met. Charlie didn't take at all kindly to such a suggestion and accused Edwin of being ungrateful for all that he had shown him and said that he didn't owe him a single thing. It was the first time they had had an open disagreement. From Edwin's point of view it wasn't the amount of a mere hundred pesetas but the principle of the matter. He hadn't even mentioned the other occasions when Charlie had claimed to be skint and Edwin had sympathetically chipped in and subsidised meals out of his own limited income.

He returned to his hostal and clapped his hands outside the ground level entrance to attract the attention of the Sereno to whom he gave the customary two peseta tip for unlocking the door. Edwin then scrawled a note to the landlady in his best Spanish saying that he would be away until the following Friday and that he would catch up with the rent on his return. He got up early the following morning and headed for the Metro from where he took trains to the southernmost station of Legazpi. He reasoned that from there he would at least be on the correct side of Madrid for a road leading out in the direction of Alicante.

Such foresight proved correct and, after a short walk through a shanty town on the outskirts of that particular side of Madrid's extremity he found himself on the right route. Standing by the roadside and holding out his thumb, he was soon offered a series of lifts that took him in the south-easterly direction of his destination. Ironically, and perhaps as a grim reminder of the previous evening's disagreement with Charlie, he was driven through the small town of Chinchón which was the home of the distillery where the syrupy aniseed firewater of the same name was made.

Later that morning Edwin was dropped off at one end of a tiny village of white stone houses in which women of all age groups were out washing clothes in a stone trough of water that ran through its middle. It could easily have been a scene from an earlier century. The setting and its simplicity seemed to have a profound effect on Edwin who felt that it captured something of the true heart of Spain. The villagers then spotted him standing there and began to comment about the fact that he had blue eyes and blond hair – evidently something that none of them had ever seen before. He walked through to the far end of the village to re-join the main road and it wasn't long before he got his next lift. The truck driver heading for Murcia insisted on stopping off on the way and buying each of them a large bread roll containing a thickly cut strip of Spanish omelette and a strong coffee. Early that evening Edwin was left at a road junction for Alicante and by ten o'clock he arrived at the hotel in the coastal town of Villajoyosa where his parents and younger brothers were staying. It was a happy reunion.

Edwin spent a pleasant five day seaside break together with his family. Although his knowledge of Spanish was still limited it was better that that of any of the British holidaymakers staying at the hotel. The fact that he could make himself understood by using certain phrases in Spanish not only boosted his own confidence with the language but also had the effect of impressing both the waiting staff and the other hotel guests. What they perhaps didn't realise what that the bulk of his vocabulary related mainly to restaurant situations because that was about the only thing that he knew.

The neighbour from Weybridge would be flying out to Madrid on the following Saturday and so in order to be back in time it was arranged that Edwin would take a train from Alicante to Madrid on Thursday evening. Concerned about the continuing saga of cash flow problem with the banks his parents had been pleased to advance him some additional funds to see him through the following week or so.

Edwin settled down into a train compartment of familiar green vinyl seats. The carriage had no couchette facilities which meant than anyone travelling all the way through to Madrid would have to spend the night sitting in a seat. When the train stopped at a place called Albacete a woman and her daughter of about Edwin's age boarded it and sat down directly opposite Edwin. He acknowledged their presence with a polite nod and said, 'Buenos tardes,' to which they both smiled and returned the greeting.

"¿Ustedes van a Madrid también?" enquired Edwin.

"Si, si," replied the mother, "¿Puedo preguntar si Usted es Ingles?"

"Si. Yo soy Ingles," responded Edwin. "¿Hablan Ustedes Ingles?"

"Nosotros no," she replied, "aunque mi hija aquí gustaría aprenderlo."

Edwin thought about this for a moment. They couldn't speak English but the daughter would like to learn it. On impulse he then suggested that he might be willing to teach her.

"Si quiere, tal vez yo pude ensenarse," he said.

The mother chuckled and replied, "Supongo que sería una posibilidad. ¿Va estar in Madrid por mucho tiempo?"

"Si. Soy estudiante y habito en un pensión cerca de la Gran Vía," he replied.

The lady then wrote down their name, address and telephone number on a piece of paper and handed it to Edwin telling him that he was welcome to pay them a visit whenever he had time. He thanked her and began to wonder whether he was even capable of teaching English from scratch should they ever wish to take up his offer to give classes to the daughter.

The following day the train pulled into Madrid's Atocha railway station. Having said "Hasta luego" to the mother and daughter, Edwin made his way back to his guesthouse.

Freddie Lea, the neighbour from Weybridge, would be arriving at Madrid Airport tomorrow and Edwin felt that he ought to put together some sort of a plan. When he got back to his hostal, however, the first thing that confronted him was that the landlady had obviously misunderstood his temporary absence and in the meantime had packed all his belongings, including a bag of dirty laundry, into his suitcase and let the room out to somebody else. That state of affairs put Edwin into minor panic mode even if it did mean that he didn't need to give her a back payment of rent money. He grabbed the suitcase and departed through the front door, down the three flights of stairs and out into the street.

Throughout the weeks that he had been staying at the Pensión Mecca he had occasionally noticed the nameplates of other guesthouses a little further along his street of Calle de Caballero de Gracia and he hoped that one of them might just happen to have a twin-bedded room available at the similar sort of price.

Luck was on his side. On the fourth floor of a rather gloomy interior with a primitive looking caged lift the door of Huespedes Havana was opened by another large landlady who showed him to a wooden-floored room with two single beds a wardrobe and a chest of drawers and explained that the shower and toilet, located further along the passage, were shared facilities. Asked about the price it turned out that she wanted 100 pesetas a night for the twin room which, split between the two of them would be 50 pesetas each – even cheaper that where he'd been staying previously. He eagerly agreed to take it, gave her some money and began unpacking his case, mentally allocating some drawers and wardrobe space for Freddie. The change of accommodation felt like a new era was dawning. The place itself was a bit basic but it would be adequate for their needs.

Edwin didn't want to bump into Charlie just yet after what had happened on the last occasion and so, when he ventured out that evening he avoided the usual haunts. Walking along the Gran Vía towards Plaza de España it felt good to be back in Madrid and he decided to treat himself to a coffee in one of the cafeterias there instead of any back street hangout. Slightly more confident with his increasing knowledge of Spanish he managed to get into conversation with two Spanish girls who were seated on bar stools adjacent to where he stood. Before leaving they agreed to meet up again at the same time and at the same place the following week.

MADRID AIRPORT WAS LOCATED outside of the city at a place called Barajas. That Saturday morning Freddie Lea stepped out into the Arrivals Hall. His hair was considerably longer than the last time Edwin had seen him in England and amongst his luggage was a large guitar case. Greeting each other they then took the Airport Bus to the centre of Madrid and the journey gave Edwin a bit of time to update him on the Spanish experience so far. The hostal seemed to meet with Freddie's approval and, after unpacking his things, the two of them set off on a sightseeing walk around the city centre. Freddie was due to join the Spanish course at the university from Monday.

Edwin told him about Charlie and explained that, although he was an interesting character with whom they were bound to meet up sooner or later, he was a bit of a scrounger at the best of times.

Acting as a kind of tour guide Edwin felt as though he had already become something of an authority on Madrid but it was also apparent that Freddie had a completely different outlook on life than he did. Freddie was a talented folk guitarist but also something of a drifter. He'd even brought some weird looking clothing out with him that was guaranteed to turn a few heads in Madrid. It fact his combination of psychedelic trousers, orange and yellow caftan, miniature green-lens sun glasses together with long hair resulted in his being stopped by the Spanish police on the very first evening. They questioned him for several minutes as to whether or not he had anything to do with drugs. After they'd gone Freddie shocked Edwin by saying that in point of fact he would love to get his hands on some hashish or some LSD. Edwin hoped that he wasn't serious.

As they continued along the Gran Vía near the cinemas of Callao, Edwin spotted the German man, Herman, and his wife who, as on the previous occasion, were sat at a table on the pavement outside one of the cafeterias in the midst of all the passers-by. Herman invited them to grab a couple of chairs and join them for a beer. Being Saturday on a hot summer's evening, downtown Madrid was positively bustling both with people and traffic. It was already getting dark and brightly coloured lights and illuminated billboards were now taking over. A massive animated neon sign on the building opposite advertised Camel cigarettes. During the course of conversation Herman asked Edwin if he had seen anything of Charlie.

"No, not for a while," replied Edwin, "But that's largely because I've been away on the Costa Blanca."

"Ah so," said Herman. "I think Charlie is quite an interesting person but he drinks far more than is good for him."

"He certainly does," agreed Edwin, "His entire life seems to revolve around glasses of Anis."

"I recently lent him money but I haven't seen him since," said Herman.

"I expect he will suddenly show up again," responded Edwin, trying not to show too much interest in the fact that someone else had parted with cash.

The subject then changed to Herman's wife, Marianna, sitting next to him and of their joint happiness at the thought of their baby which was due to be born in two months' time. Herman then went on to say that his parents in Frankfurt knew nothing of his being married let alone that a child was on its way.

"Why haven't you told them?" asked Edwin.

Herman shook his head. "No," he said. My parents are very strict and it would have been far too difficult to explain to them anything about all of this.

Later that evening Edwin decided to take Freddie to some of the various haunts. By now he had brushed off any fear about the possibility of running into Charlie. Herman's account had strengthened his own view that the man was acceptable as an eccentric and amusing friend but that one should never give him money.

They first called in at the usual hangout of the Bar Dénia with its television strung from the ceiling and a Spanish commentator's voice booming forth about the highlights of the day's football. They crossed the road to sample a tankard of cold lager in the beer bar after which Edwin suggested that they might then weave their way around to Bar Pigalle. As they did so they passed the glass-fronted entrance to Cafeteria Puri and, on glancing inside, Edwin immediately caught sight of Charlie perched on a bar stool and their eyes met. As if nothing had ever happened between them, Charlie's face broke into a broad grin.

"Come on in! Good to see you again! Let me get you and your friend a drink!" he bellowed in his theatrical voice as Edwin and Freddie lurked in the doorway. "And let me introduce you to Sidney from Lancashire here who has been staying in Madrid for a few days and who has already developed quite a liking for Osborne brandy," he said, indicating an elderly gentleman sitting beside him who smiled in response.

"Oh, aye, Oz-born-nay," said the man so as to pronounced the brand name the Spanish way.

Edwin and Freddie soon found themselves in an evening of general hilarity in which Charlie took the lead role in expressing his opinions about everything under the sun fuelled by the continual replenishment of his glass of Anis and ice cubes. He quizzed Freddie on what he hoped to gain from being in Madrid. The Lancashire gentleman's daughter then arrived to escort her father back to his hotel. Before he departed he said what an enjoyable time he'd had and how he had been glad of the English company. He insisted on paying the accumulated drinks bill for everyone.

"Well, if you must," said Charlie. "But I'll tell you what. It'll be my turn tomorrow."

The man paid and then went around saying "Box of matches" to everybody which apparently was his anglicised version of "Buenos noches."

Charlie suggested that the remaining three of them might like to call in at a small Flamenco show which was held every Saturday evening at a hall in a nearby street. It proved to be informal, inexpensive and well-performed. Afterwards they drifted on to Bar Pigalle and played the inevitable pinball machine through to closing time. Various prostitutes breezed in and out mainly it would seem to visit the toilet, accessed through the back room. There was the usual polite acknowledgement of mutual respect for each other's presence. The Egyptian diplomat, Nizam, arrived on the scene puffing on a pipe full of aromatic tobacco. Madrid life was returning to normal once again.

The proprietor of the Bar Pigalle, a Spaniard called Sancho, was a classical guitarist and some nights as his last remaining customers bade him goodnight he would sit in a corner of the front bar and pluck Spanish melodies on his acoustic guitar as he did on that night. Outside it was still stinking hot and the streets were being washed down by uniformed men wielding hosepipes. A flow of taxis moved up and down the Gran Vía stopping every once in a while either to drop someone off outside a hotel or to pick up somebody else. Edwin and Freddie sat watching this for a while before returning to their street and clapping their hands at the outer door of their hostal to summon the Soreno to come along with his big bunch of keys and let them in.

BRIGHT AND EARLY ON Monday morning the two of them made their way to the university by means of the Metro. It was rush hour and they were wedged tightly into the carriage and squeezed against the hot bodies of smartly dressed Spanish men and women.

"Talk about sardines," said Freddie, "How come no one is passing out in the heat?"

"It's always a crush at this time of day and it's the humidity that's the real problem but you get used to it," replied Edwin, "Anyway, it's only a couple more stops."

"I wish the geezer next to me would stop picking his nose," said Freddie, "I don't know where he's depositing the content every time his hand goes back down."

"Maybe he's wiping it down your trouser leg," suggested Edwin.

"It'd be a short sharp smack in the teeth for him if that's what he's up to," he replied. "I see that you've managed to squeeze yourself up against a rather tasty looking girl."

Edwin glanced at the immediate person next to him whose body warmth was gently pressed against his and saw that she was indeed an attractive looking señorita. She hadn't shown any reaction to Freddie's comments so presumably didn't speak English which saved any embarrassment on Edwin's part.

At the University, Freddie wasn't the only newcomer to the Curso de Estudios Hispánicos. There was a fresh influx of many new faces, mostly Americans, and Freddie found himself placed in a different classroom to that of Edwin. They met up afterwards.

"Well, after that, I feel as though I've learned precisely nothing!" proclaimed Freddie as he emerged into the lobby, "All we got was some lecturer pacing up and down the room in squeaky shoes jabbering away non-stop in Spanish all morning and prefixing every single sentence with the word 'Pues' which I still don't know the meaning of. It certainly was no beginners' class."

"I know. It's a major problem. The course assumes some prior knowledge of Spanish which neither of us ever had," he replied.

"I'll see if it gets any better over the next few days but if not I reckon there's more likelihood of picking up the basics of the language just by hanging out in the city of Madrid," he said.

"Yes and no," said Edwin, who felt that at least the discipline of getting up in the morning and making the effort to attend the class was infinitely better that falling into the pattern of late night escapades and doing nothing much at all during the rest of the time. He'd already experienced far too much of skipping class when his money hadn't arrived although that had been more to do with circumstances rather than choice.

THE FOLLOWING WEEK EDWIN telephoned the mother and daughter that he'd met on the train from Alicante. Having dialled the number and allowed the token to drop he recognised the mother's voice who answered the phone with the customary "Digame." In his best Spanish, Edwin asked her it would be convenient to come over and visit them early that evening and give a first English lesson to the daughter. He knew it was short notice.

"Si si, Edwin!" she affirmed with enthusiasm. "Vienes esta tarde y después tu puedes cenar con nosotros."

The unexpected invitation to have supper with them after giving an English lesson raised Edwin's spirits considerably. Food, glorious food, his empty stomach was already rumbling as he descended into the Metro station. The journey involved a couple of changes and after an uphill tunnel of twists and turns that the antiquated underground train seemed scarcely able to handle, it stopped at the station of Lista in one of the better suburbs of Madrid. Edwin had already consulted his dictionary and discovered the word 'Lista' to mean 'clever.' It struck him as a mighty strange name for a Metro station. He reasoned that maybe it meant that he himself had been clever in making friends with people who lived in such an upmarket place. It was a short walk along the Calle de Don Ramón de la Cruz to the block of apartments where he rang the doorbell.

The home of the Fernandez family was compact yet elegant. Mind you almost anything looked elegant in comparison to his run-down hostal room. Edwin was greeted at the door by the mother who ushered him down through a long passageway and into the lounge where he shook hands with her husband, a short man with a pleasant smile and then with the abuela, an elderly bespectacled plump Spanish grandmother dressed entirely in black. The girl, Isolina, appeared through a doorway and it was suggested that Edwin might like to sit at a table with her and commence tuition.

It was difficult for Edwin to know where to begin with someone who knew no English whatsoever other than the word 'yes' which she, in any case, pronounced as 'djess' and the word 'please' which she insisted on pronouncing 'eplix.' Edwin tried to get her to repeat various simple words and phrases but she was clearly demonstrating an inability to imitate anything at all. It was becoming somewhat tedious to say "Good Morning. How are you?" and then to have it repeated back as a kind of "Gooth emornin. Jau ah dju?" When he'd had quite enough of that he resorted to the use of a notepad and pen that he'd had the foresight to bring along with him and wrote out the verb 'to have' and tried getting that across in the same parrot fashion way. Still the same guttural 'h' manifested as if she was clearing her throat and getting ready to spit something out, which, it crossed Edwin's mind, maybe she was. He tried explaining things to her in Spanish but that caused added confusion. "Yo tengo," said Edwin patting his chest, "I have."

"Pero que tienes?" she asked him, somewhat mystified.

"No. Yo no tengo nada," he replied. "En español se dice 'yo tengo' y en ingles se dice 'I have.'"

"Hay caramba!" she responded as if she'd suddenly grasped it before lapsing back into something that showed that she hadn't got the foggiest idea. To help round off this hour Edwin pointed to a series of different things around the room and said their name out loud in English for her to repeat. In most cases he didn't know the Spanish word and so she provided that and they covered things in both languages. Edwin sensed, however, that he was gaining far more Spanish vocabulary out of this particular exercise than she was English and by the end of the session he discovered that he had learned previously unknown Spanish words for things such as ceiling, desk, lamp, picture and light bulb whilst she was still struggling even with simple English words which to her were like tongue-twisters. Yet it was all done in good humour and she laughed and seemed to enjoy her own apparent uselessness.

Afterwards Isolina told her parents that she had very much appreciated her first English lesson. Edwin was invited to a couple of glasses of beer as a pre-dinner drink with her father. Then half an hour later everybody sat around the dining table for a wonderful spread of hake filets fried in light batter followed by pork medallions and sautéed potatoes and salad. A wine decanter had appeared from nowhere from which Edwin's glass and the grandmother's glass were forever being topped up. Afterwards over coffee, brandy and a cigarette and whilst Isolina was clearing away the plates, her father quietly asked Edwin if he would be available to give such English lessons on a regular basis and what payment he would require. Edwin said that he'd be happy to come once a week but that the classes would be free of charge. The mother chimed in and said that even if Edwin didn't want paying whenever he came he'd always be welcome to stay with them for dinner.

Isolina's father insisted on accompanying him to the Metro station where they shook hands and parted company.

"Y entonces, hasta la próxima semana," he said.

THE FOLLOWING THURSDAY WAS the day that Edwin had arranged to meet the two Spanish girls that he'd met in a bar a week ago. He had invited Freddie to come along with him. The main problem with that little arrangement was that Edwin only had the sum total of twenty-seven pesetas to his name. He would first have to go to the bank again in the morning to check whether any payment had come through and if there was any sign of the promised chequebook. He was quite literally banking on it being there at the bank.

To his great and pleasant surprise, not only was Edwin's chequebook awaiting him but he was able to withdraw the two missing back payments. The cashier was as relieved as Edwin was with the new arrangement.

"So from now, Mr Ravensdale, when you come in each week you will always be able to receive your money," he said.

"That's excellent news," responded Edwin, completely uplifted by such a welcome change of circumstances.

When he left the bank he descended the flight of stair at the Metro station called Sevilla and stopped off at the underground coffee bar that he'd visited on previous occasions. The waitress who'd attracted his attention last time was again on duty and greeted him with a warm smile.

"Muy buenos días señor! ¿Que quiere tomar?" she asked.

He ordered a ring donut and a cup of coffee and, as an afterthought asked also for a glass of brandy. It might have been mid-morning but for the first time in ages he actually felt that he'd got something to celebrate. He even plucked up courage to ask the waitress her name which turned out to be Maria Carmen. She was probably the same age as Edwin and had a surprisingly pale complexion for a Spanish girl. The combination of her long black hair, pleasant facial features, a neatly ironed pale blue waitress outfit and white pinafore made her particularly attractive – as did her engaging smile and her ability to slip into conversation with Edwin so easily. He was just about to ask if he could meet her when she finished work when he recalled that he'd already got the other appointment lined up with the two girls in the Gran Vía on that particular evening. He reasoned that it was best to take things one at a time. Despite that, however, he ordered a second brandy and asked if he could meet with her on Friday – to which she readily accepted and said that she would be free from 4pm on that day.

Somewhat light-headed from this morning intake of spirituous liquor he stepped out into the blazing heat of the day and returned to the hostal where he was pleased to make a payment of four weeks rent in advance.

That evening the two Spanish girls were waiting at the bar when Edwin and Freddie arrived. They were both pleasant enough in their own ways and, as they got talking over cafe con leche, Edwin found himself relating to the taller of the two, Julia, whilst Freddie seemed to be making some conversational headway with the more petite Margarita. Both girls could speak a smattering of English although, certainly from Edwin's point of view, the object of the exercise was supposed to be to help improve his Spanish.

The four of them ambled down to the Plaza de España where they sat on stone benches and remained there until darkness fell. The girls then had to return to their homes but they arranged to meet again the same time the following week. It was already nine o'clock as Edwin and Freddie made their way back along the familiar stretch of the Gran Vía.

"I'll tell you what," said Freddie, "That Margarita was passionate! I thought you said that Spanish birds were all chaste and conservative in their outlook."

Edwin declined to reveal any details about his own evening sat on the bench alongside Julia. In any case he supposed that any amorous advances were in part opportunistic. After all, there were certain limitations as to where one could even meet with any degree of privacy in Spain – it was forbidden to take a girl back to a hostel room – one couldn't ordinarily visit them at their family home – and he supposed that such couples just made the most of things by groping at each other on park benches.

MARIA CARMEN, THE WAITRESS from the cafeteria, could speak no English yet seemed to enjoy the pleasure of Edwin's company. Edwin found it beneficial that he was forced to speak Spanish. Apparently she lived in a place called Campamento with her mother and three sisters. As arranged, Edwin had met her outside her workplace that Friday afternoon and the pair went for a stroll through the old part of Madrid. She was young and uncomplicated, perhaps not that well educated but not stupid either. Most of all she seemed to radiate a sense of well-being.

At the end of what had been a particularly long walk in the heat they had stopped off for a Coca-Cola and Edwin asked if he should accompany her part of the way to her home. They took the metro on the line that ventured out into the Casa de Campo and alighted at a station called Campamento.

"Aquí es donde vivo," she said, using her arms to indicate the surrounding area. Edwin looked and quietly surveyed another massive shanty town.

On Saturday afternoon Edwin stopped off at the Peña El Aguila beer bar and for a change sat at a table in the back where one had to pay a little extra for waiter service. On an adjacent table an elegantly dressed lady was drinking tea with her two daughters. During the course of conversation Edwin was asked if it might be possible for him to provide English conversation practice for one of the girls. This sudden demand for English tuition was interesting. Edwin said that he would be willing to offer conversational English on condition that an equal amount of time could then be allocated to conversion in Spanish. The suggestion met with agreement and an arrangement was made to meet up at the same place in a week's time and every Saturday afternoon thereafter.

This is becoming a bit complicated, Edwin thought to himself afterwards. It's rapidly turning into a different girl a day situation. Isolina on Wednesdays, Julia on Thursdays, Maria Carmen on Fridays and now this would be Anna on Saturdays. Admittedly, such contacts were for the expressed purpose of language exchange but at the same time Edwin couldn't help but feel a special connection with each one of them. At this rate he'd soon be able to tell which day of the week it was by the particular girl that he happened to be with.

Meanwhile back at the hostal Freddie had discovered that the landlady's son, whose room was adjacent to theirs, possessed a record player. One of the prize possessions that Freddie had brought out with him from England was the Beatles 'Sergeant Pepper's Lonely Heart Club Band' long playing record which was being played through at full blast for the umpteenth time.

> *I read the news today oh boy*
> *Four thousand holes in Blackburn, Lancashire*
> *And though the holes were rather small*
> *They had to count them all*
> *Now they know how many holes it takes to fill the Albert Hall.*
> *I'd love to turn you on.*

A few days later Freddie took his guitar with him to the university and met up with a Spanish student called Antonio Lope Gonzales who invited him to perform a couple of songs at a small concert being held in the Faculty of Science. Antonio spoke fluent English with no noticeable accent and he was sufficiently impressed by Freddie's musical talent to ask him if he'd like to join him in forming a pop group. The following Saturday a man arrived at the hostel with a pencil written note. It said 'Please go with this taxi driver who will bring you to where we are rehearsing music. The fare has already been paid. Yours Antonio'

Freddie thought that he might as well go and Edwin decided to go along for the ride too. The taxi took them to the suburb of Goya where Antonio stood waiting for them at the door. He showed them into a large room in an office building where a collection of guitars, amplifiers, microphones and a drum kit were being set up by three other young men. It soon became obvious that most of them were new to the game. The choice of music wasn't to Freddie's taste at all. He was far more comfortable with folk arrangements, many of which he'd composed himself. Instead he was now required to keep strumming three chords to a song evidently called 'Gloria' according to the out-of-tune vocalists who were repetitively chanting "Glaw-ri-ah" over and over again into their microphones and out through the amplifiers, complete with feedback and distortion. Edwin supposed that every pop group had to begin somehow. Antonio told Freddie that he thought he was beginning to get the hang of it which didn't go down too well.

Thoroughly deafened throughout the morning by goodness knows how many decibels of throbbing rhythmic noise, Edwin and Freddie took to hiring a paddle boat on the lake in the comparative tranquillity of the Retiro Gardens that afternoon. To their amusement they were pursued by some French tourists in a similar vessel and the occasion soon turned into a ramming session until an official at the water's edge started blowing his whistle.

They returned to their hostal and paused to speak with the porteria who lived on the ground floor of the building and who sat all day long in a dimly lit room by the base of the lift. To pass the time she had a sewing machine and together with her daughter, spent hours mending clothing. They had got used to the two blond-haired Englishmen coming in and out of the hostal four floors up.

They always waved and smiled.

That evening Edwin had arranged to meet up with Herman the German and his wife whereas Freddie intended going to a different part of town and taking his guitar with him to meet up with a couple of American guys he'd recently bumped into who also played music.

Although the sun had gone down it was still hot as Edwin sat down at an outside table on a terrace in front of the back street bar. There Herman introduced him to a distinguished looking elderly Spanish couple, Don Francisco and his wife, Maria. The husband had been imprisoned for his anti-Franco views whereas nowadays he had adopted the prevailing philosophy that one never discussed politics because one never knew who might be listening. "Besides, the country is not at war, we have sun, we have food and we have plenty of good red wine!" he said. Herman's wife, Marianna, looked on and smiled, as radiant as ever in her advanced stage of pregnancy.

Edwin accompanied them back to the door of their hostal on Calle del Pez. As he returned he happened to pass a corner bar called La Luna and through its entrance recognised the man Tommie Dobson who had so demonstratively referred to Charlie as the 'little shit.' Edwin couldn't resist going in.

The man recognised Edwin: "Ooh," he cooed, "I see you've discovered my little hideaway. I'm pleased to see that you haven't brought that despicable person, Charles Tennyson, along with you. Come; let me get you a drink."

Another Englishman was also present. He was a rather portly person, perhaps a few years older than Edwin, and he taught English at one of Madrid's language schools.

"That's interesting," said Edwin, "I've been teaching a bit of English myself although purely on an informal basis and I'm pretty clueless about explaining any of the finer grammatical points."

"I didn't know much about any of that either when I first started," replied the man who introduced himself as Barry. "Maybe I knew what a past participle was but I had to buy books to try to work out what things such as subjunctive and accusative meant – such terminology was a complete foreign language of its own."

As he was speaking he had picked up a leather cup containing five dice which he now shook and tipped the contents on to the surface of the bar.

"Look at that," he said, "Four aces straight away!"

The barman drew a glass of beer for Edwin who watched on as the dice game continued. It was the best out of five with the loser buying the next round of drinks.

Tommie won and took a break from the game for a bit of conversation.

"Juan," he called to the barman, "Me da una copa más cuando puedes."

It turned out that he also drank a variety of Aniseed liqueur although a different brand from that favoured by Charlie – and he drank the stuff neat and without ice cubes.

Edwin allowed himself to be initiated into the dice playing and, due to beginner's luck, ended up winning the most numbers of games throughout the evening. There was no skill involved other than occasionally having to decide whether it was worthwhile hanging on to whatever score were made on the initial throws or taking a chance to gain a few more points whilst risking the whole lot. Nevertheless it made a change from an evening on the pinball machine down the road at the Bar Pigalle. Interesting how the social life in Madrid seemed to revolve around the bars and that the way to stimulate one's mind were either chucking dice onto a bar top or indulging in several hour's worth of electronic bagatelle. But then, of course, there was also the general chit chat that went with it – albeit in English at a time when Edwin wanted to improve his Spanish.

"We're in here every night," said Barry, "Unless we're still in the litre bar a few yards further down the street."

"The litre bar?" questioned Edwin.

"Yes, it's the only place in Madrid where for eight pesetas you can get a full litre of ice cold draught lager served in a giant one litre beer glass."

"That sounds like a good deal," said Edwin, "although in the heat it might get warm too quickly."

"You just need to knock it back fast," replied Tommie.

FREDDIE DIDN'T RETURN TO the hostal that night. When Edwin awoke in the morning he saw that his bed hadn't been slept in. He wasn't unduly worried because Madrid was a relatively safe city. Under General Franco Spain was something of a police state and constant surveillance kept things tightly under the control of law and order. Freddie was probably in the company of his musical friends.

But the following day there was still no sign of him. Edwin went into class for the morning and then returned by metro to the city centre. Then, as he was making his way past the large departmental store called El Corte Inglés he spotted Freddie's mop of long blond hair coming towards him.

"What time of day do you call this?" said Edwin as they neared each other.

"Que pasa?" replied Freddie with what seemed to be a huge smirk across his face.

"I guessed that you'd show up sooner or later," continued Edwin, "but where on earth have you been for the past couple of days?"

Freddie looked at Edwin quizzically and then repeated "Que pasa?" before bursting into a fit of uncontrollable laughter. At first Edwin presumed Freddie to be drunk although there was something particularly unusual about his manner and the dilated pupils of his eyes. The explanation soon followed.

"I'm as high as a kite," he said, "Goo-goo-barabajagal."

"You've taken some kind of drugs?" asked Edwin alarmed.

"I've met some really beautiful American people down at the Plaza de Santa Anna and we have been smoking hash together," replied Freddie.

"I see," replied Edwin, "Well, I don't know about you but I am going for a cheap bite to eat at the El Centro restaurant. You can come along too if you like." He wondered whether an intake of food might help sober a person up from drug use as it sometimes did from the effects of alcohol. It was the first time he'd ever seen someone in a drug induced state and he didn't like the dreamy looking effect it had had on Freddy who was now describing the beautiful colours of the cars in the street.

Inside the restaurant the situation got worse. Freddie couldn't stop asking "Que pasa?" to other people who were sat at tables throughout the dining area and he then picked up a newspaper, rolled it up into the conical shape of a megaphone and proceeded to make trumpet-like noises through it.

"Come off it, Freddie. Quieten it down a bit. People don't appreciate it," said Edwin.

Through his rolled up newspaper Freddie then started to chant the words "F*** brain Franco! F*** brain Franco!"

"For goodness sake shut up," pleaded Edwin, "You'll have us arrested if you carry on like this."

And then it was back to "Que pasa?" all over again.

Edwin devoured a bowl of thick stew of pinto beans followed by a couple of fried eggs and chipped potatoes. Freddie didn't want to eat anything but at least managed to down a cup of coffee. He also pulled out a small Spanish matchbox which he opened and proudly showed Edwin something that looked like a largish lump of glue.

"It is cannabis resin," exclaimed Freddie, "I scored it!"

THE FOLLOWING DAY FREDDIE was seemingly back to his normal self and acted as if nothing out of the ordinary had taken place. He said that he had discovered a bar a couple of blocks south of the Puerta del Sol where a lot of like-minded people tended to hang out and that because many of them had enjoyed his folk songs he had every intention of returning there. It was called the Cervecería Alemana which even he knew meant German beer bar.

"But there's nothing particularly German about it," he explained, "It's just a large Spanish bar full of a lot of interesting young people – mainly Americans. You should come down and take a look for yourself."

"Well, maybe I'll come down for a beer," said Edwin, "although I'm content enough with this end of town."

"Well I guess the pinball machine and the company of Charlie are OK in their own way but sometimes it's good to experience something a little different." said Freddie, "I'm going down there tomorrow afternoon and you can come along with me if you like."

"OK, after class but I'll probably only stay for a short time."

The Plaza de Santa Anna was reached by narrow streets on the other side of the Puerta del Sol and it looked rather run down. The Cervecería Alemana itself was shabby on the outside with its large window frames of peeled varnish. In a thick fog of cigarette smoke the interior consisted of one large dimly lit old-fashioned room containing numerous marble-topped tables around which a lot of scruffy looking individuals were sprawled about the place. Edwin and Freddie stepped inside and made their way to a vacant table tuning in to an array of different accents as they did so. The range seemed to be from be from Queen's English to cockney and from Liverpudlian to Scottish but there was also American and Canadian drawl with a sprinkling of Australian, Swedish and French for good measure and some occasional Spanish. Almost everybody there had unkempt hair and was dressed in colourful clothing in keeping with their hippy culture. Freddie's outfit blended in well. A young American blonde with no shoes approached them at the table where they were sitting.

"Hey, Freddie!" she said with wide-eyed enthusiasm, "Great to see you again! Are you going to play here again today?"

"I don't have my guitar with me right now," replied Freddie, "Maybe some other time."

"Well gee, I really enjoyed your music, especially those home-grown compositions of yours" she continued, "and that was really cool the other night though I haven't seen anything of Dan and Donna since then. Have you?"

Freddie shrugged his shoulders. "I haven't seen anyone at all from the other night yet," he said, "but they're bound to drop in here sooner or later."

"Yeah, everyone gravitates back here – it's such an in place to hang out in."

"By the way, this is a friend of mine, Edwin, and – I'm terribly sorry but I've forgotten your name."

"It's Carla," she replied, "I'm pleased to meet you, Edwin. Any friend of Freddie's is a friend of mine – even if he can't remember my name."

A waiter then came over. There was a dark beer or cerveza negra available on draught. They both ordered one thinking it might make a pleasant change from the usual brew but found that although it might have resembled a glass of headless Guinness, it didn't taste much different to the original Spanish lager. Meanwhile Carla seemed content enough with a Coca-Cola and a packet of Winston cigarettes.

A very tall young Englishman with a mop of frizzy hair called across from a nearby table.

"Say man, any of you got some chocolate?"

It struck Edwin as being an unusual request until Carla revealed its cryptic meaning when she replied, "No, Jeff, but Sparky will be coming down soon so we should all be able to score some from him then."

She then asked Freddie and Edwin if they'd be joining her for a smoke later that evening.

"I will," replied Freddie, "although I think Edwin mentioned that he'd got to go and meet someone someplace."

Edwin was grateful for such a diplomatic way of getting out of the situation rather than being put on the spot.

"Yes, I can only stay here for a short while because I've arranged to meet up with a friend up on the other side of town," he said.

"Well, never mind," said Carla, "there's always another day."

A smartly dressed Afro-American passed by their table and greeted both Freddie and Carla by name.

"Say, I just landed some work as a film extra here in Madrid," he said, "There'd maybe be some opportunities there for you too."

"That's cool," said Carla, "Only thing is, I can't act."

"You wouldn't need to," he replied. "They are just non-speaking parts like crowd scenes and the like.

They were soon joined by five more Americans. Two bearded guys were talking about changing their accommodation because where they were staying was too hot and noisy. Three girls in tie-dyed tee-shirts sat there dreamily looking on and spoke of their recent trip to Italy and a forthcoming visit to Morocco. They were backpackers and for them Spain was just one part of doing Europe. Every now and again the conversation turned to places where they could gather in safety to smoke pot and whether anyone was interested in tripping out on acid that evening. Carla knew of someone who had his own apartment.

Edwin politely excused himself, telling Freddie that he would see him later back at the hostel. As he made his way back across the town centre up the Calle Montera towards the Gran Vía, Edwin felt shocked that people could be so enthusiastic about mind-changing drugs. He found the whole idea scary. He'd read about harmful effects. He wasn't impressed by the state that Freddie had got himself into a couple of days ago. He'd heard that it could permanently change peoples' personalities. He knew that people had sometimes died from it. Hadn't one of the Rolling Stones recently gone that way? The fact that pop groups indulged in it presumably added to its appeal like some new must-try fashion. He shuddered at the thought.

Although predictable, an evening spent with Charlie and his bunch of cronies seemed to represent a far safer social life. First a cheap meal at the Copatisan restaurant and later the usual route through the general seediness of the Calle de la Ballesta to the Bar Pigalle where, over a few drinks, they would play the pinball machine and make stimulating conversation with the others who frequented the place. Tomorrow was Wednesday and he would go again to the Spanish family in Lista to give another English lesson.

CHAPTER FIVE

AT THE BEGINNING OF October Freddie suddenly announced that he intended to move out of the hostel and into a shared apartment with two other lads. He asked Edwin if he might be interested in joining them.

"It's got its own kitchen and its own bathroom," he said enthusiastically, "and splitting the rent between four would work out even cheaper that staying here in the hostal."

"Whereabouts is it?" asked Edwin.

"It's in a place called Ciudad Lineal," he replied.

Edwin recalled the name, not least because it was one of the end stations of the Metro network and appeared as such on the destination boards of one of the lines.

"It must be at one of the outer extremities of Madrid," he said, "What about all the commuting time it would take to get in and out of the centre of town?"

"Well, there would be a bit of extra travelling, yes, but on the other hand Metro trains are pretty frequent and, after all, the flat rate fare of two pesetas to travel anywhere in Madrid means that there'll be no additional expense involved – even for getting to class at the university," he replied.

"Who are the other people moving in with you?" asked Edwin.

"Well, there's Hugo a frightfully English chap and there's also an American guy called Hank who also plays a guitar. The three of us are going over there to check it out this afternoon and if you like you can come along too if you're not doing anything else."

"Ok," said Edwin, "I guess there's no harm in taking a look but that doesn't mean that I'm necessarily going to move out there. I kind of like the convenience of being here in the centre of the city."

CIUDAD LINEAL WAS QUITE literally the end of the line. The surface of its main street had no tarmac but was plain earth and there were even a couple of horses tied to a post in front of one of the stores. There was, however, a small cinema. It had taken them three quarters of an hour on the Metro and there was now a fifteen minute walk along the Avenida de Arturo Soria. A tramline ran along this stretch which they figured might come in useful. Eventually they arrived at a small side street called Calle de Fernando Caro where the apartment was located

The Spanish landlord was already there. He ushered them in to his modern ground floor apartment through an entrance hall with a bathroom and toilet off to the left before emerging into a reasonable sized lounge with an adjoining kitchen. On the right hand side were doors to the two bedrooms, both of which were equipped with two single beds. Beyond the lounge a glass sliding door led out to a terracotta-tiled patio that could be lit at night, as demonstrated by the landlord who insisted on switching the light on and off several times as if to prove the point. The apartment was fully furnished and equipped with the basic necessities of cooking utensils, crockery and cutlery.

"It's a bloody sight better than slumming it in a pensión," commented Freddie.

"I should say so" agreed Hugo the frightfully English lad, "This has got a bit of class about it." He turned to Edwin, "What do you think?"

"The apartment itself is nice enough," said Edwin, "but the location is a bit remote"

"What about Calefacción?" the American asked the landlord, apparently having added this new word to his erstwhile limited Spanish vocabulary.

"Calefacción, si!" replied the landlord, indicating an electric wall radiator.

None of the three Englishmen could understand why anybody should be talking about heating facilities in Madrid where they'd been sweltering in the heat ever since they had first arrived. They had yet to experience a Madrid winter.

After another look around the flat the landlord asked the American if they could now go ahead and formalise its rental.

"Everyone in agreement that we take this place on?" asked Freddie.

Hugo and Hank both said "Yes" in perfect unison and then everyone stood looking at Edwin.

"Well, I wouldn't mind a bit of time to think it over," said Edwin, "I mean the flat is nice but we are rather a long way out of town."

"The thing is, the landlord wants us to agree to take it today because he has other potential tenants who will take it if we don't" explained Hank. "Three of us could take it but obviously a fourth person would bring everyone's share of the rent down to 1,250 Pesetas a month."

The landlord was looking at them and Edwin didn't quite know how to respond. Maybe it would be a good idea to move out of the rundown hostal and into the relative luxury of an apartment. And yet the decision seemed too sudden.

"I won't have any money until I get to the bank tomorrow morning," he faltered.

"Well, said Hank, I'd be able to lend you that amount of money until then if you want to share this place with us."

There was a long pause. Freddie glanced at Edwin and smiled, "Sorry this is putting you on the spot," he apologised, "but if for whatever reason you don't like it you can always move back into a hostal again."

"Well, OK," said Edwin at last, "I am willing to give it a go."

"Great!"said Hank. And with that he pulled out two thousand and five hundred pesetas from his wallet and Hugo and Freddie each produced their share and the total of five thousand pesetas was handed to the landlord.

"Pues, muy bien" he beamed, "y ahorra hay solamente un pocito de document-ación para hacer y después yo voy a dar ustedes las llaves."

"What is he on about?" asked Hugo.

"He's going to give us the keys to the place in a minute," replied Edwin.

The landlord produced a printed sheet of paper from his briefcase and asked which of them should be the signatory. He looked first to Hank as the oldest amongst them.

"If it's all the same to you, I'd rather not be the person who signs this," said Hank. "As you know I shall be here only until the end of January whereas you guys will be staying on several months longer than that as well as getting another fourth person to make up the numbers so it follows that it should be one of you who signs it.

"Why can't we all sign the rent agreement?" asked Edwin. He then asked the same question is Spanish.

"Necesito la firma solamente de una persona." replied the landlord, "a mi igual quién."

"Your Spanish is better than the rest of us," said Hugo to Edwin, "You are the obvious choice to sign."

Slightly flattered by this notion, and yet in complete naivety as to what the implications of being the sole signatory might be, Edwin took the landlord's pen and signed his name on the dotted line and then, as instructed, wrote it out in capital letters on the line underneath. The landlord thanked him and said that he would come on the 15th day of each month to collect 5,000 pesetas of rent.

Four sets of keys were then handed over and the landlord departed and left them to it. The following day a friend of Hank who had a car obligingly helped transport the four of them and their suitcases from their respective guest houses and out to their new flat.

THEY SOON GOT USED to commuting back and forth. Edwin even discovered a different route to travel to the university by tram which completely avoided passing through the central hub of Madrid. It involved changing in a place called Cuatro Caminos and then continuing by means of a further antiquated tram complete with its wooden seats. Everybody else was Spanish on these routes and Edwin's head of blond hair and blue eyes was quite conspicuous.

Every Tuesday morning he was able to collect money from the bank and on those occasions he would take the Metro into the centre of Madrid. It was invariably combined that with a visit to the cafeteria in the underpass at Sevilla Metro Station for a quick cup of coffee and a brief chat across the counter with his waitress friend, Maria Carmen.

He still continued to meet up with her every Friday afternoon after she finished work when they would again walk through the streets and public parks of Madrid together. On one such occasion they had arranged to meet each other at one end of the Puerta del Sol. Edwin arrived at the appointed hour and saw that Maria Carmen was already there and chatting to what appeared to be a gypsy woman with a maroon coloured shawl and wearing gold earrings. It turned out to be her mother. She introduced her to Edwin.

The elderly woman took Edwin's hand and fixed her eyes upon him. A smile then broke on her bronze wrinkled face which revealed two missing front teeth.

"Ingles? Ingles?" she questioned in husky enthusiasm. "y a ti te gusta mi hija?"

"Mama!" cautioned Maria Carmen.

The three of them went into a nearby cafeteria and, over large cups of milky coffee, the mother persisted.

"Entonces, tu quieres casar con mi hija?" she enquired as to whether Edwin intended to marry her daughter, Maria Carmen.

Edwin didn't want to offend this sincere woman but at his tender age of seventeen any idea of marriage simply wasn't on his immediate agenda.

The mother clapped her hands together and smiled at him. "Y mi Maria Carmen puede ir a Inglaterra para vivir contigo. ¡Que maravillosa!" she continued. She'd obviously got their whole future fully worked out.

Eventually the mother departed on her way and left them to it.

"I had told her about you. She is just curious," explained Maria Carmen in Spanish. "I couldn't stop her coming."

"No hay problema," replied Edwin momentarily intrigued by what had happened and again marvelling at Maria Carmen's good looks and pale complexion, "I enjoyed meeting her."

"We are a very poor family," said Maria Carmen. "We live in that place in Campamento and my mother is determined that we children should do better in our lives."

EVENINGS BACK AT THE apartment in Ciudad Lineal proved to be a little on the quiet side and there was often the urge to go out and explore the surrounding community. The trouble with that was that it didn't have very much to offer. A small grocery store and two bars were within easy walking distance but that was about it. The rest of the area was purely residential and consisted of blocks of apartments and detached houses set behind entrance gates. However, the four of them discovered that if they scrambled down a grass bank next to a bridge that crossed the busy main road leading out to Madrid Airport they could gain access to quite a lively cafeteria located in the back of a petrol station.

No one knew much about cooking. Edwin made a watery stew which none of them could eat because it was far too salty and the cubes of meat had ended up like hardened lumps of rubber. Hank tried to make some scrambled eggs but succeeded in making a terrible mess and burning the pan. Freddie and Hugo didn't cook anything at all but they washed their clothing in the bath and, in the absence of any soap powder, left them to soak there for days on end. Edwin began to miss the hustle and bustle of the centre of Madrid just as Freddie was missing his circle of friends at the Cervecería Alemana. In such circumstances it soon became the norm to go into the centre of Madrid most evenings and to catch the last Metro back or, failing that, share a taxi back out to the apartment.

One evening Edwin met up with Charlie at the Bar Dénia.

"I've been invited to a drinks party in Avenida de America tomorrow evening and I was wondering if you'd like to come along" said Charlie, "It's likely to be quite a sophisticated do."

"Well, that sounds as if it might be a laugh," replied Edwin. "Whose party is it?"

"It's Elizabeth Delaney's. She's an eccentric American multi-millionaire who inherited her late father's wealth from Hollywood. She's been living in Madrid for longer than I have and quite by chance I happened to run into her again a few days ago and she invited me over to a party at her rather plush dwelling place. It kicks off at six o'clock."

"Are you sure it would be OK for me to come too?" asked Edwin.

"Yes, just tag along with me and it'll be fine," replied Charlie.

ELIZABETH DELANEY PROVED TO be an overbearing, loudmouthed American of the kind that Edwin had only ever seen in films – and even that was playacting.

Yet this was real life. A Spanish maid had shown Charlie and Edwin in to an elegantly decorated lounge with plush furnishings beneath a chandelier. Various guests were dotted around, all of them American and of an older generation.

Tumblers of a particularly potent concoction of rum-based eggnog were being served on silver trays. Charlie and Edwin each took one and sipped on its frothy content as they stood at one side of the room.

"Well now, if that ain't good old Charlie Tennyson! It's damn good of you to have come along!" cried the hostess, "Oh, and who is this that you've brought along with you?"

Charlie introduced Edwin.

"OK, just you make yourself at home and make sure you grab yourself another of those eggnogs whenever you like. There'll be music starting soon" she said.

"It's a very nice drink," said Charlie.

"Yes. It's something that my butler, Marmaduke, likes to prepare from time to time. It's about the only reason I keep him on, the goddamn good-for-nothing faggot."

An elderly gentleman who had been seated in a leather armchair then rose and was hovering near them.

"Oh and please let me introduce you both to Woof," said Elizabeth, "Hey there Woof! These are two of my English friends, Charlie and Edwin."

"Charmed to meet you", replied the elderly man with a similar sounding American drawl "and what brings the two of you to Spain might I ask?"

"I've lived here for the past seven years," replied Charlie, "and Edwin is here as a student."

"I see," said the man and then turning to Edwin, "Tell me, young man, when it comes to matters of love relationships what is your preference – to have a man or a woman?"

"A woman of course," replied Edwin spontaneously, wondering whether, in addition to having such a stupid name as Woof, the old man was completely off his rocker.

"Oh, I see" replied the man whose face dropped as he returned to the comfort of his leather armchair.

Edwin quizzically caught Charlie's eye. "Bloody old queen," whispered Charlie.

Some background music then started up provided by a Moroccan man playing on a box-type stringed instrument and another round of eggnog was served.

Edwin sensed that he had nothing whatsoever in common with any of the guests although he did strike up a conversation with a couple from Haiti. Apart from that both he and Charlie got stuck into a spread of food laid out in one of the adjoining rooms, feasting on lobster and skewered lamb with coriander yogurt.

The butler, Marmaduke, turned out to be as effeminate a man as Edwin had ever met and was someone who snorted whenever he laughed.

"Oh, do help yourselves to another glass of eggnog my dears! You'll soon forget about all your worries and cares" – snort, snort, snort.

Edwin confided in Charlie, "If this gathering is meant to represent the height of sophistication, please remind me never to become sophisticated."

"I know," replied Charlie, "I've got caught up in such circles before. I'll tell you what. Let's have one more of those eggnog things for the road then I think we can politely excuse ourselves and head off to somewhere that's a bit more to our taste."

"Yes, like a down to earth, spit and sawdust bar with no airs and graces and where you can get a glass of anis and I can get myself a cold beer," said Edwin.

"Precisely," agreed Charlie.

EDWIN KEPT UP HIS weekly visits to the family in Lista. Isolina was making moderate improvement with her English. Such evenings were always pleasant and for Edwin they perfectly captivated the Spanish family's way of life. Their conversation covered all manner of things with the single exception of politics. On a couple of occasions when Edwin had mentioned that he'd heard rumours of unrest taking place in Madrid the mother would cautiously put one finger in front of her mouth and suggest that it was not wise to speak of such things.

"Ni habla!" was the expression that she used.

Sometimes, by means of a contrast to the city centre, Edwin would visit the long stretch of pleasant tree-lined walkway sandwiched between lanes of traffic and known as The Castellana. It was a popular stroll and, in many respects, was a more pleasant avenue that the Gran Vía. Part way down Edwin discovered the Cafeteria Gijon where Madrid's actors tended to hang out. It was a relatively inexpensive establishment and yet far more sophisticated than the more centrally located places that he ordinarily frequented.

But by now it was getting cold in Madrid. One evening Hugo and Edwin decided to go for an evening walk in the direction of Madrid Airport to see how far they could get to it. Although it lay on the same side of the city as their apartment, it was seven or eight kilometres further out. As they left their door snowflakes began to fall.

"You don't normally associate Spain with this kind of thing," said Hugo.

"No, there's never a mention about it in the holiday brochures. I don't know which is worse, extreme heat or extreme cold," replied Edwin turning up the lapels of his jacket.

As they walked along one side of the road the snowfall became considerably thicker. After several hours the airport became within their sight but because it was three o'clock in the morning they realised that it was time to turn around and make the trek back.

Later that day they went for a lunchtime snack at the petrol station cafeteria. They got chatting with a group of several young Spaniards there and invited them back for a drink at the apartment. Half a dozen of them came along and Edwin, who was still tired after the previous night's walk, succeeded in falling asleep at one end of the settee. When he woke up the party seemed still to be in full swing although on further inspection it was with entirely different people. Four hours had elapsed and the original guests had all departed. In the meantime Freddie had returned home with a group of his mates from the Cervecería Alemana. Music was blaring forth from a portable record player.

If you're going to San Francisco
Be sure to wear some flowers in your hair
If you're going to San Francisco
You're going to meet some gentle people there

The shoeless girl Carla was there, looking half-detached from reality and saying how everything was either cool or groovy. Edwin poured himself a glass of milk from the fridge which he quickly downed and then went out for a walk in the direction of the small township of Ciudad Lineal. There he entered the warmth of a local bar and ate a dish of paella. It was already quite late but he was in no hurry to return to the apartment with its intrusion of characters.

He lit a cigarette and quietly reflected on his current lifestyle and wondered what the future held in store. Although he enjoyed the Madrid experience and felt that he had gained a lot through being there, there remained the huge question as to what he would eventually do with his life and things such as what kind of career he would settle into. He wondered if there was such a thing as fate or whether it was completely up to individuals to go out into the world and make things happen. He felt cut out for great things but didn't know what.

The train of thought was interrupted by a short man who had been lurking near the counter and was clearly in a semi-drunken stupor. He approached Edwin whilst loudly proclaiming that he was not Spanish but something called 'Valenciano' from Valencia.

"But everyone knows that Valencia is in Spain," commented Edwin in Spanish.

The man hit the roof, "Pero No!" he exclaimed. "No somos parte de España. Somos Valencianos de Valencia."

"Have it your own way," said Edwin in English.

"Cuidado con la boca!" shouted the man.

He could already see the fervour with which the man was expressing himself and didn't what to get into an unnecessary argument about something that he, in any case, didn't give two hoots about. Fortunately the man then staggered out of the premises.

Through the front window Edwin then spotted Hugo on the other side of the street and he went to the entrance and called him over.

Hugo evidently hadn't been impressed with Freddie's hippy friends at the apartment either and had slipped out alone and taken the metro into the centre of Madrid. By coincidence he had encountered Charlie at the Cafeteria Manila in the company of Elizabeth the American millionaire and her butler Marmaduke.

"They are a weird American duo," he said taking a seat at Edwin's table, "I mean the butler is camp out of his brain and she seems to be completely off-her-head but put together as a double act they are quite entertaining. They've invited me around to their apartment for a drinks evening next week."

"Rather you than me," replied Edwin, "I felt totally out of place at their recent party no matter how luxurious the building might have been."

"Was that a party where they had some Moroccan guy playing a musical instrument?" asked Hugo.

"Yes, that's right. He provided background music throughout most of the evening. Why?"

"Well apparently he normally plays in a club from where she poached him to play at her event. But how much do you think she paid him?" he asked.

"I wouldn't have a clue," said Edwin, "but if he is a professional musician and she is a loaded millionaire I imagine that she would have paid him quite handsomely."

"Not at all," replied Hugo, "All she gave him for his entire evening's performance was fifty pesetas!"

"You're joking?" said Edwin.

"No, it's perfectly true. You can ask Charlie. He was equally disgusted. Apparently that woman is so strange that she does things like that – and she's also a racist and looks down on Moroccans."

"Well, that doubly confirms my scepticism about getting close to any of that lot," said Edwin.

After a couple of drinks they walked back home to their apartment. Although most of Freddie's friends had departed three of them were asleep in the lounge.

CHRISTMAS WAS APPROACHING AND Madrid was bitterly cold. Ciudad Lineal already had a thin layer of snow and the ice-cold winds from the surrounding mountains seemed to penetrate Edwin's jacket. Every now and again Edwin would think of his family back in England and wonder what his two younger brothers were up to. It crossed his mind that maybe he could pay them a visit. After all, there was soon going be a break at the university and classes wouldn't be resuming until mid-January. Perhaps he could go for a visit to England shortly after Christmas although the fare would be somewhat expensive. Mind you, he thought, there was always the possibility of hitch-hiking. If he could get up through Spain and then the entire length of France to Calais, the ferry fare across to Dover would be cheap enough.

But there was another problem. When the landlord came to collect the rent in the middle of December only half of it was available. Hugo and Edwin paid their share but Freddie had spontaneously decided to go to the south of Spain and across on a ferry to Morocco for a week and still hadn't returned. Also Hank had done a disappearing act although his possessions were still there in his room. Edwin and Hugo did their best to explain the situation to the landlord who had reluctantly agreed to collect the remaining half payment in the first week of the New Year.

"Let's hope there'll both be back by then" Edwin said to Hugo.

"They jolly well should be," he replied, "in fact it wouldn't surprise me if they didn't walk in the door any day now so as to be in time for Christmas."

"Talking of Christmas, I see that one can get a turkey at a reasonable price from that little indoor market just down from Noviciado Metro station. Do you think we should get one and have a crack a preparing our own Christmas Day meal here?"

"That sounds like an excellent idea. Especially if we can cook all the other bits and pieces that go with it like roast potatoes and carrots and Brussels sprouts and gravy," replied Hugo, "Any idea how to make a bread sauce?"

"None whatsoever," replied Edwin, "and I don't know about stuffing either although chestnuts seem to be in plentiful supply around here. Some of the Spanish sausages look the same as chipolatas."

"But I bet you can't get a Christmas pudding in Madrid," said Hugo, "That's a nuisance really because there's more than enough brandy to make a good sauce for it."

That afternoon, as they walked home from the metro station, they were momentarily distracted by a buzz of American conversation going on between two girls standing at a bus stop. It was unusual to find anyone other than Spaniards in the outer suburbs of Madrid but it turned out that both of them were from American Forces families and lived on a nearby American Air Base. Hugo gave them the address of the apartment and invited them over that evening. To his surprise they both showed up. At around midnight Edwin walked one of them down to a taxi rank in Ciudad Lineal and wished her Happy Christmas as she departed. The other girl remained with Hugo until the following morning.

BOTH FREDDIE AND HANK arrived back at the apartment a couple of days before Christmas. During his Moroccan trip it transpired that Freddie had simply forgotten all about his rent. Meanwhile Hank had been sidetracked by a French girl for a couple of weeks. They both agreed to settle the amount owing with the landlord in the New Year as had been arranged.

That evening Edwin and Freddie went into the centre of Madrid to make a circular tour of the various hangouts to see what kind of festive spirit was on offer whilst Hank caught up on some sleep. In the meantime Hugo set off for his drinks evening at the eccentric American millionaire's place.

People in the Gran Vía were wrapped up in heavy overcoats. There were no more outdoor tables and chairs lining the pavements. They were glad to step into the warmth of La Luna bar where they were not surprised to find Tommie and Barry still propping up the bar just as they had been the last time they were there.

"Hallo, you two. You look like half frozen to death," said Barry as they entered, "but you're just in time to join us for another game of dice."

"How very original," said Edwin.

"I Know, I know, it's all we ever do," said Tommie.

Just then a lot of shouting could be heard from the street outside and it seemed that something was going on out there. All of a sudden swarms of police were everywhere. Three uniformed officers burst into the bar and after a thorough look around ran back outside again.

"What on earth was all that about?" Tommie asked the barman.

"I don't know," he replied, "but they're obviously looking for someone."

Four middle-aged men then entered the bar and passed quickly along its length to somewhere where they would be out of sight. More police then became visible through the window.

A regular customer then stepped inside and explained that a notorious Spanish criminal was on the run and had been sighted a little further along the road of Calle de La Luna, together with some of his dangerous gang members.

Freddie then confided to Edwin in a quiet voice, "When the police burst in like that for one dreadful moment I thought they'd come for me."

"But you're hardly a Spanish criminal," retorted Edwin.

"No," he replied, "but I do happen to have a little souvenir from Morocco contained in a matchbox in my jacket pocket."

"You surely don't carry that stuff around with you?" whispered Edwin.

"Not normally but I promised to sell it to the black American guy, Jed, at the Cervecería Alemena later on this evening."

"But you've been stopped and searched by the police before so you must know that that is a tremendous risk" said Edwin.

"I know," he replied, "in fact, if you can hang around here for a while I shall nip off and deliver it and be back in less than an hour."

"What about all the police outside?" asked Edwin.

"Well if they're after some notorious Spanish criminal they are hardly going to show much interest in a blond Anglo-Saxon this evening," he said.

And with that, he politely excused himself, stepped out into the cold night air and headed off through the town.

"Where has he gone?" enquired Tommie, "It's doesn't look very safe out there and in any case I thought he was joining us for dice."

"He's just gone to say hello to a friend but he's coming back later," replied Edwin. It was about the only explanation he could think of.

The barman, Juan, poured three glasses of Anis del Mono and gave them on the house to the three remaining Englishmen.

True to his word, Freddie arrived back at the Luna Bar some forty minutes later. He looked pleased with himself and told Edwin that at least he'd now got enough money to pay his share of the rent.

They stayed until midnight before departing for Bar Pigalle where Charlie and the Egyptian diplomat, Nizam, were playing the pinball machine. At closing time, they took a taxi to back to Ciudad Lineal.

On their arrival back at the flat, the lights were on and they found a very distraught Hugo pacing up and down.

"What on earth is the matter with you?" asked Edwin.

"That American guy Marmaduke is an absolute bastard!" replied Hugo.

"Why, what's happened?" asked Freddie, "we thought you went to a drinks party.

"That Marmaduke is a bastard!" repeated Hugo.

"OK, but what has actually happened?" asked Edwin,

"Look at this!" said Hugo, who undid the buttons of his shirt to reveal three red score marks across his chest, "This, amongst other things, is what that American bastard, Marmaduke, did!"

"You must report it to the police," said Edwin.

"No, please let's not involve the police," replied Hugo, "even though the man is an out and out bastard."

"How did it happen?" asked Freddie.

"I'd rather not go into details," replied Hugo, "but I can tell you that I wish I'd never ever encountered such a perverted bastard."

THE CHRISTMAS MEAL WORKED out remarkably well, considering that no one had been sure how long a turkey should be roasted although because it was large they guessed that six and a half hours would be about right. Edwin's experimental home-made chestnut stuffing and the bread sauce were complimented as were the roast potatoes and vegetables cooked by Hank and Hugo. Freddie hadn't been involved in any of the culinary activity based on his declaration that "too many cooks might spoil the giblet broth" and so he took charge of the drinks instead.

The four of them sat together at the little table and the occasion was as formal as they could make it.

"Christmas lunch with all the trimmings – and still snowing outside," said Hugo, "I think we've got the right atmosphere here even without a tree and presents."

"In any case, I've heard that in Spain they don't give presents until the sixth of January which is to commemorate the Three Kings bringing their gifts to the baby Jesus." said Hank.

"Ever wonder what happened to that gift of gold?" asked Freddie. "I mean that must have been worth a fair bit and so they could have afforded to move somewhere a bit more comfortable that a stable."

"Yes, but then we would have been denied half of the iconic pictures," said

Edwin, "It wouldn't look the same.

"The whole nativity story has an air of mystery about it and it's rather special," said Hugo.

"It's the words to some of the carols that get to me," said Freddie, especially that bit about the baby awakes and no crying he makes. I can't believe that for one moment any more that I can believe in the biological possibility of a virgin birth. And that's despite my having had a Catholic upbringing."

IN THE FIRST WEEK of January Edwin embarked on his plan of a short visit to England by means of hitchhiking. On a crisp morning he clambered down the now familiar grass bank at the side of the bridge to the main road below where he put out his thumb and by a stroke of good luck was almost immediately picked up by someone who took him all the way to Zaragoza. That was followed by two further lifts throughout the day and by nightfall he ended up in the town of Huesca close to the Pyrenees where he stayed overnight in a pensión. The next morning a further lift took him up a mountain road to a small village called Biescas but as there was not much traffic passing through there he continued on foot in the crunchy snow and eventually arrived at the French border. Once through passport control he managed to get a lift which descended to the town of Pau. By then it was already late afternoon. At a petrol station Edwin noticed a metallic Michelin map on one of its walls and he walked over to have a look at it. He could see that his most direct route would be to Paris via Toulouse and Limoges. He asked the petrol pump attendant on the forecourt if he was on the right road to Paris and received a look of incredulity.

"Oui, c'est la route pour Paris," confirmed the man, "Mais, monsieur c'est pas possible maintenant. Ca c'est tres loin d'ici."

Undeterred by such scepticism Edwin simply said "Merci beaucoup" and stuck his thumb out once again. He was rewarded by an immediate lift from a French businessman who happened to be on his way home to Orléans, which, as luck had it, was right on Edwin's intended route and not that far short of Paris. But, even though the road was good and the car driven at considerable speed, it was a long way. The man spoke a bit of English. When they stopped off for a coffee break he made a phone call to his wife, asking her to set an extra place for dinner that evening. They arrived at his house shortly before midnight. There, together with the couple, Edwin dined on the rarest beef that he'd ever had in his life and was given a bed for the night in a spare room.

The following morning, after a shower and a petit dejeuner of coffee and croissants, Edwin felt optimistic about the possibility of making it back to England that same day. The Frenchman drove him out to the main road leading northwards towards Paris from where a further day's hitchhiking continued. Two lifts that morning got him somewhere close to the French capital after which a truck driver then took him on a ring road that skimmed around the outskirts of Paris and left him somewhere to the north at a turn off that was signposted for Calais. Although on course to his destination Edwin hadn't realised the distance through the county of Pas de Calais to be quite so far. Lifts throughout that afternoon were few and far between and only for very short distances. He thought that if he was lucky he could probably reach Calais later that evening. By about eight o'clock he'd got to a town called Beauvais where a couple in a land rover stopped to pick him up. They were intrigued by the fact that Edwin was English and chattered away to him non-stop in French, even though he couldn't understand much of what they were saying. They apparently had a friend in a place called Not-An-Gam, and it took Edwin ages to work out that they were trying to say Nottingham.

The French lady sandwiched in the middle put an arm around her husband on her left and around Edwin on her right as they continued the journey to Amiens. There they dropped Edwin off and wished him bon chance in reaching his destination of Calais.

It was already dark and there wasn't much traffic on the road that evening. For the first quarter of an hour the few cars that did happen to come along simply passed him by. Then, however, another vehicle came along and pulled over and Edwin then saw that it was the same Land Rover and the same couple who had just dropped him off. They invited him to climb back in again. They said that they couldn't bear the thought of the possibility of him not being able to get another lift that evening and had decided to drive him the remainder of the journey to the cross-channel ferry terminal in Calais. They gave him a visiting card with their address in Amiens and Edwin scribbled his address in England on the back of a cigarette pack.

The ferry departed at eleven-thirty and because of the one-hour time difference the 90-minute crossing meant that it arrived in Dover at midnight English time. Edwin intended to travel the remaining part of his journey home by train even though the next departure wasn't going to be until 4.30 in the morning. However, a station official at Dover Harbour Railway Station showed Edwin to the waiting train and told him he was welcome to get into the warmth of one of the carriages, get his head down and get some sleep.

Edwin arrived back at his family home the following morning. Rather than take everybody by surprise he had first given them a call from a phone booth at Waterloo Railway Station. One of his brothers walked to Weybridge Station to meet his train.

It was something of a culture shock to be back in the familiar surroundings of England once again. It also felt strange not to have to mentally translate words and sentences into English because everything was already being expressed in English. Even when he purchased a newspaper he had begun by asking for it in Spanish but had quickly corrected himself. He noticed that in a crowd situation where people were talking simultaneously it automatically sounded as though they were all speaking in Spanish until he listened a bit more carefully and realised it to be English.

It felt good to be home. Edwin explained that it was just a short stay and that he needed to be back in Madrid in a week's time when his class at the university would recommence. He had already worked out that he could just about scrape together a one-way air fare.

On learning that Edwin was back on a visit, Freddie's mother came over one morning. She had just received a postcard. Apparently Freddie was also taking a short break from Madrid and was in the south of Spain staying in a small mountain town called Mijas in Andalucía. Edwin hoped that he had remembered to pay his rent.

A pint of best bitter at the Hand and Spear went down well as did another at the Flintgate together with a game of darts. Having got used to the late hours of Spain, Britain's licensing laws suddenly seemed totally absurd. Invariably there would be a build-up of people cramming themselves into the pubs in the final hour before closing time. All of them, it would seem, were in eager anticipation of the ultimate anticlimax of the evening which was when the barmaid would ring a bell and shout "Time." There would then be the customary slowing down of everything, in which people would deliberately linger and drink the remainder of their glasses in slow motion, savouring every drop as they did so whilst the bar staff were anxious to get off home. Everyone would then wish each other a polite good night and the entire performance would be repeated the following evening.

During his stay in England Edwin visited a local barber's shop and emerged from it with a far more conservative-looking haircut than he'd had when he'd entered. He resisted the comments that followed from his brothers about it having got a weight off his mind.

One of the two Spanish girls that Edwin and Freddie met up with from time to time had dared Edwin to bring her back a mini-skirt from England as they were unobtainable in Spain but he'd forgotten to ask her what size. Feeling embarrassed about rummaging through a selection on display in the ladies department of C & A in Kingston-on-Thames, he purchased one that looked about right before hurriedly beating an exit. On the eve of his return to Madrid Edwin thought he might phone her on the off chance that she might be free to meet him at the airport. On a crackly line she was pleased to hear him even though the conversation was not without its surprises.

"Hola Julia," began Edwin, "Eso es decirte que llegare al aeropuerto de Madrid in Baracas mañana por la mañana a las once y media."

"Good that you're coming back to Madrid but you cannot go back to the apartment in Ciudad Lineal," she said.

"What? Why not?" asked Edwin.

"You no longer have the apartment," she replied.

"Why? What has happened?" he asked.

"First it's some problem with rent money. Then a glass window is smashed and somebody's leaving a cigarette burning on the furniture and just when the landlord came round the place was one big mess. He asked everyone to take their things and leave. He said he would make a complaint."

"My goodness," said Edwin, stunned by such a turn of events and mindful of the fact that the apartment had been taken on in his name.

"At least your things got put in your suitcase and are now stored with Antonio," she said.

"Well, thank goodness for that but what about the others? What's happened to them?" he asked.

"Freddie went to Andalucía but according to Margarita he is now back in Madrid but Hank the Yank has returned to America," she said.

"And Hugo?" he asked.

"Some girl from the American Air Base was urgently trying to get hold of Hugo for some reason but he is thought to have gone back to England. He just went without saying a word to anyone."

CHAPTER SIX

IT WAS A COLD crisp day with blue sky and sunshine as Edwin found himself walking down the Gran Vía with the intention of finding a cheap hostal somewhere nearby. He had first stopped by at the place where he had previously shared the room with Freddie but, although given a hearty doorstep welcome by the landlady, she regretted that there were no current vacancies. Eventually Edwin found an available room in a guest house on the other side of the main shopping area. As far as such accommodation went, it was a bit on the expensive side but it would do for the first few days before finding somewhere more suitable for the longer term.

Having offloaded his shoulder bag, he ventured out in the direction of the Plaza de Santa Ana in search of Freddie who, he assumed, would be at the Cervecería Alemana. Sure enough he was sitting at one of the marble slabbed table tops amongst a circle of his friends. On seeing Edwin he rose to greet him.

"Hallo haircut!" he chuckled, "How was it in Inglaterra?"

"Oh, England was OK," replied Edwin, "but what on earth has been going on here?"

"Yeah, well I'm sorry that we got booted out of the flat," he replied. "It was just one of those unfortunate set of circumstances. But there's nothing any of us can do about it now."

"I guess not," said Edwin. "Are there likely to be any repercussions? I hear that the landlord was going to make a complaint."

"Yes, he was. He was threatening to go for us through the British Embassy but he backed off when we got Antonio to talk to him who pointed out that you were still only seventeen at the time that you signed the lease."

"Thank goodness for that," said Edwin.

"Anyway," continued Freddie, "classes start again on Monday and so in one sense it's not bad being back in the centre of town again. I'm staying at a good, clean hostal very near here that charges forty pesetas a night which is a darn sight cheaper than anywhere else. They've even got some vacancies at the moment if you fancy moving in."

"Well forty pesetas a night is half the price of the place I'm in at the moment and so I might be persuaded," said Edwin, "Is it possible to take a look at it?"

"Sure," replied Freddie, "I can take you there right this instant if you like."

It was a five minute walk to the unpretentious hostal by the name of Heuspedes Las Huertas. A flight of stone steps led to an apple green front door and the owner showed Edwin to a small single inner room that would be available from Saturday onwards. It wasn't the most elegant of places but was functional and obviously economical. Edwin agreed that he would move in.

He and Freddie then went a little further down the road to a small white-tiled restaurant that served a bowl of piping hot meat and potato stew with a large bread roll for five pesetas and a half bottle of red wine for a similar price. It suddenly felt as if Edwin was back in Madrid again.

Outlining his recent days spent in Andalucía Freddie said it was a different world down there altogether. However he had gone with an American girl who on their return to Madrid had promptly been arrested by the Spanish police on a charge of drug possession and was now being held in custody prior to being deported back to the United States.

"We're beginning to reckon that someone at the Cervecería Alemana is an informer because there were only a few people who could have known much about her and it was kind of weird the way she got busted."

"How do you mean, weird?" asked Edwin.

"Well, to begin with she always looked the picture of innocence. She was always very careful and discreet the way she went about things as well as being selective with whom she mixed. Yet after paying one brief visit to the Cervecería Alemana she was straightaway arrested by two policemen when she arrived at the door of her hostal in Plaza Mayor. They were clearly waiting there for her."

"Couldn't they have been watching her over a period of time?" suggested Edwin.

"I don't know," replied Freddie, "but it happened the same day we arrived back from Andalucía. I mean, they might as well have gone for me too because I had a similar amount on me in a matchbox."

"Well, I hope you're not still carrying that around with you," said Edwin.

"No bloody fear," said Freddie, "It's stashed away where no one would even think."

THE SUNDAY TIMES COLOUR supplement that Edwin had brought back with him from England contained a selection of modern art pictures of various prominent people with deliberately distorted features. Edwin showed it to one of the bar staff in the Bar Pigalle. "Como Dracula!" she laughed. He then indicated the printed title underneath which said Generalissimo Franco. She froze and quietly suggested that he didn't show it to anyone else.

At that moment Charlie walked in through the door.

"Good grief. With a haircut like that I scarcely recognised you," he said, "By any chance did you visit a sheep shearer whilst you were in England?"

"I'd have needed to have gone and joined our two New Zealand friends for that," he replied.

Edwin went on to explain about the loss of the apartment which met with some degree of sympathy. Charlie too had changed his hostal and now stayed in a somewhat better establishment on the Gran Vía itself. Apparently his sister had increased his allowance. But he also had some more significant news.

"I have something rather special to tell you which will probably come as a complete surprise," he said, "I never thought it would happen to me at this stage of life but I've actually fallen in love."

"Is that so? Well, brilliant – and who is the lucky lady?" asked Edwin.

"Well that's just it. She's a lot younger than me and she's married and she has two little children both of whom I adore," he said.

"That sounds like a remarkably awkward way to have fallen in love, if you don't mind my saying so" replied Edwin.

"Not at all," said Charlie, "That's exactly the point. She is leaving her husband for me."

There was a brief silence. Edwin wasn't sure if Charlie was serious or kidding?

"Well, who is she and how has it come about?" asked Edwin finally.

"Angelica is a young English lady in her late twenties," explained Charlie. "I first met her and her husband at a friend's flat just before Christmas. I cracked a few jokes that had her in stitches throughout most of the evening. Afterwards they invited me back for coffee at their apartment. Well, I could tell that Angelica couldn't keep her eyes off me. Before leaving she asked me to pop back the following morning to collect some books that she'd said I could borrow. I couldn't resist going and when I got there she gave me the complete sob story about how there was no love in her marriage and how she appreciated the pleasure of my company. For some reason she kept calling me Uncle Charlie and before long she was saying "Come to bed with me, Uncle Charlie."

"And what about her husband?" asked Edwin.

"Oh, he knows and he simply doesn't care," replied Charlie. "He found out a few days later. When he came back I kind of apologised to him and even told him he could hit me if he wanted too but he declined the offer."

"And so what'll happen next?" asked Edwin.

"Well, the husband is leaving her for good and has already moved elsewhere. Angelica wants me to return with her to England and move into her home in Peterborough. And as for me, I can scarcely believe my good fortune and I'd say that she's the best thing that's ever happened to me in my life," he grinned.

"And who will have custody of the children?" queried Edwin.

"She will. It's all being arranged – and I'll be helping her bring them up," he replied.

"Well blow me down," replied Edwin.

AT THE BEGINNING OF the new term Edwin and Freddie first took the Metro to Moncloa and then walked the usual route across the university campus to the Faculty of Filosofía y Letras where their course was held. When they got there, however, they were confronted by a locked door and wondered if they'd got the date wrong. They went around to the back entrance of the building where they found some kind of a rowdy confrontation taking place. Although the cafeteria was open, a group of rather tense looking Spanish students were gathered outside its doorway and chanting anti-government slogans. One of them explained that the Minister of Education had closed the Faculty of Social Science and Economy and had confiscated the students' admission fees and was forcing them all to re-apply. Since then there had been open clashes between masked students and the police. There had also been stone throwing and some buses had even been overturned. At that moment there was loud crashing and banging that echoed from the other side of the building. More students emerged from around the corner.

"These fascist pigs are trying to close us down too!" shouted one, "Come and help us fight back!"

Rather than getting involved Edwin and Freddie slipped into a large clump of bushes at one side of the building. It gave them a reasonable vantage point from which they could get a view of what was taking place without being noticed. It turned out that the crashing and banging they'd heard was the sound of desks and chairs being hurled out of first floor windows at the police. As they watched the scene they witnessed a convoy of police vehicles and horse-mounted officers moving slowly into position. Mobile water cannons then appeared on the scene.

"Blimey, I've heard about those things," said Edwin, "They squirt blue coloured water over you and it doesn't wash off so you become a marked person and they can pick you up any time they want."

"Shit, we'd better keep out of range. What's all that smoke over there?" asked Freddie, pointing over to the right.

A black plume of smoke was rising above a clump of trees. They managed slowly to edge their way through the bushes of the landscaped area and, by pulling aside some branches, were able to get a clear view of a bus that had been set on fire. Meanwhile the police had begun moving in on the cafeteria side of the building and were chasing students through corridors and classrooms.

Students were being arrested and unceremoniously bundled into police vans.

"I think we ought to get the hell out of here," said Freddie.

"Definitely," agreed Edwin, "If we can stay out of sight and make our way through the shrubbery in this direction, we should come out somewhere round the back of the Science Faculty from where weave our way back down towards the Metro.

"OK, but let's hope the Science Faculty isn't surrounded by armed police too," he said.

It took them the best part of an hour to get completely clear of the campus and to merge back into the more normal urban surroundings of Moncloa. They stopped off at a cafeteria where, over mugs of thick hot chocolate dunked with churros of deep-fried pancake-like tubular strips, they reflected on the events of that morning.

"It's kind of ironic that on one of the rare occasions that we actually make the effort to attend the course, we find it cancelled," said Edwin.

"It is sod's law but I suspect this is going to be a long-term thing. I doubt very much if the university will be opening its doors to us tomorrow. Maybe we should watch the news," suggested Freddie.

"Yes but the problem with news bulletins over here is that they are all heavily censored and they only tell everybody what the government wants them to hear. We're unlikely to find out the real reason behind any of this" said Edwin.

"You're probably right," said Freddie, "the Spanish media is not much more than the government's mouthpiece but at least we might get some idea as to when the university is likely to re-open."

They went into the centre of Madrid and in the afternoon Edwin was persuaded to go to the Cervecería Alemana with Freddie where he had arranged to meet up with the person who knew about the possibility of working as an extra on an American film being made in Madrid. When they arrived, the usual crowd was gathered. A motley collection of colourfully dressed individuals from both sides of the Atlantic, whose main topic of conversation was either about their last drug experience or the next one that they were looking forward to. Edwin ordered a large glass of beer and attempted to steer the conversation more to their travel experiences. In this he was partially successful and got a detailed account of one group's adventures in Italy and how they'd been caught out in some back street currency exchange in which they'd thought they were wealthy with large sounding denomination bank notes of Italian Lira only to find the currency so inflated that they were worth just a few dollars.

For his part, Freddie was in popular demand to give them one of his songs and popped back to the guest house to collect his guitar. Whilst he was gone a rather withdrawn looking Norwegian girl asked Edwin if he had any hash that he could sell her. Without betraying how much he was opposed to the stuff he simply apologised that he didn't have any.

There were a couple of other English people present. The tall fuzzy-haired chap that he'd seen on a previous visit had since been referred to by Freddie as the "Missing Link." A few minutes of listening in to some of his conversation and Edwin could begin to understand the reason why. The poor soul was so stoned out of his mind that he could scarcely string a sentence together and kept saying that everything was "Far out, man." A clean shaven, short-haired Englishman called Russell looked out of place in such company. He seemed to spend much of his time working his way from table to table around the room having polite conversations with everybody whom he encountered. He would always end such meetings with a handshake and thank them for such an interesting chat. He had the air of a rather genteel church minister about him. For a while they'd half suspected him of being an undercover British police officer who was there to keep an eye on any drug-trafficking although most of them considered him harmless enough. He pulled up a chair at Edwin's table and spoke knowledgeably about Spanish history and culture. He clearly had nothing much in common with the surrounding hippy clientele although he evidently enjoyed the pleasure of their company and knew each one of them by name. There were a few Spanish hippies too. Amongst them a teenager called Pilar who made and sold coloured bangles and proved to be a useful source of information about just about anything in Madrid. But even she could throw no further light on what was going on at the university.

Freddie returned carrying his guitar case. A few moments later Jed the black American who was the main contact for the film work stepped in to the Cervecería. He glanced around the interior to see who was there and then made a beeline for Freddie.

"Hey, Freddie," he said, "About that film. Are you free to make a start at the studios? They've brought the schedule forward and want to start looking at people tomorrow."

Freddie shrugged his shoulders and replied, "Yeah. I don't see why not. There's nothing much else on and even the university is closed."

"Great," said Jed, "It'll be an early start. Get yourself out to the Metro station of Plaza de Castilla by eight o'clock tomorrow morning. I'll meet you there and we can share a cab the rest of the way."

He scribbled the details on a serviette which he handed to Freddie.

"Thanks," said Freddie, "and would it be OK if my friend came along too?" he asked, indicating Edwin.

"Are you American," asked Jed.

"No, I'm British," replied Edwin.

"Well you look as if you'd pass for an American so yeah, sure, you can come along. As a matter of fact you both look good for the parts and you'll be together with about forty others." he said.

"Just out of interest, what does everybody get paid?" asked Freddie.

"Not a lot," replied Jed, "Maybe just around five hundred pesetas a day plus they give you a lunch out there. Say, whilst I'm here in this hell-hole, do either of you have a little something I could buy?

"No, not at the moment," said Freddie.

He turned to Edwin. "What about you?" he asked.

No, I don't – don't have anything either," replied Edwin, trying to appear as neutral as possible about the subject.

"Jenny over in the corner?" suggested Freddie.

"Oh yeah, good idea, I'll go over and see her in a minute," he replied.

"Quiet everybody please. Silencio absoluto, por favour," an American director was giving commands through a loudhailer as he crossed the film set. For the fifth time that morning Edwin and the other extras sat in rows in a studio mock-up of a college classroom and looked attentively at an actor playing the part of a university professor. The camera was then repositioned and a person used a tape measure to calculate the distance of the subject from the camera's lens. And then exactly the same scene was re-enacted all over again, several times over.

"OK, everybody, take fifteen," was the next announcement which resulted in half the assembly heading off to use the toilets whilst the rest of them dispersed into an adjoining room and lit up cigarettes.

Fifteen minutes later and everyone was back and ready for more of the same. The camera had been repositioned at yet another angle and a further member of the crew was perched up on a stand and operating a boom microphone. Whatever the film's storyline was meant to be about it didn't appear to be getting anywhere particularly fast and the repetitiveness of it all coupled with the heat of the studio lights was enough to get some people nodding off who were then nudged by the person sitting next to them. That upset the director.

"Hey you, second from the end!" he bawled, "If this is destroying your beauty sleep you shouldn't be here. This is your last chance."

Cartons containing packed lunches were laid on during an hour's break from 2pm until 3pm. It was also the first opportunity for the extras to talk amongst themselves. Edwin discovered that the guy he'd been sitting next to all morning was Swedish. He introduced himself as Johan and moaned about how boring the whole exercise was proving to be.

"We've spent four hours on a scene that's not likely to last more than about three minutes in the finished film," he said. "To my mind that is inefficient."

"Ah, but isn't that the very nature of movie-making?" asked a young man from Illinois.

"Perhaps, but I just wish it was a bit more exciting that a stupid classroom scene," said the Swede.

"It's not exactly the most gripping of scenes," agreed Edwin, "although it's interesting to see the technique by which it gets filmed in small segments that are ready to be strung together into a meaningful sequence."

"Either that or a completely meaningless sequence," put in Freddie.

THE UNIVERSITY OF MADRID was supposed to re-open at the end of February. It didn't happen and when Edwin and Freddie again made the effort to go to the campus, they narrowly escaped the jet of liquid being squirted from the water cannon that suddenly opened fire on a large group of students gathered outside the Faculty of Law. Some days later a bomb exploded outside the United States Embassy in Madrid and further clashes between students and police led to several students being injured. There was a protest meeting against the American war in Vietnam in which the Stars and Stripes flag was burned and stones were thrown at the police. A number of men were imprisoned for having established a Communist Party cell in Madrid and for distributing illegal propaganda.

Towards the end of March one of the newspapers, Nuevo Diario, published an article by a student with statements about why the students are protesting. It was the first time during the unrest that the Spanish media had dared give the students a public voice. An emergency government meeting then took place and it was stated that brutal police conduct at the universities was regretted, especially that which had caused injury to professors who had attempted to protect their students. However General Franco's government took the decision to close the university in Madrid indefinitely. Apart from breaking the continuity of education for Spanish university students it also meant that there would be no more classes for Edwin and Freddie or for any of the other overseas students.

Throughout that time, Edwin had kept up his rotating schedule of teaching English to his various acquaintances. The weekly evening at the Fernandez family in Lista was always one of the high points on the agenda and he suspected that Isolina's mother went out of her way to prepare extra special food for his visit. There were always several dishes of Spanish high cuisine, beautifully prepared and presented and Edwin was treated like a guest of honour. As usual a large carafe of red wine stood on the table as did a basket of neatly cut bread. Edwin would always take time to talk to Isolina's father with whom he had developed a good rapport. Even if political matters were off the agenda he could sense that the man was no great friend of the Spanish government. A clumsy looking gold-coloured metal ashtray with a hanging circular basket in its middle was so designed that whenever the ash from the end of a cigarette was flicked into it, more often than not it resulted in a sprinkling being deposited on the surrounding table surface which rather defeated its object.

HERMAN THE GERMAN AND his wife Marianna were overjoyed with the birth of their son. They had moved out of the centre of Madrid to a small apartment in the suburb of Carabanchel. Edwin and Freddie visited them at their new home one afternoon and accompanied them on a long walk in which they took it in turns to push the pram. Their route passed a huge prison which Herman told them had been built entirely by political prisoners after the Spanish civil war.

Freddie decided to purchase a second guitar which resulted in it now being his turn to be short of money. He was already in arrears with his hostal rent. Before coming to Madrid his parents had bought him a new suit which he had never worn and he figured that he never had any real use for it. He now decided to sell it in Madrid's El Rastro Sunday flea market.

"It's in good nick and it must have cost quite a bit in England," he said. "I bet I can get a fair price for it."

Yet the reality of such expectation was markedly different and towards the end of the afternoon Freddie had parted with the brand new suit for the sum of one hundred and fifty pesetas – less that a pound.

Because Edwin had never been keen on the hippy bar of the Cervecería Alemana he tended to frequent his old stamping ground of the area around Callao. As he was making his way there he happened to bump into the Swedish guy that he had met whilst working as an extra at the film studios and stopped to speak with him for a while. The Swede mentioned that in a few weeks time he intended hitchhiking back to Stockholm and asked Edwin if he might be interested in accompanying him.

"It could be a smart move," he said, "all the more so if Madrid University looks as though it's not going to re-open in the foreseeable future. You might find Sweden an interesting place to work in."

Edwin was aware that at some stage of the game he needed to make a clear plan for his future and that finding a job played a part of it. He could return to England but he couldn't easily see himself doing that at this particular juncture. The year in Madrid had been an eye-opener and he viewed many things in a different way than before. The idea of a new country such as Sweden had a certain appeal about it. He said that he would consider the matter and let him know.

THE FOLLOWING SATURDAY WAS the day before Charlie's departure for England with his new found lady friend. He had arranged to be in the Bar Pigalle for a farewell drink that evening and Edwin had persuaded Freddie to come along too. It was also the night of the annually held Eurovision Song Contest and the event was being watched on the television set in the front bar. Because the volume was cranked up to its maximum, it could also be heard in the back bar where Nizam the Egyptian diplomat and Charlie were sat at one of the tables. They looked up as Edwin and Freddie entered.

"So this is it then? Edwin asked Charlie, "You really are leaving us?"

"My bag is packed and I fly back to England with Angelica and the children tomorrow afternoon," he said.

"Your new lady friend that we still haven't met?" asked Freddie.

"Precisely!" grinned Charlie. "We're going back to England for good. In fact the only reason I'm here this evening is because I told her that I'd just like to pop out and say goodbye to a few friends. But I mean I couldn't really bring her here with me could I? – not here."

"I suppose not," agreed Edwin, "After all, Bar Pigalle is just a place for meeting up with the riff-raff."

"Quite so," replied Charlie, "Anyway, for goodness sake let's get some more drinks in. It's my last night in Spain. The evening is on me."

"That's a first," said Edwin under his breath.

Charlie went through the swing doors to the bar whilst Edwin, Freddie and Nizam exchanged glances.

"Do you think it'll last?" asked Freddie.

" I haven't met the lady but from what I can gather she is quite a refined person and she is fascinated by Charlie's entertaining ways so I guess we'll just have to wait and see how things develop," replied Nizam.

Charlie returned accompanied by one of the bar ladies who was carrying a tray of four glasses of Anis as well as three large tankards of beer and a cup of coffee. At that moment the British entry to Eurovision could be heard. It was a song by Cliff Richard.

"Cheers and good luck, Charlie," said Edwin raising his glass, "and it seems particularly fitting that the song being sung is called 'Congratulations!'"

"Cheers," responded Charlie, "I'm going to miss all of you.

"By the way, can you get that Chinchón aniseed liqueur in England?" asked Freddie.

It was then back to business as normal as they all took turns on the pinball machine and more rounds of drinks continued throughout the evening.

The Spanish entry to the Eurovision Song Contest had a rather unimaginative title of 'La, La, La' which also comprised the bulk of its lyrics. Nevertheless the tune was reasonably catchy. Originally it was going to be sung by a male singer who had wanted to sing it in Barcelona's regional language of Catalan. That hadn't gone down too well with the Franco regime and so the entry had been withdrawn and the singer substituted with somebody called Massiel who now sang exactly the same song but in Castilian Spanish.

At the end of her performance the front bar broke into an uproar of loud applause and cheering.

A couple of hours later and it became apparent that the Spanish entry had won the song contest. Such was the celebratory mood in the front bar that everybody had to endure 'La, La, La' being played at full blast no less than eleven more times throughout the remainder of the evening.

"Never mind!" said Santos the bar's owner as they departed, "Your British entry was quite good too."

They said their final goodbye to Charlie and wished him well.

CHAPTER SEVEN

IT WAS EARLY APRIL when Edwin and the Swedish lad, Johan, set out on their journey for Stockholm. They had very few pesetas with them but at least they had been offered a ride to San Sebastian in the north of Spain by an elderly Spanish man that Johan had encountered. Edwin had left his suitcase containing his worldly possessions with Antonio for safekeeping and just had a shoulder bag with him. The Swede too travelled light with a small rucksack.

The following day they crossed into France but made little headway. Travelling as a pair didn't seem to get as many lifts as when Edwin had made a similar northward journey on his own three months ago. On reaching Bordeaux they decided to spend the night in the waiting room of the railway station where at least it was warm. They were there for an hour or so when a Frenchman entered and on seeing Johan's rucksack asked where he was going. Paris was mentioned as being part of the route and the man said that he could give both of them a lift there. At first it seemed like a stroke of luck as they clambered into his car but the man then said that they would first go to his house to sleep for a bit before driving to Paris early the next morning. They were shown into a one room flat and invited to take a nap on the one bed, together with the man. Edwin and Johan glanced at each other, and simultaneously decided that they didn't like the look of things. They turned on their heels and walked out.

"I bet you he goes back to that same railway station waiting room every night with the similar pretence of offering to drive young men to wherever they might be going," said Johan.

They found their way to one of main roads in the hope of hitching a ride that night and were fortunate in being picked up by a truck carrying fruit and vegetables which got them into Paris early the following morning. Throughout most of the journey they'd both fallen asleep. They stepped out from the warmth of the inside of the cabin. Judging by their immediate surrounding they were somewhere in the centre of Paris which would mean a long trek to its outskirts. Progress was incredibly slow throughout that day and they didn't get out to the easterly side of Paris until late afternoon. Several short lifts got them to a place called Montmirail as it was already dark and gone ten o'clock. A driver then pulled up next to them and wound down his window.

"Vous payez? Vous payez?" he asked, as he rubbed his thumb across his fingers to indicate money.

"No, we are hitchhiking," replied Edwin.

"Mais vous payez?" continued the driver.

"Look here, Monsieur Thickhead, if we'd wanted to 'payer' we'd have got a bloody taxi," retorted Johan.

The man revved up his engine and drove off in a huff.

Johan suggested that they tried to get some sleep in a communal stairway within a block of flats which apparently was something that he had done before. They succeeded in gaining access to such a place which was relatively warm and carpeted but as they stretched themselves out on the second floor and were about to fall asleep they were aroused by the noise of people entering the front door at ground level. Edwin and Johan sprang to their feet, picked up their belongings and descended the staircase in a normal manner as if they had just emerged from visiting people in one of the apartments on an upper floor. As they passed a husband and wife who were coming up the stairs they exchanged a polite "Bonsoir" and stepped out into the cold night air once again. Neither of them felt like risking it a second time.

In the morning they got a ride with a German businessman who was travelling to his hometown of Saarbrücken. Passport control took place when they crossed the border into West Germany and at last it began to feel that they were making some progress in the direction of Sweden. But they were both tired and hungry. They'd been on the road for five days during which time they'd not had a proper night's sleep and had survived on a daily ration of bread and tomatoes which had now run out. Johan still had a few Deutschmarks from a previous trip and he promised that they would eat some chips later that day.

Either hitchhiking was generally easier in West Germany or the two of them were particularly lucky on that day. They first got a lift to Kaiserslautern and then a German soldier picked them up and whisked them along a series of Autobahns all the way up to the city of Kassel. The soldier spoke good English and during the course of conversation he said how much he enjoyed his life in the army but that he hoped he would only ever experience it in times of peace.

That evening they were able to reach Hanover and both ate their first warm food since Madrid. It was purchased at a kiosk from a remarkably large German lady and consisted of two cardboard trays of chips with a generous portion of mayonnaise on top and two beakers of hot coffee. They took their time over such welcome food and drink. Afterwards whilst making their way to the main railway station where they hoped to spend the night, Johan outlined a plan. They would continue their journey north as far as Hamburg. He would then go to the Swedish Embassy and explain that he'd run out of money and needed to be repatriated. He knew from past experience that he would be issued with a train and ferry ticket and also some spending money for the journey which he would use to purchase tickets for Edwin. It sounded like a workable solution for both of them to reach their final destination of Sweden.

As it happened they arrived in Hamburg a little earlier than anticipated on account of having been booted out of the waiting room at Hanover Hauptbahnhof by the local police who didn't take too kindly to anyone being there without a valid train ticket. They had recommenced hitchhiking during the remainder of the night and had arrived in Hamburg that same morning. Although tired out through lack of sleep and walking through the city centre in a somewhat zombie-like state they were optimistic that their onward passage to Stockholm would soon be secured. When they got to the Swedish Embassy building it was arranged that Edwin would hang around in a nearby shop whilst Johan went in and pleaded his case.

It was a long wait of perhaps an hour and a half. However, when Johan finally re-appeared Edwin could see from the expression on his face that something was amiss.

"I've been caught out," he said. "The problem is that they normally give you the train fare plus some additional money but I did the same thing a couple of years ago and I was supposed to have paid them back – which I never did."

"So are they just going to leave you here stranded?" asked Edwin.

"No," replied Johan, "They've issued me with a railway warrant to travel today to Sweden where I have to go and report to the authorities but they've given me no actual money at all."

The severity hit home. Edwin and Johan would be parting company. Johan could get back to Sweden. Edwin would have to make the final stretch of the journey alone from Germany. He couldn't speak German and he didn't have any money other than a couple of twenty-five peseta coins that he'd had in his pocket since Spain. He might succeed in hitchhiking up to the north German coastline but to continue to Denmark and Sweden would require a lift from someone who was going to take the car ferry and who wouldn't mind taking an extra passenger across with them.

That afternoon, as a parting gesture Johan gave Edwin the remainder of his German money which was nearly four marks. Edwin would try and get to Stockholm as soon as possible and had written down Johan's address.

Edwin started the walk to an outer part of Hamburg to begin hitchhiking again. A cold wind was blowing and for a while he considered sheltering the night in one of the shop doorways. Some of the entrances were set back and had a small area of secluded passageway in front with window displays on either side. At least they offered some protection from the outside elements. He stepped into one of them and was just getting used to being squatted down on the concrete when, to his horror, a bell started gently chiming as a metal grill began to be electronically lowered down across the front of the shop. Edwin leapt to his feet and managed to duck out underneath the grill before it became too low to do so. Back out into the cold once again.

Throughout that night, Edwin got a lift to Lübeck where he arrived at daybreak. He then reached a town called Sharbeutz from where he could already catch glimpses of the sea over to his right and he knew that he was now on the road that would lead to a ferry service that operated to Denmark.

Sensing a breakfast time hunger he noticed some tiny apples on a tree in the adjacent field. Although they were both hard and sour he ate three of them in their entirety. And then, he wondered if he should chance his luck by ringing someone's doorbell and asking if they could give him a glass of water. Who knows, maybe they'd offer him a cup of tea or a coffee. A lady answered the door, he asked for "Wasser" and a few moments later he received exactly that – a glass of cold "Wasser." Perhaps he should have learned to have been more specific. "A cup of hot chocolate –got any freshly baked bread rolls? Oh, and a bowlful of goulash and some German dumplings wouldn't go amiss either?" But, at heart, he was too polite an Englishman and he was grateful to receive the humbly requested glass of "Wasser."

He walked on to the next village. Strains of an old German music hall piece could be heard emanating through an open doorway,

Und der Haifisch, der hat Zähne, und die trägt er im Gesicht,
und Macheath, der hat ein Messer, doch das Messer sieht man nicht.

Edwin began to wonder what his ancestors who had served in both world wars would have made of being back on former enemy territory. Ghosts from the past seemed to be becoming something of a reality but he reasoned that it was most probably due to lack of sleep.

He also realised that when you've starving hungry your sense of priorities gets a bit skewed. Passing an automatic vending machine he was even prepared to spend his few remaining coins on a couple of packets of cigarettes rather than wait for the off chance of finding somewhere to get a loaf of bread. Mind you, on that stretch of road there weren't any shops at all and in any case he was more intent of completing the remainder of his journey.

That afternoon, his third lift brought him close to the small north German seaport of Puttgarden. He had noticed a sudden stream of cars coming in the opposite direction and deduced that the ferry from Denmark must have recently docked. Unfortunately his driver was on his way to Kiel and was not taking the ferry. Edwin was dropped at a turn off and walked the remaining few miles to the ferry terminal itself. The problem now was to find a lift with someone willing to take him with them on the ferry crossing. He positioned himself on the approach to the harbour and held his thumb out to the few cars that arrived. After an hour or so in which none of the drivers showed the slightest bit of interest, Edwin began to consider a different plan altogether.

He pondered the situation. The idea of travelling to Sweden with Johan had essentially been based on the challenge of hitchhiking through the length of Europe. Edwin had pretty much achieved that and, having reached the coastline, had gone as far as he could. As far as any onward travel was concerned, he couldn't magic up the ferry fare to go as a foot passenger and it was perhaps unrealistic to depend upon someone prepared to take him over in their car. Another major stumbling block was that even if he were able to get across to Denmark he would then have to hitchhike many more miles across to Copenhagen and from there find some means of taking yet another ferry service to Malmo in Sweden before travelling up to Stockholm. Was it really worth such a gamble? After all, he had no particular need to go to Sweden at all. It had been one of those spur of the moment decisions.

What alternative options were there? Well, certainly he was exhausted and could do with a good night's sleep somewhere. He entered a prominent building called 'Rathaus' which although sounding like the name for an enclosure at a zoo was actually the Town Hall. He asked a clerk if there was somewhere that he could rest for a few hours. The man was sympathetic but in broken English gave Edwin an explanation of some strange custom dating back to medieval times in which they could assist people who arrived in town in one direction but not those who had entered it from the opposite end as Edwin had. At least, that was what Edwin thought was being said although it was possible that in his extreme tiredness he had completely misunderstood the person.

He stepped back outside and realised that if he were to abandon the venture to Sweden there was no point in remaining in this tiny German town of Puttgarden. Much as he loved Spain he had no desire to make the long return journey all the way back down there again. What if he were simply to go to back to England instead? How could that be achieved? Presumably it could more easily be arranged from somewhere such as Hamburg. If he could hitch a ride he might be able to get back there in a few hours' time. But it was already getting dark and there wasn't much traffic on the road.

Apart from the sour apples from the tree, Edwin hadn't eaten anything that day. The combination of semi-starvation and accumulated lack of sleep over the past week and a half was beginning to get to him and he started to experience mild hallucinations. He walked out of the small town and back into a dark country lane when he quickened his pace as he thought he could hear men singing somewhere behind him. It got louder and he thought it sounded like German soldiers and then it suddenly stopped. He lit a cigarette and continued his onward march. At least he had an achievable objective which was simply to get back to Hamburg and see what could be organised from there. There would be no more dilly-dallying around and any further thoughts of Sweden could be completely dismissed from his mind. Here he was in Germany and advancing on Hamburg. Somehow it felt like he was a lone Englishman marching through enemy territory and he again thought he could hear the sound of songs being sung in German. He stopped and the singing stopped.

"It must be my imagination," he said out loud.

On hearing the approach of a car he turned and held out his thumb but the driver didn't stop and the road was plunged into darkness once again. He thought that he heard more singing and even sensed he could momentarily see images of uniformed men drinking steins of beer which flashed up on either side of him but when he tried to make them out they disappeared before his eyes. It unnerved him and he decided that the best way to deal with the situation was to keep up his quick march and perhaps sing back. The only problem was that Edwin had never been much of a singer at the best of times and really didn't know the words to many songs at all. But he had to do something and in the circumstances an improvised combination of 'Land of Hope and Glory' and 'Rule Britannia' seemed to be a pretty good choice which he started belting out at the top of his voice.

"That ought to take care of the German ghosts," he thought, and suddenly felt as if he was being accompanied by an entire British regiment.

The next thing he knew he was being woken up in a car by its driver who was telling him that they had now arrived in Hamburg and were parked outside the British Consulate. Edwin couldn't even remember being picked up by the car the previous night and yet now it was morning. However, he was grateful to the driver and pleased to have arrived back in Hamburg. Alighting from the car he took in the immediate scenery of some rather elegant looking buildings and landscaped gardens, a park and a large lake. He reasoned, however, that he wasn't going to plea for the same kind of assistance in getting back to England the way in which Johan had been returned to Sweden. Instead he was simply going to ask at the Consulate if they could get hold of his father's work telephone number in England which shouldn't be that difficult because he was a bank manager.

The lady on duty at the reception desk was both cordial and efficient and after a cursory inspection of Edwin's passport and asking him why his date of birth had been smudged she soon found him the requested telephone number. He was just about to ask the whereabouts of the nearest phone box when she suggested that he might like to phone from there. He soon had his father on the line.

"Hamburg?" said the familiar voice, "I thought you were in Madrid."

"It's a long story," said Edwin, "but basically after all the recent riots in Madrid the University has closed down indefinitely and there are no more classes for me to go to. I started accompanying a Swedish friend up to Sweden and although we got as far as Germany he went on alone whilst I went as far as I could but then thought it might be wiser for me to head for England.

"Well I'm glad you're away from all that trouble going on in Madrid." he said, "When will you arrive back here?"

"That's just it. My immediate problem is that I don't have access to my weekly payments and so I was wondering if there is some means for you to transfer the train fare to me here in Hamburg."

"Well, yes, I'm sure that can be arranged although it might take an hour or so," he said. Is there a phone number where you are that I can call you back on?"

"I'm at the British Consulate. Let me ask," said Edwin.

On explaining the situation to the lady he was told that it would be fine for him to wait.

Some ten minutes later Edwin's father called back and left instructions for Edwin to go to the Commerzbank on a street called Jungfernsteig in Hamburg where money would be awaiting him. The lady at the consulate gave him a printed paper sheet showing a city map of Hamburg. She took a pen and drew rings to mark the consulate, the bank and the main railway station. Everything was centrally located and Edwin departed suddenly feeling remarkably upbeat.

The rest of the morning worked like clockwork. By half past eleven Edwin had collected an amount of Deutschmarks from the bank and then headed over to the Hauptbahnhof where he had purchased a one-way train ticket to London. The journey would involve taking the 3pm train to Brussels from where he would connect with another train to the Belgian port of Ostende. A night ferry would get him across to Dover followed by an early morning train to London. There was still quite a bit of money left over and so, with the best part of three hours to kill, what better than to find a bite to eat.

Along one outer side of the station building he found the entrance to a base-ment snack bar reached by a spiral flight of stairs. It proved to be something of a self-service affair and he eagerly loaded up his tray with a plateful of par-ticularly long sausages and chips, a bread roll and a tall glass of German beer. Edwin sat himself down at an available place at one of the many round tables set throughout the room. An elderly man already sitting on the other side of the table gave him a polite nod.

"Guten Apetit!" said the man.

"Danke schön," replied Edwin as he began tucking into what amounted to his first proper meal in ten days. As he did so a sense of well-being began to creep over him as he became adjusted to the warmth of the room, the welcome intake of hot food and the refreshing beer. The man at the table spoke again.

"Schön hier, nicht wahr?" he said.

Edwin correctly understood him to mean that the cafeteria was quite a good place.

"Ja," he responded, "It's good."

"Sind Sie Ausländer?" the man queried. Again Edwin understood the question.

"Yes I'm English," said Edwin.

"Aha, ein Engländer," he said.

A waitress who had been clearing one of the other tables stopped by and asked the man if he'd like to order another beer.

"Ja bitte," he replied, "und auch einen für meinen englischen Freund hier."

"Danke," said Edwin, who completely surprised himself that, perhaps due to his light-headedness from lack of sleep, he seemed to have acquired a sudden ability to understand virtually every word that was being spoken in German.

"Die Engländer haben einen Sinn für Gerechtigkeit, die Deutschen haben Diziplin." stated the man. „Es ist schade, daß wir miteinander Krieg hatten, denn wenn du einen Deutschen mit einem Engländer zusammen tust, ist das eine gute Kombination.

Edwin got the general gist of what the old bloke was going on about and recognised the comments to be compliments.

"Ich, ich komme hier von Hamburg," he continued. „Wir sind anders als die Menschen in anderen deutschen Städten. Wie lange bleibst du in Deutschland?"

By means of explanation "Ich take train to England" were about the only words Edwin could conjure up but he took his train ticket out from his bag and showed it to the man.

"Ah so, Sie fahren heute nachmittage um 3 Uhr nach London," He looked at his watch. „Es ist erst halb Eins. Da haben wir noch etwas Zeit."

The beer arrived.

Two rather attractive looking German girls of about Edwin's age sat themselves down at the table's remaining places and, before long, whilst eating their meal they too had joined in the conversation.

The man then insisted on buying a round of drinks and cigarettes were passed around.

Although both girls could speak a bit of English they didn't want to exclude the man so things remained in German with an occasional translation from the one sitting closest to Edwin.

Edwin then bought a round of drinks consisting of more beer for the man and himself and coffees for the girls. He was thoroughly enjoying this afternoon although, being overtired, he began to develop a slight concern about the possibility of missing his train.

"Don't worry" reassured one of the girls. "We shall make sure we get you to the right platform and onto the right train in plenty of time." She opened her handbag and wrote her name and address on a piece of paper which she handed to him.

"Here," she said. "My name is Erika Hoffmann. Please write me when you get back to England."

"I most certainly will," replied Edwin.

"Komm, liebe Leute, noch ein Trink," said the man, clearly overjoyed to see that Anglo-German relations were making such good progress. He ordered yet another round.

True to her word, the girl Erika and her friend accompanied Edwin to Platform 7 from where the train to Brussels would depart. It was already waiting there and Edwin gave both girls a kiss before clambering into a carriage. It was not crowded and he took a seat by the window. The two girls stood outside on the platform and waved and blew kisses as the train started to pull out of the station. Edwin then readjusted his position and lay across the length of two seats with his legs dangling over one edge. He slept throughout the four-hour journey. It was only the train's arrival at the Belgian frontier and the inevitable passport inspection that woke him up.

CHAPTER EIGHT

EDWIN'S FATHER HAD BEEN offered a transfer to become manager of a Brighton branch of the bank. He regarded it as a welcome opportunity to break free from the daily routine of commuting in and out of London which he had been doing for the past twenty years. The rest of the family had mixed feelings about the move due to take place later that year. They were all fond of Weybridge and didn't particularly relish the thought of being based on the Sussex coast.

By coincidence Edwin's South African friend, Henry, from youth hostelling days now worked as a chef at a hotel in Hove. In a letter he had described the place as being deadly dull. He had also said that he was seriously thinking about returning to South Africa. Edwin thought that maybe he should pay him a visit.

In the meantime, surrounded by home comforts and gently unwinding from his recent European exploits, Edwin was contemplating what to do next. That interval of calm was interrupted one Sunday morning when Freddie's mother appeared on the doorstep, clearly in a distraught state. Apparently Freddie was in a Spanish jail. He had been arrested and found guilty of possessing illegal drugs. Although the occurrence came as no great surprise to Edwin, he nevertheless felt a measure of shock and sympathy. Edwin's mother asked her what was likely to happen next.

"That's just it. They don't seem to know," she said, "We are in touch with the British Embassy in Madrid and they seem to think he will be deported which at least would mean he'd be coming back home. "

At the breakfast table Edwin discussed the situation with his parents.

"Do you have any idea as to how this whole thing might have come about?" asked his father.

"Only that he tended to keep a rather dubious circle of friends and regularly frequented a notorious hippy bar," replied Edwin. "A lot of that was to do with the fact that they appreciated his folk songs."

"And he took drugs himself?" he asked.

"Well, never in my presence but I assume so, yes," replied Edwin.

He went on to describe what he'd seen of the lure of various characters to the Cervecería Alemana on the Plaza de Santa Ana and the attraction that the place apparently held for dealing in hashish and LSD. As an afterthought he assured them that he had no such involvement just in case any such notion might have crossed their minds. They were relieved to hear it.

"Freddie's mother was also told by the embassy that an undercover informer had infiltrated their group and then had the whole lot of them arrested," said Edwin's mother.

That could well be true," said Edwin, "but because I'd already left Madrid by that time I don't know the exact circumstances."

He recalled that Freddie had often said that there was the possibly of an informer amongst those who frequented the Cervecería Alemana. The finger of suspicion had sometimes pointed in the direction of Russell, the genteel Englishman, but he had always seemed too pleasant a person to have been capable of betraying anyone at all. Someone had even asked Freddie if Edwin was 'safe' because they had noticed that he distanced himself from the drugs scene.

They went on to discuss the situation at the university. In the past week British news had reported the continued clashes between demonstrators and police on the streets of Madrid. The Spanish authorities had even started mistreating foreign journalists for reporting on such events. They had arrested the foreign correspondents from the Daily Express, Paris Match and Agence France Press.

"The whole place was cracking up," confirmed Edwin, "The day before I left Madrid the police were using batons, water cannons and horses against the students who were retaliating with Molotov cocktails and by hurling paving stones."

"By the sounds of it you were wise to get out," said Edwin's father.

"I certainly think so," agreed Edwin. "Any solution to the upheaval going on over there is only ever likely to come about if Franco gives concessions to the Spanish students," replied Edwin, "but that's extremely unlikely and of course one of the main difficulties in Spain is that there's no freedom of speech. You can't open your mouth and talk about politics or start distributing leaflets that are in the slightest bit critical of the regime. That is like holding up a red rag to a Spanish bull. Mind you, talking of red rags, there was a red flag flying over one of the university faculties before I left so presumably there was some Communist involvement in all of it too."

"HE'S NOT ON DUTY today. It's his day off but I can show you to his room," said one of the chefs at the Dudley Hotel in Hove. He ushered Edwin in through a dimly lit passageway and up a flight of stairs. "There you are. It's that second door on the left and it wouldn't surprise me if he's still asleep," he said.

Edwin rapped twice on the door. Receiving no response he turned the handle and opened the door. He recognised the figure lying in the bed.

Putting on a formal sounding voice Edwin announced, "Your early morning call, sir!"

Henry immediately sat up in bed, "What the...Good God! Edwin, it's you! Where the bloody hell did you spring from? I thought you were in Spain. Good heavens. Hey, good to see you me old mate!" He grinned.

He quickly got dressed and, confirming that it was his day off, suggested that the two of them went into the centre of Brighton. "There's not much in Hove," he explained, "just rows and rows of rather hideous looking monstrosity-like buildings one after the other. It's not the right place for me and I can't wait to get out of it. I'm off to Cape Town in a fortnight's time."

They spent the day in the centre of Brighton where after exploring an intricate maze of narrow twisting alleyways of antique shops and some rather offbeat looking coffee bars they had lunch at a Chinese restaurant whilst catching up on their recent activities. The sun came out in the afternoon which prompted a stroll along the seafront. That evening Edwin returned home to Weybridge by train after wishing Henry all the best for South Africa.

"In case I never see you again, have a nice life."

They promised to keep in touch.

EDWIN REGULARLY SCANNED THE columns of job advertisements in the press but rarely found anything that remotely appealed to him. He spent the summer months doing some casual work which involved helping with the clearance of a stretch of woodland through which the new M3 motorway was due to be built. It was teamwork and he was picked up in a van every morning and dropped back in the late afternoon.

One weekend he befriended a group of tourists from Czechoslovakia. They convinced him that Prague would be an interesting place for a visit. Edwin welcomed the idea of a short break in Eastern Europe and arranged to take advantage of an inexpensive four-day package deal which included flight, hotel and the services of a tour guide.

It was mid-August when Freddie arrived back in Weybridge having been deported from Spain. Despite his ordeal he looked well. He met up with Edwin at a coffee shop and they were soon laughing and joking about events of the previous year and recalling the numerous people that they'd met.

Freddie then spoke of his arrest.

"It was a simple strategy, really," he said, "All it took was for someone to infiltrate the group of people that used to hang out at the Cervecería Alemana and then, when the time was right, they busted the whole lot of us."

"And do you know who that person was?" asked Edwin.

"Yes," he replied, "It was that two-faced American guy who got us the work at the film studios."

"Jed?" asked Edwin genuinely surprised. "Are you sure?"

"As sure as we can be," replied Freddie. "If you stop and think about it, he knew all of the people who gathered there. He was forever asking who was where and doing what and which of them had something to sell. He was extremely well-placed to be the perfect informer and it's no coincidence that at the time of the arrests he completely disappeared from the scene. That's how these guys operate. They'll smile at your face and then stab you in the back."

Edwin then asked Freddie what he intended to do now that he was back in England and received an unexpected answer.

"Look, please don't breathe a word of this to anyone but I have every intention of returning to Madrid as soon as possible," he said

"Wouldn't that be an incredibly risky thing to do?" asked Edwin.

"I know, but it's what I want to do and what I'm going to do," replied Freddie.

"They tend to keep checks on people," said Edwin. "Even when you first arrive at a hostal your passport details have to be copied out and that information gets passed on to someone somewhere."

"To hell with the Spanish authorities," he said, "I'm missing Spain and to be quite honest I'm missing Margarita. I promised her that I'd return and I reckon that if it came to it I could earn enough to live on out there just from busking alone. I've accidentally on purpose defaced my passport in the washing machine and as soon as I've got a replacement, that's what I'm planning to do."

Freddie then asked Edwin about his future plans.

"Undecided as yet," said Edwin. "I don't know whether to return to study or plunge into some kind of job. As you know, my family is moving to Hove in a couple of week's time but first I'm going on a short trip to Czechoslovakia for a few days," said Edwin.

"Czechoslovakia?" said Freddie, "Either you are joking or you haven't yet heard today's news. The Soviet Army has just invaded that country."

THE MOVE TO HOVE took place over the August Bank Holiday. Try as he may, Edwin was unable to generate any great enthusiasm. Weybridge had been of a manageable size whereas Brighton and Hove seemed to be one sprawling mass. What's more the new family home lacked the character of the previous one. It was located in a residential area from which it was necessary to pass through rather too many identical looking roads before reaching anywhere that looked remotely different, regardless of the direction taken.

A lone green square of park boasted that it was equipped with dog toilets. Hove Railway Station and its footbridge stood alongside a row of old-fashioned shops run by old-fashioned people. Surrounding streets had pompous sounding names like Goldstone Villas, Clarendon Villas or Eaton Villas. It all struck Edwin as snootiness being inserted into a particularly dreary environment. A lengthy walk down a wide avenue to the seafront revealed a beach of brown pebbles and a grey English Channel. Even the promenade provided nothing more than an unimaginative stretch of never-ending pavement and blue painted railings watched over by silly shaped lampposts which led the way into Brighton. And as so often happens on a British Bank Holiday, the sky was overcast and it was drizzling.

In the early evening and having already walked around a large loop of identical looking streets, Edwin stopped off to capture the atmosphere of some of the public houses along the length of Western Avenue and Church Street. Most had lounge bars decorated with identical maroon and gold paisley patterned wallpaper as if it were some kind of local trademark. Elderly people sat on their own at small tables nursing their glass of drink and staring vacantly into nothingness. A jukebox played a record of piano music by Russ Conway.

Edwin ordered a pint of bitter, lit a cigarette and perched himself on a stool in quiet contemplation. The more he analysed his predicament he found himself fast reaching the conclusion that he'd like to get as far away from England as he possibly could and seek a new start and a more fulfilling lifestyle somewhere else – much as his friend Henry had done in getting the hell out of the place and pushing off to South Africa. As he mulled over such thoughts he recalled the two ladies from New Zealand that he'd met in Madrid last year, Heather and Natasha, with their distinctive accents. He could still hear them now saying "Yis" instead of "Yes" and describing anything distasteful as being "skunjee." They had seemed so self-assured and positive about everything. Perhaps New Zealand was a country worth thinking about – and that really would be as far away from England as he could possibly go.

The following week Edwin took a train to London and spent the best part of the day at New Zealand House. Back in Hove he then visited a local travel agent. He had learned that there were no visa requirements for New Zealand and that a one-way ticket to travel out there by ship would cost £250. He wondered if it would be possible to borrow that amount of money.

CHAPTER NINE

AT SOUTHAMPTON DOCKS, BRIGHT and early on Saturday 1st February 1969, Edwin caught his first glimpse of the vessel that would be taking him to the other side of the world. The Northern Star was a one-class ship belonging to the Shaw Savill line. As he drew closer he saw that its colours were a combination of dingy grey and sickly green which he hoped was not an indication of how things were going to be on the first day as it passed through the notoriously choppy waters of the Bay of Biscay.

In a crowded terminal building he handed over the larger of his two suitcases for storage in the ship's hold. Fellow passengers around him were saying emotional goodbyes to friends and relatives, young and old, with many a tear being shed. The passage to down under was generally perceived as being a one-way irreversible experience and few thought that they would ever set eyes on the northern hemisphere again.

"Bye Bye Tony, Bon voyage and don't forget to write," said one lady with moist eyes.

"Bye Auntie Dot. Take good care of my mum," was the reply.

A train then arrived at a dockside platform bringing still more people and luggage. After a wait of more than two hours some double doors were opened and an announcement was made that passengers should now make their way across the wharf to the gangway for embarkation.

As each person stepped on board they were greeted by a welcoming committee of members of the ship's company as well as the ship's photographer who was going out of his way to make sure that he got a shot of each person. Edwin weaved his way through passageways and stairways and located his four-berth inside cabin where another occupant was already there. The Australian doctor who was on his way home to Sydney introduced himself as Bruce and suggested that Edwin take his pick from the remaining bunks before the remaining two passengers arrived. Edwin opted for one of the lower-level ones and unpacked most of his clothing into a spare wardrobe.

"I don't know about you but I'm famished," said Bruce, "I'm about to go in search of some lunch. Would you care to join me?"

"That sounds like as good idea," said Edwin, glad to have some company. "How is it organised. Do we just show up at one of the restaurants?"

"At some stage of the game there will be a proper seating plan but on the first day lunch is always a bit of a free for all." He said. "Basically there are two large restaurants and they each serve two sittings for breakfast, lunch and dinner."

Meals throughout the six-week voyage to New Zealand were included in the fare and a quick scan of the menu confirmed plenty of gastronomic delights. Edwin ordered a seafood cocktail followed by a pepper steak whilst his newfound cabin mate went for smoked salmon and veal and ham pie. After taking a dessert and a cup of coffee they decided to make an exploratory tour of the ship which to all intents and purposes was a floating hotel.

Within its seven decks were spacious public rooms all of which were tastefully decorated and neatly furnished. A cinema lounge was used for concerts, dances, social events and, on Sundays, even for church services. The passenger decks outside were vast and there was plenty of scope for daily exercise. The two swimming pools might have looked rather drab on such an overcast day but their potential for when the ship reached warmer climates was obvious. An additional observational deck for passenger use was located just in front of the bridge.

There were several different bars to choose from ranging from the sophisticated cocktail variety to those with more of a pub like atmosphere. The largest and most popular one was called The Tavern at the stern of the ship. It had tables and benches set within alcoves as well as a small dance floor with an area for a jazz band to play. The length of its bar stretched wide across the ship and was already being propped up by customers, mostly Australians, who were downing pints of Tuburg draught lager at duty-free prices. Further exploration revealed a well-stocked shop adjacent to the purser's office and the added convenience of a laundrette.

Back through the maze of corridors of Formica walls and linoleum flooring

Edwin and Bruce returned to their cabin where they then met the two remaining inhabitants. Both of them were from the north of England and on their way for a new life in Australia under a scheme which was costing them just £10 per head. One was a former policemen and the other a bus driver. They were accompanied by their wives who were housed in one of the female cabins a little further along the adjoining corridor. It turned out that around a third of the passengers on board the ship were part of a similar mass exodus to Australia. The £10 passage was clearly a tempting proposition and the scheme included free accommodation on arrival and assistance with getting into work. The only stipulation was that they had to remain in Australia for at least two years but that seemed reasonable enough.

Such assisted migration to Australia had led to participants sarcastically being dubbed as the 'Ten Pound Poms.' Bruce explained to Edwin that the origin of the term 'Pommie' either had something to do with pomegranates being supplied to curb scurvy amongst convicts sent to Australia during the previous century or that it was an illiterate acronym that stood for 'Prisoner of Mother England.' Either way 'Pommie Bastards' was how many Australians referred to the British – particularly British immigrants. Although essentially a term of contempt it was sometimes used in a more jocular way too. Edwin was intrigued by that and became determined to use it on his fellow-countrymen at the first available opportunity. He would be sure to include it when writing letters to England. A long blast sounded on the ship's horn. They had set sail.

The routine of shipboard life didn't take long to get used to. Every morning an automatic overhead light in the cabin would slowly brighten to simulate daybreak and provide some indication of time for such inner cabins that had no portholes. A steward delivered teas and coffees. Someone from the purser's office would then give a weather synopsis over the ship's public address system followed by details of events that were scheduled to take place on board that day.

"And then at 2:30 this afternoon there will be a whist drive in the forward lounge and a paper mosaic design competition in the recreation room..."

A seating plan had placed Edwin at a table in the forward restaurant for its first sitting where he found himself in the thrice daily company of an Australian girl on her way back home after a working holiday in England, an accountant on his way to Adelaide and an elderly English lady who was doing the round trip.

The following week the ship docked for a full day in Las Palmas in the Canary Islands. Going ashore proved to be a pleasant reminder of Edwin's time in Spain. Contributing factors were blue sky, bright sunshine and the inevitable slice of tortilla. Some passengers arrived back at the ship with Spanish souvenirs such as dolls in flamenco dress, castanets, leather wine pouches and posters advertising bull fights, with the same enthusiasm as if they had been on a package holiday to the Costa Brava. Back on board Edwin stood at the railings on one of the decks and watched the final loading of fresh supplies being hoisted up and into the store rooms. That evening the ship set sail again and, at a leisurely pace of around 21 knots, continued to make its way down the western side of Africa.

Two Spaniards had boarded in Las Palmas. They were both heading for Sydney and as neither of them spoke much English they were glad of Edwin's company. By now the weather was becoming considerably warmer and passengers had started to make full use of the swimming pools. Many figures were soon to be found sprawled out on the sun decks wiling away the hours as they rapidly acquired a tan. Sunbathing was referred to as sun-baking by the Australians.

The six week voyage was a life of ease and the continuous cycle of meals, relaxation and social life meant that Edwin built up a large circle of new friends. For some additional entertainment Bruce the Australian doctor had acquired a large sheet of thin card left over from one of the fancy dress events. He and Edwin rolled it up into a conical shape and used it as a makeshift megaphone to make bogus announcements in competition with what came over the ship's public address system. They would open their cabin door and in a dead-pan voice say things such as, "Your attention, please. Passengers are advised that the second sitting of breakfast has had to be cancelled this morning because the ship has run out of food. We apologise for any inconvenience." Everyone in the adjoining cabins found it highly amusing but one morning the ship's hospital orderly appeared on the scene with a stern look on his face as he tried to trace the source.

Before leaving England, Edwin had written to his friend Henry in South Africa. He had given details of the ship's itinerary which included a two-day stay stop in Cape Town during which he hoped they could meet up. The ship docked very early that morning and Edwin was already out on deck. Although it was still dark a small crowd of people could be seen gathered at the dockside and Edwin could already make out the figure of Henry amongst them. Eventually the gangway was connected and Edwin stepped ashore.

"Hallo, me old mate," said Henry. "Welcome to South Africa and to this great city of Cape Town or 'Kapstadt' if you want to try saying it in Afrikaans. As you can see we are rather dominated by that particular backdrop over there," he said, pointing to a silhouette of the Table Mountain which was now beginning to reveal itself as the sun came up. Some days it has a levanter cloud hanging over it and we say that it's got its tablecloth on."

"This all seems incredibly out of context," replied Edwin, "It's good of you to have come down and met the ship."

"That's OK," replied Henry, "I thought that this morning we could take a look around the city for a bit and then, if it's OK with you, my parents have invited us to join them for lunch."

"That sounds good to me," said Edwin.

Edwin had heard of Apartheid but now, as they walked through the city centre with its blend of architecturally pleasing buildings and palm trees, he was able to experience it at first hand. Everything was duplicated wherever they went. Plush looking 'whites only' taxis, 'whites only' toilets, 'whites only' restaurants were in evidence compared with run-down amenities for the use of those of a darker skin colour. Later when they got on a train there were superior 'whites only' carriages and inferior 'blacks only' carriages. It struck Edwin as being unjust and unnecessary.

"It's just the way it is," said Henry. "I don't agree with it myself but then it's not something that can be changed overnight. They don't actually realise that they're the underdogs and they're content enough with the way in which things are."

"Surely it must occur to them that the whites have the best of everything compared to their lot in life?" replied Edwin.

"They've never known it to be anything different," he replied, "You enter a building and it'll be a black person who opens the door for you but never the other way round."

"That's exactly my point," said Edwin.

They alighted from the suburban train at a station called Newlands in time for their lunchtime appointment at a restaurant overlooking the Liesbeeck River. Henry's parents were much the same as when Edwin had got to know them in England. Well to do, well-connected, relatively sophisticated and perfectly engaging.

"I thought you'd enjoy that Rietvallei South African wine," said Henry's father, "Let's order up another bottle."

After lunch Henry and Edwin were driven around the outer extremities of Cape Town by Henry's elder brother who then dropped them back in the centre of the city where they visited several bars throughout the evening. Because Henry had to be on duty in the kitchen the following morning it was arranged that they would meet at the docks in the afternoon one last time before the ship departure time.

On his way back to the ship Edwin was determined to have one shot at voicing his concern about the politics of South Africa. To do so he approached a black truck driver and told him that the entire system was hopelessly wrong and that there should be equality between the races. The truck driver was lost for words but nodded and looked at Edwin and simply said, "What can I say, boss?"

Henry was permitted on board the ship as a guest for an hour before it sailed. Afterwards and from the vantage point of one of the upper decks Edwin looked down at him as he again stood on the wharf below. Fifty-five new passengers had embarked in Cape Town and were now finding their way around the vessel.

The next port of call was Durban. On what was a baking hot day Edwin visited its Indian Market with wafts of aromatic spices before finding an air-conditioned bar for a couple of bottles of ice-cold beer. He asked for a phone directory because he recalled that a former colleague from the architect's office of a couple of years ago had come from Durban and he was curious as to whether he could locate the family. There was only one entry of the particular surname listed and so he dialled the number and got through to the person's mother. He explained that he was from England and visiting Durban for a couple of days. Within the next twenty minutes the lady rolled up in her car and Edwin was driven to her home and introduced to her husband and another of her sons.

South Africa had no television which meant that people still held conversations with each other. But they were adamant that black people were destined to be kept in their place.

"Give them an inch and they'll take a mile," said the son, "I run a design studio in town and only yesterday I had to make sure that the coons weren't watching whilst I mixed the paints."

"Why was that?" queried Edwin, not admiring the terminology.

"Well, don't you see? If they saw how it was done, they'd soon learn how to do it for themselves and before we knew it they'd be trying to take away our livelihoods from us," was the explanation.

Edwin didn't respond but was inwardly disgusted by this admission of deliberately denying the knowhow to people just because they were of a different skin colour. No wonder the rest of the world looked down on South Africa, he thought. They had good reason to.

A black housemaid then served everybody a delicious lunch out on the veranda.

Fifty or so passengers had left the ship in Durban and a further hundred and twenty people had embarked. The Tavern Bar was like a non-stop party as the horizon moved gently up and down outside. Several New Zealanders on board gave Edwin their addresses and invited him to visit them in their particular parts of the country. All of them seemed to live on farms. He had tried to gain as much information about his new chosen country in advance so that he'd know what to expect when he arrived there. Throughout the voyage the ship's clocks had been advanced by half an hour on an almost daily basis and Edwin calculated that by now they must be about ten hours ahead of British time.

In the meantime the two cabin mates from the north of England, who for some reason seemed to be permanently at loggerheads with each other, had both been invited to a cocktail party together with their wives by the ship's captain.

"Oo, aye, I've never been to anything like that before," said the former bus driver, "I don't even know what a cocktail party is."

"You twit," responded the former policeman, "everybody knows that it's where you have to go before the captain and show him your cock."

One morning Edwin got up early and sat on deck as the new day was dawning. He had a small transistor radio with him and was able to pick up a station that was broadcasting from Perth in Western Australia. He had an awe inspiring sense of being on the other side of the world. It triggered off thoughts of the countless predecessors who'd made the same journey in far less comfortable circumstances than aboard a cruise ship.

After docking in Freemantle the majority of the ship's passengers took coaches into nearby Perth for a day's sightseeing as their first taste of Australia. Edwin and a group of others decided to remain in Freemantle for the day which was within walking distance.

"G'day" was evidently the most popular greeting and ice-cold lager was evidently the most popular form of refreshment. It was served in what at first glance looked like a glass flower vase known as a midi and filled with beer by means of a squirting device on the end of a hose pipe which resembled a miniature petrol pump. A plump Australian lady with a broad smile on her heavily made-up face and an equally broad Australian accent did the honours. After downing several glasses of this local brew they stepped outside into the blazing sunshine to see what else they could see. Quaint colonial style architecture was one feature of the town. Sunshades and canopies were the other.

When the Northern Star reached Melbourne there was a shuttle train service to and from the city centre. Arriving at Flinders Street Railway Station Edwin found some familiar sounding places displayed on the destination boards. There were suburbs of Croydon, Epping, Preston, Sunbury, Doncaster East, St Albans and there was even a Brighton.

A few days later the ship docked at the harbour-side of Sydney's inner city eastern suburb with the unlikely sounding name of Wooloomooloo. Most of the people that Edwin had befriended during the five and a half weeks since Southampton were now leaving the ship. All three of his cabin mates were disembarking. They shook hands and wished each other all the best for the future.

That morning Edwin went ashore and on realising the dock's close proximity to the Sydney Harbour Bridge he made his way to it by a route alongside some Botanical Gardens. He walked across the famous bridge to Luna Park and then back again alongside the equally famous and iconic Sydney Opera House. Back on board the ship for lunch he ran into the two Spanish passengers. They too were leaving the ship and they invited Edwin to accompany them on a brief walking tour of downtown Sydney that afternoon. They seemed to know their way around Sydney quite well. Passing through the hustle and bustle of the King's Cross district they arrived at a small backstreet building and one of them produced a key and opened the entrance door. Inside was like a club with a bar in one corner. Edwin saw that all of its walls were adorned with framed photographs of rallies of one sort or another and that there was an array of flags with a red, green and white criss-cross design. He asked them what kind of a place it was.

"Sabes, que banderas son?" Alfonso asked Edwin if he recognised the flags.

"No lo sé," replied Edwin.

"Son las banderas del País Basco," replied Alfonso triumphantly. "We are not Spanish. We are proud Basques and this is our country's flag."

Edwin didn't quite know how to respond. He already knew something of the strength of anti-Spanish feeling held by separatist organisations so he merely nodded with some degree of enthusiasm and as if to show some degree of sympathy with their cause.

"Bueno, pues primeramente tenemos que tomar una copa," said Miguel and reached for a bottle of that familiar aniseed liqueur which he poured generously into three balloon glasses.

"Salud y buena suerte!" said Alfonso as he raised his glass.

The final leg of Edwin's voyage was from Sydney to Wellington and took four more days. He was now the sole occupant of his four-berth cabin and was mentally preparing to be even more alone once he arrived in New Zealand. Quite a few new passengers had joined the ship in Sydney most of whom were bound for the United Kingdom. After Wellington their ports of call would be Rarotonga, Tahiti, Acapulco, Panama City, Trinidad, Lisbon and then on to Southampton. A dozen or so elderly passengers who had first joined the ship in Southampton at the same time as Edwin were doing the full circle back to Britain simply as a round the world cruise.

Edwin's first sight of New Zealand was of green and brown hills along the stretch of water leading towards Wellington Harbour. He could make out a few isolated single storey houses which they passed along the way before the capital city came into view.

There was an arrival procedure for those passengers leaving the vessel in New Zealand. Immigration and Customs officials had come on board that morning and set themselves up in one of the ship's lounges. Those disembarking were called over one by one to process an arrival card and a baggage form as well as to have their passports stamped. They also had to make a 'nothing to declare' statement to a customs official. Once that formality was over, Edwin was able to step ashore with his cabin bag, collect the suitcase that had been stored in the ship's hold and begin to see what life in New Zealand was going to be like.

CHAPTER TEN

ALTHOUGH EDWIN WAS PLEASED to have reached his destination of New Zealand, his first day ashore in Wellington took a bit of getting used to. Having made the fourteen thousand mile voyage he was conscious of the fact that from now on there would be no announcements over a public address system to say that lunch was about to be served. He asked a taxi driver if there was somewhere in town with affordable accommodation for a few days and after a short ride he moved into a small room in the front part of a guest house. An initial exploratory walk around the immediate area gave an impression of it being more like a provincial town rather than the nation's capital city. Edwin contemplated how best to go about things. He needed to find a job but at the same time he reasoned that if he were to start looking for some kind of employment right away, he probably wouldn't see much beyond Wellington. He wondered if there might be some way of doing a quick tour of both islands of New Zealand first. That would surely be preferable because it would enable him to familiarise himself with the country before deciding in which part to settle.

He still had a booklet of travellers' cheques and the thought crossed his mind about the possibility of a low-budget youth hostelling tour. On making enquiries, he found out that there was a reasonable network of youth hostels throughout New Zealand and that it was possible to become a member on the spot at any one of them. The idea looked promising. He went back to his room and started packing the rucksack that he he'd had the foresight to bring out with him. He came to an arrangement with the landlady that she would store his suitcases for him for picking up at a later date. He would set off on his trip in three days' time.

Edwin's first evening meal in New Zealand was a massive hamburger. He watched it being constructed. The two halves of a large bun were first painted with molten butter before the ground beefsteak was added and then topped with fried onion, a slab of New Zealand cheese, a ring of pineapple and some lettuce and ketchup. It was purchased at a kiosk across the road from where he was staying, as was the strawberry milkshake that went with it.

The Cook Strait that separated the North Island from the South Island was known to be a rough stretch of sea. The wreck of a previous inter-island ferry which had ended in a tragic maritime disaster the year before was visible near the harbour's entrance. Despite Edwin having spent six weeks at sea on the Northern Star with no adverse effect at all, on board the considerably smaller vessel he began to feel seasick almost at once. He spent the first hour out on deck for the prime purpose of fresh air and then braved it to the ferry's cafeteria for an overpriced sandwich and a cup of tea. The crossing time from Wellington to Picton was three and a half hours. He spoke with a red-haired girl who happened to be sitting alongside him. She turned out to be an Australian although she'd lived New Zealand for a number of years. When the ship eventually docked in Picton she wrote out her address and said that if he were ever passing Christchurch in his travels, he'd be welcome to drop by.

That afternoon Edwin began hitchhiking. A small country lane was actually the main highway that led down the westerly side of the South Island. He stood opposite a pastel blue wooden bungalow with a dark red corrugated iron roof. A middle-aged lady came down the driveway to collect her letters from the mailbox by her front gate. She called out a friendly "G'day!" to Edwin. He acknowledged her and asked if it was the right road for Greymouth, explaining that he had recently arrived in New Zealand from England.

"Aw, yis, you're on the right road all right," she said, "Nelson is about forty miles away and after that Greymouth is about another sixty. You say you're from England? I met someone from there once by the name of Christine Chapman.

Wouldn't happen to know her by any chance would you?"

Greymouth seemed a drab sort of a place although Edwin wasn't really sure what he had been expecting. However, the youth hostel was pleasant enough and he dutifully paid his annual subscription in addition to the small fee for a night's stay. His idea was to travel around part of the South Island in an anti-clockwise direction and then get back up to the North Island to do something similar up there.

The following morning there was absolutely no traffic on the road at all apart from two old bangers in the space of an hour and a half both of which were in any case travelling in the opposite direction. Finally a car going south arrived and pulled up to offer him a ride. The journey that followed included stretches of road that had no tarmac but with surfaces of smoothed out earth. Bridges that crossed rivers and valleys were sometimes shared with the single track of a railway line and the driver always had to make sure that no train was coming in either direction. Not that there were many trains, nor many other cars for that matter. They saw the sum total of five other vehicles throughout the entire morning. Yellow flowered gorse bushes were growing in abundance on either side of the road and Edwin asked his driver about them.

"I'm afraid that was brought over here way back by one of your fellow-countrymen," he said laughingly, "Some crazy joker got it into his head that it would make it feel more like home and then it spread like wildfire."

Occasional road signs along the route gave notice of forthcoming places. A place called Ross was 48 miles. As they got closer and passed a town called Hokitika, Ross was 19 miles, then Ross was just 11 miles, and Ross was now only 5 miles. Edwin's expectation was mounting but when they eventually got to the vast metropolis of Ross it turned out to be a tiny town left over from the gold rush days and with a population of less than 300.

The one and only youth hostel on this route was at a place called Franz Joseph which was named after the person who had discovered a glacier on the side of nearby mountain. Although Edwin had no particular interest in staring at a cavern of ice he nevertheless took the trip out to see it as it was just something that everybody was obliged to do if they happened to be passing down the West Coast of the South Island of New Zealand

Four Australians were staying at the youth hostel.

"For us it's considered part and parcel of our education to visit another country after we've finished our studies," explained one of them. "A lot of us head across to Europe or the United States on working holidays but we just fancied exploring New Zealand instead."

"What are you going to do when you go back?" asked Edwin.

'I've got a job lined up in Sydney as a civil engineer,' he replied, 'How's about yourself?'

"At the moment I just want to take a look around both islands of New Zealand and then, once I've worked out which part I want to live in, I'll start looking for some kind of work."

"Should have no probs," said the Australian, "Your best bet will be to go for one of the four main cities, Auckland, Wellington, Christchurch or Dunedin. With the kind of manpower shortage they've got over here at the moment it means you can pick and choose."

It was a couple of miles walk from the youth hostel to the nearest amenities which consisted of the now familiar combination of a post office, a church, a dairy shop and a pub. All five of them decided to make the trek for the purpose of buying some beer from the pub's bottle store. These were sold in cardboard cartons that contained twelve bottles each which they then lugged back to the hostel. They stayed up drinking and chatting late into the night.

The following day Edwin continued hitchhiking south through an area known as the Haast Pass. It took in mile after mile on breath-taking unspoiled scenic beauty. The mountains, rivers and beech forests showed no sign of human habitation at all. It felt as if time stood still and that he and the driver were the original pioneers of the country.

He was dropped off in Queenstown in the early evening. There was no youth hostel there but an out-of-season holiday camp had several rows of shacks containing twin beds and he was able to book one of them for the night. What he hadn't realised, however, was that blankets and linen weren't provided and that the huts were like ice boxes. He remained fully clothed and ended up sandwiching himself between the mattress on his bed and the mattress taken from the other bed. It wasn't very satisfactory and he was glad when sunshine of the following morning arrived.

Back on the road again a series of lifts got him across to the East Coast and the small harbour town of Oamaru. A dairy shop sold hot meat pies that had a layer of mashed potato in place of a normal pastry lid as a kind of meal-in-one arrangement. Edwin found it so acceptable that he went back into the shop and bought a second one.

It then began to rain quite heavily. For a while he sheltered in the entrance hall of the town's small railway station but the downpour persisted. There was a tavern opposite although, much to his indignation, Edwin had discovered the legal drinking age in New Zealand to be twenty-one whereas he was still only nineteen. Nevertheless, he thought he'd give it a go. Stepping inside the smoke filled bar he ordered a beer and sat himself down at a small table. The decor was bland and the clientele all male. A man sitting next to him acknowledged his presence and launched into some long winded explanation about penguin colonies which was completely lost on him. Nevertheless Edwin tried to show some interest. A reversal in the pronunciation of the vowels 'e' and 'i' in the New Zealand accent was beginning to sound quite normal and Edwin soon found himself pronouncing 'yes' as 'yis'. It turned out that the man worked for the New Zealand Railways. He told Edwin that there were no more passenger trains that day but that there would be a freight train going through to Christchurch later that afternoon and that he could easily get Edwin a free ride in the guard's van if he wanted it.

"I've never hitched a ride on a train before," responded Edwin, "but, I'd be interested in giving it a go.

"My old man was a Pom," the man continued, "although my mum is a third generation New Zealander."

He topped up Edwin's glass from the remainder of a jug of draught beer and went over to the bar to buy another. The brew had a distinctive taste, a bit on the flat side, brownish orange in colour and ice cold.

During the course of conversation Edwin observed the not so quaint kiwi custom of inserting the word 'shit' into most sentences. If it were an affirmation it was, 'Aw shit, yes!' if it were negation it was, 'Shit, no!' if it were a disappointment it was, 'Aw, shit!' and if it were something to be enthusiastic about it was, 'Shit hot!' Edwin made a mental note never to introduce any of that into his own vocabulary.

The man said that he spent a lot of his time in that particular pub. Edwin then bought a jug of beer.

"Not so long ago we had six o'clock closing time in New Zealand," explained the man. "Everyone knocked off work at five and headed straight down to the pub to get as much beer down them as they could in that one remaining hour. It was known at the six o'clock swill and everyone ended up getting as pissed as a newt. To try and make the situation more civilised the government extended the opening hours until ten o'clock."

"And presumably that has made things a lot easier," said Edwin.

"Shit no!" said the man. "The end result of it is that everybody still shoots off down to the pub straight after work but that they stay there right through to the ten o'clock closing."

"I see that they're all men in here," said Edwin.

"Some of the pubs have got a lounge bar but you have to wear a jacket and tie before they'll let you in. They are the only bars that ladies might go into – apart from the odd alcoholic women who from time to time might drift into a bar like this."

"I get the picture," relied Edwin.

"Now, there's time for another jug and it's my shout," said his companion.

They made it to the station shortly before the train pulled in. Various packages and cloth sacks were dumped on the platform. The man introduced Edwin to the guard who confirmed that it would be no problem taking him through to Christchurch.

"They're narrow gauge tracks here in New Zealand," called out the man as he waved a parting gesture, "but it'll get you there."

On arrival in Christchurch it was both dark and damp. The station was located in what looked like a light industrial area. His immediate thought was to head for the address of the Australian girl that he'd met a week ago week on the inter-island ferry. He pulled out the piece of paper from his wallet and studied the address 76 Tancred Street, Linwood, Christchurch. There was also a phone number but he figured that it might be easier just to arrive on the doorstep. If that proved inconvenient he would find his way to Christchurch Youth Hostel instead. A person came into view and Edwin asked him for directions.

"If you carry on straight down to the end of this road and you'll see that it suddenly turns into an 'L' shape over on your left," he said. "Follow that round and keep on going along there till you get to about the tenth intersection which is called Hereford Street. Turn right there and Linwood is about another ten minute walk. I don't exactly know where Tancred Street is but I guess you'll be able to ask someone else that from there."

Edwin thanked him and set off alongside various warehouses and small factories of one sort or another that stretched out alongside the railway sidings. He turned into a wide avenue with a middle island of trees which had smaller residential streets of wooden bungalows branching off on either side. Hereford Street came into view as did a further cross roads that had a public library and a small row of local shops. A dairy shop on the corner was still open and the lady behind the counter told him that Tancred Street was four blocks further up.

When he got there he saw that number 76 shared a common entrance with number 74 and discovered the place he was looking for was a long wooden hut in the back garden. There were lights shining through the curtained windows and Edwin rapped on the door. A young lady answered but Edwin saw that it was not the Australian from the ferry.

"Sorry to disturb you," he said, "but is this where Bronwyn lives?"

"Yes it is" she said, "I'm afraid she's out just now but she should be back a wee bit later."

"Oh," said Edwin, "It's just that I met her last week on the ferry and just thought I'd look her up," he said

'Well, my name's Diana. I'm her flatmate so I think you'd better come in,' she said.

He stepped into the hut and found himself directly in the kitchen.

'Here, grab a seat,' she said, indicating a small table and chairs.

Edwin took off his rucksack and jacket. The girl remained standing leaning back against the sink. She was tall and had short dark hair and a clear complexion. They got chatting. She was from a place called Masterton in the North Island but had lived in Christchurch for a year where she worked as a florist. Edwin asked whether she knew the whereabouts of the Christchurch Youth Hostel.

"I really don't know," she said, "but if you're stuck for somewhere to stay you'd be welcome to stay here with us for a few nights. We often have guests. There's only the one bedroom down the far end which is where Bronwyn sleeps. My bed is in the corner of our lounge but there's also a bed settee there where you could get a good night's kip."

The hospitality was sincere and well intentioned although Edwin had a slight worry that the Australian girl, Bronwyn, might not appreciate the fact that in her absence he had simply moved into her home. As it happened, however, his fears were unfounded. As he settled down on the bed settee, which was further along the same length of wall from Diana who by now was in her bed, they both heard Bronwyn arrive back home. She had to pass through the lounge to reach her room. Diana announced the presence of Edwin but the conversation remained extremely brief. Displaying almost complete indifference she simply said 'Hi, mate' and then added that it was fine for him to stay as long as he liked and carried on straight through to her room.

Having got off to sleep Edwin was then awoken by a loud noise a couple of hours later. It had been a crashing noise followed by some male muttering.

"What on earth was that?" asked Edwin, guessing that Diana was awake too.

"It's most probably my husband," replied Diana.

"Your husband?" said Edwin, wondering why such technical detail hadn't been mentioned the evening before and wondering how on earth he was going to justify sleeping in the same room as the poor man's wife, "I didn't realise you were married."

"Well, he's not really my husband – not yet anyway. More like my boyfriend really. He's a law student and some evenings he works in a bar in the centre of town which is what he's been doing this evening judging by the sound of things. I'd better go and see."

In her long nightdress she went out through the door and turned on a light in the adjacent connecting passage that led past the shower room to the kitchen.

Edwin could catch occasional snippets of their conversation including the words "Yes, a black coffee would be a good idea."

Twenty minutes later, Diana entered the lounge with her companion in the dark and they both clambered into her bed. Before long gentle rhythmic snoring could be heard and Edwin turned over and hoped that he could get back to sleep too. There was one further interruption that night. At around three thirty in the morning Edwin woke to the sound of Diana trying to wake up her companion.

"Oh no! Steve! Quick! Wake up! Get to the toilet!"

At first he assumed the unfortunate man to have been sick. But it wasn't that at all. After a heavy beer intake the night before and the coffee on top of it, he was urinating in his sleep.

Edwin arose shortly after eight. He'd already heard both Bronwyn and Diana get up, take showers and depart for work. Steve, however, remained fast asleep. Edwin tiptoed through to the kitchen and on the table was a spare door key and note from Diana telling him to feel free to help himself to things and make himself at home. He made use of the shower, got dressed into clean clothes and went back into the kitchen to switch on the electric jug. Something stirred in the next room and before he knew it, Steve had joined him and formally introduced himself with a handshake. He had a cultured New Zealand accent and it soon became obvious that he had absolutely no recollection of the events of the previous night. They had a cup of tea together and some toast spread with butter and Vegemite.

"I think you'll enjoy New Zealand," he said, "Some people reckon Christchurch is more English than England so you should feel at home! If there's anything you need just give me a shout."

"Thank you," replied Edwin, "I'm looking forward to exploring this city."

"Too right," he said, "I'm afraid I'm going to have to shoot through right now though because I'm already running slightly late to get to varsity in time for my lecture but what say we meet up sometime during the week and go for a few beers?"

"Sounds like a good idea," said Edwin, managing not to show any reservations that, based on the previous night's experience, it might not be a good idea at all.

Edwin washed up the few items of crockery and, taking the key with him, stepped outside to see what Christchurch looked like in daylight. It was a cold crisp morning with a deep blue sky. His first impressions were of parallel rows of single storey wooden houses with corrugated iron roofs that each stood on a quarter acre plot of land. Most were painted in pastel colours and had front verandas. Their gardens were neatly trimmed and some displayed cylindrical metal water tanks supported on a criss-cross structure of wooden stilts. Mailboxes were mounted next to everybody's front gate. Such streets were invariably straight and large gutters ran alongside the pavements. Rough-cut wooden beams supported a web of thick power cables that were hooked up to every home.

The topography of Christchurch was as flat as a pancake although some foothills could be seen in the distance. Edwin continued to walk through such suburbia for over an hour and wondered if its sprawling residential areas would ever lead to a focal point. Occasionally a small parade of local shops broke the monotony. They were accompanied by permanently fixed corrugated iron canopies that covered the entire pavement to provide shade from the heat in summer and shelter from the rain in winter. On one side of a shop an advertisement for 'Wattie's Frozen Garden Peas' had been put together using a mosaic of small coloured metallic discs that hung on pins protruding from a wooden board. The discs would change their angle with the slightest breeze and glint as they did so, which created the visual effect of an animated billboard.

Most of the car on the streets were old models that had been kept going way past their normal life expectancy. Although New Zealand had no car manufacturing industry of its own it obviously had plenty of good mechanics.

Edwin asked a passing lady if he was anywhere near the centre of Christchurch.

"The town sinta? Jeese, noey… you're headed completely in the wrong direction," she said. A single-decker red bus passed them by. "That would've got you right theer though to cutheedrul squeer."

For the sake of variety he shifted over a couple of streets over before looping back in the right direction for the town centre. Eventually he recognised the tree-lined avenue of the night before.

Several cyclists passed by. The flatness of Christchurch positively lent itself to that means of getting around. As Edwin got closer to the city centre residential housing began to be broken up by office buildings and green-grassed squares. Stopping at a crossroads to wait for the lights to change he was intrigued to see that they all turned to red simultaneously halting the flow of traffic in every direction which enabled pedestrians to cross diagonally if they wished.

The Anglican Cathedral stood in the middle of Christchurch as its central point. Wide spaces of its surrounding area served as the converging point for the city's bus routes, all of which were of the same red coloured single-decker variety that Edwin had seen earlier that morning. The tower of a Bank of New Zealand building looked down from one side of the square whilst Warner's Hotel and a takeaway food outlet run by a couple of Greek men occupied the other. The tourist office and a cinema were positioned in a far corner alongside a coffee shop whilst the central Post Office stood on the opposite side. Shopping streets radiated out from Cathedral Square in all directions and it was a short walk down to the river that meandered its way right through the city's centre.

Edwin spent a couple of hours exploring the central part of Christchurch, taking in its every detail. It was an attractive layout in which the shopping area was complemented by public gardens and riverbanks with weeping willow trees. It reminded him of certain provincial English cities – perhaps the best elements of Salisbury, Chester, Bath, Oxford and Canterbury blended together. Then, realising that he'd been on his feet all morning, he entered a snack bar which overlooked a bandstand near the river and ordered steak, eggs and chips with a cup of tea. There was a jukebox.

Those were the days my friend,
We thought they'd never end
We'd sing and dance forever and a day
We'd lead the life we choose
We'd fight and never lose
For we were young and sure to have our way

On returning to the flat in Tancred Street later that afternoon Diana had already arrived home from work and asked him how his day had been.

"It's been brilliant," replied Edwin. "I'm already quite taken with Christchurch.

It seems to have a good positive feel about it. Even though I still want to take a quick look around the rest of New Zealand it's highly likely that I'll come back to Christchurch to start looking for work."

"Well, even if you go away for a while, you know that there's always a base here for you when you come back," she said.

Edwin thanked her for such kindness and asked what time Bronwyn would be back.

"The thing with Bronwyn is..." began Diana, "Although I'm her flatmate I don't actually know her that well but from what I can see she's going through a difficult time at present and, strictly between you and me, I think she's mixing with the wrong kind of people."

"How do you mean?" asked Edwin.

"Well, some of the characters she hangs around with seem pretty unsavoury and there are also repeated demands for payment from mail order companies that arrive for her in the post on a regular basis which she never seems to pay," she replied.

Edwin spent four more nights in Christchurch by which time he felt as if he'd got to know the place quite well. Diana's boyfriend, Steve, had driven him across the university campus, around Hagley Park, along the banks of the Avon River, out to the beaches of Sumner and New Brighton, through the well-to-do suburb of Fendalton and even to Christchurch Airport. Edwin had gained a good overview of the place. He had also called in at the Gresham Arms, where Steve worked part-time. A quick lunchtime drink had lasted through the entire afternoon and ended up with deep fried oysters in batter and chips from the takeaway in Cathedral Square.

He didn't see anything further of the Australian, Bronwyn, until his final night when she had burst through the living room in an agitated state with an Italian man in a long scruffy coat who was trying to calm her down.

It was time for Edwin to move on.

IT WAS A FINE autumnal day as Edwin boarded the afternoon sailing of the ferry from Picton at the top end of New Zealand's South Island to take him back to Wellington at the bottom end of the North Island. He stayed overnight at a youth hostel in the suburb of Upper Hutt and the following day hitch-hiked to a place called Dannevirke. There was no hostel there but the landlord of an old-fashioned looking hotel provided Edwin with a room for the night at a very cheap rate. It was a farming community and all of the characters inside the hotel's bar were locals.

"Air gun?" seemed to be the most popular form of greeting which took Edwin a while to understand it as "How's it going?"

Overnight stays were then made at youth hostels in Clive, Hamilton, and Gisborne. Being out of season other hostellers were few and far between. There were some exceptions however and he did take a moonlit walk around a lake in Hamilton with a young lady who was also staying at the hostel there. He also met some Maoris for the first time. They were burly bronze men who worked at a local freezing works which Edwin discovered to be another name for abattoir. One of them offered him a native fruit called a Fijoa, demonstrating how to eat it by biting the top off and squeezing its gooey pulp up to the surface.

New Zealand had a tendency to shut down everything for the entire weekend.

Shops were closed on Saturdays as well as Sundays. During one of his lifts a horse race was being broadcast live on the car radio but, try as he may, Edwin couldn't make out a single word of the commentary. It was being delivered so fast, so nasally and with such a broad accent that it might as well have been a foreign language, which in one sense it was.

Later that afternoon he stepped foot into a roadside pub. Groups of men were noisily knocking back vast quantities of ice-cold beer and arguing with each other at the same time. They stood at tall table-like structures on which to rest their drinks. These were equipped with a built in ashtray set into the top surface under which a jam jar, half full of water, had been screwed in place to ensure that cigarettes were properly extinguished as well as aiding the by-product of a yellowish brown clear soup of swollen tobacco strands and disintegrated filter tips.

"What's this then? The Rambling Society?" jibed one of the men on seeing Edwin's rucksack.

"Thirsty work all that rambling!" roared another, "Poor bugger's dying of thirst, I reckon."

Edwin grinned and, depositing his rucksack at one side of the room, made his way to the stainless steel bar and bought a beer. When he returned he was beckoned over by one of the men.

"We can't have any ramblers drinking on their own!" he yelled, "Come over here and join us!"

The invitation was sufficiently compelling for Edwin to move across to their area.

"Jeeze, a Pommie rambler, are you?" the man said after some introductions had been made, "We don't often get any Poms in here."

"That cos we'd normally show them the door!" laughed another character called Bert.

"Don't worry, you're OK mate," reassured the first man, "It's just that a lot of folk from your country arrive out here and do nothing else but run the place down. And as far as we're concerned, if they don't like it they can push off back to England."

"I think I know the kind of people you mean," said Edwin, "but from what I've seen of New Zealand so far, I think it's a great place."

"Yeah well you can see why we wanna keep it as it is," said Bert, "It's God's own country and we're damn proud of it!"

There was more raucous laughter and two members of the group picked up all four empty beer jugs and went to get them re-filled. The session lasted all afternoon. Edwin's glass was constantly being topped up from somebody else's jug and it was a good hour before they'd let him buy a round. The conversation tended to degenerate into something of a drunken stupor for most of those gathered and in the back of his mind he was aware of the fact that he would have to find somewhere to stay for the night. He asked Bert if he knew of any suitable accommodation nearby.

"Too right, I do," was the reply, "You're stopping over with me and my family."

It was another example of New Zealand hospitality. Bert drove the two of them to his house and parked the car. He then gave Edwin a revealing pep talk.

"Look," he said, "We've all had a great time down the pub. It's something I do every Saturday afternoon together with the group of my cobbers but now we are going into a different environment and it's where I have to cut the aspect. There will be some more beer this evening, bottled beer from the fridge, but all my pub talk is now over – I have to cut the aspect!"

Stepping into his home Edwin was introduced to Bert's charming wife who was cooking in the kitchen and to his two young daughters who were playing in the lounge. Bert was suddenly as sober as a judge.

AUCKLAND WAS CONSIDERABLY LARGER than Christchurch and had the additional feature of hills – rather a lot of hills in fact. It had the distinction of being New Zealand's largest city despite Wellington being the capital. Edwin made his way to the suburb of Remuera. Two university students that he had met on the inter-island ferry a week ago had a spare room in their flat that was available for a few weeks at a low rent. Edwin took a look at it and agreed to move in right away. For the time being he thought he would stick around in Auckland and see how things developed. He had also reviewed his money situation and calculated that the sooner he could find some sort of a job the better.

An adjoining flat was occupied by four girls. The inhabitants of both flats occasionally socialised with each other and there was an extensive shared garden at the back of the property.

On Monday morning whilst scanning the classified section of an Auckland newspaper, an advertisement caught Edwin's eye. He read it through a couple of times.

Dynamic, rapidly expanding company urgently seeks new staff for exciting promotional opportunities. Immediate start. No experience necessary. Full training given. Excellent rate of pay. Apply today

If nothing else it seemed to suit his immediate requirements and he dialled the number. The person on the other end of the line didn't seem to want any details about Edwin but simply gave him an office address and asked him if he could be there tomorrow morning at ten o'clock.

Edwin arrived shortly before the appointed hour. The offices were based on the second floor of a building near Auckland's railway station. A receptionist ushered him into a large room where several other candidates were gathered. She told him that someone would be along to give an introductory overview at half past ten and that in the meantime he was welcome to grab a tea or coffee. Edwin poured himself a mug of tea and spoke with another potential recruit.

"I presume, like me, you're here in response to the job advertisement?" asked Edwin.

"Too right I am!" was his reply. "It's exactly the kind of opportunity I've been waiting for."

"Any idea what the work involves?" asked Edwin.

"I guess we'll soon find out," he said, "but from what I can gather it's supposed to be promoting something or other."

"Yes, that's what the advertisement said," replied Edwin, "Promoting what, I wonder."

"Although maybe the ad was a load of bullshit," continued the man, "just to make people show up."

"Well if that's the case it seems to have worked," said Edwin, nodding towards the growing number of people who stood opposite.

A young man wearing a suit and tie then took up position at the front of the room and having got everyone's attention asked them to be seated. He thanked everybody for coming, introduced himself as Ian Baker and explained that although he'd joined the company just nine months ago he had already risen up the ladder to the role of Supervisor.

"And if I can do it, you can do it!" he said enthusiastically. "Our particular business is in the field of educational learning systems and we have an excellent product to market. In a few moments, you'll be divided into three teams and the first part of this two-day training programme will get underway. As you'll appreciate we can't actually pay you anything during the training period but once you've been trained the income potential is virtually unlimited."

Edwin was in Team 3 which was then invited to go through to a different room in which a circle of chairs had been set up. A different supervisor arrived and asked each of them to introduce themselves one by one and to state a little bit about themselves.

"Hi, my name is Murray. I'm from Taranaki but I've been in Auckland for the past year and until just recently I've been working in a warehouse."

"Thank you," said the supervisor, "Next."

"Hallo, I'm Fiona. I live in Mount Eden where I work in a restaurant but I want to try my hand at doing something different."

"G'day. My name's Max. I come from Rotorua. I've worked four years in forestry and I have just recently moved up to Auckland."

And so it went on right around the circle including Edwin who simply introduced himself as having recently arrived from England.

With the introductions out of the way two typewritten pages of text were then handed out to each of the participants. They were then instructed to go round the circle again each reading one paragraph out loud. The content was in script form and seemed to be advancing various notions about the importance of children being able to have access to education. It was written in a conversational style. Edwin was able to deliver his paragraph with comparative ease and even applied a New Zealand accent to it. The exercise continued around the circle for the rest of the morning by which time the script had been read and re-read in its entirety perhaps twenty times over.

"…And through the learning system, children such as yours will be able to brush up on their subjects and positively excel in everything they do…"

Because it read like the words of an advertisement Edwin wondered whether everybody was taking part in some kind of an audition for a radio commercial. There was a break for lunch and he went out for a walk along the palm tree lined approach to the railway station. When he returned he learned that two of their number had departed and wouldn't be coming back. The rest were asked to continue reading the scripted piece a few more times. Then the supervisor said, "Fine, which of you thinks that by now they can remember it without reading it?" The question slightly threw everybody.

"I'll have a go," volunteered one of the men and, after a brief pause, launched into the first part of what had been recited throughout the day. He started off all right but then left out two whole paragraphs and ground to a halt shortly afterwards. Even Edwin knew the missing sentences and when they were asked who else would like to have a crack at it he raised his hand. The lines flowed forth as if he'd been rehearsing a stage performance for several months. He even got a small round of applause.

"Very well done," said the supervisor, "Now, is there anyone else who would also like to give it a go?"

As Edwin walked back to the flat in Remuera he was accompanied along part of the route by a female member of the team who was in two minds about whether to return the next day. She told Edwin that she thought that the day had been a complete waste of time and couldn't see how sitting around in a circle reading a load of drivel was ever likely to lead to any kind of a job worth doing. Edwin sympathised to a point. He too couldn't grasp the significance of having to learn such scripted words parrot fashion other than to suppose they were just testing everybody to see how well they could memorise things. Nevertheless because he'd invested a full day into the training programme, he might as well go ahead and complete the second half.

ONE OF THE GIRLS from the flat next door was a young seamstress called Caroline. She was planning a trip to Europe and had let it be known that she would like to have a chat with Edwin for any useful tips that he might be able to offer. The request was particularly welcomed by Edwin not least because he had felt some kind of a magnetic pull towards her when they'd first been introduced at the beginning of the week and since then he had been wondering if there might be an opportunity to become better acquainted. He dropped by that evening.

The four girls were sat around the dining table having just finished their evening meal. Caroline was aged eighteen and attractive with her long blonde hair that divided in two above her forehead. She had blue eyes, was of medium height and was perhaps just a little on the plump side. But above all she was talkative, bubbly and had a great sense of humour.

"Would you like some Pavlova?' There's plenty left over," she asked in her broad Kiwi accent.

"Excuse my ignorance but I'm not sure what Pavlova is," replied Edwin, slightly embarrassed, not only by such an admission but also by the shock of finding himself being addressed by the girl who had occupied his mind.

"It's just a desert," she replied, "Hang on a mo and I'll fetch you some."

Joining the others at the table, he was served a large portion of meringue filled with fresh fruit and thick cream. It transpired that Caroline came from a farming family in the South Island and that, in common with many young people from rural locations, she had moved to the city for work. She'd been living in Auckland for a year and a half but would be departing on her trip to Europe the following month together with two other New Zealand girls. However, it wasn't simply a flight to Europe. They would be travelling overland via Australia, Indonesia, Malaysia, Thailand, Nepal and heaven knows how many other countries en route to Europe. It was quite a bold undertaking and, in other circumstances, the sort of adventure that Edwin would have liked to have embarked upon himself.

After an interesting conversation for more than an hour, Caroline's flatmates disappeared off to their rooms and she and Edwin were alone. She poured them some more coffee and they decamped from the formality of the dining table to the comfort of a settee. Edwin, who felt as if he was in a dream, couldn't resist asking Caroline if she was attached. When she answered "No," their eyes met.

"Fascinating," was all he could think of to say.

She blushed slightly.

"Fascinating all right," she replied, "but actually you are the one that is fascinating." Seconds later they were locked in a passionate embrace. She was warm, huggable and enthusiastic. Edwin also discovered that she had a particularly appealing aroma of shampoo about her. Their first kiss seemed to last for eternity.

BACK AT THE COMPANY'S office the following morning Edwin began to see through the nature of the training course. Less than half of the people from the previous day had returned. The three teams were merged and he now sat in a circle of eleven people.

Some tell-tale additions to the previous day's script had been made. "Hallo Mrs Jones, my name is John Smith and I'm conducting a survey in this area on behalf of the learning division for those parents who have children of under the age of sixteen. You do have children don't you Mrs Jones? Yes, can I ask what their ages are? That's great. I'd like to make an appointment with you and your husband for this evening."

It was becoming all too apparent that the new version of the script formed the patter of a door to door salesman. New terminology had crept into the text as had some figures quoted in New Zealand dollars and the whole thing was now seen in a different context.

"Every conceivable question that you might ever get asked can be answered by referring back to the appropriate part of the script," said the supervisor triumphantly.

"I thought this wasn't supposed to be selling," objected one of the participants.

"It's a promotion," claimed the supervisor. "All we are doing is explaining the product. But of course any sales that follow as a result of that would be a good thing too – and you'll get fifty dollars for every deal that you manage to make so the earning potential is huge."

"That sounds like a commission but we were told that the job had a fixed salary," said another.

"Oh, you can have a fixed salary if you'd prefer it," chirped the supervisor. "The company will be pleased to pay you $100 a week but in return for that you must make at least three deals a week – otherwise you're out on your ear. So it stands to reason that it makes more sense to go with the other arrangement because those same three deals will give you $150 dollars."

It felt like a con. Edwin was in two minds as to whether to quit then and there having wasted two full days of valuable job hunting time. The prospect of going out and banging on doors in an attempt to flog sets of children's encyclopaedias to New Zealanders had no appeal whatsoever and he certainly hadn't come to the other side of the world be doing something like that. On the other hand, he needed some money in a hurry and if it really was possible to make some by this means then he supposed that maybe he ought to give it a try for a short while. During the coffee break he found that other newcomers took a similar view. He decided to limit the experience to a maximum of four weeks.

Later that afternoon, everyone was issued with a brief case containing pull-out display sheets to act as a visual accompaniment to the sales patter. They were then driven out to various parts of Auckland suburbia where they were deposited one by one and given a pick up time of some four hours later.

The first hour was to be spent in banging on as many doors as possible and making appointments to call back later that evening. The method was designed to gain wider coverage than simply entering the first house that invited them in. When the hour was up, Edwin had five addresses at which people had agreed for him to return to.

As luck had it, one couple sat through Edwin's presentation and without any question agreed to sign up for a set of the books. It meant that he had earned his first $50 within a very short space of time.

It wasn't until 10pm that Edwin was dropped off in Remuera. Caroline was waiting for him. Lamb chops and roast pumpkin were cooked in an electric frying pan contraption with a lid on it as they asked each other about their day.

In the three weeks that followed Edwin made only two more deals. Not only that, but it was time consuming. Everyone was expected to get in to the office in the mornings and spend most of the day practising their patter in an attempt to learn from each other before going into action in the evenings and not returning home until late.

Caroline always waited up for him and they grew closer to each other. Weekends provided the only real opportunity for them to go out together even if it was just for a local walk or the occasion in which they went to the cinema to see 'The Prime of Miss Jean Brodie.' Apart from anything else the day was nearing for Caroline's departure overseas.

IT SOON BECAME CLEAR to Edwin that the job was going nowhere. Towards the end of his fourth week he handed in his notice. It was met with some resistance. Although everybody had been told of a policy whereby anyone who suggested quitting would be unceremoniously sacked, in Edwin's case the exact opposite occurred. The company boss took him aside and told him that had he had a natural manner that came across well in sales and marketing and urged him to stay on a little longer. However Edwin dismissed the compliment as nothing more than an attempt to retain him in order to keep their numbers up. At midday he walked back to Remuera. He was content in the knowledge that he was now right out of that particular mind-set and would no longer spend his life banging on peoples' front doors. He would put it down to experience.

Caroline was due to leave New Zealand in a week's time. Maybe it was a cue for him to leave Auckland too. Their friendship had intensified to such a degree that they both knew that it was going to be difficult to say goodbye. She had even suggested cancelling her whole trip at one stage. Instead, they'd promised to write to each other.

Of the various places that he had visited in New Zealand Edwin couldn't deny the fact that he still had a preference for Christchurch. He reasoned that in his current predicament his best plan of action might be to get back down there as soon as possible and find a real job and settle down. He had one traveller's cheque left that he had been keeping in reserve. He calculated that it would provide him with just enough money for the one-way train and ferry fare to Christchurch plus a few weeks living expenses. He outlined his idea to Caroline and was pleased to see that it met with her approval.

To minimise any emotional upheaval they kept their farewell as brief as possible. Their friendship might have been short-lived and now divided by circumstances but it had been a profound experience. Edwin took the overnight train from Auckland down to Wellington. It was slow journey on the narrow gauge winding track but Edwin knew instinctively that he had made a good decision and that he was heading in the right direction. Caroline would be flying off to Australia the following morning and Auckland would have felt pretty empty without her presence.

On arrival in Wellington Edwin called in at the guesthouse where he had stayed on his first days in New Zealand. He retrieved his two suitcases which he then lugged down to the docks cursing the fact that one of them contained his heavy Spanish dictionary. The ferry crossing back to Picton in the South Island and an awaiting train got him back down to Christchurch.

It was a slow process manipulating two suitcases and the rucksack along the route from the railway station but he headed in the direction of the same place that he had stayed on his previous visit – whilst hoping that it would be all right for him to stay there again.

"MIGHT HAVE GUESSED THAT you'd be back sooner or later!" said Diana who, not for the first time welcomed him into the kitchen of the long hut.

Over a pot of tea she explained that in his absence several changes had taken place. The Australian girl, Bronwyn, had disappeared off the face of the earth leaving behind a large selection of unpaid bills and, according to press reports, her Italian friend had been arrested on drug related charges. In the meantime Diana had graduated from sleeping in the lounge and now occupied the bedroom. However she would soon be moving out of the flat altogether to a nearby studio apartment. In the meantime a young guy from next door called Gary was taking over the flat. He had already moved into the lounge and she was sure that Edwin could make use of the second bed there, as he had done during his first visit.

"So, as you can see, it's like one big game of musical beds," she said.

Edwin explained that he had returned to Christchurch with the single-minded purpose of settling there and that his immediate task was to find a job. He wondered if it would be possible for him to use the flat as his base and to start paying a share of the rent.

"That'd work out well for everybody," she said. "And it's a good job that you have arrived back just at this moment because it will even save Gary the effort of looking around for a new flatmate when I move out.

Gary was a reasonable enough lad. He was perhaps the classless Kiwi from Christchurch but easy to get along with if you could put up with the word 'shit' being inserted into every other sentence. He readily agreed to Edwin living at the flat and was pleased to take a payment of money to cover his share of the rent for the next six weeks. Although it left Edwin with a bare minimum amount to survive on for day to day necessities such as food he felt confident that now that he had arrived in his place of choice, it wouldn't take long for him to land a job.

In keeping with the manpower shortage in New Zealand, the classified section of the local newspaper was jam packed full with job vacancies of numerous descriptions. Edwin was determined not to make the same mistake that he'd made in Auckland and he went through each possibility with a fine tooth comb singly out those that were realistic. Despite his dwindling funds he felt that he had every right to be choosy about the nature of his work rather than just taking anything that happened to be available.

Over the next few weeks he attended three interviews and succeeded in getting three firm offers of work. The first was a teaching position which struck him as somewhat ironic, given his schoolboy rebellion against the entire education system together with his rather limited academic qualifications. He guessed the schools must be really short. He was also offered a job as a trainee manager at a small engineering company but the role didn't strike him as being interesting enough. On another day he took a bus journey out to the seaside suburb of Sumner to attend an interview for a job as a laboratory technician. That was more appealing but the job was not going to be available for another three weeks.

Diana moved out of the flat just as Edwin was eking out his remaining cash. Although his flatmate Gary worked in a printing works, he was still paying off a recent trip to Australia which meant that between the two of them there was very little money at all. A power bill arrived which mucked up their cash flow even further. Their meals became bare essentials in which potato played a prominent part. However, it was good humoured. They had a circle of friends who used to drop by and, as the weather was starting to get warmer, much of their social life consisted of bottled beer in the back yard.

On the same morning that Edwin was about to formerly accept the laboratory technician job he happened to have the radio on in the background. There was an announcement that the radio station was looking for a copywriter. Without even knowing precisely what a copywriter was, the idea of working in a broadcasting environment had an immediate appeal to Edwin. On impulse he made the necessary phone call and was invited along for an interview the following morning.

On his arrival Edwin was ushered into an office where two people were present who introduced themselves as the Station Manager and the TV Operations Supervisor. The interview went smoothly and Edwin even managed to throw in a few details of his brush with Sevilla Film Studios back in Madrid which he thought might be relevant. He tried not to appear too disheartened when the Station Manager said that the copywriter job would not become available until the following month.

"However," continued the man, "A new vacancy on the television side of things has quite literally arisen overnight. And we wonder if that might that be of interest to you"

"It sounds very appealing," replied Edwin, "What exactly would the work entail?"

Within the space of forty minutes Edwin was appointed as a TV Studio Assistant with the New Zealand Broadcasting Corporation and due to start in the job on the following Monday.

On his way back to the flat he stopped off at the parade of shops in Linwood and completely overspent his budget on sufficient food to prepare a decent three-course meal that evening both for Gary and himself by means of celebration.

CHAPTER ELEVEN

IT WAS 1ST SEPTEMBER 1969 and Edwin took one of the red single decker buses to Cathedral Square in the centre of Christchurch in good time to arrive at his new job with the New Zealand Broadcasting Corporation. It also marked seven months to the day since his departure from England.

He could easily have walked into town. The weather was fine, the distance was not too great and even at a moderate pace it could have been covered on foot in less than half an hour. However, on this particular first time occasion, taking a bus had felt more appropriate. Once there he lingered a short distance from the entrance to the eight storey Manchester Unity Building in which the offices of the regional television service were housed. He glanced at his watch. There was still twenty minutes to spare. He walked twice around the block before going in.

At the fifth floor reception a pleasant and efficient looking secretary ushered him through to the office of the TV Operations Supervisor, Peter Baldwin, whom he had met at the interview. Inviting Edwin to take a seat, it was explained that, as with all TV Studio Assistants in Christchurch, Edwin would first be attached to something called the Transcriptions Department for the first few months. There would then be regular occasions, particularly in the afternoons, when he would be assigned to the TV studio crew which he would eventually be joining full-time. Such an arrangement enabled more of a gradual assimilation to working on the studio floor rather than being thrown straight in at the deep end.

"That sounds fine to me," said Edwin, pleased that there would be an opportunity for learning the various ins and outs.

"And please do come and say hello to me from time to time," said the TV Operations Supervisor.

"I'm sure that I will, Mr Baldwin" replied Edwin.

"Oh, and there's no need for Mr Baldwin. Please call me Peter," he said.

With formality having given way to familiarity, he then took Edwin up two flights of stairs and into an office where he was introduced to the man who would be his first immediate boss during his time spent in the Transcriptions Department.

Mr Eric Williams turned out to be a fellow Englishman. He was a former Merchant Navy officer who had lived in New Zealand for the past ten years, married a New Zealander and adopted two Maori children. He was about forty years Edwin's senior and an interesting and engaging character. He talked Edwin through the role of the Transcriptions Department which to all intents and purposes was a despatch department that received film and videotape programmes ready for transmission by the TV channel and then, once they'd been broadcast, sent them on to their next scheduled place.

One side of the 'L' shaped office had aisles of metal racks that held a library of 16mm films in round blue plastic cases. Other containers of a more bulky nature contained videotapes. Two desks were positioned one behind the other. Eric Williams, who preferred to be addressed as Mr Williams, occupied the one in front and the one behind him was for Edwin's use. Over to one side a table used for packing up parcels was equipped with an assortment of labels, sticky tape, felt-tip pens, cutting knives, pairs of scissors and a sellotape dispenser whilst beneath it was a large selection of cardboard boxes of varying sizes.

Another TV Studio Assistant by the name of Gilbert was introduced before he departed out through the door towards the lift wheeling a low-level trolley loaded with parcelled up boxes.

"You are his replacement," explained Mr Williams when he was out of earshot, "And between you and me I hope that you will be a bit better organised. Anyway, he'll be here for a few more weeks before joining them full-time over the road at the studios."

A tea lady then arrived, as did most of the film-editing staff from a department located on the same floor. Apparently it was a regular occurrence for them to congregate in the Transcriptions Department both in the mid-morning and the mid-afternoon for a communal indulgence in caffeine and nicotine. Cigarettes were offered around and the entire office took on a blue-grey haze of smoke. Improvised ashtrays had been made from disused metallic film cans by people using their thumbs to bend in the outer rim at regular points around the circumference so as to form a decorative and functional smokers' accessory. Mr Williams introduced Edwin to everybody present and the conversation was light, informal and chatty. After the multitude had departed, he told Edwin that he found the world of broadcasting to be a wonderfully refreshing place to work because people were lively and intelligent and there was always something going on.

He went on to explain a bit more about how the place functioned. Although the New Zealand Broadcasting Corporation provided a television service to the whole country, it was divided into four distinct viewing areas in which separate transmissions were broadcast from WNTV1 in Wellington, AKTV2 in Auckland, CHTV3 in Christchurch and DNTV2 down in Dunedin. As far as this particular office was concerned, it was pretty straightforward. Head Office in Wellington issued a programme schedule for each of the regions several weeks in advance and the various films and videotapes of programmes were sent by air freight in time for transmission and then needed to be despatched on to the next place after their use.

As a general rule the routing followed a pattern from Wellington to Auckland then to Christchurch and finally on to Dunedin. However, there were occasional exceptions so one always had to refer to the comprehensive schedule and make sure that everything had arrived in time. Not only that, but it was also necessary to check that the right film was in its right container. It meant a somewhat laborious task of opening each film case and carefully removing the spool of film and reading a code number written on the head of the film to ensure that it corresponded with what was written on the can's label. It invariably did but, as Mr Williams pointed out, the one time that it wasn't cross-checked would be the one time that it didn't tally and a wrong film would be transmitted.

A van driver then stood at the doorway and Edwin was invited to go down in the lift with him and collect seven large cardboard boxes aided by one of the metal trolleys. Each box contained films that the driver had collected from the Christchurch freight depot of the internal national airline.

Back up in the office, Edwin was asked to unpack them, check that their details were correct and tick them off on a prepared list before storing them numerically in the library racks. It felt uncanny holding a reel of film that contained an episode of 'Coronation Street' in his hands. Not many other people get to do this, he thought in amazement.

It didn't take long to understand the coding system. Prefix letters from 'A' to 'E' were used to signify the size of the film reel, 'A' was the largest and could hold a one hour programme, 'B' spools were for half hour programmes and 'C' to 'E' spools were for films of shorter durations. The letters were followed by a unique reference number which denoted the title of the programme and then, after a forward slash, a final number indicated its episode number. Longer feature films contained on two or more reels were additionally labelled '1 of 3', '2 of 3', and '3 of 3'. All brilliantly logical and yet despite such detail Mr Williams told him of a couple of instances in which reels of film had actually been played out of sequence whilst on air. There were also stories of the wrong episode of a series having been broadcast in error and so Edwin began to appreciate the need to pay meticulous attention to detail so as to ensure that nothing like that ever happened during his time in Transcriptions.

Two large metal boxes were loaded up with the films for that particular day's transmission together with an assortment of programmes on videotape. By means of the van driver they had to be transported over to the TV channel building that was located a couple of blocks away on Gloucester Street. It would be one of Edwin's late morning duties to accompany such a consignment of programmes and, for now, when Gilbert returned Edwin would have the benefit of him to show him the ropes. That arrangement worked well. Edwin found Gilbert to be a very pleasant and easy going person to learn from. Apparently his father had been one of the founding members of broadcasting in New Zealand and a pioneer of its current affairs programmes.

The van driver dropped the two of them off at the front doors of the CHTV3 studios from where they manipulated their laden trolley in through a front reception area. They continued on through some swing doors that led to the TV station's operational areas. Their first delivery point was the videotape room from where a high pitched whistling noise of varying frequency was being emitted. It was there that the bulky two-and-a-half inch thick spools of magnetic tape were played on one of the three massive machines operated by the petite female operator.

"They're just giant tape recorders that can record and play back pictures as well as sound," said Gilbert by means of explanation. They neatly deposited their eleven videotape programmes on shelves designated for that purpose and moved on to the next operational area.

On the first floor they entered a darkened room called Telecine and offloaded the two large metal boxes containing the films for that day's transmission. That area was attended by two more technical operators and Edwin was shown three units, each with two film projectors and slide projectors fitted in such a way as to point into a central column where their projected optical image would be converted to the electronic image of a television picture. There was also a large contraption in the corner that could sequentially scan a series of graphic images known as captions which had been designed by the art department on pieces of card.

On a television monitor a studio based interview could be seen taking place and a voice over an intercom system suddenly burst through, "CR3 – Telecine. Two minutes to our insert on 'A'!"

"Thank you!" called back one of the girls.

"There's obviously a production taking place in one of the studios," explained Gilbert as he looked quizzically at the operator.

"It's this week's edition of 'Country Calendar," she said, "We're nearly finished. Good job too because I'm ravenous."

"Any material that's on film gets transmitted from here," explained Gilbert, 'If it's a programme for transmission like those we've just delivered it'll be put on air from here through the Presentation Control Room or if it's a film insert into a production like they're doing now it'll be routed through one of the other control rooms.

'How many control rooms are there?' asked Edwin.

"Altogether four here in Christchurch," replied Gilbert, 'One for the day to day transmission of programmes and the others are for local productions"

The intercom went live once again, "CR3 – Telecine. Stand By!"

"Standing by," she replied, with one hand next to a small panel of illuminated buttons.'

"Roll A!" came the command and the operator duly pushed one of the buttons, which set one of the projectors springing into life and, on another monitor screen Edwin could see the start of a five second visual countdown of 5, 4, 3, then dipping to black for two seconds before the first frames of the film itself. He noticed that the original screen now showed the same picture and Gilbert explained that it was because the film that was originating from Telecine had now also become the output of that particular control room. Edwin kind of understood.

Through a window in the adjoining passageway the parabolic shapes of large microwave dishes could be seen pointing in the direction of the distant hills where the transmitters were located high above the city of Christchurch

Having completed their delivery task, they were about to head back to the office but on their way out Gilbert suggested they briefly poke their noses into one of the studios. He showed Edwin its three cameras mounted on pedestals that could glide smoothly across the studio floor and the arrangement of large lights hanging from a ceiling grid. There was also a newsreaders' desk and microphones and at the other end of the studio an interview area with a blue cloth backdrop. The place felt almost sacred and the fact that it was soundproof added to its intrigue. They exited via a thick door on the opposite side of the studio to the accompanying control room from where some half a dozen people would ordinarily be seated during a production. A long operational desk contained panels with illuminated rows of buttons and an assortment of switches, faders and controls of one sort or another. Behind that a bank of fifteen television screens each served as monitors for different video sources and there was a separate booth for the sound operator.

Back at the office Edwin settled into the job in transcriptions with relative ease and it was only a matter of three weeks before Gilbert joined the studio crew on a full-time basis leaving him to handle things single-handedly although under the watchful eye of his boss, Mr Williams. By now he had learned many things about how the television station functioned and discovered the geographical whereabouts of the facilities and individuals that contributed to its operation. Along the passageway was a film processing room where cameramen would deposit their freshly shot footage. Next to that film editing took place in semi-darkened suites. Upstairs on the top floor was an open plan newsroom which bustled with journalists often under pressure to meet deadlines. Telephones rang, people were bashing out news stories on typewriters, teleprinters were clacking away in the corner and stop watches were being used to time out spoken news items.

Beyond that was the art department which, in addition to designing studio sets, also turned out all the graphics artwork that appeared on screen. Meanwhile the second floor was home to film cameramen and their film sound operators with storage space for their equipment as well as an accounts department which only ever became a popular place once a fortnight when employees visited it to collect their pay-packets.

The sixth floor was devoted to productions. An array of small individual offices housed both producer and production secretary for all of the locally produced programmes such as 'Town and Around,' 'Grandstand', 'The Ooky Spooky Club' and 'On Camera'. One floor below was reception, administration and a typing pool as well as the presentation department who were a group of people that planned and directed daily transmission. An advertising department was alongside that as well as the small office of an operations officer who assigned technical facilities and crews to meet the TV station's daily requirements. Such organisational structure within the building was in addition to the technicians, engineers and support staff who were based down the road at the channel itself.

One evening Edwin wrote to his friend Henry in South Africa and told him about the new job with the NZBC and asked if he might be interested in coming out to New Zealand. He then received a postcard from Caroline who was currently in Alice Springs, Australia. He wished she were back in New Zealand now that he had landed on his feet.

IN ADDITION TO HIS duties in receiving and despatching programme material, Edwin began to spend two afternoons a week working with the studio crew. It often involved helping set one or other of the TV studios ready for a production. From a floor plan reference, scenic backdrops, items of furniture and other paraphernalia would be positioned on the studio floor with pinpoint accuracy ready for technicians to rig their lighting and for cameras to be glided to their opening positions in preparation to what lay ahead.

Together with Gilbert and half a dozen other lads in Studio 4, he was able to gain a useful understanding of production etiquette. The first programme that Edwin worked on was a women's magazine programme that went out live for forty minutes. His immediate task was to assist one of the studio cameramen by dragging his cable behind him whilst the cameraman skilfully manoeuvred his camera across the studio floor to certain positions from where his composed shots were put on air. It had to be done at speed and in such a way as to prevent any tugging to the camera and also to prevent entanglement with other cables. Such studio camera cables were three quarters of an inch thick and it was often quite a knack to pull them around smoothly and silently. There was the additional need to avoid being seen in shot by the other cameras but it was all fascinating stuff. The programme's distinctive set, which was an aesthetic arrangement of large flat pieces of scenic material with diagonal slats across their front, was already in place. They were each held upright by means of a wooden French brace weighed down with a sandbag.

Members of the crew had each been issued with a production script. The studio cameras were manned by operators wearing headphones each with their own shot list. A floor manager, also wearing headphones, relayed instructions from the control room to the two female presenters who were making last-minute amendments to their introductory comments. An assistant floor manager ushered people in who were going to be interviewed during the course of the programme. Microphones were repositioned and a studio monitor showed the picture from whichever camera was selected in the control room and corresponded to a red cue light on the top of that particular camera.

A complete run through of the programme took place prior to it going on air. Then, as the transmission time approached, everybody's minds became focused on their tasks and the discipline of studio team work became ever apparent as the programme went out live on air. Everything needed to work like clockwork with no hitches whatsoever. At precisely 14.40 the opening titles were up on the screen and the presenter in the studio was put on standby. Then, a few seconds later the floor manager dropped his arm from where it had been held out, just below the lens of Camera 2 as the cue for her to commence speaking from the first part of her script. That had been an introduction to a pre-recorded item on videotape which was then switched to giving a three minute breathing space for the studio to adjust to the next part of the programme which was a live interview with an artist who had recently returned from an award winning event in Japan. Having worked out most of her questions carefully in advance, the presenter was skilled in bringing out a descriptive account of the trip from her interviewee. Four minutes had been allocated for the interview and when it got about halfway through Edwin was surprised to see the floor manager flash a 'V sign' at the presenter who caught sight of it out of the corner of her eye. Momentarily wondering what on earth such a gesture was doing in the middle of the production, he suddenly clicked that it signified there were two minutes left for the remainder of the interview. The assumption was confirmed a minute later when the floor manager held up one finger. Then, as the last few seconds of time allotted for the interview began to run out a slow cranking motion of the floor manager's arm was the signal for the presenter to wind it up and turn to the scripted introduction to the next item on the agenda. The 'on air' light then turned off, the microphones were no longer live and everyone was granted a few minutes grace to prepare for the next live burst.

Such was the intensity of concentration that the forty minutes worth of programme slipped by in what seemed like no time at all and the closing credits and musical theme tune brought the production to an end. It also brought with it a sense of euphoria as congratulations were handed down and the producer came through from the control room to thank everybody in person for their contribution whilst cameras were closed down and the studio set dismantled.

Gilbert accompanied Edwin across to the tea room where together with the rest of the crew they partook of a cup of tea and a cigarette whilst mulling over the rest of the week's activities.

"After doing the regional news programme in the evenings some of us go down to the pub," said Gilbert, "but this is about as good as it gets during the working day."

They chatted for some time before Edwin had to return back to the transcriptions office to make sure that the following day's episode of 'Bonanza' had arrived safely from the airline depot.

WITH A REGULAR INCOME the financial woes of the inhabitants of the Tancred Street flat soon became a thing of the past and there was food on the table once again. Between them Edwin and Gary even purchased an old car that was still in good running order even though Edwin had never learnt how to drive.

After a couple of months yet another TV Studio Assistant was employed. It meant that Edwin would soon move on to full-time TV studio work but as part of the handover he first had to train up the newcomer in the transcription office duties. Fortunately the new person was quick on the uptake and was soon able to grasp everything.

Edwin was then down on the roster for shifts that included working on news and current affairs programmes, gardening programmes, children's programmes, sports roundups, press review, car maintenance and cookery programmes. There was also the occasional outside broadcast of live sporting events and church services. Wearing a pair of headphones that provided programme sound in one ear and control room sound in the other he got used to all of the various tasks that he was responsible for throughout each programme.

On one afternoon he was given a crash course in studio camerawork. The situation came about when one of the cameramen was off sick, another was away on leave and the studio desperately needed someone to handle the third camera.

"OK, this is your focus and this is your zoom," he was instructed, "We're on air in twenty minutes. You'll need to get the camera into position and compose the shots shown on this list one after the other."

Edwin stared into the viewfinder. His immediate concern was that it would be the shakiest bit of camerawork on record but in the event it passed off OK and he realised that being plunged in the deep end like that had boosted his self-confidence.

Gilbert pointed out that Edwin was evolving into a Kiwi.

"When you first arrived here you were dressed in suit and tie but you've sure adapted quickly to the New Zealand way of doing things," he said.

With the arrival of warm weather Edwin had acquired the traditional summer wear of many New Zealand males. In addition to a sports jacket it consisted of a short sleeved shirt and tie, a pair of chequered shorts and some knee high white socks. When he had first seen men going to work in such attire he had thought that they looked like a bunch of overgrown boy scouts but by now he had to admit that such outfits were both comfortable and practical. He had also acquired a New Zealand accent within a short space of time.

By November Edwin was beginning to think in terms of finding somewhere different to live. Although he had nothing against his flatmate, Mister 'Shit-hot-bonzo' Gary, he didn't have a lot in common with him either. It had been the chain of events that had led them to share the long wooden hut for the past four months. In keeping with his new found status in the world of television broadcasting, Edwin reasoned that it was about time to move up a notch. As it happened, it didn't take much effort. A cursory glance through the classified section of a copy of 'The Press' revealed a list of all manner of flats available for rent in Christchurch, many of which were easily affordable. There was even a house to let at just twelve dollars a week which, although double what he paid for his share of the hut, sounded interesting. Edwin quickly got on the phone to arrange a viewing. It turned out that it was situated just two blocks away and although currently unoccupied he was given the address so as to be able to take a look at it from the outside.

That warm evening, as he strolled over to take a look at the house in the appropriately named England Street, Edwin had a very positive feeling about it before he even got there. A whole house! He thought, and if there was still the possibility of his old mate Henry coming out from South Africa there would even be room for him to move in too which would be a bit of a laugh.

Rounding a corner and looking at the house numbers on the mailboxes he spotted a somewhat run-down brown wooden bungalow with an overgrown front garden which he guessed must be it but, as he got closer, he saw that that was the house next door. As soon as the correct house was identified, Edwin knew instinctively that it was the place for him. It was a comparatively large pale green wooden bungalow with the usual red corrugated iron roof and a veranda on the front. A latticed fence to one side had a large imitation butterfly attached to it and, in common with most other properties, the house stood on a quarter acre section of land. Edwin opened the wrought iron front gate and walked the curve of the front garden path between rose bushes on either side. Stepping up onto the veranda, he cupped his hands around the sides of his face and peered through sash windows on either side of the front door. There, through gaps in the Venetian blinds, he could see empty, sizable, carpeted rooms.

He ventured down the left hand side of the house where, through a bay window, he was able to see into a lounge with a tiled fireplace. It was not too difficult to reach over the top of a side gate and unbolt it. A further window revealed a linoleum floored kitchen with a cooker and three adjoining doors. There was an outhouse at the rear of the property which proved to be a storage area and outside lavatory. In the back garden stood a large corrugated iron water butt perched on a sturdy looking wooden framework and a tree full of ripe peaches. Dark red grapes were growing along the fence. There were two more windows to look through at the back of the house and on the remaining side. Both appeared to be bedrooms.

Edwin retraced his steps and re-bolted the side gate on his way out. He was thrilled to have stumbled upon such a find. All that remained now was to make sure that he could secure it and that he didn't lose it to somebody else in the meantime. He would need to act fast but he was aware that the phone number he had dialled in response to the advertisement had been to an office and so he would have to wait until the following morning before he could take things any further. He determined to call them first thing. He then returned to the flat and joined Gary for a bowl of stew without mentioning a single thing about what he hoped would now happen.

The next day Edwin arrived at work a little earlier than usual. He picked up the phone and dialled 9 for an outside line and on making the call succeeded in getting through to the same lady with whom he had spoken the day before. He expressed his interest in renting the England Street house and an appointment was set up for him to call in at their office during his lunch hour. It turned out to be a firm of solicitors and on arrival Edwin was told he would shortly be seen by one of the partners.

It was a simple enough assessment in which the man jotted down various details. Edwin was asked where he worked and on saying that he was with the NZBC that in itself seemed to be sufficient grounds for him to be acceptable tenant. The house was available from the following Tuesday and all that would be required was an initial four weeks rent in advance followed by fortnightly payments thereafter. Edwin was overjoyed with such an outcome. He duly signed the tenancy document and it was agreed that he would return to the office with his payment next Tuesday when the keys would handed over to him.

Fortunately the next day was payday and as he walked over to the studios from the office some hasty mental arithmetic indicated that after clearing his share of current bills with Gary he could just about raise the forty-eight dollars even if it meant that he would have precious little to live on throughout the following fortnight. With his new home now a reality Edwin felt free to tell his workmates about it during the afternoon tea break. However his mind was wrestling to find a diplomatic way of breaking the news to his flatmate Gary. Edwin was conscious of the fact that ever since his arrival in Christchurch he had had the good fortune to have lived in the Tancred Street flat courtesy of somebody else's good will. And yet now he was about to abandon Gary and saddle him with having to pay a double rent in the process.

It turned out that he needn't have worried. Gary seemed completely unperturbed by the news and said that he knew of someone who would be able to move into the flat once Edwin had moved out. They drank a couple of bottles of beer together and Edwin felt profound relief.

The following Tuesday after work and with the keys to the house in his pocket, Edwin transported all his worldly possessions the short distance from Tancred Street to England Street. As these were contained within his two suitcases and rucksack it required just the one journey.

CHAPTER TWELVE

OPENING THE FRONT DOOR Edwin stepped into a long wide hallway that connected to the various rooms that he had peered into through the windows from outside the week before. Dumping his cases down in the first room on the left, he took a thorough look around the interior of the house for the first time. A combination of sunshine pouring in through the windows and what must have been a complete lack of ventilation over a period of time made it particularly hot. There was a slight scented odour that was not altogether unpleasant. Perhaps it was from furniture polish last used on the dark stained wooden doors.

He crossed the hallway to the other front room and found it to be of a similar size to the first although without the same recesses around a chimney breast. He would make that the dining room. Continuing through the house the lounge proved spacious and there were still the two rooms off to the right which he had already earmarked as bedrooms. One was medium sized and the other, at the back on the house, slightly smaller. "So that's two bedrooms and three large reception rooms," he said to himself. He arrived at the spacious kitchen from which a bathroom led off to one side. He gave a nod of approval at the bath and washbasin. As he'd suspected, though, the house had no indoor toilet and the only facility of that nature was in the outhouse of the back garden.

Beyond the kitchen's cooking area was an additional room with fitted cupboards and a sink – a kind of wash up your dishes area. He turned on one of the taps to check that the water was on, which it was. Then, having pulled down the switch on the fuse box, he tried one of the light switches and was rewarded with the brightness of a naked light bulb that hung from the ceiling. He'd have to get some lampshades, he thought, before reminding himself that, as he'd not got so much as one single stick of furniture, lampshades might not be the number one priority. He switched on the immersion heater in the bathroom so that at least he would have some hot water.

He felt content. It was a new phase of his life in New Zealand. Returning to the front room he began to unpack his bags, arranging his clothing in neat piles on the floor. Goodness knows why he'd brought the hefty Spanish dictionary from the other side of the world but that, alongside half a dozen long playing records, was placed in another area of the floor.

As there was no food in the house and neither crockery nor cutlery or for that matter any cooking utensils at all, Edwin went down the road to the corner dairy shop and returned with a loaf of bread, a slab of cheese, a bottle of milk and a packet of cigarettes before heading out a second time to a local takeaway for the inevitable cheeseburger and chips. He then walked a further three blocks to the bottle store of the Marlborough Tavern and in celebration of his new home purchased six bottles of locally brewed Bavarian beer, packed in a strong brown paper bag for the princely sum of one dollar and sixty-two cents. On his way back to the house, with the pack tucked under his arm, it occurred to him that he didn't even possess a bottle opener but after a series of experiments involving door handles and the sink unit, he found that by hooking one edge of the metal cap under the catch on the bathroom window, it could be removed quite easily. He had his small transistor radio as company and, stretched out on the floor. He wrote a letter to Caroline who was now in Darwin, Australia, where she collected her mail from the main post office. He also wrote to Henry in South Africa letting him know of his new address.

DESPITE THE FACT THAT he slept on the floor in his clothes and used his coat as a cover and a jersey for a pillow, Edwin managed a remarkably good night's sleep. He woke up the following morning with the sun shining in through the blinds and, reaching for his watch, saw that it was only five thirty. His joints felt a bit stiff as he stood up and walked through to the rear of the house where he ran himself a hot bath.

In fresh clothes he strolled into town ready for a day's work once again. It was another beautiful day with a deep blue sky, brilliant sunshine and a pleasant light breeze. As it was still early he made a detour to a part of town where during lunch breaks he sometimes sat on the grass next to a bandstand in public gardens that overlooked the River Avon. Within a parade of shops that ran alongside it was a showroom of second hand furniture and he was curious to take a quick peek at their window display. He had already been trying to work out some basic furniture requirements for each room of the house. If nothing else, the showroom might give him a few ideas. The interior of the shop was still in darkness but Edwin could make out a selection of three piece suites, wardrobes, dressing tables, refrigerators, beds, and tables and chairs. They were obviously well stocked but unfortunately he was unable to read any of the price tags.

During that day's lunch break he returned to the showroom once again and this time was able to go inside and view everything at close range. The prices varied considerably according to the condition of each particular item but there were certainly bargains to be had. He looked at all manner of things but assumed it to be no more than window shopping for the time being because he barely had enough money left for food and his next payday wouldn't be for another fortnight. He saw a three piece suite for fifteen dollars which he felt would have looked great in the lounge and then spotted a notice above a hatchway that said 'Ask about our easy payment terms.' On speaking with one of the sales assistants Edwin found out that it was possible to purchase items of second-hand furniture on the strength of a ten per cent deposit and then pay the balance off in monthly instalments with no interest charge. Furthermore, the store offered a free delivery service. It sounded like a solution to what could otherwise have been a lengthy inconvenience and he decided to take immediate advantage of it. The salesman took down details of Edwin's name and address and when it came to the question of where he worked, once again, the fact that he was an NZBC employee seemed to count strongly in his favour. Within the space of the next half hour Edwin had secured the three piece suite that had taken his fancy as well as a kidney shaped coffee table, a large oak dining table with six chairs and a matching sideboard, a standard lamp, a tall refrigerator, two single beds with good clean mattresses, a square kitchen table with four chairs, two wardrobes with mirrors, a cardboard box containing two saucepans, a kettle and a frying pan, a telephone table for the hallway even though he didn't yet have a telephone and, for good measure, a dark stained wooden picture frame containing a print of the Greek mythological character, Perseus, riding the winged horse, Pegasus. Edwin got the whole lot for one hundred and forty-five dollars of which he paid fourteen dollars and fifty cents as the down payment and was given a payment card showing his next instalments. He returned to work in the knowledge that he'd probably have to survive on a diet of cheese omelettes for the next two weeks. Mind you, there was a plentiful supply of peaches on the tree in the back garden.

True to their word, not only did the company deliver the furniture to his address but they delivered it promptly. That same afternoon when Edwin rounded the final corner of his walk home from work, he was greeted by the sight of his entire order distributed across the length of the house's front veranda. Getting changed into some more appropriate clothing, he set about lifting all of it inside, piece by piece.

It was the first time in his new home that he could sit down on a chair. And not just one chair. He tried all of them. In the lounge he sat for a minute or so in each of the armchairs and then along the positions of the settee whilst contemplating the coffee table. All that particular room now needed was a lampshade. Going through to one of the front rooms which had been designated as the dining room, he took turns in sitting on each of the six chairs that he had arranged around the long dining table alongside the matching sideboard and standard lamp. There was even a hook on the wall on which to hang the picture and Edwin couldn't help but think how pleasantly formal that room now looked.

To the rear of the house, the four kitchen chairs were each given a similar test of approval. The place was beginning to look more and more livable but although he had moved the beds and the wardrobes into the bedrooms, he decided to remain in the front room where he had slept the previous evening. He figured that he might as well continue camping on the floor there for the time being until he'd acquired such things as sheets, blankets and pillows.

Over the weeks that followed, Edwin gradually built up his home by adding a miscellaneous assortment of bits and pieces to it. A large round tub type of a washing machine complete with an automatic mangle took care of his laundry needs although he had yet to get an iron. An 'L' shaped bookcase now stood in the smaller of the bedrooms. It housed his large Spanish dictionary. He'd also managed to get hold of a reasonable selection of cutlery, a few cups and drinking glasses, a second-hand dinner service, two tablecloths as well as his sought-after lampshades and an antiquated manual lawnmower. Not only that, but a telephone had now been installed.

AT THE NZBC EDWIN was continuing to learn many things about television programme production. Much of it was on-the-job training. Listening to the control room through his headphones in the studio had been an education in itself. Whether working on a drama, a cooking demonstration or a press review he was intrigued by the way in which each programme was co-ordinated by its director with the smooth efficiency of a musician conducting an orchestra.

On returning home one evening, a letter with a postage stamp from South Africa lay in the mail box by the front gate. It was the news that he'd been waiting for. Henry confirmed that he would be coming out to New Zealand and that he had already booked his passage on the P & O Liner, Oriana, which would arrive in Auckland on December 3rd – in about a month's time.

The day after his twentieth birthday Edwin stood on a wharf in the blazingly hot December sunshine awaiting the arrival of a ferry from the North Island. He realised that inviting his friend Henry to join him in New Zealand would be shaping his destiny just as much as his own. The Oriana had docked in Auckland a couple of days ago and Henry had taken the train to Wellington followed by an overnight ferry to the port of Lyttelton which lay a few miles outside of Christchurch. Just as Henry had awaited the arrival of Edwin's ship in Cape Town earlier that year, in a reversal of roles, Edwin now awaited the arrival of Henry's ferry. As the vessel drew closer he soon recognised a familiar figure amongst people lining the deck.

Henry, with a freshly grown moustache, stepped ashore whilst manipulating a stereo record player and its accompanying loudspeakers, a bag containing a huge collection of long playing records, two suitcases and a camera dangling around his neck. The two of them shook hands.

"Well done. You made it!" said Edwin.

"Bloody weird place this is!" said Henry, surveying the small township and scattered houses on the nearby hills, "But I love all the old bangers that they've still got on the road. Good to see you me old mate! I hope I've made the right decision to come here. By the way, I'd better just let you know that after paying my passage and all the expenses on board the Oriana, it's left me with precisely three dollars in my back pocket!"

"Don't worry about it," said Edwin, managing to conceal any slight concern about the household budget, "At least we've got a roof over our heads and I'm sure you'll soon find some work."

They took a bus into Christchurch and alighted near the house in England Street. Henry was pleased to offload his possessions into his allocated bedroom and familiarise himself with the place. Together they set up his record player in the front room where until now Edwin had slept. He would now occupy his bedroom at the back of the house for the first time.

"So what is it actually like here in New Zealand?" asked Henry. "What is there to get up to?"

"It's mainly a good healthy outdoor lifestyle together with self-made entertainment," replied Edwin. "You can pretty much forget about the pubs. Most are men's bars where blokes go to get drunk and get into arguments with each other. Some have lounge bars where they insist you wear a jacket and tie to be admitted but even they are nothing much to write home about either."

"Oh, I'd hoped we might be back in the realm of The Coach and Horses," he said.

"No such sophistication I'm afraid," replied Edwin, "but what I'm hoping to do is to transform this front room into a kind of in-house saloon bar that we can invite friends around to. The set department at work has promised to give me something that vaguely resembles a bar which was used as the counter of a jeweller's shop in one of our productions. They should be delivering it the day after tomorrow then we'll just need to get a few bar stools, decorate the place up a bit and add some subtle lighting."

They took a stroll into town. Edwin explained that the shops were closed because of New Zealand's ban on trading both on Saturdays and Sundays. The only exceptions were some of the small corner dairies. They circled Cathedral Square and passed the front entrances of Edwin's various NZBC buildings before taking a riverside walk that weaved its way back in the direction of the house. There they prepared an evening meal of liver and bacon. Henry's insistence that each slice of liver first be dabbed in a plate of seasoned flour proved to be a useful culinary insight.

They both then sat out on the front veranda with music blaring forth through the front window from Henry's record player as bottles of ice-cold beer were fetched from the fridge in the kitchen.

HENRY HAD NO DIFFICULTY in finding a job. Three days after his arrival in Christchurch he landed himself a chef's position in the kitchens of the Clarendon Hotel in the city centre. As with many catering roles, his working week included late shifts as well as the occasional weekend.

The bar counter arrived as did an odd-shaped unit which when positioned in a corner alcove provided an ideal place for the recorder player. Two wooden beer crates that were then placed on the ledge underneath held Henry's vast assortment of long playing records. Being stored upright meant that they could be flipped through and selected at will.

Edwin joined a record club that he'd seen advertised in the newspaper. If he purchased a record from their catalogue every month he would be entitled to two additional albums for free. He opted for a selection of classical music although didn't have a clue what they would be like. By return of post he received three LP's and was pleased to familiarise himself with Khachaturian's 'Dance of the Rose Maidens' before moving on to the other records of 'Mozart's Greatest Hits' and 'Tchaikovsky's 1812 Overture'. Both he and Henry discovered that they could enjoy such music every bit as much as tracks from The Kinks, The Who, Bob Dylan, The Supremes and Fairport Convention.

Passers-by were somewhat surprised to hear classical music being blasted out into their front garden on such summer days.

Wooden stools were purchased as was a shelf unit that took up its place behind the bar area. Despite the fact that Edwin and Henry rarely drank anything other than beer it displayed bottles of whisky, rum, vodka, gin, brandy, sherry and port as well as Angostura Bitters, Worcestershire Sauce, Tabasco and freshly sliced lemons from the front garden. Colourful posters from a travel agency were affixed to some of the walls. An ice bucket and coasters were strategically put in place. A soft orange lamp was set up in one corner with further illumination originated from beneath the counter's front ridge. The overall effect was of a cosy and relaxing place to unwind. It soon proved to be an extremely popular little bar. Colleagues from the NZBC would drop by and stay several hours longer than they had perhaps intended. Some of Henry's workmates would also call in. There was no shortage of friends dotted across Christchurch that they could invite over if in need of additional company.

Edwin had told Henry about Caroline who by now had left Australia's Northern Territory and was on her way to Indonesia.

"Sure, I have since met quite a few other girls at parties and the like," said Edwin, "and I suppose that I can't help but compare but so far I haven't found anyone that comes close."

"What was it about her?" asked Henry.

"It's hard to explain it in words," said Edwin. "We just seemed to click. I suppose it was a kind of love at first sight – and probably still is."

"Do you expect to meet up with her again?" he asked.

"I hope so but there's nothing planned," replied Edwin, "I mean there are no strings whatsoever. She is off on her global exploration. We write to each other periodically but other than that she is just as free and unattached as I am."

"Does she have the same feelings for you as you still seem to have for her?" he asked.

"I really have no idea," replied Edwin. "Maybe it's just to do with the fact that she was my first love in New Zealand. Perhaps I'll meet someone else in the future. Who knows?"

"I could do with meeting a nice young lady too," said Henry.

That evening, just as Edwin thinking of turning in for the night there was a knock on the front door. He opened it and there stood the law student, Steve.

"Well g'day there," he said with a broad grin, "I know it's a wee bit on the late side but I've got a couple of sheilas sitting out in the car as well as a couple of cases of Bavarian and I was just wondering if it might be OK for us to pop in for a bit?"

"Well, I suppose that it is a Saturday night and I'm not working tomorrow," said Edwin. "Who are these people that you've got with you?"

"They are a couple of student nurses from Christchurch Hospital," he replied.

"That sounds harmless enough. Yes, come on in," he replied. "Let me just rap on Henry's door to make sure he hasn't dropped off to sleep yet."

Within a matter of minutes the house sprang back into life once again. Lights were switched back on, music started to play, laughter and jokes abounded including Steve's party piece of blowing lighter fuel out of his mouth and setting light to it. Drinks were served and Henry brought some snacks in from the kitchen as the two nurses began dancing. One was a particularly tall girl wearing bright orange trousers which made her appear to be even taller than she actually was. The other was dumpy and giggly.

By now the tall nurse was standing on one of the stools and had started to repetitively chant "Here comes the judge, here comes the judge" which apparently were the lyrics to a pop song and aimed at Steve on account of his being a Law student. She then hopped down off her perch and came over to talk with Edwin for a while. Her name was Janet and her original home town was Palmerston North. On speaking with her Edwin had a sudden realisation that she might be the ideal partner for Henry. The combination of chubby chappy and lanky lady would certainly be an interesting one if nothing else. At that moment Henry came back into the room.

"Let me introduce you to my flatmate who has recently arrived from South Africa," said Edwin.

He then left them to it and went over to change the record.

Sugar, oh, honey, honey
You are my candy girl
And you got me wanting you
Honey, oh, sugar, sugar
You are my candy girl
And·you got me wanting you

CHRISTMAS IN THE SWELTERING summer heat was a new experience. Although salad might have been more appropriate Edwin and Henry roasted a large fresh turkey along with all the trimmings. At the end of the festive meal Henry put his camera on a timer and took a photograph as they pretended to be slumped over the dining table next to the carving dish.

Edwin was then promoted to Assistant Floor Manager and worked his shifts on a wide range of different programmes. New Zealand's newly emerging soprano singer Kiri Te Kanawa appeared live on one of the afternoon programmes. Her mellow yet vibrant voice was a memorable moment. However, when the world renowned violinist, Yehudi Menuhin, was asked by Edwin if he would mind playing a piece through one more time so that the producer could modify the camera angles he strongly objected. "I often get asked that kind of thing at television stations," he said, "However, I am here to perform and I have no interest in this technical thing or that technical thing needing to be adjusted or if there might be some problem with Camera Four."

One afternoon, at the end of a recorded interview for the 'On Camera' programme a female studio guest was removing her microphone which had been positioned under her jersey. In the control room the sound operator had inadvertently left the fader up and they could hear a loud scrunching noise at the microphone was being brought upwards. The producer proclaimed, "Blimey, she's got a hairy chest!" to which all those in the studio wearing headphones simultaneously cracked up with laughter, completely mystifying everybody else who was there. Similar mirth was caused amongst the studio crew when the presenter of the locally produced gardening show told viewers that, "Now is the best time to go and root your Daphne."

Edwin was regularly involved in the studio side of the channel's nightly regional news magazine programme called 'The South Tonight.' He also got assigned to working on a new live pop music show that went out on Wednesday evenings. It involved different backdrops for each musical performance from alternating ends of the studio. Whilst one musical group was playing down at one end, the other had to be set up at speed ready for the next group to take up its position. Although this gave the impression of limitless arty scenes to the viewers, the pace at which the studio crew had to keep changing the scenery around ensured that for them at least the programme lived up to its title of 'Moving.'

On Friday afternoons at the end of the working week, those who weren't on a late shift would gather at one of Christchurch's salubrious watering holes which normally meant the lounge bar of Warner's Hotel in Cathedral Square or the Oxford Tavern by the bridge over the river. It was a time when staff at all levels and from all departments mingled together and news and views were freely expressed over copious quantities of liquid refreshment.

HENRY'S FRIENDSHIP WITH THE student nurse, Janet, was blossoming and there wasn't a spare moment when they weren't together. Meanwhile Edwin had a large circle of female acquaintances that he frequently went out with but without being attached to any particular one of them.

Because both Edwin and Henry had accumulated some holiday entitlement they decided to visit the west coast of New Zealand's North Island for ten days where, in the tradition of old times, they opted to stay in Youth Hostels in Wanganui and New Plymouth. In was an enjoyable break in which the inexpensive accommodation was combined with dining out at good local restaurants so as to experience the best of both worlds.

On their return to Christchurch a pyjama party was held at their England Street house which turned out to be a tremendous success. There was a big turnout primarily from NZBC staff, all dressed for the part, including a couple of the more flowery male members of staff who arrived by taxi dressed in nighties. Henry put on a fantastic spread of food. Crayfish Mornay was particularly popular and drinks were still flowing into the early hours.

A new production was announced for CHTV3 in Christchurch. It was to be a televised version of 'Pineapple Poll' performed by the New Zealand Ballet Company. The studio crew found themselves getting into the spirit of what was essentially a non-vocal version of Gilbert and Sullivan's HMS Pinafore. The storyline had to be explained by one of the dancers in order that they better understood what was being portrayed. The petite ballerinas all looked identical with their hair tied up whilst characters kitted out in sailors' outfits blended in with the background of wharf-side scenery and capstans depicting a dockyard. Even the studio floor was painted with a cobblestone effect.

The production schedule involved full days of sheer repetition by which time everybody involved had the music going through their heads and the images of the various dance routines in their mind's eye. When the programme had been completed a celebration party was called for. There was a request for it to be held at Edwin's house from those who had attended the earlier pyjama party there. Supplies were ordered in and Henry set about preparing another of his speciality buffets.

Members of the production crew piled into the house as did the entire New Zealand Ballet Company. The celebration went on throughout the night and into the following morning. People were to be found sleeping in the lounge, the hallway, the bedrooms and anywhere else where they'd managed to find somewhere to stretch out. Edwin had snatched a couple of hours sleep next to one of the ballerinas who happened to be sound asleep on top of his bed. When they awoke in the morning they both found it amusing to be alongside each other. A spontaneous embrace went on for the best part of an hour and led to an invitation for Edwin to visit her in Wellington. For breakfast there were various platters of savoury food and a huge box of sausage rolls still left over from the night before – accompanied by further rounds of drinks.

EVERY ONCE IN A while the TV Operation Co-ordinator went on leave and his busy office needed someone to step in during his absence. The TV Operations Supervisor, Peter Baldwin, nominated Edwin for that task which was seen as a compliment. Although the work was purely administrative it entailed the assignment of technical facilities and studios to meet the TV station's daily operational requirement, the compilation of duty rotas for the studio crew and the deployment of film camera crews to cover news events. The temporary break from studio work gave Edwin an opportunity to experience the managerial side of broadcasting.

But he was also interested in learning control room work. When the Operations Co-ordinator returned from leave he asked him how to go about that.

"One of the best ways would be for you to sit in on a few presentation shifts in the continuity control room. I'm sure that can be arranged in whatever spare time you have," he replied.

"Is presentation a natural progression into production?" asked Edwin.

"No more so than your present studio work," he replied, "although a stint in presentation can be a useful thing to have under your belt because it gives you control room experience

"I imagine that just transmitting day-to-day programmes could get a bit monotonous," said Edwin.

"Exactly," he replied, "As a stepping stone presentation work is fine but it's not something to remain in for any great length of time. I mean, just take a look at him over there," he said with a smile as he nodded through the glass window towards a senior and rather pompous presentation officer sat at a desk who apparently had been stuck in the same role for the past decade.

Arrangements were made for Edwin to spend an afternoon in the Presentation Department once a week. One of the first tasks was to go to the record library and select the music to be played before the channel went on air. He was the only person who deliberately switched on the television early the following Sunday afternoon simply to hear his choice of music accompanying the test pattern.

Perhaps more demanding was the compilation of transmission logs in which everything that was to occur within a particular day's transmission had to be mapped out in advance. The details included the titles and durations of each of the programmes on film and videotape that made up the schedule. Live programmes had their allotted time. Television commercials, trailers and scripted announcements were then added and the whole thing was timed out to the split second even to the point of adding an addition second in for the transition times it would take to go from one source to the next.

He was also given the opportunity of writing the wording for some of the various continuity announcements that would be made between programmes. That was fun because he could to introduce a bit of creativity into them so that the announcer had a lively script.

Edwin's twenty-first birthday provided yet another excuse for a party and a further opportunity for Henry to demonstrate his culinary skills. Edwin received a card from Caroline who was in Nepal saying that she expected to hit England next July. He wrote back and suggested that when she got there she might like to call in on his relatives. He even began to wonder about the possibility of taking time out to fly over to Europe for a visit himself. However, although he still had some annual leave entitlement and even had sufficient savings for the return air fare he realised that such a journey wouldn't be worth it just for a couple of weeks. Such a trip would really require a time period of about three months and the best time to depart would be at the start of a New Zealand winter in order to capture a European summer. He made a few enquiries about the NZBC's policy on granting leave without pay. It turned out that such a thing was possible and before long he put in a written request.

CHAPTER THIRTEEN

EDWIN AND HENRY SAT together in the departure lounge of Christchurch Airport. Henry was flying to Palmerston North where he would be staying at his girlfriend Janet's family home for a week. She was already there and it would be the first time for him to meet her parents. In the meantime Edwin was about to embark on the first leg of a three month break in Europe. He would be taking an internal flight to Auckland and then joining an Air New Zealand flight for the onward journey.

Henry left first. They waved to each other through the tinted glass window as he made his way across the tarmac to the small propeller driven aeroplane that stood near the terminal building. Edwin watched as it took off.

An hour later, Edwin boarded his plane. On arrival in Auckland he entered the transit lounge only to hear an announcement being made over the public address system for all passengers booked on his next flight to go to the enquiries desk. It turned out that somebody had backed a truck into the plane and the flight had been cancelled. Arrangements were being made to put passengers up in an airport hotel for the night and a new flight had been scheduled for 10 o'clock the following morning. A young man standing next to him was in a similar predicament.

"I was just heading off for my once-in-a-lifetime trip to stay with relatives in Scotland," said the co-traveller, "and yet here we all are still stuck in New Zealand!"

"I guess everyone is in the same situation," replied Edwin, "All geared up for a long-haul trip which grinds to a halt before it even gets started."

A shuttle bus ran passengers to an airport hotel where they were allocated overnight accommodation in twin-bedded rooms. Edwin shared his room with the person going to Scotland who introduced himself as Duncan McIntyre. He was from Dunedin which was the one remaining city in New Zealand that Edwin had not yet visited. Together they went downstairs to the bar for a couple of beers before finding a table in the restaurant for an evening meal.

FOURTEEN HOURS BEHIND THE original schedule the plane touched down in Fiji the following afternoon. It was humid and raining but airport personnel handed out brightly coloured umbrellas for getting across to the small terminal building during the one hour break. Edwin found Duncan standing at one end of the bar and joined him there. They were served drinks by a Fijian barman who wore a white dress-like garment with pointed tassels dangling off the ends.

A further stop in Honolulu that took place in the middle of the night was of no great joy. Passengers were required to disembark and go through a passport control and then wait in a line for what seemed like eternity before being permitted to get back onto the plane again. Once back in their seats a glass of warm Hawaiian punch decorated with flowers was served perhaps as compensation for having had their beauty sleep so rudely interrupted.

Los Angeles was the final destination of the Air New Zealand route. A connecting BOAC flight continued the journey first to New York and then on to London's Heathrow Airport where it arrived the following morning. Flying eastward had made the final period of darkness a particularly short one and Edwin's body clock reminded him that since his departure from Christchurch night had now become day, winter was summer and midnight would occur at midday. Everything felt back to front.

One of his younger brothers was there to meet him in the arrival hall. In a matter-of-fact way he said that he had got there the day before and that, on learning of the flight's delay, he had simply spent the night at the airport. They were very pleased to see each other.

The two of them took the airport bus to Victoria followed by the train journey down to the Sussex coast. Nothing much had changed. Although good to be reunited with his family again Edwin realised that he could almost have flown in, sat down, had a cup of tea and exhausted most topics of conversation in about five minutes flat and then flown back out again. However, he had three months up his sleeve and wanted to make the most of it.

The first few days were sufficient to confirm his distaste for Hove and Brighton. He walked through some of its predictably dull residential areas extremely thankful that he was now based in New Zealand. Fortunately the family also had use of a flat in Tunbridge Wells throughout the summer months which they moved into the following week. It was centrally located and a stone's throw from the quaint walkway of The Pantiles with it olde worlde shops where an orchestra played on a bandstand. People ate al fresco and tourists drank glasses of metallic-tasting water from the wells located by its entrance whilst a local pub had a large collection of chamber pots hanging from its ceiling as an added attraction to one's ploughman lunch. Lazy days of pleasant walks across the common and outdoor theatre performances enhanced their stay. One afternoon when thumbing through a display rack of long playing records at WH Smith in the High Street Edwin stumbled upon the album of 'Pineapple Poll,' the music from the ballet recently worked on at the TV studios back in Christchurch and he couldn't resist buying it. It prompted him to send a postcard to his ballerina acquaintance in Wellington.

After a brief trip to Winchester to stay with his grandmother for a few days, Edwin revisited Weybridge and looked up several former friends from the time that he had lived there. He also wanted to include a trip to Spain in his itinerary and because his mother had been invited to Valencia to stay with one of her artist friends he decided to travel out there with her. Taking a night sailing of the cross channel ferry from Newhaven to Dieppe they drove down through France and broke the journey at a small hotel somewhere near Montpellier. They then crossed into Spain the following morning and stayed overnight at the popular resort of Lloret de Mar which, being the height of the season, was jam-packed full of French, British and German holidaymakers.

Valencia had managed to keep much of its charm as an essentially Spanish city rather than becoming an international tourist resort. It was also the nearest coastal place to Madrid and many Spanish families escaped the capital by heading there in mid-summer. Throughout his time in New Zealand Edwin hadn't met a single person who spoke Spanish and he had feared that he might have forgotten the language altogether. However, he soon discovered that just by listening to it being spoken for a while it all came flooding back.

Restaurant meals brought back memories too. Edwin made a point of ordering some of his more memorable dishes as much for old time's sake as for anything else. Squid in its own ink tasted just as good now as it had done to a hungry student several years ago and so did ice-cold gazpacho soup followed by a dish of paella.

At night it was still so unbearably hot that many Spanish families sat outside their front entrance of their homes unable to sleep. Instead there would chat and drink cold beer together. Edwin was invited to sit down and join one such family and remained with them for several hours.

The main highlight of this Spanish jaunt would undoubtedly be to revisit Madrid which was where he was heading for next. After a day's railway journey he took a bus into the city centre as familiar landmarks sprang up along the way. The edge of the Retiro Park, the water fountain in the middle of the roundabout at Cibeles, the Metro entrances, the central hub of the Puerta del Sol and the shopping stretch of the Gran Vía – everything seemed still to be there. He checked into the Hotel Emperador which was a few notches up from the kinds of places that he had stayed in last time he was in Madrid. He was now seeing that city from a completely different angle.

That evening the illuminated downtown area was bustling with people. Every street corner brought back memories. It occurred to Edwin that buildings have a tendency to outlive human beings and such a stray thought bothered him for a few moments. He then turned off the wide avenue of the Gran Vía into the narrow side road of Calle Concepción Arenal. The Bar Dénia was still there on the right as was the Peña El Aguila beer bar opposite. He took a small glass of beer in each of them but amongst the clientele there was not a soul that he recognised. He ventured a little further through the backstreets and entered Bar Pigalle where one of the bar ladies immediately reacted.

"Hombre!" she exclaimed, "Hace muchos años que no hemos encontrarte!"

"Hola, muy buenas!" replied Edwin, "Si, ya lo se que es mucho tiempo porque estos días habito en Nueva Zelanda."

"Pues Nueva Zelanda es muy lejos!" she said.

"Si, es verdad," said Edwin, "Pero ahora estoy en vacaciones aquí en Europa por unas semanas."

"Muy bien. Que querías, cerveza?" She poured him a large glass of draught lager. He asked her about the characters that used to frequent the place but it seemed that just about all of them had since moved on. She'd seen nothing further of Charlie. In fact the only person from that era who was still around was the Egyptian diplomat, Nizam, who occasionally put in an appearance.

THE FOLLOWING MORNING EDWIN took the metro to the suburb of Velasquez and found his way to the apartment on Calle Castelló where his former Spanish friend, Antonio, had lived. The family name of Lope Gonzalez still appeared alongside one of the doorbells which looked promising. In the dimly lit stairway on the first floor Antonio came to the door with his face covered in shaving foam.

"Dios mío, it's you!" he said "Welcome! Please come in. What on earth are you doing back in Madrid?" They shook hands.

"I'm just on a short visit," said Edwin. "Believe it or not I live in New Zealand these days."

Over coffee they traded stories. Antonio worked in his father's printing company but was hoping to set up a business of his own. He was fascinated to learn of Edwin's career in television. They spoke at length about the previous era when they had been students.

"I suppose you heard what happened to Freddie?" he said.

"Yes, he got deported from Spain for possession of drugs," replied Edwin.

"He certainly did," said Antonio, "and I guess you know the rest of it too."

"The rest of it?" asked Edwin, "That was the last thing that I heard."

"Oh, well the fact of the matter is that not only did he break Spanish law but he also broke international law," he said. "Having been deported from Spain the stupid fool came back again. He started hanging out in the same part of Madrid and was spotted there by the same cop who'd arrested him the first time."

"Oh, I didn't know that," said Edwin, who recalled that Freddie had spoken in terms of getting a replacement passport, "so I guess he got deported all over again."

"No, not at all," replied Antonio. "He's still here in Madrid. He's locked up in Carabanchel prison and has been in there for the past three years."

THE FOLLOWING DAY, EDWIN decided to try looking up the Fernandez family where he used to teach English to their daughter. Wearing a light suit, he took a cab to the apartment in the suburb of Lista. Being a surprise visit there was every chance that they might not be at home or perhaps had even gone to the coast to escape the heat, like half of Madrid – if indeed they still lived at that same address. He took the lift up to the second floor.

Both husband and wife were home and extremely pleased to see him. They welcomed him into their lounge, which looked exactly the same as it always had done, including the brass ashtray with its swinging centrepiece that distributed cigarette ash all over the surrounding area of the dining table.

"Podemos ver que ya has cortado el pelo," commented the señora, reminding Edwin that the last time they'd seen him he would have had relatively long hair but that in recent years he had adopted a more conservative shorter style in keeping with New Zealand.

The husband poured him a beer. The wife disappeared into the kitchen momentarily and returned with a basket of fresh bread rolls and slices of cured ham. It felt just like old times. Edwin asked about their daughter, Isolina, but noticed that both of their faces seemed to drop.

"Está casada", said the mother, by means of saying that she was married.

Edwin was about to offer his congratulations but the wife went on to qualify her previous statement by adding that it was not a good marriage.

The husband tut-tutted in agreement with his wife and shook his head to confirm things further.

At that moment the elderly grandmother hobbled into the lounge. Edwin politely stood up and the wife asked the old lady if she remembered him.

She peered at him. "Pues Si, Si," she exclaimed, "Me acuerdo bien," she said, "¡Y mira que rico es! Mira su traje tan elegante!"

"Abuela!" cautioned the husband. Even if Edwin did indeed look 'rich' in his suit the husband didn't think it was the grandmother's place to be pointing it out.

"Que pena que no está casado con Isolina," continued the old lady. It was a compliment to learn that she thought that it would have been better if her granddaughter Isolina had been married to Edwin – despite the fact that such a thought had never before crossed his mind.

The week in Madrid passed quickly. Edwin revisited much of his old stamping ground. He thought back to the student days when his daily food intake often had been limited to a potage of lentils and a bread roll. He visited Bar Pigalle one more time scarcely able to believe that he had whiled away so many nocturnal hours in the back room of such a seedy establishment. There were still ladies of the night coming in and out and plenty of ghosts from the past. The latticed swing doors then opened and Egyptian diplomat, Nizam, entered.

"Edwin! Is it really you? It's so good to see you again," he beamed as they shook hands.

They chatted together for over an hour. He confirmed that their mutual friend Charlie was nothing more than a memory as was just about everybody else from the former circle of regulars that used to frequent the back room of the establishment. They recalled the two New Zealanders that Nizam had entrusted with taking bronze medallions by train to Portugal. Edwin pointed out that the encounter with the two girls had indirectly led him to the idea of going out to New Zealand. Not that he had ever met them again. Although New Zealand had a comparatively small population they hadn't exchanged addresses at the time and he had no idea which part they came from.

During the time in Madrid that Edwin had worked as an extra at the Sevilla Film Studios he had met a Spanish person who was in some way connected to the administrative side of the company and he still had his contact details written in his address book. He phoned him and they arranged to meet up in a coffee shop in the suburb of Quintana. He was well-connected in the Spanish media world and said that she would be pleased to take Edwin on a visit to the studios of Televisión Española. The national broadcaster was located in a pleasant area of landscaped parkland known as Prado del Rey over to one side of the Casa de Campo. Edwin was able to meet various members of their production staff and it was interesting to compare the operation of Televisión Española with his own studio floor experience at the New Zealand Broadcasting Corporation. Lunch was thrown into the bargain and it was a fitting end to his visit to Madrid.

Because the date of Edwin's return to New Zealand was getting ever closer he decided to save time by taking a flight back to England. Whilst awaiting embarkation of his BEA flight he noticed that the bar stocked that memorable Spanish aniseed tipple of Chinchón. Although he'd never particularly liked the stuff and although it was still breakfast time he determined to drink one down in memory of all his former acquaintances in Madrid from days gone by. Such was nostalgia.

After an uneventful flight followed by a train journey down to Winchester, Edwin arrived at his grandmother's house that evening where a surprise was in store. His New Zealand girlfriend Caroline had arrived there the day before. Although they had written to each other over the past couple of years it was a shock to the system to be face to face with her once again. He noticed that she had lost a lot of weight during her travels. They went across the road where in the cosy atmosphere to the Hyde Tavern they were able to catch up on all of their adventures. Her lively personality meant that she was still a bundle of fun to be with although her New Zealand accent didn't have quite the same novelty value as before because Edwin now had one too. She would be re-joining her two female travelling companions in a couple of days as they planned to see a bit of mainland Europe before returning overland to the Southern Hemisphere.

The reunion with Caroline was the high point of Edwin's European trip and they promised to see each other again as soon as she got back to New Zealand. On her final morning in Winchester he accompanied her to the railway station to see her off. She went to the ticket booth and in a way more reminiscent of a New Zealand Railways enquiry asked, "Do you happen to have a train that will go through to London today?"

"Every twenty minutes from Platform 1," was the reply.

Edwin and Caroline kissed each other goodbye. She boarded her train and they waved to each other until they were out of sight.

Edwin reflected on the encounter. It had all felt a bit unreal as if it were part of a dream. She was very nice. They still loved each other. What next? He wondered.

WITH HIS THREE MONTHS finally up Edwin checked in at Heathrow's Terminal 3 for the journey back to New Zealand. Fortunately no truck had backed into the plane this time round. The BOAC flight included stops in Frankfurt, Beirut, Tehran, New Delhi and Rangoon before its final destination of Hong Kong. From there he would change to an Air New Zealand flight.

Edwin didn't sleep much on the plane. The rare occasions that he did manage to drop off seemed to occur shortly before one of the stopping points with the predicable requirement for passengers to leave the plane and wait in the transit lounge before queuing up simply to get back on again.

Finally they were approaching Hong Kong. For mile after mile the plane skimmed just a few feet above the roofs of high rise apartment blocks so close that anyone with a window seat couldn't help but hold their breath. It then turned slightly before descending to Hong Kong Airport.

Edwin had five hours to kill before his onward Air New Zealand flight. It was the first time he had been in the Orient even if it was just an airport departure lounge. Announcements being made in Chinese sounded almost musical and by listening to several of them he could already imitate words that sounded like "m-goy -neh" which he deduced as being Cantonese for "thank you". He recalled that at boarding school there had been several Chinese pupils from Hong Kong and, as he now glanced around the cafeteria area, almost everybody there seemed to bear a striking resemblance to them.

Cups of coffee and cigarettes kept him awake. He'd no idea what time of day or night it would now be in England or in New Zealand for that matter. It was afternoon in Hong Kong and he felt decidedly jet-lagged but he didn't dare sit down in a chair for too long in case he fell asleep and didn't wake up in time. Eventually the comforting sight of an Air New Zealand DC-8, with its familiar teal and green colours, came into view through one of the windows. Once on board and back in tune with the familiar kiwi accent of the hostesses Edwin began to feel he was getting one step closer to home. The plane touched down in Manila then in Brisbane as well as in Sydney before the final part of the flight to Auckland. He was then on a domestic flight down to the South Island and Christchurch Airport.

The combination of four days travel and accumulated lack of sleep with constant time zone changes had resulted in Edwin being in something of a semi-dazed state but there was a jolt back into reality as he set eyes upon Henry and Janet awaiting him in the arrivals area. They grabbed a cup of tea together.

"Welcome back. Thanks for the postcards" said Henry, "How did everything go?"

"On the whole it was a very good trip," replied Edwin, "although it sure feels good to be back here. How has everything been in my absence?"

"Absolutely fine," replied Henry, "There's just the small matter of a power bill that still needs to be paid and a reminder about the account with the bottle store but that's about all. However, we do have some other significant news to tell you."

"What's that?" he asked.

"Well, actually it's quite a major announcement. Are you ready for it?" he said.

"I hope so. Go on, try me," replied Edwin.

"Janet and I are getting married next month and I'd like you to be best man," said Henry.

"Blimey – I mean congratulations," said Edwin. "I'm delighted for both of you. Amazing what goes on the moment my back is turned!"

"Oh, yes, and of course there's that too," said Henry.

"There's what too?" he asked.

"Well, what do you think? We have bun in the oven. Janet is up the spout. She's preggers. We are going to have a baby!" he exclaimed.

"Good heavens!" said Edwin, trying to process such information, "Well, I mean, that's wonderful news too – and presumably that has something to do with the early date of your wedding."

"Precisely," said Henry beaming. "I knew you'd click sooner or later."

"I think I'm still trying to wake up properly but this is all very exciting stuff. What kind of arrangements have you made?" he asked.

"Well the wedding is going to take place in Janet's home town of Palmerston North on Saturday 9th October. Now, I fully realise that you must be running pretty skint after your mammoth trip to Europe and so you don't need to worry about any costs. I have booked our flights and arranged to hire wedding outfits for both of us – and you and I are booked in at a motel for the night before."

"Amazing," said Edwin, "and what about after the wedding?"

"First of all Janet and I are going to honeymoon up by Lake Taupo for a week before returning to Christchurch. But then, and I know that this will come as a shock to you, I'm afraid that I will be moving out of the England Street house. Janet and I will still be living nearby – just around the corner in a small maisonette that we have found on Hereford Street."

In such an unexpected set of circumstances, Edwin supposed that some sort of accommodation change was perhaps inevitable. Nevertheless the news meant that he would have to try and find somebody else to share the house.

"OK, well I'm sure that everything will work out somehow," he said.

They took a taxi back to England Street, and despite his earlier fatigue Edwin suddenly became fully awake once again. They spent the afternoon playing the selection of the top ten single records that Edwin had bought back from England.

Last night I heard my mama singing a song,
Ooh we, chirpy, chirpy, cheep, cheep
Woke up this morning and my mama was gone,
Ooh we, chirpy, chirpy, cheep, cheep
Chirpy, chirpy, cheep, cheep, chirp

Where's your mama gone? (Where's your mama gone?)
Far, far away

CHAPTER FOURTEEN

EDWIN RETURNED TO WORK on Monday morning and stopped by at the Operations Supervisor's office.

"Welcome back!" said Peter Baldwin looking up from a pile of papers on his desk. "You're looking fit and well! Good trip?"

"Yes thank you. It was excellent" replied Edwin.

"Good," he said, "And now that you have returned there is a bit of a choice open to you. You've already spent a bit of time with the TV Presentation Department and there is an opportunity for you to join that department on a full-time basis if you so wish – or you can to continue to work on the studio floor, whichever you prefer.

Edwin though for moment and then agreed to the transfer to the Presentation Department. It was probably be a smart move and would certainly be a new challenge.

"Excellent," he replied, "I'll set that in motion right away. And there's one other thing that you ought to know. I will soon be leaving Christchurch. I've just been appointed Head of Television Operations in Wellington."

"Congratulations," said Edwin.

"Thank you," he replied. "I'll be holding court in the saloon bar at Warner's hotel as a kind of going away stir this Friday evening and you are welcome to come along to that."

EDWIN FOUND HIMSELF ON a learning curve. He had been asked to shadow one of the TV Channel's Presentation Directors so as to familiarise himself with the duties that the job entailed. The role was explained to him as being "Jack of all trades and master of all trades."

He already had some insight into how a day's transmission was first mapped out on paper detailing every sound and vision event that would occur and he was now invited to sit in the presentation control room from where it was put on air. In front of a bank of monitors the presentation director's position was equipped with two built-in stop clocks and an array of talkbacks to the TV station's operational areas. A technical director sat alongside at a control console whilst a sound operator was positioned next to an audio mixing desk in the far corner. There was also a technical operator who balanced the level of each video source and the duty announcer who was present in the small adjacent studio.

After a full week of observing the control room procedure Edwin was given his first opportunity to direct afternoon transmission under supervision. Most of it entailed alerting the operational crew as to the sequence of what would be coming up next, standing them by at the right times and then cueing them to carry out whatever was required. There were standard commands that soon became familiar terminology.

It was a bit robotic. There had even been speculation in the presentation department that someday in the future computers would be able to handle transmission play out. For now though, the entire operation was manual and its timing crucially important. If a live programme finished slightly early or slightly late it meant that adjustments would need to be made to compensate.

On the rare occasion of an interruption in transmission, that too could cause a major re-shuffle of things. The Network News which originated from the NZBC's Wellington studios had to be met at 7pm. That quite literally meant 19.00.00 on the dot which was when the transmitter would switch over – not a second earlier and not a second later. Everything on air beforehand including programmes, commercial breaks and announcements had to be able to meet that deadline smoothly and right on time. And sometimes there were further live links to be met later in the evening.

EDWIN AND HENRY ARRIVED in Palmerston North the day before the wedding. In the evening they visited a couple of local bars but managed not to overdo it. The following afternoon at All Saints' Anglican Church the pews were packed full with relatives and friends from Janet's family and Henry's mother had even flown in from South Africa for the occasion. The ceremony went without any hitch as did the reception held afterwards where champagne was in full flow. Edwin's best man speech not only toasted the bridesmaid but also the barmaid much to the amusement of those present.

With Henry and Janet already away on their honeymoon Edwin flew back down to Christchurch the following morning. He supposed that he would either have to get used to living alone in the England Street house or else find a suitable person to move into Henry's room. However a letter that awaited him in the mailbox effectively ruled out both possibilities. It was from the firm of solicitors through whom the house was rented. Apparently the property had been sold and its new owner required full possession of the house by the end of the following month. The timing of such notice seemed almost fateful as if it represented the end of an era. It also left Edwin with the problem of finding somewhere else to live.

Being used to a detached house the thought of moving into a flat had no great appeal. On looking through the classified advertisements of the Christchurch newspaper, however, he saw that affordable houses were few and far between. One was advertised as being available but it was out of town and remote. A week elapsed and Edwin was no further forward with the property search. The same advertisement appeared again.

Curiosity got the better of him and on Saturday afternoon a friend from the graphics department offered to drive him out to take a look at it. It was located some fifteen miles south west of Christchurch and out towards Lake Ellesmere. Edwin was a non-driver and he knew that it would be foolhardy to cycle the journey each day and in all weathers. However, when he saw the delightful house that was of the right size to hold all of his accumulated furniture he began to think in terms of taking it on and of purchasing a moped. The following weekend he moved in.

Edwin was soon directing day-to-day transmission from the control room on a regular basis. Commuting to and from work on to a Honda 50cc moped took a bit of getting used to. It also had the immediate effect of knocking out his entire social life. After the first couple of months of riding back and forth he came to regard it as one huge inconvenience. Following the late shift he would leave the TV station at around midnight after the national anthem had been played at the end of transmission but instead of being able to saunter up the road to England Street he was now lumbered with the ritual of jumping into the saddle of the moped and travelling miles out to accommodation in the middle of nowhere.

Even when he arrived back to the house there was nothing there but a deafening silence. He had rigged up the bar in one of the rooms but because the place was so remote there were rarely any visitors for company. Even on day shifts the moped factor meant that he couldn't join others for a drink after work. No matter how quaint and pleasant the house itself might have been, he would have to search again for somewhere more convenient rather than endure such isolation for much longer.

An additional role of the television presentation staff was to direct the station's regional news magazine programme called 'The South Tonight'. From its production control room Edwin was put through a dummy run and did very well. That was largely because unlike most of the other presentation directors he had the distinct advantage of having worked on the programme on the studio floor for a couple of years and was thoroughly familiar with its format. Not only that, but the studio crew consisted of all his old mates.

One Tuesday evening Edwin was told that he could direct the rehearsal in its entirety shortly before the programme went out live. After doing so he was then asked, "Would you now like to go ahead and direct it live – as well as you just did in the rehearsal?" It was a compliment and Edwin agreed to do so whilst someone rushed upstairs to telecine in order to change one of the captions that would be used in the programme's closing credits so as to read 'Directed by Edwin Ravensdale.' There were no mishaps and Edwin went on to direct the show live throughout the remainder of that week and then on a regular basis.

THE TASK REMAINED FOR Edwin to find some alternative accommodation that was more conveniently located. With such a thought in mind he arrived at the office to find a message on his desk asking him to drop in on the newly appointed Operations Supervisor who had replaced Peter Baldwin. Edwin had met the newcomer only a couple of times before and he seemed a reasonable enough chap. He wondered why he wanted to see him.

"Good morning Edwin," said Stephen Day. "Many thanks for coming by. Please take a seat. What I am about to tell you might come as a bit of a surprise although it is not necessarily a bad thing. It is something that can happen to any of us at the NZBC from time to time – and as a matter of fact it is something that recently happened to me." Edwin was curious. "The thing is," continued the man, "At DNTV2 down in Dunedin they are short of a Presentation Director and because we now have you on board as an additional member of the presentation staff here at CHTV3 in Christchurch, Head Office has decided to transfer you to Dunedin."

Edwin didn't react but simply listened as the man told him that a similar sudden transfer had happened to him when he was recently shunted down to Christchurch from Auckland. He expressed sympathy that such short notice might be a shock to the system but went on to explain that the NZBC would do everything to make sure that the transition went as smoothly as possible. They would cover all removals costs and pay for Edwin to stay in hotel accommodation in Dunedin until such time as he had found somewhere to live down there.

"How soon would all this take place?" asked Edwin.

"Well basically they're crying out for you to start down there as soon as possible," he smiled. "However, I know that from a practical point of view that it takes a bit of time to get things organised and so we can give you some extra time for that. But, ideally, if you could be down there in a fortnight's time, that would be particularly good. And again, I'm so sorry that all of this must come as a complete surprise to you."

"No, don't worry. I'm absolutely fine with it," replied Edwin.

"Well that's excellent. There's a local removals company here in Christchurch that not only transports household furniture and possessions but also does all of the packing as well. If you'd like to suggest a convenient date for that to take place we could get that part organised so that they can get your things put into a storage depot in Dunedin" he said.

Edwin was intrigued with the idea of making a new start in a new city and that such a transfer completely solved his current housing problem.

That evening he visited Henry and a heavily pregnant Janet in their new apartment. Once the removals company had done their thing Edwin would be welcome to camp on their lounge floor for his few remaining days in Christchurch.

ARRIVING IN DUNEDIN BY the one- a-day train service from Christchurch Edwin took a taxi from its quaint castle-like railway station to the centrally located Leviathan Hotel where he had been booked into a single room on the first floor.

He then strolled into the city centre and discovered it to be quite a bustling place on that warm summer's afternoon. A street map enabled him to locate the whereabouts of the Dunedin TV studios in a building called Garrison Hall whose front entrance seemed to be of a similar architectural vintage to the railway station. Turning a corner into the main shopping street he inadvertently found himself walking alongside a bearded man who was carrying four blue plastic film cases with familiar NZBC labels stuck on them. He decided not to speak to him because for all he knew it might have been anyone from the station manager to a film editor and, as he wasn't due to start work until Monday morning, he preferred to quietly check things out for himself. Nevertheless he allowed himself to trail the man to the side entrance of the Methodist Central Mission Building where, according to a stainless steel plaque, the New Zealand Broadcasting Corporation occupied six of its eight floors. Through its glass doors Edwin could make out a reception area, beyond which were lifts and a stairwell.

The front face of the building formed part of a small eight-sided central park in the heart of the city known as The Octagon. One of the features there was a musical fountain that spurted jets of water into the air synchronised with music and coloured lights which danced to the tune whilst an adjacent statue of the poet Robbie Burns looked on so as to underline the city's Scottish heritage.

Edwin walked the length of Princes Street which was the main stretch of shops and then looped back along a hilly route a couple of blocks over. Some streets veered off at unlikely angles and he recalled having been told that the original layout for Dunedin had been mapped out in Edinburgh a hundred years earlier but the planners had not taken into consideration local topography and the presence of hills had led to such unusual angles.

Back at the Leviathan Hotel dinner was served from 6pm. Edwin then went through to the lounge, lit a cigarette and watched Dunedin's local news magazine programme. It was also called 'The South Tonight' although its content reflected the different viewing area. The format was similar to its Christchurch equivalent which was a relief because Edwin realised that he would soon be in the control room directing it.

With nothing much else on his immediate agenda he decided to go out for a drink. The Leviathan where he was staying was a dry hotel. He retraced his steps back into the town centre and entered the lounge bar of the Princes Hotel. As he about to order a beer somebody tapped him on the shoulder. To his pleasant surprise it was none other than Duncan McIntyre, the person whom he had met on the flight back to Europe the year before. They greeted each other like long-lost friends. Edwin was glad that at least he now knew one person in this city. For his part Duncan was pleased to learn that Edwin had moved to Dunedin. They spent the rest of the evening together and after the ten o'clock closing time adjourned to a late night snack bar for a coffee and a cheeseburger. Duncan would be out at sea on a fishing trip over the next few days but they made arrangements to meet up again when he got back.

EDWIN WAS GIVEN A desk in an open plan office on the sixth floor and introduced to everybody. The rest of the presentation team were an upbeat bunch of likable individuals and he was soon made to feel completely at home. During the first week a couple of training sessions were laid on for him in the control room in order to familiarise him with its layout which was slightly different from its Christchurch counterpart. And then he was down on the roster for directing transmission on a shift basis.

Much as he appreciated the laid-back lifestyle of staying at the Leviathan Hotel he started looking around for somewhere to live. Listings were available for rented accommodation located mainly in parts of Dunedin that Edwin hadn't yet discovered. On his days off he explored such suburbs and looked at several flats, none of which seemed to be quite what he was looking for in areas with unlikely yet familiar sounding names such as St Kilda, Kensington and Balaclava.

Duncan came back from his fishing trip and the two of them met up once again. One of the estate agents had lent Edwin the keys to an empty house on the part of Dunedin known as the Peninsular for him to look at over the weekend. However, he had since seen on a map that it was too remote and he had no intention of falling into that kind of situation again. He mentioned it to Duncan who suggested that if only to eliminate it, he would be pleased to drive him there the following day. That evening they got talking to a couple of girls sitting at an adjacent table who said that they'd also come along for the ride.

Early on Saturday evening they all met up and hopped into Duncan's car. They took some wine and beer with them as well as disposable cups. The large, run-down, wooden house in a tiny hamlet on the Peninsula had once been a post office. It clearly hadn't been lived in for years and its surrounding garden was completely overgrown. The four of them stepped in through the front door and were greeted by a musty odour.

" And here is the delightful front parlour," announced Duncan mimicking the enthusiasm of an estate agent as he led the way into one of the front rooms that still had wooden pigeon hole sorting boxes fixed to its walls and covered in a layer of thick dust.

"You're surely not seriously thinking of living in this place?" asked one of the girls.

"No way," replied Edwin, "I was just curious to see what's on offer."

"Let's just have a quick look around and then maybe sit out in the back garden for while and have a drink," suggested Duncan.

"Good idea," said the other girl, "This house is kind of creepy."

As they went from room to room, the situation got more and more amusing. A dilapidated kitchen in which the door to what had once been a fitted cupboard was hanging by one hinge. An ancient looking cooker was covered in grime and the porcelain kitchen sink was cracked and heavily stained. On the other side of a corridor was a disgusting bathroom with a rusting iron tub and a lavatory full of brown liquid that refused to flush. Three large bedrooms each had peeling pink wallpaper with evidence of a leaking roof as demonstrated by the black dotted stains along the ceilings of mould and mildew. There was a cold stone floor throughout the entire building. Its dingy lounge was hemmed right in at the middle of the house with just one small window. An old settee with a torn cover had been left in the middle of the room.

They stepped outside through the back door into a jungle of long grass in a sizable area surrounded by conifer hedging.

"Interesting neighbours," commented Duncan as he pointed to the dim outline of gravestones in a small cemetery just visible through a gap in the bushes.

Edwin retrieved some wooden crates from an outhouse that could be used to sit on and drinks were poured. It was a warm evening and they stayed there in the garden for the best part of an hour before it started to get dark. As they passed back through the house Duncan lit his cigarette lighter to show the way. Its glow was sufficient to make out a rat that came scampering past them leading both girls to scream.

Edwin decided that he would limit his accommodation search to the town area of Dunedin.

Christmas neared and because most of Edwin's colleagues in the TV Presentation Department were married and had families to think about, it was understandable that staff members who were single would be landed with the bulk of the transmission shifts throughout the days of festivity. There was no objection to additional hours and nor to being paid double time for working on public holidays. In the meantime a pie cart was conveniently parked near to the channel's entrance which provided a welcome facility for the late shift. Some kind soul would take orders and pop outside for a few minutes before returning laden with goodies.

Early in January a spacious flat became available in the Dunedin suburb of Roslyn. It was an easy downhill walk into town. Edwin made arrangements for his furniture to be delivered from the storage depot and within a matter of a few days he had moved out of the Leviathan Hotel and into his new home. His furniture fitted neatly into the flat and yet again the famous bar unit with its associated paraphernalia was set up in the smaller of the two lounges.

AS THE MONTHS PASSED by directing transmission became almost second nature to Edwin. In common with his colleagues there were very few unforeseen problems that they couldn't effectively handle. Edwin's only concern was that although there was an undoubted thrill of being able to put the channel on air and to direct its transmission through to closing time he wasn't sure where this experience was going to lead. On some days he likened it to driving a bus or a train that wasn't actually going anywhere. Perhaps another analogy would be air traffic control. The control room was certainly a nerve centre and, although rare, there were some occasions when things went wrong. A film might physically break, a videotape might refuse to lock up and play, a live local production might overrun by a few minutes – or under-run. Lost time had to be compensated for as did gained time. If it meant having to ditch commercials so as to meet the link for the national network news they would have to be re-inserted at an appropriate opportunity later on the day's schedule in order to avoid any loss of advertising revenue.

Shift changeover could be manic. Edwin would arrive for the late duty to be informed that not only was the transmission running time a minute or so behind schedule but that there were going to be three locally originating news items to be injected into the national Network News. A long scroll of paper retrieved from one of the teleprinters provided a detailed run-down of the news programme and included the duration and last words of each news item. The transmitters would switch on cue at given moments throughout the bulletin and an audible talk-through from Wellington would spring into life over the communications system. It required a fair bit of multi-skilling to be listening in to that whilst simultaneously coordinating the sequence of events in the Dunedin control-room and alerting the operational staff of what to do and when to do it. It was common knowledge that those who directed such shifts never needed to make use of laxatives.

Transmission finished at around midnight with the traditional 'God Save the Queen' followed by the music of Bedrich Smetana's 'Ma Vlast.' Quite what such evocative music of the rolling Vltava River passing through the city of Prague had to do with the city of Dunedin was anyone's guess but the tune was a further reminder that the shift had ended and that it was time to go home. Edwin walked or sometimes grabbed a lift from the duty announcer.

Edwin also took his turn at directing Dunedin's nightly regional magazine programme. There were some occasions when just as they had finished rehearsing the programme a last minute major news story would break. It meant that half of what had been prepared would be ditched whilst politicians and other spokespersons were hauled into the studio for live interviews and the whole programme had to be reconstructed as it was going out on air. Although a nightmare scenario for the production crew, in the majority of cases what actually ended up on the screen was completely flawless and viewers watching from their homes were blissfully unaware of the mad panic that was taking place in the control room as news items were frantically being dropped and replaced whilst the programme still needed to come to its end on time.

Edwin befriended a current affairs researcher, Sara Jordan – or rather she befriended him. She first approached him after realising that they had a mutual friend in Christchurch. She invited him to accompany her to a party the following Saturday. He went along to what was a lively evening of food, drink, music and conversation. Although in many respects she was an unlikely person for Edwin to hang around with they enjoyed each other's company. Highly intelligent with her two PhDs – a wealth of knowledge about every subject under the sun, she was a few years older than Edwin. She was equipped with an amorous streak that wasn't afraid of coming into play at short notice –and often in public.

Social life was becoming quite hectic. Whenever Duncan was ashore Edwin would meet up with him for a few drinks in some of Dunedin's numerous hotels, several of which had live music and as often as not they would get talking to some of the young ladies who were out for the evening. Variety might have been the spice of life but sometimes everything seemed a bit too free and easy.

A telegram arrived from Henry. His wife Janet had just given birth to a baby daughter which they were calling Beatrice. Edwin scribbled a congratulations note. There was also a letter from Caroline. She was now in Australia but would be returning to New Zealand the following year where she would be staying with her parents near Blenheim. She said that she was looking forward to seeing him again. He thought about that and wondered how it would be.

In contrast to the centrally located bars that all too often were heaving with people and live music, Edwin and Duncan tended to drift towards a place called the London Bar which was a quieter establishment. By coincidence it also happened to be the favourite watering hole of the TV Station Manager, Rick Andrews, who used to position himself at one end of the bar often straight after work. He was an approachable and affable man with a wealth of insight into the ins and outs of the NZBC. Edwin always enjoyed the pleasure of his company and there was something refreshing about his ability to relate to people at all levels. Rick Andrews was equally skilled at knocking back the beer. Some evenings Edwin would arrive at the bar a little later in the evening and ask him how he was doing.

"I'm smashed," was his invariable reply.

When the pubs shut at ten o'clock most people either called it a day and sidled off home or perhaps found somewhere still open for a coffee. However Duncan knew of a place back along Princes Street where after hours drinks were possible. On ringing the doorbell three times an elderly gentleman would let them in with no questions being asked. The local police turned a blind eye.

On Edwin's days off long walks in and around Dunedin became the norm. He was perfectly content to walk for miles on end in a meditative frame of mind. Occasionally he took a route that passed along the dockside where various cargo ships were being loaded and unloaded. He found it interesting to encounter a ship's crew from overseas and vessels with Chinese characters written on their sterns.

WHEN EDWIN HAD WORKED in television presentation for a year and a half he began contemplating his next move. The day-to-day direction of transmission was fine if somewhat monotonous and apart from writing the continuity announcements that went in between the programmes the role didn't involve much in the way of creativity. Directing the nightly regional news magazine programme was considerably more interesting but was about as good as it got. He had joined the presentation department primarily to experience control room work as a stepping stone to programme production and coupled with his earlier studio floor experience it had added a useful string to his bow.

He was invited to attend a course in Wellington which provided an opportunity for individuals to consider where their aspirations lay within the NZBC as well as being a chance for the hierarchy to take a look at the kinds of people who had been coming up through the ranks. The thirty or so participants were put up in guest house near the waterfront. At a nearby training centre the daily talks given by a selection of departmental heads were informative and interesting.

As a sideline Edwin also managed to use the occasion to look up his ballerina friend from the New Zealand Ballet Company and got treated to a Saturday matinee performance of Coppélia into the bargain.

Back in Dunedin the weather turned bitterly cold and there was quite a heavy snowfall. He invested in an electric heater to make at least one room of the home cosy at any given time of the evening. For some reason he also purchased a book called 'Teach yourself Russian' and set about familiarising himself with the Cyrillic alphabet. He was soon able to pronounce written words as well as learn a few phrases. It was the kind of exercise that in all probability he would never have the slightest bit of use for. All the same he became quite absorbed with it.

One evening in the London Bar the TV station Manager, Rick Andrews, told Edwin that there might be some sort of a TV production role occurring in Hamilton – which could lead to bigger things. Unlike the NZBC television stations based in the cities of Auckland, Wellington, Christchurch and Dunedin, the Hamilton operation was something of a spin-off from Auckland. Edwin recalled that he had stayed a couple of nights at the Youth Hostel in Hamilton when he had first arrived in New Zealand and he remembered it as being a small provincial town with a lake. Nevertheless, he'd be interested in finding out a bit more about what the job would entail. Rick Andrews said that he'd make some enquiries.

A fortnight or so later some sketchy details began to filter through. As far as could be ascertained the job in Hamilton would involve TV production work although no specific programmes were mentioned. If he was interested Rick Andrews was willing to recommend Edwin for the post based on his studio experience and control room work. However, there was a word of caution.

"If you do transfer to Hamilton, be aware that the Station Manager up there can best be described as an out and out conman," he said.

The following month Edwin's farewell gathering took place at the Princes Hotel at which he parted company with his Dunedin colleagues prior to venturing into pastures new. His fisherman friend Duncan McIntyre also joined them for the evening.

Breaking his railway journey in Christchurch Edwin spent three days staying with Henry and Janet. They had settled into their parental role with ease and both seemed very content. Their baby daughter was delightful. Edwin felt some responsibility for their marriage. After all, if it hadn't been for him Henry wouldn't have come out to New Zealand and if he hadn't come out to New Zealand he would never have met Janet and if he had never met Janet then their marriage could never have happened.

CHAPTER FIFTEEN

EDWIN HAD HAMILTON SLIGHTLY different in his memory from the time when he had previously stayed at its Youth Hostel. Having worked in the heart of the two South Island cities of Christchurch and Dunedin, this was just a small town by comparison. A taxi from the railway station brought him to the Commercial Hotel on Sunday afternoon and after offloading his suitcase he took a leisurely stroll through the stretch of closed shops on Victoria Street. He located the small NZBC building visible down one of the side streets. At least it was within easy walking distance.

When he arrived for work the following morning, however, it became apparent that something was seriously amiss. There was confusion as to what his role was supposed to be.

He had been cheerfully greeted in the reception area by one of the news journalists who said, "Ah, so you must be the new film editor. Welcome!"

"No, I'm afraid that's not me," replied Edwin. He assumed that they must also be expecting someone else in that particular role to be arriving on that same day.

"That's strange, we are expecting a film editor to be coming up from Dunedin," replied the journalist.

"Well, the Dunedin bit is correct but I am supposed to be coming here to work in television production," said Edwin.

"That's odd," replied the journalist. "Hamilton doesn't do much in the way of production anymore. These days the television operation here is pretty much a regional extension of AKTV2's news in Auckland which is the main reason that we were expecting a film editor."

"Well I'm afraid I've never edited a piece of film in my life," replied Edwin.

The two of them realised that there must have been an administrative botch up that would need to be sorted out.

The journalist introduced himself as Gavin Grainger. He suggested that he at least show Edwin around the premises whilst trying to find some solution to what appeared to be crossed wires.

"It never ceases to amaze me that although we work in the communications industry our internal communications are often so lousy," he commented.

Although the building was equipped with a television studio and a related control-room the rest of it was essentially a radio station. On the first floor they entered a small open plan news room where half a dozen journalists were sat at their desks either on the phone or bashing out news stories on typewriters or drinking mugs of tea. Even before being introduced, there was a further wave of assumptions that Edwin was 'the new film editor.'

Gavin showed him into an adjacent room designated for the film cameramen. In one corner a film editing bench was tucked away behind two metallic storage cabinets. He suggested that Edwin might like to wait there for a while whilst he went off to speak to various managerial staff about such an unexpected turn of events.

Edwin wondered what on earth to make of it all. He would be perfectly justified in getting straight back down to Dunedin and explaining the confused situation that had occurred. However, that could be awkward. After all, he'd just said goodbye to all his old workmates down there and they had given him a really good send off and wished him well in the new job. If someone is seen to be moving on in a certain direction it might look a bit weird suddenly to re-appear. Also, from a practical point of view, he had quit his flat. His furniture and possessions had been packed up and shipped to a storage depot somewhere in Hamilton. Faced with such an unexpected development he hoped that some satisfactory solution would now present itself.

After a wait of a good half hour, during which two further staff members breezed in and out and asked Edwin if he was the new film editor, the journalist Gavin returned.

"I've spoken to the station manager. He is just as surprised as you and me about the situation. He would like to see you now but, be warned – he is a radio man and doesn't know the first thing about television."

He was shown into an office where Mr Sam Short dressed in a flashy purple and pink chequered suit sat at his desk. He invited Edwin to take a seat.

"Now what's all this I'm hearing about Head Office sending me someone with no television experience?" was his opening question.

"I've got plenty of television experience – both on the studio floor and in television presentation as well as in directing a nightly news magazine programme," replied Edwin, "but from what I can gather you are seeking a film editor."

The distinction seemed to be completely lost on the man who instead of making any constructive suggestions launched into a self-congratulatory appraisal of how he had single-handedly set up his own highly successful commercial radio station which he regarded as an entirely separate entity from the rest of the New Zealand Broadcasting Corporation. He said that he had even commissioned its musical jingles from America.

It became apparent that their conversation was at cross-purposes. Whenever Edwin tried to make the point that something was drastically wrong with his appointment there was no realisation of this on the part of the station manager. All he did was mutter things such as "NZBC Head Office – Huh."

Edwin stepped out of the office none the wiser. The journalist Gavin was waiting for him and asked if anything had transpired.

"It didn't exactly feel like the kick-start to a healthy working relationship," said Edwin, "The man doesn't seem to get the point."

"Typical," said Gavin. "But you'll probably get a far more sympathetic ear from the News Editor Pete Cornwall who'll be in later this morning."

But it wasn't sympathy that Edwin was seeking so much as a workable solution. Probing questions revealed that although the Hamilton TV studio had originally been set up with production capabilities most of the technical facilities had long since been removed and the staff transferred elsewhere. Its current use was limited to injecting local news items either into the national Network News or into Auckland's regional magazine programme called 'This Day.' Because Edwin was used to directing the entire news programme of 'The South Tonight' as he had done both in Christchurch and Dunedin a mere handful of news items each evening would be extremely mundane by comparison.

As far as he could make out through his discussion with Gavin what Hamilton needed was someone with two skills. A kind of one-man-band who could edit filmed news items throughout the day and then put them on air in the evening. He supposed that if it really came to it and if he could perhaps learn how to edit news film he could possibly endure the situation for the time being until he found the best way out of it – such as a transfer to one of the larger TV stations of Auckland or Wellington.

With such a compromise situation in mind Edwin sat down at the editing bench and throughout the rest of the day began to experiment in how to chop up 16mm film and arrange the various strips sequentially before splicing them together again. Fortunately Gavin had some basic film editing experience and was able to impart the various ins and outs of such skills. Ironically, with no formal training in film editing whatsoever, over the next few days Edwin was able to churn out some halfway reasonable pieces that were included in Auckland's news magazine programme.

AT THE END OF the working week whilst sitting in his hotel lounge, Edwin glanced up and was surprised to see the figure of the News Editor, Pete Cornwall, standing before him.

"Fancy another drink?"

"Well, why not?" replied Edwin. "A bottle of Steinlager wouldn't go amiss".

The News Editor fetched the beer and a Black Label whisky for himself and sat down opposite Edwin.

"Cheers," he said, "I understand that this Hamilton experience is not quite as you'd been led to believe."

"Well, it certainly doesn't chime with the kind of job description I'd been given in Dunedin," said Edwin. "If they'd told me the reality then I'd have given it a miss."

"I'm afraid the buggers got everything arse about face," said Pete, "but in view of the circumstances I think you've done remarkably well in getting our television news items together throughout this week."

"Thank you," replied Edwin, "but I'm afraid it's the result of self-taught editing that was probably a bit rough around the edges."

"I'm in a somewhat similar situation to you," he continued. "I'm used to being in the central hub of activity in the Auckland newsroom but for the past few months I've been stuck down here in this one-horse town trying to make things function."

"Yes but presumably you would at least have known what you were coming to," said Edwin.

"True," he replied, "but I see it purely as a temporary arrangement for now until the next opportunity crops up – and then you won't see me for dust."

"Well, to be quite honest the same goes for me," said Edwin. "This is not where I want to be for any length of time. I'd like to get into programme production in one of the larger television centres."

SOME WEEKS LATER EDWIN sensed that it was time to graduate from living in a hotel. Irrespective of how long he would be staying in Hamilton there was no shortage of affordable houses of a sufficient size to hold his accumulated sticks of furniture. He signed a rental agreement for a large detached house in Tristram Street. It stood opposite a park and a theatre and he began to feel slightly more optimistic at the thought of having access to his worldly possessions once again. On Friday morning a removals truck arrived and everything was unloaded. Edwin then spent most of Saturday unpacking and arranging things in each of the rooms. A young lady called Harriet whom he had met that morning at the local dairy shop volunteered to give him a hand. This time the famous bar unit would occupy one of the reception rooms at the front of the house together with its stools, tables and chairs and the record player. After a few hours of shifting furniture and unpacking boxes everything seemed to be in a logical place as the two of them cooked a late breakfast.

Edwin's official working hours were from 10 am to 8pm every weekday. That allowed sufficient time for most things although there were some days in which he would arrive earlier and often, in the interests of getting one step ahead he would work through meal times. He became quite dedicated to the task in hand and occasionally worked the odd weekend too.

Edwin and the News Editor, Pete Cornwall, became good friends. Edwin could learn a lot from him about news sense, what constituted a story and what didn't and he found him to be interesting company. At the beginning of each day they would discuss which of the various news stories warranted film coverage and, if time permitted, Edwin would go out and direct one or other of the film crews. However, because there were deadlines to be met and because he was aware that he'd got to get back to base with sufficient time up his sleeve to physically edit the film and then put the completed news items on air in the evening he had to plan his whereabouts carefully. If Edwin wasn't there none of it would happen.

Durations had to be agreed and there was a need to prioritise. There was a standing joke in the newsroom that if the New Zealand All Blacks were playing rugby the TV news coverage of the match might run for three and a half minutes but if the Second Coming were ever to take place they might be able to allocate twenty seconds for that.

Edwin and Pete sometimes met up after work and drove out to a tavern in one of the small neighbouring towns. There were also late night hotel bars where they were assumed to be residents. A member of the hotel staff once went around the lounge bar checking up on everybody's 'after hours' status by asking them to confirm that they were in the house. Pete had simply nodded. He then said to Edwin "It was an honest enough answer. Of course we're in the house. I mean we're not outside in the bloody garden, are we?"

After such jaunts they would then return to Edwin's in-house bar for late night coffee often accompanied by a background of Gilbert and Sullivan on the turntable.

In serving writs I made such a name
That an articled clerk I soon became
I wore clean collars and a brand-new suit
For the pass examination at the Institute.
For the pass examination at the Institute.

Mount Ngauruhoe was the most active of three volcanoes located in Tongariro National Park in the centre of New Zealand's North Island. When news came through that it had started to erupt, Edwin and Pete chartered a Cessna aircraft and together with a cameraman flew around it several times whilst filming. It might have been a nice idea but the end result of that little escapade was nothing more than some beautiful shots of white smoke and not much besides. Better pictures were obtainable at ground level.

ON SUNDAYS EDWIN GOT into the habit of taking a constitutional walk around Lake Rotoroa which was conveniently located in the park across the road. On one of its pathways he would often stop and speak to a girl with a bicycle who was present every week and although extremely pleasant was evidently on some kind of an evangelical mission to try and convert people to her particular understanding. Edwin had never had the slightest interest in religious matters but nevertheless found their weekly debate quite stimulating as he advanced his own view that if there really were such a thing as a God, religious people had been doing a pretty good job in putting people right off him. She spoke of knowing Jesus and knowing God but Edwin couldn't relate to any of that and after a while tried to change the subject to more earthly things such as whether he could take her out to the pub sometime during the week – which she always politely declined.

One evening, after another such encounter with the bicycle girl, Edwin was at home in his in-house bar listening to music by Handel and found himself wondering about the best way in which people of religious faith could ever hope to get their message across. To a certain extent he could sympathise with the difficulty that they must face. He poured himself a brandy and lit a cigarette. He tried putting himself in the evangelist's shoes and in a purely hypothetical scenario began to imagine that he would go about things in a completely different way. If ever I were a religious person, perish the thought, I'd want to go the whole hog and cause a real stir, he reasoned. He raised his glass and said out loud, "Cheers God," before shifting his thinking back into how best to go about advancing his career. He wondered what he would be doing at the same time next year, in five years' time or even in ten or twenty years' time.

In November the Hamilton broadcasting station served a useful purpose in being linked up with the rest of country for television coverage of New Zealand's general election. With Edwin directing from the control room the leader of the Social Credit political party, Bruce Beetham, was live in the studio challenging the stranglehold of the country's two-party system of the National and Labour parties. Afterwards Edwin reflected that that particular night's broadcast represented the sum total of television production work that had taken place in Hamilton other than its nightly news input.

The following Christmas was hot and humid. Edwin spent a lot of it sitting in the sun on the wooden steps at the front of his house reading a couple of books by Thomas Hardy punctuated by visits from Harriet who lived nearby and breezed in on a regular basis. In the New Year a large outdoor pop music festival was held on a farm in the small town of Ngaruawahia which was about ten miles away from Hamilton. The three-day event provided plenty of visual material both for the national network news and the regional magazine programme as well as the story of the local vendor who sold more hamburgers in that space of time than he normally did in an entire year.

One afternoon a senior executive from the NZBC in Auckland came to visit Hamilton. Edwin decided to use the opportunity to express his desire to transfer either to Auckland or Wellington. However, he learned that such a move might not be that straightforward.

"The fact that you handle both the film editing and the control room direction from here means that you could be rather difficult to replace," said the man, "It would most probably mean bringing in two people but that can't really be justified."

"That's as maybe but when I arrived here I had little choice other than to teach myself how to edit news film and yet by doing do I seem to have painted myself into a corner," replied Edwin, "and on that basis I could be stuck here forever."

"Perhaps not forever," said the man, "All I am saying is that it could prove difficult to get a replacement for you. Nobody in the corporation is supposed to be indispensable but in the case of the television operation in Hamilton, that's just the way it is."

That evening Edwin related the conversation to Pete Cornwall.

"Seems like you are doomed to remain here in Hamilton for eternity," he said.

"That's the problem," said Edwin, "There's no easy way out of it – unless, of course, I were to quit and go and work overseas and then return at a later date."

"Easier said than done," replied Pete.

"I know," said Edwin, "and I'd need to have something lined up somewhere first – but given a choice between being stuck in a rut here and the challenge of pastures new I reckon I know which one I'd go for."

OUT OF CURIOSITY AS much as anything else Edwin visited Hamilton Public Library and took out some travel books on the off-chance that they might provide inspiration for some sort of a move overseas in the event of no new opportunities becoming available within the NZBC. By a process of elimination he reached the conclusion that if he were to go anywhere at all, his preference would be to work for a television company either in South America or in the Far East. He managed to get hold of a directory of television broadcasting organisations in various parts of the world and sent off speculative letters to several that were located in far flung places. For South America he would be able to make use of his Spanish even if it was getting rusty through lack of use. For the Far East it would probably be best to stick to English speaking places such as Singapore or Hong Kong.

He was still in contact with former colleagues both in Christchurch and Dunedin although he purposely didn't reveal too much about his frustration with Hamilton. One weekend he got caught slightly off guard when his Current Affairs Researcher friend, Sara Jordan, from Dunedin arrived on the doorstep at short notice. She was en route to stay with some relatives who lived in the area. He explained the entire Hamilton situation to her and mentioned that he was contemplating working overseas. By coincidence a letter arrived from Hong Kong that same day. It was from the Personnel Department of Rediffusion Television saying that they could certainly do with someone with Edwin's experience. The letter added that if Edwin was ever over in Hong Kong he would be welcome to get in touch.

"I don't know if they imagine that I might just happen to be over in Hong Kong for an afternoon or something," he said. "If I'd made the effort of getting myself out there it would be for the sole purpose of working there."

In one sense it was a crazy idea even to think about leaving New Zealand because it had become his home and he loved the country. To all intents and purposes he had become a New Zealander. He spoke like one, looked like one, acted like one, dressed like one and felt like one. He was even eligible for a New Zealand passport if he wanted one even though it wasn't an absolute requirement to switch and so far he had got by on his British UK passport perfectly well. He cast his mind back to a day in Christchurch when in the garden he had determined that if ever he were to get married and have children that place was where he would wish to be. Despite this temporary Hamilton setback, he had a good lifestyle and enjoyed working for the NZBC which had trained him and equipped him well for his professional career. He was still in his early twenties, he had a good salary, he lived in a large house, he had an active social life and, in fact, he had so many things that other people would have yearned for. Surely he shouldn't be throwing all of it away.

Over a light lunch Edwin asked Sara what she thought of the possibility of him making the move to Hong Kong.

"There's an obvious risk involved but it's one of those situations in which you won't find out if it's been a good move until you've actually done it," she said.

"By which time it might be too late," said Edwin.

"Yes but you're the kind person who enjoys new challenges and who'll most probably do well wherever you go," she replied.

EDWIN READ UP SOME more about life in Hong Kong. 'The British have been here since 1841' said one of the books that went on to give a detailed account of the opium wars and the colony's history.

A couple of weeks later Edwin decided to take the plunge and so he put in a request for two year's 'leave without pay' to broaden his horizons overseas. To his frustration, however, it was promptly declined. That increased the pressure on him considerably. It was one thing to push off for a couple of years in the knowledge that there would be the security of some sort a job to come back to afterwards but a different matter altogether if there was no such guarantee. He wondered if it was worth the gamble. After all, it wasn't even a definite job in Hong Kong. It was merely the hint of a possible job once he got there. What if it all backfired and he had to return to New Zealand? He put the question to Pete the News Editor.

"Most probably the corporation would take you back in some capacity or other," he answered. "For all their faults they're generally good to members of staff who take a break and then return a few years later."

Edwin recalled that it wasn't without precedent. In Christchurch a producer had left the corporation to go and work in Australia but after a year or so when things hadn't worked according to plan he had returned to New Zealand flat broke. The NZBC had given him a job once again.

With mixed emotions Edwin handed in his notice and booked a flight. An advertisement placed in the local newspaper enabled him to sell off all of his furniture throughout the following weeks. It included parting with the prized bar unit. Somebody else purchased the dining table just as he had sat down to eat his Sunday lunch from it.

CHAPTER SIXTEEN

EDWIN AWOKE AN HOUR or so before the plane began its approach in to Hong Kong and for the second time in his life he was able to participate in the awesome experience of skimming just above the rooftops of apartment blocks that all seemed far too close for comfort. After watching such a never ending display of colourful washing on clothes lines and the occasional person, the plane suddenly made an abrupt turn to the right followed by a drop in height that left one's stomach in the air as it rapidly descended towards a runway that mysteriously appeared out of nowhere. Landing at Hong Kong's Kai Tak airport was still regarded as one of the most potentially dangerous flying manoeuvres in the world and a profound sense of relief was felt by everybody on board when the wheels of the undercarriage finally make contact with the tarmac.

Before his departure from New Zealand Edwin had despatched three cardboard boxes containing all that remained of his personal possessions to Henry and his wife for safekeeping and had got rid of just about everything else. His luggage now consisted of one suitcase and an Air New Zealand shoulder bag. He went through passport control and customs and in the arrivals hall followed signs for the exit. As he entered a passageway an oriental man stopped him and said something completely indiscernible. At first he assumed that the person was trying to be helpful until realising that the encounter had something to do with him wanting to measure Edwin up for a tailor-made suit. He quickly disengaged himself from the situation and stepped out into the heat and humidity of the front of the airport building and a long line of red taxis. Taking the precaution of first agreeing the price with the driver, he was then driven the twenty minute journey to the heart of downtown Kowloon.

For the first few days in Hong Kong, and until he found his feet, Edwin had booked a room at the centrally-located accommodation of the YMCA at a considerably less expensive rate than staying at one of the hotels. As the cab made its way through sprawling suburbia his first impression was that this indeed was South East Asia. He had read that in Hong Kong there were only six per cent Europeans and so it came as no great surprise to see that virtually everyone was decidedly oriental. Through the taxi window he caught sight of the sheer multitude of Chinese people thronging roadside market stalls with overhead strings of naked light bulbs that stretched down the side streets along the route. Chinese housewives were buying fruit and vegetables. Thin Chinese men in short-sleeved vests had bamboo poles balanced on one of their shoulders from which heavy goods were suspended at either end. The babble of Cantonese conversation on the taxi's radio added to the effect. Then, as they approached the central shopping area of Tsim Tsa Tsui the surroundings took on a kaleidoscopic imagery of brightly coloured lights and neon signs, the words of which were written in jumbo sized Chinese characters. On either side of the busy road that passed between a seemingly endless array of shops, restaurants, hotels, cafeterias and bars both pavements was bustling with still more people. This place was going to be some contrast to Hamilton New Zealand he couldn't help thinking to himself.

They drove past a railway station over on one side and the splendid looking front facade of the Peninsular Hotel on the other. The terminal building to the Star Ferry then came into view before which the driver made a short loop and stopped outside the front entrance of the YMCA. Although Edwin had no intention of making it his permanent residence whilst in Hong Kong, he had reasoned that such a base would provide him with a useful stepping stone until such time as he could get his work situation sorted out and presumably be able to take some sort of an apartment. After confirming the booking, the Chinese man on reception duty handed Edwin the key to room number 208 and showed him to the lift.

The room was located on the second floor at the front of the building. It was small, rectangular and rather dingy looking with dark red carpeting and curtains. A single bed lay directly alongside the window and a wardrobe and washbasin were on the nearside wall. Basic in the extreme, he noted, and a far cry from the five-bedroom house that he had just vacated in New Zealand. But this was not the time to be making comparisons. It was merely a time of transition and the start of a new adventure. He'd made the decision to take on the challenge of somewhere new and he was determined to make a success of it. Besides, he had every intention of returning to New Zealand at some stage in the future. And if, for whatever reason, things did not work out in Hong Kong the onward part of his flight ticket was valid through to London and so he could even go there for a while before making his eventual return.

A shared shower room and toilets were located a little way along the corridor.

After making use of such facilities and putting on a change of clothing he set about familiarising himself with the layout of the place. He first took the lift up to the roof garden on top of the building. There in the warm evening air groups of people sat informally at tables and drank glasses of iced lemon tea. They were predominantly Europeans. Some were watching a television that was mounted on one of the walls. The programme was in English – and it was quite probably the same channel that Edwin was hoping to work for. But it was the view over the terrace wall looking out across Hong Kong's harbour that was far more breathtaking than anything that might have been showing on television. He stood by the ledge for several minutes whilst taking in the spectacle of Hong Kong Island that lay a short distance across the water from the Kowloon side and displayed a predominance of skyscraper buildings. Before that, dotted across the harbour were numerous illuminated vessels ranging from small junks and sampans to the constant arrivals and departures of passenger boats from the nearby terminal building of the Star Ferry. Further out across the harbour he could make out cruise ships as well as the silhouettes of several large battleships.

He then went down to the ground floor where on his way in he had seen a sign pointing to a cafeteria. He wondered if he might be able to grab a quick plate of chow mein or whatever. When he got there, however, he discovered the menu to contain a selection of very plain English fare. The choice was scrambled eggs on toast, baked beans on toast, a bacon sandwich, sausage and chips, fish fingers and chips or a cheese omelette. He sat at one of the small tables from where over his shoulder he could hear an aggressive-sounding English lady with a Manchurian accent scolding one of the Chinese waiters for apparently having got something wrong and not having served her exactly what she had requested. "Bloody Chink," he heard her mutter as an afterthought.

Edwin satisfied himself with a double bacon sandwich oozing with Heinz tomato ketchup and a mug of tea after which he decided to venture beyond the walls of the YMCA. Stepping out of the air-conditioned building felt like entering a sauna bath as the waft of hot moist air hit him. Perspiration that immediately began to seep through his shirt told him that this Hong Kong experience was going to take some getting used to. As he made his way through the crowds of people, he noted the convenient coincidence of the economically affordable YMCA being geographically located next door to the sophisticated and prestigious Peninsular Hotel. He walked a couple of blocks and arrived at one end of Nathan Road which he had read about as being Hong Kong's main shopping street. Edging along its crowded pavement, he took in the window displays of carved ivory, watches and electrical goods as well as the numerous tailors and jewellers. Between each shop and sandwiched in any available doorway street vendors sold colourful shirts, cassette tapes and cigarettes as well as a whole host of other bit and pieces. Everything was still open and in full swing. Double-decker buses packed full of Chinese people passed up and down the road as did taxis and private cars. People around him were jabbering away in Cantonese. It was all noise, heat and colour. A great place for a city break, he thought, but perhaps a little different to live here on a permanent basis.

On the way back he approached the entrance to the Peninsular Hotel where the glass door was opened for him by a young porter wearing a crisp white uniform who said, "Good evening Sir." The greeting alone sounded quaint enough after the years spent in New Zealand where such formal means of addressing people was something of a rare occurrence, let alone the custom of having someone to open a door for you. The hotel's air conditioning was welcome.

Edwin was immediately struck by the hotel's splendour of ornate pillars, guilt-edged archways, chandeliers, marble stairways, rather too comfortable armchairs and evergreen plants in large copper pots that stretched forth their branches. He sat down at a vacant table and when a waiter appeared ordered a beer. To his surprise it was a bottle of San Miguel, the same brew that he recalled from his days in Spain. He studied its green bottle and noted that the brand was also brewed in Hong Kong. He remained seated in such plush surroundings for some twenty minutes and took in the hotel's atmosphere. People were coming and going. Pageboys periodically walked back and forth ringing bells and holding up the written names of those they were seeking. Having familiarised himself with the lobby, Edwin thought that whilst he was at it he might as well make an inspection of the rest of the hotel. After all, it would be an excellent combination if he were to make full use of the facilities of the Peninsular Hotel whilst using his tiny room next door at the YMCA simply as a place to sleep.

He made a whirlwind tour of the hotel's restaurants and gift shops and even managed to glance into one of the bedrooms. On the first floor he encountered a small cocktail bar where a grand piano was being played whilst guests sipped their drinks. A Chinese hostess in a black evening dress standing at the entrance asked Edwin if he'd like to come in. He did so and perching himself on a vacant stool adjacent to the piano he ordered another San Miguel beer which this time came served with a small bowl of salted cashew nuts. He struck up a conversation with the pianist who turned out to be from the Philippines. Edwin even got him to break away from his normal repertoire to play John Lennon's 'Imagine.' The bar gradually became quite full and an army captain with the British Gurkhas, who was on leave, got talking with Edwin. A group of Canadian students then arrived and the place became quite lively as drinks were flowing. Having sunk several small bottles of the San Miguel beer Edwin later visited the men's washroom, just opposite the piano bar. An elderly Chinese attendant not only opened the doors for him but also ran hot water into the washbasin for him and handed him a small bar of soap and then patiently waited alongside him with a fresh towel with which to dry his hands. Clearly it required giving the old bloke some sort of a tip and Edwin placed a few Hong Kong cents onto the saucer. The reaction was one of immense gratitude. "Oh, thank you sir, thank you sir, thank you sir," he said with a strong oriental accent. Edwin found himself mimicking the words when he returned to the bar and at one stage he even said them out loud much to the amusement of the male guests who instantly recognised where they came from.

Despite the light from the flashing neon signs outside that penetrated through the curtains and a constant noise of traffic in the streets below his window, Edwin slept soundly during his first night at the YMCA. The long day, the time difference and the different culture had all been contributing factors. When he awoke he found a cockroach in his bed.

As he got ready for the day ahead he reminded himself that he had arrived in the colony of Hong Kong with no firm offer of a job lined up. All he had was the letter from the personnel department of Rediffusion Television saying that they could do with somebody with his experience and that he was welcome to make contact when in Hong Kong. There was a telephone booth in the passageway outside his room. Shortly after nine o'clock Edwin dialled the number and got put through to the department in question. He let it be known to the person on the other end of the line that he would be dropping by at the television station that same morning. Fortunately there was no opposition to such an impending visit mainly, he supposed, because he had referred to the letter but also because he didn't think the man could properly understand his New Zealand accent. But at least he'd managed to extract an "OK, we see you later this morning" answer out of him.

Despite the intense heat and humidity, Edwin wore a suit and tie for the occasion. He stepped outside and found a taxi that would take him out to the studios which were located in the appropriately sounding street name of Broadcast Drive in an out of town part of Hong Kong known as the New Territories. Edwin learned that a government run broadcasting organisation called TVB was also based out there. At least this particular cab was air-conditioned which allowed some degree of comfort throughout the journey even if when he had clambered into the back seat it had felt like stepping into a refrigerator.

Two security guards were on duty in the booth that operated the front gate entrance to Rediffusion Television's large studio complex. Edwin explained to them that he had spoken with the personnel office earlier that morning and that they were expecting him. He was directed across the courtyard to the front entrance and the reception area. When he got there, two very young-looking Chinese girls were sat at the front desk and Edwin waited as one of them used a ballpoint pen to dial an internal phone number to let the department know of his arrival.

Some minutes later a smartly dressed Chinese man arrived and introduced himself as Eric Wing and invited Edwin along to his office. They exchanged pleasantries and he then told Edwin that although the company had no specific job vacancies, they would possibly be able to slot him in on the English-speaking channel but that he would first have to speak with the Controller of Programmes. He asked Edwin to wait for a couple of minutes and left the room. It sounded promising. Mr Wing then returned and asked Edwin to follow him to another office to meet with a Mr Thomas Chin.

Within the space of twenty minutes or so it was agreed that Edwin would be employed as Assistant Executive Producer for the General Programme Section of the English-speaking channel. His immediate boss would be an Executive Producer to whom he would be introduced later. Edwin would handle the production of a weekly children's programme and assist with the nightly news whilst helping out with staff training. It sounded straightforward enough.

There was then the question of remuneration. Edwin realised that he couldn't push his luck too far on that because it had already explained to him that his job was being newly created. Mr Chin said that Edwin would have to be regarded as local hire but that because, as a Westerner, he would probably pay a higher price for things than his Chinese counterparts his monthly pay would take that into account. The starting salary was slightly less than what Edwin had been earning in New Zealand but with a promise to review it after the first six months. From Edwin's point of view at least he had secured an interesting job and it was agreed that he would start on Monday morning. He was then introduced to his new boss who turned out to be a tiny person called Charles Yi and his Chinese secretary who by contrast was a remarkably tall young lady called Patti

Chu.

Edwin took another cab back to his accommodation at the YMCA, very pleased with the way in which everything had gone. After a quick freshen up and a change into some lightweight trousers and a short-sleeved shirt he went out to take a daylight look at the shopping street of Nathan Road. The transition from sparsely populated New Zealand to overcrowded Hong Kong couldn't have been more pronounced and wherever he went he was aware of being completely outnumbered by oriental faces. At first, all such faces had looked the same but now, even in the short space of 24 hours, he was starting to pick out distinguishing features and realised that they were all in fact quite different. He wondered if that worked in reverse and that Chinese people similarly thought that all western people looked identical. A Chinese youth then approached him and asked, "Sir? You want meet nice young girl – my sister – she very nice." Edwin politely sent him on his way. Someone then lent out of the window of a car that was stationery at traffic lights and yelled out, "Well? Did you get the job?" It was the Captain of the Gurkhas from the night before. "Yes I did!" called back Edwin giving a thumbs-up sign.

"See you again this evening at the Peninsular Hotel," was the reply, as the car moved off.

Edwin walked down Nathan Road as far as its junction with a thoroughfare called Waterloo Road. He was intrigued to see that shopkeepers used an abacus to tot up figures rather than relying on their cash register. He took a bus back to near where he'd started and decided to cross the harbour to Hong Kong Island on the Star Ferry. Transportation was inexpensive in Hong Kong. The taxis fares were cheap enough and the bus ride had been only a few cents. A cross-harbour ferry departed every few minutes and although there were plans to build a causeway and also an underground railway it was the main public means of getting back and forth across the stretch of water. On deck a sign written both in Chinese characters and in English read 'No Spitting.' Edwin considered it a cheek for it to be written in English at all although maybe it had only ever been intended as a subtitle.

The ferry made its fifteen minute crossing to Hong Kong Island or Victoria Island to give it its more correct name. A gentle breeze carried an unpleasant sulphurous smell like that of a toilet on a bad day. It seemed to be completely at odds with the concept of 'Fragrant Harbour' from which the name Hong Kong was derived.

Every first-time visitor to Hong Kong Island takes the cable car up to the peak and Edwin was no exception. He found himself amongst tourists who were mainly American. At the top a circular path offered spectacular views over parts of Hong Kong sprawled out down below. It resembled a model kit of high rise buildings. Looking back across the harbour water, Kowloon was a similar concrete metropolis of skyscrapers. After the cable car's descent he stopped off at a baker shop and purchased something called a char-sui-bau, which was a hot steamed soft bread dumpling with some sort of pork marinade mixture in its centre. More substantial Chinese meals were enjoyed at some of Hong Kong's numerous restaurants over the weekend.

Monday morning soon came around and Edwin made the first of his daily taxi journeys to and from work at the television station. He soon settled in to the job and built up a good circle of friends amongst the production staff. His weekly children's programme called 'Five o'clock Club' made use of a selection of inserts that were compiled throughout the week. Scriptwriters and acting talent were readily available for the short sketches that made up the bulk of its content as were musical performers. The programme's final recording in which each segment was introduced by a studio-based presenter was completed by Edwin on Thursday mornings ready for transmission the following day. He also lent his hand to the station's nightly news in English programme.

Because of its convenience, central location and affordable price, Edwin remained resident at the YMCA for quite some time. He had simply adapted to it. The roof garden was a popular meeting place and he got to know most of the characters that frequented it. Amongst them was an eccentric elderly Englishman who suffered from delusions of grandeur and who would occasionally go to the public telephone that was affixed to the wall and within everybody's earshot make an imaginary phone call to a fictitious office and loudly pretend to dish out instructions left, right and centre before hanging up and returning back to his glass of sweet lemon tea. A Canadian man constantly kept an eye on the stock markets to such an extent that it was the only thing he could ever hold a conversation about. An Irishman called Paddy O'Grady was another regular on the roof garden who knew the ropes about everything in Hong Kong and who could provide a whole host of useful information such as where to buy the cheapest litre bottles of Tsing Tau Chinese beer. A short man from the Philippines was something of a social climber and took every opportunity to show people a collection of correspondence he'd had with prominent members of the British Royal Family. There was an entrepreneur businessman that nobody was really quite sure exactly what he was dealing in whilst a plump lady from the Philippines purported to be able to tell people's fortunes. Snobby people were present too whose mannerisms could have been taken straight out of a story by Somerset Maugham. Many spoke down to Chinese people as if they were third rate citizens and invariably referred to them as coolies.

Because the YMCA was a Christian institution, it was perhaps inevitable that some of the people staying there were Christian missionaries. Edwin who had never had any interest in religious matters got talking to one of them. He was from the United States and Edwin first encountered him through an open door where he was sitting in a room and turning the pages of his Bible. Edwin began by gently teasing him by telling him that if he thought he was trying to turn the world to righteousness he might stand a better chance of doing so if he were first to familiarise himself with the kind of world he was dealing with instead of distancing himself from it by sitting alone in a room with a book.

The man was amused by such comment and that evening agreed to go out on the town with Edwin. Together they visited all manner of grotty bars and seedy nightclubs the likes of which neither Edwin and nor the poor missionary had ever seen before. To round off the evening Edwin at least had the courtesy to take him to the sophistication of the piano bar of the Peninsular Hotel so as to get the comparison. The two of them became good friends and the missionary insisted on giving a Bible to Edwin who said he might get around to reading it one day.

The job at the television studios continued to go well. Edwin familiarised himself with the way in which the place worked. The station was unusual in that it distributed its radio and TV signals through wired relay networks although there was some talk that it might soon be granted a free-to-air license as a terrestrial broadcaster. Amongst the staff were three other Englishmen employed by the TV station all of whom were on the engineering side of things. Unlike Edwin, however, they had been specially brought in from the UK on a contract basis and had a package deal that included their accommodation and air fares being provided as well as a far more substantial salary.

Edwin searched through the classified columns of the local newspapers to check if there might be a better alternative to living at the YMCA. He came across a spacious room with its own en suite bathroom that was available within a luxury apartment that belonged to a retired American lady. It was located on Hong Kong Island in what was called the mid-levels which was an area halfway up the peak. The rent was just about affordable and Edwin thought it to be a reasonable idea and moved in.

McDonald Road was essentially a residential area of concrete apartment blocks and the gaps in between created an echo sound of anything that was taking place. Whenever Edwin went out for a stroll in the evenings he could hear the clack-clacking of mahjong tiles being slapped onto tables as Chinese families played their favourite game. Conversely, when he departed for work in the mornings he could hear a communal throat-clearing ceremony taking place complete with intermittent spitting. Some people stood outside their homes throwing punches into the air as they practiced shadow boxing exercises to start their day.

The humidity in Hong Kong was such that if a cigarette was left outside of its pack, its white paper would turn brown with the space of half an hour. Books suffered a similar fate of mould and mildew. Edwin purchased a radio cassette player from a man in an arcade having haggled it down to half the original asking price. Background music in his room enhanced things considerably. Although the accommodation itself was fine the combination of taxi, ferry and then another taxi to get him out to the TV studios was the kind of journey that worked well if he returned home after work with no intention of going out again until the following morning. It became slightly laborious if he wanted to meet up with friends in the evenings because most of them lived back on the Kowloon side of the harbour.

Fortunately something else cropped up in Kowloon. It was a small one-bedroom apartment in the swish area of Kadoorie Avenue which was far more convenient for work. It had a tiny bathroom with a half-length bath into which Edwin could just about submerge if he brought his knees up to meet his chest. There was also a small kitchen containing some rather unfamiliar Chinese cooking utensils and an array of woks. He had already reasoned that it was less complicated and perhaps even less expensive simply to eat out. The canteen at work was fine for lunch and offered good meals at subsidised prices and on top of that Hong Kong was full of eating houses of one sort or another many of which were open around the clock.

There were multi-storey restaurants where one could sit around all day and select small dishes of food known as dim sum from trolleys being wheeled around by young Chinese ladies. The dishes were all colour-coded according to their price and the final bill was calculated simply by counting the piles of empty plates at the end. Tea was limitless and to get a top-up one simply lifted the lid of the porcelain teapot. People spent hours in such establishments.

Being left-handed was slightly problematic when using chopsticks if seated around a circular table. However, many Chinese people had never met a left-handed person before and they seemed to marvel at it and regard it as 'ho chung-ming' – a sign of intelligence.

But Hong Kong cuisine was by no means limited to Chinese food. It had often been said that the finest Yorkshire pudding is not to be found in Britain but is instead cooked in Hong Kong. The best Paella is not in Valencia but is prepared by Chinese chefs in Hong Kong and the best Chateaubriand is not in France but that too is to be found in Hong Kong.

For a bit of variety Edwin and some of his friends would occasionally dine at a Russian restaurant on Nathan Road. Pickled gherkins, cold cuts of meat and potato salad made a change from the rice bowl experience. At other times they would find themselves in places where the waiters spoke no English and the menu was printed only in Chinese characters. There it was a matter of pot luck what they got served. Half the time they had no idea what it was that they were eating other that the fact that it tasted good. Edwin inquired about one particular dish of crunchy delicacies in a sauce and was told that they were deep fried baby sparrows. He wished he hadn't asked. The Merchant Seaman's club was another place of choice for excellent wholesome cuisine. He was probably supposed to have been a member to get in but no one ever queried his presence.

Edwin had kept up his friendship with the American Missionary back at the YMCA. Instead of frequenting still more seedy bars, they often went for drinks at the Merlin Hotel where a four piece Korean music group had two accomplished violinists who played classical musical directly into microphones which created an interesting echoing effect. They also encountered a young Englishman by the name of Matthew Sherborne who as part of his university doctorate in Oxford was studying finance in the Far East and would be staying in Hong Kong for several weeks before taking a ship for Singapore.

At work Edwin was learning a lot about Chinese mentality particularly with respect to 'loss of face.' Whereas in New Zealand it had been perfectly permissible and normally quite helpful to be straight talking rather than beating about the bush, that evidently did not go down too well in Chinese culture. Instead, there was a certain protocol that was supposed to be observed. Also people were position conscious and for some reason the TV Station liked making use of abbreviations. The Controller of Programmes was known as 'CP' and the Assistant Controller of Programmes 'ACP.' Edwin had been told by one senior member of staff that behind the company's organisational structure there was also an unseen hierarchy which was described as 'being controlled by the Chinese mafia.'

Members of the presentation staff were an interesting bunch. They were hard working and loyal although one of them deliberately liked to keep all knowhow to himself rather than letting the rest of his colleagues know about various procedures which caused a few ripples of jealousy and in some cases annoyance. Edwin also learnt that although most of the junior Chinese employees were paid a mere pittance for their work at the TV station, in the evenings many of them were perfectly capable of going out and making several hundred dollars on the Hong Kong Stock Exchange

But perhaps the biggest frustration was in trying to implement new proposals. There were a number of improvements that needed to be made to the presentation of the English speaking channel and Edwin was not slow in pointing them out and providing suggestions as to how changes could be made. It normally meant sending a memorandum to relevant department heads after which a meeting would be called to go through each point one by one. Everything would be talked through in great detail and those present would nod their heads in agreement after which it was often the case that they would then return to their respective offices and do absolutely nothing about any of it.

Edwin held auditions for new announcers. When the word first went out the station was inundated with applicants from the ex-pat community. There were several instances of candidates' parents showing up on the day and urging him to select their son or daughter for the role. Meanwhile the news programme on the English speaking Channel was essentially a straight bulletin read to camera and considerably less demanding that the news magazine programmes that Edwin had worked on in New Zealand. There were three newsreaders – one Englishman, one Australian and the other an American who, on a shift basis, were the faces that appeared on the screen as well as two female continuity announcers, one English the other from Australia.

Quite by chance Edwin became friends with one of the female newsreaders from the Chinese Channel. That happened one evening when they had both been waiting for a taxi outside the building. When one eventually showed up they agreed to share it to the downtown area of Kowloon. They got into conversation and out of politeness Edwin asked her if she fancied going for a drink. To his surprise she agreed and continued the remainder of the journey with him to the Peninsula Hotel. It was all perfectly innocent but news evidently travelled fast in Hong Kong judging by the following morning when there was all manner of rumour circulating around the studios about the previous evening's liaison. Undeterred they arranged to meet again on the weekend and it was suggested that she would bring one of her female friends with her if Edwin would bring one of his male friends along with him. He said that he would put the idea to his finance student friend.

Edwin and Matthew Sherborne stepped into a bar called the Red Lion a few blocks away from where they normally hung out. Edwin told him about the proposed weekend outing and Matthew said that he would be pleased to come along for such a blind date. Perched on bar stools in the smoke-filled room they ordered two pints of ice cold lager. A juke box was playing a selection of popular music.

I remember when rock was young,
Me and Suzie had so much fun
Holding hands and skimming stones
Had an old gold Chevy and a place of my own
But the biggest kick I ever got
Was doing a thing called the Crocodile Rock

As they were talking with each other they both became aware that they had been joined on either side by two heavily made-up Chinese girls. Edwin glanced at the one on his left. She smiled at him and said, "Hallo. Is this your first time at this bar?" He nodded to confirm that it was and then on turning back to Matthew he found him now to be engaged in conversation with the young lady on his right. "You give me one cigarette?" had been her request.

After introducing themselves as Suki and Madonna, it didn't take long for the barman to ask Matthew and Edwin if they would like to buy drinks for the girls. They looked at each other and Matthew said "Why not?" After all, it was an inexpensive bar and the opportunity for some light-hearted banter with a couple of local Chinese girls might prove entertaining.

Both girls asked for a Champagne Cocktail which came served in dainty wide-rimmed glasses each with the added enhancement of a cherry on a stick. It turned out that such drinks cost four times more than a pint of beer which seemed to be a bit over the top. All the more so when the liquid content of the drink was nothing more than fizzy lemonade.

They looked around the rest of the bar and saw that quite a few ex-pat men were seated at tables and in conversation with Chinese girls who no doubt were being treated to similar so-called Champagne Cocktails, upon which the business obviously depended.

Edwin and Matthew chatted with Suki and Madonna throughout the remainder of the evening. They also moved from the bar to a table and paid for three more rounds of overpriced lemonade. It became apparent that neither girl was happy with her lifestyle but that this kind of existence was the only employment that they'd ever known. They were locked into the system. They asked Edwin if he could fix them up a job at the TV studios. They asked Matthew if he could arrange for them to move to England.

BY COMPARISON, THE WEEKEND appointment with the Chinese TV newsreader and her friend took place in more sophisticated surroundings. They first went out for a meal together at a revolving restaurant on top of a high rise building and then on to an upmarket disco at a Kowloon nightclub. TV Newsreader Shu Fang was dressed elegantly in a peach coloured trouser suit whilst her friend Sophie, who came as the date for Matthew, was in equally smart attire. It turned out that she ran her own import export ceramics business,

Whether or not the ladies thought that being in the company of two Englishmen added something to their status both Edwin and Matthew noticed that they both of them started ordering the waiting staff around like nobody's business. Although they might have observed certain ex-pats talking down to the locals it wasn't the manner in which Edwin or Matthew conducted themselves and they thought it quite odd for them to suddenly to be assuming such airs of grandeur. The dancing continued.

Hi, hi, hi, beautiful Sunday,
This is my, my, my, beautiful day...
When you say, say, say, say that you love me
Oh, my, my, my, it's a beautiful day.

The following Tuesday the sky turned a hideously dark shade of grey accompanied by strong gusts of wind. Many of the staff at the TV station went home early because they'd heard that a typhoon was due to hit Hong Kong later on that day. Edwin remained there because he wanted to complete some editing for that week's programme. Being preoccupied with the task in hand he had become somewhat oblivious of what was taking place outside the building. But when it was time for him to head off home the security guards who had come into the reception area were adamant that it was far too dangerous for anyone to leave the premises. Peering through the dark glass window he then saw several sheets of corrugated iron flying around in the air like kites which seemed to support that view, as did the fact that the usual line of taxis by the gate was non-existent.

Typhoons in Hong Kong were something of a regular occurrence and consequently the TV studios were kitted out for such emergencies. Camp beds and linen were produced from cupboards and the cafeteria remained open 24 hours. It was even possible to procure large bottles of ice-cold Tsing-Tao lager. Somebody had clearly got their order of priorities right for dealing with such a situation.

It was one of the roles of the broadcaster to remain on air and provide regular reports on the state of the typhoon. Edwin positioned himself in the continuity control-room of the English-speaking channel and got on the phone to the Hong Kong Meteorological Office for the latest information from which updated announcements could be made. Typhoons were called after girls' names and in alphabetical order. Whereas the last one had been called Typhoon Marge this one was called Typhoon Nora. There were two presentation staff present in the control room and between the three of them they kept their viewers informed throughout that night and into the following day about the status of the typhoon after which the stormy weather began to die down.

Later that day, when it became safe to leave the premises Edwin headed back into town where the most noticeable evidence of damage was smashed neon signs.

The following Monday was a public holiday and Edwin had arranged to meet up with his Christian missionary friend from the YMCA and to take a ferry out to an island called Lantau. Despite the heat it was a pleasant enough journey. When they arrived they saw a pathway leading up a hill and decided to take it. They made their way higher and higher periodically looking back to admire the view of vessels in the blue waters of the South China Sea. The route passed unfamiliar flora and fauna as pastel blue butterflies fluttered by. It was a steep climb for some distance and after a while Edwin began to notice that he was finding it to be particularly hard work.

'I can't quite understand this. Maybe I'm not as fit as I thought I was,' he said.

'Well, neither am I,' replied his companion, 'but I think we're about halfway up by now.'

But Edwin's legs felt as if they were being pulled down to the ground, almost like a magnetic force, and they would only move with a great deal of effort on his part. And then, all of a sudden he began to experience a sensation of being light headed and as if he was somehow looking down on the world below him. He tried explaining the experience to the missionary friend who was unable to throw any light on what it was. "Perhaps God is testing you," he jibed, which didn't really help the situation at all.

Eventually it passed and Edwin simultaneously regained full strength in his legs once again. There was a Buddhist Temple on top of the hill that offered a reasonably priced vegetarian lunch which they decided to take advantage of. When seated they were politely acknowledged by a western couple sitting at an adjacent table. Edwin's Christian missionary friend, who was sitting closest, spoke with them briefly but then, after a short while, brought the conversation to a halt. When they departed he told Edwin that they apparently belonged to a religious sect that held some strange belief that a new messiah had returned to the world. None of it meant anything at all to Edwin although he had noted the abrupt manner in which the missionary had terminated his conversation with them – almost to the point of being impolite in cutting them off.

MATTHEW SHERBORNE HAD DONE his dash at studying Hong Kong finance and was scheduled to leave for Singapore. Before doing so, however, he wanted to throw a dinner party for Edwin and Shu Fang and her friend Sophie. It occurred to Matthew and Edwin that neither of them had ever cooked a single thing during their stay in Hong Kong. Restaurants were so plentiful and with prices to suit all budgets so much so that it had always been far more convenient to eat out. It was also less time-consuming and less complicated than trying to understand what half the ingredients were in Chinese grocery shops.

Nevertheless they began preparing for the social evening by visiting a street market in the district of Mon Kok in search of a large chicken. They found one but hadn't bargained for it being handed over to them fully feathered. However, after a bit of wrangling and sign language the stall holder eventually understood that it would be preferable for the bird to be plucked. He took it into a tent-like structure and within a short space of time re-emerged with the plump chicken in an oven-ready state.

The soiree was a success. The apartment where Matthew stayed was elegant and real champagne cocktails as opposed to lemonade substitutes were served on arrival. The three course meal had been prepared to perfection and was thoroughly enjoyed together with a lively conversation of witticisms throughout the evening. As they settled down to brandy and coffee they joked about the cultural differences of East and West.

'What's all this about oriental loss of face?' demanded Edwin. 'I mean, realistically, have you ever gone and lost your face?' he asked Shu Fang, the Chinese newsreader, who seemed not to grasp the question which made the whole thing even more amusing.

"Where is my face? Here is my face," she said.

"So now you have found your face?" he inquired.

"And if the Chinese like to refer to westerners as white devils, can you begin to imagine what we refer to the Chinese as?" added Matthew to continued laughter.

THE FOLLOWING WEEK THE Personnel Department sent out individual letters to members of the English speaking TV channel saying that due to plans for a changeover from being a cable television network to a free to air terrestrial broadcasting station the English speaking TV channel would be forced into going off air for some considerable time – perhaps even for as long as a year. Pay would be frozen at its present level and staff could decide whether to bide their time with the company or to move on.

It was not good news for Edwin. Apart from anything else it came at a time when his salary review was already overdue and he had been anticipating an increase. The cost of living in Hong Kong was steep at the best of times and the bulk of his monthly income was taken up in rent. The rest covered the basics of food, transport and socialising but that was about it. There was never anything left to save. Other staff on the English speaking channel found themselves in a similar situation or worse. Jobs that had seemed secure now hung in the balance. On his way out of the building he walked passed an open office door where a heated argument was taking place. The topic was about his Australian colleague who read the news. "But he is a bloody good newsreader," shouted one Chinese executive to another, "We can't just get rid of him like that."

"We'll do what we have to do. There probably won't even be an English news programme for a year," replied the other and then launched into a tirade of Cantonese.

Edwin got into the first available taxi and asked the driver to take him to Wah-da-loo doh which meant Waterloo Road. He stopped off at a local snack bar to take an iced lemon tea whilst contemplating the situation. But if that break was meant to solve anything it certainly didn't work. He sat there for a good half hour as the implications of the situation began to sink in. A worry factor began to occur.

He walked up a hill in the direction of his apartment. Was there no immediate future for him in Hong Kong? The job was being taken away from him. No surely not. The letter didn't actually say that, did it? No, it didn't. But clearly something was changing and it didn't look at all encouraging as far as he was concerned.

He took a quick shower and changed clothes and then went out again. He saw that a letter had arrived for him from his friend Henry back in New Zealand. He'd read it later. Edwin headed into the centre of town and the roof garden of the YMCA. It was funny how ex-pats would always gravitate back there. It was a convenient hub for meeting up with each other. Sure enough, on arrival Edwin found a circle of friends gathered there including Matthew and the little man from the Philippines as well as the missionary and the fortune teller lady. For one moment Edwin wondered he might be in need of her soothsaying services – or perhaps the missionary's prayer.

It was something of a relief to share the details with others. It got a mixed reaction. Opinions ranged from "Stick it out – better times will come" whilst others suggested that it might be a good time for him to head back to New Zealand. Neither option felt appropriate. In any case it would be far too soon to return to New Zealand. He would really need another year or so before being comfortable about doing that – but not a year in Hong Kong if the English speaking television channel was going to be off air.

"Come on, Edwin. Cheer up", said Matthew, "It's Friday evening – it's the weekend. And what's more I'm leaving for Singapore on Monday. Let's go next door to the Peninsular Hotel for a couple of beers."

"Well I'm hardly in a celebratory mood," protested Edwin, "but yes, OK, I'll come along with you.

"There, that's more like it. Now, have you mentioned any of this to Shu Fang?"

"No, I haven't had a chance yet. The whole thing with the English speaking channel occurred just this morning."

There were not many other people in the piano bar. The hostess greeted them with her usual charm and Rauol immediately began playing 'Imagine' once again as if it were Edwin's personal theme tune.

Bottles of San Miguel arrived as did the customary brass pots of cashew nuts. Although he tried to enjoy the evening Edwin's mind was preoccupied.

Back at his flat later that evening he took a can of beer from the fridge, lit a cigarette and again mulled over the events of the day and then noticed the unread letter from Henry which still lay on the table.

On opening it he learned that Henry, Janet and the baby were going to England for a year. Their flight would include a stopover in Hong Kong for two nights where they would be staying at the Caernarfon Hotel. They hoped that Edwin would have time to meet up with them and perhaps show them some of the sights. They would be arriving in Hong Kong at 11:00 am on Tuesday 6 November and departing on the 19:30 pm flight for London two days later.

"That's less than three weeks away," muttered Edwin to himself, "Why does everything have to happen at once?"

The following morning, whilst checking out the precise whereabouts of the Caernarfon Hotel, he turned down a side street off Nathan Road. Colourful patterned shirts were on display at the stall of a street vendor and Edwin stopped to browse through them. As he did so he spotted a grubby looking Chinese tramp standing in an entranceway on the other side of the narrow road. The man beckoned him with one finger but Edwin simply looked away. It then felt as if an uncomfortable surge of something jumped on him. He looked across to the man who had now turned his back and was departing but the uncomfortable presence remained with Edwin. He'd no idea what it was. It felt almost like a clamping sensation around his head. Over the years he'd heard people mention the existence of spirits that were either good or bad that some people supposedly carried around with them. He wondered if he'd just encountered an entire legion of particularly bad ones that had been carried around by that particular man. Whatever it was, it didn't feel good and Edwin had no idea of how to get rid of it.

WHILST MATTHEW SHERBORNE WAS boarding a ship bound for Singapore on Monday morning, Edwin was getting into a taxi bound for the studios. He was still undecided about whether to remain with the TV station during its off-air period or if his days in Hong Kong were now well and truly numbered and he should simply move on. After all, he could quite easily pack his bag and push off within a very short space of time if need be. He wasn't tied down to the place. His still had a flight ticket valid through to the United Kingdom if he wanted to go there for a while and now even his friend Henry was heading in that direction – not that that should have any great bearing on things but it was an interesting coincidence. The thought occurred to him that if it really was time for him to get out of the Hong Kong experience, he should perhaps see if he could book himself onto the same onward flight that Henry and Janet were taking. That would be a bit of fun. He needn't even tell them what he was up to until the very last minute. He could make out that he was seeing them off and then collect his suitcase and make the surprise announcement that he was joining them on the same flight. The idea had a certain novelty value about it.

But what of the future, he wondered. He'd already taken a huge gamble in leaving the New Zealand Broadcasting Corporation to come to Hong Kong. He'd been fortunate in landing a job when he got there. He was already well-respected by the company for various achievements since his arrival. On the other hand, Edwin knew that his long-term future didn't lie in the colony of Hong Kong no matter how exciting its twenty-four hour pace might be. Perhaps he should go to England and see if he could do a stint at the BBC before returning to New Zealand. But the idea of England wasn't particularly appealing. He recalled how he'd longed to get out of the place and how he'd succeeded in doing so. He wasn't against the idea of visiting Britain but he had no intention of staying there for any length of time.

It had been chucking it down with warm rain during the entire morning but now the sky had cleared and the sun was shining. Edwin walked down to the nearest shopping area to go for a coffee. The deluge had left a huge puddle along one side of the road and when it was too late to get away from it a truck passed through it at speed and drenched Edwin from head to foot. It was not his day.

He found himself thinking more and more in terms of leaving Hong Kong and just putting it all down to experience. There was nothing much here to cling on to and he might just as well use the rest of his plane ticket to take that flight for London before that ran out too. Eventually he made up his mind that he would go to England for a while to see what was what over there and then make his return to New Zealand.

Once he had made his decision he began to say goodbye to colleagues at Rediffusion Television. A friend in the music department with whom he had developed a good rapport was clearly saddened that he was leaving – as was his newsreader friend Shu Fang. Some of the other members of staff went out of their way to try and encourage him to stay on.

Edwin packed his suitcase. He bought an abacus and managed to cram an entire set of porcelain bowls and cups and saucers into his shoulder bag.

AT HONG KONG'S KAI Tak Airport Edwin spotted the figures of Henry and Janet wheeling a buggy containing their daughter Beatrice. There was a problem. Their baggage had gone astray and they were left only with warm clothing in the heat and humidity of Hong Kong.

Be that as it may they managed to pack a lot into their two-day stop-over. Edwin was able to whisk them around all of the sights and points of interest. They took a sampan tour around parts of the harbour, went to the revolving restaurant, ate plenty of excellent Chinese food, took the cable car to the peak on Hong Kong Island, met Shu Fang and visited various bars including the cocktail bar of the Peninsular Hotel. But throughout it all Edwin didn't feel well. He felt tense and sometimes trembled and broke out in perspiration. He equated it with the scruffy tramp of the previous week. It was ever since that encounter that something just did not feel right.

Right up until the last moment Edwin succeeded in concealing the fact that he would be boarding the same flight as Henry and Janet and the baby for the onward part of their journey to the United Kingdom. On the final afternoon he said, "I just need to pop back to my flat for a brief moment. Then I'll come to your hotel and we can all take the same taxi out to the airport."

Janet clicked. "You're not intending to come to England with us by any chance are you?"

The Chinese newsreader, Shu Fang, came out to the airport in time to see everybody off.

CHAPTER SEVENTEEN

EDWIN FELT TERRIBLE. He was trembling and every now and again his mind seemed to race around all over the place. During the plane's early morning stop in Rome his teeth had started chattering in the cold November air and hadn't stopped ever since. He felt ill. The culture shock of suddenly being back in London's Heathrow Airport didn't help the situation. Henry, Janet and their baby had been met in the arrivals hall by Henry's mother. They had since departed and abandoned Edwin who remained leaning against a rail whilst idly observing the constant flow of passengers manoeuvring suitcase laden trolleys up a ramp.

"What the hell am I doing here?" he muttered to himself.

Nothing was making any sense. It felt like a weird dream. He lit a cigarette. An airport bus could take him to Victoria but he only had Hong Kong dollars. He made his way to a Bureau de Change kiosk and obtained some pounds at a lousy exchange rate.

His parents now lived in Wrotham in Kent and Edwin had told Henry that he would most probably go and stay there for a while to begin with. Entering a phone booth Edwin obtained the phone number from Directory Enquiries.

"Hallo Mum, this is Edwin. I don't really know how to explain this but I've just flown into London from Hong Kong and I am at Heathrow Airport."

"That's wonderful," replied his mother, "Are you going to be in England for long?"

"It could be for a few weeks or even a few months and then I intend heading back out to New Zealand," replied Edwin.

"That sounds good. And presumably you'd like to come and stay with us here in Wrotham?"

"Root-um? Ah, so that's how you pronounce it. Yes, I'm on my way," replied Edwin, "I think you mentioned in a letter that it's somewhere near Sevenoaks,"

"That's right. You can get a train to a place called Borough Green and then there's a somewhat irregular bus service from there."

Edwin took the Airport bus in to Central London and arrived opposite Victoria Coach Station. Everything along the route had looked particularly dismal and old-fashioned. It was cold, slightly foggy and the sky was grey. Red double-decker buses and shiny black taxis reminded him that this was London. Pedestrians were wrapped in coats and scarves. The all had pale complexions. Cars stopped and started at traffic lights and large groups of pedestrians made use of zebra crossings. Shiny brown tiles on the front facade of a row of buildings from a previous century added to the rather drab picture. A news vendor wearing a knitted woollen hat and fingerless gloves stood alongside a stack of newspapers calling out a repetitive chant of "Evenin' Standard!"

Whilst walking up one side of Buckingham Palace Road in the direction of Victoria Railway Station Edwin was surprised see a Greenline bus stop that prominently displayed the name of Wrotham as being the final destination for one of its routes. Could this really be the same Wrotham in Kent that he was aiming to get to? He looked at the timetable set within a glass-fronted panel and saw that the bus route went out via a whole bunch of familiar sounding places which collectively read like a print-out of a bad dream from his youth. It would pass through the suburbs of Lewisham, Eltham, Sidcup and Swanley. Certainly that was a south-easterly direction and as Swanley was already in the county of Kent presumably Wrotham was a few miles further. He reasoned that at least the journey would get him from A to B in one go and seeing that the next bus was almost due he decided to take it in preference to the train journey.

The single-decker green bus of route 719 soon arrived. Edwin boarded and paid his fare to the driver before placing his suitcase in a rack on the side. There were only two other passengers. He gazed out of the window and mulled over the recent chain of events. The first thing he needed to do was to get back to full health and then perhaps look for some temporary work to tide him over. He still felt unwell and was glad that he'd hung onto one warm jacket from New Zealand which hadn't been worn at all during the time spent in Hong Kong. He also felt utterly exhausted due in part to the time change but also the fact that he hadn't managed to sleep a wink during the flight. He tuned in to a conversation between a man with a cockney accent sitting in the front of the bus and the driver. Everything felt out of context.

"Gives me fourteen quid fifty a week clear," he was saying, "and I clocks on at seven and I'm out of it by four. I don't do no weekends. Nah, not me. Best bloody job I've ever 'ad."

The driver added his words. "Yeah well that's OK for you but see for me, I likes to 'ave me overtime. Time and an 'alf at weekends and that suits me down to the ground."

The bus stopped adjacent to a block of council flats somewhere near Elephant and Castle. A young man with a ghostly pale complexion, pimples and greased back hair stood on the pavement outside who as far as Edwin was concerned seemed to epitomise the archetypical south London lad. He was kitted out in scuff-marked, round-fronted, shoes that were completely down at heel, tight fitting blue jeans and a slightly oversized dirty-looking donkey jacket over a thick grey jersey. He was talking to a fat lady who had bright red cheeks and was wearing a green plastic mackintosh and clutching a white paper parcel of fish and chips. The lights changed and the bus pulled away in the direction of New Cross. The entire journey to Wrotham took about an hour and a half before the bus came to a halt in the centre of the small village where the driver switched the engine off and opened its doors.

Edwin spent three weeks in Wrotham. On arrival he crashed out in the spare bedroom for several hours on account of jet lag exhaustion and not feeling well. He re-surfaced in the evening and came downstairs to chat with his parents over dinner. The following morning he visited a doctor for the first time in a decade to try and get shot of the strange illness that he seemed to have picked up in the Far East. Having described the symptoms he was prescribed with two bottles of pills and advised to take things easy for a few days. Taking it easy wasn't that difficult because after the hustle and bustle of Hong Kong the Kent village wasn't exactly the most vibrant place on earth and there were pleasant country walks nearby in which to unwind. There was also a choice of four pubs – the Bull Hotel, The George and Dragon, The Rose and Crown and The Three Postboys. In the evenings Edwin generally made a circuit of the whole lot and got to know many of the regulars.

During his second week in Kent Henry phoned him. On hearing that Edwin was feeling suitably refreshed he said that he, Janet and the baby were staying in a one-bedroom flat in London and that if Edwin fancied camping on their living room floor he would be welcome to do so. It sounded like a plan and Edwin jotted down the Russell Square address and said that he would arrive there on the following Monday morning.

Although Edwin knew his way around the backstreets of Madrid, Hong Kong and every city of New Zealand, his geographical knowledge of London was limited. On arrival at Charing Cross Railway Station he took an Underground train to Leicester Square and changed to the Piccadilly Line for Russell Square. From there he was able to find the block of flats on Endsleigh Street where Henry and his young family were now based.

"My mother managed to get this place out for us," explained Henry, as he ushered Edwin inside, "It's not bad for starters. Good central location, convenient for everything and now all I've got to do is to get some sort of a job so that we can survive this working holiday."

"It's very nice," observed Edwin as he cast a glance around the neatly furnished lounge with a doorway leading through to a small kitchen. They then walked back past the entry hall to inspect the bedroom and bathroom.

"Not bad, is it?" said Janet, appearing in a doorway with the baby in her arms.

"Looks good to me," said Edwin, "and if I'm to spend a bit of time sleeping on the lounge floor I'd better chip in some money towards the rent."

"You don't need to worry about that," replied Henry, "Until I get some work the social security are giving us money to cover the rent. That's already been sorted out at their local office a few days ago."

"How on earth does that work?" asked Edwin.

"Well, basically it's a stop gap. We are a small family just arrived in the country living in rented accommodation and looking around for work. They take care of the rent and give us a small amount to live on until we can get ourselves sorted out," he explained.

Edwin had heard stories about the welfare state but the finer details were something new to him.

Over the next few days they went out and about in London behaving as if they were a group of visiting tourists which, in one sense, they were. Oxford Street and Regent Street were bustling with Christmas shoppers despite the fact that the country was apparently going through some kind of economic decline. People were working a three-day week instead of from Monday to Friday and businesses were substituting their electric lighting with candle light for certain periods of the late afternoon. Although Henry was a fully trained chef it wasn't easy to walk into a suitable job just like that and so he was thinking in terms of doing any kind of temporary work until something suitable in his profession turned up. Edwin thought that that might be a wise course of action for him to take too.

Despite his English origins Edwin had come to regard himself more as a New Zealander in recent years and so maybe he should start seeing the visit as a working holiday too. He also knew that he couldn't just walk into the BBC and expect to get a job handed to him on a plate. In Britain the procedure didn't work like that. One had to apply for BBC vacancies that were periodically advertised in the press. He was also aware that his chances of getting a job at one of independent television companies were rock bottom because of their insistence on applicants belonging to their broadcasting union. Edwin wasn't a union member and because it was a closed shop he was unable to join. Irrespective of whatever capabilities you might have had, you couldn't join the union unless you worked for ITV – and you couldn't work for ITV unless you already belonged to the union.

A sports shop in Piccadilly Circus displayed a card in its window saying that they were looking for temporary staff to work in the store in the run-up to Christmas. Edwin reasoned that it could be something to do for the time being until a more appropriate opportunity arose. He entered the shop through its glass doors and a salesperson took him up a flight of stairs to speak with the manageress in her small office. Despite indicating a willingness to learn, it soon became apparent that, in her eyes, the fact that he had no previous retail experience clearly counted heavily against him. She asked him why he wanted the job and he explained that he had just arrived back in the country from Hong Kong a couple of weeks ago and that he needed to find some kind of work. The lady then went on the offensive and asked him if he could provide references from previous employers in the UK. He replied that the last time that he had worked in Britain had been at an architect's office in Surrey but that that had been way back in 1967. That didn't seem to go down at all well. She brought the interview to an abrupt halt and said that, on that basis, there was no way that the company could consider him for the temporary job.

"If it is a matter of policy only to take on people that have a recent track record of working in England I don't see how anyone who arrives back in the country from living overseas stands much of a chance," commented Edwin, "I can't quite follow the reasoning."

The lady smiled. "Even some of the nicest people might turn out to be crooks" she said.

Edwin could scarcely believe his ears.

"That's ridiculous," he said.

She shrugged her shoulders.

Edwin walked out of her office back down the stairs and out of the shop.

What a nerve, he thought, Welcome to England.

Later that afternoon whilst strolling along Tottenham Court Road a young lady with a clipboard jumped out in front of him and asked him if he would like to take part in a free personality test. In the absence of anything else on his immediate agenda Edwin thought that it might provide a bit of amusement and agreed to do so. He was ushered through the front entrance of a nearby building and into a small hall where other members of the public were seated at desks filling out their answers to various questions on a sheet of paper.

The questions were all slightly obscure and seemed to relate to one's emotional feelings about this that and the other. Edwin scribbled his responses out and a young man collected the paper from him and then after a short wait asked him to come through to another room to obtain his result. There behind a desk a smartly dressed lady said that she had looked through his various answers and had found a certain pattern which told her that he must be an interesting person.

Edwin was bemused that in meeting two people for the first time within the space of one hour he had already made the transition from being perceived as a possible crook by one of them to being an interesting person by the other – unless of course he was now being thought of as an interesting crook.

He was asked if he'd like to do another short test that would reveal his hidden potential but that it would cost him three pounds. Well, why not? He thought. Pretty odd though, it was meant to be a free personality test but they then charge you to get the result. But three pounds wasn't going to break the bank. The lady asked him if he would take hold of two tin cans to which wires were attached, one in each hand.

"Now hang on a minute. I didn't volunteer to come in here to get electrocuted," he said.

"Don't worry. It's nothing like that. It's just a simple meter that we use for measuring reactions."

Once the cans were gripped by Edwin's hands the lady plunged into a similar set of questions to those that he had answered in the written exercise. It was more of an interrogation than a conversation and he couldn't see its purpose. Had he ever had anything to do with the occult? No, he hadn't. Was he ambitious? Wasn't everybody to a certain extent? How well did he relate to his mother? -Very well. What about his father? – Equally well. And so it dragged on for several minutes after which he was told that he was doing fine although she had detected there was a certain blockage that seemed to be holding him back from realising his full potential.

"Blockage?" he queried. "I can't say I'm aware of any."

"But would you say that you are completely fulfilled in terms of your lifestyle and your career?" she asked.

"Well, as I wrote on the form I've only just recently arrived in England and I haven't even got a job lined up yet so I'm certainly not fulfilled in that respect," he replied.

"Ah, well that's where we might be able to help you?" she said.

"Are you an employment agency as well?" he asked.

"Not exactly," she said, "although I would suggest that whilst you are here you might like to use the opportunity to meet with one of our advisors who will certainly be able to point you in the right direction with regards to your future career."

"I can't really understand that because you don't know anything at all about me and you don't even know which area I work in," he replied.

"Actually, I can already tell quite a lot about you and I honestly think that you are just the kind of person that we can really help," he asked.

"What makes you think I need any kind of help?" he asked.

"It's up to you now," she said. "You are welcome to see your personality test through by moving forward to the final stage and having a chat with an advisor for a small donation of five pounds," she smiled.

The additional fees being applied were annoying and Edwin was fast becoming convinced that this strange encounter was nothing short of a scam. Although tempted to leave he wondered if paying the further five pounds might be worth it simply to gain the satisfaction of calling their bluff.

"OK," he said, "Let's see what kind of advice your advisor is able to come up with."

He was led downstairs to a dimly lit room where two men in suits were seated behind a low coffee table. They introduced themselves briefly and thanked Edwin for having come along and invited him to take a seat. One of them then said that the organisation of something called Scientology had helped many people achieve career advancement and that it would certainly be able to do the same for Edwin.

"How is that possible?" asked Edwin.

"Where there's a will there's a way," replied the man. "We are able to help people become central in their sphere of operation and to lead the way to the very top of the ladder in their work."

It sounded far too fanciful and Edwin asked them what dealings they had with the media world. Both men then glanced at each other and appeared uncertain as to what to say.

"What we can do is to help people realise their full potential," said the other man.

"Yes, I seem to have been hearing that for the past hour," said Edwin, and then, as an afterthought, he asked "And how much would it cost?"

"It would cost you no more than the price of a small car," replied the first man.

"Well, I think I've heard enough," retorted Edwin, "I've never come across such a lot of rot in my entire life. What would you two know about professional careers? Precious little I think."

The two men again looked at each other and failed to answer.

Edwin let himself out of the room and passed back through the hall in which other people were seated doing their so-called personality tests. He was glad to get out of the place.

It was already dark as he made his way on foot back to Henry and Janet's flat. As part of improving his geographical knowledge of the surrounding area Edwin had been experimenting with different routes. He now discovered that that they lived even closer to Euston than Russell Square but that they hadn't realised it because they hadn't yet ventured up that end of their street.

THE FOLLOWING MORNING HENRY was due to pay a visit to the local social security office at ten o'clock. It wasn't far away and Edwin accompanied him there for the walk. A clerk sat behind a counter in a booth within the small office. Henry showed the man a printed card and was invited to sign his name in a space on a slip of paper attached by a clip to a small piece of hardboard. Apparently a giro cheque would be sent by post to Henry and it could be cashed at a post office to cover his rent and living expenses for the next fortnight. The clerk looked up at Edwin and asked if he was waiting to sign too.

"No, I'm just here with my friend," replied Edwin, "Although like him I am looking for a job."

"Well, if you are unemployed you can sign on as well." said the clerk.

"No thank you. I'd rather not" replied Edwin, unable to see the point of being tied down with having to report in to this place at regular intervals when all he really wanted was a job to go to.

When they got back to the flat a late breakfast of bacon and eggs was prepared by Janet. A letter had arrived for Henry inviting him to phone to arrange an interview for a temporary job in a post office sorting depot in Mornington Crescent. He popped downstairs to a call-box and then returned to say that he'd been asked to go there at 3pm that afternoon.

In the meantime Edwin had bought a copy of The Listener primarily for its page that contained a list of current job vacancies at the BBC that was headed 'Appointments.' Although several positions were advertised none of them was applicable to him. The publication came out once a week and he didn't relish the thought of hanging around for months on end waiting for a suitable position to be advertised, if indeed one ever should be.

Henry got the job at the sorting office. He was asked to start the following Monday and told that it would involve a considerable amount of shift work and unsociable hours. The pay was not brilliant but was nevertheless just enough to get by on. He could now bide his time in looking for a job as a chef and be able to switch at short notice

That evening after dinner Henry and Edwin left Janet at home with the baby whilst they slipped out for couple of pints at a pub near Euston. It was a typical London pub built of Victorian lavatory brick on the outside and adorned with thick velvet curtains and dark stained varnished furniture on the inside. It seemed to be something of a haunt for actors from the neighbouring Shaw Theatre and the best bitter was excellent. It had a jukebox.

Knock knock knockin' on Heaven's door
Knock knock knockin' on Heaven's door
Knock knock knockin' on Heaven's door
Knock knock knockin' on Heaven's door

When it was closing time a rather crusty-looking landlord circled the entire lounge bar area and let out a repetitive rasp of "Time please, time please, time please." He then drew a metal gate of the variety normally associated with an old fashioned lift shaft halfway across the door in preparation for padlocking it up for the night. He was obviously eager for everybody to push off home.

A few days later Edwin walked down Haymarket and passing New Zealand House he began to wonder if it might not be a better idea all round for him to make arrangements simply to get back out there as soon as possible rather than prolong things any further. After all there were people in the NZBC who were his friends and it would be far easier to return to work there rather than attempting to break into the world of broadcasting in Britain. On the other hand, if he could squeeze another year's television experience in before returning to New Zealand there that would also be to the good.

Entering Trafalgar Square he noticed the front entrance to the Gibraltar Information Centre. Out of curiosity he stepped inside and asked a few questions about the place to two young ladies seated at a long white desk both of whom were bi-lingual English and Spanish. They had a rather quaint accent and gave him a brochure that contained photos of the huge rock that rose from the surrounding sea against a deep blue sky. There were pictures of a shopping street, a sunny beach, some monkeys posing on a wall and a red British telephone box next to some palm trees. They told him that it was a very small place and that people from the United Kingdom were entitled to live and work there with no restrictions. It even had a small local television service. The frontier with neighbouring Spain was closed but they there were two flights a week from Gatwick Airport as well as a ferry service that sailed across the straits from Tangiers. Edwin politely said something to the effect of perhaps popping out there for a visit at some stage of the game.

He had also started to think in terms of finding alternative accommodation. Although grateful for the kind hospitality of Henry and Janet in allowing him to sleep on their lounge floor in an assortment of blankets and pillows it was a temporary arrangement that couldn't go on indefinitely. However, what should come first, a job or some accommodation?

At the end of the week Edwin phoned in response to an advertisement for a room in a flat. It was suggested that he might like to take a look at it on Saturday morning and so he now sat on a Hammersmith bound Metropolitan Line train heading for a station called Goldhawk Crescent. The underground train suddenly became more of an overground train when it emerged from its tunnel as it reached Paddington and came to a halt at a platform in the mainline railway station alongside trains heading out to various destinations in the West of England.

The journey continued out amongst the railway network's array of lines, points and signal boxes and the ancient looking stations of Royal Oak and Westbourne Park after which it separated onto a branch line of its own but nevertheless remained above ground level and perched on a viaduct. A couple of stops later and Edwin was treated to an excellent view of the BBC Television Centre through the carriage's right hand windows as the train gently passed it by. It was the first time he had ever set eyes on the place.

On arrival at the terraced house Edwin was greeted by two blonde girls both of whom had broad Australian accents. They showed him to a tiny room which was clean and furnished with a single bed, a small wardrobe and a bedside cabinet. Apparently there was one more Australian girl living in the house and all of them were over in the UK on working holidays.

"We've had several enquiries and there are three more people coming to view the room," explained one of the girls, "and so, if you want it, please phone us again this evening and we'll let you know how things stand."

"It's certainly interesting," replied Edwin, perhaps thinking more about the prospect of living with such potential flatmates than any practicalities of the room in question. He thanked them and promised to phone.

Returning to Euston he pondered about what to do for the best. In some respects the possibility of such accommodation only added confusion to his predicament. Also, did he really want to share a place with three females? That could be problematic. And apart from anything else surely his immediate task was to secure some kind of work.

That afternoon he accompanied Henry's family to the London Zoo whilst trying to think things through. The conclusion he reached was that there didn't seem to be much point in tying himself down to one particular place unless there was work to go with it. Whether or not he would be able to find immediate work was debatable. Maybe, in such circumstances, the accommodation wasn't for him and out of politeness he should phone the Australians that evening to let them know. In any case perhaps in the meantime they had offered it to someone else, perhaps even to another female. Who knows?

But when he phoned an enthusiastic voice on the line said, "Thanks for phoning back Edwin. We've been waiting for your call. You were the pick of the bunch and the room is yours if you want it."

It was exactly what he didn't want to hear.

"It's very kind of you," he said, but I'm afraid there's been a change of plan and, with regret, I'm going to have to turn it down."

"Oh, I'm really sorry to hear that," was the disappointed reply. "Well, good luck anyway."

They hung up. Part of Edwin felt relief and part of him felt that he'd just missed out on the offer of a lifetime.

Edwin's grandmother still lived in Winchester and that evening it occurred to him that, instead of sticking around in London and applying for professional jobs, he could just as easily do so from down there. He knew that she would be glad of his company. The more he considered the idea the more it began to appeal to him.

The following day after thanking Henry and Janet for his stay he headed off for Hampshire. During the course of the following week there were two advertisements for jobs to which he could apply. There was a vacancy for a temporary sales assistant in the Winchester branch of Currys electrical store which would be OK as a stop gap and there was also an advertisement for a position in the TV Presentation Department at the BBC. A brief interview led Edwin to succeed in securing the job at Currys to start on the following day and at the same time he received an application form for the job with the BBC.

The work in the shop was routine and poorly paid but after his third week of selling radios, vacuum cleaners and washing machines Edwin received a letter inviting him for an interview at the BBC Television Centre in London. Things were looking brighter.

However there then came the most devastating piece of news. Edwin learnt that the New Zealand Government had introduced a work permit requirement for British citizens. Further enquiries revealed that such permits could be granted only to people of certain professions and television broadcasting wasn't one of them. All of a sudden Edwin had no legal right ever to work there again. It was a bitter blow that completely threw his intention to return there.

Throughout his time with the New Zealand Broadcasting Corporation Edwin had always been able to live and work there on the strength of being a citizen of the United Kingdom but that now carried no weight. He kicked himself that he hadn't obtained a New Zealand passport when he had been eligible to have done so. At the time he could quite legitimately have held two passports – his United Kingdom passport and a New Zealand passport. This latest development meant that his beloved New Zealand was now closed to him.

As if to emphasise the point still further a letter then arrived from his News Editor friend, Pete Cornwall, in New Zealand who apart from providing a newsy update about things that were going on over there also drew attention to the recent change in the country's immigration policy.

THE BBC JOB IN television presentation was not really the kind of work that Edwin was seeking despite having previous experience in that field. He had already tasted programme-making which was altogether far more creative and interesting than a repetitive play out of day-to-day transmission. Perhaps the sentiment was picked up in his interview by the four-man panel. Edwin had also heard an oft-told rumour that people stood a better chance of getting a job at the BBC if they were either 'queer' or Catholic. He was neither. On the train journey from Waterloo back to Winchester he mentally re-enacted the formal interview that had taken place and felt he was in with a slim chance.

Time passed by. Christmas celebrations took place, the New Year was seen in and there was still no word from the BBC. Edwin wasn't sure if the delay was a good thing or a bad thing. If they didn't wish to take him on they could have told him shortly after the interview instead of spinning things out for weeks on end. Wondering if a letter might have gone astray he wrote to enquire about the status of his application but as there was still no immediate response and he assumed that the possibility of being offered the job was still a remote possibility.

Although he knew that the various ITV companies dotted around the United Kingdom were heavily unionised he occasionally saw interesting positions being advertised in the employment columns of the Daily Telegraph. He filled in application forms for Southern Television in Southampton, Westward Television in Plymouth, Harlech Television in Bristol and Yorkshire Television in Leeds but in each case they always contained a question that asked about union membership.

Meanwhile Henry and Janet moved out of London. Henry had found himself a job as a chef at a hotel in Kent. His family had recently moved into a spacious flat in Sevenoaks and they had written to Edwin saying that he would be welcome to visit them there whenever he had the time. They had already planned their return to New Zealand for the following year. Even though Henry held a UK passport he wouldn't encounter any immigration difficulties or work permit requirement because his wife Janet was a New Zealander, as was his baby daughter. It crossed Edwin's mind that perhaps the only way that he might ever get back to working in New Zealand again would be first to get hitched to a Kiwi.

The long awaited letter from the BBC's appointments department arrived. It was no great surprise to Edwin to read that they had decided not to offer him that particular job. He was philosophical about it. The only sense of frustration was the fact that it had been such a long drawn-out process to arrive at such a conclusion. He wondered whether the ten weeks waiting time was standard.

The outcome prompted him to hand in his notice at the shop and take the train to Sevenoaks. Once there he had it in mind to look for another temporary job but of a different nature to retail work. He wondered if working in a pub might prove to be an interesting experience. After all, such work was exactly the kind of thing many New Zealanders and Australians did on their working holidays in England.

An enjoyable evening with Henry and Janet included a slap-up meal at a local restaurant. The following morning Edwin scrutinised a copy of the Kentish Times. He came across an advertisement for a live-in trainee bar/cellarman in the village of Goudhurst. The name Goudhurst had a certain ring about it because of its youth hostel where both he and Henry had stayed back in the bicycling days of their early teens. It seemed completely bizarre that after all these years he now should be seriously contemplating going there to try and get some temporary work in a pub. In fact the more he thought about his situation the more he got the impression of being in the wrong place at the wrong time and that all he was really accomplishing was nothing more than re-visiting long-forgotten haunts for no purpose. Was there such a thing as destiny? He questioned. And besides that, what on earth was he doing back in England? He switched on the radio.

Alright, that's right, that's right, that's right
That's right I really love your tiger light
That's neat, that's neat, that's neat, that's neat
I really love your tiger feet, I really love your tiger feet
Your tiger feet

On a route through orchards and oast houses a country bus made the journey from Tunbridge Wells Railway Station to Goudhurst where Edwin alighted at the bus stop opposite the village pond.

The Star and Eagle Hotel dated back to the fourteenth century and was reputed once to have been an ancient monastery. It had also served as the headquarters for a local gang that had robbed and terrorised the surrounding area and organised smuggling raids during the eighteenth century. Edwin looked up at its front facade of attractive timbered gables and then entering through the front door found his way into a cosy looking bar area with a hint of cigar smoke from the previous evening. It was still early and there were no customers. However a cleaning lady said that she would let the boss know that Edwin had arrived.

The man wearing a blue blazer and tie soon entered and after a chat that lasted about ten minutes Edwin was offered the job. He would move in and commence work in two days' time. On the way back to Sevenoaks he wondered if he was doing the right thing. He'd been told that he'd be working split shifts so as to cover both the morning and the evening trade and that he would have a day and a half off every week. It didn't sound like much free time at all however he would have his own bedsitting room and an adjacent bathroom and all his meals would be provided. The pay was a pittance but such a live-in arrangement meant that what little he earned he could save. He would give it a go for a while. Perhaps he should put a time limit of three months on it and then move on elsewhere. What about that Gibraltar place? That could be one possibility.

Although Edwin had frequented many a pub in his life it was his first time behind the bar apart from serving at his own in-house bar in New Zealand. The array of beer pipes and torn cardboard cartons containing packets of crisps looked decidedly scruffy when viewed from such an angle. There was a sink full of tepid grey water that had been used to wash glasses and bins at either end of the narrow stretch for emptying ash trays into. A fridge tucked beneath the counter contained prawns, mayonnaise, lettuce, cheese, tomatoes, ham and cucumber was strategically positioned and ready for use for whenever customers might order a sandwich. The floor was of dark red well-worn linoleum. He took a look at the row of upside down spirit bottles clipped on to their optical measuring devices and then at the two sets of identical beer pumps for bitter, keg, stout and lager. The mechanics seemed straightforward enough.

Edwin developed a good working relationship with the boss who was called Josh and hailed from Teesside. He was an engineer by trade but together with his wife, who had been an air hostess, they had recently been on a pub management course after which they had been assigned to this particular establishment. Edwin was taught some tricks of the trade. As the end of a session it was a common practice to pour any accumulated beer that had spilled into plastic drip trays under the beer taps into a large bucket. With the aid of a plastic funnel it could then be poured back into the top of one of the barrels in the cellar thereby saving money.

"There's nothing wrong with it. It's all good beer – that." It was explained.

A problem once arose when a group of people had ordered pints of shandy and a fair bit of lemonade had also ended up in one of the drip trays. The following day one or two beer drinkers asked if the glasses had been washed properly because apparently the best bitter had a noticeable taste of lemonade about it.

Josh and his wife were working class north country people who regarded most people in the south of England as being stuck-up snobs and so much of the bar work experience was an object lesson both in a class divided Britain and in a North South divide. Most of the local clientele were the wealthy and retired and were regarded as nothing more than the essential source of money that tumbled into the pub's tills.

"Look at her, daft old booger!" Josh whispered to Edwin as an elderly lady in a thick fur coat came through the door. "Bet you she's a pink gin – you can tell them a mile off!" Nine times out of ten his predictions as to what people would drink were uncannily accurate.

Because the company that owned the hotel had done some kind of a deal with the suppliers and many of the drinks weren't proprietary brands one had to be careful under the trades descriptions act. If someone walked in and ordered a Gordon's and Schweppes by name one needed to state that it would actually be a Squires and Rawlins, although it could be quietly muttered under one's breath. It was the same sort of thing is someone requested Bacardi because that too had been substituted with some hitherto unheard of brand of white rum.

The filter coffee available at the hotel had the Belgian name of 'Rombouts' and was correctly pronounced by most customers as "Rom-boo". However, the boss and his wife were having no such highbrow foreign talk and seemed to delight in pronouncing it loudly as "Rum-boats" much to the general disgust of everybody within earshot.

Bar staff were permitted to take periodic sips of half pint glasses of beer throughout their shifts which were paid for from tips. But it wasn't nearly the same as being on the other side of the bar as Edwin soon found out. He got into the routine of constantly emptying the ash trays and wiping the bar down with a damp cloth. He knew the prices of most things and his mental arithmetic was sufficiently good to be able to add up everything as he went through the motions of serving someone's round of drinks and invariably arriving at the same figure as in the previously bought round.

He was given a lesson in what he regarded as how to provide a short-measure in a schooner glass of sherry. "If you fill it too full, you're giving away too much because, if you look, the widest part of the glass is nearest to the brim. Therefore if you just fill the narrower part the level of liquid will still look quite high and you will end up saving a fair old bit," he was told.

It was a peculiar lifestyle and Edwin got quite efficient at the work. He also attracted the attention of various admirers not least a wealthy lady from the nearby village of Cranbrook who since first encountering him used to drop by on a regular basis to subtlety flirt. But Edwin's main drive was to make plans to move on and get back into his profession.

The idea of checking Gibraltar out carried a certain appeal. Having worked overseas in both New Zealand and Hong Kong he felt that another British overseas territory might be a good idea. At least it had a warm climate and apparently a TV station – and he wouldn't mind working for very little pay to begin with.

The following week an elderly couple who were in some way connected to the BBC Symphony Orchestra were resident at the hotel. After breakfast the wife approached Edwin and in the style of a fortune teller informed him that she could see that a wonderful future lay ahead of him and that something very special was going to happen to him. Never having spoken with her before and surprised at having been singled out in such manner Edwin wondered what on earth the old dear was possibly talking about.

A few weeks later Edwin quit the pub job in order to go to Gibraltar.

CHAPTER EIGHTEEN

EDWIN MADE HIS WAY through the streets from Southampton Bus Station down to the waterside and to the start of the docks. His ticket told him to check in at Gate 9 and, because his immediate encounter was Gate 3, he figured that he had a bit of walking to do. In fact he took in a complete loop around the old fortifications of the city walls that remained from the days of a distant past and around which the ring road now passed. As long as he kept following the semi-circular route of wharf-side cranes he would be bound to get there sooner or later, he thought. And in any case he was still in good time.

The road swung around past the far end of the high street and to the first sight of the waterfront. There a dilapidated old pier stood next to the departure point for the small Isle of Wight ferries alongside the even smaller Hythe ferries, which went back and forth across Southampton Water. It occurred to him that South-ampton had been his departure point for New Zealand several years ago yet under a very different set of circumstances. Maybe this present venture out to Gibraltar would prove to be a good solution. When the situation gets dismal, there is something particularly refreshing about a complete change of environ-ment, he thought, and all the more so when it involves international travel.

He swapped his suitcase to his other hand which resulted in his shoulder bag dropping down the length of his arm. Although clumsy to carry for any great distance, he felt that the luggage combination of a small lightweight suitcase and an airline shoulder bag containing travel documents was more sophisticated than the backpacker image. He passed Gate 5, turned a corner, and breathed in from the waft of cold, slightly damp, air that greeted him. You could tell by the quality of such air that this town was a port. There was a presence of saltwater detectable in the morning breeze and even the few people that he passed on the way each had an appearance of some sort of naval connection. Some looked like retired captains whilst others might even have been retired pirates.

'Allez a Gauche', 'Links Fahren', 'Conducir por la Izquierda', said a road sign, advising continental motorists to acquire the habit of driving on the left hand side of the road whilst in Britain. He guessed that he must be somewhere near the cross channel ferry by now. On rounding the next corner, there it was. Within the wall there was a large entrance between two pillars that had 'Gate 9' displayed in bold white letters on a black plaque attached prominently to one side. A man in a uniform was seated in a wooden box-like structure, evidently on duty and monitoring all those who entered. He gave Edwin a nod.

"Foot passenger?" he asked, "Where are you going?"

"Cherbourg," responded Edwin.

"Follow the walkway through the length of the car park and you'll come to the terminal building where there's the check-in hall and waiting room," he said, pointing towards a distant edifice across the vast tarmac area beyond a block of Customs and Excise offices.

"Thanks," said Edwin.

Several other passengers could be seen making their way towards the building in question whilst those who were taking their cars with them were being parked in neat lines on the other side of a metal fence.

On arrival at the building Edwin duly showed his passport, had a portion of his ticket torn out in return for a boarding card and passed through into the waiting area that was already quite crowded. Those who were taking an earlier ferry to Le Havre were already passing through doors at the far end of the hall. The others who remained were mainly elderly couples and, judging by the voices that he heard as he walked through the centre aisle; the British/French ratio seemed to be about fifty-fifty. Although there was a bar along one side of the hall, the shutters were all down and various members of the British travellers were bemoaning the fact that you couldn't even get a cup of tea.

"Just have to wait until we're on board," muttered one, philosophically.

"It won't just be a tea that I'll need by then," said his wife, "It'll be a G & T!"

'How long does the crossing take anyway?'

"I think they said four and a half hours."

Edwin sat down at one end of a long row of orange plastic seats and mentally surveyed those around him. A French lady clad in heavy jewellery was having an overheated discussion with her daughter. An English couple were taking seasickness tablets and an elderly gentleman who was half way through the crossword puzzle in his copy of The Times, was tapping his pen on an armrest as he wrestled with the clue to sixteen down. Through the double glass doors of the check-in area a young lady entered, struggling with what looked like far too much luggage to manage. Although she appeared to be on her own, she had no less than nine different bags with her. They weren't particularly big bags but just a variety of awkward looking shapes and the fact that there were nine of them meant that she couldn't carry them all at once and could manoeuvre them only in relay stages, first advancing five of them forward and then returning back to collect the remaining four. Presumably she was with other people who would soon appear from somewhere. But she made her way across the hall and sat down alone on a bench opposite Edwin with nobody else seeming to appear from anywhere. The doors at the other end of the hall opened once again and people began to stand up and form a queue. Edwin looked up at the wall clock. It was ten fifteen and presumably boarding time. Like everybody else he rose from his seat too but then, out of gentlemanly consideration, he turned to the lady and asked if he could help her carry her bags.

"Oh gee, that's kind," she said, with a somewhat shrill voice and with an accent that betrayed her as coming from somewhere on the other side of the Atlantic. She looked down at her bags, "I guess I brought rather too many things along with me."

"Where are you from?" asked Edwin

"South America," she replied.

"Oh, that's interesting, whereabouts?" he asked, thinking it might be an opportunity to demonstrate his command of the Spanish language.

"Trinidad," she said, leaving Edwin wondering whether the Caribbean Islands really did come under the category of South America but not wishing to expose any ignorance on the matter. And then she added "But I've lived in Canada most of my life."

"You are on holiday?" he suggested, lifting four of her bags with his left hand whilst picking up his own suitcase with his right hand.

"Yes, I've been in England for a month and now I want to take in Europe before heading home to Toronto," she replied.

The queue was moving forward quickly by now and they arrived at the foot of a gangway which they ascended and boarded the vessel and found a rack for stowing luggage. She thanked him for helping with the bags. He wished her a pleasant holiday and they parted company.

Edwin went down one deck and found a quiet spot with a comfortable chair from which to digest the content of the Daily Telegraph whilst contemplating the trip that lay before him. The ferry set sail at eleven o'clock and the bar was not yet open. He munched on a Cornish pasty and an apple that he had brought with him in his shoulder bag. The public address system announced something in French followed by an English translation with a strong nasally Normandy accent. Apparently the duty free shop was now open. After a while Edwin decided to take a stroll around the ship. He climbed two steep flights of metallic steps and passed through a vestibule door out onto an outside deck. Although still fresh for an April morning, the sun was shining and its reflection on the water quite dazzling. A line of people were leaning along the rail watching as Lee-on-Solent and the rest the British mainland passed them by. Amongst them Edwin spotted the olive skinned young lady from Trinidad, which was supposedly in South America, and who was also from Canada. He managed to pass by without her seeing him. He needed to focus all his energies on getting down to Gibraltar and securing some work down there and felt it wise to remain single-minded about that. He strolled around to the starboard side of the outer deck where the passing view happened to be the town of Ryde on the Isle of Wight. There weren't as many people gathered on that side of the ferry because it was in the shade of the upper decks and a lot colder. Edwin stood there for a good ten minutes before climbing up to a wide open-deck area that had the base of the ship's funnel located in its middle around which people sat on wooden benches. He then descended two decks to the smaller of the two bars, which were now open. He ordered a large scotch whisky with ice and water together with a pint of beer then sat down at a small table and began to take periodic alternate sips and gulps from each glass. A couple seated at an adjacent table, struck up a conversation with him. They were on their way to a fortnight's self-catering holiday in Normandy.

"Not that we'll be doing much self-catering," mused the husband "We intend to spend most of our time, and no doubt most of our money, on the gastronomic delights of French restaurants and bistros."

"It's an eating holiday," confirmed his fat wife, "We just love French food and French wine."

"Did the same thing a couple of years ago," he continued, "And it was bloody marvellous."

"What about you? Are you holidaying in France too?" asked the woman.

"No, I'm just passing through it," said Edwin, "I'm actually on my way down to Gibraltar"

"That's a fair old haul! How long is it going to take you to drive all that way?' she asked.

"Well, I'm not actually driving – I'm hitch hiking," confessed Edwin, "I'm going down to the south of Spain from where I can take a ferry across to Tangiers then another ferry back up to Gibraltar."

"That sounds adventurous but a bit of a complicated route," she said.

"There's not much choice by land," explained Edwin, "Gibraltar's frontier with Spain is closed."

"Oh yes, that's right," said the man, "General Franco saw to that several years ago – Spain claims that the Rock is theirs and of course we, the British, are damned if we're ever going to give it over to them! I mean, it just wouldn't be cricket, would it?"

"Have you been there before?" enquired his wife.

"No, never,' replied Edwin, "In fact I don't know much about the place at all – yet."

"I expect it must be pleasant down there though?" she said.

"I certainly hope so," replied Edwin, "I intend living there and working there for a while and seeing how things develop."

"Well, when you get there, just make sure you keep an eye on the monkeys," said her husband, "There's a saying that the day the monkeys leave Gibraltar so will the British – and the Rock will then return to Spain!"

The couple finished their drinks, wished him luck and headed off in the direction of the ship's restaurant. Edwin went to the bar and fetched another beer. He lit a cigarette, took out a map of from his shoulder bag and thought how massive a country France suddenly looked. He studied the place names for a southerly route for a good five minutes and it was only then that he became aware that the young lady from South America, Trinidad, Canada had seated herself at the next table.

"You look well-prepared with your map," she said.

"I don't know about being well-prepared," he answered, "I just need to get some idea of which direction to head off in."

She asked him where he was going and although she'd heard the name Gibraltar before, she'd no idea where it was. As his map only went as far as the Pyrenees, he couldn't demonstrate its whereabouts on that so he tried to explain it more graphically.

"On the scale of this map, it's probably about as far as that ice bucket," he said, pointing across to the far end of the bar.

He, in turn, then asked her where she was going and it transpired that she didn't have a clue. She told him that she had a European Rail Pass, which was valid for three months and that she had a fair bit of money but, other than that, it was her first time in Europe and she didn't know anyone or have any set plan as to where she would go but would probably check into a hotel in Cherbourg for the first night and take things from there. He offered her a drink and she smiled and asked for a brandy and lemonade.

The ferry docked in Cherbourg almost bang on schedule. Over the public address system in both languages, drivers were summoned to the car decks and foot passengers advised to assemble at the disembarkation point near the purser's office. The young lady, who by this time had introduced herself as Louise Petal had retrieved her nine bags and once again Edwin found himself lumbered with carrying four or them in addition to his own things. As they walked together along the quayside and towards the town centre, which was only a stone's throw away, he thought the decent thing to do would be to escort her to a hotel, bid her farewell and then hit the road so as to be able to make some headway with his hitchhiking that afternoon. But then, the unexpected happened. Louise gave a sudden squeal of horror.

"My God!" she said, "I think I left my pocket book in the washroom on the ferry! It's got all my money in it – quick, let me check," she said as she put her bags down and rifled through the first one. "No, it's not in that one!" she said, turning her attention to the next.

"Which bag do you normally keep it in?" asked Edwin, trying to be constructive.

"I don't have one particular bag for it," she answered, unzipping the side flap of a third bag, "I keep it in any one of them – but I do remember having it with me in that washroom! It's no good; I'll have to go back to the ferry!"

Before he knew it Edwin was left standing there at the docks, guarding all nine of this Louise girl's bags as well as his own case and shoulder bag. All he could do was to wait.

He stood there for some forty-five minutes during which time all the remaining passengers and half the ship's company had passed him by until he was the sole person to be seen on the wharf. It was pointless attempting to lift the cases and transport them elsewhere and it wouldn't be right simply to push off with his belongings and abandon hers. It was a ridiculous situation that he'd got himself into and time was ticking away. Immersed in such thoughts, he then heard the shrill voice of Louise joyously calling out his name. He looked up saw her coming down the gangway waving something in her hand, which presumably was the lost wallet.

"Gee, why don't we find some place and celebrate?" she said as she approached Edwin.

"Celebrate?" he said, "I'll only be celebrating once I reach my destination of Gibraltar."

"Oh Gibraltar," she echoed, "I've just been thinking about that"

"Thinking about Gibraltar?" asked Edwin.

"Sure," she replied, "I have a European Rail Pass. What if I were to come to Gibraltar with you?"

"Well," said Edwin looking down at this young lady's nine bags, "I already told you, I'm hitchhiking there."

"I'd pay your train fare!" she said enthusiastically, "I've got plenty of money with me."

Fearing an unexpected diversion from his originally intended course, Edwin was quick to put the idea out of his mind.

"No, that wouldn't do," he said "Besides which, I'm not on holiday – my aim is simply to get down to Gibraltar as quickly as possible and to find a job."

"Well, do me one favour then," she said, "Get me to a hotel here in Cherbourg and let me invite you for dinner!"

"I'll try and find you some accommodation," he said, "but then I think I'd best be on my way."

He picked up a bundle of her bags and led the way through Cherbourg in the direction of the railway station where he felt sure there would probably be a hotel or a pension of some description where he could politely dispense of his duties. Sure enough, immediately to the right of the front entrance of Cherbourg Railway Station was a small parade of shops, in the middle of which was a restaurant with a sign on the floor above displaying the word 'Chambres.' In the tiny reception area the bags were piled up in front of a hatchway and, after ascertaining the reasonable price of a single room, Louise began imploring Edwin to stay there for the night too whilst the French landlady listened with some apparent amusement.

"It's neither in my schedule nor in my budget," said Edwin. "I need to get a move on with my journey."

"But it's already gone six o'clock French time," she pleaded. "Surely, it makes far more sense to get a good night's rest and start afresh tomorrow. And don't worry about the cost – it's on me!"

Finally Edwin succumbed. After all, apart from the hour change to continental time, wasn't it because of being delayed by this lady that the afternoon had already gone? Wasn't her reasonable suggestion a kind gesture? And hadn't he already done his good turn by looking after her wretched bags and then lugging them across Cherbourg and finding her somewhere to stay?

"OK," he smiled, "You win. I'll stay here for the night and start off again in the morning!"

"That's great!" shrieked Louise and nodded toward the landlady.

"Alors, one double room then?" she enquired, with a knowing expression.

"I think we'd better have two single rooms" interjected Edwin, deliberately avoiding eye contact with Louise. In a way he kind of surprised himself by taking such a stance but his underlying gut feeling was that it might be too easy to get horribly side-tracked and tied up with this young lady if he wasn't careful. He wasn't after a one-night stand either because, in a funny kind of logic, he felt that it might jeopardise the path on which he was now embarked. Being a healthy unattached male, he didn't normally think in such ways but then it probably had something to do with his uncompromising determination to secure a proper job at his final destination – and perhaps something to do with the fact that he didn't feel particularly attracted to her.

Two keys was handed over for the adjacent room numbers 4 and 5 and it was agreed between them that Louise would make use of the communal shower along the passageway whilst Edwin used the one located on the second floor and that they would then meet up at seven thirty.

Louise banged on Edwin's door a little before the appointed hour and was dressed in a cream coloured trouser suit and had added makeup to her deeply tanned facial features. Edwin was in exactly the same turtle necked jersey and grey jeans that he had worn throughout the day but had showered and shampooed. Together they decided to take a pre-dinner stroll in and around the immediate area. They encountered some young French children playing a version of hide and seek in which the same ones would keep reappearing in front of them at every street corner and shouting "cuckoo." One even appeared from the inside of a drainpipe.

There was a set menu available in the restaurant. A bowl of thick lentil soup with chunks of garlic sausage sitting in the middle of it constituted the first course whilst a medium rare beefsteak with a béarnaise sauce accompanied by sautéed potatoes and a side salad made up the second. A candle had been lit and a large carafe of red wine had been deposited on the blue and white chequered tablecloth as had the inevitable basket of neatly cut French bread and a pot of butter. The background music of an accordion was audible via strategically placed loudspeakers and there were about twenty or so other diners, mainly couples, seated at random amidst the rows of symmetrically arranged tables that extended through onto the pavement.

"Well, this is pleasant! Cheers!" said Louise, raising her glass of the red house wine.

"Cheers!" responded Edwin.

"Aren't you now glad that you've stopped off here?" she asked.

"I should really have been on my way," said Edwin, continuing to absorb the ambience of the restaurant and starting to feel rather content with it, "but I must admit that being here is rather good too."

"And tomorrow we'll take the train together?" she asked.

"Tomorrow I'll start hitchhiking," he replied.

"Oh come on!" she said, "You can't just abandon me! I don't speak one word of French and I already told you that I'd like to go to that Gibraltar place with you and that I'm more than happy to pay your fare."

"It's very kind of you but I couldn't allow you to do that." he said, "Besides which, I've set my heart on hitchhiking."

"You're too proud!" she said, "But I'll tell you what. Why don't we make a compromise? You can hitchhike there and I can take a train and we meet up when we get there."

"That sounds reasonable enough," said Edwin, as a waitress arrived with their first course.

"Great!" replied Louise, "What time does the train for Gibraltar leave from here tomorrow?"

"I think I'd better show you something on a larger map," replied Edwin.

As they were both quite hungry, they tucked into their potage of lentils and became lost in their own thoughts for a while. Edwin wasn't sure if it was a particularly good idea at all for this Louise lady to be thinking in terms of heading in the direction of Gibraltar. This whole encounter had been completely unplanned and had already delayed him and yet, he felt a bit sorry for her because somehow she seemed so helpless. But the overriding factor was that he knew that he had to get down there as quickly as possible, and find a job right away. Maybe he'd better re-emphasise that to her. He took a large gulp of wine.

Louise listened patiently as Edwin related the change of immigration policy that had taken place in New Zealand and some of the difficulties he had encountered in finding professional work since leaving Hong Kong and how he was hoping to find a way back into his field of television production. Because Gibraltar apparently had a small TV Station he was first going to find out if it would be possible for him to work there but if not, he'd have to take any other work that was available.

"The thing is," he concluded, "I've never been to Gibraltar before. I know very little about the place. I know that it's a tiny British colony and that I'm legally entitled to live and work there, that it's frontier with Spain is closed so you have to get there by two ferry journeys via Morocco – but I also know that once I arrive in Gibraltar, if I can't get some sort of a job right away, I'm going to be completely up the creek."

There was a long pause before Louise spoke. She had gazed at him through the flickering candle flame.
.
"You know something?" she said, "I can't help feeling that we were meant to meet!

"Really?" said Edwin, never a great believer in predestination.

"Yes!" she exclaimed, "I've got money and I can help your situation!"

Edwin looked over his shoulder at some of the other diners in case there was anyone else in earshot that might understand English. It all sounded far too embarrassing.

"Look," he said, lowering his voice, "I'm not exactly after money. I'm just after a halfway reasonable job."

"I might be able to help you with work too," she said

"How do you mean?" he asked.

"Well," she said, "I hope it all works out well in Gibraltar but if for some reason it doesn't, then you could always consider Canada!"

"Canada?" he said.

"Sure!" she replied, "We've got plenty of TV stations where I live in Toronto and I'm sure you'd have no problem working for one of them."

The French waitress removed the empty bowls and served the main course.

"Monsieur, vous voulez encore une autre carafe de rouge?' She enquired, indicating the almost empty wine jug.

"Mais oui, s'il vous plaît," said Edwin in his best schoolboy French, which suddenly seemed to be coming back to him

He couldn't quite fathom out this Louise. She seemed sincere enough but what did she expect in return? The thought bothered Edwin because he didn't want to get entangled with anybody who might prove to be a limiting factor in his freedom to do things in his own way. Similarly, although she was pleasant enough, she seemed a bit scatter-brained and wasn't really his type at all. The second carafe of wine arrived and glasses were replenished.

"Gee," said Louise, "You know this has been one of the best days of my life! I love it here in Europe."

The comment amused Edwin, who then allowed himself to loosen up a bit and to feel more relaxed about things. The wine was a contributing factor and, on balance, maybe it hadn't been such a bad thing to share his predicament with somebody else rather than carrying around the full severity of the situation just in his head. He cracked a couple of jokes and made Louise laugh. They each took a chocolate mousse as dessert followed by a cup of coffee. Edwin lit a cigarette and Louise slipped him a hundred franc note with which to pay the bill. They arranged to meet the following morning for breakfast. Then they climbed the flight of stairs up to their rooms and just as they were about to part on the first floor landing, Louise hesitated momentarily outside her door before turning and taking hold of Edwin's left elbow. Pulling him towards her, she gave him a quick peck on the cheek and wished him goodnight. He returned the compliment with a similar short kiss on the cheek, said goodnight and they each entered their respective rooms. It had been a long day and they both slept like logs.

EDWIN WOKE UP SOMEWHAT later that he'd anticipated and even that was only on account of a rubbish truck making a horrendous racket immediately beneath his window. It had already gone nine o'clock. He got out of bed and, putting a towel around him, slipped out to the upstairs washroom where he had a shave and took a shower. On his return he noticed a light shining through the gap of Louise's room.

Good, he thought. If she's getting up too, at least it means that I'll soon be able to get going with the day's journey that lies ahead.

He placed yesterday's shirt, underwear and socks into a plastic bag that had 'Sainsbury' printed on both sides, which looked decidedly out of place in France. He packed it away into one side of his small suitcase alongside his wash bag. Then, taking his map with him, he locked his room and made his way along the corridor, giving a short rap on Louise's door as he passed it.

"I'll be down shortly," said a shrill voice on the other side. "Go right ahead and order breakfast."

Edwin descended the stairs and stepped outside. It was a bright morning that was mild and dry. Hopefully, good weather for hitchhiking, he thought.

Rather than sitting down at a restaurant table he walked across to a low wall and perched himself on that instead. It was all very well being invited to go ahead and order breakfast but he'd have felt rather uncomfortable about doing that on his own, since she was the one who had offered to pay for it. In any case, in other circumstances he would most likely have opted for purchasing a bread roll from a boulangerie rather than another sit-down arrangement.

Ten minutes went by with still no sign of Louise. He unfolded his map. He'd be lucky if he could make it all the way down to the border with Spain in one day. He had hitched the journey in reverse on two previous occasions several years ago and recalled that even with good lifts it had taken him an entire day. And, of course, sitting there on a wall waiting to have a breakfast that he didn't really need wasn't aiding a prompt start for such an undertaking. He could already have been at the roadside and getting that all-important first lift of the day by now. It was another full twenty minutes before Louise finally put in an appearance.

"Gee, I'm sorry," she said, "I thought I'd lost my railcard but I found it in a different bag to where I thought it was. You've eaten already?"

"No, I was waiting for you," he said, trying to conceal any hint of annoyance at her delay.

She smiled, "That's really nice of you. But come on, what are we waiting for? Let's go eat."

They sat at one of the tables and before long fresh croissants with butter and strawberry jam were being washed down with piping hot French coffee. The talking point soon came round to Gibraltar and Edwin attempted to explain its whereabouts once again.

"Look, Honey," she interjected, "if it's such a long way, why won't you just let me pay your train ticket there and be done with it? It's that easy!"

He wasn't sure what bothered him more, suddenly being referred to as 'Honey' or having this amazing carrot of a paid-for journey dangling in front of him all the time. He remembered last night's short embrace. It had been harmless enough and yet he now already was 'Honey.'

"No," he said, "As soon as we've finished here, I'm going to get to the main road and start hitching."

"Oh, Edwin," she said, perhaps having read his mind concerning use of the word 'Honey,' "I still want to come to Gibraltar with you. If you insist on hitchhiking whilst I ride the train then that is fine but we'll need to arrange to meet up somewhere along the route. Here show me that map again."

Not for the first time he began to feel some degree of sympathy for this poor damsel in distress who seemed so lost and so adamant about accompanying him on his adventures. By the time they'd polished off all the croissants some sort of a compromise plan had been worked out. Edwin was going to hitchhike, as had been his intention from the outset, whilst Louise would take trains as far as Bordeaux where they would meet up tomorrow morning at the railway station and reassess the situation.

After giving in to the temptation of a third cup of coffee, they vacated their rooms and handed the keys in at reception before carrying the items of luggage across the road to Cherbourg Railway Station from where Louise would commence her journey. Fortunately trolleys were available on the station forecourt one of which soon became loaded up with her nine bags, neatly stacked into two piles of four with the remaining one across the top. According to a display board the next train for Paris, as the first leg of her journey, would depart from Platform 3 but not for another hour. It was agreed, however, that so as to waste no further time, Edwin would leave right away. On his way out through the large station doors he turned and gave her a goodbye wave. She waved back and blew him a kiss. Once around the corner and out of sight it felt as though he was now carrying on from where he'd left off yesterday and that the real journey was finally underway.

Edwin already had a sense as to the probable route out of Cherbourg. He'd ignore all those traffic signs that simply said 'Toutes Directions.' Past experience had shown that if you followed them you could get re-routed all over the place. After all, how was it that one direction could mean the same thing for every direction? That was a bit like the concept of 'one size fits all.' His own instinct told him that if he kept walking along the road that he was now on, sooner or later it would have to meet up with a major road and that its southerly direction would lead to Rennes, which would start him off on the route down through the length of France. Such intuition paid off and after walking through suburbia for about half an hour he arrived at a junction with a busy main road, which was signposted as leading to Saint-Lô, Fougères and Rennes.

Positioning himself at a spot that allowed sufficient space for a vehicle to pull up in safely, he then faced the oncoming traffic and adopted his familiar pose of holding out his right arm with his thumb pointing upwards for approaching drivers to see. It wasn't long before a blue Citroen drew up. Edwin was invited to deposit his suitcase on the bag seat and hop into the front.

"Moi, je vais jusque Montebourg,' said the driver, a middle aged man dressed in a suit and tie.

As Edwin had no idea where that particular destination was, he simply nodded, relaxed and felt happy to be on the road at last. As it happened it was only about half an hour's drive but Edwin, always optimistic when it came to hitchhiking, reasoned that making some headway was better than making no headway and at least he was still on the same main road.

"Merci, monsieur," said Edwin, retrieving his bag.

"De rien," replied the driver, "et bonne chance!"

Five minutes later another car pulled up, which resulted in a further lift of a slightly longer journey that ended in the middle of a town called Flers de l'Orne. Unfortunately the communication had not been that brilliant. The lady driver had turned off the main road and taken him into the middle of a town. That meant that he would first have to walk to its extremity to find a new hitchhiking point.

Edwin took a southerly road and after twenty minutes came to the start of a more rural area where to his dismay the road turned into little more that a country lane along which there was very little traffic. Sitting down on a grass verge, he tried to work out where he was on his map but the scale was far too small. A car suddenly came into view and Edwin leapt to his feet and held out his thumb. To the sound of raucous laughter from within, one of its passengers made a finger gesture through an open window and blew a raspberry. He remained stuck at that one spot for the rest of the afternoon during which time only four more cars appeared, none of which offered him a lift. Finally, however, a van came along and its driver took Edwin to the junction with the main road. Relieved at setting eyes on a constant flow of traffic once more, he vowed never again to get sidetracked in such a way. He could have been two-thirds of the way through the length of France by now and yet here he was still up in one of its northern provinces.

After two more short lifts he had by-passed Rennes. The second driver had given him some momentary hope when he had said something that sounded like "Bordeaux aussi?" For a brief moment Edwin thought he'd stumbled upon that one lucky lift that would take him right through to where he was heading. It turned out, however, that the driver wasn't going anywhere remotely near Bordeaux but only as far as a nearby village a few kilometres along the road to a place called Port Haut which had sounded similar.

The next lift was a four and a half hour drive to a turn off shortly beyond the town of Bressuire. It was the best lift that Edwin had had all day but afterwards it was already approaching midnight. The immediate problem was that there wasn't much traffic on this particular part of the route which was a connecting road between two major thoroughfares. It was quiet and the moon shone on a stone religious monument across the road surrounded by a silhouette of tall trees. The still atmosphere felt eerie and as if he was being watched by someone or something. For one fearful moment he even imagined that he could hear a distant sound of a choir like the added sound effect to an epic cinema film. He shuddered and turned around in a complete circle so as to make absolutely sure that there was no one else in the vicinity.

Picking up his suitcase he then walked briskly further along the road before stopping and lighting a cigarette. Silence again reigned, as did the ghostly moonshine on trees. He wished that he was somewhere else such as tucked up in a cosy bed for the night. Yet he knew that he had needed to be able to make progress. His thoughts then switched to that Louise lady with her nine bags. What an unusual person she had been. What a strange set of circumstances. And to think that she had actually offered to pay his fare to Gibraltar and yet here he was standing in the dark in the middle of the night, cold and isolated– and on top of that being scared stiff about something to do with that stone monument back down the road which was quite possibly haunted for all he knew.

He felt a sudden pang of sadness at the thought that Louise would be looking for him in Bordeaux in the morning and he wouldn't be there. She would assume that he wasn't coming at all and perhaps even feel that he had tricked her. They would probably never see each other again and they hadn't even exchanged addresses. She would head off somewhere else. After all, she had one of those railcard things. Why had he resisted her kindness? She'd claimed to be wealthy for goodness sake! His train fare was probably a mere drop in the ocean to her. And hadn't she also mentioned that in case Gibraltar didn't work out, she might be able to help in getting him to Canada? Such thoughts bombarded Edwin's mind.

"Get me out of here!" he said out loud.

At that point he heard the engine noise of a car and turned to see twin headlights approaching. He immediately straightened his posture and held out his thumb. The car slowed down and drew up next to him. There were four people inside and Edwin was offered a seat in the back alongside two of them, which he eagerly accepted. They were young people, two girls and two guys. One of them spoke English after a fashion and told Edwin that they would be able to take him about two hundred kilometres.

"Will it be anywhere near Bordeaux?" he asked optimistically.

"Bordeaux! Bordeaux?" Came the response, "Yes, it's in the right direction – but Bordeaux? – it is a very long way."

He spoke with the others in the car who echoed similar sentiments.

"Alors. Bordeaux! Ca c'est très loin d'ici!"

But it was good to be in the warmth of a car and good to know that he was now making some further headway with the journey. Who knows, if he kept going at this rate throughout the rest of the night, he might even make it to Bordeaux on time after all.

This particular nocturnal jaunt culminated at the home of the couple that had been seated in the front of the car. The journey had taken nearly two hours and Edwin was invited into their house for a coffee. They'd also suggested that he was welcome to spend the remainder of the night on their living room couch if he so desired but he politely declined the offer. The coffee was served as were glasses of some kind of syrupy orange liqueur after which the driver drove Edwin the short distance back to the main road and wished him good luck.

Within the matter of a few minutes he had got a lift in a lorry bound for somewhere called Angouleme, which was about an hour's drive. He asked to be dropped off next to the turn off from the main road rather than going into the town's centre. Dawn broke and Edwin pulled out his map to check where the place was in relation to Bordeaux. He saw that there was still a fair way to go whilst his stomach reminded him that he hadn't eaten anything at all since the breakfast in Cherbourg the day before.

A succession of short lifts followed throughout the day with a considerable amount of waiting time in between each of them. By mid-afternoon he'd been finding it difficult to stay awake during one of the lifts. Every now and again his eyes would shut and his head momentarily drop forward, the motion of which would then re-awaken him with a jolt. The car's driver dropped Edwin off next to a railway station in the provincial town of St. André. They'd obviously turned off the main road somewhere, probably during one of those moments when he'd been asleep. Stepping outside the vehicle the fresh air helped revive him.

He began to think that because the arrangement with the Louise lady had been to meet up that morning and it was now late afternoon it was highly unlikely that she would still be waiting at this stage of the game. She would almost certainly have given up on him by now and he wondered whether it was even worth the trouble of going into Bordeaux itself or whether it might make more sense just to continue on his route to Spain.

He went in search of a toilet in the small station building and on his way back through the booking hall he noticed on the display board that there were regular trains going for Bordeaux. He couldn't resist making some enquiries from a man seated behind the glass fronted ticket booth and found out that the next one would depart in seven minutes, the journey time was half an hour and the price was very reasonable. Before long he was seated on the train in question. He reasoned that even if Louise would no longer be waiting at the railway station, at least he would have got the whole thing out of his system. The 16.21 train for Bordeaux departed.

When Edwin alighted at the Gare de Bordeaux, the place was bustling with commuters returning from work. In the absence of any visible exit signs, he made his way via an underpass to what he assumed was the way out but found that it led only to another platform. Doubling back upon himself he returned through the entire length of the subway and up a flight of steps from where he could see people passing through an archway labelled 'Sortie.' He then heard an almighty shriek. It wasn't just the intensity of the shriek but the fact that it had shrieked his name, "Edwin!" And there standing just to one side of the barrier was a sobbing, helpless looking, Louise.

EDWIN AWOKE STILL FULLY clothed and on top of the large double bed. Lying alongside him was the sleeping Louise. The outline of bulky, old-fashioned, furniture was visible due to a shaft of light spilling through a small gap in the curtains. The room looked tatty. He slipped out of bed, went over to the washbasin with a miniature tap handle and shaved with cold water, guiding the razor across relevant areas of his facial features with the aid of a tiny wall mirror that was both dirty and cracked. Grabbing a filthy looking towel, he then crept out through the door and along the passageway where he found a small shower room with a sodden floor in which he endeavoured to complete his freshening up process. The Algerian landlady had given Louise a hard time and charged an exorbitant fee for the overnight stay in this place of ill repute. It had been a communication problem. It was the first place that Louise had found when she had arrived in Bordeaux and, when she'd tried to explain that she was awaiting a male friend, it had been assumed that she was a whore who was expecting a client.

It was still early morning when Edwin and Louise vacated the premises and, together with the bags, made their way to the station cafeteria. Edwin was famished and eagerly wolfed down a combination plate of hamburger steak, omelette and chips. Louise, content with a coffee and croissant, was quietly overjoyed at being reunited with him. Edwin had finally agreed that he would accept her offer to pay for his train fare for the remainder of the journey and for both of them it felt like a new beginning.

Louise had her rail pass and in the station's booking hall they joined a queue to buy a train ticket through to Algeciras in southern Spain for Edwin. Once purchased, he studied its printed words with a feeling both of incredulity and glee. The first train to France's border with Spain was due in twenty minutes.

Later that morning they stepped foot on Spanish soil having left the French train and passed through customs control. On studying the timetable of the RENFE train service of Spain Edwin noted the various options. Apparently there would be no through trains to Algeciras until nine thirty the following morning. However there were trains going to the Spanish capital of Madrid, which was about halfway, at regular intervals throughout the day. There would be two such departures within the next hour. One was a regular service that would arrive in Madrid shortly before midnight but there was also an express train called 'El Talgo' that would get there some three hours earlier. If they wanted to take that they would have to pay a supplementary charge. Louise had no hesitation in suggesting that they ought to travel by the faster of the two but the immediate problem was that the additional payment could be accepted only in Spanish currency and the train was already standing at Platform 1 and ready to depart in twelve minutes time. Fortunately Edwin was able to make good use of his Spanish and succeeded in persuading the man at the ticket office to trade Louise's remaining eight hundred French francs for Spanish pesetas at a reasonable exchange rate.

The express train was more like sitting in an aeroplane. It was air-conditioned and smooth running. They settled into their two large comfortable adjacent seats and coffees were ordered from a passing hostess. Louise had insisted that Edwin took charge of the money. He didn't object to that because he felt that it always looked wrong when she paid for everything.

"In any case," she had said, in her shrill voice, "I wouldn't have a clue about what any of the prices are in real money. Besides, I've got American Express Travellers cheques for a couple of thousand Canadian dollars with me and even a bank draft for five hundred British pounds, which probably won't even be needed."

"Sounds like rather a lot to me," said Edwin.

"And then if that dries up," she continued, "there's plenty more that I could draw on from my regular bank account back home."

"Did you just win a lottery or something?" he asked.

"The thing about Canada is that everybody can succeed there and really make it," she said, "All my family and relatives have done well since we moved up there from Trinidad."

When the train reached Madrid that evening, Edwin's first inclination had been to take the Metro to the Puerta del Sol to find some cheap and cheerful accommodation for the night but when he recalled flights of steps, crowded carriages and the number of bags to contend with, they opted for a taxi instead.

"Oh wow, this place looks lively," commented Louise as the cab passed through the city centre, "Is Gibraltar going to be like this?"

"I doubt it very much," replied Edwin, making a mental note to remind her not to speak too openly about Gibraltar in front of Spanish people, even taxi drivers, as it had been the main dividing issue between Britain and Spain for the best part of three hundred years and its mere mention could sometimes trigger off a heated argument. Fortunately the name was pronounced differently in Spanish.

The cab driver dropped them off outside a small two star hotel. It was getting on for ten o'clock by the time they'd checked-in and deposited their belongings in their respective rooms before heading out to eat at one of the inexpensive restaurants in the nearby street of Ventura de la Vega which Edwin knew from many years ago. They were soon seated at a small rectangular table covered by a white paper cloth, glass ashtray and a jug of water.

Morsels of meat that had been added to the pinto bean soup were either chopped up pigs' ears or tripe from a cow's stomach but Edwin didn't volunteer such information to Louise.

"Oh, I'm not really sure what it is," he told her when she'd asked, "but it tastes pretty good whatever it is."

She agreed.

Before returning to their hotel they took a brief walk around the immediate neighbourhood to soak in some atmosphere of the Spanish capital. As a finale they stopped off at a cafeteria for a cup of coffee and a glass of brandy. A man wanted to sell them a watch and to demonstrate that it was waterproof he dropped it into a glass of beer. They didn't buy it.

THE FOLLOWING DAY'S OVERNIGHT train to the southern port of Algeciras departed at 20:35 but unfortunately there were no more couchettes available. They would have to try and snatch whatever sleep they could throughout the fourteen hour journey whilst sitting upright in the confines of a compartment of eight passengers. Their fellow travellers were two Spanish ladies, three Spanish men and a Moroccan man.

It was tolerable for the first hour or so but became uncomfortable when they attempted to sleep. The train itself seemed to have square wheels the way that it bounced around and there were several occasions in which Edwin woke up to find his head banging against the glass window. Louise didn't fare much better and kept sliding forward on the vinyl seat and at one stage fell right off it altogether. They endured the journey as best they could until dawn when, with the exception of the Moroccan, the other passengers in the compartment got off at Córdoba. Edwin went out into the corridor and lit a cigarette whilst Louise lay across the length of the vacated seats as the train pulled out of the station. There was restaurant car towards the rear and Edwin made his way back there and returned with two containers of hot coffee and some Magdalenas – sweet lemony cup cakes. When he got back to the compartment Louise was sitting upright once again. The Moroccan man had been pointing towards the train's window.

"Mira esta allí!" he said in Spanish, "Es Inglaterra!"

"What's he saying?" asked Louise.

"He sounds a bit confused to me," replied Edwin, "He reckons he can see England through the window."

The Moroccan man beckoned Edwin over to take a look and repeated the same thing.

"Mira! Inglaterra!"

Edwin moved across the compartment to see what it was that the man was on about. Looking out towards the front of the train he caught his first glimpse of a massive chunk of limestone sitting on the horizon and better known as the Rock of Gibraltar.

"It's Gibraltar!" he said as Louise came over to take a look too.

"El piñón. Es Inglaterra!" said the Moroccan, proudly.

"Puede ser Inglés pero no es Inglaterra exactamente," corrected Edwin.

They peered out of the compartment window for some considerable time transfixed by the distant image and focal point of their destination. There were still a couple more hours to go before the end of line railway station of Algeciras during which the Rock looked larger still with each passing kilometre.

The train eventually came to its final halt. Doors opened and passengers began piling out. Once again Edwin and Louise performed their now familiar bag carrying ritual along the length of the platform and out through the front entrance of the small station. Despite the palm trees the weather was unexpectedly wet and windy as they transported the luggage along a run-down looking stretch of roadway which ran between some dilapidated buildings towards cranes at the waterfront that were already in sight. Once there, they located the terminal building for ferries that sailed both to Tangiers and to the Spanish enclave of Ceuta. Edwin insisted on paying for his own ticket for that part of the journey. He would have had to have done so anyway if he had hitchhiked and in any case the fare for a single crossing was only around five pounds. He and Louise joined a queue that passed through Spanish passport control and customs before being entering a large waiting room. They then boarded a Moroccan vessel bound for Tangiers with an estimated sailing time of just under two hours.

There wasn't much to do on the ferry. It was too cold to sit out on deck and so whilst one of them kept an eye on the bags Edwin and Louise took it in turns to nip out there for a breath of fresh air every now and again, mainly to keep themselves awake. Conversing in the guttural-sound of Arabic most of the other passengers were Moroccans.

The Rock of Gibraltar, which had been alongside them at the start of the crossing to North Africa, began to recede behind them. By midday the clouds had gone, the sun was shining brightly and it started to get quite warm. An official set himself up at a desk in the ship's lounge and announcements were made over the public address system that all passengers would be required to obtain a landing card prior to disembarkation. Rather than joining in the resultant stampede, Edwin and Louise decided to remain seated and wait for the queue to die down which it eventually did. Edwin then took his turn whilst Louise sat with the bags. His passport was looked at and one of its inner pages stamped. With a nod of approval, he was given an orange coloured landing card. He then returned to where he had been sitting and it was Louise's turn to undergo such processing. When she got to the desk, however, judging by the commotion that ensued, things were not nearly as straightforward. Apparently holders of a Trinidadian passport needed a visa to be able to enter Morocco and clearly that was something that Louise didn't have. When she said that she hadn't known of the requirement, the official became quite cross and, in his broken English, told her in no uncertain terms that she would not be allowed to disembark in Tangiers but would have to remain on board the ferry and be returned to Spain. She burst into tears and pleaded with him but it was to no avail.

Edwin overheard the conversation from where he was seated and, apart from being taken by surprise at this latest turn of events, he wondered how best to get round such a situation. Louise rejoined him, looking absolutely crestfallen whilst he tried to be as philosophical about it as possible.

"Look," he said, "What I suggest you do when you get back to Spain is first of all check into a decent hotel in Algeciras and then make some inquiries from there about whether it's possible to obtain a visa."

She calmed down and agreed that that was probably the best course of action to take and then reached into a side pocket in one of her bags.

"Here," she said, handing him a white envelope, "take this."

"What's that?" asked Edwin.

"It's the bank draft for five hundred British pounds," she replied, "You're going to need it."

"You've got to be joking," he said, handing it back.

"But you could use it now and then later you could even get yourself over to Canada with what's left," she declared.

"No, I'm sorry, I can't take it," he said, "It's a lot of money – your money."

"Yes but I already told you, I don't need it," she continued, "This is yours if you want it."

"No, that's completely out of the question," he said.

Half an hour later the ferry docked. Louise was still shaken by the prospect of being on her own once again. Edwin had even suggested that if it would make things easier he would accompany her back to Spain. However, they both concluded that because Gibraltar was now within his grasp, it would be better for him to continue on his set course. She gave him her address in Canada and Edwin wrote down Poste Restante, Central Post Office, Gibraltar, as the address from where he intended to collect any mail.

A different Moroccan official came over and was more sympathetic that the first one. Louise still wasn't going to be allowed to step foot off the ferry but at least things were cordial.

"Tu, tranquilo," he said to Louise.

Disembarkation began and, after a brief hug, Edwin and Louise parted company.

CHAPTER NINETEEN

IT WAS LATE AFTERNOON and still warm and sunny as Edwin made his way along the jetty. He hoped that there would be an evening ferry sailing from Tangiers to Gibraltar. Enquiries revealed, however, that there were only four such sailings a week and that the next one wasn't for two days. He hovered around the edge of a car park, not sure what to do for the best. A Moroccan man in a striped pyjama-like garment addressed him.

"Where you go, Joe?" the man asked.

"I want to get to Gibraltar," replied Edwin.

"Today ferry already go, Joe," was his reply.

"So I gather," said Edwin, "and apparently the next one is not until Saturday."

The man shrugged his shoulders "Just you enjoy," he said, "Just you can smoking." He pointed to some people across the other side of the car park.

Edwin deduced that the man probably wasn't talking about tobacco and, picking up his suitcase, headed off in the direction of some distant buildings. After a brisk walk along a dusty road, he arrived at a small township on a hill. Amongst the various shops was a travel agent with a poster in its window advertising the ferry services and he thought he'd double check on the sailing time for Saturday and find out if they knew of somewhere where he could stay until then. The Moroccan travel agent spoke fluent English and confirmed that the next sailing to Gibraltar would be on Saturday morning at nine o'clock. However, he pointed out that there were short flights across to Gibraltar and that there would be a departure that evening. If Edwin were to take a taxi to the airport, there would still be sufficient time for him to take it. Even though the price of the flight was three times as much as the ferry crossing, Edwin was sufficiently intrigued with this unexpected option that he felt inclined to go for it. The travel agent agreed to accept payment in sterling and duly issued a plane ticket. He then saw Edwin off in a taxi, the driver of which was paid in advance. Half an hour later, having checked in his luggage, Edwin was relaxing in the departure lounge with a cold beer in his hand whilst awaiting the boarding of GB Airways flight 202 to Gibraltar.

The flight from Tangiers to Gibraltar was the shortest intercontinental flight in the world. With a total journey time of twenty minutes, no sooner had the plane taken off than it was already starting to prepare for its descent again. The hostess quickly handed out boiled sweets and the 'Fasten safety belts' sign lit up. The plane touched down and from Edwin's vantage point of a window seat he was surprised to see that a road crossed the runway at which cars had been stopped in both directions much like the level crossing of a railway. There was sea at either end of the runway strip and just before the plane reached the water's edge at the far end it turned and taxied back towards the small terminal building and control tower of Gibraltar Airport. A metal flight of stairs was wheeled into place and, together with the other passengers from the flight Edwin walked across the tarmac in front of the dominating backdrop of the Rock. They passed in through some double glass doors to the baggage collection point.

A uniformed official glanced through Edwin's passport and enquired whether it was his first visit to Gibraltar. Edwin confirmed that it was and the man said that he hoped that he would enjoy his stay. Continuing on through a short corridor Edwin found himself stepping outside into a small parking area in front of the terminal building where a throng of people had gathered as they awaited others to emerge. He asked a smartly dressed elderly gentleman if it was far to the centre of town.

"No, it's not far," he replied, in a somewhat quaint version of English with a heavy Mediterranean accent of some kind or another, "You can walk it in maybe twenty minutes or so or take a bus or take a taxi."

"If it is only twenty minutes I'll walk," said Edwin, "Which direction is it?"

"Go over that way," said the man, pointing in the direction of the Rock, "You must first cross the runway and then when you come to a roundabout you keep going straight on and afterwards you pass by Laguna Estate then there's a pathway off to the left which takes you through Landport Tunnel into the centre of Gibraltar."

"Thank you," replied Edwin, "and once I get there do you know of any inexpensive accommodation like a hostel or something?"

"There aren't any hostels in Gibraltar but there are a few hotels," said the man. "The Victoria Hotel on Main Street is probably going to be the most economic. There's also the Holiday Inn but that's a bit more pricey and The Rock Hotel even more so – No, the Victoria Hotel on Main Street is probably your best bet – either that or the Montarik Hotel, which is also on Main Street."

"What about other parts of Gibraltar?" asked Edwin "Is there accommodation anywhere else?"

"No, not really," said the man, "I mean there's the Caletta Palace Hotel on the other side of the Rock in Catalan Bay but it wouldn't be cheaper than what you'll find in Main Street."

"Then is looks like it's going to be Main Street," said Edwin, "Thanks a lot for your help."

"You're welcome," replied the man, "It's not for nothing that I'm with the Gibraltar Tourist Office."

With suitcase in hand and shoulder bag swinging at his side, Edwin started the trek into town thinking how strange it was to be walking across the runway that his flight had just landed on. There were warning signs that displayed a selection of items of litter that were potentially hazardous to aircraft, amongst them bottle tops, cans, broken glass, pieces of string and cigarette packets. Pedestrians were requested to walk across the runway within two white lines on either side of the road. A gentle flow of traffic passed through its middle.

Across the runway and on the other side of the road stood a large delta-winged military aircraft belonging to the RAF and serving as a memorial to the role that Gibraltar had played in both world wars. A signpost indicated the street to be called Winston Churchill Avenue. Edwin marvelled at the impressive mass of the Rock which towered up in front of him. Parts of it were covered in green vegetation and yet there were very few buildings actually on it. The town seemed to be situated alongside its base. Passing some kind of a football ground, he reached the roundabout and the start of a residential area of some rather unattractive looking apartment blocks. They seemed to be in need of a lick of paint and the pavements beneath were caked in grime and strewn with rubbish. It was hardly the most endearing sight. In bold lettered signs, each apartment block had unusual sounding English names such as Smith Dorrien, Varryl Begg and Referendum House. The road then divided into three different directions and Edwin was unsure which one the man had meant him to take. In the absence of anyone to ask, he took pot luck. At least it was only seven thirty and still light. The road looped and passed under a road bridge and to an area of sturdy looking thick grey stone city walls which branched off in four directions and provided the historical evidence of Gibraltar's heavy fortifications. Many of the walls had names painted on them like labels in an open-air museum. There was West Place of Arms and Waterport Casemates and he now stood alongside North Bastion. He had somehow missed the tunnel entrance to the town but on asking a lady at a bus stop the whereabouts of Main Street, she told him that if he went through one of the twin archways of Grand Casemates Gate just off to his left, he would arrive at one end of it.

Edwin found himself in a triangular shaped car park alongside an old military looking grey building that had arc-shaped windows and balconies with metal railings. Directly ahead of him was the beginning of Gibraltar's long narrow shopping street known as Main Street. Although the shops were closed plenty of people were still out and about. There were young ladies wearing fashionable attire with large dangling earrings as well as some smartly dressed men and elderly couples who greeted each other. Edwin arrived at the front entrance of the Victoria Hotel, which was certainly unpretentious if not rather drab looking. However, on a limited budget cost was going to be the overriding factor and if this was going to be the cheapest place in town, he'd better settle for it. On entering he was told that a room was available on the second floor and that, without breakfast, the rate would be six pounds per night. It was more that Edwin had expected and about four times as much as in Spain but, based on the information available, it seemed unlikely that he would find any immediate alternative accommodation. He booked the room for seven nights and determined to find a job and somewhere to live within that short time scale. Unpacking his suitcase, he hung up his suit and shirts in the room's built in wardrobe and, after freshening himself with a shower and a change of clothing, his tiredness disappeared and he felt renewed optimism in the realisation that he had finally arrived at his destination.

He explored the rest of the small hotel. In the stairwell, there had been a sign pointing up to a roof garden, which conjured up memories of the roof garden on top of the YMCA in Hong Kong with its outstanding views across the harbour and glasses of iced lemon tea with syrup. Unfortunately, however, there was no comparison. The roof garden on top of the Victoria Hotel was tiny, scruffy and deserted. It was equipped with a dirty white plastic table and a broken chair and commanded no particular view at all other than the roofs of neighbouring buildings and a profusion of television aerials and washing lines. He descended the stairs again and entered the lounge cum dining room on the first floor. Four elderly people were watching a black and white television set that was suspended from the ceiling. The programme was an episode of 'The Avengers' in English and Edwin realised it to be the output of the Gibraltar Broadcasting Corporation. He gave the other guests a brief nod, sat himself down, lit a cigarette, and watched the remaining minutes of the programme. What happened at the end of the programme was a bit of a shock. It was a news bulletin so amateurishly done as to be an embarrassment. A static graphic that said 'News' remained on the screen accompanied by silence for at the best part of a minute then a burst of musical theme eventually broke through after which nothing else happened. Finally a badly lit female newsreader appeared and was seen to be reading something but unfortunately her microphone hadn't been selected so although her lips were moving there was no sound. After several seconds worth of that somebody must have found the fader as viewers were then treated to her voice. And what a voice it was. In an inexpressive and unimpressive monotone the poor soul was battling her way through the content of the news bulletin and stumbling over so many words as she went. On the occasions that she managed to look up at the camera she then had difficulty in finding her place in the script when she looked down again and twice repeated the same sentence. Interestingly enough, the other people watching with Edwin didn't seem to notice anything out the ordinary with such a presentation style. Instead their occasional comments related purely to the content of the bulletin. Three more Royal Navy frigates would dock tomorrow morning and an American cruise ship would be arriving for a 24 hour visit on Saturday. When the news summary finally ground to a halt Edwin was left with mixed feelings about what he'd seen. Clearly the television service was run on a shoestring budget for its output to have looked like that and yet, thinking on the positive side, with his professional background and expertise he would have little difficulty in helping them raise their production standards considerably. He intended to pay them a visit first thing in the morning.

For the rest of the evening he went out for a brief look around the town area of Gibraltar and to see if there was anywhere still open where he might get some sort of a meal. Although it was now dark, it was pleasantly warm outside and there were still many people around. Turning right he walked further along Main Street, where he encountered an array of small shops with window displays of electrical goods, cameras, cassette players, radios, watches as well as bottles of spirits and cigarettes and souvenirs. Everything was written in English and priced in pounds and pence.

He passed a couple of pubs both of which had the appearance of authentic English pubs and he also saw the Montarik Hotel whose front entrance was located in a short cul-de-sac with the dubious sounding name of Bedlam Court. There were branches of Barclay's Bank, a newsagent, a post office, a Lipton's food store, perfume shops, boutiques, tailors, chemists and still more of the shops that sold electrical goods and cameras. Continuing along Main Street he passed a central square and the front of a cathedral. After that were the law courts and the guarded residence of the Governor's House. A takeaway food outlet was located along the next stretch of pavement and Edwin stopped off and bought a steak and kidney pie and chips which he proceeded to eat as he walked. He came to a library and still more of the electrical goods shops which seemed to be something of a recurring theme. Passing under an archway he came to the end of Main Street. Here the road divided and a large block of flats stood out in front of him whilst the silhouette of the Rock was visible over to his left. It seemed a logical place to turn around. No doubt he would be able to explore beyond that point during the course of the next few days.

Although tired he had every intention of stopping off at a couple of the pubs on the way back to capture the general atmosphere of the place. The Angry Friar was the first of such hostelries and a pint of keg bitter in Gibraltar proved to be considerably cheaper than back in England and no tax on cigarettes meant that they too were a fraction of the price. The barmaid was not from Gibraltar but Manchester.

Another Gibraltar pub appropriately called The Rock was located on one side of the square that he'd passed earlier. Inside five men were conversing with each other in Spanish and at first Edwin assumed them to be Spaniards. That notion came to an abrupt halt when they suddenly switched to speaking to each other in impeccable English. The men all looked Mediterranean yet clearly they spoke freely in both languages and it dawned on Edwin that these were the real live Gibraltarians. He lingered a little longer and discovered that not only did they speak both languages but they possessed a remarkable ability to switch from one to the other often in mid-sentence and possibly quite unconsciously. A short spectacled man with a shiny bald head was heard to say.

"Lo que pasa es si ellos no quieren jugar con nosotros then we are going to have to beat them at their own game!"

A thin man with a moustache replied, "Si pero tenemos que continue to look on the bright side, aunque todavia hemos esperado bastante, it's still going to work out in our favour at the end of the day, no?"

"Pero, the thing is," continued the first man, "Quanto tiempo se necesita? I mean, that's the key question!"

A large third man intervened, "We'll find out the answer to that out in the morning. El tiene que decirnos exactamente lo que pasa mañana por la mañana, so we'll all know it then – one way or the other."

And so the conversation continued. Edwin listened for a while before gulping down the remainder of his drink and continuing back along Main Street. On the way he glanced up a side street called Bell Lane and on seeing the entrance to yet another pub called The Aragon he thought that he might as well give that a quick visit too. In contrast to the previous place everybody here seemed to be expats and there was little to suggest that he wasn't standing in the saloon bar of a pub in an English provincial town. The landlord and landlady were from Essex and from the snippets of conversation he gleaned that all of the other customers were people originally from the United Kingdom but who now resided permanently in Gibraltar.

His thoughts drifted to his journey down and he wondered how Louise was getting on over in Spain. Between gulps of beer Edwin yawned gently and realised that his accumulated lack of sleep was beginning to catch up on him. It was time to call it a day. Outside there were still people walking up and down Main Street and as he neared the Victoria Hotel he saw a small open-air drinks outlet called Lotti's Bar with its front counter facing out to the pavement. He hesitated. Oh, what the hell, he thought, one for the road! After all, he needed to celebrate the fact that he'd finally arrived in Gibraltar.

"You've just in time before closing," said the middle-aged lady with a heavy Russian accent behind the bar.

"Er, fine," said Edwin, handing over the money and taking the pint of beer from her.

He glanced at the wall clock behind her and saw that it was twelve minutes to ten. Turning to a man standing next to him he asked, "What time do the pubs shut here?"

"Ten o'clock," he replied, "but unlike the UK, there's no such thing in Gib as 'drinking up time'. Theoretically you are not even supposed to have a glass of alcohol in your hand when the clock strikes ten."

"Then I suppose I can understand what she was rattling on about," said Edwin nodding in the direction of the barmaid.

"Oh, Lotti? Yeah, right bloody character she is!" he said, "but it's her livelihood and she wants to keep her licence. Have you just arrived in on the flight from London?"

"No, I came in on the flight from Tangiers," said Edwin, "What about yourself?"

"I've lived here in Gibraltar for the past couple of years," he said, "I work down at the docks."

"Well, I'm hoping to find some kind of work and live out here for a while," said Edwin, "What do you make of the place?"

"It's tiny but the climate's good and the booze is cheap so what more can a man want? – apart from a good woman that is and some of the Gibo chicks aren't too bad either – except that most of them prefer to mix with Gibo blokes rather than we Brits," he said.

"But surely they are British as well," said Edwin.

"True," said the man, "and extremely patriotic at that. But if you stick around long enough, you'll see that they tend to live in a clique and there's a kind of 'them and us' mentality that exists as a barrier which is bit of a bugger."

Both of them finished their drinks within the allocated time and handed their glasses in. The man introduced himself as Tom and said that Edwin could find him at this outdoor drinking establishment shortly before closing time on most nights of the week. Edwin returned to his hotel room and was soon asleep.

THE FOLLOWING MORNING BRIGHT sunshine poured in through the thin flimsy curtains of Edwin's window at the Victoria Hotel. He had slept soundly and felt revitalised and ready to face the task that lay ahead. After a morning shower he put on suit and tie and descended to the lounge where he purchased a mug of tea. Breakfast could wait. It was a Friday, which meant that he'd have to cram as much into the day as he possibly could because offices would be closed over the weekend. The acoustics of the lounge were such that they amplified everything anyone said. An elderly gentleman seated at the far end of the table with a plate of bacon, eggs and sausage was addressing another man who had just entered.

"Good morning, Mr Reece," he said, somewhat knowingly and deliberately and in a heavy accent that echoed throughout the room.

"Good morning to you Mr Lopez," boomed back the reply, "I say, have you seen Sir Joshua's comments in today's Chronicle?"

"Not yet. What's the old boy up to now?"

Edwin thought everything sounded dreadfully old fashioned. Nevertheless if the Chronicle happened to be Gibraltar's daily newspaper, he thought he'd better get his own copy as a starting point to try and see what made the place tick. He left the two old men to get on with their British breakfast and stepping outside onto Main Street. It looked different in daylight. Shops were already open and people were passing by in both directions. There were smartly dressed businessmen, children in school uniforms, mums wheeling pushchairs, a small handful of tourists and a group of lads from the Royal Navy who had stepped ashore that morning. The numerous electrical goods shops, which he noticed all seemed to be run by Indian proprietors, had few customers. Occasionally Moroccan ladies passed by in their long distinctive dresses and headwear. The place had a cosmopolitan atmosphere about it.

Apart from the people, the external appearance of many of the buildings, despite being of a fine colonial style of architecture, looked run down and shabby with peeling paintwork of faded colours. Grey stone pavements that were both high and narrow were shiny with wear and tear and the road itself was in desperate need of resurfacing. Edwin walked back along the way that he had first entered the town's centre and on arriving at the car park he found a kiosk selling newspapers. He purchased the day's edition of the 'Gibraltar Chronicle' and sat down on a nearby bench to read it. It wasn't so much a newspaper as a newssheet. Printed on both sides of one single piece of paper it was folded in half in its middle so as to create the sum total of four pages of the latest news, views and comment about matters of importance at home and abroad for the daily consumption of the British colony of Gibraltar's population of thirty thousand. Much of the content was dedicated to local politics into which a certain anti-Spanish sentiment had been thrown in for good measure. On the back page were two short columns of classified advertisements from which Edwin could begin to gauge the price of rented accommodation and local incomes. That ratio didn't look at all promising in this particular edition.

Having digested the newspaper in approximately seven minutes flat, Edwin folded it into quarters and put it in his pocket. A young lady happened to be walking past and he asked her the whereabouts of the Gibraltar Broadcasting Corporation.

"GBC?" she said, "It's down in Wellington Front."

"Is that anywhere near here?" he asked.

'"It's not so very far away," she said, in an almost sing-song voice, whilst pointing along the road, "You go up Main Street and after you pass the Piazza you just keep on going then take the third turning off to your right. There's the millinery shop on the corner and it leads you through to Cathedral Square. On the far side of that there's a pathway that goes to Wellington Front."

"Thank you," said Edwin, as much fascinated by her accent and her strikingly good looks as in trying to memorize the directions. He'd almost been tempted to say "And please could I meet up with you later?" but when he spotted her wedding ring he was glad that he hadn't.

The problem with Main Street, thought Edwin, was that it looked pretty much the same from one end to the other. At least, that was how it seemed to him. Possibly people who lived in the place might think otherwise and could maybe distinguish one camera and electrical goods shop from another. He understood Gibraltar to be a duty free port and he supposed that to be the reason for the abundance of such stores that specialised in the same sort of thing. Maybe it was only when large passenger liners came in that they did any real trade at all. On reaching the central square where he had been the evening before he stopped to read a wall plaque which indicated that the building to the front was the House of Assembly, Gibraltar's very own political debating chamber. He had just been reading about some of the recent goings on in there in his copy of the Gibraltar Chronicle. He passed under its arched frontage to take a look at an open square located behind but found that it offered little more than a dried-up fountain in a concreted area highlighted by a public toilet block and a snack kiosk. On the ground some mosaic patterns depicting various military regiments were in a sorry state of disrepair. But if nothing else the square was a suntrap. It was a hot day with brilliant sunshine and a cloudless blue sky above.

Stepping back into the shade again Edwin continued to make his way along Main Street. He located the turn off that the lady had described. It led past a Jewish School and down one side of the Bristol Hotel before joining the enclosed square of a playground for children around which traffic flowed. The presence of an Anglican Church building with horseshoe shaped arches confirmed this as being Cathedral Square. He walked around it to the pathway on its far side. The route passed still more city walls and came to a small courtyard and some old military looking stores built into the wall itself. A black and white painted sign indicated the place to be Wellington Front. As Edwin crossed the uneven stone yard towards a door in the corner a tall man with a thick moustache emerged from it. Edwin asked him if the building housed the television service of the Gibraltar Broadcasting Corporation.

'Yes, it does,' confirmed the man, 'I am one of its engineers. How can I help?'

'I'm pleased to meet you,' said Edwin, 'I have just arrived here in Gibraltar. I have a number of years television experience working with the New Zealand Broadcasting Corporation and with Rediffusion Television in Hong Kong mainly on the production and presentation sides of things. I am wondering if somebody might be available with whom I could discuss any work possibilities."

The man shook his head. "There's no one here at present," he said, "but I can tell you that we have absolutely no vacancies at all. None whatsoever"

The blunt answer hit Edwin hard. Had he made his trek all this way to the southern tip of Europe simply to receive outright rejection? Maybe he should re-phrase things.

"I happened to watch your news programme last night and feel confident that I could contribute a lot to that particular production as well as to the station's overall operation in general," continued Edwin.

"Let me explain," said the man, "We are a small organisation with our own unique identity and a tiny budget and I'm afraid that we are not in a position to be able to take on any additional staff. It's as simple as that."

"Well I wonder if there's someone who works in programme production with whom I could at least discuss such things" pleaded Edwin, "I mean, I could come back again this afternoon, if that would be more convenient."

"I'm afraid that wouldn't be any good. We have to abide by our policy," replied the man, as he continued to walk away from the building.

Edwin felt stunned.

"I could bring a lot of expertise to the service," said Edwin.

"You could try the forces network, BFBS," replied the man, "they're also here in Gibraltar."

"Fine, but they're radio, whereas my background and experience is in television," said Edwin.

The man shrugged his shoulders. "I'm sorry, I can't help you," he said.

They came out of the courtyard and re-joined the pathway where they parted company, in opposite directions.

Edwin was more surprised than dejected by the unfortunate outcome of the encounter. After all, he reasoned, the Gibraltar Broadcasting Corporation was hardly in the same league of the mainstream broadcasters of other parts of the world. What he'd seen of their output the evening before had been downright amateurish. It was in need of a complete overhaul and yet despite that, his offer to lend a helping hand had been declined. The conversation was still ringing in his ears. Had he been too pushy? He wondered. No, he didn't think so. Had he come across as arrogant? He didn't think that either. He had been perfectly reasonable and polite throughout but for whatever reasons the man had put up barriers from the word go.

It meant that Edwin now faced the slightly different problem of looking for some other kind of work in Gibraltar if he wished to remain there. What's more, on dwindling funds, he had allowed himself just seven days in which to find a job. He was already into day one and the weekend would effectively take care of two more days. The pathway made an abrupt turn to the left and he found himself joining Main Street once again although down at its far end. He was next to the archway that he'd walked to the evening before. There seemed to be no escaping Main Street. He wandered back along its entire length deep in thought. If there was to be no opportunity with the television station what other opportunities might there be? So far he'd seen little more than shops and, having already done his brief stint as a shop assistant in Winchester, the retail experience wasn't exactly something that he had any particular desire to return to. Besides which, Gibraltar's shops were so deserted that it was hard to see how some of them made a living and doubtful if there would be any vacancies. Edwin was similarly dismissive of bar work. He had freed himself from the daily grind of that. The problem, however, was that the entire length of Main Street seemed to consist of nothing other than shops and pubs. He paused for an omelette sandwich and a cup of tea at a cafeteria and decided to return to his hotel, get changed out of his suit and use the rest of the day to thoroughly explore Gibraltar and see what else it might have to offer.

Twenty minutes later, dressed in a short-sleeved shirt and casual trousers, Edwin left the Victoria Hotel once again. Determined to avoid the predictability of Main Street, he set off along a narrow road that branched off it opposite called Engineer Lane. 'Engineer Lane?' he thought, obviously military and nothing to do that unhelpful broadcasting engineer that he'd met that morning. He passed the shuttered window of Lotti's Bar, which was closed during the daytime. The narrow road began to rise between some old and run-down looking blocks of flats with dark and dingy entrance passages that ran between them. Beneath such dwellings were occasional shops of the more essential and non-tourist variety including a grocery shop, a shoe shop, a greengrocer, a stationers and a hardware shop. There was also another four pubs. A large derelict building that had once been a theatre took up a prominent position to the right whilst off to the left was a flight of stone steps. Edwin figured that he might as well climb them because so far everything that he'd seen of Gibraltar was from a low-levelled vantage point and if he could somehow get higher up, he would be able to get some kind of an overview and work out the layout of the place.

He didn't count the number of steps but they went up for some considerable distance.

He couldn't understand why the buildings he passed were so badly neglected and in such a state of shabbiness and disrepair. Was everybody so poverty stricken that they couldn't at least afford a pot of exterior wall paint? Mind you, there was some interesting graffiti on the way up. People had written pro-British slogans all over the place. Sentiments such as 'Born British, Die British' and large union jacks had been painted on the walls. Edwin noted how different that was to anything that he'd ever seen in other places, where things like 'Yanks go home' or 'Punch a Pommie a day.' tended to prevail. For one mischievous moment he wondered what the local reaction would be if someone were to paint 'Gibraltar Español' on one of the walls.

His legs felt like jelly by the time he'd reached the top step as he hadn't used such muscles for ages and in his enthusiasm he'd come up rather too fast. It left him out of breath and wheezing slightly. However, when he stopped and turned around, his efforts were rewarded with a spectacular view out over the deep blue sea of the Bay of Gibraltar and across to Spain on its other side. He still couldn't see which part of Gibraltar was physically connected to Spain but no doubt he would discover that in due course. A narrow road ran across the top of the steps. It was lined with residential apartment blocks that obscured his view of the Rock. Edwin hoped that if he turned to the right it would lead higher still but, after walking for ten minutes, he noticed that, if anything, the road was gradually descending. Nevertheless, between gaps in the buildings he was able to catch an occasional glimpse of the near side the Rock although there didn't appear to be any access points. The road dropped down further still and eventually he arrived back at a large block of flats he'd seen on the previous evening and he realised that he was just beyond the archway at the far end of Main Street once again. There was still no escaping Main Street. An overgrown triangle of parkland littered with rubbish turned out to be a small cemetery. Edwin saw an English couple taking photographs there which struck him as being a bit bizarre. It was only when he spoke with them that he realised the significance of the place. It was called Trafalgar Cemetery and was a place where many of those who were killed in the Battle of Trafalgar lay buried.

"It's a shame they don't look after it properly," said the man, pointing to the array of beer cans, bottles and accumulated rubbish amongst all the overgrown weeds.

"It seems to me that rather a lot of Gibraltar is scruffy and uncared for," said Edwin, "Have you any idea why it's like that?"

"If you ask the locals they'll simply blame Franco for having shut the frontier and denied them the workforce of Spaniards who used to come in on a daily basis to carry out the manual tasks," he said.

"Oh, so that's it," said Edwin, "But in the absence of those Spanish workers, why can't they do such things themselves?"

"It's beneath their dignity," he chuckled, "They're a proud people and that's why they've been trying to recruit the Moroccans to fill those kinds of jobs – the kinds of jobs that the Gibraltarians don't want to do, you know what I mean?"

Edwin continued his walk around a central block of apartments and found the Queen's Hotel alongside the Queen's cinema as well as his first proper view of the side elevation of the Rock. But the main thing that grabbed his attention was the ground station for two dark red cable cars that were transporting passengers to and from the top of the Rock. Enquiries revealed that it was possible to get a one-way ticket up and then walk back down via a zigzag of roadways.

The views from the top of the Rock of Gibraltar were breathtaking even though public access was denied to a large area that belonged to the Ministry of Defence. Edwin could see the geographical importance of Gibraltar as a military base that guarded the mouth to the Mediterranean. Across on the far side of the straits was a clear view of the mountains of Morocco and looking back in the opposite direction mainland Spain was now viewable on both sides of the Rock's central ridge.

One end of the airport's runway poked out from behind an upper part of the Rock and Edwin realised that the land connection between Gibraltar and Spain must be somewhere just beyond that. Pleased at having successfully completed such reconnaissance work he wandered across to another viewing point which looked right over a top edge and down its steep side onto a small community below. Most of that far side of the Rock was covered with sheets of corrugated iron. Another sightseer explained it to be the water catchment area. Becoming better informed by the minute, Edwin then began a pleasant downhill stroll through a series of leafy narrow lanes, stopping briefly at a halfway point to watch some Barbary apes, the so-called monkeys of Gibraltar, mingling with a small group of tourists. The view from there looked out above the town's rooftops and towards the docks which now had a line of four grey Royal Navy battleships.

As he continued the descent, Edwin's thoughts returned to the task that lay ahead. He hadn't regretted the afternoon trip up the Rock even if had used up valuable job hunting time. The main problem was in not knowing what opportunities might be available. If the primitive Gibraltar Broadcasting Corporation was so short-sighted that it had no inclination to take him on, even if he was willing to work for a pittance, was it still worth his while trying to live in Gibraltar at all? Such thoughts had been nagging him for several hours and there was no easy answer. He certainly wasn't keen on the idea of returning to England. Yet, from what he had seen of the place so far, Gibraltar was small and perhaps too limited. He supposed that he would just have to take everything in his stride and see what arose over the next few days

The lane ended at a junction with a main road and he turned in the direction of the town. A group of British soldiers were jogging along the pavement on the other side. Edwin passed a casino and a convent school as well as the Rock Hotel set back in pleasant garden surroundings. Crossing the road he then walked through some public gardens that took him back to where he had started at the bottom of the cable car and at the far end of the inevitable Main Street.

Taking a detour at the central square known as the Piazza and the red brick building of the police station he entered a back street that ran parallel to Main Street called Irish Town. Pubs on either side were rowdy and packed chock-a-bloc full of young men with short haircuts downing pint after pint of draught beer like nobody's business amidst raucous laughter. Edwin realised that this must be the standard occurrence every time Royal Navy vessels stopped off in Gibraltar as their first port of call.

THE ENGLISH STYLE COD and chips were sprinkled generously with salt, saturated in vinegar and wrapped up in white paper by a man with a Geordie accent at the Main Street takeaway shop. It had seemed to be the best choice for an economical meal. The few restaurants in Gibraltar had looked decidedly overpriced and, although some pubs displayed signs indicating the availability of bar snacks, there was no way that Edwin would have been willing to battle his way through the crowds of sweaty bodies of his semi-intoxicated fellow countrymen of the Royal Navy in order to get served.

This time, rather than eat as he walked, Edwin carried the warm package with him up a side street where he discovered not only the whereabouts of the Holiday Inn but also a convenient wooden bench that overlooked it. It was a relief to sit down and he realised that he'd been on his feet for the past seven hours. He savoured the nutritional delights of his evening meal eaten direct from its wrapper and, once finished, crumpled the paper into a ball and projected it into a conveniently located litterbin with surprising accuracy.

He remained seated on that bench for some considerable time. People could be seen passing in and out of the front entrance to the Holiday Inn but because they all looked like tourists he thought there wasn't be much point in going in there in the hope of meeting somebody who could offer him a job in Gibraltar. Eventually he got up and took a look around the immediate vicinity. A white building with black doors across the narrow road behind him turned out to be the offices of the Gibraltar Chronicle and the fine, old, if somewhat dilapidated building next door was signposted as being the Garrison Library. A steep walkway of steps ran up its side. The disused theatre that he'd seen earlier stood at the far end of the small untidy square in front of him. Edwin could sense that at some stage in its historical past Gibraltar had once had all the ingredients of a sophisticated outpost of the British Empire but that, since those glorious days, the place had been so severely neglected as to give it an overriding impression of an uncared for, run-down, dump of a place. He descended some grey stone steps strewn with litter and dog's muck and, passing the entrance of a crowded pub called The Canon, he came back out onto Main Street once again. Maybe somebody should attempt to write a guidebook entitled 'A thousand-and-one walks in Gibraltar avoiding Main Street.' He could certainly use a copy.

Whilst freshening himself up with a warm shower at the Victoria Hotel he debated what to get up to for the remainder of the evening. Pubs were the obvious social life in Gibraltar although he'd need to find one that wasn't graced with the presence of the Royal Navy. With that in mind he retraced his steps to where he had bought his newspaper that morning and then followed a flow of pedestrians to a pathway along one side of an old military building which led through a tunnel. Realising that it must be the other end of where he had been directed to when he had first arrived in Gibraltar he stopped to read a placard that described the tunnelled entrance as once having been the only entrance to Gibraltar by land. The path passed a heavily guarded military enclosure before coming out at the same rather grotty estate of blocks of flats that he'd first encountered on his way in from the airport.

Edwin turned into one of the side streets where opposite the metal meshed fence of a school playground he came across a bar that was neither rowdy nor crowded. The inside was of a large rectangular shape with a pool table at one end, a television set showing a Spanish channel at the other and a portrait of Her Majesty the Queen on the wall halfway down. It was tiled throughout and had several small tables at which sat a handful of customers. Four people stood drinking at the bar and the overweight barmaid was conversing with two of them in Spanish. She turned to serve Edwin and switched into English for the occasion.

"Yes, love, what can I get you?" she asked.

"I'd like a pint of beer please," he said, surveying the row of pumps to see what was on offer.

"Well we've got Courage, Whitbread, Guinness or Heineken," she said.

"Courage would do nicely," said Edwin, "Oh, and maybe a small scotch and water to go with it."

The drinks were served and Edwin was pleased to note that the amount charged was about a third of what it would have been in England. Although his legs still ached from the day's walking, he remained standing alongside the bar as his posture of choice. A middle-aged couple seated at one of the adjacent tables smiled up at him and the landlady resumed her conversation in Spanish.

An elderly man next to Edwin turned and addressed him in broken English.

"Gibraltar – it's small – but it's nice place!"

Edwin nodded.

"No like over there in Spain," continued the man, "Over there can't trust nobody."

'When was the last time that you were able to go over there?' asked Edwin.

"Long time ago pero even they open frontier tomorrow there's no way I go Spain now. Never!" he said.

Edwin felt like saying how much he loved Spain but thought better of it.

The man continued, "Spanish people no good!"

Edwin glanced across at the couple at the table and the lady caught his eye and tried to elaborate, "The thing is," she explained, "By their actions the Spanish have created this feeling of animosity towards them."

"Because they closed the border?" asked Edwin.

"Yes," she replied, "but also by constantly claiming the Rock of Gibraltar to be theirs. No matter what people may say, it all comes back to the same thing. We don't want to lose our hometown, where we were born. It's simple." She smiled.

Her husband added, "Actually we still have many friends in Spain but we can't trust the Spanish Government at the other end. They want Gibraltar. They're after Gibraltar. They're not going to get it."

"Is there any possibility of the frontier with Spain ever being reopened?" asked Edwin.

"It depends on the way it's negotiated," he replied, "but on the issue of sovereignty there's no room for any negotiation. We are British. We want to stay British and as long as that's the will of the people everybody has to respect that."

Edwin thought how interesting it was to hear such sentiments being expressed by people who externally looked completely Spanish themselves but he thought it best not to probe further on such a delicate observation. Instead, he got the landlady's attention and ordered another pint.

"Same again, dear?" she asked, taking his glass.

"Yes please," he replied, "although just the beer this time."

"Are you from Australia?" she asked.

"No, England," he replied.

"Oh, it's just that I thought I detected an accent," she said.

"It's a New Zealand accent," he said, "I lived out there for several years."

"I knew it was from somewhere around there," she said, "The thing is when I lived in London I used to work with people who came from down under and I got so used to the way that they spoke that I can still detect it to this day."

She drew off the pint of beer and placed it on the bar in front of him.

"How long were you in London?" he asked as he handed her a red Gibraltar pound note that had been included in his change at the fish and chip shop.

"Three years," she replied. "And I enjoyed every minute no matter how much I missed Gibraltar. What about you? Are you here on a visit?"

"Well, I arrived in Gibraltar only last night. This is my first full day here. I'd quite like to stay for a while but to do so I'm going to have to find some work in a hurry."

"How come if this is your first day in Gibraltar you've already managed to find your way to my bar!" she chuckled and then, for the benefit of the other customers, repeated it in Spanish.

'Mira, este señor. Es su primero día en Gibraltar y todavía ha encontrado nosotros aquí en nuestro bar!'

They nodded their approval and Edwin couldn't resist adding, "Es que siempre cuando se llega en un país nuevo se tiene que buscar los sitios mejores!"

"Pero mira como habla!" exclaimed the landlady, "So you can also speak Spanish!"

"De vez en cuando," said Edwin.

The elderly man at the bar offered him a cigarette and the lady at the table advised him that if he was looking for work in Gibraltar the best place to go was the Employment Office in College Lane which would be open on Monday morning. Edwin thanked her for such useful information and stayed on for a third pint of beer. Then seeing that it was already past nine o'clock he bade everyone goodnight and began to make his was back into town. He had it in mind to stop off at Lotti's Bar for a final drink and to see whether Tom the dockworker was there.

When he arrived back though Landport Tunnel and onto Main Street it was still bustling with the Royal Navy. Pubs on both sides of the road were jam packed with loud merrymakers. A group of them passed him by, singing in unison at the tops of their voices,

'Auntie Mary had a canary,
Up the leg of her drawers,
When she farted, it departed,
To a round of applause!'

Turning into the beginning of Engineer Lane, Lotti's Bar had clearly been doing a good trade and a small crowd was gathered along the pavement. Tom was there and at the head of the queue. He spotted Edwin and indicated that he would get him a drink too. They then found a window ledge on which to perch their glasses and Edwin related some of the day's events beginning with the disappointment at the Gibraltar Broadcasting Corporation.

Tom said, "To be quite honest, it doesn't really surprise me. There are some Gibos who want to do things their way, no matter how cock-eyed it may be. They almost resent the idea of anybody coming in with a bit of expertise."

"Why should that be?" asked Edwin.

"A lot of it boils down to the fact that they prefer to look after their own," said Tom. "Gibraltar is such a small place that they'd rather have it badly run entirely by locals than have us lot come down and show them how to do it whilst breathing down their necks.

"But the Gibraltarians seem friendly enough people," said Edwin, "I can't see why everybody can't work hand in hand and learn new things as they go."

"Well, some of them do but others are more stubborn," he said.

"How did you get your job out here?" asked Edwin.

"My situation's a bit different," he explained. "I was hired by a company in the UK and the package included accommodation in a place called Ocean Heights for me and three other workmates."

"Oh, I walked past that building earlier on," said Edwin.

"One of the problems is that the locals regard us as people who are here today and gone tomorrow whereas they are the ones who are going to remain here for a lifetime," said Tom, "so you'll sometimes find that a lot of it is like a closed shop. If you're a Gibraltarian or perhaps married to a Gibraltarian, you're in with a fighting chance. If you're not, then nine times out of ten, they just don't want to know," he said.

"I seem to be forever coming up against a closed shop of one sort or another. From what you say, I think I'd better marry a Gibraltarian," said Edwin.

"That would certainly be your short-cut to a job with their local television service," he said, "But make sure she's got loads of money! There's a chronic housing shortage in Gibraltar and many newlyweds end up living with their in-laws!"

"And how great would that be?" wondered Edwin, "But there's something else that I don't understand. They keep going on about being anti-Spanish yet to all intents and purposes they seem to be a bunch of people of Spanish origin who for one reason or another are pretending to be British."

"It took me a while to figure that out myself," said Tom, "If you look at them, most Gibraltarians have olive skin and a Latin appearance and because Spain is so near and because they speak Spanish domestically, it's easy to fall into the trap of thinking them to be what you just said. But if you dig a little deeper into their origins you'll find that most of them are the descendents of Mediterranean trading folk, the majority of whom came from Genoa in Italy – hence their Latin features," he said.

"I see," said Edwin, "So it's essentially a British colony full of Italians!"

"That's one way of putting it," said Tom,' "But, yes, if you look down a list of Gibraltar surnames many are names such as Valerino, Bossano, Veneroni, Caruana, or Saccone and so forth – and yet those are all Italian names not Spanish. They even call that main square by the Italian word, Piazza, rather than the Spanish word, Plaza."

"That's interesting," said Edwin.

"Mind you, such trading people sailed in from other places too," said Tom. "There were a fair few Maltese and Portuguese amongst them, then there was an influx of Jews and, of course, down through the years there's been intermarriage with both the British and in some cases the Spanish. On top of that you've got the Hindu community from India who run the duty free electrical shops and Moroccans as labourers. And that's essentially what makes up the present day population of Gibraltar."

"OK, but who was here when the British first arrived?" asked Edwin.

"Certainly not the ancestors of the present population," he replied. "Gibraltar was just a poorly defended Spanish garrison town and, in 1704, when a joint

British and Dutch fleet sailed in and captured the place it was a complete walkover and the inhabitants simply fled further inland into the neighbouring hills of Spain. It wasn't until the Rock was established as a British outpost that Mediterranean trading people from Genoa and elsewhere began to arrive in their boats and found they could make a living off the backs of the British Military. Only then did they begin to settle here and so although the present day population might have somehow inherited the Rock they were not its original inhabitants at all. But they like to make out that it has always been theirs since the year dot whilst playing the British off against the Spanish."

"I think you've missed your vocation, Tom," said Edwin, "You should have been an historian!"

"Yeah, but the reality of that kind of history might not go down too well around here. Here, let's get in another drink."

They stayed talking whilst the shutters of Lotti's Bar were pulled down.

SATURDAY MORNING IN GIBRALTAR saw a particularly crowded Main Street. The American liner had docked at break of day and its passengers were already on mini-coach tours of points of interest around the Rock or were buying up things in the shops which were suddenly doing a roaring trade. Meanwhile some smartly dressed members of Gibraltar's Jewish community, the men of whom were easily identified by their skullcaps, could be seen making their way to the synagogue. Edwin had gone across the road from his hotel to a Cafeteria called the Capri for a light breakfast. Although it had started off quietly enough, the calm was rudely interrupted when what seemed like half the crew from one of the Royal Navy frigates entered the premises and began to order their bacon butties. Edwin scanned the day's Gibraltar Chronicle whilst sipping his cup of tea. It was another hot day and, in the absence of any job advertisements in the paper, he thought he might as well use the time to explore the remaining parts of Gibraltar. It wasn't his intention to become a tourist but there didn't seem to be much else to do with the weekend. He made his way to a bus stop and boarded an antiquated minibus whose destination was to an area of Gibraltar called Europa Point. It was a twenty-minute ride that passed army barracks, living quarters and a military hospital before finally reaching a lighthouse at Gibraltar's most southerly point.

On the return journey he remained on the bus which, after passing back through the town, looped around to the far side of the Rock and to an area called Catalan Bay. It was a tiny residential community that boasted a small beach, a couple of pubs, a cafeteria, some apartments and a seafront hotel called the Caletta Palace. Edwin recognised it as being the place that he had looked down on from the top of the Rock on the previous day. He now looked upwards beyond the steep face of the water catchment area and was able to work out the point along its top from where he had peered over the edge.

En route back towards the town was another small beach whose far end met the airport's runway. Gibraltarian families were out there in their numbers despite the fact that the strip of sand was covered with rusty metal cans, broken glass and litter. A small accommodation block on the beach called the Mediterranean Hotel had an adjoining shop that advertised Walls Ice Cream, Walls Sausages and Walls Chicken and Mushroom Pies. Walls definitely had the monopoly on Gibraltar's Mediterranean Beach.

That evening, instead of embarking on yet another pub-crawl, Edwin decided to try something a little more upmarket. He put on jacket and tie and went to the Rock Hotel. On arrival he positioned himself on a stool at the bar in the cocktail lounge and enjoyed an evening's conversion with people over a steady flow of drinks served by a Moroccan barman in a dark red uniform. Most of the clientele were Gibraltarians who had booked a table for dinner at what was arguably Gibraltar's most prestigious venue. There were also a number of hotel guests from the United Kingdom.

"Gibraltar provides such a fabulous playground for our forces," said a bald headed man with a red face, "I think it should be renamed Aldershot-on-Sea!"

"Oh, Gerald that's unkind!" said the lady sitting next to him, "There are plenty of other things here besides our military presence."

"All right then," he continued, "How about Weymouth stuck onto the end of Spain?

"Well, at least that shows its British character," she said to laughter.

Another man interjected, "I don't know whether you've been in the centre of town this evening but with the navy in it's more like Portsmouth stuck onto the end of Spain!"

A deeply tanned man in a dark blazer and cream coloured trousers entered through the terrace door and looked on amusedly as the banter continued. He ordered a large gin and tonic and sat on a barstool alongside Edwin.

"Lively in here tonight!" he said.

"It sure is," replied Edwin. "Perhaps it's because it's a Saturday."

"Yes, it's generally the busiest evening of the week," he said.

I take it you live here in Gibraltar," said Edwin.

"Of yes, very much so," said the man, "Let me guess. Are you on the cruise liner?"

"No, I arrived here a few days ago I'm staying at the Victoria Hotel," replied Edwin.

"I see. Well you'll find that Gibraltar is a good place to take a break for a few days," he replied, "I go to the UK quite often and although I enjoy it there I'm always glad to get back to the Rock."

"I suppose it has a certain appeal," said Edwin. "Little by little I'm discovering new things about the place."

"The fact that Gibraltar is British makes everything so easy for visitors from the UK," continued the man, "It's so convenient that everything is in English and that the currency is pounds and pence – like a home from home. We are patriots here and very proud to be British."

"Would you say that the closure of the frontier with Spain has drawn Gibraltarians closer together?" asked Edwin.

"Well, with the frontier closed many families take their holidays in the UK which they enjoy. And regardless of whatever Spain might think about it, we have chosen to remain British. We are pleased to have a strong British military presence which helps safeguard the way of life that we have chosen. I mean, don't get me wrong, I can enjoy the Mediterranean lifestyle of flamenco and sangria just like anyone else but when it comes to important issues whether it's politics, religion, current affairs or whatever, you can tell by the way that I think and the way that I talk that I have a very different view to that of a Spaniard. We are much more British in that respect – which is why we wish to keep our ties with Britain."

A party made up of four couples then appeared from the adjoining lounge. 'Ah there you are Sidney!' said one of them, 'Sorry we're a bit late.'

'That's OK,' said the man with whom Edwin had been speaking. Turning to Edwin he said, 'Enjoy the rest of your stay. It's been nice talking with you but you will excuse me, won't you?'

'Of course,' replied Edwin.

The man departed to the restaurant with his friends.

Edwin finished his drink and ordered another. As he reached for his wallet the barman told him that the man had already paid for it.

"That was very kind of him," said Edwin.

"Well, after all, he is the boss's son," explained the barman.

"Which boss is that?" asked Edwin.

"The boss of this place," he replied. "It's one big family. They own the Rock Hotel, the airline, the travel agents, the cable car, the tour buses and so many things in Gibraltar."

What a lost opportunity, thought Edwin. Perhaps I could have asked him if he knew where I could get hold of some sort of a temporary job.

Edwin remained in the cocktail bar for a couple of hours during which he got into conversation with a group of hotel guests before deciding to call it a day. On his way out through the lounge he noticed a young lady in what appeared to be an air hostess uniform sitting by herself in an armchair. She was studying a clipboard and Edwin couldn't resist speaking to her.

"Are you with GB Airways?" he asked.

"Oh, the uniform – No, it's not an airline," she replied, "I'm a tour guide."

"They actually have such things in Gibraltar?" he asked.

"Yes, of course, why not?" she replied, "We have many tourists visiting Gibraltar."

"I suppose you do. But, I mean, what can you actually do with them in such a small place?" he asked.

"Well first of all we meet and greet them at the airport and transfer them to their hotels and there's an organised schedule of sightseeing throughout the duration of their stay," she said, "and then on their final day we get them back to the airport in time for their flight back to the UK."

Edwin explained that he had recently arrived in Gibraltar and was hoping to find some means of living there.

"Are you staying here at the Rock Hotel?" she asked.

"No, I've just spent a pleasant evening here but I'm actually at the Victoria Hotel on Main Street and will be walking back down there shortly," said Edwin.

"I've got to drive that way myself in a minute or so if you'd like a lift," she said.

"That'd be great," replied Edwin, "If it's anything like it was last night the town centre will be full of the Royal Navy."

"It sometimes gets a bit out of hand on days when the ships are in," she said, "Everybody else just moves back a block or two and leaves the navy to get on with Main Street."

Edwin introduced himself and she told him her name was Sonia.

It was still very warm outside as they descended the front steps of the Rock Hotel to where her car was parked. After the short drive she dropped him off alongside the Piazza in the town centre.

"That was very kind of you," said Edwin. As he opened the car door he hesitated a little and then said, "Look, I don't really know anyone in Gibraltar yet and I wonder if perhaps we could meet up sometime."

"On Tuesday evenings I sometimes sit in the lounge of the Caletta Palace Hotel after work," she smiled, "and you can normally find me there."

"Any particular time?" he asked.

"It depends on the punctuality of the flight arrival but I normally get there at around nine," she replied.

"Then how about this coming Tuesday at nine?" he asked.

"I'll look forward to it," she replied.

EARLY THAT SUNDAY MORNING the ringing of a church bell could be heard through the open windows of the Victoria Hotel. Thank God I'm not religious, thought Edwin as he turned over and snatched another twenty minutes sleep. When eventually he did get up he went out and found Main Street completely deserted. Most of the shops had metal shutters pulled down their fronts.

It was a scorching hot day and he weaved his way through a network of narrow back streets that led by an uphill route to a tower that overlooked the town. It was a Moorish Castle built at the time in the eighth century when Arabs from across the Strait in North Africa had overrun southern Spain. Edwin read a notice explaining that the leader of the conquerors had been a man called Tarik and that the Arabic word 'gibral' meant hill. 'Gibral Tarik' later got contracted to 'Gibraltar.' History had never been Edwin's favourite subject but nowadays whenever he stumbled upon such gems of educational wisdom it was always with a certain fascination. So Gibraltar had been the Arab's first foothold into Spain and yet it was now the British flag that flew on top of the Moorish castle.

Edwin then decided to take a look at the Spanish frontier. Just past the airport the road came to an abrupt halt due to a pair of large metal gates being closed across it. Another British flag flapped gently in the breeze beneath which twenty or so people stood along the length of the closed barrier gazing across into the nation of Spain. A similar closed gate arrangement could be seen a couple of hundred yards further away on the Spanish side where under a red and yellow flag a line of people were looking across to the Gibraltar side. It was a sad spectacle. After observing it for a while he returned to the airport terminal building and as something of an impromptu late breakfast ordered a toasted ham and cheese sandwich and a cup of tea in the cafeteria.

The town centre was uncannily quiet. Edwin overheard someone saying that all four of the Royal Navy vessels had departed from Gibraltar earlier on that day as had the American cruise ship. He strolled through the parallel street of Irish Town. Pubs that had been overflowing with customers during the past few days now looked embarrassingly empty. In a side street, the dark interior of the Bull and Bush had decorative rows of bottles lining its walls, the labels of which were tarnished brown by exposure to the high level of nicotine. Elderly Gibraltarian men sat in a haze of tobacco smoke. The open fronted establishment of The Galleon had no customers at all and its bored looking bar staff sat at a table sharing a large plate of chips. Edwin interrupted them for a Coca-Cola.

The choice for Sunday afternoon seemed either to walk around all day in the heat or to sit around all day in the pubs. He decided to walk out to the dockyards and back. As usual he ended the day at Lotti's bar but on that occasion there was no appearance of Tom.

A SMALL QUEUE HAD formed in front of a counter at the Employment Office in College Lane. It was shortly after nine o'clock on Monday morning and its doors had only just been opened. Due, in part, to the large proportion of civil servant jobs Gibraltar was lucky enough to have almost zero level unemployment and there was no sign of desperation on the faces of those who were looking for jobs.

A clerk invited the next person in the line to step forward and it was the first time that Edwin had ever heard an Anglo-Spanish phrase of "Si, please!" being used. However, by the time he'd reached the head of the queue, the clerk reverted back to "Yes please!" Edwin was asked what kind of work he was looking for. He explained that his background was in television broadcasting but that he would also be happy enough to turn his hand to anything that could offer an immediate start.

"Have you tried GBC?" asked the clerk.

"Yes, but they say that have no vacancies," replied Edwin.

The clerk fanned through a handful of blue coloured cards and removed three of them which he handed to Edwin. "These all have an immediate start," he said.

Edwin thanked him and stepped outside the building before studying them. The three positions were for a sales assistant, a decorator and a barman. He could forget about the decorator job right away because it said 'Must have driving licence' whereas Edwin had never learned to drive. As regards sales assistant or barman they were the same sort of temporary jobs that he'd recently had in England but if considered purely as a means to enable him to stay on in Gibraltar it would be silly to dismiss them out of hand. After all, he thought, beggars can't be choosers and at least he had experience in such areas. He decided to explore both job possibilities.

A middle-aged, pot-bellied, Indian man was the owner of Jobanputra's Emporium which was located half way down Main Street and like so many of the other shops specialised in radios, cassette players, cameras, silk scarves and souvenir pictures of the Rock of Gibraltar. Assuming Edwin to be his first customer of the day the man greeted him with his customary "Good Morning Sir, you're very welcome to take your time looking around and if there's anything you'd like any help with, just let me know."

"Thank you," replied Edwin, "but actually I'm here in response to your vacancy for a sales assistant."

The man facial expression changed. "There is no such vacancy here," he said.

"That's odd," replied Edwin, holding out the card and showing the shop's name and address on it. "The Employment Office seems to think that there is."

"No, no, no" he replied, "That's from long time ago. They couldn't send me anyone with experience so we are bringing another one over from India."

"I've got retail sales experience," said Edwin.

"It's too late," replied the man, "First we tried to find someone here but there was nobody suitable so now we are able to bring someone."

"So is there no vacancy here at all then?" asked Edwin.

"No vacancy," echoed the man.

"It might be a good idea for you to let the Employment Office know," said Edwin, as he departed.

He continued walking down the remaining half of Main Street. The experience highlighted his awareness of the high proportion of Indian run shops. He wondered whether he had inadvertently stumbled upon the secret that enabled such a thing to be possible. Could it be that every time a shop owner needed staff they simply claimed that there was no one suitable for the job and then, through some loophole in the immigration rules, recruited more of their family and friends from India?

Edwin recognised half a dozen faces on Main Street that morning. The wife of the Gibraltarian couple whom he had met in the bar on Friday evening waved to him from across the road. The Moroccan barman from the Rock Hotel was entering the Post Office. The bloke with the Geordie accent who ran the fish and chip shop was carrying a cardboard box full of disposable napkins. The short man with the deeply bronzed face and moustache emerged from one side of the Piazza and the young lady who had given him directions to Wellington Front on Friday gave him a polite smile of acknowledgement. Gibraltar was indeed a close-knit community, he thought, and as if to prove the point further he then bumped into Tom the dockworker.

"I'm afraid I can't stop now because I'm due back down at the shipyard" said Tom, "I've been working there over the entire weekend. Mind you, it was all on overtime. What about you? How are you getting on?"

"Stagnating a bit," replied Edwin, "but I'm back to job hunting now that the weekend is out of the way."

"Well, good luck with it," said Tom, "I'll be down at the usual place tonight if you want to meet up for a jar or two."

"Okay, see you there," replied Edwin, as they both departed in opposite directions.

The Jamaica Inn was located in a back street one block behind Main Street. It was painted dark red on the outside and although the door was wide open neither customers nor staff were present. However, Edwin could hear some noises coming from a room behind the bar and he tried to attract attention first by coughing and then when that didn't work by chinking a coin on one side of a large china ashtray. A young lady then came through and, in a broad Scottish accent, apologised that he'd been kept waiting.

"That's all right," he said, "I've come about your vacancy for a barman."

"Oh dear," she said, "I'm afraid it's already been filled – by me! I started here three weeks ago."

"Oh well, not to worry," said Edwin, "Obviously the Employment Office is hopelessly out of date with everything."

"I'm sorry," she said.

"Don't worry. It's not your fault," he said, "Just out of interest though, what's it like working here?"

"Oh it's not bad," she said, "although because we're open all day I sometimes don't get to see as much of that Gibraltar sunshine as I'd like to. The pay is pretty lousy but it's a friendly enough place."

"Is there any accommodation that goes with the job?" he asked.

"Oh no," she replied, "My husband is in the military and so we get our flat provided."

Edwin departed and stepped out into the blazing sunshine once again. He was getting used to hearing such things by now. He then took one of the tiny buses to just past the Rock Hotel and, asking someone for directions, walked down a side street before reaching the curved driveway to the large colonial style building that housed BFBS, the British Forces Broadcasting Service. In stark contrast to the Gibraltar Broadcasting Corporation, Edwin was well received by the manager who gave him a guided tour of the studios, control rooms and record library. It was like stepping back into normality and a world of professionalism.

He considered it wise not to openly ask about the possibility of a job as it could cause embarrassment if there were nothing on offer. Instead, he had gone there purely as a visiting television producer and he thought that such detail would no doubt come out in the course of conversation. Sure enough, it was soon mentioned that not only was the station fully-staffed but that personnel for all jobs were recruited in the UK. Over a cup of tea, they discussed broadcasting in general and its application to the military. Apparently Germany and Cyprus both had television services for British Forces.

Having exhausted all known work possibilities in Gibraltar, Edwin realised that he wasn't getting anywhere at all. If he couldn't find anything within the next couple of days he would be left with no choice other than to take the Thursday ferry back to Morocco and then back to Spain. The thought bothered him because it wasn't part of what he had planned. Mind you the reality of Gibraltar wasn't exactly part of what he had planned either. He'd had no idea that the place would have been so limited and yet now the clock was ticking away. He glanced up at the Rock. It still fascinated him in much the same way that it must have fascinated countless people down through the ages. The Moors, led by Tarik, had used Gibraltar as the first foothold into Spain whereas he, Edwin, couldn't even get the first foothold into Gibraltar.

It was a hot evening and Edwin sat down on a bench opposite the cathedral. He wondered how many times had he walked the length of Main Street. He'd lost count. And that was just in a short space of a few days. People who lived in Gibraltar must have trampled every inch of it tens of thousands of times. He called into the Montarik Hotel. Its mock Tudor decorated lounge smelt strongly of furniture polish and cigar smoke and he was served coffee by a peroxide blonde Gibraltarian waitress. A small group of English holidaymakers on a four day package deal were the only other customers.

It was still early but Tom was already outside Lotti's bar when Edwin arrived. It was good to have someone to relate to after walking around all day long with his thoughts to himself. Somehow he could offload all the frustrations and get some feedback into the bargain. He ordered two pints of bitter from Lotti, who was talking emotionally to another customer,

"You know something? People go this way and go that way. They go here and there but you know everybody always comes back to Lotti. Everybody comes back to Lotti!"

"I don't blame them," said the customer in a strong Birmingham accent, "To be able to stand outside here on a stinking hot evening like this with a cold glass of beer in your hand takes a lot of beating. This has got to be the best spot in Gib."

She finished drawing off the two beers.

"Here," she said placing the glasses in front of Edwin and taking up the coins that he had placed on the counter. Edwin transported the drinks along to the far end of the counter where Tom was standing.

"Cheers," said Tom, "Any joy in your pursuit of a job?"

"I reckon I've explored all work possibilities in Gibraltar,' explained Edwin, 'and unless there's some grotty dive of a place down Irish Town that urgently requires a barman to look after its next wave of drunken sailors, I honestly don't think I'm likely to find anything here at all."

"That's tough," said Tom, "The Gibraltarians have got the place completely sewn up. Some have set themselves up as the representatives of companies back in the UK and can survive by being the local face of Clark's Shoes or whatever which is fine in a small place like this – except that it doesn't offer much scope for people like you."

Over the next couple of hours they analysed Edwin's situation in a light-hearted way over several more pints of beer but between the two of them they couldn't come up with any new ideas.

"On Saturday night, up at the Rock Hotel, I got chatting with a Gibraltarian tour guide and I'm supposed to be meeting her tomorrow evening. She seems pleasant enough but unless she's got some idea as to where I could work, I think that come Thursday morning I'll have no choice but to get the hell out of here,' said Edwin before taking a further gulp of beer from his glass.

At that point there was a loud enthusiastic scream from across the road and this time it wasn't the navy. In fact it was a shrill female voice and it was yelling out his name. Edwin turned around and at once saw the outline figure of Louise coming towards him.

"Edwin!" she repeated, "Oh, Edwin! Am I so pleased to see you?"

Thrown off balance by this sudden out of context occurrence, Edwin half choked on his mouthful of beer.

"Is this your Gibraltarian holiday rep?" asked Tom as Louise approached.

"No! No, not at all," said Edwin quickly regaining control of himself.

"Louise!" he said, "You've made it! That's great. Welcome to the outdoor pub. How did you get here?"

"I managed to sort out my visa and came in by ferry this evening," she said, "And boy, am I glad that you're outside or I might not have found you."

"Well, this is almost unbelievable. Oh, by the way, please meet my friend Tom. Tom, this is Louise. We travelled down from France together."

"Pleased to meet you" said Tom, "Here, let me get in one final round of drinks before they shut up shop for the night. What'll you have?"

"That's kind. I fancy something like a Bacardi and coke," she replied.

"Coming up!" said Tom as he headed off to the serving area whilst Edwin turned his attention to Louise.

"I see no bags," he said, "You've booked in somewhere?"

"Yes," she replied, "I took a cab from the ferry and he brought me to a place called the Victoria Hotel."

"That's where I'm staying," he said.

"Really?" she asked. "I'm sure these things are meant to be! Gee, I'm just so pleased to see you again."

"It's good to see you again too," he said, "How did you manage to get a visa?"

"In rather a roundabout way but I'll tell you the full story tomorrow when I'm a bit more wide awake," she replied, "But what about you? How is it here Gibraltar?"

"It's not quite as I'd expected it to be," he said, "but maybe that can best be explained tomorrow too."

"But, I mean have you gotten the job with the TV station?" she asked.

"No such luck, I'm afraid," he replied.

Tom returned with drinks and they changed the subject.

"It sure is good to hear everybody speaking in English once again," she said.

"Oh they do that down here," said Tom, "although to confuse matter the locals sometimes bung in a bit a Spanish mid-sentence too. In that way they think they can outsmart everyone."

"Gibraltar looks quaint but kind of small," she said.

"It's small all right," replied Edwin, "Two and a quarter square miles and most of that taken up by the Rock itself."

Later, when Lotti's bar had closed and they had said goodnight to Tom, they returned to the Victoria Hotel. Louise's room was one floor up from Edwin's and to the front of the hotel. They arranged to meet in the lounge at eight o'clock the following morning.

IT WAS SIX THIRTY and the sun had not yet come up. Edwin sat on the side of his bed. There was no point in trying to go back to sleep now. Complications, complications, he was wide-awake and the full picture of his current predicament had started to unfold before him. Realistically Gibraltar seemed like a dead end place of no opportunity. All the signs were there that no doors were likely to open to accommodate his aspirations. It may well be a British Colony that catered well for Her Majesty's Forces whilst its local inhabitants clung to the apron strings of Mother England, as Tom had once put it, but there seemed to be precious few openings for anyone arriving fresh from the United Kingdom. Everything was extremely limited.

Although his normally optimistic nature had served to highlight Gibraltar's potentially good points there had been certain moments over the past few days when he had found himself beginning to dislike the place. He'd even gone so far as to consider it to be the worst, run-down looking, claustrophobic dump that he'd ever been to in his life – with or without its sunshine. Yet, at the same time, he knew that much of that impression was out of frustration with his own particular set of circumstances and he reasoned that, as he had already invested quite some time and energy in pursuit of work, he still wanted to see things through to some sort of logical conclusion.

He determined to use the next couple of days to make absolutely sure there that he hadn't overlooked any opportunity in Gibraltar. He would leave no stone unturned – or perhaps no rock unturned. After all, his mind had been set on this place over the past few months and he wasn't the kind of person to accept defeat easily. But he knew that the odds were stacked heavily against him. And then there was the matter of that Gibraltarian holiday rep Sonia, whom he had loosely arranged to meet that evening. Who knows, maybe she might know of a job vacancy in Gibraltar. But then, of course she most probably wouldn't. And on top of that there was the additional complication of the arrival of Louise.

As if on cue, there was a gentle rap on his door. He opened it and there stood Louise dressed in a pink tee shirt and light blue jeans.

"Good morning Edwin!" she said in a shrill whisper so as not to disturb any other residents, "I saw the light shining under your door. I'm glad you're awake. May I come in?"

"Yes, sure," he replied, stepping aside to let her pass through, "Excuse the clutter. I was just sorting out some of my things. You're up bright and early."

"So are you!" she said, "but at least your room is quiet. Mine is right above the street and I can hear echoes of people talking down below. That's what woke me."

"I have to put up with the chiming of a church clock," he said.

"What time do they start serving breakfast here?" she asked.

"To be quite honest I don't know," he replied, "I've seen people having breakfast at around eight o'clock. I suppose we could go downstairs and take a look."

The hotel's lounge was completely deserted and in semi-darkness. Its louvred shutters from the serving hatch were still closed. They went down a further flight of tiled stairs and stepping out onto Main Street saw that the Capri Cafeteria opposite was already showing signs of life.

"So you figure there's nothing here for you after all?" said Louise, who had listened to Edwin's brief account of all that had happened since he'd arrived in Gibraltar.

"Well, it doesn't look like it," he said, "and unless by some stroke of luck I can stumble upon something today or by tomorrow at the very latest, then I'll have to leave the place."

"If it's that hopeless why don't you just leave the place anyway?" she asked.

"Because I'm not completely done with it yet," he replied.

"It seems to me that you've already had a good run for your money in looking for a job and you've found that there isn't anything here so maybe you should just accept the fact that it's the wrong kind of place" she said.

"Oh, in one sense I agree," he said. "It's just that as long as I happen to be here I might as well keep putting my feelers out in all directions in case just by some last minute fluke I actually succeed in finding something."

"And you're absolutely sure that there's no possibility of doing something with that TV Station?" she asked.

"Unfortunately that's the one thing I am sure about," he said. "I found that out on my first day. It's absurd, I know, because I could contribute a wealth of experience but they simply don't want to know. They want to do things their own way and with their own people."

A Moroccan waiter deposited two large plates of eggs, bacon, sausage, mushrooms and beans at their table together with a pot of tea, a jug of milk, some cups and saucers, a rack of toast, four sachets of marmalade and eight individual portions of butter that were still frozen solid.

"You like some ketchup?" he asked.

"Yes please," said Edwin, "and some brown sauce if you have any."

"Right away, sir," he said, darting behind a counter to fetch such essential items.

Edwin and Louise were the only customers and two members of the cafeteria staff could be seen preparing sandwiches and rolls in preparation for the day's trade which would occur a little later on.

"You know what I think?" said Louise.

"Probably, but tell me anyway," said Edwin.

"It's like I told you when we first met, that certain things are meant to be," she said.

"I guessed you'd say something like that," he said, "but if everything is always 'meant to be' or 'meant not to be' why does anyone ever bother doing anything at all? If it were already a foregone conclusion that I'd end up here in Gibraltar without the remotest possibility of a job then I needn't have bothered travelling all the way down here in the first place."

"I guess sometimes we have to explore certain avenues," she said, "but, you know, when one door closes it's often the case that another one opens."

"That's exactly my point and the reason why I'm still keeping my eyes and ears open for the remaining couple of days," said Edwin.

"But don't you see? You're already tying yourself down into a schedule," she said, as she passed him another triangle of toast.

"I've no choice," he explained, "I can't afford to stay here beyond Thursday and if there's still nothing on the horizon by then, there's no alternative but to leave."

"What I'm meaning is, rather than using your time to chase non-existent jobs, why can't you just use the remaining two days of your stay to enjoy yourself?" she asked.

"Enjoy myself? I just want to be able to do an honest day's work for an honest day's pay," he replied, "Then perhaps there might be a bit of space to start thinking in terms of enjoyment."

"I know, Edwin," she said, "but I want you to understand that help is at hand. I mean, you could just show me around Gibraltar for the two days and then we could go back to Spain together and make plans to head off to Canada."

He looked across the table at her. Her dark eyes were fixed on him. There was no doubting her sincerity. And apart from anything else, Gibraltar was tiny whereas Canada was massive. There may well be more opportunities there. He had to admit that the idea had a certain appeal. But there were still huge question marks. She might be throwing him a lifeline but what did she expect in return? Or didn't she expect anything at all?

"OK, a hypothetical question for you,' he said, "What if I were to agree to come to Canada?"

"If you were to agree it'd sure get you out of a rut!" she replied, "and besides, you'd love it there."

"That's as maybe but there are certain practicalities involved," he said, "I mean, there's your situation to think about. Apart from the journey from England to Gibraltar, you haven't had so much as a glimpse at the rest of Europe."

"Well if we can get back on those ferries to Spain I could use my rail pass to visit a few other places and then we could meet up again in England before going to Canada," she said.

It sounded too vague an arrangement for Edwin and it wouldn't solve his immediate problem of lack of work. But there was then a further incentive.

"I'll tell you what I'm going to do," she continued, "This morning I'm going to give you that bank draft of five hundred pounds. It's yours to keep. I'll never want a single cent or penny of it back. We can pay it straight your bank account and you can buy yourself a return flight ticket to Toronto and still have money left over to tide you through whilst I take in the sights of Europe."

Edwin remained silent for a long time. A return ticket to Canada would mean that he could simply return if things didn't work out over there. But could he really accept such generosity from this strange young lady? Certainly it was an interesting idea but somehow it seemed too good an offer to be true. What was she really after? The thought of a trip to Canada was intriguing. And surely there would be far more chances of finding professional work there than in this tiny colony of Gibraltar. Suddenly it appeared as a workable solution.

"You've been very persuasive," he said, "I don't really understand why or how this is happening but all of a sudden I think that I'd rather like to take you up on your kind offer to go to Canada!"

"Edwin," she said, as two tears trickled down her face, "You don't know what this means to me. Thank you."

"Would you like another pot of tea?" asked the Moroccan waiter.

"No, we're fine thanks," replied Edwin.

It was mid-morning as they entered one of the two Main Street branches of Barclays Bank and Louise asked the counter assistant if it was possible to pay the bank draft into Edwin's Barclays Bank account back in Winchester. Within a few minutes the transaction was carried out.

'Now,' said Louise, 'What about showing me the delights of Gibraltar!'

CHAPTER TWENTY

EDWIN FLEW IN TO Toronto Airport on a Sunday evening and Louise was there to meet him. After Gibraltar they had both taken the ferry back to Tangiers and then the second ferry to the port of Algeciras in southern Spain. The fact that Gibraltar and Algeciras were in such close proximity of each other had made the crossing look as if they were heading back to exactly the same point where they had been six hours earlier at the start the day's travel. It seemed an incredible waste of time to have to go to North Africa and back just to get to somewhere that was a few kilometres away. The Rock of Gibraltar again loomed large on the other side of the broad inlet of sea which the British refer to as the Bay of Gibraltar but which the Spanish call the Bahía de Algeciras.

An overnight train for Madrid had departed that same evening and couchettes had even been available. A date for Edwin's visit to Canada was worked out and the flight ticket purchased from a travel agent. Louise had bought herself a large suitcase with wheels into which she succeeded in packing the contents of eight of her nine bags. She would use her railcard to spend four weeks sightseeing in Europe on a route that took in Barcelona, Nice, Genoa, Venice, Innsbruck, Munich, Cologne, Brussels and Amsterdam. Following that she would return to Toronto where Edwin would arrive shortly afterwards.

With such arrangements having been made Edwin had seen her off on a train for Barcelona which was the last time that they'd set eyes on each other. Meanwhile he had returned to England where he stayed with Henry and Janet in Sevenoaks whilst making further written applications to television broadcasting organisations.

"Gee I'm so glad you've made it! Welcome to Canada!" said Louise in her shrill voice.

"I've been looking forward to it," replied Edwin.

"I hope you don't mind but I've booked you into a rented room that's quite near to where I live. I figured it might look better to my family rather than inviting you to share my apartment," she said.

Such a no-strings-attached arrangement suited Edwin down to the ground. "That sounds good to me," he said.

But the events of the next few days were anything but good.

It began with Louise driving Edwin around in her car to introduce him to members of her extended family. Edwin had nothing against such social visits apart from the fact that it soon became apparent that she had told just about all of them that she had been over in Europe looking for a future husband and that he was the person she had found to fulfil that role. It was acutely embarrassing. Conversation became awkward as he realised that he was being regarded in such manner. When they drove back across the city after a further such introduction to one of her brothers Edwin asked her what she thought she was playing at.

"Playing at?" she said. "No, Honey, this is no game. It's for real. But don't worry. I don't mind if you still need a bit of time to come around to it."

"Come around to what?" asked Edwin.

"To the two of us, of course," she replied, "to our continued future together."

"Well, we are good friends," he said, "and I am extremely grateful that you have enabled me to come to Canada and if I can land a professional job here that would be fantastic. But surely that's as far as it goes."

She looked at him with a disappointed look in her eyes. "You just need a bit of time, that's all," she said, "I've already made arrangement for us to take a trip down to Niagara Falls next weekend together with some colleagues from where I work."

It was not in Edwin's nature to want to hurt anyone's feelings. If she had designs on him it had not been with any encouragement on his part. It was a difficult situation to be confronted with whilst trying to remain both polite and diplomatic at the same time.

The following week Louise had to return to her secretarial work at a car accessory company. That left him free to check out employment possibilities, which was the prime purpose of his being there. He soon got the hang of the subway system as well as the bus routes that went back and forth throughout the city's grid layout. The downtown area radiated out from where the two long thoroughfares of Bloor Street and Yonge Street crossed each other at an angle of ninety degrees.

On visiting the offices of the Canadian Broadcasting Corporation Edwin spoke with a personnel officer who said that they had several positions currently available for someone of his calibre but that he would first need to obtain a work permit. The following morning he took a trip across town to the Citizen and Immigration Department but it was made plain that a work permit could only be issued once he had a firm offer of a job in writing. On returning to the Canadian Broadcasting Corporation to find out if that might be a possibility he was told that because they were a Federal Department it would be illegal for them to give him a firm offer of employment without the work permit. The impasse bore a striking similarity to what he'd experienced with the unions back in Britain. There was little he could do about it and he began to be glad that he had an open return flight ticket for London.

The weekend trip to Niagara Falls was a bit of a disaster. The couple who accompanied them could see that Edwin and Louise's relationship was purely platonic which seemed to annoy Louise. That evening, whilst staying at a motel, she stated her case.

"Even though I brought you over here you don't seem to be particularly interested in me," she began.

"You are a friend and I am grateful that you have enabled me to come to Canada," he replied.

"I may be a friend but that friendship doesn't seem to be advancing," she said.

"I wasn't aware that it was meant to," he replied.

"Don't you think I deserve something in return?" she asked.

"Look. I am extremely grateful that you kindly provided the means to get me here but it doesn't translate into anything more than just a good friendship," he replied.

"Why? Have you got somebody else?" she asked.

"As a matter of fact, yes, I have," he said, thinking that some oblique reference to Caroline back in New Zealand might at least put an end to any of Louise's false hopes – even though in reality he hadn't heard from her for months.

"Huh," she replied, "You never told me about her when we met did you?"

"It wasn't even an issue," he replied.

"OK," she said, "Well I want you to know I've got somebody else too!"

"Well that's fine then," said Edwin, genuinely relieved to hear it.

"Yes," she said, "I met him in Holland after I'd met you and I'm thinking of buying him a plane ticket so that he can come to Toronto too."

Edwin was amazed at the casual tone adopted by Louise who apparently held some concept whereby she could expect to dangle a flight ticket before the eyes of the young men of Europe as the means of drawing them into her net. The whole idea seemed pathetic. It strengthened his already held view that whenever he next accumulated five hundred pounds he would be refunding it to her in its entirety. There was no way that he wished to be associated with any idea of having been bought.

The following day the four of them visited Niagara Falls. They had hoped to drive into the United States but although the other three could have entered on their Canadian Passports, Edwin would have needed a visa. The American official at the border control who had scrutinized his passport emphasised the fact by adding, "We don't just let anyone into the United States."

So much for the so-called special relationship, thought Edwin.

When they got back to Toronto Louise seemed to have come to terms with the fact that she and Edwin were just good friends. They went out for a meal together and everything was perfectly cordial once again. Before his return to England Edwin even managed to fit in a brief youth hostel stay in Montreal, Ottawa and North Bay as well as looking up a couple of Canadians who he had first met in the cocktail bar of the Peninsular Hotel in Hong Kong. On the day of his departure Louise drove him out to the airport and they parted company on good terms. He didn't bother asking her about the next arrival from Holland.

With both the Gibraltar jaunt and the Canada jaunt now out of the way Edwin arrived back in England effectively back to square one. He had been out of his professional broadcasting career for nine months and for the time being there seemed no immediate choice other than to try and survive on a further selection of completely unrelated temporary jobs. On Saturday evening a chance encounter in a Hampshire country pub led to his renting a spare room in a flat in London's Notting Hill Gate shared by two veterinary nurses. Once there an employment agency found him a string of casual jobs in quick succession.

CHAPTER TWENTY-ONE

EDWIN WAS OFFERED A continual stream of temporary work through the Notting Hill employment agency. Most of it was perfectly mundane. The first job was with the agency itself. Acting as a kind of courier it entailed spending the entire day travelling around on Underground trains to exchange plastic wallets of internal documents at some of the agency's other branches. Edwin's specified route to be completed four times a day was from the Notting Hill Gate office to the Tottenham Court Road office where the first exchange of wallets took place. The second swap took place in Euston and finally Kentish Town was the third before returning back to Notting Hill Gate to repeat the whole exercise all over again with a fresh batch of plastic wallets. Sometimes Chalk Farm also got thrown into the itinerary. Those involved in such delivery tasks were issued with travel passes. If nothing else the job provided an interesting study of London Underground railway architecture and after the first few days Edwin was familiar with just about every air vent, lift shaft, escalator, destination indicator, and platform curvature along his route on the Central and Northern Lines. As a supposed perk of the job he could even make use of his travel pass after work – which was something that he never had the slightest inclination to do.

When this fortnight of subterranean activity was up the agency assigned him to work in a car parts warehouse. Weaving his way up through the passageways of Hanger Lane tube station he emerged at the busy intersection of London's North Circular Road with Western Avenue. It was still dark and cold as he walked briskly to get his circulation into action. An intake of traffic fumes caused him to cough and splutter which was clearly not the healthiest way to be starting the day. On the other side of the road the lit up entrance to Park Royal Underground Station was closer to where he was heading but on the Piccadilly Line which would have meant a more complicated journey. Park Royal – he considered the name as he took in the surrounding area. Industrial Park Royal might have been more appropriate. On the horizon the silhouette of three massive conical shaped chimneys looked down at him menacingly.

The Renault building adorned with yellow flags came into sight as did a pedestrian crossing that conveniently broke the continuity of metal fence barriers. On reporting in at reception a Polish man dressed in maroon overalls collected him and ushered him through to the large warehouse that contained row upon row of metal shelves. He was briefly introduced to an elderly overweight English foreman wearing white overalls who asked Edwin to go to a locker room and put on some blue overalls. Everybody needed to be kitted out in colour-coded costumes.

The job was straightforward enough. Delivery trucks arrived at an adjacent loading bay and their contents had to be stacked on designated shelves from where they could easily be retrieved for loading back onto other vehicles for redistribution. It was purely manual work that occasionally required heavy lifting. During a tea break one truck driver explained that he was a communist and that if he had his way he would nationalise all such freight delivery. Although interesting to learn of the sheer volume of goods that got shunted around Britain's clogged up road network Edwin was at a loss to follow the man's reasoning that nationalisation would provide any solution.

Because he departed for work at an earlier hour than his two veterinary nurse flatmates Edwin rarely saw either of them. Even when he got back in the evenings he would normally take a hot bath and then head straight off out again. There was a well-equipped kitchen but he didn't feel ready to start doing much in the way of cooking just yet and he had been pleased to stumble upon a two-storey restaurant on nearby Pembroke Villas which served meals at inexpensive prices. An Irish waitress with a hairstyle that resembled a large bird's nest handed him a well-worn menu. Curried eggs on a bed of rice were available for twenty-five pence and jam roly-poly and custard was priced at fifteen pence.

To familiarise himself with the neighbourhood he drank half a pint of beer in each of several local pubs. There was no shortage of such places. Some had jukeboxes.

When will I see you again?
When will our hearts beat together?
Are we in love or just friends?
Is this my beginning or is this the end?
When will I see you again?
When will I see you again?

Media jobs were advertised in Wednesday's edition of the Daily Telegraph and a publication called The Stage and Television Today had similar listings. Production jobs were few and far between and Edwin was fast accumulating a selection of polite letters saying that they would like to keep his details on file in case a suitable opportunity should arise in the future.

The next temporary job the agency came up with was serving breakfasts to nuns at a local convent. He would need to stretch his imagination before agreeing to that. Fortunately a job at Foyles bookshop in Charing Cross Road arose that same day and he went for that instead. As with the other temporary jobs the pay was basic in the extreme. After paying his share of the rent he was left with about a pound a day to cover food, transport, clothes and leisure activities. He had even been told that he would be better off living on social security rather than taking such low-paid work. Nevertheless he felt duty-bound to persevere with grotty jobs whilst continuing to apply for professional positions that were more in line with his background and experience.

From a room in the basement of Foyles book shop Edwin helped clear a backlog of overseas orders. Wading through a pile of correspondence it meant physically locating the requested books from within the store and then packing them up ready to be sent off abroad. He soon got to know the layout of the shop. He also befriended a young lady from Yorkshire who worked in the Fiction and Poetry section and they took their lunch breaks together. She lived near Marble Arch and sometimes Edwin would make his way there in the evenings and they would go out for a drink together. But with limited funds they could never manage a theatre performance or dinner at a decent restaurant. She was sympathetic to Edwin's determination to climb out from the bottom of the barrel into which he had inadvertently stumbled.

Towards the end of November some slightly better paid work was available at Barkers departmental store on Kensington High Street. During his lunch hour Edwin went along for an interview and got offered the job right away. The nature of the work was packing Christmas hampers. Laughable in other circumstances but with still no sign of a professional job on the horizon he had to take whatever was on offer.

A clocking in process took place at the store's staff entrance which was accessed from a small side street. Edwin was then shown to a storeroom where he joined seven other males to work in pairs in filling cardboard boxes with a selection of grocery items suspended in layers of straw.

The person that Edwin was asked to team up with turned out to be a New Zealander from Auckland so at least they had something in common to talk about. The rest were a mixed bunch. A Maltese guy was forever bragging about the number of different girls he'd slept with in the past week and there were two English dropouts whose main topic of conversation seemed to be about drugs. Another lad had graduated in English Literature but was forever yawning all day long. A person nick-named 'Golden boy' was a yes-man who spoke behind peoples' backs whilst another was a streetwise character already suspected of thieving from the store. A lively Irishman completed the team.

The cockney supervisor monitored the production line.

"Oi – You over there – Cop 'old of that broom an' sweep up some o' that straw would ya?" he asked of the drowsy graduate.

Consulting a clipboard he then announced, "An' nah for this next order they're also gonna need them large tins of Plumrose 'am togever wiv a jar of ginger an' two of them cans of Delmont fruit cocktail to go in as well – all right?"

The grocery items packed into the hampers were destined for a construction company and the assorted contents differed from a stack of previously packed boxes.

A West Indian lift operator forever in his element had a self-congratulatory habit of proclaiming, "The best –right!" as members of staff got out of his old-fashioned lift at their respective floor levels. In the afternoons the lift was sometimes operated by a huge African man from Ghana who professed to have some sort of spiritual intuition. On several occasions he pointed at Edwin and exclaimed, "And you, mister, are special!" much to the curiosity of anyone else who happened to be in the lift and indeed much to the curiosity of Edwin too. At other times he could be heard swearing his head off about the recurrence of a flickering light bulb.

The staff canteen on the top floor was run exclusively by disabled people. One poor soul had a permanent drip hanging off the end of his nose as he handed out plates of steak and kidney pudding, mashed potato, peas and gravy across the metallic counter. Edwin and his New Zealand colleague sat at the same table and got into conversation with staff from some of the other departments. An effeminate man from Romania who worked on the meat counter in the food hall said he would give any of them a heavy discount if they bought things from him. A French Canadian girl who worked on one of the perfumery counters found it interesting that Edwin had visited her city of Montreal.

The hamper packing task was successfully completed before Christmas and there was now a question mark as to how long the temporary staff could stay on. The streetwise lad and one of the dropouts had already been dismissed for shoplifting. The New Zealander was leaving to explore Scotland. Not for the first time Edwin wondered what he should really be doing to get out of the rut. He supposed that the London experience had been useful in familiarising himself with the geography of the place. It certainly hadn't advanced his career.

In the New Year Edwin conceded that it really was time for a change and he gave one month's notice to quit the Notting Hill Gate flat. An American friend called Chuck whom Edwin had first met at a local pub called The Sun in Splendour was going to be away in the United States for several weeks and had said that during his absence Edwin was welcome to make temporary use of his room if he needed it. The offer proved useful because although the job at Barkers was gradually being wound down a further month's work was still available. Chuck's flat was halfway down Portobello Road and shared by three young ladies who worked at the Israeli embassy – none of whom spoke much English.

THE TIME CAME AROUND for Henry, Janet and their little daughter to return to New Zealand at the end of what for them had been an enjoyable working holiday in Britain. Edwin went to see them off from the BOAC Air Terminal building in Victoria. He did so in the painful knowledge that he wished he was able be going back to New Zealand too.

The following day and perhaps as something of a compromise he sat in a train that pulled out of Waterloo Railway Station with a suitcase of his belongings in the overhead rack. He had reasoned that if he was destined to continue taking casual work whilst waiting for more applicable job possibilities to arise he might just as well do so on the Continent in order to make things a little more interesting. After all, he could still apply for professional work from there.

Edwin's grandmother had recently moved house and now lived in Bournemouth. He had made arrangements to stay there for a fortnight before heading off to Europe. The welcome break of long coastal walks to Hengistbury Head in one direction and to Sandbanks in the other made a healthy contrast to the London experience.

In the evenings a local pub called The Richmond Arms was where many of the foreign students who attended Bournemouth's English language schools tended to hang out and within a short space of time Edwin had developed an interesting circle of new friends. Most of them were from European countries such as Italy, France, Germany and Portugal whilst there were others from the Middle East and South America. One of them inserted a coin in the jukebox.

My first, my last, my everything
And the answer to all my dreams
You're my sun, my moon, my guiding star
My kind of wonderful, that's what you are
I know there's only, only one like you
There's no way they could have made two
You're all I'm living for, your love I'll keep forevermore
First, you're the last, my everything

CHAPTER TWENTY-TWO

A FORTNIGHT LATER EDWIN was once again on board a cross channel ferry bound for France. On this occasion it was to the port of Le Havre. As always, there was a spirit of adventure about heading off somewhere new coupled with optimism that he would be able to find some kind of work in France. He realised that it was a bit of a gamble but nevertheless considered it to be worth the try and better than hanging around in England.

After disembarkation he began hitch-hiking in the direction of Paris. Through-out the afternoon he got a series of lifts as far as the city of Rouen where he decided to remain. The van driver who had brought him on the final part of the journey invited him to a snack bar where they both ate a baguette stuffed full of creamy French cheese and drank a strong cup of coffee. Edwin then weaved his way through paved streets that ran between fine half-timbered houses and gothic churches and eventually found a room to rent for his first few nights.

Because of a limited knowledge of the French language Edwin knew that he could expect no more than a rubbishy kind of job. However if he could gain something in terms of language and culture at the same time, then surely the experience would be infinitely superior to doing things of a similar nature back in England. With that in mind he spent the next two days in search of any kind of a job at all. At one point he thought that he had found some work at a hotel on the outskirts of town but when he met with the manager it turned out that they wouldn't want him to start until June whereas Edwin needed something right away.

On Thursday, however, he struck it lucky in being offered a job at a large self-service restaurant located in the middle of town. He was told that he could begin the following morning at 8am.

THE LONG WIDE PASSAGEWAY that led in from the restaurant's side entrance had a tiled floor that required a thorough scrubbing every morning. Edwin soon got used to attacking it with a stiff brush, dipped at regular intervals into a large bucket of warm soapy water, until the entire surface area had received some quite vigorous treatment. He then used the same brush to drag a grey swab across everything which soaked up most of the wet and had to be wrung out several times during the operation. No doubt some bright spark would now walk through it before it had thoroughly dried and perhaps leave a long line of footprints right down its middle but for now Edwin was content. He took a certain pride in his work and had discovered that he could actually enjoy carrying out such cleaning tasks. Getting thoroughly stuck into the job was a positive way to start the day.

There was the constant buzz of French conversation as people passed by the entrance on their way to work and the nearby clock of 'Le Gros-Horloge' could be heard striking the half hour. The coffee machine hissed again and the smell of Gauloises black tobacco cigarettes wafted up the passage.

"Bonjour, Mon petit Anglish!" called out Françoise la Grosse, as she appeared on the scene.

Edwin had privately nicknamed her Françoise la Grosse as opposed to Françoise la Petite who was the precocious young wench who took care of the bar on the other side of the downstairs dining hall. By comparison, Françoise la Grosse was a considerably older lady of somewhat heftier build but was someone with whom Edwin could more easily relate.

"Mais bonjour, Françoise! Ca va?" he said.

"Ah oui, ça va!" she responded, whilst putting on a pair of rubber gloves in preparation for her particular morning chores.

Edwin had to tackle the toilets next. He'd already got used to that particular task by now. The first few days he had cleaned only the male toilet whilst assuming that a female member of staff would take care of the ladies. However, Madame Madeleine who was the wife of Monsieur le Patron had approached him and politely pointed out that it was his duty to clean both. When he had first heard her say 'pas fait' he thought he was receiving a pat on the back for his hard work and that she was saying 'parfait.' He soon realised otherwise when she pointed out that this was France and it didn't matter whether it was the gents or the ladies – both loos had to be done.

Edwin had developed a theory that French lavatories possessed a unique odour that related directly to the kind of rich food and wine combinations consumed by restaurant clientele. French cuisine might be regarded as the best in the world but on some days the after effects were hardly bearable. He had occasionally detected a similar stench in the street outside – presumably coming up from the sewers underneath. No wonder France was so heavily into perfume and that their word 'parfume' literally meant 'for the fumes.' With such associated thoughts passing through his mind, he completed the task in hand.

When he emerged from what were now his sparklingly clean toilets, the jukebox had sprung into life and was emitting a pounding rock beat accompanied by some French lyrics that didn't seem to rhyme too well. Dancing in time with the music Edwin went around the downstairs dining hall lifting down each of the chairs that had been stacked overnight on the table tops. He then went over to the bar and helped himself to a coffee under the eagle eye of Françoise la Petite. She was unpredictable. Some days she could be all over him and greet him with the familiar kiss on both cheeks as if he were some kind of a close friend but on other days she had a tendency to point the finger and wrongly accuse just about every member of staff of having done this or that wrong on the previous day. She was young, a bit vulgar and not particularly intelligent. Edwin had been able learn the whole vocabulary of French swear words just through listening to her as she went about her daily routine. Today, however, she didn't seem particularly communicative. He gulped down his tiny cup of strong black coffee and saturated sugar cubes in one mouthful of bittersweet warmth.

Edwin then went upstairs to the first floor dining hall where he collected the first of four large wooden crates filled to their brims with empty bottles from the day before. It was heavy and he hoisted it out from within its alcove with some difficulty before being able to recompose his posture and grab hold of it more securely. He found that the best way was to hold it at arm's length by the two small hand holes located on opposite sides and then to bring the whole weight of the box up against his left thigh. In that way he could hobble across to the top of the stairs before varying the angle for the descent. Some mornings he could manage to manoeuvre it right the way down the stairs without stopping at the top at all, a muscular feat which he had come to regard as a mind over matter situation. This morning was no exception and he even exceeded his own expectations by being able not only to lug the hefty crate all the way down the staircase but also right across the main dining hall and over to one end of the bar, where Françoise la Petite could now be seen drying some wine glasses with a chequered towel and serving her first customers of the day. The next stage of such daily acrobatics was to heave the crate up high and land it on the surface of the bar top itself. Practice had proved that this could be achieved with surprising accuracy just by one forceful movement of the body. He then climbed up on the bar top himself and hoisted the crate a stage further onto a little shelf just beneath ceiling level. By means of a precarious looking five-rung tapered ladder he climbed through a trap door into an attic room and then, reaching back down, he was able to pull the crate up towards him and hoist it inside. He had become so used to doing this every day that it was almost second nature to him.

Edwin gently tipped the crate onto its side and poured the empty bottles out onto the plaster floor. Oddly enough there was never one single breakage – just one hell of a noise as they came rolling out together and found their way to a suitable resting place. Edwin worked fast. He had soon collected the three remaining wooden crates and by now the accumulated mass of bottles in the attic room was considerable. They were wine bottles, beer bottles, cider bottles, fruit juice bottles, cola bottles and mineral water bottles and they all had to be sorted out into their respective cases ready to be returned with the deliveryman who would appear in about an hour's time. Edwin worked at it non-stop and most days he could have everything done and neatly stacked up in the bar below within half an hour, which allowed him some breathing space to take a welcome break.

The attic room of empty bottles had virtually become Edwin's own territory. It was tucked away out of sight and just about inaccessible to anyone else. When the bottles were cleared the room looked much larger and he could get across to the windows that overlooked the square outside. From such a vantage point Edwin could survey the passing inhabitants of Rouen and capture any amount of folklore and tradition. Small elderly ladies carried freshly baked flutes of bread from the boulangerie on the corner. The colourful display of a stall in the fish market on the other side of the street was a complete work of art in itself and there were couples sitting at outdoor tables drinking coffees or diluting their glasses of strong yellow Pastis liqueur with iced water poured from a ceramic jug. The beamed buildings of its medieval architecture and street signs such as Rue Jeanne d'Arc provided a reminder of the city's historical context whilst drivers hollering at each other and throwing their arms up in despair in the adjoining car park brought one back to the present again.

The awaited truck then came into view and Edwin returned back to the ground floor to go out and assist the driver with unloading. It was a further burst of heavy work that involved carrying not just cases of wines and spirits but hefty metal casks of French beer. It was a daily ordeal and yet somehow, within the space of just under an hour the transition was completed. Fortunately the truck driver pulled his weight and between the two of them the entire operation was performed with meticulous precision. The particular cellar where everything was to be stored was not only difficult to enter thanks to some alterations that had been made to the building but it was also hot and humid. Perspiration rolled off Edwin's body and his shirt became visibly moist and sticky. The one consolation was that once such cases full of fresh supplies had all been brought in, the remaining task of transferring the cases of empties out to the truck was really easy, as they were much lighter by comparison.

But after that, and whilst sweating like a pig, it was now time for Edwin to get changed into his navy blue trousers and white shirt in preparation for the lunch session. Unfortunately there was no shower facility on the premises.

Lunch was made available for the staff half an hour before the restaurant became open to the public. The food was excellent and there was plenty of choice. Edwin loaded his tray with a starter of celery mayonnaise, a main course of beef bourguignon, a fruit and meringue desert and a portion of ripe, runny, Camembert cheese. They were also entitled to drink in moderation and he took a small quarter litre bottle of red wine. He sat down next to Françoise la Grosse at a table in a designated area with eight or so other members of the staff who had similarly been working away all morning and who treasured this lunchtime occasion. The chef would sometimes stop by and ask what they thought of the food.

"Et tu, jeune homme de bonne famille?" He asked Edwin's opinion too.

There was a sense of being part of a team. The rate of pay was good, everybody was provided with superb meals and Edwin was already conversing in French. He had recently changed his accommodation for a ground floor room in a pleasant guest house that was both clean and affordable and all in all there was a sense of well-being.

Customers began to arrive at the restaurant for lunch and were queuing to fill their trays with entrees, main courses and desserts from the selection on display. Once they had finished their meals it would be Edwin's job to clear away their plates, cutlery and glasses and to wipe the tables clean ready for the next lot of people. It was team work and he was based in the first floor dining hall together with a French girl who seemed to spend as much time chatting with her boyfriend as she did in doing her fair share of the work. At intervals, Edwin would carry heavy stacks of dirty plates down two flights of a narrow spiral staircase to the basement where a man from the Ivory Coast was doing the washing up.

At the end of the lunchtime session Edwin never ceased to be amazed by the amount of drink that many customers had left. There were bottles that were still half full of good quality wine. If he was in the mood he would sometimes grab himself a spare glass and help himself. Nearing the end of his shift he felt as if he'd earned it.

After work he would often stop off at a local supermarket. In the early evening back at his room he would split a baguette and stuff it full of pâté or camembert cheese and accompany it by half a litre of red wine. That wine and bread combination seemed to carry a certain religious symbolism that was not completely lost on Edwin and which he found to be quite amusing. He would then go out for a long evening walk along the banks of the River Seine and perhaps on his return drop by at a local cafeteria. Back at the guesthouse the landlady obligingly permitted him to keep a few bottles of beer in her refrigerator which came in handy on the hot summer evenings as he tuned in his transistor radio to catch BBC World Service News and then Radio Luxembourg. He could get the best signal if he wedged the tiny radio behind a water pipe that ran vertically up the wall.

Far away from London town and the rain
It's really very nice to be home again
Mary-Jane, on the Coconut Airways
Now I know, she love me so
Woah, I'm going to Barbados

Although Edwin was given two days off per week there were many occasions in which he was asked if he would be able to work one or other of them. He normally agreed to do so. First he would be approached by the manageress with "Monsieur Edwin, demain est ton jour de congé n'est ce pas?"

A Saturday shift would coincide with a gathering of mainly elderly customers who came to play a French gambling game known as the PMU which was an abbreviation for Pari Mutuel Urbain. Edwin had no idea how it worked other than the fact that it entailed the use of hole-punched tickets which resulted in thousands upon thousands of very tiny paper discs being scattered all over the downstairs hall – which he had to sweep up.

One day he learned that the French girl with whom he worked on the first floor had been given the sack for wasting too much time. She wasn't being replaced. Instead the boss, Monsieur le Patron, had told everyone that there was no need for a replacement because apparently, "Monsieur Edwin – he does the work of two people."

In the meantime one of the ladies who worked at the cash register asked Edwin if one evening he might like to join her and her daughter at their home for dinner. It was an unexpected invitation and something that Edwin was grateful to accept. After work on the following Tuesday, the lady drove Edwin the short distance to her apartment in Rouen's adjoining town of Marrome. He was introduced to her plump and pleasant nineteen-year-old daughter and to their pet dog. It was an interesting chance to get an insight into a French household. The home cooking was first rate and it proved to be a thoroughly enjoyable evening. Towards the end the doorbell rang and in entered a vibrant neighbour and apparently bored housewife who despite already being half drunk had brought a bottle of Calvados with her and insisted on pouring a glass for everybody. She was one of those people who couldn't stop talking nineteen to the dozen and had few inhibitions. She was intrigued by the presence of an Englishman with whom she immediately began to flirt.

"Ooh, es ce que en peut imaginer l'amour a l'anglaise ?" she cooed as she squeezed herself on to the settee next to him.

The others were clearly used to her ways and after any initial embarrassment her various off-beat suggestions about how Anglo-French relations might be enhanced provided everybody with sufficient light entertainment for a further hour.

Throughout his time in France Edwin had continued to write letters to broadcasting organisations back in the United Kingdom in case any suitable opening arose. He even sent one to the ORTF in Paris. Although each letter was acknowledged they all contained a familiar theme of there being nothing available at present but that they would like to keep his details on file in case something should crop up in the future.

Edwin had been more than a year out of his broadcasting career and was beginning to wonder if he would ever be able to get back into it. He was also aware that much as he enjoyed the experience of the temporary job in France there was a limit as to how long he would wish to go with it. He thought that three months seemed to be the right kind of duration by which time, if there was still no professional work, he could perhaps try moving on to a different European country to further enrich such cultural studies.

The day finally came when Edwin let it be known to Monsieur le Patron and his workmates that he would be leaving France in a fortnight's time. They were sorry to see him go. Edwin planned first to return to England to spend a few days back in Bournemouth after which he intended to head off to Germany to try his luck with some casual work over there. Before leaving Rouen he was again invited for a meal with the cashier and her daughter.

On a Saturday morning he caught a train from Rouen to Le Havre which arrived in good time to take the ferry crossing for Southampton. He arrived back in

Bournemouth later that day.

CHAPTER TWENTY-THREE

THE FOLLOWING EVENING EDWIN breezed into The Richmond Arms, the local Bournemouth pub frequented by foreign students. Exactly the same group of people were there and sitting in almost exactly the same places as when he had last set eyes on them. A ripple effect of recognition resulted in his being enthusiastically called over to join them. Pierre from Limoges was impressed that Edwin was now able to hold a reasonable conversation with him in French. Meanwhile Tiziana, Hans, Pablo, Roswitha, Maria and Wolfgang took a pause from debating the finer points of their English grammar assignment.

On learning that Edwin was planning to go to Germany the following week, Wolfgang told him that if he wanted to stay in Heidelberg for a few days he would be back there by then and there was a spare room in his parents' house where he would be welcome to stay. The kind offer sounded like an opportunity not to be missed and Edwin was pleased to jot down his address.

Edwin departed from Bournemouth the following Monday. So as to get a head start with the journey he had purchased a train ticket to get him as far as Brussels. He planned to hitch-hike the remainder of the journey from there. Arriving at Waterloo Railway Station he got himself across to Victoria for a train down to Dover Marine Railway Station where, together with an army of other foot passengers, he followed a long weaving corridor that eventually connected to the ferry as it prepared to leave for the Belgian port of Ostend. It was a four hour crossing and he bided most of that time with reading the Daily Telegraph from cover to cover and in successfully completing the cryptic crossword puzzle. On arrival in Ostend it was a short walk through to the railway station where a train for Brussels was already waiting at Platform 2.

It was mid-evening by the time he arrived at the station of Brussels Midi. He checked in at a cheap hostel across the road. Leaving his suitcase and shoulder bag in the room he then went back outside in order to stretch his legs. A huge fun fair occupied a large area of closed off streets in the immediate vicinity. Coloured lights flashed and music blared forth as people queued for rides on the dodgems, the roller coaster, the roundabout, the helter-skelter, the ghost train and just about every other fairground activity that had ever been invented. A large cone of pommes frites liberally swamped with a particularly tasty cheese sauce satisfied Edwin's hunger needs and, after another stroll through the fun fair, several glasses of red wine at the bar beneath where he was staying ensured that he got a good night's sleep.

The following morning he rose early, grabbed a coffee and a croissant from the adjacent cafeteria and then crossed the busy road of commuter traffic to consult a map showing the tram network of Brussels. He found a route that would get him out to the south-east extremity and near to the entrance of a motorway from where to start hitch hiking. For much of the journey the tram was submerged in tunnels that passed beneath the city but every once in a while it burst out into the bright sunshine of the warm summer's day.

A succession of good lifts resulted in getting him down through Belgium as far as Arlon near the border with Luxembourg. A further ride with an estate agent brought him right into the city centre of Luxembourg itself. All main roads seemed to converge there many of which passed over bridges spanning deep valleys that first needed to be weaved around before finding the particular thoroughfare that went out towards Germany. Because city traffic was still a dominating factor it took Edwin a while before he was able to get a lift. Eventually a short ride got him out of the town area to a small village and the driver told him that the German frontier was near the town of Grevenmacher which was just thirty kilometres ahead.

There wasn't much traffic on the road at that stage of the afternoon. Edwin walked a little way in search of a good place to position himself in order that whenever a car did eventually come along at least there would be a safe space available for it to pull up in. He reminded himself that the prime purpose of this trip would be to learn something of German culture and hopefully a smattering of the language, in much the same way as he had done in France. He would need to find some work to earn his keep and to begin with he could stay in Heidelberg for a few days which would give him a bit of time to explore whatever possibilities might be on offer. Sometimes this kind of nomadic and adventurous lifestyle seemed even better than the thought of sitting in a television control room and directing programmes, despite the fact that it still remained his main objective to break back into broadcasting by some means or other. A butterfly flew past and the sun's rays shone brightly through the branches of a nearby clump of trees.

After twenty minutes or so a Mercedes drew up. The German driver spoke English and said that he was on his way home to his village just across the border in Germany and that he could drop Edwin off on the road for the city of Trier. The usual ritual of passport inspection took place at a tiny border control and ramshackle bridge over the River Mosel which was one of the dividing lines between the two countries of Luxembourg and West Germany.

The route continued through hills covered in grapevines. Jubilant to have arrived in Germany, Edwin was left somewhere near to where the River Mosel meets the River Saar. He walked into the small town of Konz and just beyond a small parade of shops found a convenient spot from which to continue hitch hiking. He assumed that the road he was on would join a main road for the city of Trier.

He hadn't been standing there for long before a young lady wearing a pastel blue top and bright red slacks came walking towards him along the pavement. At first glance she looked like a typical picture-book German girl of the sort that one might expect to find featured on the front cover of a glossy travel brochure – a slim neatly dressed blue-eyed blonde probably in her mid-twenties.

"Sprechen Sie Englisch?" asked Edwin.

"Yes, I speak it a little," she replied.

"Oh, good – do you know if this is the right road for Trier?" he asked.

"Trier? Yes," she said, "It is always straight on."

"Thank you," said Edwin.

"You go to Trier?" she asked.

"I want to go to Heidelberg," he said, "but Trier is on the route."

"Ah so," she said, "If you wish to go to Trier I can take you in my car."

"Well, yes, that would be very kind of you." said Edwin, intrigued by the fact that he'd managed to get a lift without even hitching for one.

"Komm," she said, "Wir laufen zu meinem auto (Come with me. We go to get my car)."

Together they walked across a railway bridge that led to a residential part of town. They introduced themselves to each other. She was called Ingrid and was a Kindergarten teacher. She asked him what he did and he explained about his background in television in New Zealand and Hong Kong but that for the moment he was taking a break in Germany for a couple of months where he intended to take some casual work whilst attempting to learn the language. Whenever she spoke to him she had a habit of saying it first in German and then providing the translation in English which for Edwin was a bit like getting an instant language lesson. They continued to walk up a hill and eventually arrived at a small modern block of apartments in a cul-de-sac.

"Hier ist mein haus und da ist mein auto (This is my home and there is my car)," she smiled as she indicated a small bright yellow Citroën parked in front.

She then turned to Edwin and asked him, "Aber bist du hungrig? (Are you hungry?)"

The surprise question caught him slightly off-balance as he had been so intent on his journey that he had forgotten all about food during the day but, now he came to think about it, he could certainly do with a bite to eat.

"Well, yes," he replied, "as a matter of fact I skipped lunch."

"Komm, first we eat something," she said. Taking her keys from her handbag she went to the front door which she opened and led him through a passageway to her apartment located to the rear of the building.

It was quite a large studio apartment and everything in it was immaculately clean and tidy. Edwin was glad to put his suitcase down in the small hallway and Ingrid invited him to be seated at a round white table in the lounge.

"Do you live here alone?" asked Edwin having noticed the single bed across on the far side of the room.

"Yes," she replied, "Once I was married but now I am divorced and so I live here by myself."

"I see," said Edwin.

"Moechtest du etwas zu trinken? (Would you like something to drink?)" she asked.

"That would be nice" he said.

"Ich habe Bier, Wein und Kaffee oder Tee. (There is beer, wine, coffee or tea)," she replied.

"Well, what are you going to drink?" he asked.

"Me? I think I take a beer," she said.

"OK. Then I'd like a beer too," he replied.

Ingrid went into her small kitchen and re-appeared with two chilled bottles of Bitburg German beer, a couple of glasses and some beer mats. She then continued to dart back and forth as she brought out food from the refrigerator. Before long the table was laid out with an appetising spread of cured ham, a variety of sliced sausage, cheeses of various sorts including one called Kamenbert spelt with a 'K', tomatoes, cucumber, a small pot of caviar, slices of dark brown bread and a dish of butter and a couple of wooden platters to serve as plates.

"Prost," she said as they both raised their beer glass and gently clanked them together.

"Cheers," responded Edwin.

She went over to a record player and put on a long playing record that contained tracks of a selection of classical music.

"Iss!" she said, "Please eat." She invited him to eat heartily on what lay on the table before them.

Feeling pleasantly overwhelmed by the chain of events taking place before his eyes Edwin chatted with Ingrid and found her to be a very pleasant young lady. The attraction became all the more evident when having fetched more beer from the kitchen she perched herself astride Edwin with her legs of bright red slacks on either side of his and put her arms around him hugging him tightly. Such spontaneity felt like a dream unfolding. He looked up into her face. She smiled as she stared back at him.

"Come, we eat some more," she said as she climbed off Edwin's lap and sat next to him on her chair at the table.

They continued with the rest of their meal laughing and joking throughout as if they were longstanding friends. Ingrid wrote out her name and address on a leaf of paper torn from a shopping list and gave it to Edwin who put it in his wallet. The coffee machine in the kitchen bleeped, cups and saucers were brought in and a bottle of Weinbrand was produced. Edwin assumed it to be brandy although Ingrid didn't know the English word for it and there was no translation on the label but whatever it was it went down well with the coffee. They replenished their drinks, smoked cigarettes and chatted for another hour or so, periodically turning the record over to its other side.

Edwin noticed through the windows on the far side of the room that it was already getting dark outside.

"It is quite late," he said, "What about that lift into Trier – or should we forget about that for now?"

"I take you there in the morning," she replied. She saw him glance across to the single bed. She smiled and nodded her head, "Yes, I have just the one bed."

The invitation was compelling. It felt dream-like and as if everything had been specially choreographed in advance. The music now playing on the record player was the first movement of Beethoven's Pastoral Symphony.

They were awakened by an alarm clock that went off early the following morning. After taking a shower and each downing a cup of coffee they stepped outside the apartment for Edwin's promised car journey to the city of Trier. As she drove, Ingrid asked Edwin what he would be doing once he reached his destination of Heidelberg.

"I can stay with a family there for the first few days," he said, "but I'll then need to find some sort of casual work and some accommodation of my own and I hope to be able to learn some German for a couple of months."

"Ich könnte dir Deutsch lehren. (I could teach you German)," she replied.

"Well, that would also be an interesting possibility," he replied, "but I'd have to come back here for that."

"You would be welcome," she said, "Und du kannst bei mir wohnen(You could stay with me at my home)."

"I will keep in touch with you," he replied.

In Trier she pulled into a lay-by. After one long kiss Edwin retrieved his suitcase and shoulder bag from the back seat of the car and Ingrid drove off to work at her Kindergarten, leaving him standing there in something of a semi-trance-like state as she gave one final wave.

Because of the convenience of the lay-by, Edwin decided that he might as well start hitch-hiking from there, even though, to the best of his knowledge, it was not on any specific route and was still part of inner city roads along which most traffic would just be local people going to work. However, a large military truck pulled over and it turned out to be a black American soldier who was on his way back to his base located somewhere near Kaiserslautern, which was more than half way to Heidelberg. Luck was on his side that hot summer's day.

Edwin chatted with the driver, who was from Philadelphia and who had been stationed in West Germany for the past three years. The soldier said that he found the standard of living in Germany to be even better than back home in the States.

"And I'll tell you what," he said. "The German people are real nice once you get to know them – even though they might come across as kind of cold or indifferent when you first meet them. I've made some great friends here and I'll be real sad when it's time to leave K-town."

"K-town?" asked Edwin.

It's what we Americans call the KMC, the Kaiserslautern Military Community. We're actually at a place called Ramstein, which is about ten miles outside of the city," he said. "Let me see now… at present we are on Autobahn 62 but I'll take you down at far as the entry road to Autobahn 6, which will keep you on the route through to Heidelberg."

"That's very kind of you," said Edwin.

"Oh, it's my pleasure," he said. "It ain't often you get to meet a Brit on these highways."

A German pop song played on the truck's radio.

Jetzt schalten wir das radio an
Aus dem lautsprecher klingt es dann:
Wir fahr'n fahr'n fahr'n auf der Autobahn
Wir fahr'n fahr'n fahr'n auf der Autobahn

Edwin's next lift was with a young driver who was delivering boxes of freshly printed Christian tracts around different parts of Germany. After they had been travelling for a while he asked Edwin if he believed that the Lord Jesus Christ was his personal saviour. Edwin had met such religious people before and had never really found the best way to answer them without sounding too offensive. However, he supposed that because the guy was giving him a lift, the least he could do was to try to sound polite.

"It's something that I haven't thought much about," he replied, hoping that such indifference might change the topic of conversation to something else.

"I believe that he died for me," said the young man with a sense of conviction in his voice.

"I see" replied Edwin.

As they approached the town of Weinheim Edwin asked if he could be dropped off near to the entrance of the Autobahn so as to continue on the route to Heidelberg. However the driver told him that there was a streetcar that ran from the centre of Weinheim right the way through to the centre of Heidelberg and that he would give Edwin a free ticket for the journey. It turned out to be a fifteen kilometre ride in a modern tram. The route passed through several small German towns and villages as well as open countryside. Edwin observed the other passengers and tried to fathom out some of their conversations but without much success.

On arrival in Heidelberg, he could understand the tourist appeal of that particular city. Whichever direction he looked in was architecturally pleasing. He alighted in Bismarckplatz, which was a short distance to the large family home of the foreign language student. The name signs of the roads were written in an old-fashioned style of writing that Edwin recalled from war films. After ringing the doorbell the front door was opened by Wolfgang.

"Hallo Edwin!" he said. "I thought that you probably would arrive sometime today. Please come in." After introducing him to his parents and an elder sister, Edwin was shown to the guest room where he was able to deposit his bags and to freshen up. That evening he joined the family for dinner after which they played cards together. It was a variation of Rummy and Edwin soon got the hang of it.

Like Oxford and Cambridge, Heidelberg had a rich academic atmosphere about it. In fact the University which had been founded in the late fourteenth century was Germany's oldest. Its baroque-style old town was within walking distance of Wolfgang's home and the following day both he and Edwin made a sightseeing circuit along the bank of the River Neckar and across a bridge of orange coloured brickwork. As with all mandatory things for first time visitors to do, Edwin was taken to the castle ruins on the hill. They also called in at several student cafeterias and bars.

"As you can see it's a little bit different from Bournemouth," said Wolfgang. He went on to explain that Heidelberg was widely regarded as Germany's unofficial intellectual capital. "Not that I am particularly intellectual, even though I studied law" he added.

"I'm not particularly intellectual either," commented Edwin, "but it's just that everybody thinks that I am."

As Edwin familiarised himself with the geographical layout of Heidelberg he wondered where to begin looking for work although whenever he pondered the question a certain thought seemed to recur. Ever since his departure from Trier on Wednesday morning he had been left with the vivid memory of the encounter with the girl, Ingrid. He recalled her suggestion that she could teach him German. Was it really necessary to go through the rigmarole of trying to find somewhere to stay in Heidelberg and looking around for temporary work of some description if at least half of that could be solved much more easily by returning there? As far as Edwin was concerned it didn't really matter which part of Germany he was going to be stay in and the thought of her company was particularly appealing.

The lure of her small Saarland town of Konz began to feel even greater than the picturesque university city of Heidelberg so much so that in the evening he went to a telephone kiosk and dialled her number.

After breakfast on Sunday morning and having thanked the family in Heidelberg for their kind hospitality Wolfgang drove Edwin to the start of the Autobahn. A series of lifts via Saarbrucken got Edwin back to Konz by late afternoon. He pressed the door bell and a few seconds later Ingrid's voice over the intercom asked him to enter as the automatic door opened.

A COSY RELATIONSHIP DEVELOPED. For her part, Ingrid was intrigued to have an English companion. The following weekend, as they strolled together, hand in hand, through a public park in Trier at which a German brass Oom-pah band was playing, she gently squeezed his arm and said, "You know something? I never thought that I could ever be so happy again."

They took it in turns to cook. She introduced him to sauerkraut, goulash and dumplings and he retaliated with poached fish in parsley sauce and a variety of curries. Sometimes they ate out. Not always knowing the English translation for certain dishes she would ask Edwin things such as "Do you like Sauerbraten with Spätzle?" He had no idea what it was although after a while he could just about work out things such as Gebratene Medaillons vom Schweinefilet.

Ingrid also phoned around on Edwin's behalf and succeeded in getting him a temporary job at a hotel in Trier. The only problem with it was that when he got there he was told that his first task would be to paint a metal fence around the perimeter of the grounds. That meant that, apart from the lunch break, he was stuck outside on his own all day long with no opportunity for any German conversation whatsoever but plenty of opportunity for quiet reflection. He wondered what on earth he thought he was doing standing in Germany sanding down the metal bars of a fence and applying orange primer and then the fresh cream paint.

Contrary to his initial expectations he didn't learn very much German from Ingrid either. She had an automatic preference to converse with him in English. He acquired a book of Hugo's 'German in Three Months' and started working his way through some of the exercise in that instead. In the evenings they would often walk down the road to the pleasant local bar and drink a few glasses of draught German beer. Whenever they did so, they were invariably treated to a repetitive melody emanating from the establishment's loudspeakers. Although Edwin recognised the words 'La Paloma Blanca' as being Spanish for 'The White Dove' the rest of the song was in German.

Oh la Paloma Blanca
Freiheit ist alles für dich
Oh la Paloma Blanca
Freiheit ist alles für mich
Was wird aus mir
Wenn ich sie verlier

Ingrid appreciated Edwin's sense of humour and often said that she would welcome an opportunity of living with him permanently in a different country such as England. However, Edwin wasn't ready to settle down or even to contemplate marriage with anyone just yet. He also knew that it hadn't been his goal simply to find a new girlfriend, however nice that happened to be. He still had to find a way to get back properly on his feet again and to get his career sorted out – and he was still just as frustrated by the fact that returning to the New Zealand Broadcasting Corporation was no longer an option thanks to that country's change of immigration policy.

In the meantime however, he and Ingrid continued to get on very well together. He noted that a British-German combination was a particularly powerful combination. German decisiveness together with a British sense of fair play contributed to such a notion. He had even begun to wonder if Germans were equipped with a kind of binary thought system in which everything was either black or white and with no room for grey which would help explain how they were able to arrive at some of their strongly held views. Conversely he could see that the quality of flexibility of the British could sometimes be wrongly interpreted as a sign of weakness or wishy-washy indecision even if it wasn't that at all. On top of that Germans were punctual. Departing at seven o'clock meant departing at seven on the dot and not at three minutes to or nine minutes past. Mind you, that aspect suited Edwin who had been used to making things happen with split second timing in the television control room.

And then there was the work ethic. It had often been said that the Germans lived to work whereas the British just worked in order to live. There was a certain seriousness and dedication in which Germans went about their daily graft. Even at the hotel, lunch breaks seemed to be regarded as an inconvenient interruption to the day's routine in which the staff would eat whatever dish had been prepared but were eager to get on with the rest of their work. And people took pride in their work. There was little of the snobby British way of looking down on the working class. Workers of all description were people to be admired rather than frowned upon. And the work was thorough.

Duvet covers were aired on windowsills, flower beds were immaculate, front steps were scrubbed every Saturday morning and it was forbidden to hang out washing on Sundays. Shops would shut at lunchtime on Saturday and remain closed until Monday. It was necessary to wait for the pedestrian crossing light to turn to green even if there was absolutely no traffic. One should never walk on the coloured part of the pavement because that was for cyclists. Keep off the grass. Even supermarket cashiers would stand up and peer into customers' trolleys to make sure they were empty as if every customer was under suspicion of theft. Edwin was becoming used to the ways of Germany.

There was no television set in Ingrid's flat which was a blessing because it meant that they could have real live conversations instead. In the mornings, as they got ready for work, the radio was tuned to SWF3 and Edwin found it interesting that in between news items and commercial breaks there was a short high pitched bleep which sounded almost like someone blowing a whistle at regular intervals as if to remind listeners to get a move on and not be late for work.

On weekends they would go for walks along the river banks of the Saar and the Mosel. Occasionally they would take a Saturday drive into Luxembourg for the sake of variety. Before returning they stocked up on cigarettes which were considerably cheaper there and filled up the car's tank with petrol for the same reason.

One evening whilst Ingrid was attending an event at her Kindergarten in Trier, Edwin ventured into a centrally located bar and was surprised to hear English being spoken. The four young men were a pop group from Sussex called White Dog Wail and were currently playing in the city as part of a tour. Edwin got chatting with them for a while before they departed to prepare for their performance.

Shortly afterwards a different group of people entered the pub and they too were conversing with each other in English. However, they were from some sort of a Christian group and one of them could be heard saying how his conversion experience had completely transformed his life. As he sat listening to them Edwin was mildly curious as to what could possibly drive people to want to be part of a religious organisation. He could think of nothing more restrictive. Also, it was one thing for them to go round saying things like, "Jesus loves you" but that was just an empty slogan that seemed to be echoed out of superstition as much as anything else. The words themselves felt pretty meaningless and rather creepy. Edwin had worked out a long time ago that such an approach was enough to put people right off God altogether. If there really was a God up there he felt sure that he would want people to do things differently if the intention was to try to drum up any kind of support or understanding. He thought back of his missionary friend in Hong Kong and recalled that somewhere he still had that copy of the Bible that he'd given him – which he had never opened.

Edwin's painting of the metal fence reached completion and the hotel's Hausmeister congratulated him in getting it done on time. By now it was the beginning of October. The summer had already gone and almost overnight the weather turned bitterly cold. The hotel had agreed to take Edwin on for a period of three months. For the final month he had hoped to be doing something inside the warmth of the hotel building but it was not to be. Instead he was required to make use of a trolley for carting numerous empty wine bottles from the events hall to an unheated outdoor storeroom and to stack them neatly in wooden boxes ready for collection. The bottles were green and he discovered that it was because they were wines from the River Mosel area as opposed to Rhine wines that were always contained in brown glass bottles. For the remainder of the working day he was asked to rake up leaves and chestnuts that had fallen onto the large area of front lawn.

Edwin had continued to write letters to broadcasting organisations on the off-chance that one of them might have a suitable vacancy. One day a reply came back from Southern Television in Southampton saying that although they didn't have a vacancy at present they would nevertheless like to invite him in for an interview in case something might crop up in the near future. He felt that he had to attend. He phoned the personnel department and an appointment was arranged for 6 November.

He explained the situation to Ingrid. "The thing is I have been out of my normal profession for more than a year and I need to find some way of getting back into it."

She could follow his reasoning although she was clearly saddened that it meant his imminent departure. He had sensed that she was very much in love with him. He was also very fond of her but the whole situation was one of wrong timing as far as he was concerned. Maybe she was the kind of young lady that he would like to end up getting married to one day but because at the moment he had no professional work, no home of his own and not much money, there was no way that such a thing could even be contemplated at this stage of the game. He had never asked her about the circumstances of her divorce. He had felt that it was none of his business. She had once asked him if he had anyone back in England and he had told her that all he had was the distant memory of someone back in New Zealand.

The following Saturday Ingrid drove Edwin to Trier railway station in time for him to take the early morning train for Belgium.

"I might return here by the end of next week if the meeting at the TV station doesn't lead to anything," said Edwin.

"Du weißt, daß du immer wiederkommen kannst, wann immer du willst. You know you can always come back whenever you like," she said.

"I know and I thank you," he replied, "Just give me a bit of time to try and get things sorted out and we'll see what we can do. I'll phone you immediately after the interview."

"Okay. Thank you," she said. They kissed each other goodbye.

Although the train didn't stop at Konz it passed right through it and as he looked out of the carriage window Edwin caught one last glimpse of the familiar hill where he had lived together with Ingrid for the past three months. From Brussels he took a train to Ostende and that night the four hour ferry crossing back to Dover which arrived at some unearthly hour of the morning and with no immediate train connection.

CHAPTER TWENTY-FOUR

THE SOUTHERN TELEVISION COMPLEX was built on land reclaimed from the River Itchen in the Southampton suburb of Northam. The receptionist invited Edwin to take a seat and said that Chris Arrowsmith from the Personnel Department would be down shortly. Several minutes later a bespectacled man wearing a green suit entered through some swing doors.

"Hallo Edwin. Pleased to meet you. Thank you for coming in," he said. "Let me give you a quick tour of the premises and then afterwards we can sit down and have a chat."

"That sounds like an excellent idea," replied Edwin as he got to his feet.

Passing through the set department they continued on to studios, control rooms, editing suites, production offices and the newsroom. Although one TV station can look much like another Edwin managed to show appreciation of each operational area. The canteen and the bar were by far the most popular places judging by the number of staff congregated in both.

After the look-around they ended up in a small office towards the front of the building where they sat down and a secretary obligingly went off to fetch them a cup of tea. Chris Arrowsmith opened a green file.

"I see that you already have quite a bit of experience on the studio floor and in transmission control as well as directing news magazine programmes and the production of a children's programme. Would you like to talk me through it?"

Edwin presented a detailed history of his broadcasting career both in New Zealand and Hong Kong. As he expounded on various aspects the tea arrived and was placed on the table between them.

"And if you were to join us here at Southern Television I presume your preference would be for a job in programme production," said Chris Arrowsmith.

"I could be willing to consider any appropriate vacancy," replied Edwin, "Although if it were a matter of choice I'd naturally favour production work and the directing of programmes."

They each took a sip from their cups of tea.

"You wrote to us from Germany," he said, "Are you based over there?"

"Until recently, yes," said Edwin. "I had been doing some completely unrelated work there for a few months."

"I see," he replied," And what about your availability? If offered a job here how soon would you be able to start?" he asked.

"I'm currently available and would be free to start at short notice," said Edwin.

"Good," he said, "And I take it that you are a member of the ACTT."

"No," replied Edwin, "As indicated in my letter I don't yet belong to the union."

"Oh, I see," said Chris Arrowsmith as he turned a page in the file. There was a pause before he went on. "That could be problematic. As I expect you know the Independent Television companies have an agreement by which they are bound to hire union members only."

"I know, I've heard it before," said Edwin, "and I've also heard that one can't join the ITV union without first having a job at ITV."

"That's correct," he said, "which for a person with broadcasting experience gained abroad must be frustrating. That I can fully understand. Let me ask you a question. If there were an opportunity for you to join the union would you do so?"

"Yes, I would," replied Edwin.

"OK, Good. Look, can you leave it with me for a while? I would like to have you on board here in some capacity. I shall see what I can do and will get back to you as soon as possible."

And with that the interview came to an end. Edwin's contact details were updated. They shook hands. Chris Arrowsmith again thanked him for coming in and said he would be in touch in a few weeks' time – hopefully before Christmas. The secretary took Edwin back through to reception and he departed from the premises of Southern Television – none the wiser.

As he made his way back to Southampton Central Railway Station he had to acknowledge that there was only a tiny number of television centres in any given country. It was not like work in something such as the health sector where there were a hundred hospitals in England alone and nor was it like education in which every town and even outlying villages had schools. And, of course, the broadcasting industry was such a sought after and competitive profession. He didn't know what his chances were with Southern Television. Not belonging to the ITV union was likely to be the stumbling block – and clearly the personnel man had only just noticed that major obstacle during the interview. Edwin supposed that he would probably have to remain in England whilst awaiting the final outcome.

There was three quarters of an hour before the next train to Bournemouth but at least the platform had a cafeteria. With a buttered scone and a cup of coffee Edwin sat down at one of its tables. A young man sitting nearby spoke to him.

"Not trying to get to Salisbury too, are you?" he asked.

"No, I'm going to Bournemouth," replied Edwin,

"Oh, you're OK then," he said. "I've been trying to get home to Salisbury but apparently they are doing something on the line to Andover and so the train that I was on got terminated in Basingstoke and I've since had to come all the way down here to Southampton to get yet another train to up to Salisbury – and now even that has been delayed. It's an absolute nightmare."

They chatted for a while. He turned out to be a post-graduate student at Oxford where he studied Biochemistry and was taking a break to visit his family in Salisbury. Edwin mentioned that he recalled Salisbury as being a pleasant place from the time when he had once stayed at its youth hostel.

"Oh yes, it still holds much of its olde worlde charm what with its market square and arched monuments," agreed the student. "Even the cinema is fashioned in some kind of Tudor style. What about you? Do you live in Bournemouth?"

"No. I'm just dropping in on a relative there," replied Edwin. "I haven't lived permanently in England for a while."

"I thought I detected an accent," he replied. "Have you been out in Australia?"

"New Zealand," replied Edwin.

"Even better still," he said, "I'd love to visit that country one day."

An announcement then cut in, "British Rail apologise for the delay of the 13:52 service to Bristol Temple Meads via Salisbury. This service is now running approximately eighteen minutes late."

"See what I mean?" he said. "It's never ending! Are you planning to stay down in Bournemouth for long?"

"I'm not sure yet," replied Edwin, "I've just been at an interview with Southern Television about the possibility of working there. I'll probably need to find some temporary accommodation whilst things get sorted out."

"If it's a temporary bedsit you are after, I might have just the thing for you in Salisbury if you're interested," said the student.

He went on to explain that he lived in the North Canonry of Salisbury Cathedral Close. There was a small apartment within the house and he was sure that his mother would agree to let Edwin have the use of it for a few weeks for a peppercorn rent. He introduced himself as Victor Horton and he invited Edwin to come to Salisbury for a dinner party on Saturday evening.

"It's very kind of you and a nice idea but as a non-driver I don't know how I'd get back to Bournemouth afterwards," replied Edwin

"Stay the night," replied Victor. "In fact you could even stay overnight in the room that I just mentioned and see if it's to your liking."

They exchanged addresses. The Salisbury train finally arrived which the student then boarded together with several disgruntled passengers moaning about having had their journeys disrupted.

That evening Edwin tried phoning Ingrid in Germany to let her know how the meeting at the television station had gone but he was unable to get through. All he got was a continuously repeated recorded message saying, "Kein anschluss unter dieser nummer" followed by three short bleeps. He tried again and got exactly the same response. Blast it, he thought. No connection under this number. Her phone must be out of order.

Over the next few days he tried calling her again from a variety of different telephones but still met with the no connection signal.

Stepping into Salisbury's Cathedral Close was like turning the clock back and entering a different world altogether. Fine looking English homes of distinction formed a square around the adjoining area of lawn with the cathedral and its tall spire set in its middle. It was early evening when Edwin arrived at the North Canonry. After introductions and an aperitif in one of the large lounges, complete with a log fire, dinner was served in an adjoining wooden panelled room. Edwin sat alongside his host, Victor Horton, at a long table of guests. Beef Carbonade was accompanied by a plentiful flow of red wine to a background of medieval music.

Towards the end of the evening Victor's mother showed Edwin to what was essentially a tastefully decorated bed-sitting room alongside its own kitchen and bathroom. It was first-rate. The latched windows commanded a spectacular view of the cathedral illuminated outside. It could easily be described as one of the most desirable residences in Salisbury – and Edwin could have it until January at a knock-down price of just five pounds per week. He couldn't resist the offer and agreed to move in on the following day.

If he was going to wait for the outcome at Southern Television he realised that he would need to do something in the meantime. By the end of the week he took a job as a temporary sales assistant in a Salisbury bookshop during the run-up to Christmas. His previous stint in Foyles bookshop had counted in his favour. The work was straightforward enough and in the weeks that followed it was actually quite enjoyable.

In the meantime, however, Edwin had lost all contact with Ingrid in Germany. Her phone still didn't connect and there had been no response to either of his two letters. He hoped that she was alright and wished that there was some other means of contacting her. He knew that she worked at a Kindergarten somewhere in the city of Trier but he neither knew its name nor its whereabouts. She had told him that she originally came from Wilhelmshaven on Germany's north coast but with a surname like Schmidt it would be difficult to trace her family. He wasn't even sure if that was her maiden name.

SALISBURY CATHEDRAL HAD THE tallest church spire in the United Kingdom. Edwin noticed it to have a changeable character in which the weather played a part. Floodlit throughout most of the evening a splattering of rain on its stone surface would create a completely different appearance from when it was bone dry. A moonlit night could also alter its appearance.

Although Christianity in the shape of the cathedral was staring the inhabitants of the North Canonry in the face on a daily basis no one there was in the slightest bit religious. That was in contrast to the person who lived further along the lane in the South Canonry who happened to be the Bishop of Salisbury. With the exception of working on outside broadcasts in New Zealand, Edwin hadn't attended a church service since boarding school but now, accompanied by Victor, he agreed to put in an appearance at the annual Christmas Carol service. The Bishop's overriding message was that 'It pays to advertise.' Edwin found it interesting that the power of advertising could even be applied to getting the Christian message out and he supposed that the Bishop did have a point. However such words of wisdom didn't solve Edwin's immediate problem. He had now been in Salisbury for several weeks and as yet had heard nothing further from the personnel department at Southern Television.

The temporary job at the bookshop would end on Christmas Eve and Edwin was due to move out of the North Canonry in the New Year. He decided to phone Chris Arrowsmith at Southern Television to ask if there had been any developments only to learn that he had since left the company. Somebody else in the personnel department said that they had Edwin's details on file and would get back to him if an appropriate vacancy were to arise. He had heard that before.

Scanning down the columns of the Salisbury Journal he saw that about the only immediately available job was as a live-in barperson at a hotel in the Wiltshire town of Amesbury. Purely as a stop-gap perhaps he could do that for a while. After all, he had previous experience.

EDWIN MOVED IN TO the Antrobus Arms Hotel in Amesbury near Stonehenge. It was supposedly the snootiest watering hole that the town had to offer. Mind you, that wouldn't have been difficult judging by some of the other dives in the immediate vicinity. He was given a pleasant enough room with an adjacent bathroom and then shown to a staffroom on the ground floor where breakfast, lunch and dinner could be taken.

Familiarising himself with the layout of the various bottles, the whereabouts of a chopping board for slicing up lemons and doing a quick run through of the prices of pints and half pints of the draught beers, he got the hang of it in no time at all. The first of the morning's customers began to trickle in at around eleven o'clock. Elderly people mainly, all of them local and, presumably, regulars. It was one of those bars in which people spoke to one another in hushed voices as if observing the code of silence of a public library. Most peculiar, thought Edwin, who for a moment felt like yelling something out at the top of his voice simply to break that convention.

The bar was closed in the afternoon and Edwin was free until its re-opening time of six o'clock that evening. He went out for a stroll around the small town and through its park to get a breath of fresh air realising that this routine would probably be repeated most days because there wasn't much else to get up to within such a limited time frame.

The evening shift started off alright with the cosiness of a log fire burning in the grate and a couple of elderly gentlemen sitting in different corners of the room each reading their own copies of the same evening newspaper. The place then began to fill up with middle class couples enjoying a pre-dinner drink or two before being ushered through to the hotel's restaurant at the back of the premises. An elderly part-time barman called Wilfred joined Edwin behind the bar for the evening. He was of the old school and kept referring to the clientele as 'Sir' and 'Madam' at every available opportunity which kind of went against the grain of Edwin's more egalitarian style. "Would sir be requiring a further pint?" "Would madam care for a drop of Worcester Sauce in her tomato juice?" "Would sir like ice and a slice of lemon with his gin and tonic?" A waft of cigar smoke permeated the atmosphere and Edwin could imagine a similar monotone enquiry as to whether madam had just broken wind.

A number of senior military personnel used the bar. They were easily detectable by the way that they dressed, the stiff upper lip manner in which they spoke and their ability to consume copious quantities of liquid without batting an eyelid. As it neared ten thirty, the bar filled up with still more people. The bell was finally rung but if Edwin had expected the place to start emptying it didn't. Instead, the majority of those gathered lingered on. The landlady then entered and closed the wooden shutters across the windows. Perching herself on a bar stool she ordered a round of drinks which were prepared for her by Wilfred. Unsure as to whether or not he was still on duty Edwin cleaned the ashtrays and shifted a couple of crates of empty bottles. The landlady caught his eye. "Edwin," she said, "Please feel free to help yourself to a drink – anything you fancy. Oh, and you might just want to serve that man at the far end of the bar – he's been waiting there for quite a while." Edwin obligingly served the man with a round of drinks whilst wondering about such unexpected extended time. Putting on a brave face he continued to serve anybody who wanted their glass replenished for the next three hours. By that time four people were left, all of whom wanted one final drink to round off the evening. Edwin and the part-timer, Wilfred, had taken to drinking small glasses of draught Guinness and both of them lost count of how many they had had. That first night it was quarter to three in the morning when Edwin finally got to bed.

It became apparent that providing the nocturnal bar service was likely to be a regular occurrence and considered part and parcel of the job. During the course of a conversation with Wilfred, it transpired that one was expected to work on into the early hours of the morning for no extra monetary remuneration other than an understanding that you could drink as much as you liked for free. Edwin also found out that his predecessor had been a middle aged lady and that she had literally dropped dead on the job as the direct consequence of following such a lifestyle.

Edwin put a time limit on this temporary job of no more than ten weeks. Because of living in and having all his meals provided he was able to save every penny that he earned and by then he would have scraped together sufficient money to push off back to the Continent. There didn't seem to be much to hang around in England for. When doing her stock control the landlady commented that the hotel appeared to be an entire barrel of Guinness down. Edwin smiled inwardly. It was quite possible that he and Wilfred had polished off the whole lot.

THE LURE OF THE Continent worked its magic yet again and Edwin was once again on the Dover to Ostend ferry. It still remained a complete mystery as to what had become of Ingrid in Germany. He had many times thought of going back there to make some enquiries but because all the indications were that for whatever reason she no longer lived at the same address he sensed that it would have been be a wasted journey. Instead he intended to stop off in Brussels and experience something of that city before deciding what to do next.

On arrival in the Belgian capital he managed to find work in a small hotel where he was able to live in a room in its basement. The duties involved a fair amount of cleaning throughout the building as well as loading crockery and cutlery into a dishwashing machine after meals were over. As with most of his recent jobs, it was the kind of mundane thing that one could easily do whilst thinking about other matters. He knew, however, that for all its faults, investing himself in such work was infinitely better that sitting around waiting for something to happen. Somehow he felt that if were to persevere even with the lowest kind of job, he would ultimately get back on track. Britain's membership of the European Economic Community had enabled the possibility of living and working on the Continent without any need for a work permit.

On Edwin's first day off he unexpectedly gained access to the Eurovision Control Centre. He had been sitting in a coffee shop opposite the iconic Brussels landmark of the Palais de la Justice – the Law Courts. A man seated at an adjacent table was reading a magazine entitled 'Broadcast' which Edwin recognised to be a weekly publication for the United Kingdom television and radio industry. It prompted a conversation with the Belgian man who spoke good English and who turned out to be Eurovision's Chief Engineer. They spoke together at some length and Edwin was then invited for a private tour of the technical facility located across the road.

To his surprise the Eurovision Centre was located inside the dome on top of the of the Palais de la Justice. It was interesting to encounter familiar looking equipment and a configuration of television monitors housed in such an unlikely place. Its position high up in the building's dome made it well placed for vision links to the rest of Europe and it came as no great surprise to learn that the centre had been equipped mainly by a BBC effort. The brief touchdown into the broadcasting world was sufficient to give Edwin the added impetus to return to it by whatever means necessary. And yet opportunities to do so seemed as rare as ever. If it wasn't a difficulty with union membership it was simply that job vacancies were so few and far between. The following week he managed to visit the studios of Radio Télévision Belge.

Edwin built up a circle of friends many of whom who worked in the European Commission and frequented the cafeterias and bars surrounding La Grande Place. He remained in Brussels for a couple of months which seemed to be about the normal time span that he allocated to each new European country. One afternoon when collecting his mail from the Bureau de Poste Centrale there was a letter in response to a recent application he had made for a job with a TV production company in London. They were inviting him for an interview next month. He hoped that at long last it might provide the opportunity to climb out of this present cycle of temporary work and get back into something that was more in keeping with his background and experience.

Throughout the entire episode of having hit hard times Edwin had skilfully avoided much in the way of contact with his relatives in England. He hadn't wanted to burden them with his situation. Although there was the old saying that a problem shared was a problem halved in his particular set of circumstances he thought that a problem shared would most likely have ended up as a problem multiplied and so he had tended to keep a respectable distance. He realised that he had been leading a lifestyle that was in stark contrast to the time when he had visited Europe from New Zealand a few years earlier in the knowledge that he then had a professional job and a home in Christchurch to return to. In the present uncertainty he considered it wise to wait a little longer before putting in an appearance with his immediate family. He would reconnect with them once he had got back on his feet again.

It was with that in mind that when the time came to leave Brussels he considered it best to rent somewhere cheap for a while much as he had done in Salisbury. This time, however, he chose Weymouth on the Dorset coast.

CHAPTER TWENTY-FIVE

EDWIN HAD FLASHED THROUGH Weymouth once before from the vantage point of a National Express Coach. At that time the place had seemed like a typical British seaside resort left over from an era before the advent of package holidays to the Mediterranean. The seafront with its crowded promenade was lined with palm trees had been basking in sunshine whilst fishing boats moored in the harbour painted a quaint picture.

On a cold March morning, however, the place was bereft of holidaymakers and everything looked decidedly bleak. Hoisting his suitcase out of the luggage rack Edwin alighted from the bus and made his way through a series of narrow streets as several seagulls overhead squawked out some kind of a welcome for him. Behind a derelict church, he found a small square of terraced houses displaying Bed and Breakfast signs. Being low-season all of them had notices in their front windows saying that they had vacancies. Edwin chose the most pleasant looking cream-coloured one. He entered the front gate to a short pathway and rang the bell. The landlady answered the door and showed him to a single room on the first floor for which the nightly rate seemed reasonable enough.

She gave him a key for the front door and another for his room and told him that breakfast was served each morning from eight until nine thirty. Thus settled, Edwin unpacked and placed the empty suitcase on top of the small wardrobe. He decided to go out to take a look around the town.

A nearby road had a railway line down its middle and Edwin watched as a diesel locomotive pulling four carriages of passengers passed slowly through the town escorted by two railway staff on foot and both wearing high visibility outfits. It was heading in the direction of the harbour to connect with a cross channel ferry. After that particular highlight of the morning Edwin embarked on a meditative walk around the streets of Weymouth which he continued for five solid hours as he inwardly digested everything that he came across. The town was a lot smaller than he'd imagined and he kept criss-crossing places that had already been passed. Beneath the dark grey skies he discovered the layout of the town centre and its shops and amenities, a small cinema, yachts moored in its marina, its bridges, a vendor of freshly caught fish, the railway station with trains to London, the remains of a disused railway station, Fortes ice cream parlour, the library, various churches, an amusement arcade, quayside inns, souvenir shops currently doing no trade whatsoever, tearooms, the so-called pleasure pier, the ferry port, a college, water meadows, takeaway food outlets, a clock tower and a blustery seafront walk to the uninspiring sight of an equally out-of-season Pontin's Holiday Camp.

By that time he had seen about as much as there was to see of the place. He then went back over the harbour bridge and followed a route up to a hill called the Nothe Fort which he had saved for last. The military looking architecture of grey walls and archways of its stone edifice looking out over the harbour reminded Edwin of a kind of Gibraltar without the sun. He stopped to read an information notice which described it as part of a network of defences and batteries that historically had been built to protect the south coast from the French. At that very moment an incoming Cross Channel ferry blew its horn signalling its arrival from France.

Edwin sat down on a bench, glad to rest his legs, and watched as a smaller ferry departed for the Channel Islands of Guernsey and Jersey. Meanwhile on the far side of the Nothe Fort hill three battleships could be seen taking part in a Royal Navy exercise in the adjacent waters of Portland Harbour.

There was a week to go before his interview in London. He was prepared to wait until the outcome of that was known before pursuing any further temporary jobs figuring it preferable to have a certain amount of continuity rather than starting something one minute and interrupting it the next. He had some savings but would have to budget things out carefully. He wished he had cooking facilities. A baker's shop sold doughnuts at half price shortly before closing for the day.

That evening, not knowing anybody in Weymouth, he did what he often did whenever he arrived in a new place. He called in on several of its local pubs where, lingering for a while over a half pint of beer in each place, he absorbed something of the atmosphere, tuned into various conversations of local gossip and generally gained a reasonably good overview of what was what in the area. Some establishments were quaint and had character whilst others were plain and boring. A repetitive chant played on a jukebox.

(That's right) Get up and boogie,
Get up and boogie,

(That's right) Get up and boogie,
Get up and boogie,
Boogie, Boogie.

Names such as The Leather Bottle and The Old Rooms Inn sounded a little out of the ordinary. In the lounge bar of The Black Dog the barmaid told Edwin of an inexpensive room in town that would soon be available to let. He was grateful and jotted down its address and the following morning went to take a look at it. The door was opened by an elderly lady who lived on the ground floor of the terraced house in Gloucester Road. She showed him to a small bedsitting room on the third floor which she said he could have for the sum of three pounds a week.

The day for the interview soon came round. The train journey into London took three and a half hours. Arriving in Waterloo Edwin was in good time to get across to Swiss Cottage where the office of Sedgley Clarke Productions was located. A panel of two men and two women sat in front of him and took it in turns to explain the role of their organization which was primarily involved in the production of television commercials. They outlined the process of first clarifying whatever it was that their clients wished to communicate. The production team would then hold brainstorming sessions to come up with ideas as to how that could best be achieved within an agreed budget. Once an idea was commissioned the scripting and storyboarding would take place and everything had to be delivered on time and on budget. They showed him some examples of the commercials and promotions that they produced.

Attention was then turned to Edwin who was quizzed on his various production skills. They seemed suitably impressed that he had experience in writing scripts, directing camerawork and editing and it was then pointed out that there were two positions available. One would be with an immediate start and the other later on in the year. They were interviewing candidates for both posts and they said that they would get in touch with him again within the next few weeks.

When Edwin got back in Weymouth that evening he was cautiously optimistic. He was aware, however, that his experience in television broadcasting, although related, was different from the film production of TV commercials. He got changed and went out to pub called the King's Arms on the harbourside for a couple of pints of beer and got chatting to a man called Joe who lived with his ageing father in a nearby village of Abbotsbury. He was glad of somebody to talk to. An invitation to Sunday lunch in Abbotsbury was offered.

Edwin was playing the waiting game yet again and with repeated speculation as to whether or not he would be offered the London based job.

The Sunday lunch in Abbotsbury was Roast Beef and Yorkshire pudding. His host Joe had collected Edwin in his car. On arrival the old cottage had a log fire crackling in the lounge. Joe's father sat in front of it reading the Sunday Times through gold rimmed spectacles. He was smartly dressed with a brown tweed jacket and tie. Joe had spoken of him during that morning's drive from Weymouth.

"He might be the oldest resident in the village but he still manages to eat like a bloody horse," he said. "I seem to spend my entire life cooking one massive meal after another for him but I suppose that as long as he's around that's what I have to do."

True to form, his father requested a second and then a third helping of the main course as he also did with the blackberry and apple crumble and custard that followed.

"Would you now like your usual cheese and crackers, father?" asked Joe.

"That would be nice, Joe," answered the old man, "and a cup of tea."

"I'll put the kettle on," he said. Then, turning to Edwin he said, "I'm going to have to drive you back into Weymouth this evening. I hope you don't mind but I'm going to have an afternoon nap before then."

"That's OK," said Edwin, "In the meantime perhaps I could go out for a bit of a walk around the village."

"Good idea," replied Joe, "and then we can have tea at around five o'clock. Father normally starts getting hungry again at around that time."

Edwin was pleased to get out of the house and glad to be on his own for a while. There was something incredibly dreary and predicable about a household routine that revolved around a non-stop cycle of cooking, eating and sleeping.

He walked through the village of Abbotsbury and its yellow coloured limestone cottages passing several shops and a couple of tearooms. Although the place was famous for a swan sanctuary there was still another month to go before that would re-open for the season. Edwin came to the front entrance of some tropical gardens but continued along the narrow lane to the coast. He arrived at the seafront with its distinctive long stretch of pebbles known as Chesil Beach leading to the westerly side of the Isle of Portland that jutted out into the English Channel. Crunching his way across the bed of stones for about half an hour he then turned back towards Abbotsbury.

An old church building perched on top of a hill came into view and Edwin decided to round off the afternoon's walk by climbing up to it. Its height commanded views over the Dorset countryside and the English Channel. Walking around the building's perimeter he saw that its walls were high and heavily buttressed under a stone vaulted roof. Once upon a time it must have had had a purpose, he thought. And then he suddenly thought of his own situation and recalled that once upon a time he must have had a purpose too. He shuddered at the realisation that his life now seemed to be heading nowhere. Everything seemed to have come to nothing. Admittedly there was still the possibility of the job in London – but even that was by no means certain. What would he do if he were turned down? It was almost as if he was being mocked by destiny itself. "Look at you. Once you had a future, a home in New Zealand and a promising career. You didn't fair too badly in Hong Kong either but you've since been blocked from going back to work in New Zealand and have instead ended up grovelling in the pits – you have no one to turn to, no future and no escape." It was as much a disturbing thought as a pretty accurate appraisal of his present situation. It was quite literally what his life had come to. For some strange reason the isolated setting of the sturdy rectangular structure of the chapel building seemed to emphasise his plight still further. Buildings might last for hundreds of years, he reminded himself, but people don't. He was glad to descend the hill which had given him the creeps.

Afternoon tea back at the cottage consisted of dainty sandwiches, homemade Cornish pasties and some freshly baked scones. Joe's father ate more than his fair share but there was plenty. He asked Edwin is he had enjoyed his walk.

"Yes, thank you. You live in a pleasant village," he replied, I went down to the beach and then up to that disused church on the hill."

"Saint Catherine's Chapel?" he asked.

"I've no idea what it was called," he said, "A square shaped building on top of a grassy hill."

"Oh, that'd be Saint Catherine's alright," interjected Joe, "but it's not normally young men who go up there."

"How do you mean?" asked Edwin.

"The young women of Abbotsbury used to go to that chapel to try and get the help of Saint Catherine to find them husbands," he said, "She's supposed to be the patron saint of virgins. Not that you're likely to find many virgins left around here in this day and age."

Joe's father added, "She's also the origin of the Catherine wheel after she got tortured on a wheel of sword points in the third century."

Edwin thought that he had experienced sufficient torture of a different nature just in visiting the chapel.

As they drove back to Weymouth that evening Edwin mentioned to Joe that as far as the future was concerned things didn't look too rosy just at present. He sympathised.

"I know exactly what you mean", he said, "and just when you reach the point at which things can't possibly get any worse – they do!"

WARMER WEATHER WAS ALREADY on its way but Edwin had heard nothing further from the Sedgley Clarke Productions despite three weeks having elapsed since the interview. He wondered whether he should contact them again or sit tight for a little longer. There was no means of knowing if a follow-up phone call might give a positive impression of indicating his continued interest in the job or whether it might be counter-productive and give them the impression that he was desperate and impatient. He decided that he would wait until the following week and then perhaps get in touch with them to ask if a decision had yet been made. In the meantime his funds were dwindling.

Walking around Weymouth Marina he happened to pass the local Employment Office. He paused for a moment and then thought that he might as well go in to check if there were any temporary vacancies available because, with the outcome of the London job hanging in the balance, it might prove wise to be one step ahead of both eventualities. On entering the building he found himself standing in a room amidst some upright display boards containing typed postcards of job descriptions of what was currently on offer in Weymouth and its surrounding area. He took his time in browsing through the whole lot of them and decided that he didn't want to be a care worker or a window cleaner and nor could he see himself working behind the bar of one particularly rough pub that he had deliberately bypassed the other night. There were several driving jobs but as he had never learned to drive they were no good and a handful of sales jobs seemed to be on a commission only basis.

He was about to leave the building when a female clerk looked up from her desk and caught his eye and smiled.

"Nothing of any interest to you on the boards?" she enquired.

"No, there doesn't appear to be" replied Edwin.

"Never mind," she replied, "but you are receiving your unemployment benefit payments OK?"

"No, I don't actually get that," he said.

"No?" she asked.

"I'm kind of between jobs and was just wondering if there might have been something temporary going to help bridge the gap," he said by means of explanation.

"I see," she said, "but if you are not actually in work at the moment your best bet might be to sign on and then consider the various vacancies as they come in.

"What would that entail?" he asked.

"You'd just need to come along to this office once a fortnight. Generally speaking the amount paid is sufficient to cover your rent and your living expenses until such time as you are back in work again."

"And what if I were suddenly to get offered a job in London?" he asked.

"Well, of course, that would be wonderful and if it were to happen you would simply need to let us know," she said.

Edwin paused. He had never done such a thing before. In one sense it felt degrading. After all, he wasn't a beggar. On the other hand such entitlement seemed to fit his current situation and any extra cash would come in handy.

"I can arrange for one of our advisors to see you right away, if you like," she persisted.

"Well OK then" said Edwin.

She wrote down his name and asked him to go through to the next room and to take a seat. Someone would see him shortly.

The small room had two rows of chairs facing three semi-enclosed booths. A woman sat smoking a cigarette and periodically flicking the ash into a metal ashtray on the stand whilst a man seated at one of the booths was in conversation with an official. After a while the man got up and came over to the woman. "All sorted," he said and the two of them then departed.

"Mr Ravensdale," a voice from the second booth summoned Edwin.

He stepped forward and entered the small enclosure and sat down on the seat provided.

"You are a new claimant?" asked a man on the other side of a dividing glass panel.

"Yes," replied Edwin.

"Right, well I just need to take down a few details from you," said the official.

After giving his date of birth and current address Edwin was asked when he had last worked.

"Friday the 12th of March," he replied.

"What kind of work was it?" he asked.

"Temporary work in a hotel," replied Edwin

"Here in Weymouth?" asked the man.

"No. It was in Brussels," responded Edwin.

"Brussels?" echoed the man, looking at Edwin somewhat quizzically.

"Yes," said Edwin.

"Why did you leave the job," he asked.

"It was only ever taken as a temporary arrangement whilst seeking work in my normal profession," he replied.

"And what is your normal job" he asked.

"Television Programme Director" replied Edwin.

The man looked up from the form that he was filling out.

"Oh, I see," he said, "And was that with the BBC or ITV?"

"Neither," replied Edwin, "I was with the New Zealand Broadcasting Corporation in New Zealand and then with Rediffusion Television in Hong Kong.

The man looked perplexed.

"Well," he said, "You come under the category of Professional and Executive. We're going to have to start somewhere but with a record like that it's not straightforward."

Edwin didn't know how to respond. It had sounded almost like having some kind of a criminal record.

The man wrote something on the front of a little booklet which he gave to Edwin.

"Whatever you are entitled to will be from today's date," he said. "Please come to the front office in a fortnight's time on Thursday 20th May at 10:00 am."

Edwin rose and departed back through the front office. He saw that a different person now sat at the desk where the previous lady had been. It must be lunch time, he thought.

ON SATURDAY MORNING A letter arrived for Edwin. The pale yellow envelope had the Sedgley Clarke logo embossed on its front. The moment of truth had finally arrived. He didn't open it right away but instead took it with him to the top of the Nothe Fort Hill. He sat down on the same bench as on his first day in Weymouth then opened the letter and read its content. The job with the immediate start had gone to another candidate however the company would be pleased to consider Edwin for the other position that would become available in September.

Well, at least he now knew which side his bread was buttered on and, above all, the torment of speculation was over. As for the job in September, he certainly wasn't going to hang around for five months waiting to see whether or not that materialised although he would reply positively and keep the line of communication open.

It was time to plan things anew. He considered the various options. He had already been in Weymouth far too long for comfort and the prospect of remaining there unemployed had no appeal whatsoever. Ever since he had wound up in this situation of going from pillar to post he deduced that the one formula which seemed to work best for him was to adopt a motto of 'When in doubt, change country.'

He glanced down in the direction of the harbour and realised that perhaps the greatest thing about Weymouth was the fact that it had a ferry service to enable him to get right out of the place. He wondered where best to head for. He could already tick several boxes. Done France, done Germany done Belgium. Spain was forever a possibility as he already spoke the language but he reasoned that he'd also effectively done that several years ago and it didn't seem wise to go back to old haunts from the past. After a while he deduced that Italy might be a reasonable choice.

There was no time like the present. Despite the fact that he had very little cash to hand, Edwin hastened down to the ferry terminal and purchased a one-way ticket for Monday morning's sailing across to France from where he would hitch-hike to Italy. There had been no formal tenancy agreement for the room that he had rented and the elderly lady didn't seem to mind at all when he told her that he would be leaving at short notice. She wished him well. The booklet from the Employment Office contained a short form for use when quitting the benefit system and signing off. Edwin was pleased to fill it out and post it. He congratulated himself on cancelling it before it had even started. He then studied a map and decided that his Italian destination would be Florence.

CHAPTER TWENTY-SIX

THE FERRY CROSSING FROM Weymouth to Cherbourg took four and a half hours. It was already mid-afternoon when Edwin walked along a road that headed in a south-easterly direction from the port and found a suitable place to stand alongside a small lay-by into which any driver willing to give him a lift would be able to pull over without much difficulty. The tried and tested strategy worked well and within the first five minutes a young French lady had stopped and he climbed into her Renault car. She was going as far as Caen which was where she lived and a distance of some forty kilometres. They had a lively conversation in French and, when they eventually arrived there, she looked slightly disappointed when he said that he didn't have time to come in for coffee but that he was going to continue with his journey down to Italy.

"Peut tête nous nous pouvons visiter à la retourne!' she suggested.

"Mais sure!" responded Edwin, who knew that if he didn't get away then and there, he might end up staying in France with this new found friend and never make it to Italy at all. He looked at her. She was attractive and seemingly uncomplicated and…no, he'd best be on his way. They exchanged addresses and he promised to look her up on his way back although he did so in the full knowledge that it was extremely unlikely that he would return there in the foreseeable future, if ever at all. They parted company.

Edwin walked through the residential streets of Caen and out to the main thoroughfare on its other side. From there he was fortunate enough to get several good lifts which later that evening had got him right around to the other side of Paris and further convinced him that his decision not to have been sidetracked in Caen had been a good one. He was dropped off at a busy roundabout which according to road signs was somewhere near Fontainebleau. It was one o'clock in the morning on a relatively warm night and he was beginning to feel tired. Walking up a grass embankment he stretched himself out and managed to get some sleep for the best part of four hours. When he awoke the sun was coming up over the horizon. He felt refreshed and ready to face the day ahead. Once again, luck was with him. First a lift with an electrician brought him to a small French village where he was able to purchase a couple of croissants from the local boulangerie as breakfast and then a lady pulled up in an open-topped car and offered to take him on a five hour journey all the way down to Lyons. Later in the day, as they neared Lyons she invited him to stay overnight in the guestroom at the house of her parents where he was wined and dined that evening.

The following morning a succession of lifts via Grenoble passed through a series of road tunnels that had been hollowed out in the mountains. Edwin finally crossed the border into Italy and was heading along a motorway in the direction of Turin.

Communication with Italian drivers wasn't easy. Edwin had assumed that there might have been sufficient similarity between the Italian and Spanish languages for him to be able to understand but he soon found out he was mistaken. He couldn't even pronounce the place names correctly let alone converse. According to his map, he needed to be on the road for somewhere called Piacenza but it was only after several attempts that the driver recognised what he was trying to say and Edwin discovered that if he pronounced it as something that sounded like "Be a gent, sir" it was understood. One driver then persisted in jabbering away in Italian even though every single word of what was said was completely lost on Edwin. He then got a lift from a truck driver who spoke a little English and who worked in an Italian ice cream factory. The man used the opportunity to lament his country's current leaning towards Communism and came close to tears in the process.

By-passing Parma, Modena and Bologna, Edwin progressed still further and finally made it to the outskirts of Florence late that afternoon. A street vendor selling water melons from a small cart pointed him in the direction of the city centre and Edwin walked a couple of miles through suburbia before arriving at Florence's main railway terminus. Two blocks further and he found a hostel where he could stay. To his surprise the dormitories turned out to be unisex and he was shown to a room with three single beds, the first two of which were already taken by an American man and his equally American girlfriend. The price was cheap enough and Edwin paid upfront for five nights. He knew that he would need to find some employment of one sort or another within a short time frame in order to survive. The set of circumstances seemed somewhat familiar.

He spent the first evening getting some idea of the geography of the centre of Florence during the course of an exploratory walk with his two roommates who had introduced themselves as Jim and Cindy. The three of them took in sights of the Ponte Vecchio, the famous old bridge that crosses the River Arno and the cathedral with the artistic dome of Il Duomo that features in just about every picture postcard from Florence. They passed through public squares lined with large white stone statues amidst crowds of tourists. Although the artistic and architectural heritage ranked it as one of the most beautiful cities in the world, Edwin's mind was already working overtime as to what work he might be able to do in such a place. As they made their way back to the hostel Jim explained to Edwin that until recently he had been training for the priesthood at a seminary in the United States but had become so disillusioned with the whole thing that he had quit and then met the love of his life, the passionate Cindy, with whom he had since been making up for lost time.

EDWIN KNEW THAT IT was never straightforward to know where to begin when looking for a job and he imagined that his best bet would be working in one of the restaurants as some kind of a general dog's body whilst he picked up the language. However, finding such a job in Florence was easier said than done. He spent the first day traipsing around from one restaurant to the next but after four and a half hours no one had offered him the slightest hint of a job. It was the same story at the various hotels and bars that he encountered on the way. In the late afternoon, despite there being an obvious language barrier, he even tried asking in some of the shops whether they had any vacancies but that too proved to be equally fruitless. He wasn't completely disheartened because past experience had shown him that as long as he kept up the momentum he would inevitably stumble upon an opportunity before long. After all, he was young and healthy and willing to do virtually any kind of work in return for very little pay provided that it would enable him to tick over whilst learning some Italian and absorbing some of the country's culture.

But the following day's search for a job was every bit as hopeless as the first. Nobody at all seemed to have a vacancy and neither did anyone know of anybody else who might happen to have the remotest possibility of one. That evening he again tagged along with his American roommates and went to eat at the university where it was possible to get a large plate of pasta and a rich tomato sauce at a heavily subsidized cheap price. Despite the fact that he would soon be running broke, Edwin remained as optimistic as ever, feeling sure that the situation would soon change.

However, as the days passed by and there was still no sign of work of any description to be found for him in Florence. Edwin was already into his eighth day of staying at the hostel. He handed the landlord some further rent money and knew that if he were to continue staying there any longer than three more nights he would have no immediate means of paying any more.

Two more days of intensive search for work took place. Even though the overnight charge at the hostel was relatively inexpensive, it was the first time in his life that Edwin had ever stayed anywhere in the knowledge that he couldn't foot the bill. He simply had to get some work right away. Similarly, he hadn't eaten more than a couple of bread rolls for the past two days and was down to his last four Italian Liras.

His American roommates would be leaving the following day but prior to doing so they invited him to join them for lunch. Whether or not they'd detected something of his predicament, Edwin didn't know but when he made some excuse about waiting for funds to arrive from England they insisted that the meal would be on them. After a brief visit to the Accademia Gallery to view Michelangelo's statue of David, they took him to one of the most intriguing little restaurants he'd ever come across. It was entered quite literally through a gap in a wall. Its interior consisted of two very long tables at which the customers, mainly American tourists, sat along benches arranged on either side. There was no written menu but for an all-inclusive price an elderly waiter delivered course after course whilst his wife kept yelling her head off at him in Italian from an open-plan smoky kitchen. Balloon shaped bottles of red wine had been placed along the table and, as soon as they were consumed they were instantly replaced and it became apparent that one was expected to eat and drink as much as one liked. What's more the dishes were of high quality cuisine. Periodically the mama chef would come through with a big smile on her face to see that everyone was enjoying their dish of Pollo alla Cacciatore or whatever course had just been placed before them. Then, turning her attention to her husband once again, she would scream at him to go and fetch another basket of bread and to get ready to bring out the next course of grilled fish, to which he humbly and meekly obliged. Their whole relationship was something of a floor show in itself. Perhaps it was intended to be. In all there were probably ten different courses, some big and some small, before the sequence repeated itself over again as dish after dish continued to be rolled out throughout the entire day. By five o'clock Edwin and his two American friends were so bloated that they couldn't manage a further thing.

The following morning when Edwin awoke he encountered the landlord of the hostel hovering outside the room.

"'ow long you wanna stay?" he asked

Edwin wondered if it was a prompt for a further payment.

"I'd like to stay for another week," said Edwin, casually, before adding "Oh, and I'll pay you within the next few days, as soon as my money comes through from England."

The landlord grunted an indication of acceptance of such an arrangement but said that Edwin would have to move into an adjacent room where there were eight single beds whilst a group of three arrivals had now been booked into the smaller room. But of course there was no money coming through from England and, having fabricated such a story, it added to Edwin's already pressurised task to find a job as a matter of extreme urgency. He went out and combed the streets of Florence yet again.

Two more days of intensive search resulted in absolutely nothing. He'd have gladly scrubbed floors, stacked shelves, served in bars, loaded trucks or cleaned toilets yet there appeared to be no opportunities even for such humdrum tasks. It had worked out in France, it had worked out in Germany and it had worked out in Belgium so why on earth was it not now working out in Italy? He entered a small café and drank a glass of iced tea, ate a pastry and resigned himself to the fact that he was now flat broke. He had a couple of packets of cigarettes left that he'd bought from the duty free shop on the ferry coming over.

That evening, for some reason, the landlord was in a jovial mood and had scooped out a watermelon and filled it with some concoction of wine and spirits which he was dishing out in small glasses to the hostel guests. It was a moment of light relief and Edwin got talking with some of his new roommates which included an Irishman and two young ladies from Texas. After the social gathering, the four of them went out for an evening walk by the river.

The harsh reality of Edwin's situation became even more apparent the following day when such holiday acquaintances had all departed for their next destinations leaving him to carry on where he'd left off in walking the sun-drenched streets in search of anyone who could point him in the direction of some work. He had already learned how to say the request in Italian but that still didn't bring about any positive outcome. By mid-afternoon, he began to feel that, as far as the city of Florence was concerned, he had covered everywhere possible in the hunt for work. He stood on the pavement opposite the Uffizi Gallery wondering how best to handle such a dire situation. At that moment he was approached by an American girl who, with air of familiarity as if Edwin was somebody that she knew, said, "Hi there!"

"Oh, hi," responded Edwin.

"You look a bit lost," she said

Presumably some sort of giveaway downcast expression about him had brought about the comment.

"Oh, no I'm fine. Thanks," he responded, trying to sound as upbeat as possible.

"Are you Australian?" she enquired.

"No, I'm from England," he said.

And her next questions took him by surprise.

"Are you hungry?" she asked, "Would you like to come back and eat with us?"

In point of fact, not having eaten a meal since that massive restaurant feast of two days ago, Edwin was ravenous but how on earth could this complete stranger know such a thing? Was she super-intuitive or was the word 'hungry' simply written all over his face? Nevertheless, he was quick to respond.

"That's very kind," he said, "Yes, I'd love to."

"Great! Then come with me," she said, "I belong to a Christian group and we are based here in Florence. By the way, my name is Melanie. What's yours?"

"Edwin," he replied.

She led the way down the street for a couple of hundred yards and then ushered him in through an entrance door and up a flight of stairs to a second floor apartment. Once inside, they passed through a hallway and into a lounge in which half a dozen people of a similar age to Edwin were sat on either side of a long dining table. A wooden cross hung on one of the walls as did a painting depicting Jesus Christ.

Edwin was introduced to everyone in the room who, it was explained, were part of a missionary group that was ordinarily based in the United States. There were a couple of spare places at the table and Melanie invited Edwin to sit down and join them. A slightly older American lady then came through from another room and welcomed him to the gathering. She said grace and dishes of chicken, pasta and salad were then passed around for people to help themselves. A basket of bread and a large jug of water made a similar circular route. The conversation at the table was somewhat formal. Edwin had always thought that it was etiquette not to speak about religion or politics during mealtimes but it became apparent that such convention didn't apply to American religious groups whose sole topic of conversation seemed to be of a biblical nature throughout the entire meal. After a cream cake desert a young man sitting at the end of the table asked Edwin what brought him to Florence. The rest of the table fell silent for his response.

Edwin gave quite an open and frank version of the chain of events. He explained something of his professional background in television broadcasting and that being unable to return to work in New Zealand he had been doing completely unrelated jobs to tide him over and was now in Italy seeking any kind of work at all. It was a sincere account of the reality of the situation and when he'd finished he was surprised when the man said, "Thank you, Edwin. And now, would you mind if I pray for you?"

Not really sure how to answer, Edwin simply shrugged his shoulders and said, "Well, if you think it might do any good, you can go right ahead."

With that, the man invited everybody present to bow their heads and join him in prayer. In what turned out to be quite a lengthy choice of words giving thanks to God for his many blessing he went on to pray that God would enter Edwin's life and that Jesus and the Holy Spirit would become his guiding force and that Edwin would be shown the way back into his professional field once again and that he would be fulfilled and that he would find new meaning in his life.

By the time "Amen" had been reached Edwin couldn't help feeling moved by such words about his own personal situation. To the best of his knowledge it was the first time that anybody had ever prayed for him or at least certainly the first time that he had ever heard anyone doing so. As he had no religious faith himself it was a completely new experience. He thanked them for the meal and as he was making his departure they told him he was welcome to return and visit them whenever he wished.

Feeling suitably nourished both physically and now spiritually, Edwin made a slight detour from the normal route back through the town. It was already five o'clock and being the gap between lunch and dinner it was not the best time of day to be banging on closed restaurant doors to ask if they had a vacancy for someone to wash the dishes. As he made his way through various backstreets he came across a small building that had the unmistakable features of being a radio station. Edwin stopped in his tracks. OK, he couldn't speak Italian and OK it was radio rather than television but surely it would do no harm at least to go in and ask if there were any job possibilities. After all, he could only get rejected and by now he was getting rather used to that so it wouldn't make much difference.

He entered through the glass doors into a reception area where he found that the Italian lady behind the desk could speak fluent English. After explaining a little of his professional background in television presentation and programme production and the fact that he was on the lookout for a job, she said that she would phone someone with whom he could speak. She dialled a number and jabbered away in Italian to the person on the other end for quite some time and then handed the phone to Edwin. 'Here,' she said, 'It's OK, you can speak in English to Roberto – he is American and he works with the television project.'

"Hello, this is Edwin Ravensdale," said Edwin, momentarily thrown by the words 'television project' and not knowing quite where to begin.

"Hi, my name's Robert Brown. I gather you have experience in television programme production," said the American voice.

Edwin repeated almost verbatim what he'd told the receptionist.

"Well," replied Robert Brown, "This is all very interesting and an amazing coincidence. The situation here is that deregulation has recently taken place in Italy meaning that small privately run television stations are able to pop up left, right and centre in most major cities. I work primarily on the technical side of things and I am in the process of setting up a new TV station for Florence. I'd sure like to meet with you with your kind of experience. Could I invite you for lunch tomorrow?"

Edwin could scarcely believe his ears and eagerly accepted the invitation. It was arranged that they would meet at 1 pm the following day at a restaurant near the Piazza del Carmine.

At the end of the phone call, he thanked the receptionist profusely and then headed back to the hostel.

What had happened was incredible. There was optimism, the likes of which he hadn't felt for months yet, at the same time he knew that he'd have to tread carefully. The following day's meeting could be a make or break situation.

ROBERT BROWN ROSE FROM his place at the table to greet Edwin as soon as he entered the restaurant. There were few other customers and the fact that Edwin had arrived bang on the dot made instant recognition that much easier. Robert Brown was a tall, thin man with a short haircut who wore spectacles and was probably in his mid-thirties.

"Welcome," he said with a smile and offered a limp handshake that felt like a dead fish. "You managed to find your way here alright?"

"Yes indeed. I'm pleased to meet you" replied Edwin, glancing around the tastefully decorated dining area.

"Grab a seat," said Robert.

"Thank you," replied Edwin sitting down opposite him, "This is a pleasant looking place."

"Well, the food here is good wholesome Italian cuisine and the service is normally excellent but because it's over on this side of the river it doesn't get crowded out like other places so at least it's possible to hear each other speak," he said. "Now, first things first, what can I get you to drink?"

Edwin saw that Robert already had a coca cola and he opted for the same thing. He needed to have his wits about him and so at this stage of the game thought it wise to resist going the route of Campari and soda, no matter how appropriate that might otherwise have been. A waitress arrived and Robert ordered for both of them. He then invited Edwin to talk him through his work in television broadcasting both in New Zealand and in Hong Kong. He listened attentively as Edwin summarised everything as succinctly as possible. It was well received.

"Wow, that's quite something!" said Robert, "you sure gained a wealth of valuable broadcasting experience in those places.

They then spoke briefly about Edwin's reason for having come to Florence. He was able to steer his way through that with comparative ease and managed to avoid any hint of effectively having hit rock bottom. He learned that Robert was half American and half French and that he had lived in Italy for the past decade. Over mounds of Spaghetti alla Carrettiera the conversation moved forward towards the topic of the new TV station in Florence. Robert explained that it was housed in the basement of a block of flats on the outskirts of the city. It was already on air and being run by a young and enthusiastic staff but the one thing that they lacked was experience.

"And that, hopefully, is where you would come in," he said, "We need someone with broadcasting experience to oversee and train up the staff in all aspects of transmission control and programme production which is why I am so interested in your background in those fields in New Zealand and Hong Kong. Let me ask you a straight question – would such a role be of any interest to you?"

"It most certainly would," Edwin replied and then added, "although presumably you are aware that I can't speak much Italian yet?"

"That wouldn't be a problem," replied Robert. "Most of the time you'd be working alongside me so that I could pick your brain about how we should be running the place."

"That arrangement sounds fine to me," said Edwin, delighted by the way things seemed to be progressing.

"OK, that's great," said Robert, 'But now we come to the more awkward bit. Although the television project is an offshoot of the radio station it is privately funded and has to make ends meet through advertising revenue. But, of course, that takes time to build up and there's not a lot of cash in the kitty. The situation will improve but at the moment and whilst it's getting off the ground those who work there do a six day week often with unsociable hours and for very little financial reward."

"I could go along with that," replied Edwin, in the knowledge that any income, however small, was going to be better that his current income of nothing at all – and ever mindful of his debt clocking up at the hostel.

"Well, let's see now' continued Robert, "The company could pay you a basic salary of thirty thousand Lira a month which isn't an awful lot to live on in a place like Florence but, to help matters, I could also offer you some rent free accommodation and there'd also be a small expense allowance."

Things seemed to take a new twist by the minute and Edwin confirmed that, on such a basis, he would be please to accept the offer.

"That's wonderful. How soon would you be able to start?" asked Robert.

"How about right away?" replied Edwin.

"You're on!" said Robert and the two of them reached across the table and shook hands. Edwin was so thrilled that Robert's limp handshake didn't bother him this time round.

The remainder of the meal was a more relaxed affair and an opportunity for them to get to know each other on a less formal basis. It was arranged that Robert would pick Edwin up by car at the Piazza Della Italia Unita the following morning and that, after a quick transfer of his belongings to the new accommodation address, they would pass by the administration office at the Radio Station to sign his employment documents before heading on out to the TV Station.

After coffee and cigarettes they went their separate ways and Edwin walked back into town wondering whether he had dreamt the whole encounter. He was also conscious of the fact that it was only twenty-four hours ago that an American missionary bloke had prayed for him and asked for God's help in getting him get back into his profession. He had occasionally heard people speak of the power of prayer before but it was the first time that he'd had anything to do with it. There seemed to be an undeniable link between the man's prayer and the seemingly impossible chain of events that had taken place afterwards – unless it was just a lucky coincidence.

He then turned his mind to the more immediate problem of how he was going to check out of the hostel whilst convincing the landlord that he would return at a later date to square his bill for the few nights unpaid rent. Maybe he needed another prayer for that. When he approached the landlord that evening, he found him not to be too happy with the idea.

"Firsta you tell me you stay another week and you awaitin' money from England, now you tell me you go away but still no pay!" said the landlord.

"What I'm telling you is that I'll be pleased to pay what I owe as soon as I have the money," replied Edwin, "You can even hang on to my passport as a deposit if you like."

The landlord shrugged his shoulders and mellowed slightly at the suggestion.

"Passport? Passport? No! No need your passport. You bringa me money soon – OK?"

"Yes," agreed Edwin, "I bringa you money soon."

AT NINE O'CLOCK THE following morning Robert's tiny Fiat car drew up beside Edwin at the pre-arranged spot at one end of the square. It transpired that the rent free accommodation was within Robert's own luxury apartment situated near the Pitti Palace and Boboli Gardens. It was also shared with a young Italian man called Andrea to whom he was introduced on their arrival. Edwin was allocated an en suite bedroom for his own use where he deposited his belongings. In addition to three other bedrooms the apartment had a large lounge, a dining room, a well-equipped kitchen and a balcony.

After a quick coffee Robert suggested that he and Edwin drive across to the television station which was located on the other side of town. As arranged they stopped off at the radio station en route where documentation proved to be a simple formality which served to ensure that Edwin was put on the company's payroll. The car journey then continued to an outlying Florence suburb where after some difficulty in finding a parking space they walked a short distance to the block of flats where the TV station was based. Robert unlocked a hefty metal door and as they entered inside he reached up to a fuse box to switch on some lights.

The medium sized studio was equipped with three cameras on tripods. Most of the technical facilities were a bit on the basic side but nevertheless functional. Polystyrene panels had been stuck to its walls and ceiling to act as the sound-proofing and Edwin could detect that improvisation had obviously played a key role in getting the place up and running.

"As you can see, there's nothing particularly sophisticated about anything in here," said Robert, "although as soon as money begins to roll in everything will be upgraded. For now, though, we simply make do with what we've got – but at least we're on air for anything from eight to twelve hours every day and the channel is beginning to attract loyal viewers."

"What kinds of programmes are broadcast?" asked Edwin.

"Italians love movies and so one of the things we do is to transmit the same movie three or sometimes four times at different hours throughout the day – just like at a cinema – and, between showing the movie we broadcast our own shows most of which are live studio discussions about topics affecting Florence – local political issues and things of that nature," he said.

They stepped into the control room.

"This doubles both as transmission control room and as the production control room," explained Robert.

'That's a bit unfortunate,' said Edwin, 'because it means that when you're on air, you've completely tied up all your programme making facilities.'

"Yes, I suppose that is true," said Robert, "but is there any easy way around that?"

'What's really needed are two separate control rooms, one for presentation and the other for programme production which in the event of it being a live programme could then be selected as a source in the presentation control room, said Edwin.

"OK," said Robert, "although I guess that means we'd need to get double the amount of equipment."

"It's definitely worth planning for," said Edwin. "And I see that here in this control room there's no separate booth for audio control which could be a bit awkward."

"Good," replied Robert, "You're noticing these things right away.

In addition to its vision mixing and audio capabilities the room also housed the TV station's transmitter in one of its corners alongside two telecine film projectors, three videotape players and a couple of fixed cameras pointing at graphic material next to some telephones – all lumped in together. Someone had clearly applied a somewhat literal interpretation of the words 'control room.'

"What I'd really like you to do over the next few weeks is to work out how we should reorganise the entire layout of the place to enable it to function more efficiently," said Robert, "but you're going to have to bear in mind that we're not in any position to race out and buy a whole lot of new kit just at the moment."

"That's fair enough," agreed Edwin. "I'll see what I can come up with."

They took their time in looking around all of the various rooms in the rest of the premises. Whilst crossing the studio floor, Edwin noticed that the soles of his shoes were sticking to a carpeted area.

"Oh, yes, we had a little disaster in here a few weeks ago with a water pipe that flooded out all over the floor," said Robert, "Some of it has still not completely dried out."

"It's a pity that the ceiling isn't a little higher – not that one can do anything about that," observed Edwin, "I'll bet you can see the studio lights in just about every camera shot."

'Yes, the low ceiling is something of a problem,' agreed Robert, It limits a lot of what we could do although we can just about get away with it in the kind of talk shows that we broadcast."

The studio was separated from its control room by a glass window. Edwin pointed out that whilst that arrangement might be fine for a radio studio it wasn't entirely necessary for television because it effectively meant the loss of an entire studio wall that could otherwise be used in productions. The control room should be able to see what was going on in the studio by looking at the monitors rather than staring through a window. Similarly the camera operators and the floor manager should be able to take their direction through headphones rather than hand signals being made from the other side of a pane of glass. Robert understood the reasoning.

Through a door off to one side of the studio there were several more rooms. A large one was used for storing scenic backdrops used in the various productions and there was a small mirrored make-up area. Five smaller rooms were not used for any specific purpose at all and were cluttered up with all manner of junk. Edwin made a note of their dimensions and thought that they could quite easily be transformed to production office, presentation control room, a small continuity studio, a videotape editing suite and a combined telecine and videotape play out area. Further along a passageway were toilets and a fire exit.

There was still half an hour to go before the duty staff would arrive to put the channel on air. In the meantime Robert locked up the building and the two of them went across the road where a conveniently located delicatessen provided both of them with a cappuccino and a salami roll.

It was suggested that they would sit in throughout that day's transmission so that Edwin could familiarise himself with the way in which the station operated in its present form and then make any suggestions for improvement to Robert at the end of the day.

Shortly before two o'clock the first staff members arrived. Stefano was the station's Chief Engineer and Maurizio would be directing transmission. Neither of them spoke English but with Robert acting as interpreter they were introduced to Edwin.

As they prepared for transmission Stefano placed an LP record on one of two turntables and faded up an Italian song.

Più ci penso e più mi viene voglia di lei
anche se nella mia mente più bella tu sei.
La mia sete cresce finché l'acqua non c'e'
Ed ora che ci sei
Io più ci penso più mi viene voglia di lei...

In the meantime Maurizio loaded up a projector with the first reel of a film. One of the fixed single cameras was pointed at a typed piece of cardboard that advertised the services of a local construction company and was then put on air by means of the small vision mixing panel. Shortly before three o'clock Fabio faded the screen out to black once again and the card was substituted for another containing the channel's name, Telemondo Firenze. Then, to Edwin's surprise and amusement, the Senior Engineer, Stefano, picked up a microphone, lowered the level of the music and did his own voice-over from the control room.

"Signori e Signore, bienvenuto alla transmissione de Telemondo Firenze per oggi. Adesso un film che sichiama 'Ogni volta en tanto.'"

And with that, Maurizio ran the projector and then leapt across to the other side of the control room in order to switch to the telecine source on the vision mixing panel thereby putting the film on air. At the same time, Stefano abruptly cut the audio right in the middle of the Italian song and selected the soundtrack of the film and hey presto, their first programme of the day was on the air.

Edwin and Robert had agreed that they would play the part of observers for the day and not at this stage offer any advice or intervene in any way. The movie trundled through its two hour duration entailing two reel changes and some further static advertising for the same construction company as before accompanied by another burst of the same Italian song.

Other people began to arrive at the TV station. Some were studio crew and others were programme contributors for a live chat show that was scheduled for after the movie. Robert introduced Edwin to the cameramen and to a female presenter, Lisa, who was to be the anchor person for the programme.

The show didn't have its own producer or any kind of a production script come to that. Once the movie was over and after another commercial slot for the same construction company a new graphics card was inserted announcing the next programme's title as 'Oggi."

Studio lights were faded up. The camera crew and uncapped their cameras and took their positions. Their composed shots were now visible on three of the monitors in the control room. The Programme participants had been arranged in two rows of chairs set in a 'V' shape with a middle chair for Lisa, the presenter.

Edwin had little idea what the content of the debate was about but it soon became obvious that whoever had selected the programme contributors had done an excellent job in choosing people with opposing views. Within a short space of time everybody was interrupting everybody else and a huge argument took place in emotional Italian with one lady guest quite literally screaming out her particular opinion. The anchor person, Lisa, could hardly get a word in edgewise.

Maurizio switched back and forth between the three studio cameras. There was no communication between the control room and the studio for any kind of direction to be given. Instead everything was very much a free for all. Cameras often had similar sized shots which made inter-cutting between them look aesthetically wrong. Half the time the cameramen didn't seem to know when their particular camera was on air and they would often start recomposing their shot as their picture was going out live. The heated debate show lasted for over an hour. Someone else then arrived over from the radio station with a bulletin of news items which was taken into the studio and handed to Lisa to read immediately after the programme had drawn to a close.

Another familiar looking commercial break then took place and was followed by the second showing of the daily movie. In the meantime the participants of the live programme had flooded through into the control room clearly elated at what they'd achieved. The crowded space soon became thick with cigarette smoke and littered with the stained plastic beaker remains of coffee brought in from the delicatessen across the road.

By halfway through the second showing of the film the assembled multitude had trickled away leaving just the operational staff behind as well as Edwin and Robert. Another lively debate show on a different topic and with different people was scheduled next. That was followed by a slightly longer news bulletin, the main highlight of which was when one of the polystyrene tiles on the studio ceiling came unstuck and fluttered down alongside the newsreader causing him to burst into uncontrollable laughter. A final showing of the movie took the channel through to its closedown at around eleven o'clock.

The one and only commercial that day had been the graphic card with details of a construction company which popped up on air at every junction between programmes. When Edwin asked Robert about that he found out that the particular construction company was owned by the man who was funding the operation of the TV station.

CHAPTER TWENTY-SEVEN

EDWIN SETTLED INTO THE flow of Florentine life. Although work at the TV station was by far the dominating factor the fact that the transmission began in the afternoon meant that the mornings were free to have planning meetings with Robert which mainly took place across the breakfast table. However there was also time to step outside and Edwin would cross the river by means of the Ponte Vecchio and go into the centre of town or simply take a leisurely stroll through the nearby Boboli Gardens. He discovered the whereabouts of local shops as well as the bustling market places and also the number eleven bus route for those days in which he would travel to work by public transport.

Between the two of them Edwin and Robert devised an organisational structure for the television project which up until that time simply hadn't existed. All told there were some forty staff members and although most of them were willing to chip in and turn their hand to anything that needed to be done, there had been no clearly defined job descriptions and that had often resulted in duplication of some areas and neglect in others.

They drew up a schedule for staff training sessions which would take place on certain mornings of the week and include all aspects of programme production and studio operations. Transmission control was another field being looked at in order to find a smoother presentation style and channel identity. Until he could learn some Italian, Edwin would be thoroughly dependent on Robert to act as a translator.

The idea of a second control room for transmission control and an accompanying small studio for continuity announcements that would free up use of the production studio had been agreed in principle although the accounts department back at the radio station had wanted to know what the additional facilities were going to cost. Because Robert was primarily on the technical side of things and had access to equipment suppliers and their price lists he would calculate that. However, if they could find some way to generate extra advertising revenue all such upgrades might stand a better chance of being advanced more rapidly.

Being purely a local television service that was broadcast from a low-power transmitter the viewing area of Telemondo Firenze didn't reach an audience of much beyond the outer extremities of the City of Florence. It meant that advertising spots in its daily transmission schedule could be offered at a knock-down price that was no more expensive than placing an advertisement in a local magazine. A problem they identified, however, was that local traders who might have been interested in taking advantage of such economical publicity could not easily do so because they didn't possess a ready-made TV commercial that could be broadcast.

"What if we were to start making low-budget TV commercials for them?" asked Edwin.

"They would have to be rock-bottom, low-budget, commercials for any small businesses to be able to afford them," replied Robert.

"Agreed," replied Edwin, "But it's something that we have the capability of doing in-house. Theoretically it should be possible to offer them a package deal of having their very own TV commercial made for them and it being placed in the schedule for broadcast on a regular basis at a price that they could afford."

"It's certainly worth running the idea past Claudia who currently handles advertising sales," he said. She would have a better idea than I do of what local companies could reasonably be willing to pay. But one thing we don't want is to spend a lot of time making an ad and then find out that the company doesn't want to pay for it after all."

Edwin nodded. "Perhaps if such companies could pay half the money up-front and the balance on completion of the commercial it would get around that. In that way we'd cover our costs and, although they wouldn't know it, the production work would double as a useful staff training exercise."

LITTLE BY LITTLE THEIR plans were implemented throughout the weeks that followed. The TV station began to be run more efficiently. A weekly roster assigned staff to the various operational roles and the studio camera crew learnt about picture composition and were equipped with headphones. Floor managers became the eyes and ears of the producer/director during live shows rather than leaving everything to the programme presenters to organise as had been the norm previously. The variety of local productions didn't change much because there was no shortage of people with strong views about local issues who would seize any opportunity to get themselves on air – and such heated debates made for popular viewing. However a history programme was introduced as was a press review. Plans were also afoot for a comedy show and a drama series. Programmes went out on time and the continuity announcements that went in between them were skilfully scripted in advance.

Within a short space of time the first five home-grown TV commercials were already being shown and there were several more in the pipeline still in various stages of production. The newly formed sales team were doing a good job and the four-person unit who produced such snappy thirty-second advertisements were sufficiently inspired to keep coming up with new ideas.

On his second payday Edwin went out and bought himself a new suit. He had noticed that people in Florence dressed elegantly and although he wore what could best be described as smart casual clothing, there were certain occasions when he felt the need to conform to a more sophisticated dress code. He hadn't brought any formal wear with him from England because it hadn't crossed his mind for one moment that he would have had the good fortune to have stumbled back into his profession in Italy.

It still astounded him how the transition had come about. It felt like a kind of rags to riches story. One moment he had been quite literally penniless, hungry and sleeping in a mixed dormitory of a run-down hostel and deeply concerned about his future and yet now, here he was, salaried, well-fed, living in the lap of luxury and completely fulfilled in his professional work. Not for the first time he recalled how things had completely turned around following the prayer that had been given for him by that American missionary. He supposed that he ought to pay a courtesy visit to that group to let them know that their prayers obviously worked – even though explaining it might sound a trifle bizarre. "Hi everybody, I'd just like to let you know that you obviously have the hotline to God."

WHILST THE REST OF Europe was experiencing severe drought throughout the long hot summer of 1976, Florence and the outlying Tuscany hills were experiencing torrential rainfall and massive thunder storms. Equipped with an umbrella Edwin found his way to the apartment where the Christian community of missionaries was based. He rang the doorbell which was answered by the lady who was in charge of the group.

"Remember me?" said Edwin with a smile.

"Sure I do," she replied, "It's good to see you again, Edwin. Please come right on in."

They passed through into the lounge where Edwin had lunched with them on his previous visit. It felt as formal a room as it did on that occasion. This time however there were only two American men present, neither of whom was the person who had prayed for Edwin's situation. Nevertheless, he was pleased to relate all that had happened to the lady in charge whose name he now remembered as Jane.

"I am so pleased that things have worked out for you," she said.

He had half expected a kind of "There, you see. Ask and you shall receive!" kind of comment but none was forthcoming. Instead they drank a cup of tea together and spoke mainly about the wet weather as lightning flashed and thunder boomed loudly outside the apartment window.

The other two Americans were rather dull looking theology students on some kind of a Bible study exchange programme that had brought them to Florence for the summer months or, as one of them put it, the Lord had brought him to Italy. Edwin thought back to the American missionary that he had befriended at the YMCA in Hong Kong who had used similar terminology in describing how he moved from one place to another. The Lord had apparently brought him there too. It sounded weird – as if the Lord, whoever he was, was some kind of a travel agent. However because Edwin was on their territory he thought it better not to show disrespect. He nodded politely. Over a further cup of tea they chatted for some twenty minutes or so by which time a lull in the storm and some bright sunshine spilling across the balcony became his cue to depart. As the lady of the house, Jane, showed him out she handed him a paperback book.

"Here, let me give you a copy of this," she said, "You might find it interesting."

Taking it from her he glanced at its title and saw that it was called 'Basic Christianity'

"Thank you," he said, "I look forward to reading it." He could think of nothing more boring.

She invited him to drop by again whenever he next had the time.

TO THE STRAIN OF Rossini's Thieving Magpie on the record player, Edwin, Robert and the other flatmate, Andrea, sat around the table late at night for dinner. It was a common nocturnal get-together after returning back home from the TV station after closedown. Andrea had invariably prepared a pasta dish in advance which would then be followed either by a beef steak or some chicken and salad together with rustic bread. The meal was accompanied by Chianti Classico red wine.

They tried to avoid talking about work on these occasions because it was intended as switch off time. Andrea couldn't speak much English but Edwin's Italian had been steadily improving and they could now hold some basic conversation with each other. Andrea studied Chemistry at the university. He was a devout Catholic. That contrasted with Robert who had no religious faith but instead was deeply into the philosophical views espoused by Friedrich Nietzsche. The three of them got on very well with each other and would often laugh and joke together late into the night.

With the exception of the female announcers and journalists and various other staff members such as the make-up artist, Edwin hadn't met any Italian girls on a social basis. He had encountered a pleasant young lady from Holland, another from Australia and still more from the United States. But they had all been tourists on short stay holidays and had long since departed.

The next day was Edwin's day off and because Andrea was also free, they agreed to go into town together. In the heat of the midday sun they traipsed around the central market of San Lorenzo with its vast array of leather handbags, ceramic bowls, fruit and vegetables, trouser belts, hats, cheeses, biscuits and salami. Edwin was somewhat shocked that there was even a stall selling second-hand pornographic magazines. Some inner pages had become detached and were strewn along the paved walkway adjacent to Florence Cathedral providing a selection of hard core images that could be seen by any passer-by.

The cathedral itself was the thirteenth century building that towered above the city centre on account of its massive red-tiled dome and tall tower. Its outer walls were artistically designed in geometrical shapes of circles, triangles and arcs of coloured marble in various shades of pink, green and white. A queue of tourists was waiting to go inside and so, as cameras clicked all around them, Edwin and Andrea joined its tail end.

The gothic interior of pillars and arches and three wide naves ending under the octagonal dome was surprisingly bare and Andrea explained that many of the decorations of the church had been transferred to a nearby museum. However, there was no shortage of artwork in the form of large frescos depicting biblical stories and a total of forty-four stained glass windows. The place had a certain atmosphere about it. Above the main door was a large clock face surrounded by still more fresco portraits.

Afterward they stopped off at a small restaurant for a late lunch of Spaghetti Carbonara oozing with cream, eggs, cheese and diced bacon. Three young ladies were sat at an adjacent table eating ice cream sundaes. They were looking at a map and speaking with each other in German. The position of Edwin's chair meant that he was in direct line of sight with one of them who happened to glance in his direction.

"Are you from Germany?" he asked, realising that such a question wasn't exactly the most original chat-up line – if that was what it was meant to be. However, it was met with some enthusiasm.

"Yes. We are coming from Germany," she replied, "And you, are you American?"

"No. I'm English and my friend here is Italian," replied Edwin.

"He is Italian? Ah so, maybe he knows. We want drive to Valdelsa Valley. Is it a nice place?"

"I've no idea where that is," said Edwin and turned quizzically to Andrea who said that Val d'Elsa was somewhere in the province of Siena.

The girl brought her map over to their table. "Here," she said pointing to an area a few miles south of Florence, "This town of Poggibonsi." She had pronounced it with a hard 'g' which Andrea corrected. "Is just small town," he said, "is in wine region."

"Is that where you are going to be staying?" asked Edwin.

"No. We stay at the campsite here in Florence but we just want drive out there and look and then come back," she said, "My neighbour in Germany says it's a nice place."

"I see," said Edwin and then cheekily added, "Can we come with you?"

"You like?" she asked. She turned to her two friends and said, "Sie wollen mitkommen."

One shrugged her shoulders in a way that indicated that she didn't mind two additional passengers on their excursion. The other nodded.

"You can come with us if you like," said the first girl.

The friendly exchange had been somewhat lost on Andrea and so Edwin explained to him in his broken Italian that they would be going on a car journey with the German girls for a couple of hours. He liked the idea.

Their green Volkswagen beetle was parked in a car park just around the corner in Via dei Fossi. The five of them climbed in.

The yellow walls and red tiled roofs of the buildings in Poggibonsi were much the same as in many towns in Tuscany and didn't strike any of them as being of any unique distinction. They got out of the car and walked through its narrow streets. The German girls introduced themselves as Katrin and Hedda who were both from Munich whilst the car belonged to Ursula who was from Bonn. They were all in their mid-twenties.

Two men and three women wasn't the kindest combination for pairing up. However Edwin found himself walking alongside Ursula who was the one that he had first spoken to in the restaurant. In the meantime Andrea had seemed to attach himself to Hedda who was the most petite of the trio. And that left Katrin walking on her own – somewhere between both of the newly formed couples.

Edwin got talking with Ursula and learned that she was a secretary with an insurance company. She asked him if he had ever been to Germany.

"Yes I have," he replied, "First with a school trip when we visited Cologne. Then in 1968 I travelled up from Spain through France into Germany and finally ended up in Hamburg – and more recently I visited Trier."

He didn't elaborate about painting the railings of a hotel or mention anything of his former German acquaintance, Ingrid, whose abrupt disappearance off the face of the earth still baffled him.

"I have not been in England," continued Ursula, "but I think one day I like to visit London."

"Well, London is an interesting place," replied Edwin, "though in many ways it's not typically English. It's a cosmopolitan centre within England. It's also good to visit some of the outlying places to experience the real England."

"Yes, this I heard also," she said.

She asked him why he was living in Florence and he explained that he worked with the local television station. He also gave a brief summary of his New Zealand and Hong Kong experience.

"Neu Zeland," she said, "So many of those farm animals – how you call them in English? Mäh, mäh!"

"Sheep," he replied and then added, "Schaffe, viele Schaffe."

"You can say it in German!" she said.

"Yes but I still don't know how to say it in Italian," said Edwin.

She laughed. "You know something? I cannot say it in Italian also!"

Ursula was quite attractive in a slightly dumpy Teutonic way. It turned out that she had first got to know the other two girls the previous winter whilst on a skiing holiday in Austria where they had been staying at the same hotel. They had spoken then of the possibility of the three of them making a camping holiday in Italy which had now become a reality. They had been there for a week and a half and would be returning to Germany in two days' time.

A shop front advertised Tè Freddo in its window. Edwin knew that to mean iced tea and the two of them stepped inside to quench their thirst. There were no tables and chairs – just a small area of tiled floor space and a serving counter. You had to stand up to drink it.

So much for Poggibonsi, thought Edwin.

Afterwards they continued their walk around the town in a loop that passed a thirteenth century palace and a wishing well into which they both dropped a shiny silver one lira coin. The road led them back to near where the car was parked.

"Look those two," said Ursula, "They become friends quick, no?"

Edwin turned his head and saw that Andrea and Hedda were walking hand in hand.

"We can do that too if you like," he said jokingly. "Here, give me your hand."

She obligingly held out her right hand which Edwin took and began to rapidly swing their arms back and forth in such a way as to be sure to grab the attention of the couple behind. They heard some appreciative laughter.

The fifth member of the group, Katrin, then appeared from around a corner just ahead of them. She was holding a straw bag containing a large bottle of locally produced olive oil and an even larger bottle of locally produced red wine.

"Souvenirs from Poggibonsi," she said.

As they drove back to Florence it was suggested that they might all like to go for a drink at the terrace bar of the campsite. It was already beginning to get dark but because neither Edwin nor Andrea was pushed for time they agreed that they would be pleased to wind up there as an end to the day.

The Michelangelo Campsite was located high on one of the hills that overlooked Florence and the River Arno. They drove in through the front entrance and parked in a designated spot alongside a vast array of tents that nestled between trees. The terrace bar was crowded mainly with Dutch, German and French campers and a fair few Australians. Cold beer and slabs of pizza went down well and they stayed there for a couple of hours.

You can dance, you can jive
Having the time of your life
Ooh see that girl, watch that scene
Diggin' the dancing queen

Friday night and the lights are low
Looking out for the place to go...

Shortly after midnight Edwin and Andrea had intended to walk back home. However, they first escorted the three German girls to their tent but just as they as did so an almighty storm broke out. The sudden downpour of torrential rain sent all five of them scrambling in through the flapped entrance of the tent as quick as could be.

Lightning flashed through the canvas and thunder crashed all around them as the rain beat down relentlessly outside. Katrin switched on a small battery operated lamp which dimly illuminated the tent's small floor space. At least the tent wasn't leaking. Edwin asked Ursula if it was alright for him and Andrea to remain there until the storm passed.

"Of course," she said, "or I think you become very wet!"

The girls then unrolled their three sleeping bags. The lamp was switched off and they fumbled around in the darkness for a while as they removed their outer clothing and found their way into their quilted bedding arrangement. Occasional flashes of lightning lit them up during the process.

The entire plastic floor of the tent was lined with some spongy material to make the ground feel considerably more comfortable than it would otherwise have been. The three girls lay along its length. Katrin was in the middle and the others were on either side of her. Edwin positioned himself alongside Ursula who invited him to lay his head on the edge of her pillow. He was not surprised to realise that Andrea was on the other side of the tent alongside Hedda.

The storm showed no sign of abating. Instead, everybody was treated to a sound and vision performance that went on for several hours. During one particular episode of bright flashes of fork lightning each of which were followed by earth-shaking booms of thunder Ursula reached over and put her arm around Edwin. She was scared. He reciprocated by hugging her through her sleeping bag. They did manage to get some sleep as the next thing they knew they were waking up to bright morning sunlight beaming down on the tent's roof and it was already nine thirty.

The campsite had a shower facility in a nearby hut and using shared towels they took it in turns to go there and freshen up for the start of the day. Hedda and Andrea visited the store and returned with some fresh bread rolls and quark and strawberry jam. A white plastic table and chairs were located next to the tent. Meanwhile Edwin fetched five large disposable cups of coffee from the terrace bar. Ursula came back from the shower wearing a bikini and with a towel wrapped around her head. Edwin didn't recognise her at first until she came over and sat down next to him.

Mindful that he had to get ready for work in the afternoon and that he was still unshaven, there was nevertheless sufficient time to enjoy a leisurely breakfast with their German friends. Hedda asked if they would see each other again before they returned to Germany.

"Andrea has to go to his university and I have to work from 2pm until midnight for the rest of this week and so the only available time would be tomorrow morning," explained Edwin. "We could meet up with you then if you like."

"Maybe we visit you at your home?" asked Ursula.

"Yes, if you like," he said. He turned to Andrea for confirmation "Va bene si domatina vene a casa nostra?"

"Si, si," he replied, "Anchora colazione!"

"It's fine with him. He says you can all come for breakfast if you like," said Edwin.

After a second cup of coffee and a cigarette it was time to leave the girls to their own devices. Edwin and Andrea walked down the hill to the riverside where they took a bus to St Trinity Bridge which was near their apartment.

"Well, that was an interesting experience," said Edwin.

"Yes," sighed Andrea, "I like Hedda very much."

"Well I found that Ursula girl quite nice too but the trouble with holiday romances is that they are too short lived. They are here today and gone tomorrow."

"Yes, it's problem," said Andrea.

THE FOLLOWING MORNING THE doorbell rang and in trooped the three German girls. They were intrigued by the luxury apartment of the three bachelors who lived there.

"Can we looky-looky?" asked Katrin who seemed intent in exploring each of the rooms.

"Sure," said Edwin who opened the various doors for them.

There were murmurs of approval as each area was visited.

"You live in a very nice apartment," commented Ursula.

"Yes. It actually belongs to Robert whom you have not met. But we are really pleased to live here too," he said.

Teas and coffees were served and a large selection of pastries that Andrea had bought from the local bakery earlier that morning was eagerly attacked. Addresses and telephone numbers were exchanged together with promises to keep in touch. Edwin then suggested that they might like to take a brief walk through the Boboli Gardens which were just a stone's throw away.

They sauntered through its wide gravel avenues admiring the statues, fountains, temples, courtyards and grottos of the sixteenth century Italian gardens. Although the adjacent Pitti Palace had once been the main seat of the Medici grand dukes of Tuscany, these days Edwin used the place as if it were his own personal back garden. The five of them then sat for a while on the stone steps of the amphitheatre.

"I wish we had found this place before," said Hedda, "It has such a wonderful atmosphere."

"I know, I try to visit it every day," replied Edwin. "It's a great place for inspiration."

An hour or so later they returned to the apartment for a final cup of coffee. Andrea who had already missed his morning lecture at the university had a tutorial that afternoon which he had to attend. Edwin would need to get changed ready for work. Robert returned clutching a boxful of new microphones. The eventual goodbye involved a round of hugs and kisses before waving as the green Volkswagen drove off into the distance.

EDWIN AND ROBERT ARRIVED at the TV Station shortly before the start of afternoon transmission. The duty crew were already there but in a state of mild panic because the newsreader hadn't shown up and there was only a couple of minutes left before he or she was supposed to be on air. The newsreaders were shared with the radio station whose journalists also put together the news bulletins.

"Sputanatura!" exclaimed one of the technicians and then with a grin removed the printed bulletin from the telex machine and sat down in front one of the cameras and made preparations to deliver it himself. He managed to get through it OK.

That afternoon Edwin directed one of the chat shows from the control room. He did such things from time to time. It was an interesting experience to be directing a live programme whilst not being fluent enough in the Italian language to understand the finer details of whatever topics were being debated. However, he could sense the general gist of the discussion as he cut back and forth between cameras and gave instructions to the studio crew. The programme, which had been about the plight of homeless people, reached its inevitable crescendo of heated argument but was brought to a conclusion on time. The film of the day was then rolling on the telecine projector.

The people who had taken part in the live programme drifted through into the control room and were thanked for their participation. Such local debate ensured that the TV station's output was different from anything that the national broadcaster RAI could provide. The programmes were deliberately about topics that a local audience could easily identify with and because they were to do with things happening on their own doorstep they tended to attract an audience of loyal viewers.

There was some degree of competition from another local television service, Channel 48, whose signal covered most of Tuscany and the province of Perugia. That particular service was run by a friar but it had been taken off the air following the broadcast of late night strip shows. It had since re-launched and was trying to find its way. The coastal city of Livorno also ran a local TV station although most days its signal barely reached Florence and so posed no great threat.

Later that evening Edwin sat with Robert and Andrea for their evening meal.

"Oh, I nearly forgot to tell you," said Robert suddenly, "One of those girls who were here the other day phoned from Germany."

"Really, which one?" asked Edwin.

"The one from Bonn," he replied.

"Ursula," said Edwin, "That's interesting. What did she want?"

"I'm not sure if it was for anything specific. She just wanted a chat with you I guess," he replied. "I told her you were at work. She asked when you would be back and I suggested that she might like to try again tomorrow as it's your day off."

"Thanks," said Edwin.

THE FOLLOWING MORNING ANDREA hurried into the lounge to fetch Edwin.

"Issa for you! Is Ursula in Germania!" he said.

Edwin went into the hallway and took the phone. "Hallo?" he said.

"Hallo, here is Ursula!" said a familiar voice.

"Oh, Hi! It's nice to hear from you. I take it you got back to Germany OK?" he asked.

"Yes thank you," she said, "But now all the time I think of you. I miss you"

"Well it's gone a bit quiet around here since you left," he replied.

"I hope we can see us again soon, yes?" she said.

"That would be nice," replied Edwin.

"Yes, very nice," she said.

"Are you planning to come to Italy again next year?" he asked.

"Next year is too long time. I hope we can see us before then," she replied.

"You can come back down here next week if you like," he said jokingly.

"Next week no," she said, taking it literally, "but in November there is a weekend when I have the Friday free and the Monday afterwards free. Maybe you can get the same time free.

"And you would come back to Italy then?" he asked.

"Not Italy," she replied, "Maybe we can meet us in Germany? München is half the way between Florence and Bonn on the train line and we can stay some days in Katrin's apartment there."

She clearly had it all worked out.

Such phone calls from Ursula in Germany became something of an everyday occurrence. Often it would be Robert who was first to answer the phone and he would stand in the hallway with his hand clasped over the mouthpiece saying, "Germany calling, Germany calling!"

The phone was then handed over to Edwin and the conversation would normally start with, "Ach, Edwin! I just wanted to hear your voice again." A chat of some twenty minutes or so would then ensue about nothing in particular after which she would end each call by saying, "Tschüs" and briefly whispering "Ich liebe dich." It was all very flattering and Edwin became increasing intrigued by the way in which this friendship seemed to be growing. He looked forward to seeing her again and started making arrangements to be able to take the long weekend off work.

WHEN THE DAY FOR the visit to Munich finally arrived things started to go wrong. Edwin had wanted to iron a pair of trousers before his departure but the iron decided to overheat and break in half whilst doing so. The hot base became completely detached from the handle and dropped onto the floor. It wouldn't have been quite so bad were it not for the fact that he had borrowed it from a neighbour. He could hardly hand it back in that condition. And it also meant that he would have to make do with a different pair of trousers which wouldn't match the colour of his shirt and so he would end up having to wear a different shirt too. The train was due to depart at eleven o'clock that morning. In the meantime Ursula would be driving down from Bonn and she planned to meet him at Munich Railway Station that evening.

It was an uneventful train journey. Edwin used the time to work out the format for a new quiz programme which would probably work in Italian. On arrival at München Hauptbahnhof he spotted Ursula dressed in a blue denim jeans skirt with a red jersey waiting on the main concourse of the station. She waved and started walking in his direction. On nearing each other, however, he sensed that something didn't seem to be quite right. Admittedly he didn't know what his expectations had been but whatever they might have been were soon shattered. They went to a coffee shop where Ursula confessed that she was married. All that glistens is not necessarily so brilliant, thought Edwin. He had no particular interest in having an affair with a married woman and he wondered why she hadn't told him of her status when they'd first met each other in Florence.

"It changes things?" she asked.

"Well, yes, I'm afraid that for me it does," he replied.

And that set the tone for the weekend. As far as Edwin was concerned there seemed no point in attempting to develop their relationship any further in the knowledge that come Monday morning she would be driving back home to her husband in Bonn. They remained on friendly but cordial terms with each other. Edwin decided to sleep on the settee in the living room. On Saturday they went into the centre of Munich together and afterwards spent a couple of hours visiting a beer marquee that was still trading after the annual Oktoberfest. On the Sunday they went out to a restaurant for lunch.

They vacated the flat on Monday morning. Once Ursula had departed in her car Edwin spent the rest of the day walking around the city centre and going into several shops and cafes before making his way back towards the railway station to catch the evening train back to Florence.

On his way there he was stopped by a lady who handed him a leaflet. She said something to him in German which he didn't understand and then, on realising that he spoke English, she asked, "Do you know that Jesus Christ is your Lord and Saviour?"

"Is that so?" replied Edwin. Not another religious fanatic, he thought. They seem to turn up all over the place. He spoke with her for a while. She was Swedish and said that she was on some kind of a Christian mission for a few weeks in Germany.

"What about you? Are you just visiting Munich?" she asked.

"Kind of," said Edwin. He felt he might as well outline the whole story. "I live and work in Italy but I came here for the weekend to meet up with a German acquaintance but when I arrived she told me she was married – which kind of brought things to an abrupt halt."

"Then she was the wrong person for you," said the lady.

"Yes, I worked that out for myself on Friday. It's been a pointless trip," he replied.

"Maybe God has another German girl for you," she said.

"Well, who knows? But I think I'll believe that when I see it!" he said.

He bade her farewell, wished her good luck in her efforts to save people's souls and continued the remainder of the walk to the station.

THE TRAIN FOR ITALY pulled out of the station at nine o'clock that evening. Edwin had the whole compartment to himself and it was one in which the seats could be pulled out into the middle to enable passengers to have a nap during the nine hour journey if they so wished. That would come in handy for later but right now Edwin was in no mood for sleep. He mulled over the friendship that had developed with Ursula and how it had now been so unexpectedly crushed. He also recalled the disappearance of his previous German friend Ingrid and wondered why things in life could sometimes be so complicated.

He was nearly twenty-seven years old. He had a relatively stable job at the TV station and for the first time in his life he actually felt like settling down and getting married and starting a family. He thought back to the numerous girlfriends that he had had in the past. They must have run into several hundreds. Each of them had been pleasant in their own way and he liked to think that if ever he were to meet up with any of them again the friendship would still be just as alive as it had been at the time. In those days he hadn't been thinking along the lines of getting married to any one of them – and neither, to the best of his knowledge had they. They were just encounters. They were young ladies whom he had often met by chance in various parts of the world and in which there had been some kind of mutual attraction. He had rarely developed any long-term relationships because he hadn't felt ready to be tied down to one particular person. Variety had seemed to be the spice of life. He supposed that it had all been rather casual.

But when it came to thoughts of a marriage partner, that was a different matter altogether. He had often wondered how one could know if somebody would be the right person to get hitched to. Was it just down to that emotional thing called love that he had so often felt for a great many people? Edwin thought that he would like to meet someone pure and innocent for a wife rather that someone who'd been around. Given his own track record he knew that to be completely hypocritical and, apart from anything else, he didn't know where to meet such a person. Based on his personality it was easy enough for him to continue to bump into new people wherever he went. He had an address book crammed full of names, addresses and phone numbers of people that he had met from all over the place and yet there was no one in particular that leapt from the pages as being a potential wife. His thoughts momentarily returned to Caroline in New Zealand. In all that had happened in recent years he had completely lost contact with her. He was sure that by now she would already be married and most probably had children. In many ways he would rather not know because it might have shown him something that could have been. It occurred to him that if he had ended up marrying her he would have regained his right to work in New Zealand once again. Too late for that now, he thought.

He prised open the ring pull on the first of the cans of cold German beer he had purchased from a kiosk at the station. By now the train had left the lights of Munich suburbia behind and with darkness outside there was nothing to see through the window other than his reflection in the glass.

Reaching into his pocket for a cigarette lighter he came across the leaflet that had been handed to him by the evangelist earlier that evening. It was written in German and he didn't understand it. However, he recalled that zipped up in the front panel of his bag was the book that the American missionary in Florence had given him. He had brought it along with him in case it would come in handy for whiling away the hours of the long train journey. Because it was a relatively thin paperback Edwin thought he might as well read it through from cover to cover so as at least to be fair to whatever its content might be and to gauge whether or not anything in it could be of any remote relevance. The front cover claimed that over a million copies had been sold. The back cover said that the book investigated basic Christianity.

He skipped the preface and went straight to the first chapter which was entitled 'The Right Approach'. There was a fair bit of assumed knowledge and some of the terminology was slightly indigestible for a newcomer but Edwin worked his way through it. There was even a suggested prayer included which began:

'God, if you exist (and I don't know if you do), and if you can hear this prayer (and I don't know if you can), I want to tell you that I am an honest seeker after the truth…'

That element of doubt contained within such words seemed to reflect Edwin's own position on the issue and to make an even stronger case than if it had just been a plain assumption about the existence a Supreme Being. However he wasn't sure that he was 'an honest seeker after the truth' because he didn't know which truth was being referred to although for the purpose of the exercise he supposed he could go along with it.

The next three short chapters all tended to rely on biblical understanding of which Edwin was largely ignorant other than some vague recollection of stories from Religious Education classes in secondary school. However, the following pages dealt with the reality of the world lived in today and was something he could relate to more readily. It spoke of mistrust. Doors not being enough; we have to lock and bolt them. Payment of fares not being enough; tickets have to be issued, inspected and collected...

At that moment the compartment door slid open and an inspector asked to see Edwin's ticket and clipped it with a metal implement that resembled a pair of pliers.

"Firenze?" said the man, "Va bene. Grazie."

"Grazie," responded Edwin and then managed to find his place on the page once again.

...Law and order is not enough; we need the police to enforce them. And all of that, the book said, was due to humankind's sin.

It seemed a reasonable way of looking at things and the reader was then invited to consider the Ten Commandments so as to see how very far short of them every person falls – and hence understand a need for a saviour.

Five cans of Löwenbräu beer, half a packet of cigarettes and two cheese and ham rolls later, Edwin had finished the book in its entirety. By then it was two thirty in the morning. It had been quite an interesting read and had expressed things in simple terms that were easy to grasp. Edwin could relate to a lot of what was being said and, however out of character it may have sounded, he even wondered if perhaps he should make the effort to develop some kind of religious faith.

One chapter had explained that if anyone repented for their sins and invited Jesus and the Holy Spirit into their heart they could have a so-called rebirth experience and become what was referred to as a born-again Christian. Well, either that was true or it wasn't – and what would be the implications of doing such a thing? He had met people before who had enthusiastically said that they had been saved. Would there ever come a time when he would wish to have such a conversion experience himself? Certainly the book had stressed it was important for everyone to do so. But then it would say that, wouldn't it?

After a brief trip along the corridor to make use of the train's lavatory Edwin returned to the compartment and pulled four of the seats forward so as to form a horizontal area like one large mattress. Turning off the lights he then settled into a deep sleep for the remainder of the journey to the Stazione di Santa Maria de Novella – the terminus railway station of Florence.

IT WAS STILL EARLY and before his flatmates woke Edwin had purchased some butter, a packet of plain flour, a bag of sugar, a dozen eggs, four litres of milk and half a dozen lemons. The resultant pancakes for breakfast proved to be a great hit with Robert and Andrea. Both demanded the simple recipe. Robert, whose mother was French, was familiar with the thinner variety of crêpes.

They asked Edwin if he had had an enjoyable stay in Munich and he simply replied that it had been a pleasant enough break. He had decided not to mention the finer details of what had occurred in his friendship with Ursula.

In the mornings before work Edwin began re-reading parts of the paperback book on Basic Christianity. He absorbed its content at a more leisurely pace than on the train journey and in the genteel surroundings of the Boboli Gardens. Although he had had no religious upbringing other than the attendance of morning services at school, he supposed that, if anything at all, he was Church of England. That had always been the most convenient term to use if ever there was a requirement to specify one's religion. After all, the entire country of England was nominally Christian and so even if one never actually went to church at all one could still reasonably describe oneself as being Church of England with some degree of legitimacy. Being Church of England, it seemed, could cover a multitude of sins.

He vaguely knew the history of how the split from Rome had occurred under King Henry VIII and that the Anglican Church was in some way different from Catholicism. He even remembered reading an account about the small British colony of Gibraltar that he had visited the year before in which, after its initial capture, Englishmen had delighted in the place as being "a plaguey Protestant thorn in the side of Catholic Spain." Presumably it was that kind of thing that had made the British Empire so great.

A couple of evenings a week Edwin tended to visit some of Florence's social venues. It was useful to step outside of his work environment every once in a while. One of his usual haunts had live entertainment in the form of a musician who played a lute-like instrument and sang along with it. One evening Edwin met an Australian girl there and spent his next day off showing her around the local tourist spots. The recent German encounter became almost forgotten. But, like so many others, the Australian girl was a tourist who was only going to be there for a week before moving on.

In a place such as Florence with its cathedral, churches, art galleries and regularly held festivals the age-old question of religious faith cropped up almost wherever one looked. Edwin read the book's chapter on re-birth once again. He could relate to the sentiment that was being expressed that mankind was in the pits and that a lifeline was apparently at hand. Curiosity was getting the better of him and one evening he decided to try reciting that prayer to see what would or wouldn't happen. It was the first time that he had ever prayed formally but in accordance with the instructions from the booklet he repeated the short prayer of repentance and invited Jesus and the Holy Spirit to enter. Having said such words he felt what could best be described as a surge of warmth run through his entire body, almost like electricity. At the same time he wondered what the implications were. He recognised that such a do-it-yourself conversion experience to Christianity was just like it said in the book but what on earth did it all mean? Perhaps he should visit the American Missionary group to ask them for some kind of elaboration and yet he somehow doubted that he would get much further forward by going back to them. Although that group had contributed to putting him on this particular path it might even be preferable for him to try and work out the experience for himself rather than being unduly influenced by other people's views.

Over the days that followed he sensed something of a benevolent spiritual presence on a daily basis. It was a totally new experience. He even considered the possibility of taking a bit of time off work to go on a short search to see if he could make some sense of what it all meant. However, now that he had been fortunate in getting back into his career he would need to organise things in such a way that there would be no risk involved to that.

EDWIN DIDN'T KNOW ONE end of the Bible from the other apart from the fact that it was divided into Old and New Testaments. Even the word 'Testament' sounded so off-putting that it was probably one of the reasons why he had never bothered to try reading it before.

Apart from anything else, the text didn't exactly read like a novel and nor as a particularly concise reference book. Much of its content seemed long-winded and consisted of endless accounts of various individuals from way back when in history. It became tedious in trying to understand their relevance at all. It just didn't flow.

In the evenings Edwin was able to speak with Andrea about religious matters. The discussions took place as they prepared their evening meal together which they then ate and washed down with a balloon-shaped bottle of Chianti Classico. Andrea understood something of Edwin's recent conversion experience. He also suggested that if God called somebody for a specific purpose all other things in life became of secondary importance.

"I feel that it was God's guidance that led me to my job here with the television station in Florence," explained Edwin, "So it would seem a bit strange if, after all that effort, I'm on some kind of a spiritual quest instead."

"You have to combine the two things," advised Andrea, and then added, "If you have faith then everything will work out."

Well, it is a new faith and I'm not used to it yet," replied Edwin. "I'm torn between hanging on here in Florence and perhaps taking a little time off to try and make some sense out of Christianity."

"But Edwin, this is Italia! You are surrounded by Christianity right here," said Andrea.

"Surrounded by its architectural heritage," replied Edwin. "Why are there so many unmarried priests and unmarried nuns in Florence who stay single out of some strange notion that they are married to the church? That seems very odd. Wouldn't it make more sense if they simply married each other and raised nice families?"

"You have some interesting ideas," said Andrea with a smile.

"I don't even know how to pray properly but I do seem to get some pretty strong impulses – and I don't think all of it is just my imagination," replied Edwin.

"It's up to you to decide what's best," said Andrea, getting up to put the coffee percolator on the stove in the adjacent kitchen. "If it were me, I'd simply follow."

"But follow what? And to where?" asked Edwin.

"Just go where the spirit leads!" was Andrea's answer.

Edwin lit a cigarette. If arrangements could be made for his job to be left open he might be persuaded to shoot off somewhere for a couple of months to satisfy his curiosity as much as anything else. Andrea returned with a tray containing two mugs of coffee and two goblets of Amaretto liqueur. They played a game of chess before deciding to call it a day.

A WEEK LATER, EDWIN put in a request to combine his accumulated holiday entitlement with some additional unpaid leave, which was granted. He couldn't bring himself to explain the real reason for taking such time off in winter months because no matter how he might have worded things it would have sounded highly peculiar. Instead he simply let his work colleagues know that there were several matters that he had to attend to in England but that he would be back soon.

"You've been offered a better job there!" suggested Fabio, to which Edwin shook his head.

"Sure you're not going in pursuit of that German Fraulein?" asked the sound operator, Claudio, who knew about the recent trip to Munich although not of its outcome.

"Cheeky!" replied Edwin, "But no, I'm not."

Only his flatmates, Robert and Andrea, knew of the strange reality that Edwin was about to embark on some kind of a spiritual search and even they thought it would be just a passing phase which he would snap out of sooner or later.

CHAPTER TWENTY-EIGHT

A WEEK LATER AND Edwin was back on the familiar platform of Florence Railway Station but this time for the evening departure of a train bound for Amsterdam. His initial idea was to head up to England to seek someone who could provide him with a clear understanding and some guidance concerning his recent Christian experience. He felt that if he could understand the theory he would then be better equipped to apply the practical side of it to his day-to-day life and at his workplace. The train slid out of the station and, as there was nobody else in the compartment, he began reading the continuing adventures of the Acts of the Apostles. Twenty minutes later he was sound asleep.

The journey time to Amsterdam was nineteen hours. The train followed the same route as that disastrous weekend in Munich and would then continue right up the length of Germany and into Holland.

When Edwin awoke it was already daybreak and he saw that he had been joined by three passengers who must have got on the train at intermediate destinations during the night. A visit to the end of the carriage for a quick splash of cold water from a washbasin completed the rise and shine process. He was aware, however, that the old chunky sweater and flared green trousers he was wearing made him look like a bit like a tramp. He had also borrowed a fine chequered overcoat from Robert which simply didn't match. Clothing left behind in Florence was of a short-sleeved summer variety.

Throughout the rest of the day there was a considerable turnover of passengers as the train made its journey northwards through Germany. In the afternoon Edwin found himself conversing in English with a German couple who joined it in Cologne. They introduced themselves as Wilhelm and Kerstin who were on their way home to a place called Emmerich which was one station before the Dutch border. When Edwin mentioned that he had no fixed schedule, he was promptly invited to break his journey and stay overnight at their home. Such an out of the blue offer was most welcome. Edwin could do with a proper night's sleep and because his train ticket to Amsterdam had two month's validity he could simply continue his journey the following day.

Edwin was shown to a guest room before joining his hosts for an evening meal. During the course of conversation it turned out that the husband, Wilhelm, was desperately short-staffed and on the lookout for temporary workers for a night shift at a local factory. He asked if Edwin might be interested in this. The pay would be good – even if he could only do it for a fortnight.

"I don't speak German," was Edwin's first reaction.

"That doesn't matter. It is manual work," said Wilhelm. "It's at a margarine factory."

It was all very fascinating although Edwin wondered what on earth he was doing there at all. Was this an example of being led by the spirit or was it more a case of being led up the garden path?

Edwin ended up staying the two weeks at the couples' home. It seemed completely bizarre that he had momentarily substituted his professional job in Italy for working night shifts at a margarine factory in Germany but he figured that doing something completely different for a fortnight might be beneficial. He worked as part of a team and the job entailed tearing off large squares of thick paper filter from a roll and placing each leaf between hefty metal frames that hung on a rack, all of which were then screwed together tightly before a flow of liquid margarine was pumped through them. Then the plates would be unscrewed, the now oily papers discarded and substituted for clean ones and the whole process would start all over again. It was repetitive work that required no conversation and no particular skill. He started at 10pm and went through until 6am.

On his final day at work Edwin was really surprised by the large amount of money he received in the form of a wad of crisp German banknotes. The rate of pay had been excellent and working night shifts had made it even more so. He offered some of it to Wilhelm and Kerstin as gratitude for having stayed with them but they wouldn't hear of it. They drove him to the railway station and wished him well.

EDWIN FOUND HIMSELF SITTING in an identical train to the one that had brought him up from Florence. For all he knew it was exactly the same train. He was more than two thousand Deutschmarks better off and now knew what a margarine factory looked like. The train stopped at the border with Holland and officials clambered on board to inspect passengers' passports. Edwin would be in Amsterdam by midday and he was wondering whether to continue straight to the cross-channel ferry for England or first to look up a Dutch schoolteacher he'd befriended earlier on that year in Florence. He decided that he would at least phone her but that if for whatever reason it wasn't convenient to meet up, he would continue on his way to one of the cross channel ferry ports.

On arrival at Amsterdam Railway Station Edwin changed a fifty-mark note into Dutch guilders, rummaged in his bag for his address book and headed for one of the phone booths.

"Isa Zijlstra," answered the voice on the line.

"Hallo Isa!" he began, "I don't know if you remember me but we met each other in the summer when you were on holiday in Florence? My name is Edwin."

"Edwin? Oh yes, sure I remember you," she replied, "You're English and you work with television in Italy."

"That's right," continued Edwin, "The thing is, I'm on leave at the moment and I'm just passing through Holland. As a matter of fact I'm at Amsterdam Railway Station."

"You're here?" she asked.

"Yes," he replied, "and I was just wondering if perhaps we could meet up."

"Yes of course we can," she said, "I've had so much going in my life recently but that's another story. You say you're at the Railway Station now? Just wait there by the main front entrance. I'll be there in about fifteen minutes!"

"Okay, that's wonderful," he said and they both hung up.

He waited and she arrived, not in a car as he had assumed, but on a tram. He recognised her straightaway and, suddenly aware of his attempted beard and the chunky jumper under Robert's smart overcoat, he stepped forward to greet her.

"Oh, there you are," she looked at him quizzically.

She was a few years his senior and aged around thirty. She was tall, slim and good looking with her clear complexion and light brown hair that she wore tied up in a triangular headscarf. She was also sophisticated, well-educated, talkative and engaging. They had met each other one hot Sunday afternoon in Florence during the course of a riverside walk and had then gone for a cappuccino together in a cafeteria where they had exchanged addresses.

"Have you been in Amsterdam before?" she asked.

"No, it's my first time. I'm actually on my way back to England but couldn't resist looking you up on my way through," he said.

"That's really nice of you," she said, looking down at his suitcase. 'How much time do you have to spare in this great city of mine?'

"Oh, I'm completely flexible," said Edwin, "As a matter of fact I haven't even bought my ferry ticket yet."

"Well, if you want to stay for a few days, you're welcome to sleep on the couch in my lounge," she suggested, "It's quite comfortable according to other guests who have used it."

Edwin thought for a moment, unsure as to whether or not to accept the kind invitation. Mind you, he really was flexible and there was also the slim possibility that he might be able to further his spiritual understanding whilst here in Amsterdam.

"It would be great to stay for a couple of days if it's convenient for you," he said.

"Then come on," she said, "Let's get your bag back to my place and then we can come back out again and I'll show you round the street markets."

They took a tram and after a journey of some fifteen minutes which passed through a stretch of shopping streets, canals and bridges, they alighted in a leafy suburb where Isa pointed out her flat across the road on the first floor above a bakery. It was a cosy one person flat and consisted of a lounge with a curtained off bedroom area, a small kitchen and a bathroom. It was tastefully furnished, immaculately clean and tidy and equipped with sufficient books to envy a local library.

The phone rang. She answered it and spent a few minutes conversing in Dutch. "Just sorting a few things out," she said afterwards. "That was my former husband. He has re-married but we remain friends. My father passed away on Wednesday and my sister is making all the arrangements for the funeral."

"Oh I'm sorry to hear that," replied Edwin. "It's probably not the most convenient time for me to be here at all."

"No, no, it's fine that you're here," she replied. "Having someone around that I can talk to is really helpful."

Edwin stayed in Amsterdam for three days. During that time Isa asked him if he thought that there could be such a thing as life after death. He said that he would like to think that there was and he told her that he had recently begun to explore Christianity and that he was currently on a search to try and find out what it all meant.

"The problem with religion is that even if you pray you never get a straight answer," she said. "I used to be quite a religious person but I can't say that I am anymore. Having faith in something invisible is difficult."

Edwin then attempted to relate something of his recent spiritual experience but it didn't seem to mean very much to her and even he was aware that the way in which he had described it must have sounded pretty weird

"That kind of thing is alright for some people and I can admire you for doing it," she said, "Maybe I'll get to experience something similar some day but for now I prefer to take things just as they are."

He recalled that she was seeking comfort in her moment of bereavement rather than anything else. That evening they went out for a meal at a restaurant which helped lighten things up. When they returned to the flat she produced a bottle of apricot brandy which served as a nightcap.

Edwin slept a good night's sleep under a duvet in the comfort of Isa's settee in the lounge. Her bedroom was behind a curtain drawn across the rear end of the lounge from where he could hear gentle snoring.

The following day they spent an enjoyable time out and about in Amsterdam. That night, however, Edwin awoke to see that a light shone behind the curtain divided apartment room and heard some shuffling of papers.

He called out to her.

"Are you OK Isa?"

"Yes, I'm alright," she replied, "It's just that I have too many things going round in my mind that I'm finding it difficult to sleep. I think I'm going to make myself a cup of hot chocolate, would you like one too?"

"Yes, I'd love one," replied Edwin.

Five minutes later they both sat on the edge of Isa's bed sipping from large steaming mugs. It was three o'clock in the morning and Edwin could tell from her tear stained face that she was upset. He put his arm around her and there was no resistance. There was little conversation as they had finished their chocolate drink after which they lay down together and cuddled up to each other. They didn't have sex. He had no idea if it would even have been an option and in any case it would have been unfair to have taken advantage of her emotional predicament. They slept alongside each other.

The third night was Edwin's final night in Amsterdam and he now felt ready to advance on England.

THE OVERNIGHT FERRY FROM Vlissingen sailed to the port of Sheerness, located in the eastern area of Kent known as the Isle of Sheppey. There was a railway connection to London and the train's route happened to pass through familiar places from Edwin's childhood. Chislehurst Woods brought a flood of memories of being in the Boy Scouts. It also triggered off recollections of his friend Henry who, mainly due to Edwin, now lived in New Zealand where he was happily married to Janet.

At Waterloo Station he bought a copy of the Daily Telegraph. It was the first English newspaper that he'd seen in a while and for old time's sake he also queued at a kiosk for a cheese and tomato roll and the inevitable polystyrene cup of tea.

Edwin thought that the easiest thing to do would be to visit Salisbury again. After all, the Cathedral Close had some sort of an ecclesiastical air about it which might be conducive to his spiritual search – although not that he had particularly felt it last time round. On arrival he checked in at the Red Lion Hotel.

The following morning he arranged to meet up with Victor Horton at the North Canonry and they went out for lunch at the Haunch of Venison together. Edwin tried to outline something of his spiritual search and although Victor listened it soon became obvious that he couldn't relate to it.

"By the sounds of it, I think you could do with another beer, old chap!" was about the only thing that he could say.

Edwin was fast learning that other people didn't want to hear about religious experiences. There was the danger of it sounding strange or fanatical, or both. He resolved not to initiate such conversations again unless specifically prompted to do so. In the meantime he deposited most of the money that he'd earned in Germany into his bank account.

He then stayed a couple of nights in Bournemouth where as always, his grandmother was pleased to see him. In the morning Edwin went for a bracing walk along the seafront. The weather was overcast and windy. As he walked back through Boscombe he noticed a church with its side door open and decided to venture in. The place was deserted and smelt of furniture polish. He sat down in one of the pews and wondered if there might be a minister there to whom he could go to for some kind of clarification or guidance. At that moment the sun must have broken through the clouds as the whole church lit up with strong rays of light shining in through its stained glass windows. On his way back out he passed the adjacent vicarage and went up to its front door and rang the bell. The lady who answered fetched a desk diary and made an appointment for Edwin to meet with the vicar at ten thirty the following morning. At last, he thought. Some of this recent upheaval would now begin to make a bit of sense – or so he hoped.

Next day, in anticipation of the meeting with the vicar, Edwin wore suit and tie for the occasion and was determined to listen intently to any advice that would surely be given. The same lady opened the door and ushered him into a study where an elderly minister complete with black clerical shirt and white dog collar sat as his desk.

"Do come in Mr um…?'

"Ravensdale", volunteered Edwin, "But you can call me Edwin if you like."

"Right then, please take a seat,' said the vicar, indicating the chair alongside his desk.

The lady went out and shut the door behind her. Edwin sat down and momentarily felt as if he were in a doctor's surgery.

"What can I do for you?" asked the vicar.

"Well, the thing is, I've come to you to seek some advice" said Edwin, not quite knowing how to get to the point.

"Advice?" queried the vicar, "Why, what seems to be the problem?"

"Well, it's to do with my future really," said Edwin, "You see I've recently become a Christian."

If he was expecting any cry of "Praise the Lord" or even any hint of congratulation or welcome into the fold, he was to be disappointed. There was an uncomfortable silence and then the vicar responded by saying flatly, "Well, we've always been Christian here."

Edwin didn't know how to react to that. "Yes but, I mean, I need to find out what direction I should be taking now that I've effectively joined the club, don't you think?"

The vicar was nonplussed. "I think you should just carry on living your life," he replied.

Realising that to be the sum total of this particular Christian minister's guidance, Edwin rose from his seat, thanked him and that was the end of the meeting. As he walked back through the long rows of red-bricked houses of suburban Bournemouth he began to recall reasons why the established church had never had any particular appeal to him. The words "We've always been Christian here" echoed in his mind in the same tone that they had been given. Blast the Church! He thought. That institution has probably done the most to put people right off God altogether. The sun burst through the clouds once again.

EDWIN STAYED WITH HIS parents in Wrotham over Christmas. As far as they were concerned he was simply on leave from his work in Italy and he didn't mention a thing about his current spiritual quest which he knew was out of character and would have sounded most odd. He did, however, attend midnight mass in the local church on Christmas Eve which was something that he'd never done before. It was a traditional service attended by a small congregation of mainly elderly people who had braved the cold night air. But for Edwin, the service seemed to provide more questions than answers.

With no hint as to how he should be going about his so-called spiritual search Edwin began to question whether he'd done the right thing in returning to England. It many respects it was feeling like a step backwards whereas he wanted to venture forth into a clearer understanding. He came to the conclusion that he might be better off spending the remainder of his leave back on the Continent. He could slowly meander his way back down towards Italy and if something were to turn up along the way he would simply stop off and check it out. On the other hand if nothing materialised he could always re-visit that American missionary group once he arrived back in Florence. The thought of being on the move again was far more appealing than stagnating in England. It just felt right.

AS SOMETHING REMINISCENT OF a déjà vu experience Edwin once again found himself walking along Buckingham Palace Road from Victoria Coach Station towards Victoria Railway Station which he then entered through a small side entrance. He purchased a one-way train ticket to Essen in Germany which he would use as the first leg of his journey. There was no particular reason for such a choice. It had simply been one of several destinations listed on a leaflet as being available at a discount price. When the train arrived there the following morning everything in that part of Germany was covered in a thick blanket of snow. He booked into a nearby hotel for one night. It was expensive but would do for now.

Things then began to happen in quick succession.

In the confines of his hotel room Edwin tried praying a simple prayer, "Dear God, just out of interest, please can you show me where should I go to tomorrow?"

That evening he went out for a walk. As he stepped outside into the snow, a German lady came up to him out of the darkness and, speaking in English, she said, "Hallo, you're from England, aren't you."

Edwin confirmed that indeed to be the case and the lady said, "You are welcome to come along with me. My husband and I are going for a meal at a restaurant near here and we'd like to invite you."

Sensing the encounter to be directly related to his prayer, Edwin deliberately didn't query anything but just agreed to go with her. He didn't even ask how she knew that he was from England.

The restaurant looked cosy and had a low hanging light suspended above each neatly laid table. The lady's husband was already there and studying the menu. He rose from the table and shook hands with Edwin and invited him to take a seat. A waitress came along and took orders for drinks and handed over two further copies of the menu. The lady translated what was on it. Edwin chose a schnitzel with mushroom sauce and the three of them enjoyed a very pleasant meal together. The lady then turned to face Edwin.

"You're looking for somewhere to stay, aren't you?" she said.

"Yes I am," replied Edwin, still managing not to show the slightest sign of any surprise at her uncanny perception.

She scribbled something on a piece of paper, folded it in two and handed it to him. "You must go here, tomorrow morning," she said, "They will show you where."

Edwin placed the paper in the breast pocket of his shirt and thanked her.

'Nicht zu Danken!' said her husband with a smile and asked the waitress to bring them some coffee.

Edwin returned to his hotel and slept well.

The following morning he went to the address that had been given to him which turned out to be some sort of a Catholic-run mission centre located at the city's central bus station. He asked the two people at the counter if they knew of some inexpensive accommodation but they both shook their heads. However, as he was departing one of them called him back. In broken English she said that he needed to take a tram somewhere. He had no idea what she meant but she bought a ticket from a machine and gave it to him and then saw him onto one of the trams. She told him to stay on it until it reached its final destination.

Edwin looked out through the tram's window at the passing suburban scenery. He thought, well, that's great. Here I am in Germany, sitting on a tram with a ticket in my hand and heading off for somewhere – and I've absolutely no idea where. Talk about a magical mystery tour!

The final stop turned out to be Essen University campus. Edwin walked up to the front door of one of the buildings which was a hall of residence and rang the bell. A man in charge opened the door and Edwin simply asked him if there was accommodation available. The man said that there was but that it was quite expensive. Edwin replied that he was on a limited budget and the man said, "Please come in. We have a guest room where you can stay for free and you are welcome to stay here for as long as you like."

By now Edwin was getting used to such things happening and so once again he didn't query any of it. The Hausmeister showed him to a warm room equipped with a single bed, a table and a wardrobe and en suite bathroom. He said that Edwin should make himself at home. "Oh, and by the way," he added, "Because of Silvester we shall be having a little party in the room at the end of the corridor and you'll be very welcome to join us."

"Thank you," replied Edwin, wondering who on earth Silvester was.

The man gave Edwin a door key and then departed.

What an amazing way to have found somewhere to stay, thought Edwin. Having unpacked his belongings he decided to go back out and familiarise himself with the locality. It was still early afternoon and the sky was dark with snow clouds. A modern building opposite turned out to be a Catholic Church. Edwin took the road that led in the opposite direction to the way in which the tram had come. He continued walking for a kilometre or so before reaching a small commercial area of shops and restaurants. A cosy looking bistro was called 'The Oliver Twist' and, on impulse, he went inside and asked the man behind the bar whether there were any job vacancies that might come in handy. As it happened they did have a vacancy for two shifts a week and Edwin was asked if he would be able to commence the late shift from 4pm on Sunday.

Things were obviously on the move. All he now needed to do was to pray about what to do next. He would be due back at work in Florence in a few weeks' time but was still none the wiser about his spiritual path. However, he felt that if he remained sincere in his search then surely some form of guidance would come his way.

That evening, back at the student hostel of the university he went along to the party and realised it to be New Year's Eve which the Germans refer to as Silvester. He had lost track of the date even though Christmas had only been a week ago. There were about a dozen others at the gathering and four crates of beer had been deposited in the centre of the room. Edwin drank a couple of bottles and chatted with some of the students, most of whom spoke English. Glasses of Champagne were handed out at the midnight hour and a small firework display took place outside. Meantime a cassette player provided a musical background.

Sailin' away on the crest of a wave, it's like magic
Rollin' and ridin' and slippin' and sliding, it's magic
And you, and your sweet desire
You took me, higher and higher
It's a livin' thing,
It's a terrible thing to lose
It's a given thing
What a terrible thing to lose

On Sunday morning Edwin went across the road to the Catholic Church to attend their service. Smartly dressed people were there, elderly couples mainly, and he found it hard to follow much of the German sermon. He had assumed that there would some kind of Christian fellowship afterwards. With that in mind he had lingered at the end but it soon became obvious that the entire congregation was pushing off back to their homes and that they didn't go in for such things as a cup of tea and biscuits at that particular church.

That afternoon he started work at the bistro. A lady called Gertrud was on duty with him and between the two of them they had to run the place until midnight. It was easy work and Edwin soon became quite proficient at it. Customers were perched on stools around the perimeter of the rectangular shaped bar. Edwin served at one end whilst Gertrud took care of the other.

AFTER A COUPLE OF weeks of living in the university's hall of residence Edwin woke up abruptly at five o'clock on two consecutive mornings. On both occasions he experienced a strong intuitive feeling that he should go once again to England. However, on both occasions he resisted the thought and dismissed it as his imagination. Why should he now return to England? It made little sense. He'd already tried that and what had been the outcome? He had gained no clarification there other than the words of that pompous oaf of a minister in Bournemouth telling him that they had always been Christian down at his end of the beach.

Having had his sleep interrupted at such an early hour Edwin was so wide awake that he got up and used the time for some bible study. In fact much of his daytime activity seemed to consist of trying to understand biblical passages and in going out for long meditative walks. He also met with up with some of the students every once in a while and had gained a small circle of friends. The difficulty remained that he was still seeking spiritual guidance but that he hadn't yet found anyone suitably qualified to provide it.

To his annoyance that same crack of dawn experience as on the previous two days occurred yet again. He woke up at exactly five o'clock and once again an intuitive feeling told him that he had to go back to England.

"But I don't want to go back to England!" said Edwin to himself. "Besides, I'm already part of the way back down to Italy."

"But listen, Edwin," the nagging thought persisted, "first you need to go back to England where you will be able to learn something and then later you'll be able to return to other countries."

"But I really don't want to go to England," reasoned Edwin, "I've just been there and it was completely useless."

After a light breakfast he went out for a long walk in the snow and by mid-morning he found himself to be in the vicinity of his work place. It was sometimes the case that staff, on their day off, would pop in for a free cup of coffee and on this occasion Edwin did just that. Inside the warmth of the bistro and, whilst sipping a cup of freshly filtered coffee, the boss appeared from a back room and came over to speak with him.

"Ah, Edwin – good that you come!" he said, "We have a problem. Stefan, who was going to leave us, is now going to stay. It means we will have one person too many and so because you are temporary I'm afraid we won't be able to keep you on anymore."

Such news didn't bother Edwin who took it calmly and philosophically. There'd be something else to move on to – and if need be he could even return to Florence earlier that anticipated. As Edwin finished the remainder of his coffee the boss went over to the till and returned to hand him 40 marks pay for the one shift that he had already worked that week.

"Hier," he said, "Vielen Dank für alles und macht's gut." They shook hands.

Edwin left the premises and first went back to his room at the university campus to take a hot shower and freshen himself up before heading into town to see about the possibility of alternative work.

As he was making his way through the building a Turkish student called Nesrin with whom he had spoken on several previous occasions ran up to him by the lift and said, "Edwin, I can't explain now but take this!" and she thrust a twenty mark note into his hand and ran off down the corridor.

Edwin called after her, "Thank you, Nesrin, but I don't need it!"

But she had rounded a corner and disappeared from sight. How embarrassing, he thought. Oh well, I'll just have to find her this evening and return it.

Stepping outside again he followed the main road down the long hill that led in the direction of the city centre. He knew that there was a large Inlingua language school there where perhaps he might be able to teach the odd English class for a few weeks. It was a forty minute walk and as he neared the main shopping area he passed Essen Hauptbahnhof Railway Station on the opposite side of the road. He glanced over at a large advertisement on a billboard which said:

'Farhren Sie nach England mit Zug und Schiff – nur DM 62.50.' This one-way fare to England had a picture of Big Ben seen alongside a train and a cross channel ferry.

The English Tourist Board obviously doing its thing, he thought.

The language school was approached by an outdoor escalator and after waiting in the warmth of the reception area for ten minutes or so Edwin was shown into a small office for an interview with one of its administrators. It transpired that it was something of a plus not to be able to speak much German as the school insisted that all of its teachers were to converse purely in the language that they were teaching. Edwin's details were taken down and the man then said that although he felt that he was well suited to the job there was no immediate vacancy but he would keep him posted. There could be some available classes in the very near future. A nice idea but it wouldn't solve Edwin's immediate needs.

Whilst in the centre of town he had also wanted to change some of his English pounds back to German Deutschmarks but by now it was mid-afternoon and the banks had already closed. He would have to come down a little earlier tomorrow.

In the crisp winter air, Edwin again began to wonder about his strange quest. It might have felt right at the beginning but now, in retrospect, didn't the whole thing seem perfectly ridiculous? He wrestled with such thoughts yet came to the conclusion that, as illogical as though it might have seemed, he was definitely on some kind of spiritual path and that before long all would be revealed. Try as he may he couldn't deny the sensation of some kind of benevolent spirit that appeared to be accompanying him along his path.

As he made his way back in the direction of the university he again passed the railway station he glanced once more at the same poster that advertised England. Then a stray thought struck him. The advertisement displayed the one-way fare for the journey to England as being DM 62.50. On pulling out his wallet and going through his pockets, Edwin made the startling discovery that the amount of money received from his shift at the pub plus the twenty marks that had been thrust on him by the Turkish girl,together with some coins in his pocket, came to exactly DM62.50. Not a pfennig more, not a pfennig less.

He knew straightaway that he had no choice in the matter. It even tallied with his early morning experiences. He entered the station and, with the entirety of his German money, bought a ticket for travel that same evening. The train would depart at 17.46 which meant that he had just enough time to return to the university halls, collect his things and hand back the keys. He'd also hoped to see the Turkish girl, Nesrin, to tell her what had happened but she wasn't in her room.

And that was the end of that particular German escapade. He felt as if he was in good hands as he settled down into one corner of a compartment on the train bound for the Dutch seaport of Hook van Holland. An elderly Englishman with horn-rimmed spectacles stood smoking in the adjacent corridor and on having a brief conversation with him Edwin realised that whatever else there might or might not be in England, at least there would be no language barrier. By eleven o'clock that evening he was on board the overnight sailing of the Sealink Ferry service to Harwich.

EDWIN AWOKE FROM HIS slumbers with the discomfort of a fluorescent light shining directly into his eyes. Nevertheless, having used a rolled up shirt as a pillow and Robert's borrowed overcoat as a blanket, he had slept flat on his back on the carpeted floor which had helped straighten out his spine and he felt pretty good as a result of it. There would still be a couple of hours before the ship's arrival in Harwich so he freshened himself up in the washroom and then went out on deck for a breath of fresh air. It was a cold January morning and he could just about make out the coastline of England. As he stood there he felt a sense of well-being. Equipped with such inner strength there was a renewed sense of optimism and he was confident that this time round he would find something meaningful.

Apart from a childhood memory of a family holiday spent in a caravan somewhere near Great Yarmouth, Edwin was not at all familiar with the East of England. After the ferry had docked he disembarked along with the rest of the foot passengers and went through the passport control and customs areas. Once outside the building he then took a pedestrian route that passed under a railway bridge which seemed to represent the dividing line from the dockland area. It was still only eight o'clock in the morning and Edwin thought that his best course of action would be to try and get to a larger town that could serve as his immediate base. He continued walking along a main road to the outskirts of Harwich and, as on numerous previous occasions, found a suitable spot where he could face oncoming traffic and held out his left thumb to indicate that he would appreciate it if some kind soul would stop and give him a lift. It didn't take very long at all before a car pulled up and he was able to place his suitcase along the rear seats and then hop into the front.

"Where are you heading for?" asked the driver.

"To be quite honest, I'm not really sure," began Edwin, simultaneously realising how strange it felt not having to search for German words but also how peculiar his answer must have sounded. He qualified it by adding, "I'd really just like to get to the nearest large town."

"Well, the first large town is Colchester and I'll be passing by there," said the driver.

"Then Colchester it is," agreed Edwin as enthusiastically as if he'd just received a revelation from God on high, which maybe he had.

The journey took about half an hour. They drove passed a row of drab terraced houses in the middle of nowhere and Edwin found himself thinking how pathetic they looked standing there all alone and disconnected with the rest of the world. Other visual reminders that he was back in Britain were the flashing orange beacons of a zebra crossing, a grubby looking newsagent and three fish and chip shops all in close proximity of each other. Further along the route a Chinese takeaway and a red telephone box added to the sightseeing as did public houses, farm houses and council houses. He made polite conversation with the driver. When they reached the outer perimeter of Colchester a roadside sign described it as 'The oldest city in England.' He was duly deposited somewhere near the centre of town by the driver who wished him all the best.

First things first, reasoned Edwin to himself. Clearly this was the town where he was somehow destined to be for the remainder of his break from Italy and so he'd better find somewhere to stay and take things from there. A lady was out walking her dog and he asked her if she knew if there was any bed and breakfast accommodation in the locality. She directed him to a road that lay on the other side of a roundabout just beyond a small railway terminus. He trudged down the entire length of that road with his suitcase and eventually came across a row of bed and breakfast places but they all had signs up in their windows saying 'No Vacancies'. At a main road another house also displayed a no vacancies sign. Edwin entered the front gate and rang the doorbell. A pleasant lady answered it and he asked her whether she happened to know of any accommodation in Colchester that might actually have a vacancy. She paused and thought a bit and then said, "Well, there is a Mrs Sticks at number sixty-six a bit further along and she sometimes takes in lodgers. It might be worth asking there."

Edwin continued to number sixty-six which was a large semi-detached property with an overgrown front garden and a broken blue metal gate. The bell drew no response and so he rattled the letterbox. A bubbly landlady with peroxide blond hair answered and said that she had one single room spare but that she only ever let it out on a half-board basis – that is to say inclusive of breakfast and an evening meal. However, her rates were reasonable enough and Edwin had little hesitation in agreeing to move in and was glad to dump his suitcase in the room. She provided him with two door keys and he went off in search of a Barclays Bank to withdraw some cash. Everything worked like clockwork and within a couple of hours Edwin had paid four weeks rent in advance, had taken a rather tepid yet refreshing bath -"the hot water only comes on in the mornings and evenings, love"- had a change of clothes and was enjoying a chat with the landlady over a pot of tea. Outside it began to snow heavily.

He spent the afternoon in his small bedroom writing a couple of letters mainly to have his mail forwarded to Colchester. Then, as a plan of action, he determined that he would make a point of visiting as many local church groups as possible once he knew where to find them in the hope that, by so doing, it might lead to a better understanding of what everything meant.

The evening meal was served in the dining room at six o'clock. The food was pretty basic yet adequate. That night it was liver and bacon with fried onion and gravy, peas and mashed potato followed by jam sponge and custard. Two of the other lodgers introduced themselves. They were both railway engineers who were working on a nearby stretch of track. Also present was a youth who delighted in making smutty suggestions most of the time much to the amusement of the landlady's fourteen-year-old daughter, Sharon, who was still in her school uniform and who had a habit of non-stop sniggering about anything and everything. On being asked by one of the railway workers why he had come to Colchester, Edwin said something about having just returned from Italy and needing to get a few things sorted out. It was not far from the truth.

After dinner he went upstairs and fetched the chequered overcoat before stepping out of the front door into the cold night air. Two inches of snow had settled and crunched under each footstep. This was his first night in a new town and in keeping with his time honoured tradition he intended to drink half a pint of beer in several of the town's pubs in order to capture the overall atmosphere of the place. As always he deliberately walked past the first two pubs because he figured that he would call in on them last on his way back to his lodgings. He passed the entrance to some kind of military establishment and under a pedestrian subway leading to a more central part of the town where there was a variety of such establishments to choose from. He didn't really care whether or not he got into a conversation with anyone at the bar as he was perfectly content simply to take in the atmosphere and occasionally tune into other peoples' conversations.

The following morning, after what turned out to be a full English breakfast, Edwin explored the streets of Colchester in daylight. Set upon a hill, its layout appeared relatively straightforward apart from a slight confusion of two parallel shopping streets which at first glance seemed identical. The public library was equipped with a reading room with free access to all the daily newspapers. It also had a whole section of reference books about Christianity including several leather bound hefty volumes of heavy reading. He browsed through some of the pages but soon realised the archaic terminology used did little to throw much light on things.

Edwin continued with his exploration of Colchester. He simply kept on walking. Amongst his various discoveries were the whereabouts of the three Anglican Churches of St Botolph's, St James the Great and St Peter's. He also located the Colchester Baptist Church, The United Reformed Church, the Castle Methodist Church, the Seventh Day Adventist Church and the Catholic Church of St James. He jotted down the times of their services. He again wondered why there were so many divisions of Christianity if they all stemmed from the same Jesus and the same Bible. Need it be so complicated? He wondered. There was also a Pentecostal Church that had meetings every Wednesday evening and, as the day happened to be Wednesday, he determined that he would return there that at seven thirty that evening.

Edwin had never been to a Pentecostal Church before. It was well attended and led by a Canadian Pastor who gave a sermon that described his days at a Bible College in which he had to chop down a driveway of trees which he somehow equated with his spiritual mission. A couple of hymns were sung and then, much to Edwin's surprise, the entire congregation suddenly erupted into making some most peculiar noises of indiscernible utterances that supposedly were examples of speaking in tongues. As he could make neither head nor tail of such a phenomenon he simply sat there in silence and tried to work out what the couple sitting nearest to him were actually saying. It sounded complete gobbeldy-gook. Suddenly the voice of somebody stood near the front rose above everyone else's and, in English, started trumpeting something about the cross at Calvary. The rest of the room fell momentarily silent and then, after a while, everybody began to verbally exalt the name of Jesus for several minutes. And that was it. It had been a meeting that left Edwin somewhat bewildered and, once again, none the wiser.

IT WAS WHILST LOOKING through the window of the town's Christian bookshop that Edwin first encountered Vicky who was inside and looking through various books that were on display. When she emerged and started looking at the window display Edwin asked whether she thought there was anything in the shop worth reading.

"Oh, every now and again there's something," she replied, "If you can sift it out from amongst all the rot."

"Is there any book on Christianity that you would recommend?" he asked.

"Not really," she said, "I think I'm happy just with my New Testament, let alone this lot!"

"I take it you are a Christian?" he said.

"Yes I am," she replied, "I became a born-again Christian five and a half years ago. What about you? Are you a Christian too?"

"Yes," he said.

"But are you born again?" she asked.

"Yes," replied Edwin, "and believe it or not you are the first person I've ever met in the same category."

"Really?" she queried, "When did you have your experience?"

"Just a couple of months ago whilst in Italy," he replied.

"Praise the Lord!" she said.

"Fancy a coffee?" he asked, in the knowledge that there was a cheap and cheerful cafeteria just around the corner where he had sat for over an hour earlier that morning.

Well, why not?" she said, "I'm not due back on duty for a couple of hours.

They sat in a back corner of the cafeteria and chatted over two mugs of frothy Nescafe. Vicky was a nurse at Colchester Hospital and she lived in the nursing home. She'd been raised in Essex and had never been out of England. She was in her mid-twenties. She attended the United Reformed Church in the centre of town and explained that she went there primarily because its vicar could generally be relied upon to deliver interesting sermons although she doubted whether many of its congregation were similar born-again Christians.

"The problem," she said, "is that far too many people only pay lip service to the Lord."

"So I hear," replied Edwin, and then, thinking of his own situation, said, "And yet not everybody who experiences Christianity necessarily knows what they're supposed to do about it."

"Oh, I think that they do," she said, "After all, they're the ones who've been chosen to bring the message to the rest of mankind. Everybody has to come to Christ sooner or later. Jesus himself made that plain when he said that "No man cometh unto the Father but by me."

"That's going to be a monumental task then isn't it?" he said, "Especially when you consider the Jews, the Muslims, the Hindus, the Buddhists and all the rest."

"That's why God needs workers in the field. But don't worry, brother, we've both been saved!"

"That's one way of putting it," he said but not without wondering how, from a practical point of view, such status could be extended to the rest of humanity.

Edwin escorted her to the front entrance of the nursing home and they made arrangements to meet again on Friday afternoon. "Praise the Lord," mimicked Edwin as he walked back to his digs. Mind you, a bit of female companionship in the equation might make some sort of difference.

Edwin met up with Vicky on an almost daily basis. She knew her way around the Bible and could quote chapter and verse, which was helpful in trying to locate various reference points that seemed to keep cropping up in their conversation. Unlike his room, the nursing home was centrally heated right around the clock and there were occasions when he would stop over for the night. Although completely different both in their outlook and in their personalities they found a certain comfort in each other. She was content simply to know that she was 'saved' and yet he sensed there had to be a lot more to it than that. By definition he too had had a born-again experience but surely it didn't end there. He wanted to unravel the mystery and get the message out in a way that could be understood by the public at large. But that didn't mean that he was about to stand on a street corner bearing a placard saying that the end was nigh and nor was he going to approach every Tom, Dick and Harry with some half-baked slogan. The problem was that he didn't know what he was going to do.

One Sunday lunch time he was sat in a cafeteria near to where he was staying and, as was usual in these days, engrossed in thought. He had been reading from the Book of Genesis earlier that day and noted that it had referred to several generations of individuals as indicated by frequent use of the word 'begat.' Someone had begot Mahaleet, Mahaleet begat Jurad, Jurad begat Enoch and so on and so forth. It had occurred to him that since everybody in the world has two parents and is therefore the end product of their ancestors, to work upwards on family trees and multiply them to the power of two for each generation was a mind blowing exercise in which everyone ended up with common forebears. He thought that perhaps it underlined the fact that all members of the human race are in some way related and that in some way they all needed to be returned to God. He tried making some mathematical calculations but gave up in the end.

Throughout the weeks that followed Edwin went to a variety of church meetings and study evenings in Colchester. On Sundays he attended at least one if not two church services. He'd also joined up with a group that met at someone's home once a week where they discussed a particular biblical theme and occasionally had a guest speaker. On one occasion an elderly minister turned up with a two thousand year old coin from Israel and the entire evening was spent in some pointless speculation as to whether Jesus himself might possibly have handled it. At the end of such evenings they read a prayer out loud from a book of prayers.

Edwin attended Sunday services at different churches on a rotation basis. The congregations varied, as did the sermons. But as far as he was concerned each of them seemed to be saying more or less the same thing. A couple from the United Reformed Church invited him back to their home for Sunday lunch.

During the course of conversation Edwin mentioned he had never been baptised and he asked them whether they considered such a thing to be important.

"Oh yes," said the wife, most emphatically, "Baptism is very important and you know it's never too late. It's not only something done for babies. I've seen adults baptised."

The husband agreed.

"It's one of the central planks of the Christian faith. It's like membership of a club. Without a card one can't fully participate. But Joan's right, it's never too late to be baptised."

Edwin then put the question as to whether they were born-again Christians and they didn't seem to know what he was talking about.

"We were both brought up in the Christian faith from birth so I suppose one could say that we were born into it," the husband said.

Edwin thought it might be wise not to elaborate and instead harped back to the previous subject.

"So, you think I ought to make arrangements to get baptised?" he asked.

"Yes, I think that would be an excellent idea. Why don't you go and have a word with Reverend Lawrence and see what he can arrange?"

BY NOW EDWIN HAD been in Colchester for just over a month. Although he had felt guided to the place he still hadn't stumbled upon any clear understanding in his spiritual search. He would soon be due to return to his job at the television station in Florence. In many respects he was looking forward to that although it did beg the question as to why he had gone on this jaunt at all if it hadn't achieved anything. He glanced at his reflection in the mirror and thought that he resembled a down and out tramp with his scraggly beard, long hair, chunky woollen sweater and Robert's chequered overcoat. If he'd arrived in Colchester a couple of months earlier someone might have been inclined to have given him a 'penny for the guy'.

But of course that was just the external appearance. Internally he had entirely different sensations. He had felt what he believed to be the presence of a benevolent guiding spirit on a daily basis. He knew beyond a shadow of a doubt that there was something beyond this small phase of physical life. Realistically, however, try as he might, he didn't seem to be getting any real answers from any of the various church groups that he visited and nor from Vicky and all her biblical knowledge. He again wondered if that could have anything to do with the missing baptism factor. Picking up his copy of the Bible that had been given to him by his missionary friend in Hong Kong he thumbed through the pages until he arrived at a passage in Matthew's gospel where Jesus was baptised by John the Baptist, an act that apparently triggered off the heavens opening and the Spirit of God descending like a dove and lighting upon him. Edwin pondered over it. So, even Jesus was baptised. He made up his mind to visit Reverend Lawrence that very afternoon.

A pathway through the small graveyard led to a side door of the church and to Reverend Lawrence's office. He welcomed Edwin in like a friend and made him a cup of coffee from a freshly boiled kettle. He was very easy to relate to. He asked Edwin what he thought of the United Reformed Church.

"Well, let's put it this way," said Edwin, "Since arriving in Colchester I've attended other churches on several occasions but somehow I keep coming back to this one."

"Do you understand what differentiates us in our doctrine from other denominations?" he asked.

"I've absolutely no idea," replied Edwin, who was far most interested in what the various branches of Christianity had in common than what divided them.

Reverend Lawrence went on to explain some technical detail relating to whether Jesus was perceived to be God incarnate or not. Edwin sipped on his coffee and couldn't really grasp much of what was being said not least because he didn't know the meaning of the word 'incarnate.' Rather than admit to such ignorance he just nodded out of politeness every now and again whilst waiting for an opportunity to change the subject to the prime purpose of his visit. Eventually the conversation swung around to Edwin's situation.

"The problem is," said Edwin, "that I believe God has called me for something but I don't know what."

"Well, of course the ministry is vast," replied the vicar, "and I can see you as being particularly well cut out to be a fighter on the front line rather than just taking on a low-key role."

"I'm inclined to agree," said Edwin, "but there is something I'd like to ask you."

"Fire away," he replied.

"Well, it's just that as a child I was never baptised – and I was wondering if arrangements could be made for me to get that done."

Reverend Lawrence breathed an audible sigh and looked Edwin in the eye.

"Baptism?" he said, shrugging his shoulders, "Baptism – is purely psychological, really. But I can tell just by looking at you that you know more about such matters than I do."

Edwin was quietly flabbergasted but managed not to show it. He thanked the Reverend Lawrence for his time and made his departure. He walked down the length of a hill whilst digesting what had been said. Here he was, a new convert to Christianity, and yet when he'd gone to somebody in supposed authority for advice he'd been told that he supposedly knew more about such things than the person in authority did. It made no sense at all – or did it? Could he for one moment imagine that he was better equipped or more prepared for carrying out God's will than an ordained vicar? He supposed that if he stretched his imagination he could just about imagine it despite having such a shallow biblical knowledge. But God would have to show him what to do next. That was all there was to it. Edwin had asked everybody else.

Edwin wrestled with ideas throughout the rest of the day. At dinner he ate his meal unconsciously and couldn't even recall what it had consisted of. That evening he walked across to the hospital to see if he could get any fresh insights from Vicky but it turned out that she was on night duty. He instead walked around the entire circumference of Colchester. On returning to his room he knew that it was pointless trying to sleep. Instead he sat on the faded yellow candlewick cover of his bed and, in the dimness of the low-watt bulb in his overhead light, attempted to pray to God.

"I've been here in this town of Colchester for five weeks and even though I've done the rounds of the local churches I still don't know what I'm expected to do or even if I'm expected to do anything at all. Please can you show me? Presumably there's some purpose to it all but please could you show me what that purpose is? I seem to have exhausted just about everything here and it will soon be time for me to return to my job at the TV station in Italy– but unfortunately I am none the wiser."

Edwin stayed awake all night and repeated variations on the theme at regular intervals. Sometimes he said it in a serious way. Other times he said it in a more light-hearted jocular way. But the general gist of it was the same on each occasion.

CHAPTER TWENTY-NINE

HE SPOTTED HER AS soon as he came around the corner. She was standing outside the Co-op grocery store and offering what looked like small booklets to the various shoppers who came along the pavement in her direction. An elderly lady stopped and reached into a handbag to purchase one before continuing on her way. Edwin knew intuitively that he had to speak to that sales girl but, rather than going straight up to her, he first went to the reading room of the library to digest the content of the day's press. After an intake of news he then made his way back to where she had been located and, sure enough, she was still there.

"Good morning," he said as he approached her.

"Good morning," she replied fixing a pair of bright eyes on him, "Can you spare ten pence for missionary work?"

"I think I can just about manage that," said Edwin, stopping and handing her a coin.

"Thank you," she said.

"Which organisation is it?" he asked, determined to enter into some kind of a conversation rather than go on his way with nothing more than the literature.

"Our full name is the Holy Spirit Association for the Unification of World Christianity but because all of that is a bit of a mouthful it normally gets abbreviated to Unification Church," she said.

"Can't say I've heard of it," said Edwin. "What are its aims?"

She smiled at him and responded, "Well, we are an international faith group with an important message for this particular time that we are living in."

"Oh, and what kind of message is that?" he asked.

"Well, one of the problems facing mankind today is that everybody would like to live in a world of truth, beauty and goodness – but they don't know how to bring it about," she said.

"That may well be true," said Edwin, "but how do you think it could be brought about"

It can only be realised with God's help," she replied.

"You're probably right about that," he agreed, "Are you a Christian group?"

"Yes and we favour Christian unity. There are about four hundred mainstream denominations of Christianity which can be confusing."

The comment was of particular interest to Edwin who, on a smaller scale, had reached a similar notion himself about the various divisions.

"But if there are that many different groups and if each of them is set in their own ways how do you think that unity between them could ever be achieved?" he asked.

"Historically God has always revealed certain things to certain people at certain times," she began, "and now is one such time when he is doing just that."

Edwin was becoming more and more intrigued with what this young and not unattractive lady seemed to be saying.

"And of course there all the other religions throughout the world." she continued, "They fit into the plan of things too."

It was the first time Edwin had ever met anybody else purporting to be Christian who openly showed respect for the other major religions. Others had tended to dismiss anything but their own as being false, misguided or in some cases the work of the devil.

He quizzed her a little more and seemed to be getting some quite sensible answers to his various questions. He also asked if she was based in Colchester but found that she was there only for the day. She had driven up from London with three other people who were similarly positioned outside shops for a day's fundraising activity.

He told her a bit about of his own recent conversion experience and how he was on his spiritual search. She responded by saying that she felt he was just the kind of person that she had been praying to meet. He could sense her sincerity in this and found it more than a coincidence that he'd been awake throughout the previous night pretty much pleading for some direct guidance through his own maze of religious experience.

"If you're free later this afternoon, I could invite you to come back with us to our headquarters in London" she suggested. Edwin reasoned that because the whole encounter had seemed to be a matter of divine intervention he ought to follow it through to some sort of conclusion.

"London?" he said, "It would take a bit of time to get down there and back."

"You could stay overnight. We have a guest room. We can drive you there today and bring you back up here tomorrow morning," she replied.

Edwin had the fleeting thought that it wasn't every day that a young lady invited him back to her place in London to stay overnight but then, recalling the religious context of the conversation, was able to dismiss any idea of possible romance. On the contrary, the invitation sounded perfectly in tune with his spiritual search and was straightforward and reasonable enough.

"OK," he said, "How should we go about arranging that?"

"Well, perhaps we could meet right here at four o'clock? By the way, my name's Debbie, what is yours?" she asked.

"I'm Edwin," he replied, "Yes, that'll be fine – here at four."

"I wonder…" she started and then asked, "Do you believe in Satan?"

Edwin nodded. From his limited study of the basics of Christianity, it had been one of the first things that he'd learned.

"Then please be sure you're here," she said, "I mean, don't go and break your leg or something in the meantime."

Assuring her that he would be there at the appointed hour, Edwin then headed back to his guesthouse intrigued by what had taken place. Because he hadn't slept the night before, he set his alarm clock and took a nap for two hours followed by a tepid shower. He then packed a few essentials into his shoulder bag as preparation for the overnight stay before returning to the centre of Colchester. It was still only three-thirty when he passed a young man outside a newsagent handing out pamphlets and receiving donations in much the same way that he had seen Debbie doing that morning. Edwin called out to him "I'm meeting up with Debbie in about half an hour!" The young man looked up at him and smiled "Ah, so you're the one. Great! OK, see you then!"

As the clock struck four the fundraisers gathered at the meeting point and

Debbie formally introduced the other three of them to Edwin. They all seemed pleasant enough, he thought, and all in their early-twenties. There was a girl called Sarah with a radiantly engaging smile, the tall bloke, Bob, whom he'd seen earlier and then Neville, a young bespectacled lad with a North Country accent. It became apparent that Debbie was in the capacity of co-ordinator or team leader. Together they walked across the town to a car park and clambered into an estate car. Jeff took the wheel and they headed off in the direction of London. One of Edwin's first reactions was to reach for his packet of cigarettes but he checked himself as no one else was smoking and they all looked rather clean cut and, in any case, it would be rude to ask if he could smoke in what was obviously a non-smoking car.

The journey got underway and after some polite exchanges the conversation came round to taking turns in how each of the four had first encountered the group. It transpired that Debbie had been a university student in Exeter who on the strength of an invitation in a leaflet had gone on an introductory study weekend held at a farmhouse where she had apparently discovered many answers to hitherto unanswered questions – so much so that she had decided to devote her time to the cause. Neville had been working as a decorator in Sheffield and had met up with one of the Unification Church members who'd invited him to some locally held events at which he had evidently been suitably impressed to the extent of chucking his job in and committing himself to the group on a full-time basis. "We don't get paid for doing what we do," he explained, "I mean, our expenses for things like food and somewhere to live are taken care of but we don't actually draw a salary." Debbie clarified, "It's certainly a different kind of lifestyle from more conventional work. The movement is a registered charity and one could say that we work for God."

The driver, Bob, then gave his story of how he'd been through a long spiritual search which took in considerable European travel, smoking marijuana, working on a kibbutz in Israel and trying to make sense of the Bible before finally, in common with the others, he had met someone on a street corner who had pointed him in the direction of the Unification Church. Sarah, who sat in the front seat next to Bob, had similarly bumped into someone who had brought her along to a series of lectures, which she had found inspiring.

There was a sense of wellbeing that Edwin detected amongst the co-passengers who seemed genuine and sincere. It felt as if he had been guided to meet them. Perhaps this entire spiritual journey hadn't been completely in vain after all.

The London Headquarters of the Unification Church was situated in a corner of Lancaster Gate in two adjacent buildings one of which had been the Norwegian Embassy. Edwin instantly recognised the square as a place that he had occasionally walked around during some of his evening meditative strolls when he had lived nearby in Notting Hill Gate.

The five of them passed through the pillared front entrance of number 44 into a reception area where a lady operated a telephone switchboard and five or six other young people lingered. They greeted each other and Edwin was introduced as a guest who would be staying for the night. He was informed that he would be on the second floor and that the room number was 208. Well, that was easy enough to remember, he thought – 208 had been his room number at the YMCA in Hong Kong. Surely that was just a coincidence although at this stage of the game nothing much surprised him. He deposited his shoulder bag in the room and returned to the reception area where Debbie was waiting to give him a brief tour of the premises.

"Dinner will be ready in half an hour," she said, "so there's still a bit of time to show you around."

They went down a flight of stairs to the basement where a small team of people were preparing food in a large kitchen. Once again, everybody seemed to be in their early twenties and very friendly and polite. The front of the basement housed a laundry room and Debbie deposited a carrier bag of clothing there.

They then went upstairs to the first floor where there were some administrative offices and still more people to shake hands with. There was also a ballroom on that floor which was apparently used for meetings rather than for dancing.

They descended the stairs to the dining room where some forty or so people were gathered and standing alongside tables. Debbie ushered Edwin to a vacant spot. "We normally sing a song or two before we eat," she told him which helped explain why green books had been laid out between the cutlery arrangements on each table. And, as if on cue, a young man with a guitar strapped around his neck addressed the assembled multitude as "brothers and sisters" and suggested that they all sang song number fifty-two. Everybody picked up a book and turned to the appropriate page and, after a countdown of "one, two, three, four", the room burst into such lively song that Edwin suspected that it could be heard for miles around.

Edwin wasn't much of a singer himself. He never had been. Even in recent attempts at hymns in Colchester church services his voice had sounded decidedly flat and invariably triggered off a bout of smokers' cough. Half the time he found it more convenient just to mouth the words without any sound actually being emitted at all. But the singing here was different. It was as if everybody was giving of his or her best simultaneously and succeeding in harmonising it in a truly professional sounding way. He recognised the song as having been one of the tracks on an LP by the Seekers that he once used to play on his turntable in New Zealand.

There's a new world somewhere, They call the Promised Land
And I'll be there someday, If you will hold my hand
I still need you there beside me, No matter what I do
For I know I'll never find another you

Just when he thought it had come to an end, they started singing the first verse and chorus all over again.

"Thank you everybody and now let's sing song number twenty-eight," said the guitarist. That turned out to be 'Top of the world' which had been popular on juke boxes in the bars of Hong Kong at the time when Edwin had lived there.

Something in the wind has learned my name
And it's telling me that things are not the same
In the leaves on the trees and the touch of the breeze
There's a pleasing sense of happiness for me

There was a third song that evening. It was called 'Streets of London.' It felt almost as if someone had deliberately selected the three songs to correspond with three different phases of Edwin's life. But of course that had to be coincidental. At this rate, had there been a fourth song it probably would have related to his travels in Europe. Instead of that, however, a fresh-faced rather chubby looking young man with a decidedly French accent invited everyone to join him in prayer in which he gave thanks that they could be gathered together and asked for God's blessing on the meal.

With the pre-dinner sing-song over and done with, everybody then sat down and tucked into a generous helping of shepherd's pie and vegetables followed by stewed pears and custard. Edwin listened in to the conversations of those sitting alongside him. Perhaps the first thing that struck him was the diversity of those present. There was a Swiss girl opposite and some Japanese chatting amongst themselves over to his left. On the other side a Sri Lankan man in a pin-striped suit could be heard explaining something about architectural heritage. He could also detect a Scottish accent and an American accent somewhere nearby. Without exception everyone looked radiantly healthy and clean and seemed to have a certain confidence about them. They sounded intelligent and were dressed conservatively. Within a rich spiritual atmosphere Edwin soon found himself engaged in conversation with those around him. He probed a bit and discovered that in his immediate vicinity one person came from a Catholic background, another had had a Methodist upbringing and yet another had lent more towards the Church of England. And yet somehow they had all wound up under the same umbrella.

A tall man entered the room and Debbie beckoned him over and introduced him to Edwin. "This is Blaise and, if you like, he will be able to give you a bit of an introduction to the movement after dinner," she said.

"Please to meet you," said Blaise, as they shook hands, "and I gather that you work in television broadcasting."

"Yes that's right" replied Edwin, mildly surprised that such detail was already known.

"Actually that's a bit of a coincidence," continued Blaise, "I used to work for the BBC myself."

"Oh, that's interesting. What did you do there?" asked Edwin

"I worked in graphic design at the TV Centre in White City."

"Well, it's good to know that I'm in good company," replied Edwin.

"Absolutely," he said with a smile, "See you a little later."

Edwin sensed that here at last was someone who could probably help him understand the chain of events that he'd been through during the past months. As the meal continued he was able to further quiz some of the people at his table and it seemed like they'd all given up whatever it was they'd been doing before to come and join this particular religious organisation. An Irish lady was a qualified doctor, a young man had left a promising career in a bank and another had been an aircraft design engineer. Whether such apparent zeal to join a religious group was strange or noble it was too early to say.

Teas and coffees were then served after which Debbie ushered Edwin to a small lounge where Blaise was waiting for him. She then departed and left them to it.

Edwin's notion that Blaise might be able to shed some light on his situation was an accurate one. Blaise was open, approachable and sensitive and he seemed to possess some insight into spiritual matters as if they were a perfectly normal everyday occurrence. Edwin's brief summary of all that had happened to him including his Christian conversion experience in Florence didn't sound quite as bizarre as it sometimes did when he'd tried to tell it to other people. Blaise listened patiently and seemed to understand every detail.

"So," concluded Edwin, "although I somehow felt guided I didn't really want to be back here in England at all."

"Well, there are still some wonderful qualities here in England," said Blaise, "It's not all gloom and doom – and maybe there's a good reason for your having returned here at this time."

Edwin recalled that back in Germany he'd had that early morning intuition that it was important for him to return to England in order to learn something. And now what this man Blaise was saying seemed to echo that notion. A young lady entered and asked if they would like a further tea or coffee. She returned shortly afterwards with a tray containing two glass mugs of tea, a sugar bowl and a plate of biscuits.

In the meantime Blaise had asked Edwin if he would like to hear the first part of the group's theological understanding. Edwin had agreed to do so but it was not without an inbuilt mechanism alerting him to be on the lookout for any kind of distortion. Why did this group apparently have to have its own teaching? Maybe it was like the Mormon's who had their own teaching too – all about someone with the totally unconvincing name of Joseph Smith – no offence meant to him but how could anyone know if his version of things was correct? Presumably it was all to do with discernment. And if there really were four hundred different denominations of Christianity from the same Jesus and the same Bible maybe this Unification Church group would prove to be nothing more than denomination number four hundred and one – thereby compounding the problem further.

And yet this Blaise character, who had previously worked at the BBC and with whom he now sat seemed sincere enough. Edwin resolved to listen attentively to whatever was going to be explained but if he felt for one moment that it was deviating from his own limited understanding he would have no hesitation in saying so.

Blaise stood up and positioned himself alongside a white board equipped with felt tip pens and all of a sudden looked like a schoolteacher about to give individual tuition to a new pupil. He took a quick slurp from his mug of tea and began an easy to follow theological talk which he illustrated by drawing diagrams on the board as he went. The content of the talk was interesting and periodically he asked Edwin if he was able to follow it. In fact, Edwin soon discovered that not only could he follow it but every now and again he found that he was one step ahead and would interject at various points. Blaise had spoken about the relationship between a painting and its artist as being similar to that of the relationship between the creation and its creator. It was then suggested that if one wanted to find out more about the nature of God one could take a look at the things of the creation and realise that everything had been designed in a system of pairs. These were man and woman of the human race, male and female of the animal kingdom stamen and pistil of the plant kingdom right through to the smallest things such as protons and electrons. He elaborated on this at considerable length and said that ideally each half should have a harmonious relationship with its counterpart.

Edwin interrupted, "That's all well and good," he said, but the reality is that we don't always find such harmony."

"Precisely," said Blaise "and, even if there really is a God, many people don't experience him in their daily lives and a lot of people even doubt his existence altogether which implies that some sort of separation seems to have taken place."

'And presumably that's due to the fall of man,' contributed Edwin, having understood that much from his Christian literature.

"That's right", replied Blaise, "and the next part of the teaching gives a very clear understanding of how that fall of man came about.

They took a short break and chatted about the Unification Church in general. It had been founded in Korea by somebody with a name that sounded to Edwin like "some young man" but after querying the pronunciation, it proved to be someone by the name of Sun Myung Moon who was also referred to as Reverend Moon. Edwin didn't think that he had heard of him before. It was explained that the group's structure was like one big family in which the female members were all regarded as sisters and the male members were regarded as brothers. Apparently they had numerous centres throughout the world where members lived and carried out missionary activity on a daily basis.

"Do members form love relationships with each other?" asked Edwin, wondering about segregation of the sexes.

"Not until marriage," was the reply.

"Oh, so the group does believe in marriage, "said Edwin, relieved to hear that lifelong celibacy as advocated by some religious groups at least didn't apply to this one."

"Oh yes, very much so" replied Blaise, "Marriage is central to our faith. In fact the Unification Church could even be described as a preparation school for marriage. In the meantime, though, brothers and sisters work together in their various mission fields but don't have any physical relationship until such time as they are married."

Edwin began to get the picture.

Tutor and pupil positions were then adopted once again as Blaise went on to deliver his next talk. Once again the content was easy to follow and logical in its presentation although this time it contained some things which were quite shocking. It consisted of the biblical explanation about how the first human ancestors had been cast out of the Garden of Eden but with explicit details as to how that situation came about. Apparently it had had nothing to do with eating a literal fruit but it seemed that the Archangel Lucifer seduced Eve both spiritually and sexually and became what is known as a fallen angel or Satan. Eve then used that newly acquired knowledge, hence the knowledge of good and evil, to seduce Adam. The Fall of Man was all to do with wrong and premature sexual relationships. Edwin gulped. Somehow he could identify with a lot of what was being said – he had a quick flashback to some of his own previous relationships and the main thrust of this startling explanation seemed to relate to him personally rather than to any distant Adam and Eve characters. The lecture concluded and Blaise asked if he had any questions.

"But does this mean that sex is actually sinful?" asked Edwin, "I mean, surely the sexual act is a normal and natural occurrence otherwise how could anyone ever be born?"

"Originally the act of sexual intercourse between husband and wife should have been the most pure and beautiful expression of love in which God would have been present throughout," clarified Blaise, "The problems brought about by the fall were the result of a misuse of love. Firstly, there should never have been such a relationship between the Archangel and Eve and secondly, Adam and Eve had been still growing up as brother and sister at that time and had not yet entered the married relationship and so their sexual relationship was premature."

Blaise then went on to further explain that because everybody is descended from that first family, successive generations have inherited a contradiction in which they all have both an original mind and a fallen mind and that humankind has never reached its full potential as true sons and daughters of God, hence the need for a messiah.

It wasn't too far removed from the basic Christian understanding of the need for a messiah due to mankind's sinfulness, thought Edwin, and yet the explanation had contained more hard-hitting detail. He'd sensed a tremendous amount of spiritual power behind each of the points that had been made. It felt as if he was being let in on age-old secrets and he now sensed more than ever that he had been guided to this place specifically to hear such things.

Blaise then suggested that Edwin had probably digested enough of the teaching for one evening but said that there was still more things to come that could be explained at another time. He also mentioned that there were courses held every weekend that newcomers could attend and study such matters in more depth and at a more leisurely pace.

DESPITE THE RELATIVE TRANQUILLITY of the guestroom Edwin found it difficult to sleep that night. The atmosphere felt alive and buzzing. He sat up in bed and went through the events of the day. Although he felt as if he'd done the right thing by coming to this place he wasn't quite sure what to make of it all. He ought to have all kinds of questions but, when he put his mind to it, he couldn't think of a single one. They were nice enough people, he thought. They were obviously Christian yet they were somehow different from other Christians. He'd have to find out more. That explanation in the lecture about what had supposedly gone wrong at the beginning of human history had hit a raw nerve. So it was all to do with premarital sex and the involvement of angels, was it? he asked himself and sensed that there could be some degree of truth in it. He prayed and asked God to show him if he was on the right path.

When he awoke the following morning, a distinct sound of singing could be heard emanating from somewhere in the building. Edwin got dressed and made his way down to the ground floor reception desk where a short-haired, clean-shaven, young man greeted him and asked if he'd had a good night's sleep. He ushered Edwin through to the adjacent dining room for breakfast and invited him to take a seat at a table with a small group of church members. The dozen or so people, all in their early twenties and of various nationalities, were discussing their planned schedule for the day. They politely acknowledged Edwin who devoured a bowl of cornflakes and was then offered some scrambled eggs and baked beans on toast. A rather debonair looking man dressed in suit and tie entered the room and, pulling up a chair alongside Edwin, introduced himself as Stephen Holder.

"I gather that you are from the media," he said.

"Well, I work in television broadcasting if that's what you mean," replied Edwin.

"Is that with the BBC or ITV?" asked the man.

"Neither," replied Edwin, "I've been based overseas, first in New Zealand, then in Hong Kong and now in Italy."

"Oh I see," he said, "What is it that you actually do?"

"Mainly programme production," replied Edwin.

"That sounds interesting. Any kinds of programmes in particular?" asked the man.

"I've worked across a range," replied Edwin, "News, Current Affairs, Children's programmes, Drama, a Women's magazine programme – I even worked on the production of a ballet once upon a time."

"I see. And this is the first time that you've come across the Unification Church?" he asked.

'That's right," confirmed Edwin, "I just happened to bump into some of your companions yesterday in Colchester."

"Ah yes – Debbie mentioned it," said the man. "Incidentally, she should be along to collect you soon. She's probably rounding up the rest of her team."

And with that Stephen Holder politely excused himself and left the dining room.

A blonde lady at the table looked up from her scrambled egg and with a distinctly Scandinavian accent said, "It's because the media can be so terrible. That's the problem."

"Sorry, I don't quite follow," said Edwin.

"The media," she repeated, "Most of the people who work in it can't be trusted. They've really got it in for us. It's no offence meant to you but the media reports always distort things and get everything completely wrong about us. It works completely against God's providence."

It was the first time Edwin had heard such a sweeping generalisation about the media being applied to coverage of a religious group. If she'd been talking about a political party, then maybe one could expect such criticism, but religion? He'd always had the impression that the media treated religious matters with a certain sensitivity and respect. He cast his mind back to the times when he had worked on religious programmes and on outside broadcasts of church services in New Zealand. Certainly religious broadcasting could be downright boring. Everybody knew that. The best thing about it was being paid time and a half for working on a Sunday and the inevitable booze up that took place once transmission was out of the way but he could recall no cynicism about religion itself. He was about to ask her to elaborate when Debbie arrived and announced that it was time to depart.

THEY WERE BACK ON the road again shortly before eight o'clock. The five of them occupied the same places in the estate car as they had done the day before. Today the team would first drop Edwin off in Colchester before continuing on to Ipswich where they would do another full day's fundraising with their magazines. As the sluggish journey of stop start traffic out through London's East End got underway, Debbie asked Edwin what he had thought about his visit to Lancaster Gate. He replied that it had been interesting but that he needed a bit of time to fully digest it. She asked him about the lectures from Blaise and he told her that he had found them to be both revealing and thought-provoking. She said that after she'd heard the teaching for the first time everything around her seemed to acquire richer colours and that she'd then attended a weekend study workshop on a Wiltshire farm.

"Oh yes, Blaise mentioned something about a farm," he said.

"It's a place where newcomers can come along and hear an introductory overview of the teaching in its entirety." She explained, "We hold them every weekend and they're very popular."

Edwin thought that he'd quite like to meet other newcomers to see what they made of it. He was also curious as to whether there could be those amongst them who had gone through a similar helter-skelter spiritual ride in a completely out of character search.

"Does it cost anything to go on such a workshop?" he asked.

"Yes but it is just three pounds for the entire weekend which runs from a Friday evening through to the Sunday afternoon," she said, "and that includes the lectures, the meals and dormitory type accommodation."

"That sounds very reasonable," said Edwin, wondering whether or not he ought to commit himself to spending a whole weekend with these people. "But if it's down in Wiltshire, it would be to be a bit complicated getting there from Colchester."

"Well," she said, "Let's see, it's already Thursday and, if you wanted to come along this weekend, I daresay we could arrange to pick you up tomorrow evening and take you there."

It all seemed a bit too convenient for comfort but he didn't want to appear ungrateful. "How many other people would be there?" he asked, changing the subject slightly to allow for some thinking time.

"It varies," she said, "but there are normally around twenty to thirty or so new guests."

Edwin knew deep down inside that he needed to go and check it out and recognised that, because he had grown so used to assuming that here was a catch to most things in life, perhaps he was coming across as a little over-suspicious. Mind you, he thought, he'd only just met these people and he still hadn't fully worked out what they were trying to achieve, apart from standing on street corners all day long and flogging magazines.

"Well, what actually happens on these weekends?" he asked.

Bob the driver answered. "Oh, they're quite well organised," he said, "There's a schedule of lectures, meals, entertainment and a chance to look around the farm and breath in some good country air."

"The thing is," said Edwin, "I'm always a bit wary about getting involved in something without knowing much about it."

"That's perfectly understandable," said Debbie, "and that's why the weekend is really designed just as an opportunity to find out a bit more about it."

Edwin's eyes met with hers momentarily and again he sensed her sincerity.

"OK then, I'll come," he said.

"That's great!" she said.

Back in Colchester, Edwin dropped the overnight bag off at his lodgings and strolled into town. Although it was a bit on the chilly side there was a clear blue sky and bright sunshine. He headed to the centre of town and then out towards the hospital on the other side. He'd visit Vicky and tell her all about the Unification Church. When he arrived at the nursing home, however, she wasn't there and another nurse who lived in the room across the corridor told him that Vicky had gone to visit her parents for a couple of days but would be back on Saturday. That's unfortunate, thought Edwin, because he would have liked to have bounced some bits of those lectures off her before going on the study course. After all, she was extremely well versed in the Bible and knew her way around it far better than he. He'd be especially interested in hearing her take on the Adam and Eve story and what she thought about the version that he'd now been given – if he could remember it properly. If the explanation was true, it presumably meant that they'd have to put an end to some of their amorous antics too. But, at the same time, he wondered how anybody could reasonably be expected to give up what was generally regarded as a healthy sex life. Had he got that bit right? Certainly the group seemed to attach a lot of importance to marriage so presumably abstaining from sex was just something of a temporary arrangement after which a full loving relationship would be developed within matrimony. That progression would make some degree of sense. He spent the rest of the day deep in thought and took a long riverside walk out to a place called Rowhedge. By the time he got back via the same route it was already getting dark. Although it was Thursday, he decided to skip the usual evening meeting at the United Reformed Church. He needed a break from religion.

THE FOLLOWING DAY EDWIN was picked up by the fundraising team at the appointed hour from a spot near the gated entrance to the public park. Debbie got out of the car to greet him and suggested that he place his bag in the boot.

"I hope you don't mind," she said, "but although we'll end up at the farm we're going to do a bit of fundraising on the way."

"That's fine by me," replied Edwin, "but it'll be dark in an hour and all the shops will have closed so I don't know suppose you'll be able to do much more after that."

"Oh no," she said, "We won't be standing out on the streets any more today. In the evenings we go round the pubs."

The thought of a pub crawl had a momentary appeal to Edwin until he quickly realised that they weren't going to be drinking in such establishments. Instead, with the landlords' prior consent, the church members would go around the bar areas offering copies of their magazine to the pubs' clientele in return for donations whilst Edwin remained seated in the car outside. It reminded him of the occasions when he had bought a copy of 'The War Cry' from the Salvation Army who could normally be relied upon to put in an appearance on a Friday evening round about the time that he was on his philosophical fourth pint. He saw that the smaller pamphlet-like magazines being distributed by the Unification Church were entitled 'One World'. Edwin asked if he could look at one and Neville pulled one out of a shoulder bag and handed it to him. It had a bible quote of the front page 'Blessed is he who washes his robe.' He turned it over and on the back it gave a registered charity number and contact details. He opened the eight-page booklet and read one of its short articles about missionary work in Kenya. It seemed reasonable enough.

For an early evening meal they stopped off at a roadside cafeteria. It was something of a greasy spoon affair in which they all ended up with sausage, eggs, peas and chips together with sliced bread and butter and mugs of tea. Debbie paid the bill and asked for a receipt. Edwin was impressed by the fact that she paid for him too. They continued their journey in the direction of Reading but as they reached Maidenhead they took a more cross-country route and two of them started leaping out at every pub along its way. They alternated with each stop which lasted anything from five to fifteen minutes. The pair would return to the vehicle several magazines lighter whilst the side pockets of their shoulder bags were beginning to bulge with coins. Apparently most people donated the suggested cover price of ten pence although, every once in a while, they would be given fifty pence or even a pound note and told to keep the change. At the fourth stop that evening Bob returned to the car and said that someone in the pub had asked him a bit about what the group stood for and, when he'd explained, had insisted on giving him a ten pound note as a donation. Such was the generosity of the British public. Each time they got back into the car Edwin caught a waft of cigarette smoke and realised it to be due to the pub fumes having permeated their clothing.

"Does anyone ever offer you a drink?" he asked.

"Sometimes," replied Bob "But, we wouldn't ordinarily accept alcohol and because of the time factor in trying to get around as many places as possible we wouldn't really have time to stop off for a soft drink either, especially knowing that we were keeping everybody else waiting."

The evening seemed to last a long time. The team took full advantage of the pubs' licensing hours right the way through to the eleven o'clock closing time. By then they were somewhere in the vicinity of Swindon and Debbie said that they would now continue direct to the farm. For some reason Neville began to sing a song. The lyrics said something about having a story to tell to the nation.

Despite it being shortly before midnight when they arrived there were still signs of life at South Farm in the Wiltshire village of Stanton Fitzwarren. Two young guys were outside carrying out some maintenance work on a white van and another estate car. Edwin was ushered into a large kitchen with a range cooker to one side around which six or seven people were gathered with green plastic beakers of hot chocolate. Two of them were Portuguese. He was introduced as being Debbie's guest and before long was also supping on the warm cocoa liquid. It transpired that everybody there was a Unification Church member and that the other guests had already gone to bed for the night. A thin young man with a ski-jump nose wearing a jacket and tie entered the room and asked if he might have a word with Debbie. She excused herself and said she would be back shortly. They were gone for some five minutes whilst Edwin hovered around feeling slightly conspicuous. When they returned, however, the man was introduced as Trevor, who would be teaching the weekend workshop.

"It's obviously been quite a long journey for you all the way from Colchester," he said.

"Yes it has," agreed Edwin.

"Well, as it's already quite late, what we're going to do is whisk you straight off to bed now so that we can all make a fresh start with everything in the morning."

"That sounds fine to me," said Edwin.

"And Debbie tells me that she stopped off several times on the way for her team to do some fundraising," he said.

"That's right," agreed Edwin.

"Ah well, at least it's given you the chance to see some of the ways we go about doing things," he said. "Now, if you'd like to follow me, there's a bed awaiting you in the upstairs side room."

AT SEVEN O'CLOCK THE following morning somebody switched the light on and announced that breakfast would be served in an hour's time. Edwin sat up in bed and saw that there were seven other occupants in the room. He had slept reasonably well. He made his way along the landing to a door marked 'Brothers' Washroom,' where he took a hot shower and dried himself as best he could on a communal damp towel only discovering afterwards that a freshly laundered towel had been placed at the foot of his bed. He went downstairs and mingled with the numerous people who were now congregated there. Almost all of them looked to be in their early twenties. Some were Unification Church members and others were guests although he had no means of knowing which were which. There was no sign of Debbie or any of her team. Not that that necessarily mattered, apart from the fact that most people seemed at least to know somebody. Before long everybody was ushered into a dining room through a doorway on the far side of the kitchen. It had a horseshoe arrangement of long refectory tables lined on both sides with wooden benches. Individual places had been set with cutlery and cereal bowls were in evidence as were plastic containers of muesli, glass jugs of milk and stainless steel sugar bowls. Edwin noted that songbooks had been strategically placed along the lengths of the benches.

Those present stood in rows around the tables and a so-called workshop co-ordinator arrived on the scene tuning a guitar that was strung around his neck. "Great everybody!" he said, with a smile as he acknowledged the assembled multitude. "Let's begin by singing song number 15, 'I'm on my way to the Promised Land.'" And before Edwin knew it, it was a bit of a repetition of what had happened in London and the whole room burst into enthusiastic song. This time, however, some of them provided an additional percussion input by accompanying it with loud rhythmic clapping. Edwin found it all a bit overwhelming but in some way managed to mouth the words. There were two more such songs and then the room fell silent as one of the Unification Church sisters gave a prayer in which she asked that God be with all those attending the workshop and that they would be able to open their hearts and minds to better understand the significance of the time in which we lived. She ended the prayer by asking God's blessing on the food. She had prayed in Christ's name.

It was a hearty farmhouse breakfast. After the muesli came a plateful of bacon, eggs, mushrooms and grilled tomatoes with plenty of toast and marmalade to follow. Someone from the kitchen then came in and asked for a show of hands as to who wanted tea and who wanted coffee. Edwin had struck up a conversation with a young man and his guest who had arrived from Birmingham. He was intrigued to learn that, like himself, the guest had met the Unification Church for the first time just a few days ago. However, on talking with him over a further slice of buttered toast, Edwin found that he hadn't experienced any of the ups and downs that he had gone through. The man worked in one of Birmingham's departmental stores and had simply met a Unification Church member in the park during his lunch break and had been invited along to visit their local centre. How very uncomplicated, thought Edwin, compared to his own long drawn-out process.

A walk around the farm was organised. As it was muddy a large assortment of wellington boots had been provided as well as some polythene food bags to first put over one's socks in case the insides of the boots were damp. The group of thirty or so people then trudged off to look at chickens, cows, fields of barley and woodland led by an attractive looking lady with a strong Australian accent. Edwin found himself to be walking next to a church member called Peter who seemed genuinely interested to learn how Edwin had first come into contact with the group. He then gave a little insight into how he had become involved. Apparently he was a primary schoolteacher by profession and although from a strong Catholic background he had discovered that he still had a lot of questions concerning faith that the traditional church seemed unable to answer satisfactorily. One day, after experiencing a period of certain emptiness in his life, he happened to bump into someone fundraising on a street corner in Bath and had subsequently attended his first workshop just as Edwin was now doing. He'd been with the group for two years and apparently never looked back. "Somehow everything just slotted into place," he said, "and all those unanswered questions became answered."

"So what is it that you actually do now?" asked Edwin.

"I have a mission as leader of our centre in Plymouth," he replied.

"Oh, I see. And what does that entail?" asked Edwin.

"Well basically we have centres in most major cities throughout the country," he said. "Members live there as part of their missionary training and they also serve as bases for our regional activities and outreach. We're still in a kind of pioneer stage yet slowly but surely becoming more and more established as we expand."

"What kinds of day to day things do you do?" asked Edwin.

"Well, of course, much of our work is educational. That's because we have an important message to share with people from all walks of life and so we need to have the facilities in place for them to be able to come and study it," he replied, "but we also have other things like a printing works, a couple of bakeries and various businesses. And as you can see, even this farm is a working farm."

The route around the outer extremities of several fields and through an area of woodland completed a full circuit and they had now arrived back in the village itself once again. One of the guests, an oriental girl from Macau called Suzie had begun to sing a repetitive chant of 'Jesus is my Lord, Jesus is my Saviour' over and over again to the apparent annoyance of the Australian lady leading the walk.

"What is that you're singing?" she asked.

"Jesus is my Lord, Jesus is my saviour," replied the guest.

"And why are you singing that now?" she was asked

"Because Jesus is my Lord and Jesus is my Saviour." answered the guest.

"Well, I've nothing against the sentiment," said the Australian, "but I'd appreciate it if you'd stop because it's getting a bit repetitive."

"But Jesus really is my Lord and Saviour," she protested.

"I don't doubt it," replied the Australian, "but there's no need to let it dominate the entire atmosphere."

On returning to the farmhouse building the guests assembled in the back lounge and along the length of the hallway to be given some words of welcome from a suave Italian gentleman in a tweed jacket.

"What we are going to study throughout the weekend is a brief overview of the Divine Principle, which is the teaching of Reverend Sun Myung Moon who is the Korean founder of the Unification Church," he said, "but please understand it is not our aim to try and convert you our set of beliefs – it's simply an opportunity to explain the teaching to you and it's then up to you as individuals to decide whether or not it's of any particular relevance to your own lives."

He went on to say that they would be divided into two groups for lectures which would commence at ten o'clock. Half of the guests would remain where they were and make use of the back lounge whilst the others would go through to a front lounge. Both rooms were then set up like classrooms each with a whiteboard and easel and several rows of plastic backed chairs.

Edwin found himself in the front lounge along with seven other guests including the two people from Birmingham and Suzie from Macau. The five remaining guests of the team consisted of three young ladies, two of whom were from London and the other from Basingstoke, and two young men who had driven over from Cardiff. They spoke amongst themselves for a while and were then joined by the workshop's leader, Trevor, of the previous evening, who in turn was accompanied by four other Unification Church members who planned to sit in on his lectures.

"And to get the ball rolling, what better way than to sing the song number 23? 'When all the Saints come marching in,'" announced one of the helpers strumming yet another guitar. Edwin, along with the other guests, suddenly found themselves back into warbling mode once again.

Trevor's lectures were very good indeed. He managed to include humour within his in-depth theological presentation and to get the balance exactly right. The first two lectures covered pretty much the same ground that Edwin had heard from Blaise in London a couple of days ago, namely the so-called Principle of Creation and the Fall of Man. Despite being a repeat, however, the talks were not boring. On the contrary, it was interesting to hear everything through again, being expressed by a different person and in a slightly different way. There were fresh insights that came to Edwin's mind as the talks unfolded although the overall message was exactly the same, as was the overriding implication of the explanation of the biblical story of Adam and Eve.

"After lunch" said Trevor, as he concluded the morning session, "we'll be taking a look at the life of Jesus and at some parallels of history."

There was free time in the early afternoon for some general chit-chat with Unification Church members and, for those who wanted it, a further opportunity to take a look around the farm. Then everybody assembled once again for the inevitable pre-lecture song before Trevor the lecturer plunged into the next part of the teaching.

Ever since Edwin's initial brush with Christianity Jesus had been a main point of focus and so he could readily identify with the content of that particular lecture despite the fact that it contained several unexpected details. The lecturer clearly knew his Bible well and was able to quote chapter and verse in support of the various points that he was making whereas Edwin, who was still biblically illiterate in terms of where to locate individual passages, would need to crosscheck things afterwards.

For reasons beyond Edwin's immediate comprehension, a lot of the lecture was about the historical figure of John the Baptist. The main gist of what was being put across was that he was meant to have played a pivotal role in connecting Jesus to the religious leaders of that time. John the Baptist had apparently been identified by Jesus as being the return of Elijah, an occurrence that had been prophesied in the last book of the Old Testament. It seems, however, that difficulties arose because John the Baptist himself denied being the return of Elijah which tended to contradict the claim made by Jesus.

There was a pause in which Trevor the lecturer asked if everyone followed the point he'd been making. No one actually said anything but as several heads politely nodded he continued on into the next part. For the following twenty minutes or so it transpired that it was not God's desire for his son, Jesus, to have been crucified at all – that unfortunate situation had only arisen as a result of the Jews' disbelief in Jesus. Apparently Jesus was the second Adam and, if he had been accepted during his lifetime rather than rejected, he would then have taken a wife as the second Eve and together they would have recreated Adam's family that had gone astray at the beginning of human history – and would then have grafted mankind onto that family.

After such information overload it was time for a tea break.

Edwin popped outside for a breath of fresh air. When he returned, there was a question and answer session going on and Suzie from Macau was saying that at far as she was concerned the crucifixion had been absolutely necessary otherwise Christianity couldn't possibly have started. Trevor, however, was suggesting that if Jesus had been welcomed rather than rejected, Jesus would have been able to establish the foundation for the kingdom of heaven during his physical lifetime and that there would have been no need for a new religion of Christianity to emerge at all.

"The parable of the vineyard makes it clear that God didn't send his son simply to watch him get killed," he said, "The way of the cross and the subsequent emergence of Christianity was a secondary plan that came about only after Jesus had been rejected."

"Was this true?" Edwin wondered. It sounded plausible although he couldn't really see where it was leading to because surely history was history and whatever had happened had happened. Why were they analysing the past when we lived in the present? On the other hand though, he had to admit that the explanation about the fall, which was also something that had happened in history – right at the beginning of human history in fact, did seem to have some sort of a bearing on things of the present so maybe learning hitherto unknown things about Jesus would relate to present day things too.

Trevor then drew an intriguing comparison between certain events that had taken place in the Old Testament and the history of Christianity. There were periods of time involved, often of 400 years, in which certain eras appeared to directly correspond to others. The 400-year period of the Jews' slavery in Egypt, for example, was put alongside 400 years of the early Christian persecution under Rome. The next period, of church patriarchs, culminated in the year 800AD when Pope Leo the third anointed King Charlemagne. This was said to match the earlier era of Old Testament Judges up until King Saul.

The two calendars of Jewish history and Christian history were mapped out alongside each other on the board as the explanation continued. History had never been Edwin's strong point and whilst he was unable to verify anything of what was being said, he could understand what Trevor was driving at and found the whole thing extremely fascinating. The parallels continued right up to the four hundred years of preparation for the Messiah of the Jews, which corresponded to a four hundred period of Christian history since the Reformation of 1517. And then the real shock.

"And so you see," explained Trevor, "if you add up all of these years, which correspond to time periods of both eras, you get one thousand, nine hundred and thirty or alternatively, if you simply add four hundred years to the time of the Reformation in fifteen-seventeen, you'll arrive at nineteen-seventeen. So, if such parallels are anything to go by; we can say that the expected return of Christ is likely to take place sometime between the years of nineteen-seventeen and nineteen-thirty."

"But those years have already passed," blurted out Edwin.

"Yes they have," agreed Trevor, "and it means that if the Messiah were born between those years, he could already be here and already be in his late fifties."

Gareth, one of the lads from Cardiff, intervened. "You're saying if the Messiah was born – but I thought we were talking about Jesus returning."

"Well, we're certainly talking about the return of Christ," said Trevor, "and we'll be covering that in depth in tomorrow's lectures, but for now let's suppose it happens in an unexpected way. The Book of Revelation mentions a male child born of woman."

"So you reckon it won't be Jesus coming back then?" asked Gareth.

"Clearly the hope of all Christians is in the return of Christ," said Trevor. "That was the promise that Jesus left. But there is a very real danger that they might fail to recognise him when he comes – especially if he were to come in an unexpected way – just as the chosen people of an earlier era, the Jews, failed to recognise Jesus as the Messiah."

Suzie from Macau put up her hand. "I'll recognise Jesus when he returns!" she exclaimed. "I'm going to meet with him up in the sky because I've been saved!"

"Many people have their own expectations about the second coming," said Trevor, diplomatically.

"I still don't follow why you think the Second Coming won't be Jesus himself," continued Gareth from Cardiff, "and as a practicing Christian I find the suggestion rather offensive."

"I'm certainly not trying to offend anyone," said Trevor calmly, "but individuals don't just step out of history. It's something that just doesn't happen. For example, as we discussed earlier, John the Baptist was considered to be the second coming of Elijah. Yet he was a different person but with exactly the same mission."

"But who said John the Baptist was the second coming of Elijah?" challenged Gareth.

"Jesus did," was Trevor the lecturer's reply, 'In Matthew's Gospel, Chapter 17: Verse 13 as well as in Matthew's Gospel, Chapter 11: Verse 14."

"I'm going to have to check that out," said the guest.

Despite such debate, Edwin could understand the implications of what had been taught that afternoon and felt as though he'd learnt something. Although he was still grappling with the concept of the first coming of Christ, could it be that he now found himself slap bang in the time of the Second Coming? It raised a lot of questions that he didn't really want to ask – not just yet, anyway.

After the formal content of the lectures, the evening provided a contrast of light-hearted moments between members and guests alike and there was plenty of opportunity to engage in interesting conversation. The atmosphere was relaxed and most people looked radiant. Dinner of Spaghetti Bolognese and Apple Crumble was followed by an evening programme of home-grown entertainment that included music, poetry and amusing sketches. The lecturer, Trevor, took part in one of them that was supposed to illustrate mind and body co-ordination.

With a towel draped over his shoulders, an assistant behind him provided a different pair of hands that were instructed carry out various tasks such as combing his hair, brushing his teeth and applying shaving foam to his face with disastrous consequences. The evening closed with a prayer given by the farm manager and everyone went through to the kitchen where yet again the inevitable green plastic mugs of hot chocolate had been prepared.

Edwin caught sight of himself in the bathroom mirror of the brothers' washroom. He still resembled a tramp in his chunky sweater and the way he'd let his hair and beard grow over the past couple of months yet he looked more at ease with himself. He went to bed and slept soundly through to the seven o'clock switching-on-the-light ceremony, as had occurred the day before.

SUNDAY'S LECTURES WERE EQUALLY absorbing. They delved into events of more recent history, including the world wars and the emergence of Communism, which was explained as a Godless ideology. Edwin found it interesting that theological reasoning could be shown to overlap with politics in that regard. There was mention also of things that were likely to occur in the biblical last days with Trevor pointing out that many of them seemed contradictory.

"On the one hand we can read in 2 Peter that 'the earth will be destroyed by fire' and yet on the other hand we can read in Ecclesiastes that the 'a generation comes and goes but the earth remains forever'. Clearly such statements can't both be right, so one of them must be literal and the other symbolic and, in this particular case, the world being destroyed by fire can best be interpreted to mean that the sovereignty of evil will be destroyed by the word of God."

Although Edwin wasn't in the slightest bit familiar with any of the prophecies concerning the last days, he nevertheless found the explanations being given to be both clear and logical. By the time they reached the mid-morning tea break he felt positively privileged to be hearing such teachings.

The final talk of the day was all about the Korean founder of the Unification Church, the Reverend Sun Myung Moon. Trevor provided a detailed biographical account of a man of deep faith and yet Edwin found himself at a loss as to see it in any kind of context. The overall picture being painted was that of an oriental man who had had many direct experiences with God. After a spiritual encounter with Jesus he had developed a new insight into religious matters but his teaching had been rejected by Christian churches in Korea and so he had set up his own group. Whilst treading a path of truth and righteousness he underwent the most terrible ordeals at the hands of the Communists and was sent to work in a harsh labour camp where the life expectancy was zero but from which he was miraculously freed. It all sounded perfectly honourable but Edwin couldn't for the life of him see how it followed on from the previous lectures. The connection came during the course of the question and answer session that followed.

Gareth's hand shot up first. "So you're saying that this Moon person is the new Messiah!" he said.

"Well, I didn't actually say that," replied Trevor. "All I've been doing is explaining some of his teachings but at the end of the day it's up to each individual to find out for themselves who Reverend Moon is."

"But do you believe he's the Messiah?" asked Gareth.

"Well, as a matter of fact, yes I do," was Trevor's response, "although I wouldn't necessarily expect anybody to arrive at that same conclusion right away."

His admission of holding such a view shocked Edwin, who could scarcely imagine anyone believing such a far-fetched idea. There was a brief silence whilst the full severity of this startling notion crept in.

A Welsh lady called Doreen, who had been sitting next to Edwin throughout the last lecture, turned to him and asked, "Did you realise that we were living in the end times?"

"I'd not really considered such a thing before," he confessed, still not used to the terminology let alone its meaning.

There were further questions from the guests. Did Reverend Moon himself claim to be the Messiah? Evidently he didn't make the claim directly but instead asked people to pray and ask God or Jesus Christ as to his position. And apparently he'd also said that everybody should strive to be the Messiah. Where was Reverend Moon? He was currently in the United States. Had he visited Britain? Yes. He'd even been on this farm.

It was lunchtime and Edwin was still absorbing the content of what they'd been taught. In one sense he wished he hadn't heard the last lecture. Things had been going well up until that point and yet now he felt burdened with the difficult task of trying to decide whether this Moon character, about whom he knew nothing at all, could possibly have anything to do with his new life of faith or whether he'd been completely misled into coming to the workshop and it was all a load of old cobblers. Suzie from Macau hadn't exactly helped the situation by approaching him on the way into the dining room and saying that she thought that Reverend Moon was the Anti-Christ. Edwin felt the need for time and space rather than rushing into any opinion on the teachings one way or the other. It was almost with relief that they started singing a song about an island in the sun and he could focus his mind on that instead. Everybody then sat down to a lunch of vegetable soup and roast chicken. Edwin found himself sitting opposite a female member of the kitchen staff who turned out to be a New Zealander. It was good to hear a kiwi accent again. She hailed from Taranaki and had been a member of the Unification Church for about a year having first been introduced to the group by a member in London who'd invited her to an event. She'd then heard the teachings over a period of time and decided to join. In common with the other members that Edwin had met, she seemed so sincere and pleasant.

After lunch everyone assembled in the front lounge where a projector had been set up and they settled down to watch a film. It was about the British branch of the Unification Church and showed members going about their daily activities of travelling around the country and speaking to people on the streets and at Speakers' Corner. It also included footage of the Korean founder Reverend Moon himself, first planting a tree and then standing at a podium in front of a large audience in a stadium and delivering a speech. Unfortunately the presentation style seemed reminiscent of a Hitler rally. However, each burst of animated oratory, delivered in the preacher's native Korean language, was followed by an interpreter who stood alongside him and spoke in American English. The content had something to do with a new future for Christianity.

The film came to an end, the curtains were re-opened and Trevor the lecturer rose from his seat and addressed the guests one last time. He thanked everybody for having attended the weekend workshop, which he hoped they had found interesting. If there were any further questions people were welcome to get in touch. Teas and coffees would shortly be available in the kitchen after which transport would begin departing in four different directions.

Edwin mingled with everybody else in the kitchen area. Debbie had finally put in an appearance for the first time since Friday evening and, after asking how he had got on, had told him that they would soon be ready to drive him back. In the meantime Edwin was approached by Trevor the lecturer who said he realised that the content of the weekend study had been quite a lot of new things for people to digest. He told Edwin that it was possible to study everything in depth and at a more leisurely pace on one of the 21-day study workshops that he currently ran in Cardiff and that they were free of charge. Out of politeness, Edwin asked him when the next one was due to start and was told that as they were ongoing and that new people could join them at any time they liked. He gave Edwin his Cardiff phone number and said that he was welcome to contact him there whenever he wished.

Although glad that such an intense couple of days had now drawn to a close and although still stunned by some of its content, it felt almost sad to be saying goodbye to the people he'd met. They'd unconsciously developed a bond of friendship even during the short time spent together and yet now on the Sunday afternoon they were all going their separate ways. One by one they got into vehicles – the two from Birmingham, Gareth and the others from Swansea together with Trevor the lecturer who was getting a lift back as far as Cardiff in the same white van, Suzie from Macau who was heading back to London and the rest in still more cars.

Rather than drive Edwin all the way back to Colchester that evening, it was agreed that Debbie's team would get him as far as London from where he would take a train from Liverpool Street Station for the remainder of his journey.

Still digesting the weekend's theological presentation the car ride provided an opportunity for Edwin to ask various questions. He tried to make it sound as hypothetical as possible when he asked about the procedure for anyone wanting to join the group.

"Well, what normally happens is that people first come along and study an overview of the teaching, as you have just done." said Debbie, "and then, if they want to, they can go on a twenty-one day study course. That is really the entry point at which they decide whether or not they wish to join. Those who wish to do so then move into one of our centres and either get assigned to one of the teams or given a specific mission."

"And what if they then decide that isn't for them after all?" he asked.

"Oh well, they'd just simply get up and leave," she replied, "There's no compulsion in any of this. But because joining requires a certain level of commitment it's important that people first find out if it really is the right thing for them to be doing which is why they attend the twenty-one days study course."

"Is there any significance in it being twenty-one days? I mean why not nineteen days or perhaps twenty-three days?" he asked.

"It's structured on some providential numbers," replied Debbie. "It's seven lots of three that represents the stages of formation, growth and completion – but that kind of thing gets explained in detail on the workshop."

Another thought crossed his mind. "Supposing someone were to go on the course in Cardiff and then decided that they wanted to join your movement," he said, "Could they move in right away or would they first have to return to wherever they'd come from?"

"It's normally possible for people to move into one of our centres and join us right away if that's what they want to do," she replied, "and that's certainly what most of us did."

"I see but how do things work from a practical point of view? I mean presumably there must be some sort of structure to the organisation – some chain of command," said Edwin.

"The movement is run like one large extended family in which everyone is regarded as one's brother or sister," replied Debbie, "In addition to team leaders such as myself we also have centre leaders like the chappie you met from Plymouth and also each country has national leaders which in the case of Britain happens to be an Anglo-American husband and wife called Mr and Mrs Blake."

Although it hardly seemed relevant anymore Edwin then harped back to the topic of baptism and asked if the Unification Church offered such a thing.

"Yes, we have our own form of baptism," replied Debbie, "and our own marriage ceremonies too."

THE TRAIN JOURNEY BACK to Colchester might ordinarily have provided some welcome breathing space but Edwin found his mind working overtime about having to make a major decision that he knew lay before him. Should he return to his job in Italy or should he go to Cardiff? Having been in the non-stop company of people throughout the entire weekend he had hoped that being on his own for a couple of hours might be an opportunity to gently chew things over in his mind. He smoked his first cigarette since Friday afternoon. On arrival at Colchester Town Railway Station it was already sufficiently late for everything to be closed. He walked back to his guest house.

CHAPTER THIRTY

WHEN EDWIN AWOKE THE following morning the sun was streaming in through his room's small rear window. Images of the people he'd met on the weekend workshop were still fresh in his mind. He recalled Trevor the Lecturer's kind invitation for him to join the study course in Cardiff from where he could then team up with them if he so desired. He looked around his shabby bedroom in the Colchester guesthouse with its dingy dark yellow candlewick covers and reflected on the long and winding road that had brought him from Italy through to this present situation.

He was due back in Florence the following week but there was now a pull in a different direction altogether. Whichever way he looked at it, it felt as though he had been led to this particular group of people. The chain of events spoke for themselves. A profound spiritual experience in Italy had led to a search which had become a process of elimination and, having exhausted the main stream churches, he'd finally stumbled upon this unknown Unification Church that seemed to offer a far clearer explanation of things than all of the other churches put together. Not only that but they were young and vibrant as opposed to stuffy and old-fashioned. They seemed to have something that the others lacked. Mind you, there was still the Korean aspect to look into and there was all that singing. He still had songs from the weekend workshop buzzing through his head.

Throughout the morning Edwin kept thinking that, in all probability, attending this so-called twenty-one day workshop was his obvious next move and there were moments when he felt quite uplifted at the thought of it. However, doubts and worries about making such a move also came to his mind. Was he not blindly rushing into something that he didn't know much about?

The move would inevitably mean lifestyle changes. For a kick off, no one there seemed to smoke so presumably that would be one of the first things that he'd have to quit. Mind you, on health grounds alone, that wouldn't be such a bad thing to do. He wondered whether it would still be permissible to occasionally pop out for a couple of pints of beer. And as for girlfriends and relationships, it was interesting that the Unification Church lived as brothers and sisters with no sex before marriage. They all seemed happy enough to endure that and it had been emphasised that marriage was central to their faith. But how soon could he get married and to whom? Many such questions arose.

Deep in thought, he'd walked across Colchester and arrived at the nurses' home where he found Vicky in the process of filling her kettle.

"Hallo stranger!" she said, "I was beginning to think that you might already be back in Italy. Would you prefer tea or coffee?"

"Hallo Vicky, it's nice to see you again." he said, giving her a customary kiss on the cheek. "A cup of tea would go down well, please, especially if you've got any of that Earl Grey left. Actually I came looking for you last Thursday morning but that little blonde nurse with the Liverpudlian accent who lives in the room across the way told me you were out of town."

"I popped up to visit my parents for a few days. I hadn't been to see them for quite as while and so I thought it was about time to show them my face," she said, "but it's been a while since I last saw you. Have you been up to anything interesting?"

"Well actually I've been up to rather a lot," said Edwin, "and I don't really know where to begin."

He sat himself down in the small armchair and a few minutes later, with his hands clasped around a steaming mug of Earl Grey tea, began relating the whole story of his encounter with the Unification Church. Vicky listened patiently and without interrupting. At the end of the entire story she commented that she knew of many Christian groups who lived communally but that personally she valued her own independence. She had never heard of the Unification Church before and asked Edwin if he was sure that it wasn't called the Unitarian Church, which was something that she had heard of.

"No, it's definitely called the Unification Church," said Edwin, "and they have an interesting view on things which, if you'll bear with me, I'll try and explain if you've got some paper and a pen."

"Sounds complicated if whatever it is needs to be expressed on paper," she said, "but, if you really need it, there's a block of A4 up there on that shelf behind you and there's a biro on the table."

Edwin attempted to draw some of the diagrams that he'd seen during the lectures but couldn't remember exactly how they went. He also tried to explain the version of the Genesis story of Adam and Eve but soon discovered that he couldn't fully recall the way that had been taught and so it came out in a somewhat disjointed and unconvincing manner which eventually came to a grinding halt.

"Well that's all Old Testament stuff," said Vicky, "As Christians we've moved on from that because we have Jesus and the New Testament."

"There's a whole lot of new information about Jesus too," said Edwin.

"Well, you need to be a bit careful about that," she said, "It's clearly stated in the Book of Revelation that new words should not be added."

"Yes but, it's not new words being added so much as an interpretation of the existing words," he said.

"You need to be a bit careful about that too," she said.

"Here, let me try and show you something else," he said, returning to the notepad.

This time he reproduced a diagram showing the positions of God and Satan with respect to Jesus, the Holy Spirit and Christians. It had seemed so logical in the lectures yet now he had to confess, he couldn't quite work out exactly what it was trying to demonstrate. Again he faltered and apologised. Vicky commented that she thought he'd been listening to some pretty weird doctrine and suggested that he should only trust the word of God as expressed in the Bible and forget about anyone else's interpretation of it.

"That's as maybe but why do you think Adam and Eve were expelled from the Garden of Eden?" he asked.

"I don't know why you want to keep going back on the Old Testament," she said, "but, since you ask, it was disobedience to God. They ate the fruit when they'd been told not to."

"Ah – but do you think it was a real fruit or did the word 'fruit' symbolise something else?" asked Edwin.

"I've no idea but I can't see that it would make much difference," she replied, "After all, disobedience is disobedience no matter what kind of fruit it was."

"Do you think sexual relationships and an angel might have something to do with it?" he persisted.

"I've certainly not heard anything along those lines before." she said, "and you already know my views on sexual relationships. As far as I'm concerned God is love and therefore there can't be anything particularly wrong with an act of love between two consenting adults. Marriage is more of a binding commitment that comes when people are ready for a more permanent arrangement and I've nothing against that either."

"But is sex wrong outside of marriage?" he asked.

"Well, it is the first time I've heard any such reservations coming from you," she said, "I suppose that in some peoples' eyes, and technically speaking, we've probably committed sin each time we've had it off because we're not married but on the other hand one would have to ask the question as to why something as beautiful as making love could possibly be regarded as evil or sinful."

"But might it have been a premature sexual relationship that brought about the Fall of Man?" he asked.

"I don't really see how that could be because without any sexual relationships there'd be no population of the world," she replied, "Besides, as I've already told you, it was disobedience to God's commandment not to eat the fruit that brought about the Fall of Man but, in any case, I think we need to be dealing with the good news of Jesus Christ."

"Of course," agreed Edwin, "but isn't it possible that 'not eating the fruit' could have had a double meaning. Even the Bible says that after they did whatever they did, they then covered up their sexual parts with leaves. If the sin had been eating wouldn't they have been more likely to have covered up their mouths?"

"Perhaps," she replied, "but we must never forget the one who died for our sins and the fact that it's through him that we are saved – and our sins can be forgiven."

"Sure," said Edwin before asking, "And what about the Second Coming? How is that likely to occur?"

"For me, the Second Coming of Christ has already taken place," she replied, "It's the oneness we feel in being together with Jesus and the Holy Spirit. Even though Jesus died on the cross for us two thousand years ago, he's here with us now – that's what's meant by the Second Coming."

She had to go back on duty at four o'clock but before doing so she was determined to get some fresh air into her lungs and they decided to go for a walk in the park together. It was still cold and crisp outside but with a cloudless blue sky. Edwin was tempted to tell her that rather than returning to his job in Florence he might head off to the Unification Church in Cardiff instead but he resisted mentioning it. She had been a good companion to him during his time in Colchester and he suspected that she might put up some opposition to the idea. She might even succeed in talking him out of it altogether. No, it was best not to say too much right now. Instead they spoke of other things as they made a large circular route around the park that brought them back into the town. He then accompanied her back to the entrance to the hospital from where he stood and watched as she walked down its long pathway and eventually out of sight.

"Goodbye, born-again Vicky," he whispered to himself.

He sneezed and realised that he was developing a cold.

His route back through the town took him past the National Express coach station. Out of curiosity he enquired about travelling to Cardiff and found out that it could easily be accomplished from Colchester with one change at London's Victoria Coach Station. He also asked the price of a one way fare.

In possession of such details, he crossed the road to a fish and chip shop where he purchased a takeaway and returned to the park to continue the mental debate with himself about whether he should take the plunge or not. He realised that there was no one else he could ask about such a major, potentially life-changing decision just as there'd been no one to ask when he'd first embarked on this strange spiritual search.

Vicky's input had only confused the situation although in one sense it was typical. She was a Christian who was perfectly content with her life as a nurse at the hospital whereas he felt he needed a slightly more meaningful purpose than walking around a Colchester park eating from a warm pack of vinegar-soaked fish and chips. She hadn't experienced the weekend workshop and just because he didn't yet know how to explain the things that he had been taught it didn't mean to say that they were flawed. On the contrary, most of them had seemed to make sense at the time.

He still felt dubious about the Korean bloke though. How come someone from that part of the world was suddenly so central to Christianity? And what about Trevor the lecturer's admission that he even thought the man was a new Messiah? How could anyone who had just delivered a perfectly plausible series of theological lectures possibly end up with such a strange idea? It made no sense whatsoever. He recalled the guest Suzie from Macau's thoughts on the matter. Mind you, she was Oriental too. Not that he'd anything against Orientals. It was just that the whole bizarre suggestion had sounded like sheer heresy.

And yet here he was seriously contemplating joining them.

Looking back over the past few months, however, everything had been out of the blue and unexpected. He couldn't deny the conversion experience in Italy and he couldn't deny that he felt as though he'd been led in his search on a daily basis. That alone implied that he had been led to this particular group. But had he been led to them because he was supposed to join them? – Or just to be aware of them? But the main worry seemed to be a question of commitment. What was on offer seemed like an all or nothing situation. And there were also economic considerations. If he were to let his job go that wouldn't be wise. He supposed that he ought to write to Robert in Florence and lengthen his leave of absence by three weeks just to keep the option open of returning there.

By the end of the afternoon, he walked back to his bed and breakfast accommodation clutching his coach ticket. He'd booked the one-way trip to Cardiff for Wednesday which was in two days' time.

THE JOURNEY TO WALES should ordinarily have been a simple matter involving two coach trips but the debate that had started to take place in Edwin's head made it much less straightforward. He vacated the Colchester accommodation and after boarding the first National Express coach some feelings of concern were beginning to set in as he considered what he might be letting himself in for. This was going to mean commitment. But did he actually want commitment? No, was the short answer. But if it was God's Will then he supposed that it might be tolerable. He really didn't know. The stark reality was that he was heading off on a coach journey to spend time with a religious group. Who could possibly have imagined such a thing even three months ago? Had he gone mad? He didn't think that either. He still had his wits about him and could think things through in a perfectly objective way. He lit another cigarette. He was smoking heavily that morning because for all he knew it might be his last chance to indulge in that pleasurable but disgusting habit. He might as well get as much last minute satisfaction out of it as he possibly could. He gave a chesty cough, perhaps in sympathy with the situation.

At London's Victoria Coach Station there were three hours to spare before the next coach departure for Cardiff. It occurred to Edwin that being in possession both of his passport and his luggage he could just as easily walk up the road to Victoria Railway Station, take the next train down to Dover, hop on a ferry and head back down to Florence where he was expected and where his job at the TV Station and his room in the apartment were awaiting him. Instead, however, he purchased a picture postcard of Tower Bridge and wrote a brief line to Robert saying that he would be extending his leave of absence by three weeks and looked forward to seeing him soon. He included the Cardiff address on it.

Feeling under slightly less pressure as a result of having posted the card, he then crossed the road from the coach station and went for a snack in the pub opposite. But he was still dominated by the recurring question as to whether or not he was doing the right thing. He wrestled with such thoughts right up to the last minute when, almost reluctantly, he dragged himself back across the road to climb aboard the coach bound for Cardiff just before it left. Feeling torn down the middle about this venture, his cold was getting progressively worse which didn't add to the situation. He ate an entire packet of Jaffa Cakes almost unconsciously whilst tackling the cryptic crossword puzzle in his copy of the Daily Telegraph.

It was a four hour coach journey along the M4 motorway and the final destination was a bus station adjacent to Cardiff's Central Railway Station. On arrival it was dark and raining. Edwin clambered out of the coach and collected his suitcase from the storage area underneath. He had resigned himself to the fact that having made the effort to get there he was at least going to join the study course and see how things went from there. With the phone number to hand a row of four telephone boxes was conveniently located nearby.

Trevor the lecturer arrived to pick up Edwin by car. It was a short drive to the local church centre which turned out to be a former corner shop on the end of a row of Victorian red-bricked terraced houses in the Cardiff suburb of Grange-town. They entered through a door in the side of the building and passed through a hallway into to a brightly lit room where a dozen or so people were seated. Edwin was conscious of the fact that they all looked young and healthy whereas he felt bedraggled, washed out and exhausted as well as being aware that his cold had gone to his chest. A lady at the far end of the room got up to welcome him. Edwin recognised her to be Doreen, the same Welsh lady that he'd met on the farm towards the end of the weekend workshop.

"Glad that you made it," she said with a warm smile, "Did you have much difficulty getting here?"

Edwin resisted the temptation to explain the battle he'd experienced in deciding whether to come at all. Instead he said, "Well, it has been quite a long journey but at least I got here in the end."

Someone appeared from the kitchen and asked if he'd like a cup of tea or coffee. He settled for a tea and was introduced to each of the others in the room whose names he instantly forgot. Shortly afterwards he was shown upstairs to the so-called brothers' room where he got changed into his pyjamas, climbed into bed and within a few minutes fell into a deep sleep.

IN THE MORNING THE light on the landing at the top of the stairs was switched on and a voice called out "Good morning brothers and sisters. It's six o'clock and time to get up!" Another light then went on in the bedroom and to Edwin's surprise he discovered that in addition to the occupancy of the two single beds, one of which had been himself, a dozen or so young men had been sleeping alongside him in sleeping bags on the floor. In fact the entire floor space was a sea of such bodies in the process of waking from their slumbers and getting up. Edwin got dressed too and, having received a friendly "Good Morning" from the person next to him, he asked what was first on the agenda.

"We have a morning service at seven o'clock in the lounge on the first floor," he was told, "but if you want to make use of the bathroom first, it's probably best to get along there now because unfortunately in this house there's only the one and it's the brothers' turn to use it at this particular time."

The bathroom proved to be crowded and rather too communal for comfort. Five young men were simultaneously shaving in front of one shared bathroom mirror. Two more were brushing their teeth, one was taking a shower and another was using the toilet whilst three more were waiting for their turn. The steamed up room had the smell of a combination of soap, toothpaste and the lavatory.

Edwin learned that there was an additional toilet outside in the backyard which provided a little more privacy so he headed off there. On his return one of the members politely suggested that he might like to leave his shoes by the door and explained that, as a general rule, outdoor footwear wasn't worn in the house. He'd wondered why everybody else had been walking around in their socks.

A girl called Christina led the morning service. Everybody sat cross-legged in a large circle on the carpeted lounge floor and began singing several songs from the distributed books accompanied by her guitar. Edwin attempted to sing along with them but immediately developed a bout of coughing so he mimed his way through everything instead. Periodically glancing up from the songbook he was able to count twenty-seven people assembled in the room. Christina then prayed, giving thanks that everybody could be present at what was apparently a significant time in history. She then gave a short talk about different kinds of love which she described as passive love, mutual love and unconditional love. She spoke also of God's love and true love. After another song there was something called a unison prayer in which everybody prayed their own personal prayers out loud simultaneously. For one dreadful moment the idea was reminiscent of the speaking in tongues phenomenon that Edwin had come across in the Pentecostal Church but he realised that at least everybody was praying in their own language and that he could even listen in to some of them if he wanted to. Nevertheless he found the mix of voices and emotions a little confusing and realised that the best he could do to quietly ask God for guidance for the day. Christina then played a music cassette for everybody to listen to.

It's all a dream, an illusion now
It must come true, sometime soon somehow
All across the land, dawns a brand new morn
This comes to pass when a child is born

After that, a closing prayer was followed by announcements about the day's activities.

There would be half an hour's housework before breakfast and it was emphasised that everyone should not simply regard that as being just another boring chore but instead carry out the task as though they were cleaning the house for God. After breakfast fundraising teams would depart to various destinations in their vehicles whilst an outreach team would head off to the pedestrian precinct in Cardiff's main shopping area where they would hand out leaflets inviting members of the public to come and hear introductory lectures. Those attending the 21-day workshop would be walking into the centre of town to the building where the course was being held. At that stage Trevor raised his hand.

"I'd just like to say one thing," he said, 'Please can we give a warm welcome to Edwin who has come to join us for the workshop?"

There was a spontaneous round of applause.

The meeting then broke up. Edwin was handed a dustpan and brush and asked if he would like to tackle the stairs. Taking on board what had been said he really put his heart and soul into making a thoroughly good job of it whilst feeling somewhat guilty that any grain of dirt which might have had happened to find its way onto the stair carpet was probably due to him as he was the only person who had stepped foot on the stairs in his shoes.

At breakfast time there wasn't enough space at to fit everybody around the already elongated table and so several of the members sat on the floor to allow the eleven workshop guests the privilege of eating in a civilised manner. Once again, there was no faulting the food which in this instance was a full-blown British breakfast prepared by a slightly older lady called Maggie. Edwin tucked in. Doreen sat at the head of the table and, judging by the courteous way in which the members addressed her or asked her advice, he assumed that she held some kind of leadership position within the group – probably like the Mother Superior or something.

Although informal, the conversation felt a little bit stiff. No one seemed to speak unless they were spoken to. Some of the members were asked specific questions that related to what they hoped to achieve throughout the day. A Danish girl then described the content of a dream she'd had the previous night in which she's seen people queuing up in their thousands to hear Trevor's lectures.

Christina then brought Edwin into the conversation.

"So I guess the weekend workshop must have been sufficiently inspiring for you to want to come and join the 21-day workshop?" she said.

"Well, yes in many respects it was," admitted Edwin, "even though I don't think that I can go along with the bit about that Korean bloke."

If he'd thought that such an honest appraisal might have offended anybody he was surprised to note that it didn't have that kind of effect at all. No one seemed in the slightest way put out by what he'd said and Christina responded by saying that it was a perfectly understandable.

"Don't worry," she said, "the workshop will give you a good opportunity to study the teachings in more depth and then everything will begin to fall in place."

Trevor then entered the room and handed Edwin something in a paper bag.

"Here," he said, "You've got a bit of a cold. These might help."

Edwin looked inside and found that it contained a packet of Lemsip.

"Thank you", he said, impressed by such a thoughtful gesture.

When breakfast was over, the Unification Church members departed from the house to go about their daily activities and the workshop guests were escorted across town by Trevor and a Welsh brother called Dylan. It was a twenty-five minute walk. The route made its way through Cardiff suburbia then across a bridge over the River Taff, under a railway bridge, and along a commercial stretch of road that led to one end of the main shopping area next to where the premises were located.

The second floor office contained half a dozen rooms of varying sizes. The largest had been set out as a kind of reception area with a desk and some comfortable seating as well as tea and coffee making facilities. It was explained that the outreach team made the most use of this particular room as a place to bring their guests when offering them the opportunity of coming along to hear one of the introductory talks. They continued along a corridor to the room at the far end which had been designated as the lecture room for the current twenty-one day workshop complete with whiteboard and two rows of blue plastic chairs.

"Now, before we begin this morning's lectures and for the benefit of our newcomer, Edwin, I think we'd better go round the room and each briefly introduce ourselves," said Trevor, "Penny, perhaps we could begin with you and then move on down the line?"

"Hallo, my name's Penny," said the curvaceous young lady with a strong welsh accent and the most delightful of smiles sitting on the end of the front row, "I'm actually from here. I trained as a nurse at Cardiff Hospital. I first met this movement about three months ago as a result of talking with the Maltese sister, Samantha, and since then I've been coming along to meetings and have just recently decided to join."

"Thank you," said Trevor, who nodded towards the next person in the front row.

'Hi, I'm Andy and originally from Stafford,' said the quietly spoken young man. 'I met the church whilst studying Politics and Sociology at Bristol University last year.'

The introductions continued along both rows.

"My name's Jeremy and I come from Hartlepool," said the next person, a thin lad with a somewhat olive complexion and a mop of curly hair. "I'm an electrician by trade and my sister has been a member of the Unification Church for two years and so I suppose she's the one who introduced me to it. Before that we were both Methodists."

"Hello, I'm Dawn. I'm from Eastleigh in Hampshire where until recently I'd been working as a sales assistant in a chemist shop," said a young lady wearing a pink mohair cardigan. "I became a Christian five years ago and met the movement just a couple of months ago when I bought a magazine from a fundraiser. I went on a weekend workshop and realised that the principles being taught were in line with my own beliefs, which is why I'm here and why I'm about to join as a full-time member."

"Hallo. I'm another Andy. I'm from the West Midlands and I work in a hotel as a chef." said a heavily built young man sitting on the end of the back row. "I had many questions about the way the world seems to be going and a few weeks back I went for a weekend on the farm and found it interesting – so I've come here for another dose!"

"I'm Natalie," said a plumpish looking West Indian, "I was born in Birmingham, I'm a cellist and last year I graduated in Music from Lancaster University. My family are Pentecostals and just before Christmas I happened to meet one of the Unification Church members who invited me to come on a workshop."

"Thank you," said Trevor, "And now, Peter."

"Hallo, I'm Peter," said the person in a jacket and tie sitting alongside Edwin. "I'm from here in Cardiff where I'm currently training to become a Solicitor. I first met the Unification Church a little over a year ago and in many respects I'm already a member although, because of still being tied to my job, I still have to go off and do that during the working week. I'm on holiday at present so I'm able to attend this course. In the past I used to go to chapel once a week on Sundays but that was about it."

It was now Edwin's turn and, following the pattern that had been established by the previous speakers he said, 'Good Morning, my name is Edwin. I'm originally from the London area but have spent much of my life overseas – Spain, New Zealand, Hong Kong and Italy. My professional background is in television broadcasting. I had no religious upbringing whatsoever yet three months ago I had quite a dramatic conversion experience to Christianity. It was so unexpected and yet so profound that I have taken time away from my job in Italy to go in search of what it all meant and so, in many ways, I feel that God has actually led me here.'

"Thank you," said Trevor, "It's interesting to see the ways in which Heavenly Father works in peoples' lives."

"Hallo everybody, my name's Mike. Although I'm English, my parents live in Portugal so I've been living out there myself for several years. I was brought up as a Catholic and attended Catholic schools but it was only when I first started to hear the teachings of the Unification Church that I realised how shallow my understanding of things had been. I met the movement in December and I've been on two weekend workshops so this is now my third visit."

"I'm Jed and I live in Catford in South London. I believe in God, I believe in Jesus and I believe that the Bible is the word of God. The only real reason I'm here on this workshop is because of a guy I met in the street a couple of weeks ago who took me to one of the weekend courses. Anyway he reckoned it would be a good thing for me to come on down here. I do office cleaning in London and because it's casual work I was able to take the time off."

"My name's Kate and I come from Scotland – Greenock to be precise. I've been unemployed for the past year or so. I got witnessed to by a South African sister about two weeks ago and went first to the farm before coming here. Last week was tough but I'm getting into it a bit more now."

"Thanks, Kate" said Trevor. "And now last but by no means least it's Nicola."

"Hallo. Well, as you just heard, my name is Nicola. I have been a Unification Church member for the past year and a half,' she said. "I've just been given the mission to pioneer a new centre in Ipswich and so the reason that I'm attending this workshop is as a refresher course so that, hopefully, I can brush up on how to teach it. I grew up in Gloucester and worked as a secretary there for several years. I'd always believed in God although never belonged to any specific church before. When I first met the Unification Church, the teaching showed me the significance of where we all stand in history and, since joining, it's been great working together with all the other brothers and sisters."

"Thanks everybody," concluded Trevor, "As you can see there's a broad range of differing backgrounds and yet the one thing we have in common is that we're all here to take a look at the way in which God is working in the world today and to find out how that relates to our own lives. Believe it or not I was actually on my way to drama school when a chance encounter on a train journey led to my own introduction to this movement. I've been a member of for the past three years. Anyway, before we get going with the first of this morning's lectures let's all sing one song together."

The course was a far more comprehensive version of what had been taught on the weekend. At one stage Edwin's thoughts started drifting slightly whilst listening to the final part of a talk about the life of Moses. He recalled the words of Vicky in Colchester who had questioned the need for new insights into events from the Old Testament. But because Edwin wasn't particularly familiar with the original biblical stories it was like hearing them for the first time.

Throughout most of his life he had avoided anything that sounded remotely religious and yet now, against all the odds, he was willing to absorb a whole series of talks on topics with ferociously religious sounding names such as The Creation, The Fall, Noah, Abraham, Isaac, Jacob & Esau, Moses, The life of Jesus, Parallels of History, Resurrection, Spirit World, Second Advent and Last Days. Fortunately, however, there were generous pauses for questions and answers as well as plenty of breaks for cups of tea.

Although taught in a manner that was by no means fanatical, the content was intensive and there seemed to be no end to hearing that God had wanted this to happen, God had wanted that to happen, God had called this person and God had raised up that person. Sometimes during the breaks some of the guests commented amongst themselves about how immersed they were becoming and how they could do with an ordinary conversation that didn't involve the word 'God' coming into every single sentence. But it was said good-humouredly because there was little to fault in the actual content of what was being taught. Presumably if it had been an intensive course in pure mathematics the need to have breaks from the subject would have been similar. It was difficult to say whether that analogy was wholly true, however, because Edwin and the others detected that it wasn't purely the knowledge that was being imparted but that there was a spiritual dimension to learning such things too. They could feel something of an atmosphere that was being generated.

In the days that followed Edwin began to feel more at home with things even though the scheduled daily trek to and from the centre of town along its now familiar route was the only part of Cardiff that he ever got to see. He had befriended the other workshop guests and most of the local members whom he now regarded as brothers and sisters and was beginning to learn something about how the Unification Church functioned. Once at morning service during a talk about working together in unity there was mention of the importance of a so-called Cain and Abel relationship. Edwin raised his hand and said that he didn't know what that meant. It raised a gentle chuckle and an assurance from Trevor that he would explain all about it.

It transpired that the Cain and Abel relationship was something of a chain of command. In the biblical story both brothers had made an offering to God but although Abel's was accepted Cain's was rejected. It was explained that the reason for that was that after the fall of Adam and Eve, God sought to separate good from evil and had set up the brothers to represent both respectively. Instead of killing Abel, Cain should have humbled himself to him which would have enabled God to have worked a restoration process. In a nutshell, however, it translated as meaning that in order for things to progress one should unite with one's team leader, who was regarded as being in an Abel position.

In addition to studying the theory there were also practical exercises to be carried out as part of the twenty-one day training. One of these was standing in the middle of the Cardiff shopping precinct and lending support to one of the members who gave a short public speech by effectively becoming his or her main audience. The gathering attracted the attention of several passers-by who stopped to listen to what was being said. The content of such speeches was essentially that the Unification Church had a new message from God to share with everybody and that the public were all invited to come and hear an introductory lecture.

"Bloody religious nutters," muttered one elderly gentleman who turned on his heel and walked away.

"Moonies!" shouted another.

Others who remained were handed leaflets by members of the outreach team.

By now, in common with the other guests on the course, Edwin had heard the Unification Church's central teaching several times through and although he recognised it as being a powerful and revealing message, he still couldn't come to terms with the inference that Reverend Moon might be the second coming of the messiah. During free time one afternoon, he found himself discussing the matter with some of the others.

"Accepting it wasn't exactly instantaneous for me," said Penny, the nurse. "In fact I was shocked the first time I realised what was being suggested. I mean, it seemed like blasphemy! But I went home and every time I prayed about it I felt such a strong presence of God that suddenly I just knew it to be true."

"That's the thing about it," said Andy, "It's a personal spiritual experience and has nothing to do with anybody else believing that it's true or false. For me, it was similar. I doubted the whole thing to begin with but then one afternoon whilst thinking it through it all fell into place and made sense."

"I wish I could experience something like that just for my own peace of mind," said Dawn. "For me the teaching is logical and it throws a lot of light on things that we Christians refer to as mysteries but I still can't come to terms with a belief that suggests anyone other than Jesus is coming back at the time of the Second Coming."

Trevor the lecturer came into the room and after listening for a while entered into the conversation.

"There is a bridge of faith involved in accepting Reverend Moon as Messiah," he confirmed, "and it's very healthy that we can question the idea and pull it to pieces and analyse it because no one is asking anyone just to swallow everything in blind faith. At the end of the day everybody has to find out for themselves if it's true or not."

"And what made it seem true for you?" asked Edwin.

"Actually, the answer came to me whilst in prayer," replied Trevor. "When I first heard the final part of the teaching, like most of you, I was pretty shocked and just kept thinking "These people are saying that this man is the Messiah!" – It seemed so absurd at the time. Also, because of my staunch Catholic upbringing, I'd been warned about false messiahs appearing but because I felt that I already had some sort of a relationship with God, I simply had to pray to him and ask if this claim was correct. I spent a lot of time in deep prayer over it. I had to humble myself and the answer I got was "yes"."

"One thing that I don't understand is the way some members keep referring to Reverend Moon and his wife as 'True Parents' said Jed.

"Yes, the terminology is widely open to misinterpretation," said Trevor. "Try looking at it this way. The first human ancestors, Adam and Eve, would have been the original 'True Parents' of mankind. However, because of the events of the fall they lost their direct connection with God the creator. Throughout history God worked through various individuals to try and restore that situation. Eventually he was able to send Jesus as the Messiah who is even referred to biblically as the Second Adam. Had Jesus been welcomed and not killed he would have married and raised his bride up to the Second Eve position. In other words Jesus and his wife would have become the new 'True Parents' and they would then have been able to engraft the rest of humanity on to their family thereby establishing the foundation for the Kingdom of Heaven on Earth."

"Okay but how does Sun Myung Moon fit into that?" asked Dawn.

"Well, although the crucifixion of Jesus brought about the new religion of Christianity, Jesus left the promise of the Second Coming of the Messiah. Sun Myung Moon is said to have been given that new messianic role when he was 16 years old whilst praying on a Korean mountainside at Easter – where he had a spiritual encounter with Jesus who asked him to complete the unfinished work."

"Just supposing Reverend Moon really is the new messiah," said Mike, "What does he actually expect to achieve in setting up this church?"

"Let's be clear on one thing," replied Trevor. "It wasn't Reverend Moon's original intention to set up his own church. He'd wanted to be accepted by the established Christian churches in Korea but they rejected him and didn't even bother listening to his message. It parallels what happened at the time of Jesus who came as the fulfilment of Judaism. This time round Reverend Moon comes as the fulfilment of Christianity. The mission of the messiah is to establish the foundation for the Kingdom of Heaven on Earth and that's what he has to do in his physical lifetime. The Unification Church is not just another denomination but is equipped with a God-centred ideology that can embrace people of all faiths and even bring people of no particular faith to a clear understanding of God. In a sense it's the mirror image of Communism, which is a God-denying ideology. Reverend Moon has even talked of a march on Moscow. Apparently that's due to take place in 1980 and, as that's only three years away, I guess many things are going to have to change in the world before then."

During the second week of the study course, in addition to further lectures on topics which included current affairs, one of the practical exercises was to shadow a member of the outreach team and see how they approached members of the public. Edwin had been paired off with Christina whom he accompanied out onto the area of the shopping precinct and observed how she went about things. She was armed with a handful of leaflets and they stood together near the entrance to the British Home Stores whilst observing shoppers walking through the area.

"See that girl in blue over there?" she said to Edwin, "Let's talk to her."

Edwin looked across the paved area and saw a girl dressed in a pastel blue blouse and jeans skirt walking towards them. When she was within striking distance Christina stepped forward and said, 'Excuse me, I wonder if you could spare a moment. Are you concerned about the way in which the world seems to be going?'

Edwin thought it was a bit of a wide open question but the girl stopped and answered with a sing song Welsh accent.

"Well of course I'm concerned. Everything seems to be going from bad to worse with so many people out of work and the spiralling prices of everything. I don't know where it's going to end. I don't think our politicians have got a clue let alone a solution."

"Are you interested in new ideas?" asked Christina.

Again it seemed to be a wide open question.

"Well I suppose it depends what they are," replied the girl.

"We're inviting people to come and hear a talk about the way in which God is working in the world today," said Christina.

"Oh no, not religion," replied the girl. "No thanks. That's not for me. I don't believe in such things."

She'd lost her. The girl continued on her way.

For the best part of an hour Edwin remained alongside Christina as she approached still more individuals on the shopping precinct. The response was much the same. A young man said that he was perfectly happy with his own religion and therefore didn't see any need for new messages. A lady coming out of Woolworth said that she thought Christina was brainwashed. A female university student turned out to be a self-declared atheist and a smartly dressed young man proclaimed that all religion was nothing more than superstitious rot. Although Edwin didn't say anything, he noted that the stumbling block was every time the topic of religion was raised. It was the phrasing of the questions that needed modifying and he thought back to the sales pitch script that he'd once had to learn in Auckland when he'd been involved in a book selling experience and of how it had the ability to turn a negative response into a plus factor in such a way that the person had no choice but to end up agreeing with everything. He was sure that if he put his mind to it, he could adapt such patter into something that could be applied to something as straightforward as an invitation to a talk. After all, he thought, coming to a lecture was free whereas buying a set of children's encyclopaedias involved a financial outlay. Anyway, now was not the best time to do it. He was supposed to be there to see how Christina handled the task.

"Excuse me. Can you spare a moment?" Christina asked a tall thin girl with glasses who stopped in her tracks. "Are you concerned about the way in which the world seems to be going?"

"As a matter of fact, I am," responded the girl.

"Are you interest in hearing new ideas?" continued Christina.

"Yes,' she replied.

"We're inviting people to come and hear a series of lectures about the way in which God is working in the world today," said Christine.

"That sounds interesting. When are they going to be held?" she said.

"Well, we have a meeting place just along the road from here," said Christina. "If you'd like to come there now, you'd be welcome to sit in on an introductory talk. It won't take up too much of your time."

The girl glanced across at Edwin then back at Christina, shrugged her shoulders, smiled and said, "Well, OK, why not?" Before they knew it all three of them were walking together in the direction of the lecture rooms. General chit-chat took place along the way. The girl's name was Madeleine and she came from Guildford but had lived in Cardiff for the past six months where she was a care worker at an old peoples' home. They ascended the flight of stairs and entered the reception area. There they each drank a cup of coffee after which Christina ushered her new guest through to one of the smaller lecture rooms where a brother called Max was available to deliver the first part of the teaching.

At the end of that afternoon when those attending the twenty-one day workshop began their customary walk back to the Paget Street Centre, it occurred to Edwin that he hadn't smoked a single cigarette for the past fourteen days. It was the first time in a decade that he'd gone without and even though he could still feel the bulge of a packet of Benson and Hedges in his coat pocket, he had no desire for one. Nor for that matter had he experienced any of the cravings or withdrawal symptoms normally associated with giving up.

During dinner Doreen suggested that Edwin and another of the workshop participants, Jed, might like to accompany Trevor to the farm the following day where he was scheduled to teach another weekend workshop.

"I know that might seem a bit repetitive," she said, "but it won't do either of you any harm to hear everything through once again only this time you'll be there in more of a supportive role to Trevor, rather than complete newcomers."

It seemed a reasonable enough suggestion and in the early evening of that

Friday a white van transported them along the M4 and across the Severn Bridge in the direction of Swindon. Cardiff had found four new guests for the weekend workshop and they were accompanied by four Unification Church members. Amongst them was Madeleine, who sat alongside Christina. It turned out that it was a normal practice for guests to be taken to a workshop and looked after by the particular member who had met them. Such members were even referred to as the guests' 'spiritual parent.' Edwin supposed it meant that Debbie, as his first point of contact, was, in effect, his spiritual parent even though as soon as she'd got him as far as his first workshop three weeks ago, she'd pushed off elsewhere for its entire duration. But maybe that was because she was a team leader and had had more pressing things to attend to.

On this particular weekend the farmhouse was packed solid with far more people than the one that Edwin had been on previously. In all there were thirty-two new guests who had been driven in from various parts of the country together with a similar number of Unification Church members. The overall format was exactly the same but this time everybody was divided into three separate teaching groups. By the time the weekend was over no less than nine of the new guests had indicated that they would soon be joining the twenty-one day course in Cardiff.

On the return journey Edwin was sat in the van opposite Madeleine who had been moved by the whole experience. She asked him various questions about the Unification Church and Edwin found himself speaking almost authoritatively about it as if he'd been a solid member for a good many years.

There was one week left of the twenty-one day course. Time was running out and he would need to decide if he would stick around with this group, if invited to do so, or to return to his job with the television station in Italy. On the Monday morning Edwin asked Trevor why members sometimes prayed in the name of True Parents rather than in the name of Jesus if the Unification Church was a Christian organisation.

"It's just that it's one stage further forward," replied Trevor. "When people come to understand the identity of Reverend Moon and his wife they can begin to pray in the name of True Parents. The reason being that if Reverend Moon really is the living messiah on earth at this time, then that's got to be a very powerful way of praying. There's nothing wrong with praying in the name of Jesus. You might have noticed that whenever we have guests present we tend to pray in the name of 'Christ' which in one sense covers both possibilities and at the same time sounds more acceptable to other Christians."

That night Edwin had a profound dream in which he saw Reverend Moon's face smiling at him as if in complete understanding of Edwin's uncertainty as to who he was. When he awoke he was left in no doubt that Reverend Moon was indeed a man close to God. It was a spiritual confirmation and had little to do with lectures. Suddenly things were beginning to move into place as never before. The name Reverend Moon no longer sounded strange. The term True Parents no longer sounded alien. Even referring to Reverend Moon as 'Father' suddenly seemed natural. It felt like he had now made a personal connection with this extraordinary man.

Edwin's new realisation didn't go unnoticed. At morning service the centre leader, Doreen, commented on how radiant he had suddenly become and greeted his new appearance with a hearty "Hallo and welcome!" Edwin felt good within himself and amongst the others. Moreover, he felt full of benevolent spirit.

Despite such exhilarating feelings, however, several thoughts still bothered him. If he really had inadvertently stumbled upon the second coming of the Messiah, he wondered why the news of such an historical occurrence hadn't already been brought to the attention of the wider world through the media and why so many people had never heard of the event.

That morning, one of the lectures took a look at some of the criticisms that had been levelled at Jesus during his lifetime and also at some of the criticisms that were apparently been meted out on Reverend Moon. In their respective times both men were considered controversial.

"Just as Jesus was widely regarded as being nothing more than the ringleader of the 'sect of the Nazarenes', in much the same way the Unification Church was being characterised as a sect commonly referred to as the 'Moonies'," explained Trevor.

It seemed to be the case that throughout history virtually all religious movements of any significance had tended to meet with considerable misunderstanding and persecution at their inception and that even the early Christians were assumed to be cannibals and vampires because rumour had it that they ate flesh and drank blood.

"In today's world the media has an important part to play in all of this," he said. "The media is powerful and can make or break many things and so it has to show responsibility in reporting things accurately."

Edwin raised his hand.

"Up until a few weeks ago I'd never even heard of Reverend Moon or the Unification Church at all. But is that the fault of the media or the fault of the Unification Church?" he asked.

"Probably both," replied Trevor, "but it's certainly easier for the media to dismiss us as a bizarre cult rather than a serious religious movement. We used to get the occasional good press report in this country but nowadays the only stories that ever appear in print are of a more sensationalist nature. As long as the media has no understanding of the reality of what's going on, they're actually missing out on what is arguably their biggest news story ever."

During the tea break that followed, Penny had removed a large limp-covered book from a shelf at the back of the room and, together with some of the others, was flipping through pages containing pictures of numerous young couples dressed in wedding attire.

"Don't they look lovely?" she said. "If you look at the husbands and then at their wives, you can almost feel that they were made for each other!"

"What's that you're looking at?" asked Jed.

"They're pictures of the mass wedding of 1800 couples," replied Penny, "I always get inspired when I look at them."

"Mass wedding?" he echoed, "What kind of thing is that?"

"It's when the brothers and sisters in the Unification Church get married," she replied, "Hundreds of them do so at the same time."

By now everyone else in the room was gathered around the book looking at the photos of rows and rows of brides and grooms standing together in pairs with all the men dressed in navy blue suits and all the women wearing white wedding dresses.

"It's amazing. And it must have taken so much organising," said Natalie.

"How does it come about?" asked Andy.

"You'd best ask Trevor," said Peter, "but I've been told that Reverend Moon actually makes the suggestions as to which brothers would be suited to marry which sisters and then, if the couples are happy with that choice, Reverend Moon and his wife then officiate over the marriage ceremony."

"Do you mean he actually chooses their marriage partners for them?" queried Edwin.

"That's right. He matches the couples," said Nicola.

Edwin was intrigued by the very thought of it. Admittedly in London they had told him that the Unification Church was a preparation for marriage but he'd had no idea that this was how they went about it.

When Trevor returned to the room they seized the opportunity of quizzing him about the mass wedding phenomena which in Unification terminology was known as 'The Blessing.' One of the conditions of eligibility to take part in such an event was to have been a member of the Unification Church for at least three years. Edwin calculated that by such reckoning he would be at least thirty if he were going to get married by such means. Mind you, he thought, if he was going to end up with some gorgeous, uncomplicated, pure and holy wife as a result of it, surely it might be worth the wait. He had long considered the difficulty that he would one day face in knowing who he would ultimately want to settle down with. And yet now, if he could trust the method involved, it seemed that the whole process could be taken care of in a completely different way. It was intriguing and mind-blowing at the same time.

EDWIN WAS NEARING COMPLETION of the three week study course. Most of the others had arrived on it before him and had already decided that they were going to join the movement full time. They were already being assigned to various church missions. Jeremy and Dawn would both be joining the Cardiff-based fundraising team. Andy was going to apply his culinary skills to the kitchens of the London headquarters. Kate was going to work on the farm whilst Natalie and the other Andy were both joining a business team selling health food products. Jed was the only one who wasn't intending to join and he was simply returning home to South East London.

On Thursday evening Edwin made up his mind that he would like to join the movement. He knew that it would require a fair bit of adaptation and that in the past he had never considered himself remotely cut out for a religious way of life at all. Nevertheless it felt as if he had somehow been guided to it and there was the challenge that he might even be able to help it advance.

The following morning two letters arrived for him. The first bore a German stamp and had been forwarded. It turned out to be from the language school that he had visited in Essen a couple of months ago and said that they were now able to offer him a job teaching English classes. Somewhat irrelevant at this stage, thought Edwin as he crumbled it up and tossed it into the bin in the kitchen. The second letter was from Robert in Florence. He thanked Edwin for having notified him of his delayed return. He looked forward to seeing him again soon and said that, as a result of recent investment, the television station was now in a position to be completely upgraded and to implement many of Edwin's proposals.

Edwin felt momentarily torn. In his heart he felt he should stay with the Unification Church. After all, based on the content of everything that had been revealed throughout the past weeks, just about anything else paled into insignificance. And yet, he recalled his enthusiasm for the development at the TV station and all that went with it.

He thought that he would at least mention both letters to the centre leader, Doreen.

"Well, of course it's entirely your choice," she said, "but I know from experience that from time to time things do crop up that try to lure us away from this movement and on those occasions I tend to see it as a test of our faith and our resolve. I can't actually make the decision for you other than to say that you are welcome to join the movement if you wish."

It was sufficient comment for Edwin.

"Don't worry," he said, "I've no intention of disappearing off back to Italy just at the moment. I've already made up my mind to join. But maybe you could tell me what I'm going to be doing now that my twenty-one days is just about up."

She smiled at him and said, "I'm sure that God will find something fulfilling for you. First though I'd say that you're about ready for Chapter 13 this morning."

"And what exactly is that?" he asked.

"Well, the Divine Principle teaching is actually divided into twelve chapters but we also offer a thirteenth chapter to some of those who successfully complete the twenty-one days and who want to join," she said.

"Is that what Trevor's going to teach today?" he asked.

"No," she replied. "Chapter thirteen is a haircut. If you'd like to come through to the first floor lounge in about five minutes time, Christina and I will be there with a pair of scissors and we'll give you a trim."

It was an unexpected suggestion. He'd noticed that the brothers all looked clean cut as if in some kind of conformity. He reflected on the idea for a brief moment and reached the conclusion that a new look probably wouldn't do him any harm.

"What about my beard?" he asked, realising for the first time that none of the other young men had one.

"I'm sure one of the brothers will provide you with a razor and some shaving foam," she said.

The so-called trim turned out to be the shortest haircut that Edwin had had for many a year. Neither Doreen not Christina were especially skilled in administering it and they took in turns to hack off large clumps of his blond locks that fell first onto the towel that had been draped around his shoulders and then onto the floor. They had said that something about cutting it in a style of three layers out of some symbolic reasoning but when the end result of that didn't look quite right they'd simply chopped the rest off. It wasn't just a short back and sides but a short top and short fringe as well as a short back and sides. Edwin looked at himself in the mirror and wondered how he could possibly thank them for their kind efforts with any degree of sincerity.

The shaving operation came next. Armed with a can of foam and a disposable razor he set about removing his beard. He finished the task by washing his face with warm soapy water and noticed that, together with the short haircut, the overall effect highlighted his rather baby-faced features. Feeling somewhat self-conscious, he then rejoined the others for the morning walk across Cardiff but if he'd been at all concerned about their possible comments, he needn't have been. He received nothing but compliments.

There were only five people left to attend the lecture that morning because the others were already moving on to start work in their new missions. There was also news that five new replacement guests would be arriving in the Cardiff centre to join a further 21-day workshop immediately after the weekend. .

Trevor told the diminished group that as a practical exercise, they would be given an opportunity to experience the delights of fundraising that coming Saturday. They would each be assigned to a member of the fundraising team for the day and driven out to a specific location where they would offer magazines to passers-by.

"Technically, it's not selling," said Trevor, "It's simply asking the public if they can spare a donation to support our missionary activity. We always work within the law and we are a registered charity."

"What happens to the money that's collected?" asked Natalie.

"First it's counted and sorted into money bags and then sent through to our Accounts Department in London," replied Trevor. "As with any other charity, the books are scrutinised by external auditors to make sure that everything is completely above board and the funds are then allocated to our missionary activity in various countries throughout the world."

IMMEDIATELY AFTER BREAKFAST ON that bright sunny Saturday morning those who were going fundraising, which meant just about everybody, got into white Bedford vans and were driven to various shopping high streets of towns located in the Cardiff area. Edwin had been assigned to a member called Mike who had been in the Royal Air Force before joining the Unification Church. He was a decent enough person who found Edwin a suitable spot to stand in on one side of the entrance to a bakery and advised him that the cover price of 10p that was printed on the front of the magazine was purely a suggested asking price but if people could only spare 2p they could still have a copy of the magazine.

"What if they can't spare anything?" asked Edwin.

"Well, you'll find that most people will completely ignore you and just walk right past you as if you don't exist," he said, "but if they actually stop and are interested yet have no money with them, then I'd still be inclined to let them have a copy of the magazine for free. The chances are that someone will then come along afterwards and give a twenty pence piece and tell you to keep the change so the amount of money that actually gets collected tends to average itself out. The main thing is to be as pleasant to everyone as possible because throughout the day we are the ones who are representing the movement."

It was nearly nine o'clock and the shops along the stretch of road were already opening their doors as early shoppers began to arrive. It was arranged that Edwin and Mike would do an hour and a half before taking a tea break. Mike would be stationed outside the Post Office on the other side of the road and just within sight of Edwin.

"Well, good luck!" he said, "You'll probably feel a bit self-conscious to begin with and you might find it takes a while to get into it but then the time will fly past. I'll come back over and collect you at ten thirty."

Edwin had been issued with a beige shoulder bag that contained a large neat bundle of the 'One World' magazines. He removed a handful of them that he could hold out in front of himself for people to see what he was offering and then he stood there for a few minutes before plucking up courage to start saying to people, "Excuse me. Can you spare ten pence for missionary work?"

Mike was right. Edwin's words fell on deaf ears as everybody trooped past him and continued on their way. Mind you he wasn't particularly enamoured himself with the wording of what he was asking. On the one hand it sounded almost like the plea of a beggar and on the other hand the word 'missionary' seemed to conjure up all kinds of old fashioned religious connotation. He was about to try a different approach altogether when an elderly lady came up to him and said, "Missionary work, did you say, dear? Oh, yes, I'll have one of them," and handed him a 10p coin. He recalled the lady to have been one of the passers-by who had ignored him earlier and the fact that she had now returned meant that obviously something must have registered after all. From that moment on he regarded his words as more of an advertisement than a request and found that, on that basis, it made the whole experience seem far less daunting. Two more people stopped and bought a magazine and three more returned to get one from him after having initially passed him by. There was a slight confusion when Edwin offered the booklet to somebody who had already bought one from him ten minutes ago and he realised that to avoid such things happening again he would need to keep a mental note of everybody who received one.

One man reacted angrily to Edwin's request by shouting at him, "That ain't missionaries – that's Moonies! The money goes to keep your Mr Moon living in the lap of luxury! You lot shouldn't be allowed, you shouldn't!"

Edwin didn't know how to respond to this outburst. On the course they'd been taught that there was a fair bit of prejudice against the Unification Church and now he seemed to be experiencing it at first hand. Fortunately the man carried on up the road.

By the time of the tea break Edwin had raised £7.20. In a cafeteria a couple of blocks away from where they'd been fundraising, Mike bought two mugs of tea and two jam doughnuts across to their table. It was good to sit down and chat for a while.

Before long, both were back on their original spots plying their magazines once again. The crowds had thickened by now and Edwin found that he had to raise his voice in order to be heard. In a sense it felt like being an actor on a stage but with just the one well-rehearsed repetitive line and he experimented a bit by putting the stress on different individual words. 'Excuse me. Can you SPARE ten pence for missionary work?' or 'Excuse me. Can YOU spare ten pence for missionary work?' which he thought sounded far too accusing. He then tried 'Excuse me. Can you spare TEN PENCE for missionary work?' but when someone asked him what kind of 'machinery work' it was, he realised that he'd better put a bit more stress on the word 'missionary.'

"Thankless task isn't it?" suggested one man who gave him a pound and didn't want the change.

A lady then approached. "If it is missions then I'll give to it!" she said.

Another returned "What, are you still here? I saw you when I came past at nine o'clock this morning! Do you mean to say you been stood here all that time? Anyone who can do that gets my 10p!"

A fat woman then stopped and said, "Bloody missionaries? No thank you very much! Half the problems of the world are caused by what the missionaries did in those countries!"

A young man said, "I'll tell you what. We could do with having a few missionaries in our own country, not abroad."

A smartly dressed lady then stopped and asked if it was Christian missionary work.

"Yes it is," replied Edwin in all honesty.

"Which church is it?"

"The Unification Church," he replied.

"Oh, that's all right then. I do hope you didn't mind my asking. It's just that you get so many people out collecting these days that sometimes you have to make sure what it is that you are giving to. Some Saturdays you'll get the Socialist Worker being sold up that end of the pavement and then the Children of God and those Hare Krishna people in their robes a bit further along and the Save the Whale people just around the corner. But yes", she said, handing over her ten pence and taking one of the magazines, "I'm pleased to donate to this one."

"Thank you," said Edwin.

"That's quite alright," she continued, "It's a good cause and you're a fine young man doing a fine job."

As she moved off into the crowd she turned once again and called back to him one last time, "At least it's not for those dreadful Moonies!"

Before he could say anything, she was gone.

Edwin was surprised at the completely unpredictable reaction of the people. He found that it was often the case that the people who looked most likely to donate simply didn't whilst many who looked the least likely were only too pleased to do so.

A huge scruffy man who looked like a real thug heard Edwin's request, "Missionaries? Yeah?" he growled. He thrust his hand into his pocket and pulled out a five pound note. "There you go mate!" he said, handing it over.

Conversely some of the more conservative-looking prim and proper types that one would easily have imagined as willing to donate a few pence often proved to be the tightest ones of the lot. Edwin got used to the more standard responses of individuals of which "Sorry I've got no change." "I bought one off you last week." "Not today, thanks." and "I've already got one." were the most common.

Every once in a while an attractive young lady would stop and engage in conversation with him. This happened with such frequency that he seriously began to wonder if he'd discovered the ultimate way of meeting people, which was simply to ask them if they could spare a donation for missionary work. Within the space of three hours he'd had more conversations with interesting females than he might have met in an entire month by conventional means. He knew, however, that such were the rules about love relationships outside of marriage that the only real option was to try and introduce such people to the movement and to dismiss any romantic ideas. One had already given him her name and phone number.

Mike appeared again shortly after one o'clock and they took another break and went for lunch together. He'd apparently been having a much harder time than Edwin. It had begun when a man had bought one of the magazines and returned twenty minutes later accusing Mike of not having said that it was for the 'Moonies'. Mike had responded by saying that he had quite openly made plain that it was for the Unification Church but that the term 'Moonie' was a derogatory label. Even after Mike had refunded him his ten pence the man didn't leave but instead hovered around and kept calling out that the Unification Church was just a front organisation for the 'Moonies' and that Mike was practising deception by not telling everyone that he was a 'Moonie.' Such taunting had disrupted Mike's fundraising for some twenty minutes, which was about the last thing anybody needed when carrying out this kind of activity. When a lady eventually stopped to make a donation the man implored her not to by yelling, "Don't give him anything – the money goes to the Moonies!" Fortunately for Mike the lady had the strength of character to respond. She had turned to the man and said, "I'll thank you not to tell me who I should or should not be giving money to. I'll donate to whomsoever I choose."

"But it's the Moonies," the man had protested.

"So what!" said the woman, as she pressed a 50-pence coin into the palm of Mike's hand and told him to keep the change.

The man had then departed in a state of disbelief.

After a cafeteria lunch Edwin and Mike returned to their positions to see what the afternoon would bring. Edwin found it interesting to note that because he had been stood on the one spot throughout most of the day he could relate to almost everything within sight. The layout of the guttering and drainpipes on the building opposite, the cracked paving stone three slabs down to his left and the pillar box a bit further on all seemed incredibly familiar to him by now as did the shop names of Boots the Chemist, Jane's the Florists, The Bread Basket and Eric's Electronics which faced him. That annoying advertisement on the bus shelter saying 'Drink Milk' which had been staring at him all day and the configuration of housing details displayed in the window of Stephen Dale, Estate Agents.

Edwin had little difficulty in getting started again. However, the afternoon was not without its challenges.

A man tried to prove that the Unification Church couldn't possibly be a Christian organisation. However, his logic was so flawed that Edwin soon had him tied up in knots.

Needless to say there were the odd moments in which Edwin would question himself as to what on earth he was doing. The experience was certainly a far cry from the television station. Shouldn't I now be rehearsing tonight's news programme instead of arguing about religious matters? He wondered. It all seemed so unlikely.

And then there was the added irony that as a result of having bumped into someone fundraising on the street just a few weeks ago, he had now ended up fundraising on the street himself.

And what was the collection of money for? There were more questions.

On the other hand, there was a certain feeling of spiritual elation that was hard to describe.

By the end of the afternoon, they returned to the Cardiff Centre. Others would be continuing to fundraise in pubs throughout the evening but, for as far as those on the twenty-one day course was concerned, it was the end of the exercise which had been a taster. Mike and Edwin each counted their coins by making one pound piles of silver and ten pence piles of copper. Edwin had raised the sum of thirty-three pounds and thirty-seven pence which was about eight pounds more than what Mike had made.

"You did really well," said Mike, "You want to watch out. There'll be putting you on a mobile fundraising team next."

"Well. It was certainly an interesting experience but I don't think it's something that I'd want to do on a daily basis," replied Edwin. "But, now that the course is drawing to a close, who actually decides who's going to be doing what?"

"As far as I know there'd be some consultation between Trevor and Doreen and then I guess their recommendations are passed on to the National Leader, Mr Blake, for his approval,"

"And what kind of a person is he?" asked Edwin.

"Oh, he's a man of God if ever there was one," replied Mike. "I've only met him a few times but I've always been impressed. He's dynamic and straight-talking. His wife is a deeply spiritual person who has spent a lot of time with Reverend Moon and is able to give internal guidance to members. She's American so she comes across in a different way."

The other members of the course returned to the centre from a similar day's fundraising activity. Andy had evidently had a terrible day. However, he was relieved that no one passed judgement on the comparatively small amount of magazines that he had been able to shift.

That evening Trevor joined them and explained that the following morning everybody was invited to attend an early morning service known as the Pledge.

"Every Sunday morning and also on the first day of every new Month, the Unification Church holds a simple ceremony known as the Pledge. Basically members put on their best clothes such as a suit and tie and gather for a special service at five o'clock in the morning. It was explained that together they would first recite some words on a printed card and that the Centre Leader, Doreen, would then be giving a talk."

As he was getting off to sleep that evening Edwin carried an image of the stream of people to whom he had offering the magazine. Certainly some members of the public had made it clear that for whatever reason they despised the Unification Church. Mind you, it had been explained on the workshop that the group was considered controversial. Why was that? He wondered. He presumed that everything was completely above board and legitimate. And what was all this business about having to get up at some unearthly hour of a Sunday morning? Having just got used to getting up each morning at six o'clock it now seemed that they were going to be woken a couple of hours earlier to prepare for the occasion. Surely it was right to question such things.

At the gathering in the lounge the following morning the inhabitants of the terraced house in Cardiff looked extremely smart. In some cases the transformation made them difficult to recognise. The brothers were all in their suits and ties and the sisters wore their best dresses. Edwin had put on the suit that he'd had in his suitcase since Italy. Coupled with his new haircut, a glance in the mirror showed that he looked considerably more conservative than a few days ago.

A framed photograph of Reverend Moon and his wife had been placed on a low table at the front of the room. At precisely five o'clock the centre leader, Doreen, broke the silence by announcing "Today is Sunday 20th March. Let us begin this new week by making three full bows before Heavenly Father and True Parents." That was evidently the cue for everybody to put their hands to their foreheads, drop down onto their knees and then complete the action by lowering their heads down to the floor. Such a motion was repeated twice. Back on their feet once again, cards were handed around that contained the printed words for reciting the so-called Pledge. The content had seven points that at face value sounded reasonable enough even if the terminology was poorly translated from its original Korean. A reference to the cosmos was vaguely reminiscent of something from outer space.

The centre leader, Doreen, prayed and then gave a brief sermon about love as being the purpose of creation and a suggestion that God Himself wanted to experience love through each and every person. She said that individuals needed to experience love to become happy and that the purpose of the Messiah was to reconnect mankind with God's love. Reverend Moon and his wife, as the True Parents, were apparently doing that by giving divine love to everyone as well as proclaiming the truth. They needed people to help spread the message and also to spread true love.

She said that if people just proclaimed the truth on its own, that wouldn't bring about the victory but that it was necessary to develop a culture of heart to realise the Kingdom of Heaven on Earth. In other words, the truth was not the end in itself. It meant that the truth should set people free to give love and to embody love. Edwin could more or less catch the drift of what was being said.

When Doreen had finished everybody joined hands and sang a short Korean song and made a half bow from the waist before being asked to sit down on the floor once again.

It was now time to congratulate all those who had successfully completed the twenty-one day course. One by one the names of Peter, Mike, Kate, Edwin and Penny were called out by Doreen and each person came forward to be presented with a certificate by Trevor the lecturer. There was a round of applause for each of them.

When the meeting came to a close, Doreen came over to Edwin.

"Well done Edwin," she said, "It's been decided that from tomorrow we'd like you to join the outreach team here in Cardiff."

CHAPTER THIRTY-ONE

AND SO THERE HE was, Edwin Ravensdale, to all intents and purposes a fully fledged member of the Unification Church and all within the short space of five weeks of having first encountered it. There had been no application procedure for membership, no system of registration and nor had he been required to sign anything or pay anything. In many respects the transition had felt like a natural follow-on from his three month spiritual search. His new lifestyle was unexpected, definitely out of character and yet at the same time it was all completely fascinating. However, he could see that there were no half measures – one was either in this movement on a full-time basis or had nothing to do with it. Any concept of part-time involvement or associate membership didn't seem to exist. He supposed the reason for that was that whenever anyone came to an understanding that the Second Coming of the Messiah was at hand there was little else they could do with a clear conscience other than drop everything and team up. And that's what people were doing.

He got used to the routine of early morning worship, household chores and breakfast, the trek across Cardiff to the town premises. From there he would spend most of the day in the adjacent shopping precinct asking almost anyone who happened to be there if they might be interested in coming to an introductory talk about the movement. In the reception area hot drinks were readily available that could be offered to them and a light lunch was served at one o'clock. At the end of the afternoon the outreach team would then return to the centre in time for dinner, occasionally accompanied by new guests. Evening activity tended to take the form of teaching practice and finished with a short prayer meeting before bedtime.

The immediate task in hand was to bring the message of the return of the messiah to the attention of the world. Edwin still wondered why such a significant event hadn't already been cottoned on to by the media which had the obvious capability, if not the responsibility, of bringing the matter to the attention of the world in one foul swoop or perhaps in one foul scoop.

As far as he was concerned, apart from any amount of bad rumour, the main difficulty facing the Unification Church seemed to be that the theological explanation wasn't something that could easily be imparted in the space of a couple of sentences. It had taken him a three week study course even to understand the basics. Also, if looked at purely from a marketing or promotional point of view, the Unification Church really didn't sound that attractive. "Roll up! Roll up! Come and join us for a lifestyle of no salary, no alcohol, no smoking and no sex!" They were never going to be the best of selling points. But, of course, that completely ignored the spiritual dimension of the whole thing and the news of the messiah having arrived in an unexpected way.

By now Edwin had got to know all of the brothers and sisters in the Cardiff centre. Each of them was unique in their own way and the one thing they all had in common was their shared faith. Despite the fact that some of the sisters were exceptionally good looking, intelligent, witty and good company, Edwin found it interesting that he felt no romantic attraction towards them. Somehow they seemed too precious for that and instead he detected a certain innocence and sincerity in all of them and felt protective towards them.

He'd reasoned that doing without a girlfriend could be endured in the knowledge that one day he would be rewarded with one of the sisters of the Unification Church who would become his wife. Even if that was going to take the stipulated three years, it seemed worth the wait. Nevertheless, he glanced at one particular sister and, although he didn't mean it unkindly, he sincerely hoped that he wouldn't end up being paired off with her. But he took comfort in the fact that the Unification Church was international and vast so much so that the chance of landing someone who was currently based in Cardiff was extremely remote.

On the study course Edwin had been taught a few things about the influence of the so-called spirit world, where one was apparently destined to go to at the end of one's physical life on earth and where one's ancestors apparently already were. Even the theory of reincarnation could be explained as the effect of spiritual beings communicating with certain people on earth and thereby giving them an impression of being able to remember something from a supposed previous life. He was also becoming increasingly aware of an awakening of his own spiritual senses and could feel a benevolent presence around him. It was similar to the surge of energy he'd experienced at the time of his initial conversion to Christianity only this time it stayed with him and perhaps had a reassuring effect on those people with whom he came into contact out on the shopping precinct.

When he'd watched Christina's approach to people in the shopping area a few weeks ago he had thought he could come up with a suitable patter that would work better. After a few days practice he devised what he considered to be a foolproof script and had just about memorised his lines. A lot of it was to do with finding a point of universal agreement. For example, after a brief introduction he could throw in the leading question as to whether the person had a particular religion. If they said "Yes", he could build on that and move on to the next point but if they said "No", he would say, "No, but I expect you believe in God, don't you?" to which it was almost guaranteed that the person would say "Yes". However, in the event that they'd said "No" to that too, a sympathetic line would come into play, "No, I know what you mean. It's hard to believe in a God when you see the turmoil going on around us, isn't it?" to which they would agree. That was always the first stage of the exercise – to find a point on which they could agree and then, almost as an afterthought, it seemed perfectly natural to ask whether they could spare twenty minutes to come for a coffee and an introductory talk at the conveniently located base nearby.

There were no false pretences and it was always made plain that the prime purpose was to hear a talk of a religious nature. Often he would end the formal part of his pitch with, "The movement's founder comes from Korea and claims to have had a new revelation from God for today's world but, of course, all we can do is explain the content of that message and people can then decide about it for themselves."

Somehow, as a method it seemed to work. Whether it was the words, his sincerity, some help from the spirit world or a combination of all three, Edwin soon found that he was able to bring many people back for cups of tea or coffee and introductory lectures during the course of the day. Not only that, but he enjoyed doing so and felt elated and full of the spirit. By the end of the week he'd introduced seventeen individuals to the movement, two of whom had been sufficiently moved by the introductory talk that they'd decided that they wanted to attend the next weekend workshop on the farm.

In the weeks and months that followed, Friday evening trips to the farm with new guests became something of a regular occurrence for Edwin. That was because he invariably had at least one guest and he was obliged to accompany them. The format was always the same. The workshop staff was the same and Trevor's lectures were delivered in exactly the same way as they had been when Edwin had first heard them. What made each workshop refreshing, however, was that the guests were different every time as were many of the members who brought them there.

But regardless of how many guests came to the study courses, the percentage of those who ended up joining the movement was disappointingly low and Edwin felt that there had got to be a better way of getting the message out than this. The teaching was powerful and the general consensus of opinion amongst the brothers and sisters was that the entire world needed to be equipped with such theological understanding. But, if that was the case, the method being used was a bumbling inefficient way of going about it. Of fifty-three weekend guests, seven had gone on to the twenty-one day course but only three of them had ended up joining. It made him wonder if it was really worth the effort of pounding the area of the shopping precinct on a daily basis looking for still more people to bring to lectures.

On one particular weekend so many new guests converged on the Wiltshire village to attend the weekend workshop that a marquee had to be erected adjacent to the farmhouse simply to accommodate them all. Afterwards only a couple of them went to the 21 day course whilst others showed no wish to take it any further. Edwin discussed this numerical intake with Trevor the lecturer who referred him to a biblical passage in the book of Matthew in which it said 'Then shall two be in the field; the one shall be taken, and the other left.'

"Yes, but surely that implies a fifty-fifty ratio?" said Edwin.

"Well, maybe," agreed Trevor, "But what more can we do? New guests keep arriving; some of them are obviously prepared by God – others not. All we can do is to introduce people to the teachings."

"Yes but, I mean, it's not going to make much headway if so few respond to it," replied Edwin.

"It might seem like a slow process but at least the movement is expanding," he replied, "We are constantly opening up new centres throughout the country such as Bristol, Norwich, Maidstone, Hull, Grimsby, Coventry and now Oxford. But I agree, I wish we could hit upon a better way of getting the message out to everybody'

"The media," suggested Edwin.

"I'm afraid I don't hold out much hope with the media," replied Trevor, "They only distort things."

"I seem to have heard that view expressed before but I don't entirely go along with it," said Edwin, "Surely the media is neutral and it could be playing a significant part in all of this. It may have distorted certain things in the past but it still has the capability and even the responsibility for correcting any misconceptions."

"I'd like to think that at some stage in the future it will," replied Trevor, "but at the moment it's set in the wrong direction."

Edwin discovered that the movement's policy of an all-or-nothing commitment had already caused considerable disquiet amongst the relatives and friends of some members who had thrown in their jobs or abandoned their university studies in order to become full-time members of the Unification Church. A Member of Parliament, speaking under privilege of the House, had aggravated the situation further by making allegations that the movement brainwashed people and broke up families. Unsurprisingly the British press had seized on his comments and the Unification Church was fast becoming headline news for all the wrong reasons. A small pressure group of self-appointed, fanatical, cult-watchers had sprung up and it purported to be able to provide information about the church's supposed activities. Most of their claims were disturbing, inaccurate and largely untrue and yet they were widely reported as if fact. Against such a backdrop of adverse publicity it was hardly surprising that the faith group received the occasional mouthful of verbal abuse from members of the public. However, most of the members could stand their ground and found that in such confrontation they could generally do quite a good job in defending both the movement and its founder.

A total of twenty-two brothers and sisters from France, Germany, Austria, Italy and Malta then arrived in Cardiff to join local activities whilst similar numbers were assigned to other towns throughout Britain. To Edwin that was a breath of fresh air and he was pleased with the cosmopolitan atmosphere that their presence created. It did mean that the availability of floor space for everybody's sleeping bags was in short supply but, because the weather was getting warmer, he and two other brothers opted to sleep in the loft of a small outhouse in the back yard that was ordinarily used for storage purposes.

The singing of songs seemed to be a regular feature of the Unification Church. Gathered in the first floor lounge the Cardiff members sang to the assembled audience of their continental cousins. That was then followed by an hour's worth of French songs, German songs and Italian songs from representatives of the various countries. One of the French sisters couldn't seem to take her eyes off Edwin, which, in such a church environment, felt slightly unnerving. She was a good looking young lady and he wondered how she could dare get away with what looked like blatant flirtation. As it happened, her smiles had been completely innocent. It transpired that she was a spiritually sensitive person and had simply tuned into what she described as Edwin's bright aura.

"God has blessed you with such spiritual antennae," she told him over a cup of tea afterwards, "You are so fortunate because you can use this to find many good people."

He breathed a sigh of relief that his initial notion had now been defused.

It wasn't the first time that reference to some kind of spiritual presence had been expressed. Whilst waiting to cross a road in the centre of Cardiff, a young man standing in front of Edwin started twitching and kept turning around to look at him. Finally he could contain himself no longer,

"Excuse me but are you some kind of religious person or something?" he asked.

"Yes I am," replied Edwin, "I belong to the Unification Church."

"Wow," he had said in admiration, "That sure is some powerful presence you've got with you!"

There was another occasion in which Edwin had walked up to a girl at Cardiff Bus Station one Sunday and for some reason said "Hallo. You're from Melbourne, Australia, aren't you?" He didn't really know why he had said such a thing but the response was equally surprising.

"How the hell do you know that?" asked the wide-eyed girl with a broad Australian accent.

Edwin explained that sometimes these things simply happened and he invited her back for a meal at the centre to which she readily came. She returned on a couple of occasions to hear some of the lectures and said that she would be making a point of looking up the local branch of the Unification Church on her return to Australia the following month.

Some weeks later a group of church ministers arrived in Cardiff for a conference. One of the topics on their agenda was the perceived threat of new religious movements or cults as they liked to call them. A group of a dozen or so ministers were gathered outside one of the church venues and Edwin couldn't resist jumping right into the middle of them and asking what it was that they'd got against the Unification Church. A war of words lasted for a good ten minutes. It became apparent that not only were the ministers prejudiced in their viewpoint but they knew very little about Reverend Moon and the movement other than a string of unfounded allegations. Edwin wasn't shy in pointing out the flaws in their argument. Raised voices amongst such a gathering of clergy attracted an audience of onlookers.

ONE SUNDAY EVENING IN September, having just returned from the farm to Cardiff and dropped off three workshop guests at their respective homes, Edwin, Trevor and two other church members returned to their Paget Street centre and sat down to a late supper. The centre leader, Doreen, who had been away in London for the weekend entered the room.

"I have some interesting news for you, Edwin" she said with a smile, "Our National Leader, Mr Blake, who has just recently returned from America, spoke with me today and he is giving you a change of mission."

The announcement came as a complete surprise to Edwin. Did it mean that the six month era of pounding the Cardiff shopping precinct in search of people to introduce to the Unification Church was finally coming to an end?

"What kind of mission will it be?" he asked, hoping that it wouldn't mean transferring to one of the full-time fundraising teams.

"Well, Mr Blake thinks it would be a good idea for you to move to London to handle Public Relations from the movement's headquarters in Lancaster Gate," she replied.

There was a pause to allow the words to sink in before Edwin responded, "Well, what can I say? It certainly sounds like an interesting opportunity," he said.

"He'd like you to be there from tomorrow," she continued, "We've got Andy and a van going up to London in the morning so if you could please have your things packed ready to depart shortly after breakfast that would be great."

Talk about spontaneity, he thought.

CHAPTER THIRTY-TWO

THE LEADERS OF THE Unification Church in Britain were Daniel and Carol Blake who were always addressed by members in the more formal manner as Mr and Mrs Blake. There was no question of using their first names. Mr Blake himself proved to be a portly Englishman who had a keen sense of humour. He came across as likeable, dynamic, knowledgeable and deeply religious. He was also well-travelled, having spent the earlier part of his adult life in the Merchant Navy and somewhere along the line he had acquired the knack of being able to make people feel far more confident about their various abilities than perhaps they did themselves.

"Great, Edwin!" he said, his face beaming as they shook hands in a small tastefully decorated office, "Please take a seat. Welcome to what can best be described as 'God's Strategic Planning Centre' from where, with your help, we're going to make things really happen!"

It turned out that he already knew of Edwin's background in television broadcasting. He'd also been told about his success rate in bringing new guests to the weekend workshops and even about the confrontation with the church ministers in Cardiff.

"God needs a champion like you to help straighten everybody out!" he said, "and the more I look at it, the more I can see that there's still a lot more straightening out that needs to be done – especially in the media, right!"

He said that Edwin would be working to a brother called Dave Taylor who was in overall charge of Public Affairs and that he could also make use of a small office in Bouverie Street, just off Fleet Street, which he would be shown to later.

"In that way you'll be right there on the spot for the media," he said, "and in addition to dealing with any negative press articles what I'd like you to do is to try and cultivate a few journalists and broadcasters to see whether we can begin a more positive advance along the media route. And I'd also like you to help out with the content of a new magazine called 'New Tomorrow' that we've got planned and to lend your support to the various cultural events we hold each week here in Lancaster Gate."

The job description, if you could call it such, sounded comprehensive enough and a welcome challenge. It was certainly in line with Edwin's own view that if the message of the Second Coming was ever to stand any chance of reaching the wider world it would need to move beyond study courses held at remote country farmhouses. In recent months the tabloid press had done little more than spread suggestions that the Unification Church was a sinister cult that brainwashed people and broke up families yet it was easy enough for Edwin to see for himself that that simply wasn't true. He felt that if editors, journalists, producers and other representatives of the media could somehow be given the same opportunity as he had had to study its theological understanding, they would form an entirely different impression of it altogether.

Although he had stayed overnight at the Lancaster Gate headquarters on the day that he had first encountered the group earlier that year, this time round he found that he could relate to the place more easily and better understand its administrative function. It had an organisational structure of departments that included publications, business, general affairs, secretarial, reception, accounts, catering, transportation, security, cultural activities and planning. The headquarters staff struck him as being similar to civil servants. There were also fundraising teams that breezed in and out on a daily basis and the arrival of regional leaders from different parts of the country that came to London for meetings of one sort or another. Several foreign missionaries were visiting from overseas in addition to the ever-present, multi-lingual groups from mainland Europe whose sheer numbers helped ensure that the place was as chaotic as possible.

Edwin had been allocated a bed in a small dormitory with four other brothers. One of them was his immediate supervisor, Dave Taylor, a pleasant enough young man with a strong Catholic upbringing who had a degree in History from Cambridge University and was extremely well read. Having slept in a sleeping bag on the floor of the attic in the Cardiff outhouse for several months, to be suddenly granted a bed seemed like something of a luxury.

Edwin peered out of the sash window. There was a view across to a block of flats opposite and somewhere right down below, perhaps behind the darkened yellow-bricked wall, lay a short open stretch of the Circle and District lines of the London Underground whose passing trains were audible as they made their way to and fro between Bayswater and Paddington stations.

The day's schedule was similar in format to what took place in Cardiff. Members got up early and gathered for a morning service which, in the case of Lancaster Gate, was held in the ballroom on the first floor. There would then be a brief period of theological study before descending to the dining room for breakfast after which people would commence going about their daily activities. In addition to those who worked in the various offices throughout the day there was a team of brothers and sisters who brought back new guests to hear introductory lectures in a room adjacent to the front entrance.

After a brief discussion with Dave Taylor over a second cup of tea, Edwin would normally commute across London to the Bouverie Street office which was housed in the United Press International building, immediately opposite The Sun and the News of the World. It took a bit of adjustment to be going about things alone once again. Throughout his time in Cardiff he'd rarely ventured beyond the defined route from the house to the town centre and daily activity had been in the company of a team. Now, however, he silently contemplated the other passengers who accompanied him on the Central Line underground train to his stop of Chancery Lane knowing that not a single one of them was remotely aware of the new understanding about the Second Coming. It was a bizarre sensation and there were moments when he even regretted having such knowledge himself because, in all honesty, life might have been a lot simpler without it. He reasoned, however, that knowing what he knew had a certain responsibility attached to it and that there was some kind of obligation to help bring the message to the attention of the rest of the world. As he made his way out of the tube station, the never-ending flow of people on the escalators served to highlight the massive task that still lay ahead. Numbers – so much of this depended upon how to reach numbers of people.

The office itself was small and equipped with a desk, four chairs, a telephone, an empty book case, a coffee table and a hot water jug. It was lit by a single florescent tube that emitted a low buzzing noise and the one and only window looked out across a dingy gap in the building and into three similar such offices opposite. Edwin scoured the building and found it to be something of a rabbit warren of foreign journalists working for obscure sounding publications.

"If you're going to fight, fight with a plan." he recalled such words of wisdom having been read from the text of a speech given by Reverend Moon. "OK," thought Edwin. If the task was to reach the British media he'd begin by compiling a list of relevant press and broadcasters and then systematically find ways to approach them. There was a small Public Relations expense allowance available for his work and he began by acquiring a copy of Willing's Press Guide as well as yearbooks for both the BBC and ITV. From such publications he drew up a list of individuals and departments that he felt ought to be contacted. The main problem was going to be that the Unification Church was already widely perceived as being an unsavoury cause. However, it was reasonable to assume that somewhere in the vast British media there would be certain individuals who might be more receptive than others and that therefore it was just a case of finding them. He also figured out that it would probably be more effective to meet journalists face-to-face in order to make any headway at all rather than sending out letters, which would have only a limited impact.

One morning the phone rang and a journalist from the Sun wanted to know if he could ask a few questions about Reverend Moon's arms deals in South Korea. Fortunately Edwin had heard about that particular allegation and was able to respond accordingly.

"Look," he said, "In South Korea the threat of a Communist invasion from the north is a very real threat and so it's the law of the land that any manufacturing industry based in the south has to contribute something of its product towards the national defence. Reverend Moon's engineering company is no exception to that rule and so, yes, it's perfectly true that it supplies gun parts to the military."

There was a moment's silence.

"You mean every factory in South Korea has to contribute?" asked the journalist.

"Yes, that's right," replied Edwin, "Even if someone was to manufacture paper clips, my understanding is that they'd still be required to help out in that way."

The explanation apparently satisfied the journalist who thanked him for the information and hung up.

Although Edwin might have felt more at home dealing with reporters from broadcasting organisations rather than the world of print journalism as he was based in the heart of Fleet Street he would have to see what could be done from there. He spent a couple of days on a reconnaissance tour of the area to familiarise himself with the geographical whereabouts of such institutions as The Daily Telegraph, Daily Express, Daily Mail, Evening Standard and Daily Mirror then continued a little further to the Gray's Inn Road premises of The Times before doubling across to Farringdon where The Guardian and The Observer lived.

He also poked his nose into several Fleet Street pubs where many of the journalists hung out and stumbled upon an incredibly cheap Italian-run restaurant where a number of them ate, as he now did. By the end of the week he knew the layout of the area and was already on greetings terms with a few journalists but had not, as yet, found an easy way of introducing the topic of the Unification Church. After all, people in normal circumstances don't start spurting off about religion unless they were some kind of a fanatic and Edwin sensed that a more measured approached would be necessary. Applying the patter that he'd used on the streets of Cardiff to bring people to introductory lectures was unlikely to work with hard-nosed journalists, most of whom were extremely busy and up against deadlines. He learned of the existence of the London Press Club and thought that it might be a useful starting point for coming into regular contact with some of the media.

EVERY NOW AND AGAIN, Edwin was invited in on some of the planning meetings that took place in Lancaster Gate in which he noted that democracy seemed to play little part. Although the Unification Church spoke of 'give and take' much of what took place was more like 'take and take'. Mr Blake, nice guy though he was, would invariably chair such discussions and in something akin to the style of a benevolent dictator, would spell out the details of things that he would like to see accomplished, with precise instructions as to how everybody should go about it. Such meetings provided an opportunity for him to display his leadership skills and such was his charisma that even if some of his numerous ideas might not have been particularly brilliant ones, no one openly challenged them. Instead there was normally a universal acceptance and willingness to carry out everything decreed. It was generally understood that maintaining unity with the leader was every bit as important as daily prayer. Amongst the British membership the words, "Mr Blake says…" or "Mrs Blake says…" carried a lot of weight.

However, Mr Blake always gave Edwin every encouragement.

"It's definitely a good idea for you to get yourself well in with that Press Club," he'd said. "At the end of the day we need the media to be on our side, right? And I think it's very important that you pursue that by all possible means. If we can get some decent newspaper coverage and perhaps one or two reasonable television programmes made it'll transform the whole nation and we'll have won the battle."

Dave Taylor pointed out that the movement was holding a media conference in Japan and that although invitations had been sent out to several London-based journalists no one had responded. It was suggested that Edwin might like to phone some of the individuals concerned and find out whether they intended to go or not. They went on to speak about the New Tomorrow magazine and Edwin agreed to try his hand at writing the odd article as well as interviewing various people that could perhaps be featured in it.

Meanwhile, disturbing stories about the 'Moonies' continued to boost newspaper sales. It was inevitable that there would be phone calls from journalists wishing to push the boundaries still further. Edwin fielded such calls and could invariably detect what they were up to. Nine times out of ten they had already written their story and were only now contacting the Unification Church for the first time to get a quick quote to include somewhere in the article to make it look as if it had been properly balanced. They normally began by sounding friendly enough over the phone but before long some of their questions would become completely absurd. Edwin realised that merely responding to a string of outlandish claims that simply weren't true led only to a kind of defensive public relations that served no useful purpose. If one wasn't careful one could waste an awful lot of time in discussing all the things the Unification Church wasn't rather than in explaining any of the things that it was. Bad rumours were plentiful. They'd been there before Edwin had met the movement and yet he now had the awesome responsibility of trying to deal with them.

During the course of what had started out as a polite telephone enquiry from a Christian magazine, the caller suddenly said, "So what's it feel like to be completely brainwashed?" Edwin took delight in assuring the caller that it was she who had clearly been brainwashed by the tabloid press.

And then a journalist on another publication said, 'You sound to me like a nice and normal person but I am told that you must have been trained in something called 'heavenly deception.' In other words, he assumed that members of the Unification Church had a licence to tell lies – which, if he really believed that, would have made the whole point of the conversation pretty well futile in the first place.

But Edwin was already sufficiently battle-hardened from his experience of face-to-face encounters with the public out on the streets. By now he was familiar with most of the common accusations levelled at the Unification Church and its Korean founder and he was able to respond sincerely and convincingly to such things with comparative ease. He could anticipate the line of questioning and knew the kinds of things they were hoping to unearth. But as far as he was concerned there was nothing to hide and he simply spoke the truth about the reality of the situation. His answers weren't necessarily what the journalists wanted to hear although few attempted to twist his words.

The Daily Mail published an article saying that Japanese members of the Unification Church were banned from entering Britain. It was untrue and Edwin wrote to the Editor to say so. A reply came back requesting him to provide evidence. He sent back a snotty letter saying that surely the Daily Mail had sufficient resources at its disposal to check the authenticity of claims that it had made in its own article but that, if it would help matters, a copy of a letter from the Home Office was enclosed which clearly stated that there was no such ban. A few weeks later the Daily Mail dutifully published an apology for its misleading report. It was a postage stamp sized apology tucked away on an inner page. Although the climb-down might have been a small victory, it didn't alter the fact that the damage had already been done.

At the same time Edwin could understand the Unification Church's unfortunate public perception. The messiah claim sounded preposterous to just about everyone. If members of the Unification Church believed such a thing then that, in itself, was regarded as sufficient evidence that they must all be misguided. Lack of adequate research had completely omitted any of the reasoning as to how such a conclusion had been reached by so many people.

Everyone seemed to have something against Reverend Moon. The political left disliked him for saying that Communism was the anti-Christ. Meanwhile Christian groups were saying that said he was anti-Christ. Some had incorrectly understood that the Unification Church was teaching that Jesus had been a failure which, understandably, added yet more fuel to the fire. However the most common allegation was that Reverend Moon was a conman who used religion to get rich and that he did so by brainwashing young people and breaking up families.

Public Relations for the Unification Church must surely have been one of the worst jobs for anyone to be lumbered with. The two things didn't seem to equate.

The journalists from the Daily Telegraph and The Guardian, who had been invited to attend the media conference in Japan, both declined the offer. Despite the fact that the five-day event was a freebie complete with prepaid flight tickets and that it included full-board accommodation at one of Tokyo's most prestigious hotels, both said that they didn't have the time to get away from their work. They wished it well and that was that.

ON SATURDAYS IT BECAME the norm for the entire headquarters staff to go out for a day's fundraising. Edwin was grateful for the balance that such activity provided. After all, standing outside Woolworth in multicultural Harlesden with a bagful of 'One World' magazines provided a contrast to the rest of the working week.

Mr Blake was a skilled orator and his Sunday morning sermons were every bit as engaging as they were deep and powerful. He could combine wit with tales of his own personal experiences with Reverend Moon and demonstrate the way in which he claimed to experience the hand of God at work in almost any situation. He would draw interesting parallels between current affairs and biblical passages of old and his talks would normally last for over an hour. Some of it was in a bit of a rant mode, some of it judgmental, but a lot of it was in good humour and most of it was inspirational. Afterwards the majority of members felt uplifted by what he had said. Yet he also had his own overbearing style of prayer which every now and again would include what amounted to commands to God such as "Move your mighty hand…!" and, another slightly more theatrical favourite, "Break the back of Satan!"

Edwin was often invited to join both Mr and Mrs Blake for breakfast in their flat on the first floor during which time all the latest news, gossip and insights about how the Movement was progressing was given an airing. The Blakes had bold opinions on just about everything and by virtue of their position they enjoyed a certain air of infallibility. Mrs Blake's dramatic pronouncements upon even the smallest of occurrences tended to leave everyone in awe at her apparent deep insight into the whys and wherefores of the world of spirit, with which she purported to be in tune. She was an impressive American lady in many respects. Together they made an interesting combination.

Criticism of their leadership was rare because it was widely understood that, whatever faults they might or might not have had, they stood in the position of the appointed national representatives to Reverend and Mrs Moon and occupied a parental role to British members of the church. As such, any whisperings were invariably quashed.

"One of the problems with the Unification Church in Britain is that it seems largely to be run on a 'follow my leader' basis," complained one of the workshop staff, who had just been on the receiving end of some of Mrs Blake's pointed comments.

"But it needs strong leadership to keep it together," said another, anxious to display loyalty.

Any direction received from Mr and Mrs Blake was generally thought of as motivated out of love rather than an attempt to demonstrate any kind of superiority. They were regarded as inspirational people and most church members found their words of wisdom uplifting and beneficial.

One morning everybody was summoned to a meeting in the ballroom. There Mr Blake explained that the movement was going through something of a financial crisis and that he would like everyone to temporarily stop whatever mission they were engaged in and go out and do a fortnight's fundraising instead. The news was calmly accepted by one and all.

"Where's Edwin Ravensdale?" demanded Mr Blake suddenly.

Edwin, who was sat near the back of the room raised his hand and said, "I'm over here, Mr Blake."

"OK, Edwin. You don't need to go fundraising. PR is kind of important, right? – and I therefore think it far better for you to carry on with what you are doing."

Such unique exemption from the fundraising drive took Edwin by surprise. He nevertheless thought that he'd better use the time wisely to help justify such an endorsement.

IN KEEPING WITH THE aim of trying to get a television programme made about the Unification Church, Edwin drew up a list of religious broadcasters and began contacting them to set up meetings. Over the months that followed, it resulted in a tour of television stations throughout the United Kingdom. He was in his element at being back on familiar territory once again.

However, at each of the various meetings the response was somewhat predictable. Due to bad press reports, the Unification Church was widely regarded as being a weird cult. Although some producers expressed a passing interest they felt that, for the moment, it was far too controversial a subject for them to involve themselves in and something that they would be unlikely to get past their channels' religious advisory committees. They nevertheless assured Edwin that were they ever to take the view that coverage of the Unification Church was warranted, they would be pleased to contact him as a first port of call.

"One of the problems we face is that if we open the gates to the Unification Church we'll be under a tremendous amount of pressure to open up the gates to everyone else too," explained an executive producer in Plymouth. "It wouldn't just be the Moonies, er sorry the Unification Church. It'd be the Children of God, the Divine Light Mission, Scientology, the Hare Krishna Movement and goodness knows what else."

"Well, I can't speak for any of those groups," said Edwin, "but I can see that there'd be some pretty good mileage for a television programme about theological aspects of the Unification Church."

"But surely you can understand that from our point of view, all of these new religious groups are pretty much one and the same thing," he persisted.

"Therein lies the problem," replied Edwin.

Dave Taylor was available to accompany Edwin to a meeting at the BBC's Religious Broadcasting Department at Richmond House in Shepherd's Bush. On arrival, and before meeting the person they had come to see, they encountered somebody else in the reception area that was openly hostile to their mere presence in the building. All the usual allegations of brainwashing and breaking up families were being spat out by this individual in front of several startled onlookers. It was a remarkable phenomenon in which the person had set himself up as an apparent authority on the Unification Church but with no research or first-hand knowledge of it at all. Edwin reached the conclusion that ignorance might be one thing but that sincerely-held ignorance was highly dangerous – and slap bang in the BBC of all places.

A few weeks later he travelled up to Birmingham to visit the studios of ATV. At last he stumbled upon a religious broadcasting department which was interested in the idea of making a programme about the Unification Church. They asked if it would be possible for one of their researchers to visit the movement on a regular basis and to explore the various possibilities for treating the subject matter.

Details of the meeting were related to Mr Blake in Lancaster Gate who was pleased with such a breakthrough in gaining media interest. It was arranged that an ATV Researcher, Kevin Jackson, would come to the headquarters the following week and, in the meantime, Edwin put together a schedule that would enable him to gain a good comprehensive overview of the Unification Church in the United Kingdom together with its beliefs and its activities.

By now Edwin had got to know everybody at the Lancaster Gate headquarters. Each one of them had an interesting story to tell about how they'd first encountered the group. Most could sense that the teaching offered a clear insight into solving the ills of the world and many had gone through some sort of an exercise in trying to pull it to bits in an attempt to find flaws before reaching the conclusion that it was, in fact, true. Interestingly, many of the backgrounds of the members bore little resemblance to the work to which they had now been assigned. It was quite common to find a former schoolteacher working as a business representative, a university graduate on one of the fundraising teams, a musician working in the accounts office or a kindergarten teacher doing the laundry. Such roles had not been advertised as vacancies as such but they were regarded as missions to which the individuals had been assigned by the leadership, normally after a brief discussion. It was a voluntary movement and no one expected a penny for their work.

Such was the rich spiritual atmosphere of the Unification Church that many members had what could be termed 'spiritual experiences' on a regular basis. Decision-making was invariably done with a considerable amount of prayer and intuition together with what was perceived as guidance from the spiritual realms. It was and felt like a religious movement. It also felt like one large family in which each individual really felt like one's brother or sister. There was a collective sense of belonging and a collective sense of caring for one another. Doubtless some of it was the result of all having wound up in the same boat together. After all, most members had joined as a result of hearing its in-depth teaching. One thing they had in common was that at some stage they had all experienced the initial shock in discovering that the Second Coming of the Messiah had actually taken place – and in such an unexpected manner.

There was no such thing as a stereotyped member. Everybody came from a broad cross-section of society across all classes and from every continent of the world. The variety of backgrounds that Edwin encountered included doctors, solicitors, teachers, nurses, social workers, business managers, bankers, postmen, retailers, librarians, and drivers and there were also factory workers, tradesmen, builders, students and a handful of those who had been unemployed. Generally speaking they were people of high calibre who were good, honest and hard-working and had pleasant personalities.

However, it wasn't all lovey-dovey. There were occasional clashes as one would expect to find in any large organisation irrespective of its nature. Some team leaders could be insensitive, some members thought they knew how to do things better than others and there was occasional argument. In most cases such conflict was quickly resolved as each became reminded of the common sense of purpose and the all-important emphasis on team unity. It was generally acknowledged that the Unification Church was never intended to be the end goal in itself but a mere stepping stone towards the establishment of a better world. The speed with which that better world could be realised was largely dependent upon the public response to its teachings.

It was also inevitable that some people who joined the Unification Church either lost the plot or found that they weren't really suited to its lifestyle and decided to quit – as was their right. To help avoid a large turnover of such people, however, the word went out that members should concentrate on seeking 'people whom God had prepared' as opposed to dragging just anyone off the streets. That was always going to be problematic, however, because of the underlying notion and widely held understanding that God loves everybody. Similarly, Unification Church theology had the potential to transform peoples' sometimes dubious backgrounds and lifestyles, as it had already done so for many people, and so pre-judging whether someone was the right kind of individual was not a particularly easy thing to do.

Apart from the religious side of the movement, the Lancaster Gate headquarters served as the venue for cultural events which were held on Wednesday evenings. These took the form of classical music concerts or poetry readings and attracted an audience of loyal followers from the neighbouring area. They were organised by a Sri Lankan brother who also co-ordinated the UK's input to the International Conference on the Unity of the Sciences run by the Unification Movement. In doing so he had built up a wealth of contacts in the world of academia and frequently headed off to its organised events accompanied by professors with disciplines ranging from economics to medicine and from entomology to physics.

THE ATV RESEARCHER, KEVIN Jackson, arrived by train from Birmingham the following Thursday. Edwin met him at Euston Station where they sat in a snack bar and chatted over coffee before going on to Lancaster Gate. He proved to be an amiable character. Edwin had reasoned that the best way for any researcher to understand the movement's theology would be to attend a study course in much that same way that he had. But he wasn't sure how he would react to an invitation to spend a weekend on the Wiltshire farm. Another slight complication was that the object of the exercise wasn't to make a convert out of him but simply to allow him to get a better understanding of the teaching. How would that be possible? After all, the prime purpose of the study courses had been to educate people about the Second Coming of the Messiah and there was every possibility that the explanation would take on a personal meaning to the person hearing it and yet now, almost in complete contradiction, the idea was to study the theology but remain completely objective.

Edwin explained to him that whilst it was common knowledge that Unification Church members regarded Reverend Moon as the Second Coming of the Messiah and that that might sound heretical, remarkably few journalists or broadcasters had ever bothered to take the time to study the teachings to see how such a conclusion could possibly have been arrived at. The researcher was pleased to accept Edwin's invitation to a weekend study course and a date was arranged to do so.

In the meantime, Mr Blake decided to embark on an intensive tour of Britain in which he planned to deliver a public speech in most major cities. He asked Edwin to go to each place a day or so in advance to help prepare the ground and deal with any local media enquiries. Mr Blake's spirited speeches tended to fluctuate between accounts of his own personal understanding of world affairs, a potted history of the Unification Church and its core beliefs coupled with an occasional blast of hellfire and brimstone proportions. Throughout the day local church members would go out leafleting to help ensure that at least some sort of an audience would come along to the evening's event. There was occasional hostility whenever the word got out that the event had been organised by the dreaded 'Moonies,' with some people turning up who were intent on disrupting things. Such gatherings were normally held in a centrally located hall that had been hired for the purpose. On a couple of occasions there had to be a last minute change of venue because the owners had received malicious phone calls urging them to cancel the booking or being warned of possible trouble.

Despite any lingering scepticism about the Unification Church, such meetings went off reasonably well. It was, after all, an opportunity for many people to meet this notorious group at first hand for the first time. A Unification Church choir, whose angelic voices were enough to melt many a person's heart, set the atmosphere prior to the talk itself. At the end of each meeting questions were invited and Mr Blake would answer them in his own inimitable way by verbally demolishing any opposition. Most of the time, the local press weren't interested in covering such events. A church meeting was a church meeting and the general feeling about that was that one couldn't ordinarily get a more boring topic than that at the best of times. However, whenever word got out that it was to be a 'Moonie event,' that did sometimes trigger off interest in the newsrooms. Journalists were occasionally present in the audience with the sole intention of getting yet another sensational story on what was generally thought to be a sinister cult. However it tended to backfire because, despite whatever preconceived ideas they might have had, much of the content of the speech was about new interpretations of the Bible and unless they happened to be biblically literate themselves, which few of them were, they had no idea if what was being said was significant or not. Most ended up writing nothing at all whilst a few headed a brief account of such events with things such as 'Moonies hit Grimsby' or 'Moonie Recruitment Campaign Reaches Coventry.' If journalists made themselves known at such events Edwin would endeavour to speak with them to help put whatever prejudices they might have had into proper perspective.

This tour continued for several weeks in cities throughout the length and breadth of Britain. One afternoon, when Edwin had arrived at the next scheduled venue of Norwich, he was met by a startling piece of news. Reverend Moon had apparently arrived in London. Not only that, but the entire British membership was being invited to meet with him in Lancaster Gate the following day. It was a shock to the system. It was one thing to have some sort of an understanding about the Second Coming of the Messiah but quite another thing to have the possibility of meeting him in person. Edwin's first thought was that he didn't feel pure enough and that he was burdened with his own sin and there was a worry that presumably a messiah would be able to see all of that. For a moment he even started to wonder whether his life of faith had been little more than pretence. After all, wasn't it completely out of character that he had ever 'gone religious' in the first place? He felt a curious mixture both of apprehension and reassurance and it was only when he spoke with some of the other members that he realised that they were going through exactly the same kinds of concern themselves.

On the train down from Norwich to London's Liverpool Street station the following morning, Edwin took to quietly reading a paperback book of a selection of speeches that had been made by Reverend Moon. He felt that by doing so, at least he might feel more in tune with the man by the time he arrived. Very few Unification Church members in Britain had ever met Reverend Moon in the flesh before and it was going to be a new experience for just about everybody. They crossed London by tube to Paddington and walked the remaining short distance to the Lancaster Gate headquarters. It was already packed full of people from here, there and everywhere who had converged on the place and the mood was one of quiet anticipation. After an hour or so, as the time drew near, one of the members then turned to those sitting alongside him and optimistically summed up the situation by saying "Come on brothers and sisters! Let's go and meet him!"

Everyone had been asked to gather in the first floor ballroom which soon became crammed full. The brothers sat on one side, the sisters on the other and there was a small gangway way through the middle. Edwin found himself to be approximately two thirds of the way back on the right hand side. There was a prelude to the meeting in which several of the Unification Church Holy Songs were sung and Mr and Mrs Blake took their positions at the front of the room after which in marched Reverend Moon accompanied by two of his aides. Everyone bowed their heads in respect and Edwin sensed many things simultaneously. Firstly there was a sense of relief that setting eyes upon the man himself had actually happened. Secondly he seemed to hear a voice telling him, "Look, there's old Moon!" which he reasoned hadn't come from his own thinking and was probably the intuitive voice of some spiritual being but thirdly and most significantly, he felt an undeniable surge of warm love that seemed to fill the entire room. There's no denying the spirit, he thought, I mean, what do you think that is, Scotch mist? He asked himself. Indeed, if there had ever been the slightest lingering doubt about Reverend Moon, it was now swept away. The audience were asked to please be seated.

Reverend Moon was dressed in jacket and tie. Edwin first impression was of someone who was authoritative, interesting and amusing. He spoke in Korean into one of the microphones that had been strategically placed at the front of the room and would then pause for his Korean interpreter to provide a translation in English. The double act of performer and interpreter took a bit of time to get used to but, once attuned, Edwin found the content of what was being said to be uplifting and inspiring. Reverend Moon's undoubted sense of humour became immediately apparent through his anecdotes and keen observations.

There was occasional reference to historical matters about Britain and what was perceived as its quaint customs and general politeness and also a suggestion that it tended to fare better under a queen than under a king. Reverend Moon went on to ask how many thousands of dollars the audience thought that he spent on providential matters in a day and then estimated some astronomical figure which he found to be highly amusing. He also came out with unexpected and amusing stories from which one could begin to understand something of his personality. One day he'd come across a row of restaurants that each offered a set lunch menu. Reverend Moon had reasoned that he was quite an important person and had wondered if it would be possible for him to eat all seven lunches one after the other. He indicated just how bloated he became after such a feat and how he could almost have rolled home like a barrel afterwards. The story wasn't intended to indicate greed but an example of how he challenged limitations.

After speaking for an hour or so he asked whether the members had any questions and several raised their hands. Amongst them Dave Taylor asked why so much of the members' time was taken up with fundraising activity. Instead of replying that the movement couldn't survive without being financed by such means, Reverend Moon explained that fundraising activity was part of one's training in being able to discern things easily. For example, after fundraising, if one were to go into a supermarket one would know exactly what items on the shelves to buy. It was an interesting thought and based on Edwin's own experience not without accuracy.

The meeting came to a close but the warm embracing spirit remained and most of the young familiar faces of brothers and sisters looked radiant through having experienced Reverend Moon for the very first time.

The Lancaster Gate premises soon became more crowded than ever with further arrivals of members from across Europe who, on hearing that Reverend Moon was in London had made an immediate effort to get over to see him. Everybody set up camp in the building wherever they could find the space and that evening bodies in sleeping bags were to be found occupying almost every corridor, office or hideaway.

The following morning was a Sunday and, as per usual, people woke up at the crack of dawn, got dressed in their best clothing and prepared themselves for the five o'clock Pledge Service. This time, of course, instead of the sermon coming from Mr or Mrs Blake, the man himself, Reverend Moon, was there to deliver a speech in person, which he did – for several hours. Although he didn't make use of notes and his talk was completely spontaneous, it was deep and meaningful and touched on many aspects of events in biblical history that seemed to have some bearing on events taking place in today's world.

Afterwards Edwin bumped into Mr Blake in a corridor who, instead of his usual authoritative self, seemed to have become completely humbled by the presence of Reverend Moon.

"Were you here at Father's speech this morning?" he asked Edwin quietly, "Wasn't it brilliant! The living Lord! And you know when he first arrived here yesterday; he'd scarcely had time for a shave before he straight away wanted to talk with the members."

A MONTH LATER THE ATV researcher, Kevin Jackson, came down to London once again and, accompanied by Edwin and some other members with their guests, was driven down to the Wiltshire Farm to attend the weekend study course. The schedule followed the same tried and tested formula as on previous occasions and Trevor was still there as its lecturer. The researcher listened to the theological presentation over the two days yet displayed no noticeable reaction to the implication of the Second Coming of Christ. However, he took an interest in the members who were there and asked them if they'd found anything in the Unification Church that they couldn't have found in the more established churches.

"Well there's youth, for one thing," suggested one, "Most of the established churches have dwindling congregations mainly made up of elderly people but I think that our average age is around twenty-four."

"For me, it provides answers to many questions that other religious groups just can't explain," said another, "The teaching makes all those mysterious stories in the Bible come to life and take on new meaning."

At the end of the weekend the researcher returned via train to Birmingham. He and Edwin arranged a time for their next meeting in which they planned to visit several Unification Church centres and take a look at the movement's various activities.

MARRIAGE WAS CENTRAL TO the Unification Church and excitement spread amongst the members as it became known that Reverend Moon would officiate over a wedding ceremony to be held in Lancaster Gate. To be eligible one had to be at least twenty-seven years of age and to have been a member of the Unification Church for at least three years. That ruled Edwin out because, despite the fact that he had already turned twenty-eight, he had been a member for little more than one year. It was a blow to him in many respects because the one thing he knew to be missing in his life was a close partner of the opposite sex.

A couple of hundred brothers and sisters were willing and able to take part in the planned joint wedding. Prior to the event itself a so-called matching ceremony took place in Lancaster Gate in which, after speaking about the importance of the marital relationship Reverend Moon had then set about the task of making suggestions as to which particular church brother would be suited to which particular church sister as potential marriage partners. It was then left entirely to those individuals to discuss the matter and decide whether they wished to go ahead and become engaged to each other. The right of refusal was available to either of them.

In all two hundred and thirty-six brothers and sisters were paired off in such a way thereby creating one hundred and eighteen couples. It was a private ceremony and Edwin could only glean the details of it as the various participants emerged and some of them spoke to him of their individual experiences. In an atmosphere of something approaching euphoria, most of them appeared to be overjoyed. Many of the members who participated were well known to Edwin and it was fascinating to find out how they had fared in such an intriguing lottery of life. Dave Taylor had been matched with a Korean university student whilst another brother who shared his room was with a Canadian. Trevor the lecturer was with a Scandinavian sister and one of the secretarial staff from the accounts department was together with a German. Sometimes Edwin knew both the brother and the sister individually and it was interesting now to view them as a couple.

Wherever he turned people kept introducing him to their new partner. Some asked Edwin with whom he had been matched and he had to explain that he hadn't been long enough in the church to be eligible. He passed a Swedish sister on the stairs that he knew to be similarly still single. She asked him if he'd been matched and he jokingly said "No, not this time. I'm still waiting for you!" At least she laughed.

News of the mass wedding ceremony got out to the press and the telephone rang non-stop. Edwin found it somewhat odd to be the church's media spokesperson for an event that he hadn't been directly involved with and hadn't even been able to watch. He didn't have much detail but still had to handle the various press enquiries. However, most newspapers were more interested in acquiring pictures of the newlywed couples and during the course of conversation several journalists wished the marriages well. The News of the World had picked up on some misinterpretation of the event and asked if it would be possible for them to interview a 'perfect couple.'

As far as he could tell previous attempts at Public Relations had always been on the defensive. However Edwin was far more interested in trying to develop a healthy relationship with the media rather than being caught up in an endless cycle of waiting to respond to the next instance of poor press coverage. He thought it could best be achieved through face-to-face meetings with producers, editors and journalists, the hope being that sooner or later that would lead to opportunities for the kind of media coverage that accurately portrayed aspects of the movement in a way that was sufficiently intriguing to the audience.

After floating the idea on several occasions he finally got the go ahead to hold a one-day research seminar for journalists at Lancaster Gate. A schedule was drawn up that would include a brief overview of the Unification Church and an outline of its teaching followed by a look at the various criticisms that were being levelled against it and an explanation as to how misunderstandings had arisen. There would be a mid-morning coffee break and plenty of time for questions and answers. At midday a hot lunch would be served and followed by the showing of the film about the British Unification Church. Afterwards there would be time allocated for further questions and answers and a media pack of literature about the movement would be handed out.

Although the object of the exercise was intended to be a step forward in relations with the media, there was a surprising amount of opposition to the event by some of the members.

"Why should we even be contemplating talking to those people after all the problems that they have caused?" seemed to be the most common complaint.

"It's the newspaper reports that have caused us so much conflict with our families and friends so what on earth are we doing inviting journalists along here?" said one.

Another put it more bluntly. "Surely it's the same as inviting Satan into God's house."

At that time, Edwin received a letter from Pete Cornwall, his former news editor colleague from New Zealand. Apparently he was being seconded to the United Kingdom for a period of three months. He would re-contact Edwin as soon as he'd arrived in London, got over his jet lag and found somewhere suitable to stay.

THE NEW TOMORROW MAGAZINE was a smart looking publication and Edwin had even persuaded a couple of Fleet Street news vendors to take some copies on a sale or return basis. Edited by Dave Taylor, the content was a blend of features, interviews and comment mainly on topics of a religious nature. Some of the articles had been written by Mr and Mrs Blake who had both used a nom de plume. It would have been hard to say who the target audience was. For his part Edwin had equipped himself with a tape recorder and been developing new skills in the art of interviewing people. Although previously experienced in editing filmed interviews for television news it was a challenge now to be taking hold of a microphone and becoming an interviewer himself. He discovered that as long as he prepared a list of questions well in advance of each interview he could conduct them quite well and extract the kinds of answers that would be usable in his magazine articles. He interviewed the military, he interviewed members of parliament, he interviewed authors, he interviewed the police and he wrote accounts about the plight of the elderly. He found the whole experience exhilarating and that it added a new dimension to his activities.

The magazine found itself in hot water on one occasion however. At a Press Club function Edwin had got chatting to Count Nikolai Tolstoy, who was there to launch his new book entitled 'Victims of Yalta.' He agreed to be interviewed for the New Tomorrow magazine and invited Edwin down to his Somerset home for that purpose. The interview went well. As usual, Edwin had recorded it and was already transcribing its content on the train journey back from Castle Cary to Paddington. Count Tolstoy had made various claims about what he regarded as British complicity in sending people back to Russia after the war apparently in the knowledge that they would be killed on arrival. An article was shaped and duly published in the following month's issue of the magazine. If there had been curiosity as to the kinds of people who read the New Tomorrow magazine it was interesting to note that the article was pounced upon by certain members of the House of Lords who took offence at what Count Tolstoy had said and demanded a retraction. After some discussion with Count Tolstoy the magazine thought it wise to publish a brief clarification in its next issue along the lines that the claims had been speculation rather than known fact.

PETE CORNWALL LOOKED EXACTLY the same as when Edwin had last set eyes upon him in New Zealand. Wearing a brown suit he was a short man with a conservative short back and sides. His wry wit was the same as ever.

"G'day, you old bastard!" was his customary form of greeting, which he again used on this occasion.

"Good to see you again, Pete!" said Edwin, as they shook hands.

They were stood inside the entrance to West Hampstead underground station, which was a five minute walk from where Pete had now rented a flat.

"Now, as it's absolutely pissing down with rain out there we can either get ourselves soaked to the skin or there's a coffee shop across the way that we could dive into until it eases off," he suggested.

They sat with two large mugs of frothy cappuccino and Pete explained that the prime purpose of his stay in London was to spend time at Viznews from where television news items were pumped around the world as well as liaising with the BBC for an update of technology and know-how relevant to the broadcasting operation in New Zealand. It was also the dawn of so-called Electronic New Gathering cameras that had newly arrived on the market and he was keen to see their performance and perhaps persuade the powers that be back home to purchase some.

"And what about you?" he asked after a while, "What's all that stuff you told me about in the letter about getting involved with some religious outfit?"

"Well, I know it might sound strange but it's perfectly true," said Edwin. "I took time out to go on a bit of a spiritual search and eventually stumbled upon one particular group that seemed interesting and at the moment I'm involved in doing Public Relations work for them."

"And that's the Mr Moon organisation that you mentioned?" he asked.

"Yes, that's right. I guess you've heard about it in New Zealand?"

"Yes. Although nothing good about it, that's for sure," he said. "By all accounts he's a devious oriental man who acts like some pied piper figure in taking young people away from their families. At least that's what seems to be the general opinion."

"Yeah, I know all the things that have been said about him but you know as well as I do that there are many sides to a story," replied Edwin "I've come across so many press articles full of the most outlandish claims about Reverend Moon and the supposed activities of the Unification Church which I know from firsthand experience are simply not true."

"So you reckon he's whiter than white? – apart from being yellow, of course?" asked Pete.

"All I can say is that I've studied the theological reasoning, I've met him and I've listened to his talks. I'm suitably impressed and I believe him to be a man of God if ever there was one," said Edwin.

"And all of that coming from such a worldly person as yourself," said Pete.

"Well exactly, that proves the point," said Edwin. "You know me. I'm not exactly the most gullible person."

"At least that's for sure," he said, 'Mind you, back in New Zealand we've got those other buggers going around called deprogrammers. If you listen to what they've got to say about the Moonies and other such groups you just end up not knowing who's who at the zoo."

By now the rain had stopped and so they made their way to Pete's flat which turned out to be a tastefully furnished, up-market, first-floor conversion within a large Victorian semi-detached house. They whiled away the remainder of the afternoon chatting about people they knew back in New Zealand and recalling events before going for a meal at a Greek restaurant nearby.

"Now, I hope you're not going to tell me that this new found religious calling of yours is going to prevent you from coming along to the pub for a jug of beer," said Pete.

"Oh, I'll happily drink a pint or two if the occasion demands it, although perhaps not quite the same amount that we used to get through back in New Zealand," replied Edwin, momentarily recalling late nights at the Matamata Tavern, blazingly hot summer weekends, pleasant female company, good music and a fridge stacked full of Waikato 4X.

They headed down to a West Hampstead pub called 'Ye Old Black Lion' and sank ice cold lager for an hour or so. A group of three girls with green and blue coloured hair sat at a table whilst Edwin and Pete were perched on stools at the bar. The jukebox blared forth.

You're the one that I want
(You are the one I want, want)
Ooh, ooh, ooh, honey, the one that I want
(You are the one I want, want)

Before their departure Pete agreed that he would come along to the one-day research event for journalists scheduled to be held in Lancaster Gate in a fortnight's time.

THE FOLLOWING WEEK NEWS came through that the Member of Parliament who was chairman of the pressure group, Family Action Information and Rescue, would make a public apology in the High Court for comments he had made about the Unification Church. His oft-quoted allegations of brainwashing and breaking up families had been the source of many of the sensationalist claims in the British media and so the apology was clearly something to be welcomed. Such adverse publicity had caused untold concern to many parents, relatives and friends of church members.

Whilst the retraction might act as a useful point of reference, it was perhaps inevitable that people's suspicion would continue to work on a 'no smoke without fire' basis. The son of one of the senior staff at the Daily Mail had recently joined the Unification Church in California and as a consequence that highly popular newspaper had now been persuaded to embark on a relentless campaign against the movement.

Most of the brothers and sisters in the UK visited their parents on a regular basis and were able to reassure them that despite what certain newspapers had been saying about the Unification Church everything was perfectly OK. A small handful experienced some conflict in which their parents were more inclined to attach credibility to the disturbing press reports rather than listen to the first hand experience of their adult son or daughter. That was an unfortunate situation. Former acquaintances would drop by and look them up and down presumably in search of evidence that they had been undernourished or were in some way psychologically disturbed. Concerned relatives would crawl out of the woodwork and attempt to persuade them that they'd been led astray. However, the vast majority of members of the Unification Church enjoyed full parental support.

"I'd rather my son were a Moonie than a punk rocker," said one prominent member of the House of Lords, whose son had joined the movement in America.

THE DAY'S MEDIA RESEARCH event went off without hitch and to all intents and purposes was deemed a success. It was held in one of the back rooms at Lancaster Gate and a total of seventeen media professionals attended including Edwin's friend Pete from New Zealand Television and the ATV Researcher from Birmingham. Invitations had been sent mainly to religious affairs correspondents although those who showed up on the day were from a broad cross section of Fleet Street.

Edwin gave a short introduction to the Unification Church in which he openly acknowledged that it had taken a hammering in the press and suggested that now was an opportunity to consider the reality of the situation. He then handed over to Mr Blake who began his slot with a condensed presentation of theology.

"Great everybody, our critics might call it brainwashing but for the next half hour let's take a brief look at what the Unification Church is actually teaching and you can then make up your own minds about that."

The format worked like clockwork and there could be no doubting the willingness of the Unification Church to answer questions on anything at all. In addition to its theological explanation and the concept of the Second Coming, there were questions about the church's funding and about why there was so much opposition to it by the established churches. Some were surprised when they got back perfectly reasonable answers. Perhaps for the first time the assembled journalists realised that maybe the Unification Church was a significant religious movement after all rather than the kind of weird cult that so many had assumed it to be.

The problem in journalistic terms, however, was that there was no story to be told. Once the controversial issues about the Unification Church were removed there was nothing much that one could say about it other than that they were a nice group of people. There was no hook on which to hang a story. Although grateful for the insight that the event had provided, the journalists returned to their respective newsrooms and wrote absolutely nothing at all. From the Unification Church's point of view, however, that wasn't necessarily a bad thing. If such meetings could have the effect of neutralising the British press then surely they were worth holding. It also meant that if and when something newsworthy about the church next occurred, the journalists who had attended would at least have some knowledge about the subject from which their storylines could be developed.

Edwin's News Editor friend, Pete from New Zealand, commented that the meeting's content had been well within his tolerance level and that, from his point of view, the overall message of its teaching was perfectly in tune with a commonly held belief that 'God is Love.'

It was decided that such media events would be held on a regular basis, perhaps every couple of months.

CHAPTER THIRTY-THREE

MANY UNIFICATION CHURCH MEMBERS in Britain were being encouraged to learn to play musical instruments and to form bands. The UK's Lancaster Gate headquarters started to sound like an elementary music school as scales were being rehearsed on flute, saxophone, trumpet and clarinet in just about every available room of the building.

Reverend Moon had departed from the United Kingdom and was due to return again shortly but there was some speculation as to whether or not he would be permitted to re-enter the country. That was because a small pressure group of people opposed to the Unification Church had been making the claim that he was a bad influence and were suggesting that once he was back in the country it was his intention to remain and never leave.

For his part Mr Blake had been having a war of words with the Home Office about Reverend Moon's visa status and an appointment had been made with the Immigration Department in Croydon for the following morning at which a decision on his right of entry to the UK would be made. Because the outcome would almost certainly be favourable it was suggested that Edwin might like to set up a press conference that Mr Blake would address. In keeping with the idea, Edwin checked out the facilities at the Press Club in Shoe Lane but their hire rooms were already booked out. He phoned several alternative venues and ended up booking a large upstairs room of the Masons Arms pub, which was located near Chancery Lane Underground Station and within easy walking distance of Fleet Street.

Next day whilst Mr Blake and a couple of other church members went down to Croydon, Edwin let it be known to London newsrooms that a press conference would take place at 3pm. He and a Scottish sister called Heather made their way across to the venue in plenty of time. It had been arranged that details of the Home Office decision would be phoned through to the church's Lancaster Gate headquarters by midday and that Mr Blake would return to London in time to give the afternoon press conference. Neither thing happened. There was no message left at Lancaster Gate and by half past two still no appearance of Mr Blake.

"This is cutting things a bit too fine for my liking," said Edwin returning from the payphone, "We still have no news of the outcome and the press will be here soon."

"I suppose it's possible that not that many will show up," replied Heather.

"I'm beginning to hope they won't," he said, "but one or two are bound to come and I'm blowed if I know what we'll be able to tell them."

"You could just tell them all to go back to their offices" she suggested with a smile.

"Yeah, thanks a bunch," he said.

Shortly before 3pm a final phone call to the Lancaster Gate switchboard confirmed that there was still no news regarding what had happened in Croydon or on the whereabouts of Mr Blake. In the meantime journalists were beginning to arrive and the room allocated for the event soon became quite full.

"Well, it's now three o'clock so here goes nothing!" whispered Edwin to Heather. He then strolled out to the front of the room as the audience fell silent.

"Good afternoon," he began, "First of all I'd like to welcome you here and thank you for coming along. My name is Edwin Ravensdale and I currently handle Public Relations for the Unification Church here in the United Kingdom – that notorious group that everybody seems to have heard so much about – and what I'd like to do right away is to take any questions about it that you may have."

In the circumstances it was about the only thing he could think of doing that might bridge the gap before the arrival of Mr Blake – always assuming, of course, that Mr Blake was in fact going to arrive at all.

A couple of hands went up.

"In your opinion is Reverend Moon the Messiah?" asked a journalist from The Times.

It was an easy enough question for Edwin to answer because he had been asked it so many times before when meeting people on the streets or explaining the position to guests. To help pad out time he gave a comprehensive reply about such confirmation ultimately relating to one's personal relationship with God and not being dependent solely on one's opinion. Pens were busily scribbling in notebooks.

"What about the mass weddings in which people are married to complete strangers?"

And so it went on. In fact it went on for 40 minutes yet the interesting thing was that despite the wide range of questions being asked from the floor, not a single one was about that day's Home office decision as to whether or not Reverend Moon was being allowed back into the country. Edwin guessed that permission had probably been granted but he was nevertheless relieved that no one asked him a direct question about it.

At the end of the ordeal a journalist from the Mirror stood up and thanked him for his efforts.

"You've done well," he said, "It takes some guts to stand up there and defend your beliefs the way that you just have."

It was a welcome comment.

Later that day Edwin learnt that the Home Office decision had indeed gone in favour or granting Reverend Moon re-entry to the country for a limited time period. Apparently negotiations with the Home Office in Croydon had become such a long drawn-out process that had completely tied everybody up for most of the day to such an extent that Mr Blake's scheduled appearance at the press conference in London had been completely overlooked. Nevertheless, the following day's newspapers contained reasonable coverage.

Reverend Moon was shown a copy of The Times article and he asked the meaning of the words 'public house' in which the press conference had taken place. He was highly amused when it was explained that it was a bar where people ordinarily socialised over drinks and he commented that the movement was now making its presence felt in all kinds of places.

A NEW INITIATIVE CALLED 'Home Church' activity was introduced in the Unification Church. It amounted to each member being encouraged to take on a small parish of three hundred and sixty homes as their special territory in which they could provide practical service to the community. It was a welcome development for a variety of reasons – not least because it would enable members of the Unification Church to be seen to be doing something beneficial rather than a common assumption that they didn't do anything other than sell magazines on street corners all day long. It was also an opportunity for many members to experience a new form of outreach that put a greater sense of purpose in their life. The various Unification Church leaders from continental Europe had arrived in Britain and the country was divided up geographically into regions for teams of members brought over from their respective countries. South Wales became the Austrian region; Devon and Cornwall were Portuguese whilst Yorkshire went to the Spaniards.

There were also plans to purchase another property and to Edwin's surprise, three houses that were under consideration were located in Chislehurst, Weybridge and Salisbury – all of which were towns in which he had previously lived. They eventually settled on a former convent building near Chislehurst Caves. It was in a road that Edwin had often cycled up and down as a child. In fact, he could even remember the actual house. Shortly after it had been purchased, Reverend Moon returned to the United States and there was a certain emptiness experienced by many church members in Britain. However, the Home Church activity was now in full swing and there was healthy competition between the various regions.

Despite the public apology from the former chairman of the pressure group that campaigned against new religious movements, The Daily Mail published a further article which claimed the Unification Church to be 'the church that breaks up families'. Mr Blake believed that part of the report referred to him in person and sought advice from a lawyer. Edwin was not personally involved. He had little knowledge of legal matters and took the view that any differences between the Unification Church and the British media could best be resolved by calm discussion rather than resorting to courtroom battles. Besides, much of the article in question had seemed to be about the church's activities in America rather than in Britain. However, Mr Blake was adamant that he would win a court case and that it would put an end to such unfortunate media reports once and for all.

In the meantime Edwin took the ATV Researcher on a tour of the country. They visited an evening gathering in Newport to which local guests had been invited and where a Swedish sister gave a powerful and engaging talk about the changing world in which they lived.

"She's good," admitted the ATV Researcher, "In fact she's the kind of person who would come out on top in an interview with Robin Day."

They then drove down to Falmouth to take a look at the new restaurant which was being run by a group of church members. A fishing business and a boat building business were based nearby and it became evident that church members were engaged in a range of diverse activities. They stopped overnight at the church centre in Plymouth before heading up to Reading the following day to visit the church-run printing works where the New Tomorrow magazine was being put together. The rest of the week took in three more centres as well as church-run bakeries and a health food business.

As far as the television programme was concerned, there was no shortage of visual material that could be gathered. Similarly various members who would interview well on aspects of the movement were being pencilled in as potential programme contributors. Perhaps the most difficult point to deal with was the fact that Reverend Moon didn't himself give media interviews.

A further one-day research event for journalists was held in Lancaster Gate which, although not as well-attended as the first, was successful in imparting information in a palatable way. The Daily Express gave it a short write up.

ONLY ONE PERSON EVER snubbed Edwin at the Press Club and he was a narrow-minded accountant from a Christian publication who having cottoned on to Edwin's connection to the Unification Church always made a point of turning his back on him whenever he was in the vicinity. But for everybody else it was no big deal and Edwin developed a good rapport with many of the regulars including a correspondent for the Irish Times, a journalist from the Telegraph and the editor of the Daily Mirror as well as the club staff who ran the place. Edwin had even handed a copy of the New Tomorrow magazine to Prince Charles who had dropped in on a visit.

In Lancaster Gate there had been occasional talk about the possibility of setting up an in-house television production unit. Edwin had stumbled upon an affordable building that was available in Banbury which, with a minimal amount of conversion, could have housed studios, control rooms and editing suites and related offices. It would have required considerable investment in technical facilities but, in terms of personnel, there were probably enough church members around who could be trained up to run it. The property was viewed and further enquiries made but somewhere along the line the local newspaper in Banbury got wind of the fact that the prospective buyer was the Unification Church and the sale fell through. How dare the 'Moonies' think for one moment that they should ever start making their own television programmes.

Meanwhile in Exeter a public meeting had been organised to warn people about sinister cults and because the advertisement had included the term 'Moonies' on its list, Edwin decided to go to it in order to find out precisely what they were saying about the Unification Church. He arrived early and got chatting to a man who was also there for the event.

"It's good that people are beginning to see the reality of all these cults," said the man.

"Well yes," agreed Edwin, "Getting to the reality is very important, there's so much misinformation and disinformation going around."

"The public are being deceived left, right and centre," continued the man, "what with all these weird groups appearing and luring them into their net with all kinds of empty promises."

Edwin was aware that they were speaking at cross purposes.

"And then of course there's the Moonies," continued the man, "They're all completely brainwashed and have been programmed to put on false smiles and are so incoherent that they can only speak like automatons."

"Oh, that's not my experience of them," countered Edwin.

"Well, maybe you don't know as much about them as I do," replied the man, "And what about their leader Mr Moon? He's got ten Rolls Royce cars!"

"I think you'll find that's not true," said Edwin.

"Oh, it's true alright," said the man, "I've even got the newspaper article with me to prove it."

"Well I know it's not true and I happen to a member of the Unification Church," replied Edwin.

"What?" he exclaimed, "You don't mean to tell me that you're one of them?" he asked, with a look of horror appearing on his face.

'Yes, I am,' replied Edwin.

"But you can't be!" said the man, "What right do you think you would have to be coming to a meeting such as this?"

"It's a public meeting," said Edwin.

"Well I never!" he said, "Such are the deviant ways of the Moonies that they've even programmed someone to behave like a normal human being!"

On another occasion a village church near Maidstone became packed to capacity for a meeting that was billed as an exposé about the 'Moonie Cult.' The picturesque village church normally attracted a tiny congregation for its Sunday worship whereas on this occasion people had arrived in their droves eager to hear an evening's criticism of the infamous Unification Church. The event began with a film which consisted of a selection of out of context quotes from Reverend Moon's speeches which were read by an actor endeavouring to impersonate an oriental accent in the style of, "Confucius, he say…". It was a mud-slinging exercise as much as anything else.

A man at the front of the church then got up and proceeded to launch into a verbal torrent of all the common accusations against the Unification Church referring to press articles as his sole source of authenticity. Apparently Unification Church members were so brainwashed that they had no minds of their own. They were deprived of sleep and fed only on starchy foods with no protein. They had been indoctrinated into believing that their parents were false parents and it was therefore forbidden for them to return to their homes. They were programmed like robots to stand on street corners for long hours and dishonestly obtain money from the public. They worshipped the Reverend Moon. They prayed to Reverend Moon and had been hoodwinked into believing that Reverend Moon was God. They kidnapped children and made converts of them. They forced members into marrying complete strangers against their will. They relieved people of all their worldly possessions and drained their bank accounts. In short it was an evil cult that should be outlawed forthwith.

The picture being painted bore no resemblance to the reality of the Unification Church and at various junctures some of the members in the audience began to call out in protest. The man responded.

"Ah, it would appear that we have some of the cult members here with us this evening," said the man, "Kindly don't interrupt. This is our meeting not yours."

With that the father of one of the members was so outraged that he stood up on his pew and demanded the right to reply to what was being said. He said that he was an army officer and that when his son had first joined the Unification Church he had been concerned by what was being said about it in the media. However he had got the army to carry out its own investigation into the group and they had given it a clean bill of health and dismissed the hysteria surrounding it. He continued to see his son on a regular basis and had found nothing strange about his behaviour whatsoever.

By this time Edwin had squeezed his way forward to the front of the church and asked if he might be permitted to speak. The request was declined and so he climbed up into the pulpit and told the audience that he was a member of the Unification Church and asked them if he might be permitted to speak.

"Let him speak!" shouted several people from below and so, very reluctantly, the floor was given over to him.

Although unscripted, unprepared and unrehearsed, Edwin managed to give a convincing performance in which he effectively pulled to bits all the unsavoury suggestions that had been made that evening one by one. He did so in a reassuring manner and with the voice of authority leaving no doubt in anybody's mind that far from being some kind of a brainwashed zombie, he was perfectly reasonable and rational and had a clear grasp of the facts of the matter. At the end of his input of ten minutes or so, the audience gave him a round of applause, much to the embarrassment of those who had organised the event.

When the meeting broke up a reporter approached him and asked if he would be free for an interview with Radio Medway the following morning. Fortunately it was a live interview which meant that it couldn't get mucked around with in editing and that Edwin had as much editorial control over it as the interviewer. The usual trip-up questions were there and Edwin simply bridged them and plunged into the positive aspects of the Unification Church and the vision of Reverend Moon for bringing about a world of peace. The interviewer was taken by surprise and clearly out of his depth on the subject matter. However he quoted the Bishop of Tonbridge as being deeply concerned about the activities of the Unification Church. Edwin responded by saying that he felt truly sorry that the Bishop of Tonbridge had evidently been so misinformed about what the faith group stood for and for good measure threw in a conveniently recalled bible quote of "Judge not lest ye be judged". The interview had been useful in setting out the Unification Church's side of things.

But the Church of England persisted in being one of the prime scaremongers. Its ministers would frequently denounce what they called the 'Moonie cult' based on press reports. The state of affairs was regrettable because if looked at from an historical point of view Christian institutions such as the Church of England with its infrastructure and theological base were in so many ways far better placed to be receiving the Second Coming of Christ than the group of individuals that made up the Unification Church in the United Kingdom. Instead, however, just as the Scribes and Pharisees hadn't for one moment thought that Jesus could be the long-awaited messiah, the Christian ministers thought it impossible for Reverend Moon to be part of the Second Coming equation.

Edwin even took a small team of members up to York where they attended the Church of England Synod at which many of the old unsubstantiated claims were voiced yet again by prominent clergy who should have known better. The presence of the five Unification Church members at the Synod became known when one of them bumped into her former local vicar and said good morning to him.

"We're going to have to be on our guard," one minister was later heard to say to another. "I have just found out that this event has been heavily infiltrated by the Moonies.

"How can we recognise them?" asked the other.

"Oh, they will be easy enough to spot," replied the first, "They all have fixed smiles on their faces."

Edwin, who happened to be sitting alongside them, could scarcely contain himself from smiling at the very idea.

THE ATV RESEARCHER, KEVIN Jackson, attended a full week's study course on the farm. An outline for a proposed documentary programme was beginning to take shape and the producer then came down to London and sat in on a weekend workshop. The bulk of the programme would consist of illustrated interviews with members in which visual material would be used to relieve the monotony of talking heads.

Chris Southgate would be interviewed on Unification Theology, Dave Taylor was willing to be interviewed about any of the controversial issues surrounding the movement, Karen White would explain what it was like to be in charge of a Unification Church centre, John Chivers would outline the business side, Blaise would elaborate of the production of publications such as the New Tomorrow magazine, Cynthia and Malcolm would be pleased to give personal testimony as to their reasons for having joined the movement and even Mr and Mrs Blake had agreed that they would be interviewed about the role and mission of Reverend Moon. There was no shortage of willing programme participants.

A date was set for filming to commence. There was a quiet optimism about the project and its potential to portray the movement in a more favourable light that had been achieved before. It was understood that the success of the programme would very much depend upon the performance of each individual participant and there was a general feeling of confidence. After all, this was going to be a golden opportunity to explain what the movement was really about and also to set the record straight regarding any misrepresentation.

A problem arose. The day before filming was due to commence Mrs Blake had begun to have serious reservations about whether the whole thing should be taking place at all. Whether it was last minute nerves about her being interviewed was not clear. But it became evident that she had had a difference of opinion about the project with Mr Blake who, up until that time, had been eager to see it go ahead.

"We're doing the television programme and the filming starts tomorrow," declared Mr Blake.

"But how can we be so naïve as to trust the media?" she demanded.

"Look love," he said. "Our media coverage has been rock bottom and there's every possibility that this programme could make things a lot better."

"It might make things a whole lot worse," she replied, "I really think it's best just to call it off. You know what a television programme did to them in Germany – the same thing could happen over here."

She glanced across to Edwin, "What do you think?"

"Well, this TV programme is something that we initiated. It's been planned for over a year and both the researcher and the producer have been on study courses and have a reasonable understanding of the movement," replied Edwin, "It's definitely worth giving it a try."

She turned back to her husband.

"Daniel, why don't you just call those television people in and tell them that the programme can't possibly go ahead unless they are willing to hand over complete control of its content?" she persisted.

Mr Blake looked at Edwin somewhat meekly and asked if it would be possible to arrange for a meeting with the production team that afternoon.

"I expect I can set up a meeting," replied Edwin, none too pleased at the hint of last minute non-cooperation. "They might be willing to give some further reassurance about the programme's content but that's as far as they will be able to go."

Late that afternoon, over tea and biscuits, in a small office in Lancaster Gate, Edwin and Mr Blake sat down together with the programme's producer, researcher and presenter.

Mr Blake proceeded to present them with what amounted to a demand for full editorial control of the programme to be signed over to the Unification Church. The producer was completely taken aback by the request and politely pointed out that with the best will in the world such an arrangement was simply not possible under the rules and regulations that governed ITV programme-making. He emphasised however that the programme would be impartial and that it would provide an excellent opportunity for Unification Church members to put across their point of view.

"I can't get much fairer than that," he said.

"But you must be aware of all the negative allegations that has been circulating about the Unification Church," said Mr Blake.

"Yes, but throughout our research we have found nothing that supports such things," he replied.

Mrs Blake then put in a brief appearance and the female presenter caught her eye and said that she was looking forward to talking with her.

"Well, maybe. We'll have to see about that," answered Mrs Blake who then departed from the room.

The meeting ended in stalemate. Mr Blake had said that he would make a decision first thing in the morning and added that in the meantime he would compile some basic safeguards in a document for their signature prior to any filming taking place. The production team were surprised that after their detailed planning the programme now seemed to be hanging in the balance.

"Oh well, time to stand the crew down," sighed the producer to Edwin.

The female presenter then asked Mr Blake, "Could I just ask you why there is all this sudden suspicion?"

He stared at her straight in the eye and replied, "It's because I believe that the forces of evil could be at work."

"Doesn't that strike you as a bit paranoid?" she asked.

The production team departed but had agreed to return the following morning at 9.30am.

Edwin saw nothing more of Mr and Mrs Blake that evening. He reflected on the year's work that had taken place with the production team and the fact that he had been encouraged by Mr Blake to follow it through. Surely, after all the effort that had gone into it, the movement wasn't going to completely blow things now by backing out of it. It made no sense whatsoever.

THE FOLLOWING MORNING THE same people were assembled once again in the same room and it soon became obvious that they were up against exactly the same stumbling block. Mr Blake, true to his word, had gone ahead and prepared a document but it contained the same impossible demands of the previous day for complete editorial control of the programme to be handed over to the Unification Church. To compound matters further, Mrs Blake had said that if the television company was not prepared to sign it, it would be a clear indication that their intentions were bad and that no co-operation was to take place.

Probably even Mr Blake realised that there was no room to manoeuvre. For his part, the bewildered producer again explained that it was simply not within his power to grant editorial content to anybody else. Mr Blake then declared that the programme would not be going ahead and he asked everybody kindly to leave the premises right away.

As far as Edwin was concerned the chain of events had unfolded like a bad dream. Opportunity given, opportunity declined. All the headway that had been made was now being shoved down the drain right before his eyes. What on earth was the point of encouraging engagement with the media if at the end of the day the Unification Church wasn't prepared to follow it through? Didn't the movement have an important message that it wanted to get across to as wide an audience as possible? Then why suddenly block the chance to do so? And why had they waited right until now to decline? Had they got something to hide? And, if so what? Any amount of good will that had been generated with ATV had now been reduced to nothing. Edwin was left to usher the production team downstairs and out through the front door.

"I'm really sorry about this," he apologised to the threesome of producer, presenter and researcher.

"I still can't understand the reason for the u-turn but I can see that it's not your fault," replied the producer, "As you know, we've got a film crew on standby and we are still committed to making the programme."

Edwin then retraced his steps to the first floor. As he did so could overhear the words of a telephone conversation being made by one of the headquarters staff who had been instructed to phone around every Unification Church centre in Britain and relay a short message to each of them.

"Hi, John, it's Stephen in Lancaster Gate. This is just to let you know that there's a particularly nasty television crew going round the country at the moment and if they contact any members where you are on no account should you have anything to do with them."

That's ridiculous, thought Edwin. Right up until yesterday the intended production had been regarded in a completely different light and as the main hope of a media breakthrough. He knocked on the door of Mr Blake's flat and entered. He had never openly disagreed with him before but this time he felt he ought to say something.

"I'm sorry, Mr Blake, but I think we've just lost an opportunity and that the decision not to have gone ahead with the programme was wrong."

Mr Blake was annoyed.

"How dare you come in here with that attitude!" he said. "Maybe you should come of off your Public Relations mission and go back down to Cardiff or somewhere and join one of the teams!"

Edwin began to wish that he'd never entered the room. Mr Blake was someone who didn't easily take criticism no matter how well-founded that criticism might be.

Edwin departed in silence and went upstairs to his room where he pondered over the entire situation. It was nothing short of a complete nightmare in which none of it seemed to make sense any more. He'd been encouraged to seek media opportunities and yet now that he'd found a potentially useful one it was as if he was being punished for it. He sat there on the edge of his bed in quiet contemplation. It was difficult even to find the right words for a prayer in such circumstances. What would God make of such a mess?

He wondered if there was any remote possibility that Mr and Mrs Blake were right and that he had been wrong about such a media opportunity. The fleeting thought passed through his mind. But, if that were the case, why had every encouragement been given to him to foster relations with the television company in the first place? It would have been far easier to have banged the idea on the head right at the beginning rather than have him spend more than a year's worth of time and effort in helping bring about a potential programme – only to see them pull the plug on it at the last minute.

CHAPTER THIRTY-FOUR

IT TOOK ABOUT FOUR months for the relationship between Edwin and Mr and

Mrs Blake to return to some semblance of normality.

With some justification Edwin could have left the Unification Church altogether over the TV programme fiasco but he still had sufficient faith in the movement as a whole that enabled him to persevere. Even if its media outreach was temporarily put on hold he knew that that situation couldn't last forever for the simple reason that such activity was vital in ensuring that the movement's voice got heard by the wider world. However, the matter was not helped when one of the members told him in confidence that Mr and Mrs Blake apparently had some hunch that Edwin was a media plant who had infiltrated the movement. The suggestion was ludicrous and Edwin wrote a lengthy letter to Mr Blake and told him so. However he thought it wise not to make further mention of the ill-fated TV programme.

Edwin hadn't been sent back to Cardiff but had instead been put in charge of a team of eight new members who had recently joined the Unification Church. He was also given the task of finding a house to buy in London to accommodate them. After a fortnight of visiting estate agents and viewing a selection of properties he found a suitable house for sale in the north London suburb of Hendon and negotiated a purchase price of £25,000. A mortgage was arranged but it was going take some time before they would be able to move in. In the meantime the team stayed temporarily at a house in the Berkshire countryside near Reading and had the use of a transit van.

The letter to Mr Blake obviously had some effect because Edwin received a reply that invited him to drop everything and participate in the first European Leadership Course which was scheduled to begin in the Lancaster Gate headquarters. That sounded promising.

The intensive leadership course was run under the guidance of Reverend Moon's very first follower, an amiable Korean gentleman by the name of Reverend Kim. The content was comprehensive and interesting and members who took part experienced a sense of renewed optimism at the way in which the movement might progress. There was also speculation as to which nation would be the first to completely embrace the movement's teaching.

One morning Mr Blake had been invited to address the assembled group. He gave an upbeat and amusing talk.

"OK, the Second Coming takes place. He's the hope of Christianity. So what should he do? Drop in at Lambeth Palace and notify the Archbishop of Canterbury of his arrival? Go down to Rome and tell the Pope? You can imagine the likely response. There is no straightforward way. It's the likes of you and me that have been called for the task of getting the message across and so we all have a responsibility on our shoulders. But the battle is not going to be won in this country until we're all sitting on the lawn celebrating at Buckingham Palace, right?"

The course came to an end the following month. The participants were all given new missions including Edwin who was appointed Centre Leader of Oxford. It was something different. On his arrival at the semi-detached house in the suburb of Cowley, he met the brothers and sisters. Seventeen were from Germany, two were from Japan, one was from Ireland and yet another was from New Zealand.

They were a nice enough bunch. Each of them visited their home church areas on a daily basis where they offered to help people with any odd jobs that might need doing as a free service. It was a kind of bob-a-job activity but without any need to be paid the bob. In that way they befriended many people in the community and found themselves actively engaged in all manner of tasks such as shopping errands, painting walls, vacuuming, cleaning, gardening and cooking. They also found themselves acting as mentors and even as shoulders to cry on for some of the people as well as providing them with good company and quality time. Their efforts were widely appreciated and word soon got out about the good deeds being done by this particular group of young international people who were quite upfront about being members of the Unification Church. There was also the usual ongoing drive to find new members. A team went to the shopping area in the centre of Oxford and handed out leaflets inviting people to come for an introductory talk whilst others did their share of fundraising.

One of the disadvantages in Oxford was that the movement didn't have a downtown base to invite people back to for an introductory talk over a tea or a coffee. As a compromise solution they would end up inviting people to chat in one of Oxford's cafeterias instead. Depending upon the clientele at any given time of day it didn't always provide the most conducive atmosphere for discussion on faith matters.

A cultural event was held every Wednesday evening at a rented hall in town. It was essentially an evening of musical entertainment that was normally combined with an uplifting talk given by a guest speaker. A visiting Unification Church band performed and many of the local home church guests came along on a regular basis. One week the guest speaker was Mrs Blake. It was the first time Edwin had seen her since the unfortunate episode over the TV programme. When she arrived, however, she was clearly impressed to see that everything was well-organised and that the event was so well-attended. She thanked Edwin profusely for such an enjoyable evening and was charming throughout.

As centre leader, Edwin got used to a schedule of giving early morning talks to members and delivering a sermon at the public Sunday Service. It was the first time that he had ever done such a thing but, if he decided on a particular theme and made notes in advance he found he could handle it reasonably well. He frequently surprised himself how some of his personal observations on topical issues were eagerly digested by his small but loyal congregation. So as to be more accessible to the public the Sunday Services moved to a multifunctional building in the centre of Oxford where a Sikh gathering took place at the same time in an adjacent room. On realising such a simultaneous occurrence the Sikhs very kindly offered their hand of friendship to the Unification Church by inviting them to share a prepared curry lunch on the premises immediately after both of their respective events had finished. Such inadvertent interfaith activity soon became one of the highlights of the week.

Sunday afternoons offered a bit of relaxation time for the church members to unwind. If the weather was fine they would often stroll over to Oxford's Magdalen Bridge Boathouse and hire punts, rowing boats or pedalos to enjoy a couple of hours on the River Cherwell.

One day one of the members had spotted an advertisement displayed on a notice board outside a hall which said that an 'Anti-Moonie' meeting that was being organised in Oxford. The text was full of the usual venomous rhetoric about the group being a cult and a threat to society and included the familiar list of recycled allegations. Edwin said that because the wording of the poster contained claims about the Unification Church that were not true he hoped that next time one of them was passing that way they would have no hesitation in removing it. Later that evening two rather over-zealous German members triumphantly arrived back at the centre with the offending poster. What Edwin hadn't bargained for, however, was that they brought back the entire uprooted wooden notice board on which it was pinned. After removing the poster he at least got them to return the notice board back to its rightful place.

SOMETIMES A REGIONAL MEETING was held to discuss progress. One of the barometers used in measuring a success rate was the number of new guests. That was occasionally accompanied by goal-setting which didn't go down too well in Edwin's thinking. He could meet people, he could teach people, he could uplift and inspire people and he could invite them to come on a study course. That was all well and good but being expected to fill some kind of quota was not the way that such things worked and it seemed to take away the entire motivation for doing so in the first place. Such numerical expectations were often set by individuals who were pretty useless at gaining new members themselves. And as often as not the targets were completely unrealistic.

Edwin sat through one such regional meeting where someone was systematically going around the room asking everybody to pledge how many new guests their particular church centre would bring to the following weekend's study course. The truth of the matter was that despite their best efforts nobody could possibly know. They each hazarded some kind of a guess that sounded vaguely achievable. Most aimed for two guests, one suggested three. When someone said that they expected that they could bring one guest it was met with a comment of "Come on, surely your centre can do a bit more than that." When it came to Edwin's turn he casually said "Seven" which was greeted by a gentle but audible sigh from someone sitting nearby. Oddly enough, however, the Oxford centre managed to bring seven new guests to the workshop the following weekend.

But just as Oxford was gaining momentum Edwin received a phone call saying that Mr and Mrs Blake would like him to join them for breakfast at a house on the farm estate near Swindon the following morning. It was an out-of-the-blue request although two significant words had occurred during the course of the telephone conversation. They were the words "Television" and "America."

"GREAT EDWIN, DO COME in and take a seat!"
Mr Blake was back to his normal self and in fine form.
"If you have faith, you'll have breakfast!" he quipped as a clattering of dishes could be heard from the kitchen.
It wasn't long before they settled down to bacon, eggs, sausages, fried bread and mushrooms and Mr Blake began to convey the purpose of their meeting to an ever inquisitive Edwin.
"The thing is," began Mr Blake, "It would seem that the movement is now ready to start a television station in America and that they need you there to help run it."
The prospect of being centrally involved in such a relevant project was just what Edwin needed. Throughout his two years as a member of the Unification Church there had been occasional mention of the possibility that one day the movement would have its own television station, just as it now had its own daily newspapers, but it had always been couched in terms of being in the future and with no clear time schedule. Now, however, according to Mr Blake, that

time had arrived.

"I'm afraid I don't have any details other that the fact that they'd like you to be there in a couple of weeks' time," continued Mr Blake, "and that you'll be based in New York."

Edwin returned to Oxford and broke the news of his impending departure to the church members there. Some found it ironic that the move should occur just at a time when the centre had started to generate a steady flow of new guests.

It took Edwin a couple of weeks to tidy up various loose ends and transport some of his accumulated possessions to relatives for storage. As with most of his earlier trips abroad he would be equipped with one single suitcase and his ever faithful Air New Zealand shoulder bag.

The day before his departure Mr and Mrs Blake invited Edwin to London to accompany them to the Royal Tournament, a military tattoo and pageant held by British Armed Forces, at Earl's Court. Afterwards they wined and dined him at that rather plush, best of British, establishment of Simpson's-in-the-Strand where in a setting of wooden panelling and chandeliers, Scottish beef on the bone was carved at the table from an antique silver-domed trolley. It was a pleasant parting gesture. The following day Edwin was aboard his flight to New York.

TRAVELLING WEST AT A speed that more or less paralleled the earth's rotation meant that the plane which took off from Gatwick at six o'clock in the evening landed at its destination six hours later also at six o'clock in the evening, although local time. It was the first occasion that Edwin had stepped foot in the United States of America despite having come close to doing so on his earlier trip to Canada. On this occasion, however, he had a visa stamped in his passport even though it was valid only for the duration of three months. In the Arrival Hall of JFK Airport another member of the Unification Church was holding up a sheet of paper with Edwin's name written on it in felt tip pen. He turned out to be an Australian called Matt Duncan who had originally joined the Unification Church in England but who had been based in New York for the past few years.

He seemed to be a decent enough guy although as they drove towards Manhattan there were several things that emerged in their conversation that were not as Edwin might have expected. To begin with although Matt had been asked to work together with Edwin, he seemed not to have heard of any plans for a TV station. He was under the impression that Edwin's role in New York was to make some video recordings of members giving lectures on theology. That was different to what Edwin been told in England and was something that would need to be clarified as soon as possible.

They parked the car and the two of them walked a couple of blocks to the thirty-six storey building of the New Yorker Hotel on Eighth Avenue which was owned by the Unification Church.

A revolving door took them through to the lobby and a check-in procedure at a reception desk. Matt introduced Edwin as being a new addition to the World Mission Department staff. They then took one of the lifts up to the 19th floor. The dimly-lit passageway led along a well-worn stretch of carpet past a row of identical dark green doors. On turning a corner Matt announced, "And this is where your room is located."

Unlocking the door and stepping inside revealed it to be an en suite double bedroom that looked as if it hadn't been touched for about fifty years. Wallpaper had faded with age and in some places was stained. An electric power socket was hanging out from the wall. The room had thick velveteen curtains of a pale green colour behind which the window view overlooked an inset corner of the high-rise building. There was a fitted wardrobe and even a bedside table and lamp. It was the kind of place that might have featured in an old American movie. Edwin put his suitcase down next to the bed. Matt said that because they had arrived too late for an evening meal in the dining room he would be pleased to invite him to pop out to an Italian restaurant on 34th Street.

Throughout the following day Edwin was able to gain a better understanding of what he had come to. Much was familiar but in an American setting. First of all, there were the Unification Church members who were international and from a wide range of different backgrounds. As in Britain the majority of them were in their twenties. Numerically there were a lot more and needless to say they spoke with an American twang and had a slightly different approach to things than their European counterparts.

The movement in the United States was structured into various departments. The World Mission Department, as the name implied, was the central co-ordinating point for its foreign missionaries around the globe. Edwin would be sharing an office with Matt on the 29th floor of the New Yorker Hotel but nobody seemed to be able to throw any light on the TV Station project. Enquiries on the matter were invariably met with comments such as, "Ah, the television station. Yes, that's certainly something for the future" but that was as far as it went. It all seemed a bit of a mystery.

Nevertheless there was an immediate project to record a series of the Unification Church's theology lectures on videotape as Matt had outlined to Edwin when he had first arrived. It was intended to coincide with the publication of a new study guide from which the text and diagrams were expected to feature in the video version. The two of them discussed the brief and numerous limitations soon became apparent.

"There's one huge difference between the written words of a textbook and a script suitable for television," pointed out Edwin, "The wording needs to be completely re-phrased to make it flow properly and be more easily understood."

"We cannot do that I'm afraid," replied Matt, "We are under strict instructions to stick to the original text, word for word."

"Well a lot of the terminology is going to be mightily difficult for anyone to follow. It'll sound as through whoever presents it has just swallowed an encyclopaedia for breakfast. Not only that, but what about the visual content? Pointing a camera at someone giving such a talk and illustrating it with graphics is not particularly imaginative and many of the diagrams are so detailed that viewers won't get much of a chance to retain the information."

"I know. I've been worrying about that myself," he replied, "but again we've been told that these images prepared by the art department have to be used."

"Some of them are complicated enough even to look at in the book let alone on a television screen" observed Edwin, "And who is going to be delivering the talks"

"There will be a different person for each lecture" replied Matt, "They have already been selected. Some of them are from the Unification Seminary.

It seemed that things had already been pretty well set in concrete. However, Edwin had strong reservations as to whether this was the best use of the television medium. A rotation of individuals stuck in front of a camera, each reading passages of complicated terminology out of a textbook with occasional cutaway shots to highly detailed diagrams could be pretty dull and boring rather than uplifting and inspiring as it presumably was meant to be. And since everything was so completely inflexible he questioned what his role should be.

"Well, I guess you are the one who can make it all happen," explained Matt. We can have the use of New Future Films equipment and the newly built studio on the top floor of the Manhattan Center which is located just around the corner from here."

Together they spent the rest of the day checking out the studio space and technical facilities as well as meeting with other church members who would be directly and indirectly involved in the project. They soon gathered a small team of volunteers who were willing to give up some of their time to help out with the production.

Because of the necessity for graphics to be prepared on time and the availability of technical facilities from the in-house production company run by some Japanese church members, Edwin determined that the best way to get the project done would be to bash out the recorded lectures at a rate of one a week. He opted for a multi-camera arrangement and a vision mixer so as to avoid the necessity of editing and to simply record the control room's output as if live. Because it would be a twelve part series with a bit of luck they'd have the whole thing wrapped up by the end of summer which then might be a good time to pursue the real issue of a television station.

Edwin was introduced to the Korean director of the World Mission Department. He was clearly a busy man who was just on his way out of the building to go to Washington DC. Nevertheless he welcomed Edwin to America and said that he was sure that Matt would cater for his needs. It would have been inappropriate for Edwin to have raised the TV station question on that occasion.

Midtown Manhattan was every bit as bustling and noisy as Edwin had been led to believe it would be. Together with Matt he took in Times Square and after cutting across to Fifth Avenue walked up to Central Park. They then took the subway south and the ferry across to Staten Island and back passing the Statue of Liberty en route. After a MacDonald's lunch they took a lift to the top of the Empire State Building and got a further idea of the magnitude of the city of New York or the Big Apple as it was sometimes called.

Back at the New Yorker Hotel the dining hall proved to be the best places for meeting other Unification Church members. Meals were a self-service arrangement. For some reason the Japanese members preferred to sit together along the entire length of one side or the room but everyone else intermingled. Although the vast majority were Americans there was also a good mix of members from all corners of the earth. A Unification Church owned newspaper had recently been launched in New York and some members had taken jobs with that as journalists and support staff. A Spanish language publication was also in the process of being set up and there were even a couple of British members who were working on a project designing fishing boats. Reverend Moon himself was a keen fisherman and would often go out on the ocean for hours on end. A fleet of vessels would enable teams of members to get involved too.

The videotape recording sessions became a regular feature every Tuesday. The studio was arranged with a desk and a rear projection screen. As well as the studio cameras a fixed camera was available for shots of full-screen diagrams whenever they were required. The control-room layout allowed for a sound operator, vision mixer, camera control unit, and director and production secretary. A videotape operator was positioned behind. For Edwin it was a throwback to the past. For everybody else the set-up had a novelty value.

Edwin and Matt enlisted one of the World Mission Department's secretaries to take on the role of anchor person who would each week introduce whoever was delivering the talk. In that way, at least there was some sort of continuity to the videotape series.

Some presenters came across better than others but they too recognised the fact that the text they were being asked to read wasn't the most conversational way of engaging an audience. Although the content provided an overview of the church's teachings the way in which it was being expressed was not that easy to digest. Viewers would need to be exceptionally keen to want to sit down and try to understand the over-complicated way in which it was being presented.

ONE OF THE ADVANTAGES of being based in New York was that Unification Church members could attend talks given by Reverend Moon every week. These never failed to be inspiring even if they did sometimes go on for hours on end. As often as not such gatherings took place at the crack of dawn on Sunday mornings at a large estate a few miles outside of New York City for which coach transportation was laid on. Sometimes, however, they would be in the ballroom of the New Yorker Hotel. Such encounters kept members on a kind of spiritual high that would carry them through the week and beyond.

A small budget was available for day-to-day activities and Edwin was able to join the New York Press Club which he found useful in making new contacts within the media world. He also made a point of visiting the television broadcasting stations of NBC, ABC and CBS. That was easier to arrange based on his professional background. The NBC studios were housed in the midtown Manhattan building of the Rockefeller Center and Edwin was invited to sit in their control room as their main news programme of the day was put on air. Similar hospitality was given by the other broadcasting organizations too. He even spent an afternoon at the Children's Television Workshop from where the ever-popular programme 'Sesame Street' was made. He recalled the numerous occasions when he had put episodes of that particular programme on air whilst poised to jump into action for the next commercial break during afternoon transmission shifts back in New Zealand.

The Unification Church in America was well-established and reaching out into a great many places. Quite a few congressmen, dignitaries and academics were now speaking out in its favour. But there was also evidence of bigotry in some quarters. The contemptuous term 'Moonie' was flung around so frequently that in an attempt to defuse its impact some members had ordered a selection of drinking mugs and badges that had 'I'm a Moonie and I love it' printed on the white background together with a red heart. One member went a step further and took to wearing a tee-shirt with 'Brainwashed Zombie' splashed across his back.

Generally speaking the members in New York were decent, educated and idealist young people who were actively involved in doing their bit to help advance the cause. Quite a few were of a Jewish background. Some worked within the movement in roles such as lawyers or accountants whilst others included musicians, fundraisers, secretaries, maintenance staff, drivers and cooks.

Most of those that Edwin worked with, including Matt Duncan, were married. They had already taken part in one of the infamous mass weddings of the Unification Church. Their marriage partners had been suggested to them by Reverend Moon at a matching ceremony held beforehand. Matt's wife was Japanese. She was a good looking young lady with nice smile and she had a degree in Economics from Tokyo University. She spoke English reasonably well apart from a common tendency to pronounce the letter 'l' as an 'r' sound.

"We had a rubbery time."

Even if such couples lived in just one room of the New Yorker Hotel at least they had each other for company. For single people such as Edwin, it could be a lonely existence. Visiting contacts in his newly acquired home church territory on the East Side of Manhattan provided some kind of social activity. He also did many things that one would ordinarily be advised not to do in a place like New York such as travelling on the subway late at night and walking alone through the South Bronx. However he never encountered a single problem – until one sunny afternoon.

He arrived at a subway station in Brooklyn where he had arranged to meet a guest that he was bringing to the weekend study workshop. Having skipped lunch he ventured down the road to a fast food outlet. It was a scruffy joint in run-down surroundings and the first thing Edwin noticed was a bullet-proof barrier between him and the vendor. To obtain a cheeseburger it was necessary first to deposit the money in a small hatch with a sliding door. It was the kind of security arrangement that one might reasonably have expected to find at a jewellers shop or perhaps at an all-night petrol station but hardly at a hamburger bar in the middle of the afternoon. Stepping back outside, he devoured his cheeseburger and started making his way back towards the subway station. As he did so, however, he was approached by three men. "Hey, mister!" one of them called out in a threatening voice as the other two moved in on either side of him.

Sensing danger Edwin leapt forward between them and started running along the length of the sidewalk in the direction of the subway station. But he was pursued. One of them caught up with him and wrestled him to the ground. When the others arrived they began kicking his body relentlessly. Edwin thought that was it and he was going to be killed. However, he then felt the metal strap of his watch being wrenched off his wrist and suddenly it was all over. The men beat a hasty retreat leaving him sprawled out on the concrete. He climbed to his feet. A large hole had been ripped in the left leg of his suit trousers and his knee was bleeding. There were cuts to both hands as well as a bump on his head and various other aches and pains to his rest of his body where the boots had come in. He wondered why such violence had been necessary just for the sake of a watch. It would have made things a lot easier if they had simply asked him to hand it over in the first place. In such circumstances he would readily have done so and probably would have included his wallet into the bargain if they had asked for that too. There was no need for them to have beaten him up and ruined his suit in the process. The loss of his watch which had served him well since its original purchase in Hong Kong was a minor inconvenience.

His guest Mandy arrived at the subway station and on hearing what had happened she was more upset than Edwin was and insisted on telling the subway station official who expressed his sympathy.

'Do you have a good description of the three men?" he asked.

His first impulse was to say that they looked much the same as every Afro-American man in the area but fortunately, and in view of the ethnicity both of the subway official and of his workshop guest, he managed to stop himself from making such a sweeping generalisation.

THE VIDEO LECTURE SERIES was finally completed. Edwin was still not entirely happy with it as being the best example of an educational aid but its content had been beyond his control. He had merely co-ordinated all of the pre-determined elements and the small production team had effectively fulfilled its brief.

Every three months Edwin took a train to Canada for the weekend for the sole purpose of renewing the validity of his visa to the United States. Such journeys from New York's Penn Station to Montreal provided a bit of breathing space and an opportunity to reflect on the way things were going. On the occasion of the third such trip Edwin had drawn up plans for setting up and running a TV station and Matt had printed them out on a recently installed word processor. As yet, however, there were still no clear signs as to whether the project would ever get off the ground. An African member from Namibia whose room in the New Yorker Hotel was adjacent to Edwin's had added his input by saying, "You are ahead of your time. This movement is not yet ready for television."

The following week one of the Korean elders took Edwin aside and asked him how a television station could be set up. Edwin sat down with him and proceeded to give a quite detailed outline of the required technical facilities and suggested organisational structure. A few days later, however, he was called into the World Mission Department director's office and asked why he had been speaking of such things.

"I was asked how a television station might be set up and I simply gave him my opinion," replied Edwin.

"What about attitude?" he asked.

"Attitude?" queried Edwin.

"He belongs to a different department," he said.

"Oh yes, I realise that," replied Edwin, "I was just trying to be helpful. That was all. "

"I see," he replied, "Well, Father has not yet given the go-ahead for television."

"Yes, I realise that and it is something that I have been meaning to ask you about," said Edwin. "What is the future regarding a television station?"

"My advice to you is to please make research in television possibilities ready for when it happens," he replied.

Edwin then asked if he might take a trip to the West Coast to attend the National Association of Broadcasters annual convention in Las Vegas which could normally be relied on to gather fifty thousand or so media professionals from around the world. Permission was granted.

EDWIN FIRST FLEW TO Los Angeles and then hopped on to one of America's notorious Greyhound buses for the remainder of the journey to Las Vegas. Arrangements had been made to stay in the local church centre which was walking distance from the Las Vegas Conference Center where the convention was being held.

The NAB Show was widely regarded as an incubator for excellence within the ever-changing broadcast industry. Edwin soon found himself completely at home amongst the numerous guests attending the displays, talks, demonstrations and social events. He befriended many people attending the event and accumulated a wad of business cards. One of the British visitors was a Fellow of the Royal Television Society in London who said that he would be pleased to act as a sponsor for Edwin to join it as an overseas member.

As a town renowned for gambling, its mega-casino hotels and associated entertainment tended to dominate downtown Las Vegas. One-arm bandit slot machines were to be found everywhere, even in unlikely places such as the men's washroom and at petrol stations. It was also possible to get a three-course steak meal for an all-inclusive sum of 99 cents. The knock-down price was to keep people gambling around the clock without the necessity for them to go anywhere else. A full American breakfast was similarly available at 49 cents. The city's tolerance of numerous forms of adult entertainment had earned it the nickname of Sin City. Edwin walked along the boulevard known as The Strip where a high concentration of hotels, casinos and dramatic architecture was lit up at night in a dazzling display of colours.

On his return to New York, Edwin was summoned to a further meeting with the director of the World Mission Department. However, this time, it wasn't to tick him off for revealing media plans to somebody else but instead to offer him some degree of flexibility regarding the future. He said that he had spoken with Reverend Moon and it was suggested that it would be a good thing for Edwin to keep one foot firmly planted in professional television broadcasting until such time that the movement was ready to launch its own TV station.

"Therefore you are free to work in television in whichever country you like," he said, "Your future is guaranteed. Please make a good experience in television and please keep in touch."

The development was unexpected but most welcome. Edwin had been away from professional work for the past three years yet now here was the chance to return to it. He nevertheless wondered where to begin at this late stage of the game. His first choice would have been New Zealand television had it not been for the changed immigration rules of that country. Even if there were openings in the United States he was not completely enamoured with the thought of remaining there. There was still the television station back in Italy but a more mainstream broadcaster would be preferable. Perhaps the most logical starting point would be the United Kingdom where the government was thinking in terms of enabling a fourth national television channel.

CHAPTER THIRTY-FIVE

ALTHOUGH IT WAS THE month of May, London was bitterly cold.

Edwin stayed for a few nights at his brother's flat in Streatham. It was a good opportunity to unwind, catch up on things and to begin to work out some sort of strategy for the future. On the third morning he took the tube from Clapham Common to Lancaster Gate and dropped in at the Unification Church's British headquarters. With a mug of tea nestled in his hands he relayed some of his New York experiences to a group of familiar faces in the front lounge.

The fact that Edwin was planning to take an outside job raised a few eyebrows. It was unheard of at the time when fundraising and Home Church where the main activities of the movement in the United Kingdom. Even the idea of living in accommodation other than in one of the church centres sounded revolutionary.

Edwin nevertheless faced the task of finding some way of getting back into professional television broadcasting yet he knew from past experience how difficult that was likely to be. He had already glanced through UK media publications and seen that no applicable jobs were currently being advertised. It crossed his mind that he might stand a better chance of immediate work if he was prepared to carry out more menial tasks and that a lesser job within the industry might be easier to obtain – even if it would mean playing down some of his previous television experience.

Because the BBC Television Centre was based in Wood Lane it seemed logical to live somewhere nearby. After flat hunting for several days he managed to find a small self-contained attic apartment in a place called Brook Green which was about halfway between Hammersmith and Shepherd's Bush. The rent was reasonable and he was able to move in the following afternoon. During a brief chat with the landlord who lived on the ground floor a chance comment gave Edwin a new idea. Edwin had mentioned the fact that he'd recently returned from the United States and was now in London and looking to work in television.

"Well you're in the right place for that what with having the BBC right on our doorstep," replied the landlord, "I tell you what, I've been up to that Television Centre quite a few times myself. I've had some smashing evenings up the BBC Club."

"The BBC Club?" queried Edwin.

"Yes. It's the social club they have up there in the Television Centre. It's a lively place. There's plenty of cheap booze sloshing around and no shortage of famous people that you get to see."

"That sounds interesting. Can anyone go?" asked Edwin.

"No. It's strictly BBC staff only. The only way around it is to get invited there and signed in by a club member. I've got a mate who works at the BBC as a carpenter in the scenery block and so he's the bloke that takes me along with him as a guest and gets me in."

That evening Edwin took a stroll around the backstreets of the surrounding area and surprised himself by emerging behind the exhibition centre of Olympia. He pondered what he had been told by his landlord and how it seemed to tie in with his earlier notion of being prepared to take a lesser job to begin with. He wondered if there might be a job available at the BBC Club that could serve as a useful stepping stone. After all, when he'd been between professional jobs in the past, he had done a bit of bar work and was actually quite good at it

Bright and early the following morning two phone calls led to a same-day interview at a BBC building near Edgware Road. Jill Wolseley who had overall responsibility for BBC Club staff asked Edwin various questions and listened attentively as he described working in country pubs in Goudhurst and Amesbury. As it happened there was a vacancy for a full-time barperson at the BBC Club and within twenty minutes she said that she would be pleased to offer him the job. He would be able to start in two day's time. Arrangements were made for Edwin to pay a visit to the Television Centre the following morning to meet with the bar manager who would explain the rota.

"He's a bit of a rough diamond but he knows his stuff," she said.

THE BBC CLUB WAS located on the 4th floor of the central block of the Television Centre. Its manager, Vince Nero, emerged from a tiny office in the back of the entrance hall and gave Edwin a quick tour of the premises.

"Two bars, one large one small. Both open twice a day seven days a week," he said, "At closing time we push off home and all the clearing up gets done first thing in the mornings. But at least there's no washing glasses by the bar staff because another department collects them from us in racks and wheels them away to a room down the passage where they get machine-washed and then brought back to us squeaky clean."

The decor of the large main bar, deserted at that time of day, looked surprisingly drab. Dimly lit, it had split level flooring on which dark red chairs were positioned around small tables. Alongside one of several pillars was an area of tall tables for those drinkers who preferred standing. At the far end, French windows opened out onto a patio area of wooden benches and picnic tables. The direct view from there was to a silhouette of the conical chimney stacks on the horizon that Edwin recalled from his earlier experience of working in London. Some of the club's staff members were going about their morning chores in preparation for opening time. They did so to the background music of BBC Radio 1 which blared forth from a strategically positioned ghetto-blaster radio.

And how she was before the years fly by,
And how she was when she was beautiful.
She signed the letter
All yours, Babushka, Babushka, Babushka-ya-ya!
All yours, Babushka, Babushka, Babushka-ya-ya!

"Low prices the likes of which you'll never have seen before," continued Vince Nero indicating the vast array of bottles and pumps along the length of the bar. "And whilst on duty all barpersons each have their own cash register" he added, "In that way we don't get any confusion." Edwin noted that six tills were evenly spaced along the mirrored back wall.

He was told that he would be started off in the smaller bar until he got to know the ropes and that his working hours would be from 9am through to 9pm with one hour for lunch and three hours off in the afternoon.

"See ya tomorrow morning then," said the bar manager.

FOR THE FIRST FEW days Edwin was on duty alongside an Irishman, a dreamy English girl and a chap from India. The small bar attracted its own regular BBC staff customers. Once he knew where everything was located and had familiarised himself with the prices of such things as a pint of Ruddles County the work itself was easy. Edwin didn't drink whilst on duty and so kept a clear head throughout each shift. However, being plunged into a thick fog of cigarette smoke which permeated clothes and hair and caused irritation to eyes and lungs left a lot to be desired.

Towards the end of his second week the bar manager, Vince Nero, praised Edwin. He said that his work was good and that from Saturday onwards he'd like him to work in the larger bar.

It was often said that the BBC floated on a sea of alcohol and Edwin soon began to see why. From quite early on in the day the club would begin to fill up. Before long every nook and cranny was crowded out with groups of people who tended to congregate in their own specific areas. News staff would gather together at their self-designated spot just beyond one end of the main bar whilst engineers laid claim to the other. Production staff and secretarial staff occupied the middle area and newsreaders gravitated to one of the tall tables. It was almost as if there were demarcation lines.

A group of workers from the scenery block had just finished their night shift and were buying their first rounds of drinks for the day.

"Two points of 'olstein, three points of Guinness an' a loight an' bitter," had been their order.

Four men from the wardrobe department then positioned themselves daintily in front of the bar. They each sipped from tall glasses of vodka and tonic that were replenished at regular intervals throughout the morning. Meanwhile some of the secretarial staff avoided the daily alcohol intake by opting for something called a St Clements which was a bitter lemon mixed with orange juice.

During his first shift in the large bar Edwin ran into two former acquaintances both of whom had acquired their respective jobs at the BBC as a result of someone they knew. Edwin had been at boarding school with one who now worked on a Saturday morning live children's series called 'Multi Coloured Swap Shop' which was normally on air for the best part of three hours. There was mutual recognition of a familiar face and then a recollection of both of their roles in a school play.

The second character, who turned up later that morning, was a large bearded man who had helped train Edwin in studio direction several years earlier at the TV station in Christchurch, New Zealand, and who now worked for BBC News. Interestingly there were no disparaging comments about the fact that Edwin was now doing bar work. On the contrary, as a stop gap, it was considered to be a smart move. Although a far cry from programme making at least it got him into the building and before long he would have the right to apply for the internal vacancies that occurred within the BBC. There was a method in his madness.

At the end of the morning shift there were three hours spare until the club re-opened at six o'clock. It wasn't worth going out. Edwin soon got to know his way around the Television Centre which began with the squeaky swing doors to the right of reception. Its layout consisted of a six-tier stack of doughnut rings adjoined by a dozen studios of varying sizes together with engineering areas and additional offices. The architect who came up with the design in the 1950's was said to have retreated to a pub to try and work out how best to fit eight to ten studios on the area of land in White City in such a way that would allow easy access to scenery as well as for all of the people who would be using such facilities. The story goes that after giving the matter some thought but not reaching any firm conclusion he had apparently drawn a question mark on an envelope and then realised that a question mark shaped layout would be perfect.

The circular corridor arrangement of the main block meant that it was easy enough to walk around a complete circuit of any particular floor. The lower levels were taken up with wardrobe, makeup, cameras, sound and lighting. Above them were production offices for drama and light entertainment programmes. At the back of the building was the scenery block where designers and their assistants were based. In the basement Edwin found that he could make use of a shower facility if he first poached a towel from makeup. He also discovered where to obtain a polystyrene cup of tea and, depending upon which shift he was working, he frequented the heavily subsidised BBC canteen for lunch, dinner and occasionally for breakfast.

Being gainfully employed once again was welcome in many respects. Edwin found that it represented a kind of reference point from which he could gauge things more clearly. He still had his faith and his understanding of the Second Coming. The fact that he'd moved out of a church centre and had become self-sufficient didn't knock that in any way at all. In fact if anything it strengthened it. By the same token, however, such was the lousy public perception of the Unification Church that it would have been futile mentioning his involvement to any of his BBC circle of friends. It would have required far too much explanation and the risk of it backfiring was too great. On Sundays, Edwin would hop on a bus to Lancaster Gate and attend the morning service. It was all a matter of balance.

Membership of the Royal Television Society enabled him to attend evening talks held regularly at the headquarters of the Independent Broadcasting Authority in Knightsbridge. That helped him keep abreast with the latest developments both in production and technology. It was an interesting time for the broadcasting industry in the United Kingdom. ITV's franchise was up for renewal meaning a shake-up of regional television stations and a new company called TV-AM had won the contract to provide a breakfast-time television service. But perhaps of greater curiosity to Edwin was that the Broadcasting Act had widened the remit to include the setting up of a fourth national television channel. That would surely create many new job opportunities and there might even be a way round the union impasse.

Back at the BBC Club the word got out that there were a few more strings to Edwin's bow than serving people with their double brandies or large sauvignons and that he had a background in TV production. A middle aged lady who handled the club's accounts from the same small office as the bar manager approached him,

"I knew there was a bit more to you right from the moment you arrived," she beamed, "I can see the intelligence."

It was all very flattering. However, at a meeting with a helpful personnel officer the following afternoon, it emerged that before being eligible to apply for any of the BBC vacancies that were advertised internally Edwin would need to have been in his present job for at least a year. That was considerably longer that he had anticipated.

BREAKFAST IN THE BBC canteen included a multi-choice of elements. Regular customers were already lined up when it first opened its doors at eight thirty each morning. "I'll 'ave two eggs, two bacon, a froid sloice, black puddin', mushrooms, beans, toast an' butter an' a cuppa tea." Edwin joined the queue and selected a similar combination for the princely sum of ninety pence paid to a cashier whose till emitted a high pitched peep every time an amount was entered. It sounded like a bird chirping.

He then went over to the BBC Club by means of a connecting bridge to the main block in time to join the others in preparing for the day that lay ahead.

They were the usual team of two guys from Northern Ireland, a lad from Zimbabwe, a Glaswegian and four English staff.

As usual the radio was on full pelt once again.

Upside down you're turning me,
You give your love instinctively,
Round and around you're turning me,
I say to thee respectfully,
Upside down, boy you turn me,
Inside out, and round and round...

Bar manager Vince Nero emerged for a quick check of the bars and then returned to his tiny office for the rest of the morning. No one was quite sure what he actually did there apart from keeping his eye on stock control and getting through a considerable amount of gin and tonic. His train of thought was interrupted by the club's elderly doorman who had a habit of groping the young blonde Polish barmaid whenever she entered the premises.

An efficient barperson soon becomes everybody's friend in an institution such as the BBC. Edwin dealt with everyone on an equal footing. He could cut through departmental barriers and relate equally well to staff at all levels whether managerial, technical or creative. Amidst the general buzz of conversation he frequently found himself in discussion with individuals about their forthcoming drama series or a newly-hatched programme format, an installation schedule, recently introduced policies, the running order of news items or the rigging of studio lights for that week's 'Top of the Pops.'

In September he took a few days off to attend an International Broadcasting Convention being held in marquees alongside the Grand Hotel in Brighton. It was a biannual event for European media professionals and a smaller version of what Edwin had attended in Las Vegas earlier on in the year. At one of the evening receptions he was seated next to somebody called Malcolm Barnes whom he knew from the BBC Club. It transpired that Malcolm had recently left the corporation and was in the process of setting up a TV production company in Southampton. After a lengthy chat he offered Edwin a job with the new company as a Producer/Director to start in the New Year.

A formal letter of appointment was typed up the following morning.

Although extremely pleased to have got a job in TV production Edwin realised that moving to a small company in the south of England was going to be very different from being at the hub of life at the BBC Television Centre. Realistically, though, it would have taken a further six months of bar work before being able to apply for internal vacancies at the BBC and the Southampton opportunity was more in line with picking up the threads of his career. Besides there was still the prospect of Britain's new national fourth television channel due to start in the following year and that might then enable him to return to London.

Ironically, just as Edwin was about to hand in his notice at the BBC Club, the bar manager Vince Nero called him into his office. He wanted to promote Edwin to Assistant Bar Manager. It would have been a step up the ladder but unfortunately it was the wrong ladder.

CHAPTER THIRTY-SIX

EDWIN SPENT CHRISTMAS WITH relatives in Bournemouth where much of the festive celebration entailed doing the cooking. He had found that time spent in the kitchen was one of the most enjoyable ways of getting through the way in which the event is traditionally celebrated in Britain. The preparation of chestnut stuffing, bacon-wrapped chipolatas, bread sauce and a free range turkey, roasted to perfection, had been a fulfilling exercise in his culinary skills. And that was just the Christmas Day meal.

On Boxing Day, however, he received a surprise telephone call from the Unification Church in London. Apparently Reverend Moon would be holding a 'matching ceremony' in New York in three days time and, as Edwin was eligible to participate, he was invited to attend if he so wished. The implications were immediate. Marriage was central to Unification Church faith and ever since he had first encountered the group Edwin had been intrigued that Reverend Moon made suggestions regarding one's potential marriage partner. He had long ago decided that he would be willing to participate in such a ceremony whenever the opportunity arose. But right now – in the middle of mistletoe and mince pies? And in three days time in New York? He quickly calculated that the practicalities of being able to get there on time might just about be possible.

Caught up in a whirl of running around trying to find someone who would cash him a cheque on a public holiday and the unfortunate fact that no trains were running, Edwin succeeded in getting himself up to London on a National Express coach, obtaining a tourist visa from the American Embassy and in purchasing a return flight ticket for the United States. He had had little time to prepare for the trip other than to throw a change of clothing which included a suit and tie into a bag and hope for the best. On top of that he seemed to be coming down with a heavy cold which didn't exactly help matters.

Two days later, together with a large group of single brothers and sisters of the British Unification Church he sat on board a British Airways afternoon flight to New York.

It had been explained in a pep talk that it was best to keep a completely open mind about the kind of person that one would be introduced to in the matching ceremony. In fact, the explanation had often gone a step further by saying that, as part of an historical process of restoration, members should be prepared to meet the worst possible kind of person imaginable. But it was also understood that there was no compulsion involved. If an introduction were made it would then be left entirely to the couple to decide whether or not they wished to go ahead and get engaged. The right of refusal was available to either of them.

It was snowing in New York. They took the JFK Express Subway from the airport to Sixth Avenue and walked the remaining couple of blocks. On arrival at the New Yorker Hotel, the brothers from Britain were told that were being assigned to a room on the 17th floor. When they got to it they found that although it was a useful dumping ground to offload their bags it was otherwise empty and had no heating. Some were regretting that they hadn't had the foresight to have brought a sleeping bag with them. At that stage an American member knocked on the door and politely informed them that Reverend Moon would like to meet with everyone that same evening in the grand ballroom in one hour's time and that the dress code was jacket and tie.

Literally hundreds of members queued to enter the ballroom. An usher was doing his best to organise things. "OK everybody, brothers to the left and sisters please sit to the right – but leave an area free in the middle of the room."

The singing of several Unification Church songs took place and then Reverend Moon arrived amid cheers and applause. Edwin was momentarily choked with emotion. It felt good to be setting eyes on him again. Through his translator Reverend Moon gave a brief introduction to the proceedings and amusedly pointed out that everybody who was gathered there in some way needed him. And then, he plunged straightaway into matching people which, apart from anything else, was an education to watch. He began by asking if it was anybody's birthday. A young man raised his hand and was asked to come forward. He was asked his nationality which was Spanish. Reverend Moon looked across to the female side of the room and asked which of them were from Spain. Several raised their hands. One was beckoned to come forward and she was paired off with the brother. The two of them then walked through to an adjoining room that had been specially set aside for the newly-matched couples to discuss their introduction and decide jointly if they wished to go through with it.

The process gathered momentum as Reverend Moon began to ask certain individuals to stand up and come forward to the central area of the ballroom and be positioned in a row of several brothers on one side and a parallel row of several sisters on the other. Although they were facing each other it was by no means obvious which of them would end up with whom from the opposite row. Reverend Moon would beckon one forward and, sometimes directly opposite or sometimes in a diagonal direction, guide them across to the person that he was suggesting for them. This was done with some speed and was interesting to observe. Edwin began to relax and enjoy the phenomenon as it continued throughout the night occasionally wondering when it might be his turn.

Most of the couples matched in this way were pleased to accept the person that had been found for them. After all, they had a common faith in the man who was making such introductions and in the process as a whole. Because of the sheer number of participants who had travelled in from around the world it was normally the case that the paired individuals were meeting each other for the very first time. Others might have met previously at some stage during their years of work within the church. In such an international movement it was also inevitable that some of those introduced to each other didn't share a common language although that proved to be of little or no hindrance in their agreeing with their match – and various translators were available in the side room if need be. As couples reached agreement concerning their wish to go ahead and get engaged, it was customary for them to indicate their acceptance by returning together to the main ballroom and, in oriental tradition, making three full bows. That received a round of applause from the rest of the onlookers.

In the meantime Reverend Moon continued in his creation of such new couples one after another. Edwin sensed the rich spiritual atmosphere of such a joyous event. Every once in a while he would see that a person being matched was someone that he knew. Still more single Unification Church members from around the world were on their way to New York and keen to take part in the event.

Sometimes Reverend Moon would ask the assembled participants various questions. "Please raise your hand if you had a college education." He would then plough ahead and invite those that he selected to come forward to be matched. Edwin had lost track of time as probably had most of the others. Everyone was so absorbed in what was taking place that nothing else seemed to matter any more and any fatigue simply vanished.

By about four o'clock in the morning Reverend Moon asked the gathering if he should continue or if they'd like to have a break. It was agreed to go on for a short while and then to resume later that day.

During the break the British brothers lay across whatever space was available in the coldness of their 17th floor room and attempted to grab a bit of sleep whilst they could. One of them had been matched to a Japanese sister and another to an Italian. The rest were still unattached. A few hours later and after a quick shave and shower and a bite to eat in the dining room they returned to the grand ballroom in the hope that they might be meeting their eternal partner on that day. The session was just getting underway. There were some members such as foreign missionaries or those behind the Iron Curtain who for one reason or another couldn't easily get to the United States but they had been able to submit a full length photograph of themselves in order still to be included in the matching process. Every now and again Reverend Moon would match a person to one of those photos. It seemed that everything had been thought of.

Many of Edwin's friends were matched that day. But there were still new arrivals to the ceremony and so the ballroom felt just as crowded as it had done from the beginning. Day seemed to merge into night and night into day as the matching process continued seemingly without end but with occasional breaks.

In accordance with the way things had been explained Edwin had kept a completely open mind about the kind of person he would like to end up with. However at one stage of the morning, and with still no match in sight, he began to wonder if it would improve his chances if he allowed himself to think in terms of a few specifics. After all, he reasoned, this unique religious movement didn't really make any sense at all unless Reverend Moon was the messianic person that members believed him to be. And yet because of the Korean aspect and an obvious cultural difference it wasn't always easy to grasp certain things. Edwin wondered if that might be improved if he could speak Korean. And then he thought that perhaps the easiest way for that ever to happen might be to have a Korean wife. However, it was merely a floating thought and he was quick to remind himself that he was prepared for receive anyone and wasn't going to limit things by stipulating anything such as a preferred nationality. It was just at that moment when Reverend Moon turned to the male participants and said "Put your hand up if you would like a Korean wife." The shock timing of the question was such that Edwin's hand shot up and he was immediately beckoned forward by Reverend Moon to stand alongside some other brothers and opposite a row of sisters. Although he had stood at close hand to him on previous occasions, on this particular day Edwin sensed that Reverend Moon towered way up above him. He watched as some of the participants alongside him were paired together and then in anticipation of a Korean he was somewhat surprised when Reverend Moon glided a young lady over to him who was certainly not an oriental at all. However, he quickly realised that this was his intended match. The two of them walked together towards the side room during which the young lady turned to him and introduced herself.

"Hallo, my name is Helga. I come from Germany," she said.

"Oh, hi, I'm Edwin and I'm British," he replied.

They found a vacant coffee table in the side room and both sat down. Edwin was still momentarily stunned by the fact that he'd put his hand up for a Korean and ended up with a German. He didn't think it had been a mistake but he needed a little time to gather his thoughts properly. He glanced across at the young lady. She looked a fair bit younger than him. She caught his eye and smiled.

"Well the thing is..." he faltered slightly. "I mean – back in the ballroom it was a bit odd because one moment I put my hand up for a Korean..." He then broke off and reasoned that it probably wasn't the best way to start explaining things. Maybe he should play for time a little bit so as to digest the situation before seeing the way in which things might go. He continued by casually asking,

"What do you think about this entire matching process?"

"I think yes!" she replied nodding enthusiastically. Edwin was shocked to realise that she was already one step ahead and was answering what she thought about their particular match rather than the more general question about the matching process that he'd intended.

"Well, I don't really know..." he began and then stopped as he realised how terrible that must have sounded. "Yes maybe... I mean, please tell me a bit about yourself. What is it you do?"

"I do mission as a team leader in Germany," she replied, "And what about you?"

"Mainly PR and media," he replied. "I guess the movement is still trying to find a way of getting its message out to the wider world in a way that they can understand it – and the media has its role to play in enabling that."

"That's very important," she replied.

"I'm glad you think so," he said, "Do you mind if I ask your age?"

It turned out that she was eight years younger than Edwin and that she'd joined the movement almost straight from her school days. She came from a place called Darmstadt. He told her that he'd lived all over the world and she told him that this trip to New York was her first time outside of Europe. As she spoke Edwin quite suddenly felt captivated. He saw in her a beautiful sincerity and innocence in her face and she also had an obliging laugh. His heart melted.

For the sake of any doubt he thought he'd better just clarify her position one more time.

"So you think we should go ahead with our match?" he asked.

"I think it's what God wants," she said.

"Well, you know what? So do I," replied Edwin. And they took that as their cue to rise from their chairs and re-enter the grand ballroom together where they made their three bows signifying their acceptance.

As each of the newly matched couples left the hall they emerged onto a balconied area where they were greeted by a mass of eager onlookers, photographers and well-wishers. The familiar faces of Mr and Mrs Blake were amongst those who congratulated Edwin and his fiancée Helga.

THE FOLLOWING DAY WHEN all of the matching had been completed, the couples were invited to gather in the ballroom one more time to share a cup of holy wine which, it was explained, symbolised their engrafting into God's lineage and effectively completed the process. As engaged couples they would now have to wait to jointly attend one of the church's mass weddings but the date for the next one was still to be announced.

It was time for a breath of fresh air and, together with a small group of other couples, Edwin and Helga took a whirlwind trip around New York City. Coffee and cheesecake were to follow.

Edwin was booked on his flight back to England. Helga would be returning to Germany one day later. They had exchanged contact details and both had promised to be in touch soon. Exhausted but never having felt so content in his entire life, Edwin fell fast asleep whilst the plane was still on the tarmac in New York and didn't wake up until shortly before it landed in London. After a brief visit to Lancaster Gate, where many of the newly-engaged Unification Church members had gathered to compare notes about their experience of the matching process, Edwin headed across to Waterloo Station and took a train back down to the South Coast.

EDWIN WAS DUE TO start work with the TV production company in Southampton in one week's time. He had waited outside the offices of the Evening Echo to get a copy of the newspaper as soon as it came out so as to be one step ahead of everybody else in scanning its columns for rented accommodation. With a ballpoint pen he then ringed the five possibilities on offer and headed to the nearest telephone box. There was no reply from the first two numbers. A lady answered the third and explained that her self-contained flat had been let the previous evening but that there hadn't been time to cancel the advertisement. The fourth call sounded quite promising and the landlord asked if he could meet him at the property at 3pm that afternoon. The final phone number turned out to be an estate agent who asked Edwin if he wanted to be put on a list.

With just the one appointment having been made, Edwin arrived at the address in the Southampton suburb of Shirley. The landlord unlocked the door and explained that the place had previously been lived in by someone who had fancied himself as some kind of a musician which was why the ceilings and walls of the sitting room were painted dark blue and all of the woodwork, including the floor boards, was of a shiny black gloss. It was part-furnished with corresponding black furniture and blue curtains throughout. The rent was about half what Edwin had been paying in London and he agreed then and there to take it. He wrote a cheque for his first month's payment and the landlord handed him two door keys.

Bargate Productions in Southampton employed just six full-time staff but had access to a pool of local freelancers. Its manager Malcolm Barnes, whom Edwin had first met at the BBC and then at the broadcasting event in Brighton, had a good track record in factual programmes. The St Mary's Road premises was equipped with TV cameras, a small studio, two videotape editing suites and a row of tiny offices for production staff and administration. The set-up was simple and it worked. Thanks to the efforts of the company's dynamic marketing lady, who was particularly skilled in securing deals with local businesses, there was no shortage of work coming in, most of which was local advertising, promotions and training videos. There would be occasional commissions for documentary programmes.

Edwin had been assigned to an educational series about the geology of the New Forest. The presenter was an authority on the subject from Southampton University's Faculty of Natural and Environmental Sciences. It meant that they were often out and about with a camera crew and that Edwin was gaining a lot of knowledge about shark's teeth, molluscs and corals.

Several weeks after settling in to his new role he became aware that there was another Unification Church member based somewhere in Southampton and he decided to pay a courtesy visit. It turned out to be a French sister called Yvette, whom he knew by sight. Over coffee she explained that in a couple of month's time she would be departing for Spain to join her Spanish husband. In the meantime she had a daily schedule that normally began with a short burst of fund-raising. After that she would get across to her home church parish to help out with odd jobs and run errands for anyone there. In the evenings she visited local contacts who had showed an interest in the movement's theological teaching, in the hope that one or two of them might wish to attend one of the weekend study courses.

Whilst they were chatting, there was a knock on the door. Yvette went to answer it and Edwin could overhear the conversation.

"Is this the Unification Church?" asked a young man's voice.

"Yes it is," replied Yvette.

"Oh good, I'm glad I've found the right place," he said. "My name is Sam Brookes. I used to be a member in Leeds. I've been right out of it for a while but I've now decided that I'd like to come back."

"You'd better come in," said Yvette.

After introductions had been made the person gave a brief account of himself.

"It was a bit daft really," he said. "Because of all the bad publicity in the newspapers my parents were upset and annoyed that I'd ever got involved with the Unification Church in the first place. I later found out that they'd got on the mailing list of an outfit called FAIR, that sends out negative material about it. Anyway, to cut a long story short, there was a heated debate and for the sake of harmony I agreed to pull out of the movement for a while, get a job and then reconsider the matter. They were very pleased with that because they thought that I had somehow seen the light of day and come to my senses and that I would never have anything more to do with the church. So, I joined the Royal Navy, from where I really have seen the light of day and come to my senses and my inclination is that I'd like to re-connect to the Unification Church."

"That is really interesting. You are most welcome," said Yvette, "but why have you come to us here in Southampton?"

"It was the nearest centre," he replied. "I'm still in the navy and the ship that I'm on is docked in Portsmouth, so it was an easy enough train journey to get here."

It transpired that the following morning he would be sailing on a tour of duty for several months but would like to get in touch again on his return. Edwin gave him the address of his flat, in case Yvette had already left Southampton by that time.

ON HIS DAYS OFF Edwin took to helping Yvette in her church-related activity. In that way he was able to strike some sort of a balance between work life and church life. He took on a home church area of his own in Southampton's Inner Avenue. After a few weeks of helping people out with the odd chore at weekends the attitude of a man at one particular house was most strange and his utterances seemed to be verging on regimental commands.

"Right – at least you're on time. Come in." barked the man one Saturday morning. "It's painting today. There are two rooms to be done. Use that pile of newspapers over there to cover the floor area. Where the walls are flaking use the scraper then sand them down to a smooth surface. Use the stepladder to paint the ceilings with white emulsion then do all the walls with the magnolia and afterwards the wooden skirting boards with the white gloss."

Having issued such instructions he then withdrew to another part of the house leaving Edwin to get on with it. A paint roller and tray and a couple of paint brushes had been left out for him as had an assortment of cloths, a paint stirrer and a roll of masking tape.

Edwin made quite a good job of it. The worst bit had been smoothing the walls down but once he'd started applying the new paint he could see that he was making headway. In all it took six and a half hours to complete both rooms. Throughout that time there had been no communication with the man or his wife although he could hear that there were still in the house. He could have done with a cup of tea but none had been offered. Having stuffed the remaining sheets of newspaper into a black bin liner, he opened the door that led into the hallway and called for the man to come.

A brief inspection of Edwin's work took place and the man said. "OK, fine. That'll be all for today then. Now, if you can be here next Saturday at nine o'clock sharp, there's an attic to be cleared which will take you most of the day."

As Edwin was walking home he tried to fathom out the man's attitude. When he'd first visited the house the man's wife had also been present. Edwin had been totally upfront about it being a community project initiated by the Unification Church. Since then, however, the wife was kept out of the way and the man dished out the tasks almost as if he they were intended as some kind of punishment.

A chance conversation with another contact in the same street revealed the reason for the man's seemingly unreasonable behaviour. The words 'community project' had been misinterpreted as 'community service' of the kind that got handed down to offenders in place of a prison sentence. The man and his wife had assumed that Edwin was a criminal who was making reparation to society by being required to do a certain number of hour's unpaid work in the community.

Mr Blake's libel action against the Daily Mail had trundled on for six months and involved numerous witnesses from both sides of the Atlantic. When the court ruled in favour of the newspaper it came as a bitter blow to the church's membership. The end result of such costly legal action seemed to set the status of the movement back rather than forward. Mr and Mrs Blake then transferred to a new role with the Unification Church in Germany.

Lurking in the back of Edwin's mind, however, the problem still remained as to how to get the theological reasoning about the occurrence of the Second Coming out through the media in a way that could be easily understood. It was a fascinating story to be told that so far had been misunderstood, misrepresented or completely ignored. But even if a limitless budget were available, it was not easy to know where to begin or the kind of content that would be required to turn it into riveting viewing because so much of it was conceptual and it was difficult enough to pack an overview of the teaching into a weekend study course let alone trying to condense it down to a single programme.

Several other Unification Church members in the UK had similar views about the need to make use of the media. Edwin thought it might be worthwhile to get them together and explore a few ideas and so he set up a meeting. Twelve of them duly arrived in Southampton early one morning. They included Trevor the lecturer, several of the staff who worked on the New Tomorrow magazine, a brother who had once been a professional photographer and some other interested members. They sat together and enthusiastically bounced ideas around for the entire day and came up with several suggestions for potential documentary programmes about aspects of the Unification Movement. Yvette cooked a hearty French meal of Boeuf Bourguignon for everyone.

BRITAIN'S FOURTH NATIONAL TELEVISION channel was due to be launched the following year. Edwin attended a preliminary interview in a temporary office in London. Despite its remit to encourage innovation and experimentation the channel was to be the world's first publisher/broadcaster. It meant that rather than making any of its programmes itself, it would instead be commissioning outside TV production companies to supply all of its programmes. That limited the number of creative jobs at the channel itself although there could be the possibility of work in TV Presentation.

Closer to home as part of ITV's franchise arrangements Southern Television in Southampton was giving way to a new company called Television South. As a member of the Royal Television Society, Edwin was able to attend regional meetings held at their studios. Meanwhile the BBC's presence in the city continued to be housed in the disused railway station of Southampton Town.

IN THE FIRST WEEK of June Edwin took a week off work to visit his fiancée Helga in Germany. Although they had written to each other on a regular basis they hadn't seen each other since they'd first met in New York five months ago. She was waiting for him in the Arrivals Hall of Frankfurt Airport and, in keeping with the church's tradition of not getting intimate until after marriage, they politely shook hands and smiled at each other. She looked lovely and, as a couple, there was a certain magnetism that seemed to exist between the two of them. They first took the S-Bahn to Frankfurt's main railway station where in German tradition she suggested going for coffee and cake at a nearby cafeteria.

Edwin found it strange to feel very close to somebody and yet still not know so many little things about them. Did she take sugar in her coffee? Yes, quite a bit by the looks of it. And her eyes – were they actually blue or greenish blue? But he didn't want to stare at her. At least she chuckled at some of his comments. It also felt a little odd being back in Germany again after his previous experiences in that country.

Helga spoke reasonably good English albeit with a detectable German accent. Shortly after she'd joined the Unification Church at the tender age of seventeen her parents had been so concerned about bad press reports that initially they'd feared that they might never see her again. However, she had remained in regular contact with them and returned home for visits on many occasions so much so that they had changed their opinion. They had even visited a church centre and been impressed with the calibre of the members. More recently Helga had told them all about Edwin and they were looking forward to meeting him.

Following a half hour train journey to Darmstadt they walked the short distance to her parents' home where the four day visit proved to be an enjoyable occasion for one and all.

Afterwards Edwin and Helga went to Berlin for a few days. Helga was busy there with some church-related activities whilst Edwin took the opportunity of going behind the Iron Curtain into East Berlin. That was a slightly nerve-racking experience. To get there he took an underground train from the brightly lit modern S-Bahn station of the Hauptbahnhof in West Berlin to a dingy looking station called Friedrichstrasse in the East. After then walking through a long dimly lit passageway he arrived at a glass encased passport control. There a young East German officer opened Edwin's British passport and took a considerable amount of time in looking back and forth between Edwin's photo and at Edwin himself. After a while the official began shaking his head. Not a single word had been spoken throughout this ritual and Edwin thought that he wasn't going to be allowed into East Berlin at all. Suddenly, however, the official turned to a different page of the passport and stamped it with the green and re-inked mark of the Deutsche Demokratische Republik before handing it back. Edwin continued through the remainder of the passageway before emerging into daylight.

His first impression of East Berlin was that it looked as if the Second World War had finished only yesterday. So many buildings were in a state of disrepair. The next thing that became apparent was a total lack of advertising. There were no billboards, no posters or signs of any description. Streets were lined with unnamed buildings of drab, grey concrete with no indication as to what any of them were. One of the entry stipulations had been to exchange a minimum of twenty-five West German Deutsche Marks for East Germany Marks at a one to one exchange rate. The irony was that it was virtually impossible to spend that amount of money during the course of a single day and that any unspent money had to be handed over to the East German authorities on the way back out. There was nothing much to buy other than a three-course meal in a hotel restaurant which cost only four marks. But at least Edwin could say that he had stepped foot in a communist country – even if only for a few hours.

WITH MR AND MRS Blake no longer at the helm of the Unification Church in Britain one of the early British members had been put in charge. He let it be known that if anyone wanted to change their mission they should get in touch with him. Unbeknown to Edwin some members expressed an interest in moving to Southampton to join forces in building up a media team.

It resulted in Edwin receiving a curt phone call from one of the church administrators.

"One by one, members have been asking if they can join you in Southampton," she said.

"It's the first time I've ever heard anything about it," he replied.

"It all seems a bit unprincipled," she continued.

"Well, a few weeks ago a small group of us got together for the day to discuss some programme making ideas," he said, "but that's all there was to it and there was no suggestion of anyone relocating down here to Southampton."

"I see," she said, "but you belong to the World Mission Department and you should continue to relate to them in New York whereas we are the British Church."

With the dividing line explained in such a way, Edwin hung up. He was more surprised than annoyed.

Old Matey from the Royal Navy then put in an appearance. Sam Brookes had arrived back in Portsmouth and made his way to Southampton. He had a few weeks leave and Edwin told him that he was welcome to stay at the flat whenever he was ashore. He was a sincere lad with a keen sense of humour who proved to be good company. He bought a second hand car which enabled them to transport some guests to the weekend workshop.

Towards the end of his leave the phone rang early one morning and the person on the line asked to speak to Sam Brookes.

"Yes, sure," replied Edwin. "Who's calling?"

"The Navy," was the reply.

Argentina had invaded the Falkland Islands and Sam was being requested to return to his ship right away.

BY NOW EDWIN HAD been with the TV production company in Southampton for a little over a year. Although he remained in written contact with the World Mission Department in New York there was still no news of the Unification Church setting up its own television station. He had a fortnight's holiday due and fancied a complete change of scene. He had noticed an inexpensive package deal to Gibraltar advertised in the window of Thomas Cook. Although his previous visit to that place had been in circumstances that were quite bizarre he now saw things in a different light. He went ahead and booked the trip.

Back at his flat he then received a telephone call from Channel Four Television. Following the informal discussion which had taken place there a couple of months ago he was told that they could offer him the job of Assistant Editor in the Presentation Department. He said that he would be pleased to accept the position and it was agreed that he would be able to commence working there in one month's time. A confirming letter would be put in the post to him right away.

Things were looking up. He walked back into the centre of Southampton and called in at the office to hand in his one month notice. His boss, Malcolm Barnes, congratulated him of his new appointment and set about organising a farewell gathering to be held at a local Italian restaurant called The Pizza Pan.

WHEREAS EDWIN'S FIRST VISIT to Gibraltar had been at a time when he was desperately seeking work, this time it was a far more relaxed state of affairs. He could use the time to recharge his batteries before getting stuck in to his new job.

Blue sky and Mediterranean sunshine greeted him on arrival. He was booked into the Bristol Hotel which was centrally located and a minibus had driven him in from the airport. He soon found himself retracing the steps of his previous visit which was not a difficult thing to do in a small place like Gibraltar. He passed the front entrance of what had been the Victoria Hotel where he had stayed on that occasion. It had since closed down and the inside of the building was completely gutted and awaiting reconstruction. Opposite he saw that the open air pavement bar of Lotti's no longer existed.

However, the duty free shops of Main Street and their Indian proprietors were just the same as before. He even passed the one where the man had been unable to offer him a job. It seemed amusing now but had not been quite so funny at the time when he'd staked his future on finding any kind of work in Gibraltar. He recalled the strange twist of fate and encounter with the Louise girl who had lured him to Canada. He wondered whatever had become of her and if she had finally succeeded in finding the husband of her dreams that she'd been looking for. She should have tried the Unification Church.

The Royal Navy was present throughout most of the town area. Although Sam

Brookes was on board HMS Fearless which as part of the task force was already well on its way to the Falklands other vessels were being re-fitted in the Gibraltar shipyard. At his hotel Edwin overheard the telephone conversation of one of the naval officers. "Don't believe a word of what it says in the newspapers, Mum, and don't you worry about a thing. We know what we are doing."

In keeping with his plan to use the time in Gibraltar to get healthy Edwin began each day by walking a zigzag route up to the top of the Rock. It was a bit of a climb but well worth the effort both in terms of accomplishing it and in being rewarded with the spectacular view of North Africa across the Strait and of Spain's Andalucía on the other side. The frontier was still closed.

An overgrown and neglected walk called Mediterranean Steps lay just over the far side of the Upper Rock which provided a further challenge to the day's fitness exercise. Its worn pathways were originally built by the British military as a means of getting from one of their defence posts to another. With so many stones, rocks and steps to negotiate, which in places were very steep, it took Edwin the best part of two hours to get round the circuit on his first attempt. He gradually speeded that up on subsequent days even though his legs felt like packing up by the time that he got to the end. The combination of native flowers, warm sunshine, a gentle breeze and the odd military remains such as gun emplacements left over from the Second World War created a unique atmosphere. And yet nobody else was ever there on any of the days. He was alone with such fantastic views and a peace and quiet that was only interrupted by the occasional cries of yellow-legged gulls.

Edwin realised that he now saw Gibraltar differently than on his first visit. He loved the place. Sure, it still had its shabby exterior but there were many qualities that seemed good. The local television station was now housed in different premises on the south side of the Rock near BFBS. One afternoon Edwin dropped in for a courtesy visit and a chat with its station manager.

The fortnight in Gibraltar passed by quickly and Edwin was beginning to wish that he wasn't returning to the UK at all – job or no job at Channel Four. Even from a religious perspective Gibraltar was an interesting blend. Within its small area of two and a quarter square miles Christians, Jews, Hindus and Muslims lived alongside each other in perfect harmony. He could quite happily have pioneered a branch of the Unification Church in such a setting.

On his way back into town through the Alameda Gardens Edwin bumped into a lady whom he recognised. And she recognised him. They both stopped in their tracks. She had been one of the staff at the Gibraltar Information Office in London that Edwin had visited some six years ago but she now lived back in Gibraltar with her parents.

They chatted for a while and arranged to meet up for a coffee the following day at the airport cafeteria which was normally a quiet place as there were so few flights. There, throughout the afternoon, Edwin was able to explain about the Unification Church and give an overview of its teaching which she patiently absorbed. She grasped the general gist of everything even if there was some confusion over terminology.

"Oh, I see, yes, the Second Coming," she said, "And so presumably that must be the Reverend Moonie?"

"Well that's not exactly his name," clarified Edwin.

CHAPTER THIRTY-SEVEN

CHANNEL FOUR TELEVISION WAS located in the trendy setting of London's Charlotte Street around which there was no shortage of places to choose from for a slap-up gourmet lunch. However, Edwin also discovered the whereabouts of the Indian YMCA just up the road which did an authentic curry sufficiently hot enough to blow one's brains out at a considerably cheaper price.

As with any start-up situation there was a lot to be done in preparation for the new television channel to go on air in a few months' time. The technical installation was more or less complete and there were plenty of training opportunities to learn how it was all going to work. Edwin recalled that in the days when he had directed transmission in New Zealand he and his colleagues had realized that so much of what they did in the presentation control room would one day be carried out by computer. Evidently that future had now arrived as advances in technology had enabled precisely that for the play out of programmes on Channel Four. However Edwin also learnt that the writing of continuity announcement scripts, which had always been one of his strong points, was instead going to be carried out by the announcers themselves. That didn't leave very much in the way of creativity other than making trailers for the various programmes that were beginning to arrive at the channel.

Viewing sessions of such newly arrived programmes were held several times a week at a small theatre in Soho Square from which it was possible to gain a flavour of the kind of thing that the new channel would be offering. Many productions showed originality. Some were over the top and a good few were clearly boundary-pushers stemming from a liberal interpretation of the channel's mandate for the untried and the untested in television.

"That last one was a bit risqué," commented Edwin to a group of colleagues after they had finished viewing an episode of a drama series that had been peppered throughout with foul language.

"It most certainly was," agreed a young lady recently arrived at Channel Four from Tyne Tees Television, "There'll be complaints when that gets broadcast."

"But if viewers don't like it they can just switch to a different channel," reasoned another.

"That's all well and good but it's a bit late then isn't it – after it's already been delivered into peoples' living rooms," she said.

Edwin realised from the outset that, although the run-up to the new channel's launch would be an interesting experience, the role in the presentation department was then likely to become predictably repetitive. He had already tasted programme-making whereas Channel Four Television didn't make any programmes at all but merely transmitted those supplied by outside production companies. But because the new channel had created new jobs within the industry Edwin had finally been able join the ITV union of the Association of Cinematograph Television and Allied Technicians, normally abbreviated as the ACTT.

The presentation department occupied the middle area of an open-plan office from where it was possible to tune in to everybody else's unrelated conversations even from some considerable distance. As far as Edwin was concerned it might just as well have been located on the forecourt of Euston Railway Station but he supposed that he would get used to such a clamorous working environment.

An influx of presentation editors from the BBC then arrived. They tended to favour a rather old-school style for the channel's identity so as to make it look 'professional' which presumably meant to make it look not that much different from the presentation style of the BBC. There clearly wasn't going to be much in the way of innovation or experimentation for the on-screen look of the new television service as far as they were concerned.

Commissioning Editors occupied offices around the building's perimeter. They were an interestingly diverse bunch and, although well versed in their particular fields, some had no previous broadcasting experience at all. Each of them was responsible for a specific programme genre which included Arts, Drama, Comedy, Music, Sport, News and Current Affairs, Multicultural, Film, Education, Documentaries, History and Religion. It was their job to arrange for independent TV production companies to make programmes for the channel within an agreed budget. It had crossed Edwin's mind that the channel's policy to embrace diversity and cater for minority groups might even lend itself to an explanatory programme about the Unification Movement. For that to happen, however, it might be better first to have a television production company banging on the door with an enthusiastic idea for making such a programme.

For his accommodation needs Edwin was staying in the spare room of the Victoria flat of an American sister who worked as the London correspondent for the recently launched Washington Times newspaper which was owned and operated by the Unification Movement. She was invariably as busy as a bee and forever up against deadlines. Meanwhile Sam Brookes still commuted from Portsmouth dockyard to Southampton where he bought a small terraced house in Lyon Street. At weekends Edwin often took the train down there and every once in a while, if there was nothing much else on the agenda, they would hop aboard the Friday night sailing of the cross channel ferry to Le Havre and spend Saturday in that French town before returning in the evening.

NEWS CAME THROUGH THAT the next Marriage Blessing Ceremony of the Unification Church would take place in New York that summer on Thursday 1st July 1982. Edwin phoned Helga in Germany and they made plans to attend. He went out shopping for a dark blue suit, white shirt and maroon tie as well as having a finger measurement for a gold ring. He also managed to negotiate four days off work which, taken alongside a weekend, would allow him sufficient time to take part in such a significant event. The mass wedding was scheduled to take place at Madison Square Gardens, located just a block away from the New Yorker Hotel. The day before the event a full rehearsal took place for all the engaged couples who had arrived there to be wed in such an unorthodox yet meaningful manner.

On the day itself the spectacle of two thousand and seventy-five couples dressed in identical wedding clothes and making their way along the sidewalk to the venue was a real eye-opener to New York City. Local restaurants took it upon themselves to offer half price meals to any of the couples married that day.

The ceremony was presided over by Reverend Moon and his wife and went without hitch. Holy water was sprinkled over the participants, prayer was offered, marriage vows were made, rings were exchanged and congratulations were given to all of the participants. It was an uplifting occasion and Edwin thought Helga looked positively gorgeous in her wedding dress. Numerous photographs were taken and the event featured prominently in news bulletins throughout the world.

The following morning something known as an indemnity ceremony was held in small groups. Widely open to misinterpretation, it was a tradition in which the newly-wed husbands would whack their wives on the backside with a stick three times and then reverse roles so that they were on the receiving end. It was carried out fully clothed and was not some kind of a sado-masochist exercise but its purpose was to symbolically signal an end to sin and to prepare for a new beginning.

There was still several more months of separation to go before the couples would consummate their marriages. There was a sound spiritual reason behind that although it was pointed out that in the future such separation period would be of a much shorter duration. There was also the fact that Unification Church marriages were not acceptable in law. To obtain marriage certificates each couple would also need to make arrangements to get married legally at a registry office back in their own countries. Edwin and Helga had already decided to do so in Darmstadt the following spring.

Edwin slipped back into the office at Channel Four on Monday morning. No one there knew that he had been in New York let alone what he'd been up to. After a meeting with the Commissioning Editor for Education he sat down in front of a monitor and set about the task of viewing time-coded VHS copies of several newly arrived programmes and jotting down the durations at which extracts could be lifted for making trailers. Such logging was the means by which the various in-points and out-points of scenes from a drama or clips from a documentary were identified as being usable for trailers and the exercise was about as creative as it got.

The new television service went on air at 4:45pm on Tuesday 2nd November 1982 and celebrations took place throughout the Charlotte Street building in the form of one huge office party as each of the evening's programmes was broadcast. However, despite its mixed-bag offering of new independent productions which extended the viewing choice to the British public, The Sun newspaper decided to label it 'Channel Bore,' 'Channel Snore,' and 'The Channel That Nobody Watches.'

For Edwin the prospect of working on endless transmission shifts was likely to become his only 'Channel Bore' and he was already missing hands-on programme production work. It had been fun working on the channel's launch but now that it was up and running it could easily become too monotonous. Nor was he interested in the office politics and empire building that seemed to be occurring as a result of some rift between the presentation department and the technical division. He had friends in both camps.

He had already begun to keep his eyes open for an opportunity in programme making and had even been interviewed for a TV production job based in South Africa. He was also in touch with the World Mission Department in New York regarding any new developments for a proposed TV station. He received a letter back from them saying that unfortunately things were still not at that stage. They also said that if he was contemplating a change of country to work in television broadcasting overseas they would favour it being in a Middle East country if that were at all possible. With that suggestion in mind Edwin then succeeded in landing a job as TV Station Manager of a small cable television station on the Gulf in Saudi Arabia.

Once the contract had been signed he handed in his notice at Channel Four Television and used the remainder of his leave entitlement to spend a few weeks down in Southampton where he helped redecorate Sailor Sam's terraced house.

Shortly before his departure for Saudi Arabia the Unification Church let it be known to all members that Reverend Moon had asked for forgiveness ceremonies to be held throughout the world and that those of them who had made mistakes during their church life were invited to attend one. It was the first time that Edwin had heard of a mechanism within the movement for offloading things of a personal nature and he felt that the opportunity was applicable to him. There had certainly been occasions in which he knew that he had overstepped the mark. Up until that time he had simply carried the burden of such situations around in his head because, apart from an occasional repentant prayer, there hadn't seemed to be anybody obvious to turn to. But he had also realised that it wasn't a healthy situation to be bothered by feelings of guilt or accusing thoughts or to live a life in denial. Therefore such a ceremony, although daunting, was clearly something to be welcomed.

The process entailed making a written confession of whatever it was that one had done and submitting it in confidence to an officiating church elder whilst attending the short ceremony. On arrival at the Chislehurst property where the event was being held Edwin was surprised by the large turnout. He had assumed that there would only be one or two other members present. During an introductory talk about the granting of such grace it was mentioned that some of those attending might be asked to make some token retribution which would be announced a few days later. In Edwin's case that amounted to an additional separation time of four months being applied before consummation of his marriage to Helga. He felt that that was fair enough and he was grateful to have got things off his chest.

CHAPTER THIRTY-EIGHT

EDWIN HAD ORGANISED HIS schedule in such a way that his flight out to Saudi Arabia would include a two week stopover in Frankfurt. That fitted in neatly with the arrangements that he and Helga had made for their civil marriage to take place at the Town Hall in Darmstadt which had involved a bit of a last minute run-around.

"The registry office here in Germany says that it will need to see your birth certificate and your residence registration document and that they both need to be officially translated into German," explained Helga over the phone.

"The birth certificate is easy enough to get translated but the other thing is going to be difficult," replied Edwin. "We don't even have a system of residence registration in England let alone a document to go with it."

"Surely there is some way," she said.

"I guess there must be," replied Edwin. "Let me phone the German Embassy in London in the morning because they must be used to providing information for British people intending to marry Germans in Germany."

"Good idea," she replied.

The inquiry resulted in Edwin having to pay a local solicitor to type up an embossed piece of paper containing a solemn declaration that he had lived at Sailor Sam's Southampton address for the past three months. The translation then had to be done through the German Embassy as the only recognised means.

On payment of a somewhat hefty fee and a wait of several days the document was duly issued with an official stamp and on Edwin's arrival in Germany at least it satisfied the registry office in Darmstadt.

In contrast to the enormity of the Unification Church wedding in New York, it was a short, simple ceremony attended by some of Helga's relatives. It seemed a trifle odd to be getting married all over again but at least they would be issued with a marriage certificate this time round. As there were still some months to go before completion of their separation time they still slept in separate beds and didn't yet go charging off on a honeymoon. Nevertheless they made the most of the occasion by forest walks, a trip into Frankfurt city centre and a couple of good restaurants.

EDWIN'S LUFTHANSA FLIGHT FROM Frankfurt to Dhahran took four hours. On arrival the first thing to hit him was the intense desert heat. However, it wasn't a humid heat such as he had experienced in Hong Kong but a drier kind of heat which he found more tolerable. The plane's passengers walked across the tarmac and into a construction that was more like a hanger than a terminal building. That provided a first glimpse of Saudi men dressed in their white gowns with their red and white chequered cloth headdresses. Edwin's passport was stamped with a multi-coloured entry permit in Arabic writing that took up a full page. On retrieving his suitcase he noticed that the customs area didn't have such a thing as a 'Nothing to Declare' exit. Instead everybody's bags had to be opened and painstakingly gone through with a fine-tooth comb. Such an inspection process took ages and there was already a long queue of people waiting.

When Edwin eventually reached the arrivals hall he was met by a driver. The car journey took a road northwards that ran parallel with the Persian Gulf coastline of Saudi Arabia. There wasn't much to see along the route other than miles of sand, oil pipelines and the occasional small cluster of palm trees. Such monotony was broken only by road signs written both in Arabic and English and a particularly large number of wrecked cars that lay by the roadside perhaps as an indication of local driving standards. Edwin then caught sight of some of the living quarters for those who had come to work in Saudi Arabia. They consisted of row upon row of white mobile huts that resembled a massive caravan site. Further along the highway they approached something that looked like a large factory by the water's edge.

"Is that part of an oil refinery?" asked Edwin.

"No. It's a desalination plant," replied the driver. "It turns seawater into drinking water."

"That's interesting and rather useful out here I would have thought," said Edwin.

The Rezait Motel lay a few miles short of the town of Jubail and was to be Edwin's accommodation throughout the duration of his contract. To get to it the driver turned off the main road and drove along a dusty bumpy track for about half a mile before arriving at a gate house where a security guard crossed off Edwin's name on a list and gave a nod for the vehicle to enter the compound grounds. The driver then showed Edwin to a reception desk.

The motel was plush and Edwin's en-suite studio apartment was tastefully furnished. It came with the convenience of air conditioning, a television, a telephone and a refrigerator. He unpacked his clothing and transferred it to the fitted wardrobes. The man on the reception had told him that breakfast would be served in the restaurant from 5am and that the normal working day commenced at 7am. There would be an induction course for those people who had just arrived in the Kingdom.

ALTHOUGH EDWIN HAD SET his alarm clock he might as well not have bothered. The early morning call to prayer emanating from a minaret in the immediate vicinity of the motel was of a sufficient volume to rouse anybody from their slumbers. He took a shower, got dressed and then made his way across to the restaurant block where he joined a queue of men who were mainly Americans and waiting to be served with breakfast.

It turned out that there were twenty or so other British people who, like Edwin, had newly arrived for the start of their employment in Saudi Arabia. The first morning consisted of orientation. After a brief welcome by an American personnel officer some various dos and don'ts were explained. "One of the worst insults to an Arab is to show him the sole of your shoe," he explained, "So it's important always to keep your feet pointing downwards in the company of the Saudis. We are guests in their country and we have to show respect to them at all times. During the holy month of Ramadan, for example, it is not allowed to eat, drink or smoke in their presence." The list went on. "Your security passes are now being processed and will be issued shortly. The motel's restaurant is open three times a day and your meals there are free of charge. The food is of the highest standard and the menus offer plenty of choice. A shuttle bus service will be laid on at various times of the evening for visiting the nearby township of Al Jubail which was also an hour's walk through the desert if any of you prefer doing that but taxis are also available."

The assembled group were then given a guided tour of the on-site recreational facilities which consisted of a library, a games room for table tennis, billiards and darts and a large outdoor swimming pool. Edwin spoke with the other newcomers from the UK and found out that most of them were there to work in computing. Everybody was then taken by coach into the town of Jubail which was their first real taste of Saudi Arabia.

Edwin teamed up with four other British men and made an exploratory tour of the small town. Its two main streets were both lined with shops, a few restaurants, a massive indoor bazaar and a meat market. Kerbside traders sold pirated copies of music cassette tapes. Saudi men sat together on stools whilst puffing on hubble-bubble pipes from which they smoked a blend of sweet smelling molasses. The bulk of the shops stocked luxury items such as jewellery and electrical goods. Grocery stores had their own Middle East aroma of herbs and spices. There were also a number of outlets selling glasses of hot black tea or freshly squeezed orange juice and serving rolled up kebabs known as schuwamas. It was an all-male environment. The few women in town were dressed in identical black robes and had full veils that entirely covered their faces. There was little means of knowing whether they were young or elderly but apart from anything else it was not permitted to converse with them.

It was a well know fact that alcohol was strictly forbidden in Saudi Arabia. However cans of non-alcoholic beer were readily available and some of the British contingent eagerly stocked up on them by the caseload with which to fill their refrigerators back at the motel.

Later that day Edwin's new boss, the Head of Communications, made himself known to him. Jack Simpson was American, amiable and in his sixties. He had been based in Saudi Arabia for the past twenty years yet still preferred his hamburgers to his kebabs. He had a technical background and was glad that Edwin had arrived to take charge of the new television station. He told Edwin that the rest of the television staff would be from Pakistan and from the Philippines.

The following morning with a newly issued ID card clipped to the left lapel of his light beige jacket Edwin joined three new friends who together formed a car pool for the ten minute ride out along the bumpy track and then on the main road to the Royal Saudi Naval Base where they would be working. On arrival they each went off in search of their respective functional areas with an arrangement to meet again back at the car at eleven thirty for the trip back to the motel's restaurant for a one hour lunch break.

Edwin entered the building of the Communication Department. It was luxuriously decked out in black marble. As he waited in reception he glanced up at a large map of the Middle East on the wall and noticed that Israel didn't exist on it. That geographical area was indicated as being part of Arabia.

Edwin's American boss, Jack Simpson, took him on a tour of the TV station which was brand new and hadn't yet transmitted a single programme. It had a small continuity studio as well as two good sized production studios with control rooms for each. Judging by the state of the art technical facilities it was obvious that no expense had been spared.

But there were potential difficulties. Throughout the Kingdom of Saudi Arabia it was not permitted to go out and about with a still camera let alone a television camera. Most local productions would therefore need to be studio based. Also, although much of the transmission schedule would include imported movies they would all have to be censored. Even if an actor in an American film was to say something like "goddammit" that would have to be edited out straightaway. Scenes of kissing similarly had to be removed. Any references to religion other than respect for Islam would not be tolerated. A small team of dedicated staff would need to go through the footage and chop it down to size even if that might result in the storyline becoming hopelessly confused or, in some cases, completely lost.

Edwin was then shown to his plush office and introduced to the person who was to be his secretary who was a male Filipino.

"Sir, I am very pleased to meet you," said Pablo as they shook hands.

Throughout the remainder of the morning Edwin met the rest of the all-male technical and production staff. As TV Station Manager he was already being referred to by them as "Mr Edwin." A Saudi man then stepped into the office. He shook hands with everybody and touched his heart before picking up the phone and holding a conversation in Arabic. Afterwards he shook hands with everybody once again and departed.

"That's him done for the day," explained Jack Simpson. "He's supposed to be in training here with the communication department but he prefers to leave everything to those of us that have been hired to do the work."

SAUDI ARABIA HAD A rich spiritual atmosphere. The call to prayer emanating from the mosques five times a day enhanced Edwin's own devotional activities rather than acting as any kind of hindrance to them. Although religious literature other than the Koran was banned, Edwin sat down and wrote out the words of various Unification Church songs from memory as well as the Sunday Pledge.

The first six months passed by very quickly. Edwin's staff worked well together as a team. They were helpful and enthusiastic and the television station was soon fully functioning. The day was used for the videotaped recording of local productions and there was then an evening transmission of programmes from 5pm to 10pm. It was easy to immerse oneself in the work because outside of it there wasn't an awful lot else to get up to. Social life was limited to a walk into town through the desert with a group of friends. Sometimes they would opt to go for a spicy hot Mutton Masala curry at one of the Pakistani restaurants which made a change from the routine of dining at the motel.

There was even a Korean restaurant in Jubail to cater for a workforce of Koreans who worked mainly in construction. They were pleasantly surprised when Edwin greeted them with "Anyonghaseyo" or thanked them by saying "Kamsamnida." Although their presence served as a reminder of Edwin's link with the movement, it wasn't appropriate to speak openly about faith matters in Saudi Arabia. Islam was the country's religion and nothing else was permitted. By the same token, however, Edwin was aware that Muslims regarded Jesus as a prophet who was expected to return to earth near their so-called Day of Judgement. For its part the Unification Movement had respect for all major faiths and some of its members even came from a Muslim background. The theological understanding could be taught from a Muslim point of view drawing on the Qur'an and Hadith and including the life of Muhammad and the providential role and history of Islam, thereby providing sensitivity to Muslim spirituality.

EDWIN SOMETIMES FOUND HIMSELF acting in an advisory capacity to some of the other expats at the Rezait Motel. Life in the desert wasn't everybody's cup of tea and some were clearly struggling with the lifestyle which many felt was like a cross between a prison and a holiday camp. In addition to providing a counselling service they would ask his advice on all manner of things.

"Where should I go for my leave next month?" asked an American friend.

"Have you ever been to Europe before?" asked Edwin.

"No, is it worth a visit?"

Edwin sat down and worked out an entire three week itinerary for him.

An English friend from Portsmouth wanted to know whether to buy a house in Petersfield without first viewing it. Edwin helped organise someone in the area to take a look at it on his behalf after which he did actually go ahead and buy it.

An Indian friend who worked as a systems analyst came to Edwin with a different concern. "Whilst I am here slogging it out in Saudi Arabia my wife back in Harrow is frittering away all of my money, the bitch."

Friday was the one and only day off. Most of that was spent in letter writing, relaxing around the motel's swimming pool with a good book or playing games of darts and table tennis. A car parked in the forecourt had left its radio on.

All we hear is Radio ga ga
Radio goo goo
Radio ga ga
All we hear is Radio ga ga
Radio blah blah

Radio what's new?
Radio, someone still loves you!

On such Fridays Edwin and a group of friends would sometimes drive to the beach and immerse themselves in the coolness of the sea. It was about the best place to be in the intense heat. Others would head for one of the large towns such as Damman. But they had to be careful where they parked the car when they got there because public hangings were also held on Fridays and it was compulsory for them to be watched by anyone in the immediate area.

If Edwin had thought that he'd be able to learn much Arabic and absorb something of local culture he was going to be disappointed. Things were segregated and the Saudis tended not to socialise with the expats. In fact he'd previously had more light-hearted banter with Saudi Arabian students in a Bournemouth cafeteria than in their own country.

One exception was somebody called Ahmad Karim who was originally from Bahrain and who invited Edwin to his house. It was his first visit to an Arabic home. The house was divided into two. There was a front door for men and a separate entrance for women. Without his headscarf Ahmad looked considerably older than with it on. He welcomed Edwin into a lounge. There were no chairs but cushions were arranged on the carpeted floor. He banged on the wall and called out something in Arabic to which a reply could be heard by a female Arabic voice. Before long a hatch opened and a tray of glasses of mint tea and some sweet pastries was passed through by his wife who remained completely out of sight throughout Edwin's visit.

Some of the American expats working in Al Jubail were there on 'married status' which enabled them to have their wives with them living in a closely guarded compound of bungalow housing just up the road from the motel. Not that it was much of a lifestyle for them as it was forbidden for women to drive and they were not permitted to venture out alone. By contrast, however, the Europeans, although living well in their first class motel accommodation, had to get by on 'single status' contracts. At the beginning that was no great problem for Edwin because it happened to coincide with his separation time from Helga.

The Filipinos lived in a separate shanty town area of small mobile homes each shared by up to six people and with a canteen that served their particular cuisine. The Pakistanis, despite being Muslim, also lived in similar such camps with a canteen that provided them their daily dose of curry. And as for the Sri Lankans, conditions were even more basic. Few complained about such a tiered arrangement however because everything was relative and people knew that they were earning far more money than they could ever manage to do in the same space of time back in their own countries. Nevertheless it could sometimes feel as though the Saudis had purchased a period of one's life and that they effectively owned the individuals during their stay.

Most expats managed to survive without alcohol for the entire duration of their time there. However there were some who managed to pick up the odd bottle of whisky on the black market whilst others tried fermenting fruit juice with yeast and sugar. A few got hold of a surgical spirit from the hospitals and mixed it with ice cubes and lemonade.

EDWIN HAD BEEN COUNTING the days down to his first annual leave.

With Saudi Arabia's strict ban on alcohol as well as not having set eyes on a female for the past six months it felt quite surreal when a German air hostess wheeled a trolley through the aisle of the Lufthansa plane and stopped to ask Edwin if he would like something to drink.

The first part of his break was spent in Frankfurt with Helga. Apart from holding hands and a brief hug they respected the fact that there was still a little more time to wait before getting any more intimate. But it was pleasant to be together once again. Helga then had to return to Bremen where she was now the Centre Leader. Meanwhile Edwin had arranged to use the remainder of his leave first for a trip down memory lane in Madrid and then for a visit to Istanbul where he would be meeting up with Sam Brookes who's Royal Navy ship would be docking there at that time.

RE-VISITING MADRID PROVED INTERESTING. The airport bus into town passed the petrol station in Ciudad Lineal near to where Edwin had lived as a seventeen-year-old student. He then took the Metro which had been modernised on some lines but still had the familiar antiquated red carriages on others. Alighting at Puerta del Sol he walked up to the Gran Vía. That main shopping area had become far more cosmopolitan than before when it had been distinctly Spanish. The buildings were much the same and Edwin had no problem at all with the geography of the place. He could easily have afforded to stay at any one of the plush Madrid hotels but instead chose to book into a cheap and cheerful hostal on Calle de La Luna which would do for his one week stay.

That afternoon Edwin went to visit the Madrid headquarters of the Unification Church which was on the top floor of an apartment block located near the bullring in the suburb of Ventas. The movement in Spain was numerically small but the members were all very pleasant. The French sister, Yvette, who had previously been in Southampton, was there with her Spanish husband, Manuel, and they spent several hours together exchanging news and views.

When Edwin got back to the city centre later that evening, curiosity got the better of him as to whether any of the old faces might possibly still be around in any of his old haunts. It was shortly after midnight when he decided to make a quick circuit of the local bars.

In Calle de la Concepción the Bar Dénia was still there but he could see through the glass doors that there was no sign of anyone he recognised, not that he really expected there to be. The Cervecería Peña el Águila across the road was bustling but yet again it was with none of the former regulars. Bar Puri had closed down and a new place had opened on the street corner. He even ventured down the notorious street of Calle de la Ballesta in the red light district and turned off into the first side street to the front entrance of what had once been the Bar Pigalle. It was now derelict. Everything was just ghosts from the past, he thought.

However, a small bar situated directly beneath his hostal was still in full swing and when he glanced in there he immediately recognised the two figures of Tommy Dobson and Barry Smith, both playing dice with a leather cup on the bar top just as they had done so many years ago. He went inside and clapped both of them on the shoulder.

"I guess some things will never change," said Edwin with a grin.

"Blimey, is that really you," asked Tommy. "How many years has it been? Twenty?"

"Nearly," replied Edwin.

"You seem to have moved on from your student days." said Barry.

"I certainly hope so," said Edwin, "although it looks as if life has stood still for you two."

"Which indeed it has," replied Tommy, "but what's with the accent?"

"I spent a fair bit of time in New Zealand and every once in a while it manifests," said Edwin.

They chatted together. Barry, whose front teeth could be seen as half rotten, had married a Spanish girl whilst Tommy Dobson was more content with a daily intake of aniseed liquor.

EDWIN REVISITED MANY PARTS of Madrid. Every street corner seemed to bring back a flood of memories from the time that he'd lived there. He went out to the university, sat in Plaza de España and walked in the Retiro Park. He again caught up with former Spanish friend, Antonio, who now ran his own business of collecting unwanted items of furniture for next to nothing, stripping down the woodwork and then re-painting them in bright glossy stylish colours. Such arty looking products were sought after in Madrid and they fetched a good price. He had a small workshop and a showroom in the city centre.

Edwin also thought he might also pay a courtesy visit to the parents of Isolina whom he used to teach English. Her mother answered the door and was overjoyed to see him. He was invited into the apartment and through its long corridor to the lounge which had remained completely unchanged since the days of his previous visits. Her husband rose from his seat and enthusiastically shook Edwin's hand

"Bienvenido Edwin! Sientate," he said indicating a chair.

"Vale, Gracias" said Edwin

"Quieres fumar?" asked the husband.

"No gracias. Es que ahorra no fumo," replied Edwin who had quit smoking when he'd joined the Unification Church.

Coffee was served and a conversation ensued in Edwin's now rather rusty Spanish. The elderly grandmother had passed away.

The last time Edwin had visited the Fernandez family was when he had been on a visit from New Zealand. At that time they had told him that their daughter Isolina was married but that all was not rosy. They now told him with a detectable degree of optimism that she had since divorced and was now single once again and completely free and unattached. It was Edwin's turn to tell them that he was the one who was now married.

THE FOLLOWING MORNING EDWIN took a flight to Istanbul where he had arranged to meet up with Sam who was aboard his Royal Navy ship. By coincidence one of Edwin's previous workshop guests was in the Nigerian Navy and his ship was also going to be in Turkey at that time. Edwin arrived the day before their arrival. He checked in to a centrally located guesthouse opposite the British Embassy and then started exploring the city. Istanbul had been described as a place that looked as though everybody was still living back in the nineteen-fifties which seemed pretty accurate. It also proved easier to get by in his limited German than in English

One of the things about the Unification Church was that because its members were quite literally dotted all over the world, there was always someone that one could call in on no matter which country one visited. Turkey was no exception.

Edwin recalled Safiya as being a Turkish sister who had joined the movement in England. He had seen her again in New York at the time of the joint wedding ceremony. Together with her American husband they lived on the Asian side of the city and worked together as foreign missionaries to Turkey. Edwin took the ferry across the Bosphorus, the stretch of water that forms part of the boundary between Europe and Asia. When he arrived at their apartment he was warmly welcomed. Another foreign missionary was also there and temporarily biding her time in Turkey due to the political upheaval taking place in her mission country of Iran.

Sam's Royal Navy ship docked in Istanbul the following morning as did Bonny's Nigerian Navy ship. It was a happy reunion. The three of them took a sightseeing tour and from the vantage point of a double-decker bus they were able to enjoy panoramic views of the city's points of interest including the famous Blue Mosque and some of its palaces. After visiting the Grand Bazaar and stopping off for some Turkish coffee and pastries, they then took the ferry to visit the foreign missionaries where they had been invited for dinner.

Edwin's flight back to Saudi Arabia was delayed by five hours. That had a knock-on effect of missing the connecting flight from Riyadh to Dhahran which was a nuisance. He arrived back in Jubail one day later than originally anticipated.

IN THE RUN-UP TO Christmas the expats had it spelled out to them that no celebration of the occasion would be tolerated in Saudi Arabia. There was one religion in Saudi Arabia which happened to be Islam and that was it. They certainly didn't want their land infested with any other belief system and there was an outright ban on all religious literature other than the Koran. There was also no visual presence of any other religion, no churches of any description and certainly nothing of any reciprocal match for the large mosque in London's Regent's Park. Saudi Arabia itself was recognised as a Holy Land for Muslims and they intended to keep it that way.

In keeping with that, a notice went out to all employees advising them that, out of respect to the host nation, Christmas was not to be celebrated in any way, shape or form. It was to be nothing other than a normal working day. Furthermore, special Saudi police would be patrolling to make sure that no one stepped out of line in this regard.

And that's how it was. Some of the expats phoned their loved ones back home on Christmas Day. Tales were recounted of how their families had attended nativity services at their local churches and that their children had hung up their pillow cases for Father Christmas. Presents from under the tree had been opened on Christmas morning and everybody had sat down to a lunch of roast turkey and Christmas pudding – and of how they all missed not having Daddy home for Christmas. For those in Al Jubail, it had been the usual routine of getting to work at seven o'clock, a normal working day and a normal menu at the motel's restaurant.

Some of the British joked amongst themselves. "Let's not get too emotional about it," said one. "What is Christmas in England anyway? It's just a meal! When you stop and think about it that's all it is. Perhaps a bit of a piss-up to go with it but realistically it's just a meal! And not only that but they'll all end up with hangovers – which we won't!"

Edwin tucked into his beef pie and chips and finished off his cup of tea.

A Korean American couple from the Unification Church lived in the compound of the Arabian American Oil Company known as Aramco. Edwin had been given their phone number. He gave them a call and they asked if he'd like to come over and visit them the following Friday. Aramco was like an American town that had been transplanted into Saudi Arabia. Once through the security check it was a world of its own and a rather western world at that. The vast residential area included tennis courts, shops and parkland. Men and women were out jogging or riding bicycles. The couple and their young daughter lived in a well-appointed house. Over a Korean meal of bulgogi, chap-chae, kimchee and rice they spoke of the difficulty of doing much to advance the cause of the Unification Church whilst in Saudi Arabia.

The latest buzz of conversation about the movement was that Reverend Moon had been found guilty of tax evasion in the United States and was currently serving time in an open prison. No one really knew how that had come about because the amount of money involved was a mere seven thousand dollars spread over three years which he had claimed was a church fund. But perhaps the most interesting fact of the matter was that the case had caused an outcry amongst many Christian leaders in America and other faith groups who regarded it as religious persecution. They were now coming out in full support of Reverend Moon.

Edwin and his wife Helga were in regular contact with each other by post. She had recently started working as the PR secretary in the German headquarters of the Unification Church in Frankfurt. The time was nearing when their separation time would be over. Edwin booked another flight to Europe for the occasion. He made himself a cup of tea and switched on the radio.

I stay, I pray
See you in Heaven, far away
I stay, I pray
See you in Heaven one day
4 am in the morning
Carried away by a moonlight shadow
I watched your vision forming
Carried away by a moonlight shadow

IN THE TRADITION OF Unification Church marriages there was a special ceremony that would take place in private between husband and wife to mark the beginning of their family life. It was an enjoyable experience that entailed the couple making love on three consecutive nights with the wife taking the dominant position for the first two nights and the husband on the third night. Normal marital sexual relations would then continue thereafter.

After a prayer meeting at the church's Frankfurt headquarters, Edwin and Helga headed off down to a hotel on Spain's Costa Brava for their ceremony which to all intents and purposes was a honeymoon. Perhaps the sensation of the sexual act is heightened if people have abstained from such activity for any length of time. And for Helga, who was still a virgin, it was a completely new experience altogether. Certainly they felt part of each other as they now entered into full union and they could sense a spiritual dimension too. Perhaps the only embarrassing thing was at breakfast when Helga was overheard by other hotel guests asking Edwin if he took sugar in his tea. It was indicative of how little time they'd spent together.

Throughout the days they went for long beach walks together. Although February it was still comparatively mild in Catalonia and certainly a notch up from the frozen conditions of Frankfurt. Most evenings they dined out at one of the resort's numerous restaurants.

The ten days of Edwin's leave passed by all too quickly. After they'd returned to Germany he departed back to the Gulf alone, with just pleasant memories. He wished that Helga could have been with him but there was no escaping the fact that his contract was on 'single-status.'

ONE OF EDWIN'S TECHNICIANS at the TV station was a Filipino called Ernesto who openly expressed his views on faith issues to Edwin as long as nobody else was in earshot. In a similarly hushed up way Edwin had explained some of the Unification Church's teaching to him and he had became so intrigued that arrangements were made for him to go to England where Sailor Sam put him up in Southampton and accompanied him on a study course. On returning to Saudi Arabia he said that as soon as he returned home to the Philippines he would make a point of contacting the Unification Movement in Manila.

A reminder not to engage in religious debate in Saudi Arabia came about one morning when Edwin happened to have a copy of the UK broadcasting industry's magazine 'Broadcast' on his desk. It had been left open on the appointments page. A somewhat oversized Pakistani man who worked in the administration department sauntered in and a particular job advertisement caught his eye. It was for a cameraperson at London Weekend Television. The heading said 'Wanted – Cameraman/woman'

"How can this be?" he objected. "How could there ever be any such thing as a camerawoman?"

"Oh, it's quite common back in my country," replied Edwin. "We don't have discrimination in the workplace. Men and women have equal rights."

"That is something that is completely wrong," he retorted.

"Well, it works quite well in Britain and even our Prime Minister happens to be a woman," replied Edwin.

"That shows how wrong Britain is," he continued.

"Why's that?" Edwin asked.

"Because it goes against what it says in the Koran," was the reply.

"Oh, does it really?" queried Edwin somewhat indifferently.

The man turned on his heel and stomped out of the office.

Later that week, when taking an after-dinner stroll along some of the dusty tracks near the motel Edwin was passing a mosque at a time when men were emerging from it. One them was the same Pakistani man who had taken offense at the advertisement in Edwin's magazine. The sight of Edwin was something akin to a red rag before a bull and he stepped forward and began shouting in Urdu. That in turn started three or four of the other men shouting too.

It was a potentially dangerous situation to be in. Even though nothing in the least bit offensive had been said by Edwin the fact that there were people shouting loudly at him was not the best set of circumstances in a country such as Saudi Arabia. Edwin remained completely calm. Fortunately that seemed to have a calming effect on the others who suddenly thought that perhaps for their own sakes it might be wise to stop their shouting.

AS A NEWLY MARRIED couple the prospect of starting a family could not easily be achieved if the husband was out in the Saudi Arabian desert and the wife stuck in Frankfurt. Edwin's employers wanted him to renew his contract and were offering him a substantial salary increase as an incentive. However the only incentive that Edwin wanted was 'married status' to enable Helga to be able to join him but it looked increasingly doubtful that he would succeed in negotiating that.

He then received an unexpected telephone call from an English newsreader who worked at Saudi Television's second national channel which was based in Riyadh. Edwin knew the man's screen appearance having watched the channel's news bulletins on many occasions. Whenever there had been a news item about someone being punished for a crime the newsreader had been instructed to end the piece with such words as "And let that be a lesson to everyone in Kingdom to uphold and respect Sharia law." The national broadcaster was controlled by the country's Ministry of Culture and Information.

"We have heard about your work in Jubail," said the newsreader on the phone, "and we would like to meet you with an eye to offering you a position here with the TV Station in Riyadh."

"It sounds like an interesting opportunity," replied Edwin, "although it would need to be on 'married status' to enable my wife to join me."

The stipulation didn't meet with any objection.

"If you are able to come and visit us here in Riyadh next Tuesday at 2pm we shall see what can be arranged," he said.

"OK" replied Edwin, "Let me first book a flight from Dhahran and then I'll get back to you to confirm my arrival time."

Under Saudi law expats can't switch jobs easily because there is first the formality of having to obtain so-called release papers from their current employer. In Edwin's case, that opportunity wouldn't come about until the end of his contract in April, provided that he didn't renew it in the meantime. So he still had a bit of time for negotiation up his sleeve.

The Riyadh buildings of the Broadcasting Services of the Kingdom of Saudi Arabia made Edwin's TV station in the East Province seem like a very small operation indeed. On his arrival, however, he was told that the newsreader had unexpectedly been called elsewhere and so it was a different person who gave Edwin a tour of the television complex. It was one of the few institutions in Saudi Arabia where females were also permitted to work and he noticed several Saudi women employees on the premises which made a welcome change from the all-male environment of just about everywhere else. He sat in on the production of a Saudi press review programme that was being recorded. Afterwards during a chat with the show's producer they joked about how the format used for such a programme was pretty much identical the world over regardless of whatever language it was broadcast in.

Although Edwin would have quite happily fitted into such an environment the main object of the exercise, as far as he was concerned, was to ensure that whatever could be negotiated would enable Helga to be able to accompany him. Later that afternoon Edwin was shown into a boardroom where he was introduced to three Saudi Executives. One of them explained that they would like Edwin to join the production staff of Saudi Television. However, he mentioned a salary that was approximately half of what Edwin currently earned in Jubail.

Not only that, but there was no accommodation being provided with the job.

Edwin had been advised that it was never a good idea to try and bargain direct with the Saudis other than the ones in street markets and that to do so could be interpreted as an insult. And yet, here he was in a face-to-face situation with three high ranking Saudi executives trying to secure an acceptable deal. He managed to slip details of his current remuneration package into the conversation but it seemed to fall on deaf ears. However, when he asked about the possibility of his wife being permitted to accompany him in Riyadh that wasn't ruled out and it was suggested that maybe she could teach German in one of the local schools.

It was left to Edwin to consider the offer which he was told would be sent to him in writing as soon as his current employer provided his release papers. On his flight back to Jubail, however, he could see that based on what had been offered the position in Riyadh would not be particularly sustainable.

There seemed to be three options facing him. He could renew his contract in Jubail and remain there in his current job as TV Station Manager but still on 'single status' which meant that he and Helga would remain living in different countries. Clearly that was a hopeless situation. Alternatively he could accept the job in Riyadh and try to find some way of making it work but no matter which way he calculated things that would be problematic. Or he could simply pull out of Saudi Arabia altogether and seek pastures new. He had heard on the news that during that same month of February 1985 Gibraltar's border with Spain had now been fully re-opened. There might even be new opportunities there for all he knew.

In keeping with his relationship with the World Mission Department in New York, Edwin sent them a brief update.

As the day for Edwin's departure from the Jubail TV station drew closer few members of his staff could believe that he was really going to leave them. In fact he could scarcely believe it himself. He was pulling out of what was an excellent job. However, everybody could understand his reasoning. He was newly married. He had a young wife and they hadn't yet had the chance to set up home together.

CHAPTER THIRTY-NINE

EDWIN FIRST SPENT A couple of days with Helga in Frankfurt. However, because his contract stated that the final flight back from Saudi Arabia could be to the employee's nearest UK airport, he had deliberately chosen Southampton Airport even though it meant being routed via Paris. A taxi then brought him back to the small terraced house in Lyon Street where he let himself in through the front door. Sam Brookes was still at work in the Portsmouth dockyard but would be back that evening.

Helga would be arriving the following month but it was still by no means clear if she and Edwin would then be going to Riyadh. That hung in the balance. Although Edwin had been given a glowing reference by the Head of Communications, Jack Simpson, in Jubail and had obtained the sought-after release papers and letter of no objection to him taking further employment in Saudi Arabia, the TV station in Riyadh had told him that things would now proceed through the Royal Saudi Embassy in London. The only problem with that arrangement was that nobody there seemed to know anything about it.

If, for whatever reason, the position in Saudi Arabia on married status was not going to materialise Edwin had a contingency plan of finding some way for them to live in Gibraltar instead. Ideally he'd like to have everything sorted out before Helga's arrival rather than vague possibilities that might or might not be realistic. With that in mind he thought that a quick fact-finding trip to Gibraltar to see what the situation was like down there now that its frontier with Spain had opened might be a worthwhile idea.

Edwin felt decidedly peckish and not having cooked anything at all throughout his time in Saudi Arabia he found the effort of making a cheese omelette to be thoroughly unfamiliar. And then there was the additional task of washing up. He realised that he had been thoroughly spoiled by the motel's restaurant meals served three times a day.

Shortly after six o'clock Sailor Sam arrived back home.

"Hallo there! Welcome back to Blighty," he said.

"Thank you," replied Edwin, "It's good to see you again Sam."

Over a pot of tea Edwin outlined the slim possibility of making a return to Saudi Arabia to work in Riyadh and also mentioned making a brief trip to Gibraltar in the meantime.

"Well, I've got the remainder of the week off and I wouldn't mind coming down to Gib with you for a few days," said Sam.

"That'd be great," replied Edwin. "Let's see what we can arrange first thing in the morning."

Two days later Edwin and Sam had checked in at the Caletta Palace Hotel on the opposite side of the Rock from the town area. Having offloaded their bags they then retraced their steps back to Gibraltar Airport and continued further to the frontier with Spain. After a passport control and customs check they stepped into the adjacent Spanish town of La Linea conscious of the fact that until recently such access had been denied to people on both sides of the border throughout its thirteen years of closure.

The first impression of the neighbouring community was of a poverty-stricken run-down looking town. The fact that the weather was overcast made it look even worse than it actually was. Blocks of social housing gave way to backstreets of single story terraced houses with crumbling walls and weeds growing between the terracotta tiles of their roofs. A long stretch of concrete promenade was cracked in many places. It ran alongside numerous colourfully painted fishing boats set out on a stretch of sandy beach and a distant cluster of buildings turned out to be fish restaurants. Edwin and Sam stopped off at one of them for a remarkably cheap lunch of seafood soup and grilled hake.

Returning to Gibraltar they went to the shopping area of Main Street which Edwin noted was far more crowded than on either of his previous visits. Hoards of people had come across the border for the day to take advantage of goods that were either cheaper or less obtainable than in Spain. Spaniards stocked up with sugar, butter, cheese and cigarettes by the bag load whilst British expats who lived on the Costa del Sol seemed more interested in Marks and Spencer clothing, Cameras, Radios, Colman's mustard, Clarks shoes, English books, and Patak's Curry Paste. The shops were doing a roaring trade.

The following morning Edwin and Sam sat in the hotel dining room for breakfast.

"What do you reckon we should get up to today?" asked Sam, "I expect that you'll first want to check out the Gibraltar television station in case they have a job for you."

"I'm not holding my breath on that," replied Edwin. "Past experience has shown that the first requirement to work there is either to be a Gibraltarian or at least be married to one."

"But you've got tons of experience and have just this minute returned from managing a TV Station in Saudi Arabia," he said.

"Such things don't count for much in this place," replied Edwin. "Sure, I don't mind putting in an appearance at the Gibraltar Broadcasting Corporation but I can almost guarantee that it won't lead to my getting a job there."

"I'd have thought they would have welcomed you with open arms" he said.

"Yes but you've got to understand that because Gibraltar is such a small place the locals wish to run their media themselves rather than having outsiders coming in," said Edwin.

"But what other kind of work could you possibly do in such a small place?" asked Sam.

"There's probably some way of earning a living out here. There's certainly renewed optimism now that the frontier is open and there must be a media related opportunity somewhere," replied Edwin.

Despite his earlier reservations Edwin's first visit that morning was to the local television station. He was shown into a small office where he explained his availability to a senior member of staff. It was a cordial meeting and the man was clearly impressed by Edwin's background and experience. He jotted down several notes and assured him that this application would be discussed with the powers that be and that they would get back to him as soon as possible.

A few days later Edwin phoned the television station from his hotel room to see if there had been any further developments but drew a blank. "It's still being discussed – I'll let you know as soon as I hear anything," said the man.

Edwin and Sam returned to Southampton the following week. Shortly afterwards Helga arrived in England with bulging suitcases that weighed a ton. They grabbed a coffee at the railway station cafeteria and somebody put a coin in the jukebox.

I just called to say I love you
I just called to say how much I care
I just called to say I love you
And I mean it from the bottom of my heart

In the weeks that followed a considerable amount of time was spent in making phone calls both to the Royal Saudi Embassy in London and to the Gibraltar Broadcasting Corporation. Neither place was coming up with anything promising. The man at the embassy was forever waiting for a response from Riyadh whilst the person that Edwin had met at the Gibraltar TV station could only say that the matter had been passed to the people upstairs, whoever they were, and that they hadn't yet got back to him. In the meantime Edwin and Helga had little choice other than to wait.

It crossed Edwin's mind that it might not be a bad idea to take Helga down to Gibraltar for a few days so that at least she could get a flavour of the place at first hand. If they were there on the spot he could even pay a further visit to the Gibraltar Broadcasting Corporation now that he'd set the ball rolling there as well as checking out any alternative opportunities.

THE NATIONAL EXPRESS COACH from Southampton to Gatwick Airport departed in the middle of the night and arrived just in time to check-in for their early morning flight. On arrival in Gibraltar they crossed the frontier into Spain. Edwin wanted to try staying somewhere in La Linea this time. In brilliant sunshine Helga sat on a stone bench in the central square with a view of the Rock of Gibraltar in the background whilst Edwin scouted around for some suitable accommodation. He returned some twenty minutes later having booked a room at a guesthouse called the Hostal Sevilla which was a short walk along one of the shopping streets and adjacent to a church square. As with many places in La Linea it was a slightly run-down building although an inner patio of ornamental tiles, plants and a small fountain gave it an air of Spanish authenticity and the landlady was a charming person.

After a quick freshen up they took their passports with them to enable them to get back across the frontier into Gibraltar. Helga then got her first look at the small British colony beginning with the road that cut across the airport's runway as they made their way to the town centre.

"The shops all looked the same from one end to the other," she commented after walking the length of Main Street, "It's all electrical goods, cameras, cigarettes, perfume and bottles of whisky."

"The essentials of life," said Edwin as they approached the entrance to the cable car, "but now that we're down this end do you fancy being uplifted?"

Helga was impressed with the spectacular views from the top of the Rock. Across the Strait the Reef Mountains of Morocco were plainly visible. Together with the Rock of Gibraltar they formed the so-called Pillars of Hercules. Ancient mariners believed that if they were to sail through them they would have fallen off the edge of the world.

After their whirlwind look at Gibraltar, Edwin and Helga returned across the border to La Linea where a tiny restaurant run by three very large Spanish ladies offered a very economical three course lunch. Afterwards, when stepping back outside in the sun-drenched street Helga wasn't feeling quite so bright.

"The food in there was really good and whether its tiredness or the heat I don't know but I'm completely washed out," she said.

"Could be a combination of both," replied Edwin. "Why don't we head back to the hostal? You can take a nap like the Spaniards do at this time of day whilst I sit in that patio downstairs and see if I can do any more of the Times crossword puzzle that I started during the flight."

The arrangement seemed liked a good one. When it got to six o'clock, Edwin went back up to the room and was pleased to find Helga very much recovered. She had been able to relax even though she hadn't managed to sleep.

"I don't know if you realise it," she said "but although this place is quaint it's ever so noisy. It's too hot to close the windows and we are right above a taxi rank with an extra loud outdoor telephone bell that keeps ringing. Also, that church clock opposite not only chimes every quarter of an hour but for some reason it repeats itself and does its chimes twice over."

"It's all to do with the beauty of Spain," replied Edwin, "Everything is designed to be as noisy as possible."

"Well fine but have you studied the bed yet?" she asked, "It sinks right down into the middle."

"Maybe it's specially designed to keep us together?" he suggested, "Just out of interest are there any further complaints about this salubrious establishment?"

"Just the small factor of the mosquitoes but, other than that, none at all," she smiled.

"And might this be a good time for us to test out the bed?" he asked.

"As long as we don't both break it," she chuckled.

WHEN THEY AWOKE FROM their late siesta it was already getting dark outside. La Linea was beginning to come to life and everybody was out and about in the streets. Later that evening Edwin and Helga went out too and spent an hour or so exploring the town and looking around its selection of shops. Over dinner at a cheap and cheerful restaurant called La Esteponera they attempted to work out what they would do for the remainder of their stay.

Edwin would again visit the Gibraltar Broadcasting Corporation first thing in the morning. Helga could accompany him there and wait in the nearby snack bar called The Matchbox until he returned. Sunday was bound to be an unproductive day as offices were closed so they could perhaps use that time to make a day trip by ferry to the Spanish enclave of Ceuta on Morocco's coastline. Then, for the remainder of their stay they could also look around to see if there might be other possibilities for living and working in Gibraltar.

It turned out to be a night of continuously interrupted sleep caused by a combination of the taxi telephone that rang repeatedly just beneath their window, the church clock that really did repeat its chimes in case anybody had missed them the first time, as well as the heat and the mosquito attacks.

Crossing back into Gibraltar the following morning, they took a tiny antiquated bus to South Barrack Road where the Gibraltar Broadcasting Corporation was located. When they got there Helga again said that she felt unwell.

"I don't know whether it's the heat that is causing it," she said. "Perhaps it's just the change of food but I was actually sick in the bathroom this morning," she said.

As soon she had said such words a realisation hit both of them simultaneously.

"Do you think I could be pregnant?" she asked.

"Well, I'm no doctor but I suppose it could be morning sickness associated with that," he replied.

"How can we find out?" she asked.

"Well, the best thing would be to go for a check-up, maybe not here but as soon as we get back to England," he said.

Unsurprisingly the visit to the Gibraltar television station revealed no advance on any possible job there. The person with whom Edwin had been dealing was apologetic about the delay in getting a decision but said it was out of his hands. He felt sure that they could use someone with Edwin's professional experience but said that he would have to wait a little longer.

"It's the way they do things here, I'm afraid, "he said apologetically, "It's very difficult to get a straight yes or no answer out of anyone."

"Would there be any chance of knowing one way or the other by this time next week?" asked Edwin.

"I'd be more inclined to give it a fortnight," the man replied.

"I'll be back in the UK by then but I can phone you again from there," said Edwin. He sensed that nothing would ever become of it.

AT THE HOSTAL SEVILLA on Sunday morning Edwin and Helga got up shortly before five o'clock to hold the traditional early morning prayer service to mark the start of the new week. Shortly afterwards an almighty explosion shook the whole town of La Linea. People rushed outside into the streets to try and find out what on earth had happened. Emergency services vehicles then began to sound their sirens and to speed through the town.

Edwin and Helga took a bus into the neighbouring town of Algeciras and then a ferry for their day trip to the Spanish enclave of Ceuta. It was an enjoyable outing to North Africa even if the place itself was much like any other Spanish town.

On their return journey as the bus passed alongside the oil refinery near La Linea a fellow passenger explained the cause of that morning's explosion. Apparently a Japanese ship docked there had been unloading highly flammable liquid. It had blown up and caused a Spanish tanker to catch fire and sink in a slick of burning oil whilst the Japanese ship had broken in half, leaving its burning bow and stern visible above the waterline. In all thirty-three people had died at the refinery and another thirty-six were injured. It was a sad day for Spain.

Throughout the remainder of their stay Edwin and Helga took time to look at the property situation in Gibraltar. A few flats were for sale on short leaseholds. An over-enthusiastic Gibraltarian estate agent gave them a viewing of three such properties. The first was an attic apartment in the side street of Bell Lane and the other a poky ground floor flat on George Street. A better possibility was a first floor flat in College Lane.

Mr Smoothy the estate agent was on form with his helpful suggestions, "You could rip down this wall, put in a new bathroom over here and create a small balcony over there and then transfer the kitchen across to that end of the property." From what he was saying one might as well demolish the entire flat and build a new one in its place.

But the whole thing was an academic exercise for the time being because Edwin didn't have a job lined up in Gibraltar and there was still the Saudi possibility that might yet materialise.

THE DAY AFTER THEY got back to Southampton Helga registered with a local doctor and made an appointment for a pregnancy test. The result was positive. Both she and Edwin were overjoyed but at the same time it meant that they would now need to include that in the equation regarding their future plans.

They stayed on in Southampton for several weeks during which time they found a new guest whom they accompanied to a Unification Church weekend workshop on the Wiltshire Farm. They also went for picnics in the New Forest, a trip to the Isle of Wight and to a theatrical performance of HMS Pinafore. Edwin continued to phone the Royal Saudi Embassy on an almost daily basis but it was the same old story. They weren't any further forward with the job in Riyadh.

In the meantime Sam had decided to leave the Royal Navy and join the Unification Church on a full-time basis. Together with his resignation letter he enclosed a large lollypop purchased from a local sweet shop. It had the words 'Hallo Sailor' written across it in brightly coloured lettering. He also put his Lyon Street house on the market and various potential buyers started coming round to view it. He had offered to sell it to Edwin and Helga. However, because they didn't see their future as being in England they declined his kind offer. Instead they went to the Polygon Hotel and over a pot of coffee tried to work out their next move.

I walk into an empty room
And suddenly my heart goes boom
It's an orchestra of angels
And they're playing with my heart
Must be talking to an angel. Must be talking to an angel.
Must be talking to an angel

"I don't mind trying Gibraltar a few more times especially because we already have the go ahead from the World Mission Department to be based out there but it might take a bit of time to get some appropriate work lined up." said Edwin.

"Yes but what if Sam sells the house before then as now looks increasingly likely?" she asked.

"In that case maybe we could go to Germany and bide out time there for a while," he suggested.

"Germany?" she said, "Well, yes, I suppose we could go there for the baby's birth but if we are going to do that we should get over there soon."

Edwin nodded, "The sooner the better as far as I'm concerned."

Within the next couple of weeks, Sailor Sam had sold his house and a completion date had been arranged.

The three of them went out to a Southampton restaurant called Oliver's for a farewell meal together.

CHAPTER FORTY

A BROWSE THROUGH THE inner pages of the Frankfurter Rundschau led to Edwin and Helga finding a place to live in the Frankfurt suburb of Heusenstamm. The small one-bedroom apartment in a block that had once been a hotel would serve its purpose well. It was cosy and within easy commuting distance to the centre of Frankfurt. They went to Sunday Services at the German headquarters of the Unification Church and began to meet up with a circle of friends from that community on a regular basis including an Austrian/English couple called Manfred and Diana Lerche. Manfred was an electronics engineer by trade but he also had some experience in videotape editing.

Edwin attended classes at the Volkshochschule in order to get some grasp of the German language and he and Helga bought a baby bed, a pram and a second-hand car. As the weeks passed by the weather turned to winter which brought a layer of thick snow. Germany was used to such occurrences and geared up for it in the form of double glazing, central heating and snow ploughs. Christmas was spent with Helga's parents in Darmstadt. On New Year's Day, which was also one of the Holy Days of the Unification Church known as God's Day, they stayed at home and were joined by another couple from the movement who were similarly awaiting the birth of their first child.

Edwin had been flitting through the pages of a slim booklet entitled The Gibraltar Annual that had been purchased during their last visit to the Rock. In doing so he came across a full page advertisement for an advertising agency in Gibraltar called Impact and decided to drop them a line. In his letter he let it be known that he had already been making enquiries about some sort of a job with the Gibraltar Broadcasting Corporation although not getting much response and that he was curious as to whether his relative skills and experience might be of interest to their company instead.

The following morning Helga began to experience contractions. They took a taxi to the hospital and after a brief inspection at the maternity ward she was advised to go outside and walk around the town for a few hours. It was snowing again as they stopped off at an Imbiss for a German Bratwurst. They returned to the hospital in the evening and their baby son was born shortly after midnight. Absolutely delighted by his arrival into the world they named him Leon which seemed to work in both languages and realised that their lives would never be the same again. Mother and son remained in the maternity ward for several days whilst Edwin put in regular appearances during visiting hours.

On the day that Helga and the baby returned home a letter arrived from Gibraltar. It was a remarkably positive reply from the advertising agency that Edwin had written to. Its Managing Director said that he was well aware of the mentality of the Gibraltar Broadcasting Corporation and that its sluggishness came as no great surprise to him. He went on to say that he was interested in Edwin's background and experience. The Impact advertising agency was planning to branch into TV production. Would Edwin like to phone him to arrange a time for coming out to Gibraltar to talk the matter through?

A meeting was fixed for the following week. Edwin flew from Frankfurt to Malaga followed by a coach journey down the length of the Costa del Sol to La Linea. There he crossed the now familiar frontier into Gibraltar and took a taxi up to The Rock Hotel where the company had booked him in for the duration of his stay.

The Impact advertising agency was based on the second floor of Don House, which was a building in Main Street that had a small arcade of shops running through its middle. Its Gibraltarian receptionist turned out to be the wife of the Managing Director, Aiden Macdonald.

It wasn't a formal interview at all. Instead it was more of a laid back meeting of the "Hi, hello, great to see you! – thanks for dropping in on us, have a mug of tea" – kind of encounter. There was an instant rapport between Edwin and Aiden. A show reel of low-budget TV commercials that the company had already made for clients in Gibraltar and in Spain was played followed by an arty compilation of shots of staff members, the females of whom were on the beach clad in bikinis, which had been edited to a pop song.

I come home in the morning light
My mother says when you gonna get your life right
Oh mother dear we're not the fortunate ones
And girls they want to have fun
Oh girls they want to have fun

Aiden expressed his own frustration in the various dealings that he'd had with the Gibraltar Broadcasting Corporation for whom he had little regard. He came across as being a very reasonable and considerate person.

"I first arrived in Gibraltar on a yacht with very little money to my name," he explained. "Having worked as a graphic artist in London, I recognised the potential of setting up an advertising agency in Gibraltar and two printers back in the UK have helped finance the initiative in return for putting work their way."

The re-opening of the frontier with Spain after so many years of closure had created a demand for advertising of a high quality. That applied both to the design side of the business as well as to the production of local TV commercials and promotional material. They went on to speak about the possibility of putting together a television documentary programme about aspects of Gibraltar.

Aiden then told Edwin that he would be pleased to make him a formal offer of a job as a TV Producer/Director with a reasonable enough salary to go with it. His secretary typed up a letter of appointment which Aiden then signed and handed to him. Edwin could commence work as soon as possible although it was understood that he would first need time to sort out accommodation and bring Helga and the baby down from Germany. Just about everyone else who worked for the company was from the UK and they all lived across the border in Spain where apartments were more plentiful and considerably cheaper. However Edwin wanted to be based in Gibraltar itself.

Very content with finally getting his foothold in Gibraltar, Edwin spent the remaining two days of his visit in checking out what accommodation available – or at least checking out what accommodation wasn't available. There was a chronic housing shortage. The high demand and low supply meant that rents were similar to London prices. The main estate agency in town was run by a genteel Jewish man to whom Edwin had first written to from Saudi Arabia the previous year.

"I'm really sorry. I have absolutely nothing on my books for rent at the moment," he explained. "We don't keep a waiting list because when flats do become available they do so all of a sudden and so it works easier if you keep phoning in every day."

It was a similar story at Gibraltar's other two estate agents. Rather than the familiar "Don't call us. We'll call you," the local policy seemed to be one of "Call us – We won't be calling you."

There were some flats for sale in Gibraltar. Although Edwin had sufficient funds for a hefty deposit equal to three quarters of the purchase price of one of them, research revealed that none of the banks would give him a small mortgage. He was told that it was only possible to get a mortgage for a Gibraltar property if one had been a resident in Gibraltar for a minimum of three years. Even the estate agents were unaware of that.

Edwin returned to Germany where Helga was delighted with his success in securing work in Gibraltar. In the short space of a few days the baby seemed to have grown. Edwin held him in his arms.

They began to phone all three estate agents in Gibraltar each and every weekday morning for an entire fortnight but strange though it seemed there were no flats available for rent. However it was always emphasised that something would be bound to become available sooner or later and that they should keep on phoning in.

"It's the 'or later' bit that I'm worried about," said Edwin as he put the phone down for the third time.

"You'd think that there'd be at least something to rent somewhere in Gibraltar," said Helga.

"Yes, it's getting a bit ridiculous," he said, "I suppose we could start off by staying at one of the hotels down there. In that way at least I could be going in to work each day."

"Gibraltar hotels aren't exactly cheap," she said.

"True and I'm not suggesting we return to that place in La Linea with the taxi rank and church bell to contend with – not to mention the mosquitoes. However, another idea would be to stay temporarily a little further up the Spanish coastline yet within striking distance of Gibraltar, perhaps somewhere such as Marbella."

They decided to take the plunge. It felt sad dismantling the baby bed and putting it into storage. However they would be able to take the pram with them on the flight. They gave away their car to their friends, Manfred and Diana, from the Unification Church.

Arrangements were made to stay temporarily at a complex of self-catering apartments called El Coronado located halfway between Fuengirola and Marbella. On arrival it was such beautiful weather and the beach was just a five minute walk that it felt as if they were on holiday. Everybody else staying in the apartment block really was on holiday. Throughout the first week Edwin continued to phone the three Gibraltar estate agents each morning. He let it be known that he was staying nearby and would be able to move into Gibraltar at the drop of a hat as soon as anything was available. Each time, however, it came to nothing.

"Why don't you ask your new company if they know of somewhere in Gibraltar?" suggested Helga.

"Well, I doubt if they'd know," he said, "They all live in Spain and commute in and out of Gibraltar each day in their cars. Besides which I haven't yet let the boss know that I'm a non-driver. Sure, we could live in the adjacent town of La Linea but, as you know; it's kind of run-down and grotty there and not the safest of places. But apart from anything else, from a spiritual point of view its better for us to be based in Gibraltar itself."

"I agree," she replied, "but how on earth can we find somewhere to live there when everybody keeps saying that there's absolutely nothing available?"

"I don't know if it will change the situation in any way but I think that I'd better go into Gibraltar on my own tomorrow and run around the three estate agents, scan the Gibraltar Chronicle and simply ask around," he said, "You and baby Leon can remain here and I'll see what I can come up with."

Two slow bus journeys that stopped everywhere along the route got Edwin to the border town of La Linea. He walked the short distance to the frontier and arrived in Gibraltar in mid-morning accompanied by a massive crowd of day-trippers who had got there at the same time. Grabbing a copy of the Gibraltar Chronicle he was disappointed to see that that day's edition contained no advertisements at all for any rented accommodation. He progressed up the length of Main Street amidst the crowds of shoppers taking advantage of duty-free goods on offer. When he reached the offices of Joshua Cohen Estate Agents he was told that by a stroke of good fortune they had just been informed of a fully furnished two-bedroom apartment on Main Street that would be available from the following day. The rent was a bit higher than Edwin might have wished but nevertheless it was something that was available.

"Unfortunately I can't show you inside it today," said the estate agent. "The owner is away and I won't have the keys until first thing tomorrow morning. But I can tell you that it's quite a nice flat. It is centrally located near the Piazza and on the second floor above Chaplin's Restaurant. It has two bedrooms, one big and one small, a large lounge-cum-dining area, a kitchen and a bathroom."

Being the only available flat in Gibraltar meant that it was very much a 'take it or leave it' situation. All the indications were that it would be best to agree to take it there and then – even unseen.

"Just pay four weeks rent in advance and the place is yours," said the agent.

"Can I pay with a British cheque?" asked Edwin.

"Sure," he replied.

Edwin then returned to Marbella content in the knowledge that they would move into the Gibraltar flat the following day which was a Friday. He also phoned the Impact advertising agency to let them know that he would be starting work in his new job with them on Monday.

THEY FIRST STEPPED FOOT in to their new home on Friday afternoon. Manipulating the pram up two flights of narrow stairway had been slightly problematic but fortunately it was one that could be taken apart which enabled Edwin to accomplish the task in two stages whilst Helga held the baby. The accommodation itself was functional and would serve its purpose. There was tiled flooring throughout and the windows in the lounge and both bedrooms overlooked the bustling Main Street down below. The furniture was pretty basic although the kitchen area seemed to be reasonably well equipped.

After a quick look around Helga put the baby in a sling and they went back out again to pay a visit to the nearby Lipton's store to stock up on food supplies that would see them through the weekend.

It was realised from the outset that because Gibraltar was such a small close-knit community in which everybody knew each other, they would need to be selective over whom they spoke to concerning the Unification Church. It was one of the unfortunate paradoxes of the minority faith group that it was still widely regarded as being some sort of a weird cult and there was no easy means of telling how people would react to its mere mention. Although both Edwin and Helga could easily counter any of the popular misconceptions and enjoyed sharing its theological understanding with as many people as possible to do so too openly or too soon could run the risk of backfiring. It seemed wise for Edwin first to establish himself in Gibraltar on a professional level and to identify any potential opportunities for discussion on faith matters along the way.

The Impact advertising agency had recently taken delivery of a Betacam television camera and a related videotape editing suite which had been installed in one of the a back rooms of the building that had been designated for its TV production activities. Since Edwin's previous visit the builders had been in to knock a hole in the wall through to some adjacent offices which now accommodated the graphic design team. The company was expanding in more ways than one.

An office next to the edit suite had been assigned to Edwin. The TV production unit was already being referred to as 'Impact Productions' so as to distinguish it from the graphic design side of the business. It had taken on a further two full-time staff members comprising a cameraman and a sound operator as well as a part-time assistant. Although it lacked a hands-on videotape editor the managing director, Aiden, said that he would be able to step in and push the right buttons whenever he wasn't tied up with other matters. There was also secretarial back-up, the availability of in-house graphics and a growing client base of local companies that had been notified of the advertising agency's new TV production capability.

Aiden mentioned to Edwin that unfortunately the cameraman and the sound operator didn't always see eye to eye and that he might sometimes have the additional task of trying to bring some sense of unity into their working relationship. James the cameraman was a young English former public school boy who was highly skilled and enthusiastic at camerawork but who tended to be arrogant with it. That contrasted with Albert the sound operator who was a down-to-earth Gibraltarian with a Latin temperament. Edwin took both of them to a local coffee shop.

Every breath you take
Every move you make
Every bond you break
Every step you take
I'll be watching you

Although the main source of income was from the production of TV commercials Aiden was particularly keen for Edwin to start work on a documentary programme about Gibraltar. Because the project would require a considerable amount of research Edwin was glad that they'd chosen to live on the spot in Gibraltar rather than somewhere up the Spanish coastline. There was a wealth of topics that could be touched on in such a programme. The Rock's geological origin as a massive chunk of limestone at the mouth of the Mediterranean would feature at the beginning. A brief summary of its history could include the Moors arriving in boats from North Africa and conquering much of Spain. The later period during the Spanish war of succession when a combined British and Dutch force had captured Gibraltar in 1704 and it being ceded to Britain by Spain ten years later would be highlighted. The sovereignty issue, which was forever a talking point in Gibraltar, would feature in the context of the various sieges that had taken place as well as the more recent closure of the frontier with Spain for a period of thirteen years.

To enable the story to be told Edwin would need to find a selection of local people who interviewed well. The documentary would also include the presence of the Royal Navy, the housing situation, the workforce of Moroccans and the blend of different religions on the Rock. Gibraltar was now trying to establish itself as a finance centre. The tax advantages of setting up off-shore companies there were currently being emphasised. Somehow Edwin would need to weave together such content together in such a way as to capture a flavour of the place.

Living just a five minute walk from work meant that Edwin was able to go home for lunch every day. It was an opportunity to catch up with Helga and baby Leon. For her part Helga had invariably been out shopping and was getting to know her way around. She had discovered a supermarket called Peralta located under a road bridge and also the whereabouts of the John Mackintosh Library, the Moroccan greengrocers, an indoor market and the military retail store of NAAFI. Many of the smaller shops stocked specific products that were in demand by the day trippers and locals alike. Whole red cannon balls of Dutch Edam cheese could be purchased for one pound fifty. Tins of butter were popular as was corned beef. Neither Edwin nor Helga smoked but they noticed that a pack of Rothmans could be purchased for forty-five pence. An American brand called Winston was particularly popular with Spaniards some of whom tried to smuggle cartons of them into Spain either by stuffing them up their trouser legs or under their skirts. They could be resold there at a considerably higher price.

Eating out in Spain was a lot cheaper than in Gibraltar. Sometimes Edwin and Helga would wheel the pram across the frontier at around nine o'clock in the evening and go to the Spanish restaurant called La Esteponera that they'd stumbled upon during their first visit to La Linea. It was almost as cheap to eat there as to cook a meal at home.

Meanwhile back in Gibraltar on the opposite side of the tatty looking square from the Holiday Inn a tiny pub called The Pickwick was where the journalists from the neighbouring offices of the Gibraltar Chronicle used to hang out after work. As such it was a good source for local gossip and to learn of things going on in Gibraltar. The paper's editor was normally there for an hour of so as was a highly amusing elderly English photographer who had lived in Gibraltar for many years and knew as much about its nooks and crannies as he did about its crooks and grannies. He could be relied on to add a shaft of wit to any occasion. Edwin tended to socialise with newspaper staff more than with the broadcasting staff from the Gibraltar Broadcasting Corporation with whom he seldom had much contact. Maybe that was because the TV Station was out on the south side of the Rock rather than in the town centre.

The documentary programme started to take shape. At weekends Edwin would do a recce of places around the Rock to work out camera angles and put together a location schedule for use when directing the camera crew during the working week. They had already gathered considerable footage that could be used to illustrate various points that would be raised in the programme. Some of it included coverage of traditionally held events such as the Changing of the Guard and a local Keys Ceremony. All of the recorded tapes were logged in such a way that individual shots could be accessed with relevant ease whenever they were required for use in the programme's compilation. Interviews were conducted by Edwin himself rather than finding somebody else to employ as an interviewer. He interviewed every contributor to the programme including Gibraltar's Chief Minister, Sir Joshua Hassan, and one of the Rock's most vocal critics who was an eminent barrister by the name of J E Triay QC who, on his own admission, was the most anti-Gibraltarian Gibraltarian. The manager of one of the newly arrived financial institutions discussed the tax advantages of doing business in Gibraltar. Even Mr Smoothy the estate agent agreed to take part as did a local sociologist and a pleasant Gibraltarian husband and wife who expressed the overriding local sentiment that although Spain wanted the Rock back, it was never going to get it.

A day out on a Royal Navy frigate proved to be a memorable experience for Edwin and his production team. All four of them threw up as the vessel, equipped with a Concorde engine, sped out into the Mediterranean for a training exercise. However, once their stomachs had settled they succeeded in getting excellent camera shots of HMS Ambuscade in action that could be edited with an interview that Edwin had recently done with one of the officers back at the Naval Base. Throughout their day at sea they had been shadowed by a Russian submarine.

The following Saturday three Gibraltarian ladies stood in front of the House of Assembly street preaching. As they loudly proclaimed that Jesus Christ was Lord, a line of smartly dressed Jews passed in front of them on their way to the synagogue. That was captured on camera as was the prayer-call at the mosque in Casemates and an interview with the local Hindu priest who ran a shop down an alleyway that stocked a selection of Indian herbs and spices.

"We have got here, you see, Hindu Merchant Community," he said, "They don't enter politics or secretarial work or anything like that. They just make money and are just happy to be happy in making money. But we don't forget our religion – you understand?"

The programme commentary would also make mention of the fact that the Catholic Community Centre had been built by a Jewish construction company using a Muslim workforce of Moroccans from across the Strait who had been on overtime in order to get the job finished by Christmas.

When all of the material for the documentary had been gathered editing was becoming a drawn out process. Edwin was reliant on Aiden being available to operate the editing suite but all too often he was too busy with other things. On top of that Aiden liked a drop of duty free whisky at odd hours of the day which didn't exactly lend itself to the process. Although Edwin had previously edited film for television news in New Zealand and the basic production grammar of shot sequences was identical, he had yet to master the controls of the videotape editing suite. Having already worked out all of the various in points and out points for each of the shots that he wanted to use in the programme from the vast array of recorded videotapes it would be preferable to have a hands-on videotape editor to work alongside him. To help speed things up Edwin asked Aiden if it was OK to invite his Austrian friend down to Gibraltar for a couple of weeks to get the project done and dusted. The suggestion met with approval and arrangements were made for Unification Church friend Manfred to fly out the following Tuesday.

That idea worked very well. The programme's editing was finished in its entirety in a fortnight of solid work that had included several late nights. A professional announcer was then flown in from London for the voice-over commentary which was then added together with music, titles and closing credits.

Initial viewing sessions were organised and the programme received an excellent review in the Gibraltar Chronicle. The company would now begin marketing it to English language television stations in countries great and small throughout the world.

Like so many British couples who reached pensionable age in the United Kingdom Edwin's parents decided to retire in Spain. They moved into a pleasant villa in the small resort town of La Cala de Mijas on the Costa del Sol and there was now an open invitation for Edwin, Helga and the baby to stay with them at weekends. Whenever they did so it felt almost as if they were going abroad on holiday. A Friday evening bus from La Linea would take them to Estepona where there was a connecting service to Marbella followed by yet another bus to the final destination. The journey was always something of an adventure in itself and the weekends enjoyable although it always felt good to get back into Gibraltar on Sunday afternoon ready for work the following day.

Helga had taught an overview of the theological understanding of the Unification Church known as the Principle to a young lady from the Philippines who worked as a maid in a home on the opposite side of Main Street. She was fascinated by the whole thing until her English solicitor fiancé arrived on the Rock and planted a few seeds of caution in her mind based upon some of the things he had read in the UK press.

One of Impact advertising agency's new clients was a financial company called

Langley Blundell which had recently set up offices on the Rock. It dealt in gilt-edged Government bonds that were purchased and sold in order to create tax advantages. Investors were told that their money was risk-free. The company would be holding a lavish launch party in the gardens of the Rock Hotel to which anyone who was anyone in Gibraltar had been invited to attend. The graphic design side of the advertising agency had put together all of the invitations, brochures and publicity. Aiden and Edwin had produced a thirty second television commercial that was already playing on GBC Television. As part of the lucrative deal there was now a request for Edwin and his camera crew to record the launch event. On the day they were down at the airport to gather shots of the gilt company's chief executive, Paul Blundell, arriving there on his private jet. That evening, however, at the party in the grounds of the Rock Hotel and just as he was delivering his speech a loud siren went off somewhere in the vicinity which lasted throughout its entire duration effectively drowning out just about every word, much to the frustration of Albert the sound operator. It meant that although the production team had plenty of pretty pictures of Gibraltarians drinking quaffs of champagne and gorging themselves on smoked salmon and cream cheese canapés on that warm summer's evening, the only usable footage of the main speech was limited to shots of the man with his lips moving accompanied by a voice-over commentary which summarised what he had been saying.

A MAJOR RIFT OCCURRED at the Impact advertising agency. Its head of marketing was an amiable Englishman called Bill Woodley who had been going out to what he referred to as 'creative meetings' that took place at eleven o'clock each weekday morning in Saccarello's coffee shop. There was nothing wrong with that were it not for the fact that the occasion was being used to plot and scheme about breaking away from Impact and creating a rival media organisation. He had already found a wealthy man willing to help set him up.

Before long the day arrived when members of staff were asked to gather in the graphic design studio for Bill's farewell at which Aiden thanked him for his work.

"Competition is a good thing and on behalf of everyone here at Impact I'd like to wish you well in your new venture," said Aiden.

"Thank you very much," said Bill, "It's been great working with all of you and it goes without saying that given the small size of Gibraltar we shall still keep bumping into each other."

What Bill Woodley didn't reveal was that arrangements had also been made for other members of staff to defect and join him over the next weeks. One by one there were absent places around the design studio and offices. Within a short space of time they had poached four graphic artists as well as a runner, a copywriter and the editor of the Gibraltar Annual.

Aiden was understandably furious. They were all valued people that he had provided with the stability of salaried jobs. The company had always been a happy place to work in and yet now everybody on the graphics side seemed to be deserting him. Not only that but some clients were switching sides too.

Aiden flew to London to recruit some replacement staff. He returned the following weekend with news that new people would be arriving within the next couple of weeks.

In the meantime the documentary programme was being purchased by broadcasters in various English speaking countries and had almost broken even. The amount that could be charged varied with different television stations. Countries such as Iceland had been willing to pay a reasonable price whilst Kenya got the programme for an amount that barely covered the postage cost. It demonstrated the fact that programmes made purely on a speculative basis needed to be sold to a large amount of outlets to make much money. The tried and tested way would have been first to get the programme commissioned but that was would have been a time consuming process that ran the risk of it not being made at all. As Aiden pointed out, the project had not only kept the TV production team going for many months but the company had accumulated an enviable library of local video footage at the same time.

There was now a television commercial that needed to be made for a merchant bank that Edwin put his mind to. He came up with a concept that played on the perception of off-shore banking. A boat would be out at sea with a banner strung across its side that read 'Off-Shore Bank.' A supposed customer would be seen in a smaller boat rowing his way out to it. The voice-over would say that something about people seeming have a strange idea as to what off-shore banking was all about but that the merchant bank could make things a lot simpler for them. There would then be some throw-away line about wishing everybody else a bon voyage.

It was a simple storyline. The bank manager liked the idea and had no hesitation in giving the go ahead for the commercial to be made. Three boats were hired for the day, one of which was for the camera crew. Aiden got to play the part of the guy in the rowing boat. Later in the editing suite the theme music to 'Desert Island Discs' was added to the final shot of him rowing off into the distance.

EDWIN, HELGA AND THE baby visited Germany for Christmas. They stayed in Darmstadt for most of the time most of the time but also visit various friends from the Unification Church and attended the celebration of 'God's Day' at a farm house in a place called Bad Camberg. They also met up with their Austrian friend Manfred again. He was currently in the process of setting up a small video production unit in Frankfurt mainly to handle church-related events but also available for anything else that came his way.

When they returned to Gibraltar Edwin and Helga were still interested in the possibility of buying a flat there rather than seeing the bulk of their income disappear into a landlord's pocket every month. They had heard that there was even a way of getting around the earlier stipulation of having had to live in Gibraltar for three years before being able to get a mortgage. They viewed a small flat above a cafeteria in Engineer Lane.

However, just as they were contemplating the idea uncertainty about the future of the Impact advertising agency suddenly arose. Aiden had been approached by a financial institution in London which for reasons of its own was interested in buying him out and he had recently received visits in Gibraltar by two London executives.

"They're clueless about graphic design, advertising or TV production," he told the staff. "In all probability it's some tax avoidance thing for them to want to own a company here in Gibraltar – but it might be an offer that I can't refuse."

Before long it became official and a date for the company takeover was announced. Some weeks later and after a fair bit of wrangling with a Gibraltar based legal practice that went on late into the night the deal was signed. Impact had been taken over and the company would now trade under the less attractive sounding name of Houndsditch Advertising. It would be moving into new premises in Gibraltar's Marina Bay. Meanwhile Aiden and his wife left Gibraltar to purchase a house in the UK on the Norfolk Broads.

Two weeks later the cameraman James had a blazing row with the sound operator Albert.

"You have always been such a pain to work with you stuck up little twat," said Albert. "Didn't that expensive school that you went to ever teach you anything about respect?"

"I don't have respect for amateurs," replied James, "Your entire knowledge of audio work seems to be limited to cranking up the volume on the radio."

"See what I mean? You always think that you're so damned superior," he said.

"It's probably because I am," replied James smugly.

"I've had enough of your puffed up nonsense," said Albert.

"The feeling is mutual," replied James.

"Well then, why don't you just piss off – Gibraltar doesn't need people like you," said Albert.

"I'm only here out of a professional reason which is more than can be said for you," he said.

"Then you'd better see how you can go about by yourself because I quit!" responded Albert.

And with that he walked out the building.

The following morning a hand-delivered letter lay on the doormat that confirmed Albert's resignation together with a few choice words as to what he thought of James the cameraman.

Edwin was sad to see Albert go as they had always got on very well together.

An accountant from the London headquarters of Houndsditch Finance now occupied Aiden's office. When Edwin mentioned that he was about to advertise for a replacement sound operator, he received an unexpected reply.

"It won't be necessary," said the accountant, "We are planning to transfer the TV production side of the business to London and just keep the graphic design operation here in Gibraltar."

From a personal point of view Edwin was appalled at the idea. It had taken him so many attempts to get into Gibraltar. He and his young family had been there for almost exactly one year and had enjoyed every minute of it. They had become quite well-known within its close-knit community and had even managed to introduce the teachings of the Unification Church to several of their friends. He had no desire whatsoever to be based in London and neither did Helga. In any case they were now expecting their second child.

Edwin was still in regular contact with the World Mission Department in New York and willing to drop everything as soon as the long-awaited television station got underway. But despite occasional hints there was still no news of that project taking off.

One afternoon Edwin received a phone call at work from Manfred in Frankfurt who had now set up his small TV production company called Lerche Media Services. Apparently the student wing of the Unification Movement known as CARP was planning to stage a major convention in Berlin that summer and

Manfred had been asked to provide video coverage of the various events taking place and to make a documentary programme from it. He asked Edwin if by any chance he might be available to work on the project as its production supervisor.

Edwin discussed it with Helga. Certainly it would fit neatly into the schedule of things in the light of what was happening to the company in Gibraltar. Perhaps they should temporarily return to Germany.

Two months later Edwin, Helga and the baby were booked on an Air Europe fight to Gatwick which would connect with a Malaysian Airlines flight for Frankfurt. It felt sad to be leaving the Rock but circumstances dictated that there was no alternative at that particular juncture. Having checked in their luggage and the pram they waited in the cafeteria. One of the graphic designers happened to be present.

"We'll be back," Edwin assured her.

CHAPTER FORTY-ONE

IN SOMETHING OF A repeat performance Edwin and Helga moved back into the same block of flats in the Frankfurt suburb of Heusenstamm that they had lived in previously. This time however the apartment was on the top floor rather that at ground level.

The same bakery across the road sold the same selection of sesame-seeded and poppy-seeded bread rolls each morning whilst the same East European man wearing the same leather hat drank the same brew of bottled German beer whilst standing outside the same kiosk a little further along the same stretch of road. The recent Gibraltar experience began to feel like a figment of the imagination. Perhaps the most noticeable difference was that whereas Gibraltar and neighbouring Spain had a continuous bustle of people most of Heusenstamm looked pretty well deserted.

They purchased a second-hand Volkswagen Polo and after visiting Helga's parents in Darmstadt re-contacted their circle of friends from within the Frankfurt community of the Unification Church. Like themselves, many had also become young families and had moved into their own apartments rather than living in church centres. There had been further mass wedding ceremonies. Another Anglo-German couple and their young daughter lived quite close by in Offenbach, the husband of which worked on the American air base across from Frankfurt Airport.

They also met up with Manfred and his English wife Diana at the premises of his new video production company in Frankfurt. He explained what he knew about the forthcoming project in Berlin and Edwin suggested that it might be beneficial to take a trip there as soon as possible to get a better idea of exactly what would be involved.

Later that week Edwin and Manfred boarded an overnight train from Frankfurt to Berlin. They were met at Berlin's Wansee Railway Station by a German member of the student branch of the Unification Movement. He provided a comprehensive outline of the series of events that would be taking place that summer. In additional to conferences, entertainment and sporting activities its theme would also entail a campaign for the removal of the Berlin Wall, that forty-two kilometre stretch of concrete and barbed wire that separated East and West Berlin.

An outline of the proposed schedule was studied. Venues such as the Philharmonic Concert Hall and International Congress Hall had already been booked for the occasion as had a sports arena and several hotels where conferences and banquets would be held. They spent the day visiting each place one by one.

All of the various events would need to be captured on camera and a documentary programme made from the material gathered.

"Coverage on this scale is going to require a multi-camera set up for everything that takes place in the larger buildings together with sufficient lighting and sound facilities," said Edwin.

"Yes, I can begin to realise that," replied Manfred, "I'm afraid that my small company has nowhere near enough equipment or staff to handle it properly but there are plenty of hire companies here in Berlin that we can check out."

"Okay. Well it would be best to get a few quotes from them and book a Berlin production company for the main interior events. From what's shown on the agenda the rest of the production could probably be carried out with the aid of three separate camera crews," replied Edwin. "Presumably there's sufficient budget to cover all of that?"

"The money side of it is no problem," replied Manfred, "as long as such expenditure is justified.

On their train journey back to Frankfurt they set about putting together a production schedule.

Three more planning trips to Berlin took place in the months of May and June during which time they succeeded in securing the services of a local TV production company to cover the major venues. It nevertheless became clear that for filming the remaining activities they could do with some additional production staff. Manfred managed to recruit some interested members from the Frankfurt headquarters although they were still short of a sound operator.

"Remember my former sound operator, Albert, in Gibraltar?" asked Edwin.

"Sure I do," replied Manfred. "Why? Is he likely to be free for a few weeks?"

"I could try him," replied Edwin. "He already knows a little bit about the movement."

"Well, give him a go," replied Manfred.

Albert jumped at the opportunity. He would be free throughout the entire month of August and welcomed the chance of coming to Germany to lend a helping hand.

AT THE BEGINNING OF July when preparation for the convention was nearing completion a major disaster struck. A group of people who for reasons of their own were opposed to the Unification Movement began making threats that it intended to disrupt the event so much so that the Philharmonic Concert Hall announced that it had no choice other than to cancel the booking. To make matters worse that then had a knock-on effect in which there was an outright ban on the Unification Movement using any hall at all in the city of Berlin.

The situation prompted an outcry from professors, theologians and politicians who protested about the treatment of a minority faith group and the way in which its democratic rights of free speech and free assembly were being disregarded. Within a matter of a few weeks a skilful lawyer was able to reverse all of the cancelled venue contracts. It meant that things were back in business once again and that the show would still be able to go ahead as planned.

Unification Church members from across Europe began to converge on Berlin for the CARP Convention including many who were university students. CARP was an acronym for Collegiate Association for the Research of Principles.

The opening ceremony was held at Berlin's International Congress Centre and drew an audience of just over three thousand people. Representatives from eighty different countries took part in a colourful display, much to the surprise of the forty or so journalists present, who hadn't quite known what to expect. Meanwhile three hundred demonstrators gathered outside were ranting and raving about the 'Moonies' apparently being a fascist organisation. In addition to shouting abuse they threw paint and stink bombs and wrote graffiti on hotel walls. They also slashed the tyres of twenty vehicles and set fire to a bus and a car. The brothers and sisters of the Unification Movement had to travel around in groups and a heavy police protection was provided at all of their events.

Reverend Moon's son, Hyo-jin, then arrived in Germany from the United States and gave a speech in which he expressed his sympathy for the divided city of Berlin and connected its hope for unification with his father's work to unite the two Koreas. Conferences and sporting events were held as were evenings of musical performances.

On the final day of the convention two thousand people took part in a seven kilometre march from the city centre to the Berlin Wall near Checkpoint Charlie. It was the largest international demonstration against the presence of the wall ever to be held in Berlin since its erection in 1961.

The march was accompanied by a repetitive chant of "Die Mauer muss weg!" which translated as "The wall must go!" A group of left wing individuals tried to destroy placards. They even hit some church members who then formed a human wall and pushed them towards Checkpoint Charlie into East Berlin. The East German police stopped them and pushed them back. A stone hit a Japanese brother who had to be taken to hospital. The police arrested nine demonstrators and the incident was reported in newspapers all over the world.

The question was raised as to why there should be so much violent opposition to a worldwide movement that had come to Berlin for the cause of freedom and to protest against the presence of the Wall.

EDWIN RETURNED TO FRANKFURT in time for Helga to give birth to their second child. It was another boy and they decided to call him Peter.

From the videotape material that had been gathered in Berlin the remaining task was to create a documentary programme from it. Time coded VHS copies of the footage were made which enabled Edwin to sit in the comfort of his lounge and begin the process of working out the shot sequences jotting each reference point down on paper as he went. The method was an efficient way to ensure that time spent in a costly editing suite would be kept to a minimum.

During his time on the production team in Berlin, Albert from Gibraltar had befriended many members of the Unification Church some of whom had suggested that he might like to pop across to England to go on one of the workshops to study the movement's teaching. Arrangements were made for him to do so and he departed from Frankfurt Airport.

In the meantime Edwin and Manfred drove up to the Bonn suburb of Meckenheim where they had hired an editing suite for as long as they needed it in order to compile the programme. Edwin had calculated that in all probability it would take them a fortnight. Another Unification Church member had been asked to bring a first copy of the completed production down to Frankfurt where a Korean elder was waiting to take it to South Korea for showing to Reverend

Moon.

Edwin and Manfred worked well together just as they had done on the Gibraltar documentary the year before. They were used to putting in long hours which enabled them to make good headway with the production. At the end of each shift they snatched a few hours sleep in a nearby guest house. Although under time pressure they were bang on schedule with editing the programme's visual content. They had also organised a session for recording the voice-over commentary. Every once in a while they would get a frantic phone call from the Korean elder wanting to know if the programme would be ready by the end of the second week. They responded by saying that provided they didn't get any interruptions it most probably would be.

WITH THE BERLIN PROJECT over and done with Edwin and Helga were contemplating what to do next. In many respects they both missed Gibraltar and often wondered if there might be some possibility of further professional work there in such a small place.

Edwin still had the contact details of Bill Woodley, the former marketing manager from the Impact advertising agency who had left to set up a new company called Smart Media and who had poached half the staff from the original company in the process. He decided to give him a ring.

"We could certainly do with having you here," said Bill, "I have a number of clients both in Gibraltar and up the coast who want TV commercials made if you're interested."

"Who is handling them at present?" asked Edwin.

"No one," replied Bill. "That's exactly the problem. I keep on having to give away the work to other companies like GBC or to an outfit called Alpha Productions up in Torremolinos."

"But presumably Smart Media has no camera or editing facilities?" asked Edwin.

"No, nothing at all," he replied, "If you do come down you'd have to dry hire kit although there are a few cameramen dotted around and editing suites that can be hired come to that."

Edwin began to get the picture. He explained that he'd welcome doing another stint in Gibraltar but that with a young family to support he needed to make sure that it was viable.

"It's a chicken and egg situation," replied Bill. "I've got a good client base and if there was suddenly the capability of being able to make the TV commercials ourselves there would be plenty of new work coming in."

"OK but would it be a continual flow of work?" asked Edwin.

"As far as I can see, yes," he replied, "I've got several lined up now and there are more in the pipeline. We would need to come to some arrangement as to how the finance would work though because I'm afraid that I wouldn't be able to offer you a fixed salary."

"Well, how might it work," asked Edwin.

"Look at it this way," said Bill. "I can drum up the business and secure all the deals and you can do all the production work. We then split whatever profit we make fifty-fifty. How does that sound?"

In the absence of anything else, it sounded like a reasonable arrangement. It was a bit of a gamble and would be like working freelance but it would include having daily use of the office and a flow of projects coming his way. Even with all its possible drawbacks it still felt like something worth doing.

"OK, that sounds interesting," replied Edwin, "Give me until the beginning of next month to get things sorted out here in Germany and then I'll be down there and ready to start work," said Edwin.

"That's great. You won't regret it," said Bill.

After they'd hung up Edwin discussed the situation with Helga.

"The thing is," he said, "There's still nothing on the horizon regarding the setting up of a TV station for the Unification Movement. In the meantime, I need to keep my hand in and get back into related work as soon as possible but my German is not good enough to do that here and neither you nor I have any burning desire to return to England."

"True," she said, "and I'd like very much to live in Gibraltar again but if Bill Woodley's company can't even afford to pay you a salary I'm not sure how we could do it bearing in mind the cost of renting a flat down there."

"In all probability we'd have to live across the border in Spain this time round," he replied. "Compared to Gibraltar, apartments are about half the price and double the size on the other side of the frontier."

"OK, but I wouldn't want to live in La Linea," she replied.

"No, me neither. It's far too druggy and grotty. No, we'd have to live up the coast or slightly inland but it would need to be on a bus route to La Linea bus station for the short walk to the frontier with Gibraltar. I'd have to commute in and out every day the same as countless other people. It could easily be done."

"Not quite the same thing as living in Gibraltar itself," she said.

"No, I know. Bill Woodley lives half an hour's drive from the frontier in a village called Guardiaro but then his wife is Spanish and so that kind of makes sense."

"Could you generate sufficient income for us to survive down there?" she asked.

"Well, that depends almost entirely on how many clients he has got up his sleeve," replied Edwin, "And bear in mind that his company has no TV production facilities whatsoever and there'd be no TV production staff other than myself. That means that for every project I'd need to hire a cameraman and a small production crew for gathering the material and then hire an edit suite somewhere to put the things together. There aren't too many of them around in that neck of the woods. Even at Image Productions we used to boast that we were the only Betacam team south of Madrid. I'll need to check and see what editing facilities are available in the area. I do know that there's at least one place in Fuengirola."

EDWIN, HELGA AND THEIR two little boys made the journey down to southern Spain by train. With a travelling time of forty-two hours, it entailed two nights of sleeping in couchettes which were folded up during the day. When the train reached the French border town of Hendaye its carriages had to pass through a changer which adjusted their wheel span to meet the wider gauge of Spanish railway tracks.

Arriving in Algeciras on Friday morning the Rock of Gibraltar could be seen across the bay as a bus ride took them to La Linea where they rented a room at the Hotel Paris for the first couple of days. That lunchtime they sat in the familiar surroundings of the Esteponera Restaurant located next to the meat and vegetable market

Edwin used the callbox to phone Bill Woodley and let him know that he had arrived.

"That's brilliant," said Bill, "So that presumably means that you'll be in at the office on Monday morning."

"It sure does," replied Edwin, "though I'm going to need a bit of time to get some proper accommodation sorted out. At present we're staying temporarily in a hotel in La Linea."

"There's a self-catering holiday flat in my village of Guadiaro that you could have for a few days if you want it," he said. "It's vacant at the moment and might be OK as a starting point. That way you could get a ride into Gibraltar with me each day."

"That sounds like a good idea," replied Edwin.

"Well, come out here on the bus on Sunday morning and you can move in," he said.

"OK, we'll see you then," replied Edwin.

THE APARTMENT IN THE small Spanish village of Guadiaro was spacious and available for the next couple of weeks. That would give Edwin time to scout around for somewhere more permanent. At first it seemed a bit weird living on the Spanish side and having to show passports to get into work but after all it was an international frontier.

Smart Media didn't exactly live up to its name and the office turned out to be an untidy tip of a place. Its open-plan room had two graphic designers at their drawing boards positioned next to the windows whilst five desks were piled high with back copies of magazines and newspapers. A wooden screen split the room in two and attempted to hide a photocopy machine and numerous stacks of cardboard boxes. Both telephones were ringing simultaneously.

Bill Woodley, who despite the heat and lack of air conditioning, was immaculately dressed in a pinstripe suit and tie, took his place behind the largest desk and offered Edwin a chair to one side. He asked the Gibraltarian secretary, Mimi, if she'd finished typing the last batch of invoices.

"They're all ready to go," she replied.

"Good, it's about time we got a bit of dosh coming in," he said. "Has anyone else phoned at all?"

"Toby and Josephine, to say they are planning to come in on Wednesday afternoon," she replied.

"Not until Wednesday. Good," he replied and then turning to Edwin asked, "Fancy coming down the road for a coffee?"

The two of them spent an hour or so at Saccarello's Coffee House in Irish Town during which Bill outlined the set-up of the advertising agency. In the past year he had lost a lot of staff and now retained just two graphic designers, a receptionist and a still photographer who doubled as an errand boy.

"Oh, and there's also a British couple who breeze in periodically to do the accounts. He's a chartered accountant and she's a lawyer. They sometimes act as if they own the bloody place but you'll soon get used to them. They've helped me out in the past and it's fair to say that the company might have folded without their input."

Later that day Bill succeeded in securing a deal to make a local TV commercial for Banco de Bilbao that had recently opened a branch in Gibraltar. It was now up to Edwin to come up with some ideas and to work out the budget. Once approved by the client, he would then get the go ahead to make it. He grabbed a pen and some paper and spent the next few hours working out a few ideas for the content of a thirty second television commercial. He also began to phone around in search of technical facilities. Fortunately there was an English chap in Gibraltar who had his own professional television camera and recording equipment who could be hired at a reasonable day rate. He lived on a boat in the Marina.

ON WEDNESDAY BILL HAD to depart from Gibraltar early to attend a meeting with a client up in Malaga and so after work Edwin took a bus from La Linea to get back to Guadiaro. Its route passed through the small Spanish town of San Roque perched upon a hill. As the bus drove around the perimeter of a central square of parkland with a fountain in the middle he caught sight of many families sitting outside with their children. Being closer to Gibraltar than Guadiaro the place also had the convenience of an additional and more frequent bus service to and from La Linea. That evening he told Helga of his attraction to San Roque and it was arranged that after work the following day he would go there again and see if he could find an apartment to rent.

As with so many things in Spain, word of mouth was the best way of going about it. A young lady in a boutique directed him to one of the town's landlords. Impressed that Edwin spoke Spanish the man said that he had an apartment available right away for a period of two months after which a slightly cheaper one would then be available. He took Edwin to a large modern block of flats adjacent to the central square which he mentioned was generally regarded as being the best accommodation in town. The three-bedroom flat was in many respects too large for their needs. It was tastefully furnished and the rent was approximately half what Edwin had paid in Gibraltar. There were mountain views in the distance. Edwin agreed to take it and it was arranged that they would move in the following day.

Edwin took that morning off work and ordered a taxi to make the move. It was such a hot day that a plastic tub of margarine taken from the fridge had become a tub of liquid by the end of the journey. Very pleased with their new base, Edwin then departed for work by bus leaving Helga and the children to discover the whereabouts of a local grocery store in the small town of San Roque. When he returned in the evening they ate together and then went out to the square in the cooler evening air.

Over the weekend they explored their new town of San Roque. Its cobbled streets and white houses were quaint. Oranges grew on trees and a panoramic view of Gibraltar could be seen from the top of the hill. A bull ring lay in the town centre. Venturing out after breakfast on Sunday morning they saw that a large market had been set up just a couple of blocks away. Vendors were selling articles of clothing, sunglasses, sandals, music cassettes and earthenware bowls but there were also fruit and vegetable stalls. It attracted people from far and wide.

Throughout the working week Edwin commuted to La Linea by the twenty minute bus journey and then continued on foot into Gibraltar. One Saturday morning he took Helga and the children in with him. As they wheeled the buggy across the airport runway they ran into three people whom they knew from when they had lived there before – which was not a difficult thing to happen in such a small, close-knit community. They then took the familiar route into the centre of town via Landport Tunnel.

"It feels like we never really left the place," observed Helga as they reached Casemates Square at one end of the inevitable Main Street.

"Doesn't it just," agreed Edwin, "Same shops, same people, same buildings all under the same blue sky and sunshine."

They made their way to Cathedral Square where there was an enclosed children's playground for Leon to run around in whilst being amusedly observed by baby Peter from his buggy.

Bill had given Edwin a key to the Smart Media office in Secretary's Lane. He had acknowledged that the place was untidy. The layout was illogical and every available space seemed to have become a dumping ground for accumulated piles of newspapers, brochures, magazines, cardboard boxes and disused artwork. It had been agreed that Edwin might re-arrange things a little.

Whilst Helga and the children played in the park, Edwin spent the entire day completely changing around everything in the office in such a way that it was barely recognisable from its previous state. Desks and drawing board were now placed in a more sensible configuration. The receptionist would face the front door entrance instead of being hidden away around the corner. Archive material was neatly stored on shelves. The wooden screen that had divided the room in half was done away with altogether apart from two of its panels that were now used to concealed the sink unit and coffee making area. Everything looked smart and inviting. Seven large bin bags full of rubbish were taken to a nearby disposal area.

On Monday morning the new-look workplace of Smart Media seemed to go down very well with everybody – staff and visiting clients alike. Bill Woodley could be heard overheard enthusiastically describing the transformation on the phone to his part-time accountant who lived up on the Costa del Sol. Edwin had noticed that Bill reported many things back to that accountant at various times of the day.

THE BANCO DE BILBAO advertisement was given the go ahead and Edwin assembled a small production team to set about making it. The storyline required the use of twenty or so extras that were required to play the part of bank customers. As a local production on a relatively low budget he needed to grab hold of anyone who was available for an hour or so for that purpose. As luck had it he was able to poach some willing staff from the adjacent tax office after which he handed each of them a ten pound note by means of a token appearance allowance.

Edwin took the recorded videotapes with him on a coach journey up to Fuengirola where he had booked the use of an editing suite to compile the sequence. The facility was housed in a room at the back of an electrical appliance store. In the absence of a videotape editor, Edwin had no choice but to teach himself its hands-on operation which wasn't too complicated. Although television commercials had never before been Edwin's speciality, they were easy enough to make and the editing part was not far removed from the style of programme promotions that he had put together whilst working in television presentation.

The bank was pleased with the finished commercial and settled their invoice right away. Having taken the gamble of working with Bill Woodley on a profit share basis, Edwin calculated that there would need to be a steady flow of such work coming to generate a sufficient income and some semblance of stability.

He had a good working relationship with Bill who was in daily contact with company bosses both in Gibraltar and southern Spain, many of whom were expats. Bill wined and dined with them at lunch times and played cricket with them at weekends. He had the sales knack of being able to go out and bring in the business. He would arrive back in the office and say to Edwin, "Just had lunch with Norwich Union. They'd like us to make a TV commercial to coincide with the press ads that we're doing for them. See what you can come up with will you?"

Within a fortnight three new TV commercials were waiting to be made.

In the meantime the headline news in the *Gibraltar Chronicle* was all about the collapse of Langley Blundell, a financial company dealing in gilt-edged securities that had brought its business to Gibraltar a year or so ago. Edwin recalled the launch party held at the Rock Hotel when, by coincidence, the Chief Executive's key speech had been drowned out by police sirens. Paul Blundell was now facing charges of fraud on a massive scale. A misprint in the *Gibraltar Chronicle* article referred to him as head of a 'guilt company.'

BILL WOODLEY WAS GREAT at drumming up business but had never been so hot on the accounts side of running a business. He explained to Edwin how he had first got the accountant involved. They had initially met in a Spanish bar a couple of years ago when Bill had casually mentioned something of his own financial shortcomings. Toby happened to be an accountant who had taken early retirement in Spain and he suggested that if he and his wife Josephine were to visit the Gibraltar office of Smart Media to look over the books perhaps they could offer some advice. They did so and discovered that most of the company's assets lay in payments still not received for work that had already been carried out. A list of all outstanding bills was compiled and individual members of staff were sent out to collect payments and before long the books began to balance once again. Although their names never appeared on paper they effectively controlled the purse strings of the company from the comfort of their apartment up the Spanish coast in Puerto de la Duquesa. Apparently they had struck a deal with Bill that in return for their services they would take the same amount of money from the company as he did. For his part Bill maintained that it was a worthwhile arrangement that took the pressure off him and had kept the company going at a difficult time in which many clients had been delaying the payment of their bills.

However, it had since become obvious to the graphic designers and the receptionist that Toby the accountant and his wife, Josephine, were only really interested in milking the system rather than any wellbeing of the advertising agency. They had taken control of the invoicing and would deliberately charge over the odds for most of the work that the company carried out by adding a huge mark-up. They didn't posses much in the way of diplomacy and had a general dislike of Gibraltarians. But the most annoying aspect was their assumed right to try to talk down to the staff at Smart Media.

Often at about midday there would be a phone call from Toby the accountant who invariably sounded as if he had a monstrous hangover. He would demand to know what was going on at the office and whether this, that or the other thing had been done and whether any cheques had been collected. The receptionist would be heard giving him a blow by blow account of what everyone was doing including each person's arrival times. Such remote monitoring was not welcomed.

The company's photographer then discovered that despite Toby's undoubted financial expertise he had been struck off as an accountant in the United Kingdom some years ago following alleged involvement in some dodgy deals and had been living on the Costa del Sol ever since. His wife Josephine combined her extensive legal knowledge with an ability to consume vast quantities of Rioja in competition with her husband's daily intake of San Miguel beer. Despite having been in Spain for many years, neither could speak a word of Spanish. They socialised in bars frequented by British expats and dined at the best restaurants.

Some of the staff at Smart Media asked Bill why he put up with them and he just said that without their financial guidance the company would have gone down the tubes.

Although they never interfered with Edwin's production work, Toby had nevertheless suggested that the Norwich Union commercial could be filmed at a large Spanish house owned by one of his friends and located in the opulent millionaires' private estate of Sotogrande, about half an hour's drive up the Spanish coastline. After an initial recce of the place, the one-day shoot went like clockwork. The segments were edited together, music and voice-over were added and the manager of Norwich Union in Gibraltar was very pleased with the result. The new TV commercial was scheduled to go on air in a couple of weeks' time. Before it did so, however, the Gibraltar Broadcasting Corporation received a complaint from the homeowner, saying that he had not given permission for his premises to feature in the commercial and threatening legal action if it was shown. It was a disaster for everybody concerned and of considerable embarrassment to Toby. Edwin rescheduled everything and shot the entire commercial again at different premises in a place called Miraflores, where a more accommodating homeowner not only gave his written consent but remained on hand throughout the day's filming.

THE TOWN OF SAN Roque was essentially working class and had none of the tourist trappings and inflated prices that existed a few miles away up on the Costa del Sol. Historically it was the place that the Spanish inhabitants of Gibraltar had fled to when a combined force of British and Dutch ships had captured the Rock in 1704. A large sign on the main road described the immediate area as 'Campo de Gibraltar.'

Edwin and Helga's second apartment there was not nearly as nice as the first. They endured it for a short while but after suffering mosquito bites, power cuts, the odour of the drains and one particular morning in which the water supply cut out immediately after Edwin had applied shampoo to his hair, they decided to seek another.

The Bar Deportivo on the Calle Malaga was where an elderly Spanish gentleman could be found who acted as a go-between with local landlords. He showed Edwin to a large flat close to the area of the Sunday market. The rent was £150 per month which included electricity, water and community charge. Within the next few days they moved in.

One evening on his bus journey home Edwin got chatting to an American concert pianist who was staying in San Roque for several months and who went to the John Macintosh Hall in Gibraltar every day to make use of its grand piano.

They became good friends and Edwin even found an opportunity to explain something about the Unification Church which he seemed to be able to grasp quite well. He was particularly interested to learn that Reverend Moon had predicted the downfall of communism and that at the height of the Cold War he had funded a controversial conference in Geneva entitled 'The End of the Soviet Empire.' At the time that notion had seemed so unlikely that even some of the distinguished academics who attended the conference had been somewhat sceptical about such a prediction.

THE FOLLOWING SPRING AFTER the next batch of television commercials had been successfully completed and made a welcome boost to his bank balance, Edwin took the family for a fortnight's break in England primarily to visit his brothers who both lived in Somerset.

Not having been in the UK for several years they stayed at a self-catering holiday flat in the town of Glastonbury. Once there they did touristy things such as climbing the famous hill known as the Tor, drinking water from the Chalice Well and walking in the grounds of the Abbey Ruins. It was an unusual town full of ageing hippies left over from a previous generation and who still dressed in weird outfits. One overcast Sunday afternoon Edwin and Helga watched some kids jumping off a wall on a skateboard in what seem to be the sole social outlet for local youth. They couldn't easily imagine themselves living in England and were pleased to be going back to the Mediterranean.

You can tell that you are back in Spain when your toothbrush tastes of garlic, thought Edwin as he prepared to take the early morning bus from San Roque to La Linea and then to cross the frontier into Gibraltar. Back at the office he was pleased to learn that during his absence several more of Bill's clients had expressed an interest in having TV commercials made for them. One of the graphic designers switched on the radio.

Let me sail, let me sail, Let the Orinoco Flow
Let me reach, let me beach, On the shores of Tripoli
Let me sail, let me sail. Let me crash upon your shore
Let me reach, let me beach, Far beyond the Yellow Sea
Sail away, sail away, sail away
Sail away, sail away, sail away

By now Edwin had several cameramen to choose from both in Gibraltar and in Spain, three of whom had their own kit. He continued to use the editing facilities up the coast in Fuengirola and whenever he was going to be there for a few days he arranged to take Helga and the children with him. They stayed together at one of the hotels and there was plenty going on in the resort to keep them occupied throughout the day whilst Edwin tended to his videotape editing. They would then meet up in the evenings and eat out in one of the numerous restaurants. If Edwin needed a voice-over he would normally hire announcers from BFBS Radio in Gibraltar who were only too pleased to oblige.

Edwin's production team felt motivated and enjoyed working together. He tried to look after them well and made sure that the schedule always included provision for coffee breaks and meals. On completion of a shoot it was traditional to take them to a Gibraltar pub called The Star Bar for an hour or so to unwind which they appreciated. They had invariably had their share of fun and games.

When making a promotional video featuring The Rock Hotel the management had insisted that everyone at the outdoor swimming pool was first asked if they objected to the presence of a camera because, it was explained, some of the men might be there with their mistresses. There had then been an occasion when they'd been interviewing the Gibraltarian manager of Banque Indosuez and he had begun pronouncing it as 'Bonk Indo-sway' which succeeded in having the film crew in stitches much to the poor man's puzzlement.

The storyline for a Marks and Spencer advertisement included an open-top car first getting clamped for parking outside its Main Street store and then getting stuck in a long traffic queue at the Spanish frontier, the implication being that some shoppers were prepared to put up with anything just to get their hands on some decent things from Marks and Spencer. Filmed from an open window above street level the staged clamping of the vehicle parked in front of the shop became slightly problematic. Hostility was shown by several passers-by towards the actor dressed in a uniform and seen to be clamping the hired open-top Mercedes. It took several takes to get an uninterrupted version.

By now Edwin had produced a range of local TV commercials and promotional videos for clients such as Norwich Union, Banco de Bilbao, Marks and Spencer, Young Sparks, Sunseeker Power Boats, GB Airways, Hambros Bank, The Danish Furniture Centre, Bland Travel, Credit Suisse, Spicer and Oppenheim, The Rock Hotel, Abbey National, Coopers and Lybrand, Banque Indosuez, Praga Housing Development, NatWest Bank, Taylor Woodrow, Exchange Travel as well as the Gibraltar Chamber of Commerce.

ONE DAY A LETTER arrived at Edwin and Helga's post office box in Gibraltar from the World Mission Department in New York saying that Reverend Moon had recently spoken again about the possibility of a television station being set up. It went on to say that they would be in touch with Edwin again as soon as there was any further news.

Their elder son, Leon, started going to the local Spanish nursery school in San Roque. Not to be outdone by this, his younger brother, Peter, who was now aged two, had promptly stepped into the house with him. Helga tried to get him back but the Spanish lady who ran it shrugged her shoulder and said that it was fine for him to attend too.

July was the season of the Feria. The annual fair travelled around Andalucía with towns taking it in turns to be decked out in banners and floral displays announcing that they were 'en fiestas.' Such celebrations were week-long street parties. In San Roque the fair occupied the entire Sunday Market area. During the heat of the day nothing at all happened but once darkness fell all hell broke loose. People took to the streets, the women in flouncy flamenco dresses, to dance, drink and, generally, make merry. Large booths had been set up for entertainment and refreshments where young and old met up amidst swirling dancers whilst waiters rushed back and forth topping up porcelain goblets with fino sherry and serving tapas. Meanwhile the dazzling lights and deafening music of the fairground went on until four o'clock each morning. Being in the close vicinity of Edwin and Helga's apartment the chance of getting any sleep before then was pretty much impossible.

The nearest branch of the Unification Church was in Madrid which they visited a couple of times. They also managed to return to Germany twice a year and were able to re-visit members there.

Meanwhile the technological knowhow of a Dutch company led to the implementation of a major land reclamation project on some of Gibraltar's shoreline which would provide sufficient extra land area for building apartment blocks and effectively solve the housing shortage problem. The ambitious scheme was already getting under way. Although Madrid might have been annoyed at the thought of any territorial expansion of Gibraltar many local Spanish construction workers from just across the border were glad of the job opportunities it provided as they began to commute in and out each day.

EDWIN AND BILL RARELY encountered anyone from the former company of Impact which now traded as Houndsditch Advertising. They supposed it was partly due to the fact that it was based in Marina Bay which was geographically remote from the town centre as well as being considered a rival to Smart Media. News emerged, however, that Houndsditch was closing down its operation in Gibraltar.

"Far be it from me to gloat about another company's downfall," said Bill Woodley, "but when they pull out it can only be good news for Smart Media because many of their clients will now turn to us for their advertising."

"I suppose that'll mean an additional workload of glossy brochures, booklets, flyers, restaurant menus and posters," commented one of the graphic designers.

"Most likely," replied Bill, "and there's bound to be the need for some innovative advertisements to be devised and inserted into local magazines and newspapers and there could well be additional TV commercial spin-offs for Edwin to get stuck into," he said.

"I've got quite enough on my plate with this latest project for the Gibraltar Chamber of Commerce just at the moment thank you very much," replied Edwin, "but yes, I do take your point."

Bill was already thinking in terms of taking on a couple more staff and moving into larger premises. He had got his eye on some prestigious offices in a newly built block called Centre Plaza on Main Street. The accountant Toby went to look at them and gave it a grunt of approval as did his wife Josephine who saw it as a sign that they were going up in the world which, in one sense, they were. The building even had a lift.

A fortnight later, Edwin organised the office move. It took four members of staff an entire working day and the use of a van to transfer all of it across to the new building in stages. The large bright premises were laid out in an aesthetically pleasing way and several new items of office furniture were purchased for additional enhancement. If first impressions were supposed to count for something the office looked sufficiently plush and up-market to impress many a client. Edwin had his own corner down at the far end devoted entirely to TV production.

Everybody at Smart Media had predicted that some sort of a confrontation with the accountant was bound to happen sooner or later. Shortly after moving into the new office in Centre Plaza one of the graphic designers, Felipe Humphries, had a difference of opinion with the accountant's wife. She had asked him to drive some artwork up to Marbella and he maintained that he wasn't employed as a deliveryman and pointed out that because she and her husband lived up near Marbella it would make more sense for them to deliver it. As a result of the disagreement, Toby and Josephine instructed Bill to give Felipe the boot from the company.

"But he's a good little worker," protested Bill.

"You'll just have to find someone else," said Toby.

"It took me long enough to find him," replied Bill, "and his artwork is excellent."

"His attitude in not excellent," replied Toby. "We want him out."

"Yes, for goodness sake get him out," echoed Josephine.

The following morning and with a great deal of reluctance Bill had the task of taking Felipe to a coffee shop and giving him the news of his dismissal. His notice period would allow sufficient time to finish off some graphic artwork that he had been preparing for a TV commercial that Edwin was making.

Felipe Humphries was in his twenties. He mother was Spanish and his father was English and they lived in the town of Jimena which was several miles inland. His father was a wealthy man and, on hearing what had happened to his son at Smart Media, he decided to set him up in business by starting a new advertising company from an office a little further along Main Street. However, as Felipe was quick to point out, it was one thing to have been employed as a graphic designer but quite another to attempt to run a business from scratch and with no client base.

THE LOCAL TELEVISION SERVICE in Gibraltar broadcast it programmes in English and was watched on a regular basis by the numerous English speaking ex-pats who lived on Spain's Costa del Sol. Its free to air signal could be received as far up the Spanish coastline as Fuengirola. However transmission ended shortly before midnight which although a reasonable time for those people who had jobs to go to in the morning in Gibraltar did seem a bit on the early side for the late night hours kept in Spain.

Edwin was aware of this lifestyle difference and wondered about the possibility of an extension of its broadcasting hours. He discussed the idea with Bill.

"What if we could broadcast a selection of television programmes via the transmitters of the GBC for three additional hours after their transmission had finished?" suggested Edwin.

"If the three hours had a good selection of British programmes I'm sure it would be watched by numerous residents living up the coast in Spain," he replied.

"Precisely," said Edwin, "And I guess the main question is whether or not such a late night audience of viewers would be of sufficient interest to advertisers to make such a service viable."

Well, if there's a captive audience it should be easy enough to sell commercial spots," said Bill.

In the weeks that followed they set about researching such a project.

To check out the legality of such an enterprise Bill and Edwin first met with a Gibraltar government minister who gave the initiative his nod of approval. They then met with the current managing director of the Gibraltar Broadcasting Corporation who was clearly interested in the money that the corporation would be able to generate for hiring out use of its transmitters for such a late night play-out of pre-recorded material.

Edwin and Bill thought that they might have stumbled upon on an interesting opportunity. It seemed like a workable idea. The question was whether such a three-hour service of late-night television could generate sufficient advertising revenue to cover its running costs, pay for programmes and staff and make some kind of a profit. Edwin was not a business person but was fortunate in having friends in Gibraltar who were.

Details were worked out. A trip to London to visit Thames Television who could supply the bulk of the programming was fruitful. A London-based advertising sales company were interested in selling international TV commercials for the late night TV service whilst Smart Media would deal with local advertising. Flow charts were drawn up showing income and expenditure.

"It's obviously going require the financial backing of an entrepreneur," pointed out Bill, "and I can think of one or two wealthy individuals up the coast who might be interested."

Meetings were set up with several such people. In each case, however, the one stumbling block was the Gibraltar Broadcasting Corporation's insistence on being paid a full year's fee in advance. Although there were people in southern Spain and Gibraltar who had a fair bit of money to play with and even if the advertising revenue figures stacked up none of them was willing to fork out a full year's advance payment for transmitter hire for such a venture. They suggested that a rolling four-weekly fee that would be renewed every four weeks would be a far most attractive and less risky option.

The accountancy firm Coopers and Lybrand looked the figures over and was suitably impressed. "If you can go and kick the shit out of the Gibraltar Broadcasting Corporation and get them to agree to a one month renewable arrangement you've got a workable business," said one of its managers, who also lived in San Roque.

But the TV Station wouldn't budge. Edwin and Bill lunched at Strings Restaurant with one of Gibraltar's prominent lawyers who let slip that the Gibraltar Broadcasting Corporation had even had the nerve to write the income that it expected to receive from the Night Time Television project into its budget for the forthcoming financial year before anything had even been signed and sealed.

It was only after Edwin and Bill had exhausted their entire list of potential backers that the TV Station finally said that it might be prepared to agree to the one month rolling rent after all. But their climb down had come too late for any of the original punters who had since lost interest.

So there it was – a business venture that was never going to get off the ground.

CHAPTER FORTY-TWO

ONE NOVEMBER MORNING WHILST listening to the news on BFBS Radio, Edwin and Helga were fascinated to hear that crowds of East Germans had been permitted to cross the Berlin Wall where they had been joined by West Germans in making large celebrations. The report went on to say that souvenir hunters were chipping away at parts of the wall and there was speculation that it marked the first stage of its complete demolition. It felt as if the campaigning activities of the Unification Church and others that had taken place there in recent years had not been in vain and might even have played some part in helping pave the way towards an eventual German re-unification.

Meanwhile in the Soviet Union the political movement of Perestroika for reformation within the Communist Party had emerged and was widely associated with President Mikhail Gorbachev and his openness policy reform of Glasnost.

Such events were significant to the Unification Movement insomuch as Reverend Moon had forever sought to bring about the peaceful end of Communism. He had endeavoured to do so through a spectrum of initiatives in education, culture, conferences, rallies and the media. He was also a person who had experienced Communism at first-hand. Having begun his public ministry in communist-held North Korea he had been arrested, tortured and imprisoned in a hard labour camp for three years. Despite such treatment he had nevertheless taught people to love the people of Communism and to help bring about its end by teaching that their Marxist/Leninist ideology was fatally flawed and could never bring about an ideal world.

EDWIN AND HELGA WERE delighted to find out that they were expecting yet another addition to their family. The baby was due to be born at the beginning of July. They worked out that if Edwin were to take a couple of month's unpaid leave at around that time arrangements could be made for the birth to take place in Germany.

Following the abrupt dismissal of the graphic artist Felipe Humphries from Smart Media some months ago he still kept in touch with Edwin. They occasionally met up for lunch at a Moroccan run snack bar adjacent to the Piazza. Felipe now worked from an office a little further along Main Street and traded under the name of Casemates Design. His father had set him up in business by first renting an entire floor of offices and then sub-letting most of them which brought in sufficient money to cover Felipe's rent-free presence there. He had taken on two female school leavers on work experience who spent most of their time running errands for him. So far his workload had been limited to the design of run-of-the-mill letterheads, business cards and compliment slips but being bi-lingual meant that he could get the printing done across the border in Spain at a discounted price.

One Saturday morning, when Edwin, Helga and the children were in Gibraltar shopping for items of clothing at the British Home Stores they happened to run into Felipe who was there with his father.

The father was quite an elderly man and known to be mildly eccentric. Originally from the Midlands he had made his money working for many years in the United Arab Emirates. He had married a Spanish lady and they had eventually retired in Spain where they owned a sizable amount of agricultural land near the Andalucían village of Jimena. Felipe was their eldest son.

The old man turned to Edwin and said that he'd heard from Felipe about the proposed Night Time Television project and that he thought it was an excellent idea and that he would be prepared to put up the necessary working capital to finance it.

Edwin could scarcely believe what he was hearing because he had all but given up hope on that particular enterprise. Nevertheless it was suggested that they meet for a pub lunch the following Wednesday to talk things through. Bill Woodley would ordinarily have accompanied Edwin to such a meeting but because it was he who had had unenviable the task of dismissing Felipe from Smart Media that would have felt too awkward.

Edwin arrived at the appointed hour and Felipe showed up with his father ten minutes later.

"With a project such as this we're going to need to act fast before somebody else cottons on to the idea," said the man to Edwin with a sense of urgency, "How many other people know about Night Time Television proposal?"

"There were four potential investors who gave it serious consideration a few months ago but each of them declined to get involved because of the GBC's insistence on wanting a year's payment in advance," replied Edwin.

"Sounds like a case of Gibraltar Television shooting itself in the foot," he said, "but I gather they are now willing to accept payments on a rolling monthly basis?"

"That's right," replied Edwin.

"Well that's very good indeed," he replied. "Just this morning I have been on the phone to Saatchi and Saatchi in London and I've made arrangements to visit them there next week."

Edwin was at a loss to see how that connected to the Gibraltar project and so he gave an outline of the way in which the Night Time Television service would function and of how each evening's transmission of programmes including commercials and continuity announcements would be recorded during the day and delivered on videotape to the TV Station for replay that same evening.

"I see," replied Archibald Humphries, "Well, there are four spare offices next door to Felipe's that I have now set aside to house Night Time Television. Let me know the technical equipment you're going to need."

Edwin didn't know quite what to make of Archibald Humphries but was relieved to learn that he didn't want a hands-on role in the company. The man said that he would be pleased to finance the enterprise if his son, Felipe, could be involved with it which as far as Edwin was concerned would be OK.

"Felipe is going to be the new Robert Maxwell," said his father proudly, perhaps oblivious of the difference between print media and broadcast media and presumably not knowing much about the Mirror group boss either.

Edwin detected that even the son Felipe had certain reservations concerning his father's involvement in the project. When they were alone Edwin asked him what he thought.

"My father might have his own ways of doing things but he always gets there in the end," said Felipe, "He is a shrewd investor – although admittedly sometimes he bites off far more than he can chew."

"I can't fathom out what he expects to achieve at Saatchi & Saatchi in London," said Edwin.

"He'll have something worked out," replied Felipe. "Once started, there's no stopping him."

'That could be a problem,' thought Edwin.

Back in the office of Smart Media Edwin kept Bill Woodley and the rest of the staff up to date with the latest developments. They realised that if this new nocturnal television service were ever to get off the ground it would mean Edwin departing to join forces with Felipe and his father – and they joked about what strange business partners they'd make. Meanwhile Toby the accountant and his wife, Josephine, were sniffing around to see if there was some way in which they might benefit financially from any deal. They had already emphasised that Smart Media would be well placed to handle all of the advertising sales for the new television service.

NEWS ARRIVED THAT THE Unification Church would be holding a media conference that April and that it would be taking place in Moscow. Edwin and Helga were invited to attend. The event represented the long-awaited breakthrough into Russia that had been spoken about so often when Edwin had first encountered the movement. What had once seemed like a distant dream was now becoming a reality. Up until that time the movement's activities in East European countries had been limited to a number of its missionaries working underground and coordinated in secret from Austria.

Edwin and Helga realised that if they were to go to Moscow they would need to make arrangements for the two children to stay with their grandparents for the duration. That didn't pose any problem and although pregnant, Helga would still be able to fly. Unfortunately, try as they may, they discovered that it was not going to be possible for them to obtain the necessary visas for the USSR in time and so with regret they were unable to attend.

Instead they had to make do with reports of the event. They learnt that the Media Conference was a great success. Despite having spoken out against the ideology of communism throughout his public ministry Reverend Moon and his wife had been invited into the Kremlin by President Gorbachev.

A FAX FOR EDWIN came through to Smart Media from Archibald Humphries. It was in handwritten scrawl and made little or no sense.

'Still in London awaiting important information from Saatchi & Saatchi but cannot understand why they have not been in contact with me since my meeting there last Tuesday. Do you happen to know where the name Saatchi originates? That information could be helpful. Night Time Television will succeed. I see also that the pound is up again against the peseta. I have more meetings today. Archibald Humphries here in the United Kingdom of England, Scotland, Wales and Northern Ireland'

The content caused considerable mirth around the Smart Media office until later on in the day when Edwin received a phone call from the international advertising sales company located near Tower Bridge.

"Hi Edwin – It's Jack Jones at International Advertising. I've just had a visit here from a Mr Humphries purporting to be connected to your new television company in Gibraltar. Is he in some way involved with it?"

"Well he is a potential investor in the project," replied Edwin. "I met him for the first time only recently."

"I see. Well I hope you don't mind my saying so but he came marching into my office with some pretty opinionated views about how he thought I should be running my business which didn't exactly get us off to a good start."

"Oh, I'm sorry to hear that," said Edwin. "I didn't even know that he would be calling on you."

"I think I would rather deal with you or your secretary in future, if that's OK," he said.

"Yes sure," said Edwin.

"Great, thanks Edwin," he replied, "Talk again soon."

Edwin hung up and relayed the conversation to the rest of the office much to their amusement.

"That's made a dent in your public relations. I wouldn't hold your breath on the Night Time Television service ever taking off if that's the way that doddery old fool is going about things," said Bill.

"I'm inclined to agree with you," said Edwin, "He seems to be in a world of his own."

"It's a shame that thanks to the initial greed of the Gibraltar Broadcasting Corporation none of the original investors is still involved," said Bill, "The new television service might have already been operating by now."

Toby the accountant then chipped in "Let's first see if old man Humphries is prepared to put his money where his mouth is."

Irrespective of whether the Night Time Television project was going to happen or not, Edwin and Helga had made plans to go to Germany throughout June and July for the birth of their baby after which their eldest child, Leon, would be of school age. For a while they wondered about the possibility of moving back into Gibraltar itself so as to take advantage of local schools. However, after looking at the few pokey places currently available for exorbitant rents, they had thought better of it. Because they were resident in Spain the only legitimate option for Gibraltar schooling was the fee-paying Catholic-run school of the Loreto Convent where various other ex-pats sent their children. Enquiries were made and following a guided tour of the premises both boys were enrolled to start there from September.

Archibald Humphries eventually returned to Spain and announced via his son Felipe that he would be coming into Gibraltar the following Wednesday to meet up with Edwin again. It was another pub lunch, this time at The Clipper in Irish Town.

"Here is a copy of the complete list of technical equipment that needs to be purchased," said Edwin, handing him a plastic wallet containing documents, "Obviously once the working capital is there the company needs to be registered. After that it's just a case of signing the deal with the TV station, purchasing the necessary technical equipment, recruiting some additional staff, ordering the first batch of programmes, agreeing a workable launch date, advertising the new service and starting to sell commercial spots within it."

"Yes, all of that must happen," said Mr Humphries, "I shall get the ball rolling so that as soon as you return from Germany it'll be all systems go."

And things were left at that.

It was still anybody's guess as to whether Edwin would remain with Smart Media or if the Night Time Television would actually get off the ground. If Archibald Humphries could get his act together and stump up the working capital everything might fall into place.

Edwin discussed the situation with Bill, Toby and Josephine.

"You haven't got much choice other than to see it through with old man Humphries if this TV venture is going to happen at all," said Toby. "Let the bugger cough up the money and then make sure he leaves you in peace to get on and make a success of the project."

"And don't forget that Smart Media will still be on hand to sell local TV commercial spots for the new late night viewing service," said Bill, "In return for our usual hefty commission of course," he added with a smile.

HELGA WAS IN AN advanced stage of pregnancy and unable to take a flight and so the trip to Germany was made by train. For the two month duration of their stay they had use of an apartment in the Frankfurt suburb of Bad Vilbel, courtesy of their Unification Church friend Manfred. With split-second timing their baby daughter, Anna, was born slap bang in middle of the two month break on 1st July which also happened to be Edwin and Helga's wedding anniversary.

They spent the remainder of their time in Germany meeting up with Helga's relatives as well as with a circle of friends from the movement. Edwin, Helga and their three children then flew back from Frankfurt to Malaga and took a taxi down the length of the Costa del Sol and back to their flat in San Roque.

On his first day back in Gibraltar Edwin purchased a white buggy from Mothercare and wheeled it across to Smart Media. When he got there, however, he was surprised to find the office locked and although it was already nine-thirty there was no sound of anybody inside. He pulled out his key and unlocked the door only to find the room completely empty. For one moment he thought he might be on the wrong floor but, no, this was definitely the same office where Smart Media had been located for the past few years and from where it now seemed to have evaporated.

Puzzled and concerned by such an unexpected occurrence Edwin took the lift back down to the ground floor where the caretaker was standing outside the building's entrance.

"What's happened to Smart Media?" asked Edwin, "Have they moved office or something?"

"Ceased trading last month," replied the man.

"Ceased trading?" said Edwin, in case he hadn't heard correctly.

"Went bankrupt," said the man.

"Good heavens," said Edwin.

Feeling somewhat conspicuous wheeling the empty buggy back down the length of Main Street, Edwin made his way to Felipe's office to see if he knew what was going on.

"Congratulations on the birth of your baby daughter," said Felipe.

"Thank you," replied Edwin. "What on earth has happened to Smart Media?"

"Didn't they tell you?" he asked.

"No. I just arrived back to an empty office and that bloke who takes care of the Centre Plaza building told me that the company had gone bust," said Edwin.

"That's right. They shut up shop a few weeks ago," said Felipe.

"How did that come about?" asked Edwin.

"Well, it's what comes of Bill Woodley entrusting his company's finance to those two scroungers Toby and Josephine who, as everybody knew, were creaming off large chunks of whatever money came in. My guess is that it reached the stage in which the rent and office overheads could no longer be met."

"So what's become of Bill?" asked Edwin.

"At home in Guadiaro and looking to work in Spain, so I hear," replied Felipe, "and mightily pissed off with Toby and Josephine who apparently did nothing to help save the situation."

"I see," said Edwin. "Well, I suppose that in the absence of Smart Media it really is time for us to get going with the Night Time Television project,"

"My father is away in Birmingham at the moment but he left this letter for you," he said, handing Edwin an envelope which he opened.

To his surprise the typewritten letter was a job offer for Edwin to work as a TV Producer/Director for Felipe's company until such time as the Night Time Television was ready to go ahead.

"I don't understand this at all," said Edwin. "It's got nothing to do with what was agreed."

"I'm afraid I'm as much in the dark about things as you are," said Felipe. "My father told me that he'd like you to work here with me until the Night Time project is ready to begin and that in the meantime I am supposed to pay you a basic salary of £700 a month – which I don't even know how I'm supposed to find."

"That's all well and good but why the delay with Night Time Television?" said Edwin. "I need to know whether or not your father is going to be true to his word in putting up the working capital to set up the project."

"I think he will," responded Felipe, "He had already registered the new company."

"Really?" asked Edwin.

He then learned that Archibald Humphries had indeed registered the company. Night Time Television was now a wholly owned subsidiary of the son's company, Casemates Design. Edwin pondered on this latest twist. At least registering the company indicated some positive intent. He supposed that it didn't really make much difference who actually owned the company provided the new television service could go ahead and that Edwin could run it according to what had been laid out in the business plan.

"So can we now go ahead and order the technical facilities from the UK?" asked Edwin.

"That I don't know," replied Felipe. "As you can appreciate, I'm kind of caught in the middle here. My father only tells me certain things."

Edwin weighed up the situation. The fact that Smart Media had packed up was a disaster because it had been his livelihood for several years and represented a safety net that he could always have returned to. Unless the Night Time Television could begin right away he didn't relish the thought of being tied to Felipe's office. The offer of a token salary was a kind gesture but in return for doing what? Felipe had no client base worth speaking of and even at Smart Media Edwin had been totally reliant on Bill Woodley going out and bringing in the business for making local TV commercials.

Edwin re-read the letter. In a small place like Gibraltar there was nothing to turn to.

"OK," he said to Felipe, "I'll go along with this as a temporary measure but I'd like to emphasise that it's the Night Time Television project that I'm here for rather than anything else."

"Yes, I realise that," replied Felipe, "and I'm sorry that you have been mucked around but you can see for yourself how my father does things – but I think he'll get there in the end."

"Let's hope so," replied Edwin.

That evening back in San Roque Edwin told Helga all that had occurred throughout the day. It was a bizarre set of circumstances and Edwin didn't like the thought of effectively being at the mercy of the unpredictable Archibald Humphries. Be that as it may, there was still a tiny shred of hope that the television project might eventually be realised and, who knows, being present in his son's office might actually speed the process up.

On collecting the accumulated mail from his Gibraltar Post Office box Edwin saw that there was a letter from the World Mission Department. For one moment he thought it might have been news about the long-awaited TV Station but it wasn't. Various members of the Unification Church were being sent to different parts of the world for a few weeks and a couple who worked at the seminary in upstate New York were wondering if would be convenient for them to stay with Edwin and Helga. He wrote back to them to say that they would be most welcome. There was also a letter from his old friends Henry and Janet in New Zealand with whom he had kept up contact over the years. They had decided to move to Australia where Henry's prospects as a chef were considerably better. They were in the process of buying a house in Brisbane.

Over the weekend Edwin and Helga bought a second hand car for the prime purpose of doing the school run in and out of Gibraltar each day.

SOMETHING WAS AMISS. In the weeks that followed Archibald Humphries didn't put in an appearance at all. Any communication was conducted entirely by fax and his scrawled messages were becoming increasingly vague and confused. Edwin went in to Felipe's office each day and sometimes sat at a desk in the adjacent room but with continued stagnation it became obvious that things were going nowhere at all. Enquiries as to the current state of play began to come through from the programme suppliers and the advertising sales company in the UK as well as from the Gibraltar Broadcasting Corporation.

By coincidence a company based in Marbella contacted Felipe's office of Casemates Design and asked if he knew of somebody who could make a television commercial for their carpet showroom. In the absence of anything else, Edwin set about working out the content, schedule and agreeing the budget. At least it would solve the immediate cash problem. It kept Edwin busy for a month. Filming and editing took place and the client was pleased with the result and made out a cheque to Casemates Design.

That would have been fine were it not for the fact that once it had been banked Felipe received strict instructions from his father not to pay Edwin or his crew anything for the work that they had done.

"That amounts to daylight robbery!" said Edwin.

"I don't understand it either," responded Felipe, "but my father told me to follow his instructions or he would take steps to close down my business."

"I've never heard anything quite so ridiculous," said Edwin.

"Well I always thought he shouldn't have got involved with your TV project," said Felipe.

"He isn't even involved in that," replied Edwin, "The service should have been up and running by now. Tell him he can forget all about that so-called basic salary which in any case has still not materialised – but I do want paying for the carpet advertisement as well members of my production crew."

"I can't get hold of him by phone until this evening," said Felipe.

"Well make him understand that I have had enough of this nonsense and that I want nothing more to do with him. I am clearing out of here but I will call by first thing tomorrow morning to collect my money from the carpet commercial and to ensure that the rest of the production crew gets paid," said Edwin.

"OK. I will talk with him and see what can be arranged," agreed Felipe.

Edwin grabbed his few belongings from the adjacent office and left the premises. He took a bus to the frontier and, after passport control, walked the short distance to La Linea Bus Station, where he boarded another bus that took him back home in San Roque.

Helga was feeding the baby. Edwin related all that had happened that morning.

"Surely he can't just withhold payment for the work that you have done – especially now that the client has paid in full," she said.

"I know," replied Edwin, "but you have to realise that we're not dealing with a normal person at all. Archibald Humphries is a law unto himself. Anyway, Felipe has said that he will speak to him tonight and I have said that I will drop by tomorrow morning."

"So that really is the end of the Night Time Television project?" she asked.

"I can't see it happening now," replied Edwin, "Even if by some fluke Archibald Humphries were to come up with the money tomorrow morning I'd still find it hard to deal with such a person. He is nothing more than a lot of hot air with delusions of grandeur and it wouldn't surprise me if he never had any real intention of funding the project despite having registered the company name."

"It's best not to have any more dealings with him," she replied, "but what comes next?"

"Good question," replied Edwin. "I'll have to scout around and see if I can find something. I don't think we should pull out of Gibraltar though – especially now that the boys have started in school there."

FELIPE HUMPHRIES WAS CAUGHT in the middle of crossfire and confused. On the one hand he was being asked to obey his father's commands or face the risk of no longer having a design company at all and yet on the other hand he could see that what his father was demanding was totally unjust.

Edwin arrived at Felipe's office mid-morning.

"I spoke to him about payment for the carpet advertisement," said Felipe, "but I'm afraid that he doesn't fully get it.

"Meaning?" asked Edwin.

"I am authorised to pay your cameraman but nobody else." he replied.

"Well hang on a minute. It took a small team of us to produce that commercial and not just the cameraman. Everybody still needs paying for what they did. That has to include me who just happened to be its producer/director, the cameraman and hire of his kit, the sound operator, the hire of the editing suite in Fuengirola, the videotape stock, the voice-over announcer, the assistant as well as the transport and overnight accommodation. Even after everybody has been paid in full your company will still be left with more than two thousand pounds," explained Edwin.

"I know – and I entirely agree with you," he said. "It's just that my father seems to want to charge you for rent of the four offices that had been set aside for Night Time Television and, in his strange way of doing things, he calculates that it is you who owes us money and not the other way round."

There was a long silence as the absurdity of such a notion sank in.

"Why do you think you father is behaving like this?" asked Edwin.

"I didn't understand it at all at first," said Felipe, "but now I realise that a lot of it stems from when I was ousted from Smart Media," said Felipe "My father didn't take at all kindly to that and I suppose that in his own way he decided on some form of revenge."

"Revenge on whom?" asked Edwin.

"The original intention was revenge on Smart Media," he said. "I guess that poaching you from them and then leaving you in the lurch was seen as retaliation for what that they tried to do to me."

"But I had nothing to do with your dismissal from Smart Media," said Edwin.

"I know that and you know that and I am truly sorry," said Felipe. "Unfortunately you got caught up in my father's confused way of thinking and yet you should never have been targeted at all."

EDWIN NEEDED TO FIND a way forward fast. Over his years spent in Gibraltar he had occasionally come across sales people of one sort or another. One such person was Lou Jones who was about the most aggressive sales person that Edwin had ever encountered. Although he was undoubtedly highly skilled in the pitching, negotiating and closing of deals, much of his abrupt manner grated with a more diplomatic approach to things.

Nevertheless, in Edwin's hour of need, it was this aggressive sales person who came to his rescue by offering him a desk in his office and a small salary in return for helping out on several media related projects. It was better than nothing and would help tide things over at least for a few months – hopefully at least until the end of the school year.

New apartments were springing up in Gibraltar on land that had recently been reclaimed from the sea and Lou Jones had begun publishing a magazine full of household tips and handy hints which he succeeded in cramming full of advertisements for electrical appliances, hardware, furniture, kitchen utensils, pot plants, curtains and anything else associated with people setting up a new home. Edwin helped on the editorial side of the magazine and with its distribution. He also put together a TV commercial and several promotional videos about the new apartment blocks which had effectively solved Gibraltar's housing shortage.

At that time a war began in the Middle East following Iraq's invasion of Kuwait and as Edwin followed events on BBC World Service Radio he thought back to his cable television station on the Royal Saudi Naval base in Jubail and wondered as to its current use.

After an absence from Gibraltar of five years Albert, the former sound operator arrived back in town with a Scandinavian wife on his arm. Having helped out on the production in Berlin he had attended a Unification Church study course in England but had subsequently met a Danish girl in the check-in queue at Luton Airport whom he had ended up marrying. They now lived in Copenhagen and were just visiting the Rock for a few days. Edwin joined them for a cheese and ham toasted sandwich at the Copacabana snack bar accompanied by the sound of Radio Gibraltar.

Turning and returning
To some secret place inside
Watching in slow motion
As you turn around and say
Take my breath away
Take my breath away

The American couple from the Unification Church Seminary arrived the following week. They were very pleasant people. They stayed with Edwin and Helga in San Roque and went into Gibraltar each day where they did their best to connect with ministers of different faith groups. News had recently come through that Reverend Moon had visited North Korea and met with its notorious Communist leader Kim Il Sung. Such a meeting between two Koreans with such opposite ideologies was an amazing development.

AFTER THE COUPLE FROM the USA had departed Edwin and Helga took the children on a short break to Madrid. Whilst there they arranged to meet up with the French sister Yvette and her Spanish husband Manuel who now had two young children and lived in Moncloa near the university.

"Actually we are thinking of moving south to Sevilla," said Yvette.

"Well, that's good. We shall be neighbours," replied Edwin.

"It would certainly be nice to have other members living nearby," said Helga.

"Sevilla is where Manuel comes from and most of his relatives are there," explained Yvette. "I don't know if you've heard this yet but all Unification Church members are now being encouraged to live and work in their home towns. The era of living communally in church centres had finally come to an end."

Although Edwin and Helga hadn't lived in a church centre for years it was good to know that the movement was evolving in such a way.

"That will probably help make the movement much more acceptable in the eyes of the public," said Edwin, "although if anyone asked me where my home town was I'd be hard pushed to come up with an answer having moved around such a lot – and apart from anything else I always felt most at home in New Zealand."

"Whatever became of the movement's planned TV station?" asked Yvette.

"Unfortunately nothing at all and I've given up asking about it," replied Edwin. "Mind you, the Washington Times seems to be doing OK. Some of their reports even find their way into the British press such as The Times and the Daily Telegraph."

At the end of the week Edwin, Helga and the children took the overnight train back south.

The following day when shopping at the large Spanish supermarket of Continente alongside the main road that runs between San Roque to Algeciras they joined a check-out queue behind an oriental man. Glancing down at his hands Edwin spotted a Unification Church wedding ring. He tapped him on the shoulder and showed them his own similar wedding ring. The person was highly amused by such an encounter. It turned out that he belonged to a Japanese fishing team that was temporarily based in southern Spain. He invited Edwin, Helga and the children to visit them at their apartment in Algeciras for a meal of freshly caught tuna enhanced with a horseradish sauce dip.

As the end of the boys' school year neared Edwin and Helga began weighing up their future options and reached the conclusion that in the absence of much in the way of TV production work it might soon be time for them to leave Gibraltar.

"Realistically with Impact Productions gone and with Smart Media gone I reckon it's about time for us to be gone too," said Edwin. "It's sad but hanging on down here for another year is not really sustainable even with the projects that Lou Jones puts my way and in a tiny place such as Gibraltar there's little else to turn to."

Through one of his contacts Edwin had received an invitation to attend some sort of a media briefing being held at a tennis club in a mountain village near Mijas. However because he and Lou Jones were busy in getting the latest edition of the household magazine out on time he had to give it a miss. That was unfortunate because the event turned out to be an initial planning meeting for a new BBC drama series about British ex-pats living in Spain with production taking place a few kilometres inland from Marbella. It was an opportunity missed as they had been short-staffed and willing to take on additional people locally. Even though Edwin wasn't particularly impressed with the storyline of 'Eldorado', it might have been fun working on it.

Later that summer a van parked outside Edwin and Helga's San Roque apartment was being loaded up with boxes of their possessions for delivery to Germany by a removal company. The family flew back to Frankfurt the following day.

CHAPTER FORTY-THREE

THE RETURN TO LIVING in Germany started off well enough. Edwin and Helga purchased what could be described as a gingerbread house that was for sale at such a low price that they had been able to afford it outright. It was located alongside the river Rhine in the small and picturesque township of Sankt Goarshausen. The area was associated with the legends of Lorelei whose singing, whilst combing her golden hair, had lured many a passing boat to its peril on rocks just below the waterline.

The three bedroom house had small rooms that were stacked on four floors. It took them a while to work out why there was nothing much on the ground floor other than a tiled storage area and why there was a massive drop down to the back yard from a heavily bolted door of their first floor kitchen. They soon learned that, in common with the rest of the houses in the quaint cobble-stoned street known as Burgstraße, the property was not 'Hochwasserfrei' meaning that every once in a while if the Rhine burst its banks the lower parts of the buildings would get completely flooded out. The back kitchen door was for the sole purpose of being able to board a boat in such conditions.

Sank Goarshausen was a place that depended on seasonal tourism as its main source of income. As such there were three hotels one of which was called the Adler that catered for the weekly arrival of visitors on a coach holiday from England. Geography had dictated a linear development of the small town which was hemmed in between the river Rhine on one side and the Wiesbaden to Koblenz railway line that ran behind. The ground then rose up high and a castle stood on the hill. There were several cafeterias and pubs, a couple of restaurants, a supermarket, a newsagent, a bakery and even a tiny cinema. A car ferry across to the other side of the river operated throughout the day.

An Imbiss kiosk next to the railway station selling hot Bratwurst and chips seemed to be a central hub of activity. There was also a late night venue called Second Life where local youth tended to gather. The more elderly residents frequented the Reblaus wine cellar which was right next door to Edwin and Helga's house as confirmed by the periodic bursts of raucous laughter that emanated from it most evenings. In his best German Edwin ticked a man off for urinating down one side of the house.

In addition to their worldly possessions having been sent up from Spain, Edwin and Helga also had a cellar full of things that had been in storage with Helga's parents for years. Now, for the first time, everything was gathered in Sankt Goarshausen. Sealed cardboard boxes left over from Southampton days and from the two occasions when they have lived near Frankfurt were unpacked. There were beds that needed reassembling as well as numerous suitcases stuffed full of clothing, boxes of books, a set of winter car tyres, electric heaters, an ironing board, radios, two televisions, tables and chairs, pots and pans and several cartons marked fragile.

"I must have put on weight whilst living in Spain," said Helga, "None of these items of clothing fit me anymore."

"Funny you should say that," replied Edwin. "Take a look at this." He demonstrated the impossibility of doing up the button on a Harris Tweed sports jacket.

"Never mind, there's a Red Cross charity collection point next to the river ferry where some of the clothing can go," she replied, "and I've noticed there's also a refugee hostal just past the petrol station. They might be glad of some of the other bits and pieces."

THE FOLLOWING WEEK EDWIN began commuting in and out of Koblenz where arrangements had been made for him to work at Manfred's TV production company which had recently moved there from Frankfurt. It was a thirty minute train journey. Manfred and his English wife Diana now had two children. The TV production facility was housed in the basement of their apartment.

"I've filmed loads of material for this tourism project but I'm not really sure about the best way of putting it all together," explained Manfred. "They are expecting a one hour documentary programme on the highlights of Koblenz which they then want dubbed into several languages,"

"Let me look through the footage and I'll see if I can come up with some sort of a sequence for it," suggest Edwin

"I was hoping that you would say that!" replied Manfred, "There are still a few more things to be shot such as a music festival in October but you'll find that most of it is there."

JUST AS EDWIN AND Helga were beginning to enjoy living in a home of their own in Sankt Goarshausen it became apparent that there was going to be a problem with the continuity of the children's schooling. Both boys could already read and write quite well in English and German as well as being able to speak a little Spanish. In Germany, however, schooling didn't begin until the age of six and the elder son had been put into a class where the teacher wasn't actually going to teach anything at all and in which the days would instead be devoted to playing games. Meanwhile their younger son could theoretically have gone to the local Kindergarten but the administrative staff apologised that because of a recent influx of refugees from the East there were simply no more places available. So for the time being he was destined to stay at home.

As the weeks passed by this clearly unacceptable situation with the schooling was proving to be a major bugbear. One Saturday Edwin sat down with Helga and they discussed the situation yet again.

"We're momentarily stuck with this," he said, "but we are going to have to do something about it soon.

"I know," replied Helga, "The system is different even though it's said that a few years later German schoolchildren catch up with and often overtake British children despite having had their later start."

"Fine, but that doesn't exactly solve the immediate situation," he replied.

"No," she agreed, "What do you suggest we do?"

"I'm not yet sure," he replied, "Probably hang on here until Christmas and then make fresh plans for the New Year. Whatever we do I first need to finish off the production with Manfred which is going to take a few more weeks."

The doorbell rang and Edwin went downstairs to answer it. A young Turkish lady stood on the doorstep.

"Guten Tag. Ist dieses Haus zu verkaufen?" she enquired as to whether it was the house that was for sale.

"Es tut mir leid, es ist schon gekauft seit drei monate," replied Edwin who explained that it was no longer on the market because they had bought it a few months ago.

"Ah so, Schade," said the lady, who went on to explain that she was pregnant and wanted to move on this side of the Rhine to live closer to her parents. She then said that if Edwin and Helga would consider re-selling it she would happily buy it. She even named a price of several thousand Deutschmarks higher than what they had paid for the place. Edwin called Helga down so as to double-check the lady's offer. They told her that they would consider the matter and let her know one way or the other in a week's time.

Edwin and Helga soon reached the decision to sell the house to the Turkish lady and the date for the move had been set for the beginning of February. However, there was still no fixed plan as to where they might head off to other than the criteria that it needed to have a work possibility for Edwin and immediate schooling for the children.

They even contemplated returning to Gibraltar even if that would mean Edwin taking any kind of a job, however unrelated, to begin with. That idea was quashed, however, when a letter arrived from the Gibraltar Tax Office with a demand for the best part of three thousand pounds that they claimed Edwin owed them. He knew the figure to be wrong. If anything it was the tax office that owed him a rebate as he would be able to prove in correspondence. Nevertheless the letter had the effect of putting them off making an immediate return to Gibraltar. Perhaps they should consider the United Kingdom.

THEIR FORD FIESTA CAR was loaded up and topped by two large suitcases strapped to the roof rack and protected with a sheet of plastic wrapped around both. It was snowing on the cold February morning of their departure. They took the Autobahn to Aachen and then up through the length of Belgium to the ferry port of Ostend. A late evening sailing of the cross-channel ferry got them across to Dover. From there they continued the remainder of the journey to the same self-catering holiday accommodation in Glastonbury that they had stayed at a few years ago. It had been about the only place that Edwin could think of to use as a base whilst seeking somewhere to live on a more permanent basis. He had phoned the landlady and, being off-season, the accommodation was available.

Tired from the journey they didn't do much for the remainder of that day other than visit the adjacent Safeway supermarket.

"Well, now that we are here I guess we had better use the first few days to decide which town to live in on a more permanent basis," said Edwin.

"Do you have any particular preference," asked Helga.

"No apart from the fact that I have read some quite horrendous accounts of inner-city schools in Britain so it'd be best to avoid moving back into somewhere like Southampton much as I have fond memories of the time when I had lived there," he said.

"I enjoyed Southampton too," she replied, "but I agree about schooling."

As they walked up Glastonbury High Street they paused to look at an estate agent window display and were shocked to see the rise in house prices that had taken place in their absence. Everything was now three times as much as it had been at the time of their departure. Throughout the rest of the week they drove to other places such as Salisbury, Romsey, Winchester and Dorchester where property prices were even higher still and they reached the grim conclusion that they were right out of the UK housing market altogether.

"It looks as though we are going to have to rent," said Edwin. "The problem with England is that people buy homes as an investment rather than just as a place to live in and so you tend to get artificially inflated prices."

"Well, never mind. I suppose that we are used to renting," said Helga.

Another day trip took in Ringwood, Wimborne, and Blandford Forum but they discovered that even affordable rented accommodation was in short supply. That evening they considered the possibility of remaining where they were in Glastonbury which, although small and a bit off the beaten track, at least had local schools that were within walking distance.

"It's certainly an option," said Edwin, "It's not exactly the most convenient of places. It's too small to have any suitable work for me and it hasn't even got a railway station but I suppose that Bristol, Yeovil or Taunton could be commuted to by bus."

"OK, but we can't stay forever living in this holiday accommodation. We'd need to find somewhere in the town that's slightly more permanent," said Helga.

"Agreed," said Edwin, "but in the meantime and in fairness to the boys let's take them over to the local school tomorrow morning to see if we can get them started there.

St John's Infants School was located immediately behind St John's Church halfway up Glastonbury High Street. A pathway led to a gate then in through the playground on the other side of which was the headmistress's office. Explaining their sudden arrival in the United Kingdom, Edwin and Helga provided the pleasant lady with relevant details of the boys' previous schooling in Gibraltar and an outline of the situation in Germany. She warmly welcomed them to her school and accompanied them to their two respective classrooms where introductions were made to their teachers.

It took another week to stumble upon a small house in Glastonbury that was available to rent. It had been advertised on a postcard placed in the window of a corner shop and was a modern furnished home. The house had only two bedrooms, one of which was tiny, but they figured that it would do them for the time being. It had its own back garden which, not having had such a luxury in Gibraltar, Spain or Germany, was something of a novelty value and an electric lawnmower was also provided.

Glastonbury was a strange place. Identifiable from miles around by the iconic landmark of a hill with a lone church tower perched on its top the town was equally famous for its abbey ruins where these days an admission fee was charged for the privilege of entering its grounds. Edwin and Helga had already been there and done that on their previous visit to Glastonbury. The High Street shops catered for those in search of crystals, lucky charms, psychedelic clothing, incense and books on the occult. Apart from a Woolworth and couple of newsagents there was little else as far as retail went. The town was still regarded as a latter day hippie centre as evidenced by the multi-coloured attire of many of its residents. Edwin looked decidedly out of place in jacket and tie as if he were the alternative one. An abundance of unusual spiritual groups of one sort or another seemed to be in evidence. People sat under a pyramid in one shop window whilst others banged bongo drums on the street outside. It all made the Unification Church seem very tame.

Now that they had a UK address and a telephone number Edwin set himself up as a freelance producer/director and before long landed himself a project with a television production company in Bath. He had never learned to drive and the bus journey time of an hour and three quarters each way took a large chunk out of the day.

ONE SATURDAY EDWIN AND Helga thought it about time to look up the Unification Church. A few phone calls revealed that a couple that they both knew from several years ago were now living in a Bristol suburb.

Dominic Higgins was born and bred in Bristol and so it had been the natural place for him to go to with his family in the context of returning to his home town. His wife Brigitte was from Salzburg. They had four children and now lived in a council house near the Wells Road in Bristol. They welcomed Edwin's family inside and put the kettle on. Both sets of children were introduced to each other and ushered into the front lounge to play together with an assortment of games.

"We've been here nearly a year," said Dominic as a plate of bourbon biscuits was passed around. "I have managed to get a job as a school teacher which I thoroughly enjoy. In that respect the movement has become much more normalised rather than having its members living in centres and spending most of their time standing on street corners fundraising although since getting here I can't say that we feel as if we are doing very much in terms of church-related activity."

"What about the weekend workshops?" asked Edwin.

"Oh, I'm afraid they are no longer held every weekend," replied Dominic, "In fact they've become something of a rarity. The demand just doesn't seem to be there anymore."

"I think it's because the movement has evolved and that so many of us have now got young families to think about. We can't just drop everything and be out and about all hours of the day like we used to a few years back," said Brigitte.

"But that must mean less intake of new members," said Helga.

"It's certainly dwindled. It might sound strange but I think that the main increase in membership is probably the number of babies that have been born," said Brigitte.

"There's a different emphasis these days," interjected Dominic. "Things have moved on from the individual level to the family level. Even the transition of moving out of church centres and into homes of our own was easy for some but a major upheaval for others. Some church members had become so institutionalised that they found it difficult to start doing things in the real world. A few who had money were able to buy houses but for many it has been something of a struggle to get back on their feet."

"What about your situation?" asked Edwin.

"Well, as you can see we don't exactly live in a palace," replied Dominic. "A council house on a Bristol estate might not be everybody's idea of the Kingdom of Heaven on Earth but it just happens to be our starting point."

"It's a similar situation for many members," explained Brigitte. "In our case we have been lucky because at least Dominic has been able to find a job and I now work a couple of evenings a week down at the supermarket. When you think of it though, most members gave their young adult life to the movement on a voluntary basis and yet now, suddenly, they are in their forties with no work, no home and no savings. It hasn't been an easy situation to adjust to."

They asked about other church members living in the area and learned that they were a few dotted around although they lived several miles apart from each other. The greatest number of families was in London and Birmingham.

THE FOLLOWING WEEKEND EDWIN and Helga decided to take a trip into London. There they attended a Unification Church Sunday Service held near Wembley and were surprised to note that they recognised just about everybody gathered in the hall. There seemed to be no new members at all. The couple in Bristol had suggested that the movement in Britain had become inward-looking rather than reaching out to the world. Such a notion was confirmed when Edwin spoke with one of his former friends after the service, who told him that for ten years there had been a policy in Britain to have no contact with the media.

"How short-sighted is that?" said Edwin.

"Absolutely crazy," said Bob Jamieson, who had worked as a researcher for BBC Scotland before joining the movement. "Even when interesting conferences are held with some quite prominent guest speakers, the membership in Britain is told not to inform the media. It is a huge contradiction because on the one hand there is the desire to show the world what we're about and yet we are being discouraged from doing so by the most logical means – and all because of some bad media experiences of the past."

"Do you still get enquiries from journalists?" asked Edwin.

"Every now and again," said Bob, "but to give you one example of something that happened recently, the phone rang in my publications office one morning and a sister happened to answered it. When she found it to be someone from the press she screamed down the phone at them that after all the things that the media had done she wouldn't be giving them any information – and then hung up."

"So much for trying to establish good media relations," commented Edwin.

"Precisely," said Bob. "And there's another thing too. As a consequence of that lost libel case against the Daily Mail the government investigated the Unification Church for four years in an attempt to remove its charitable status and yet all of the various allegations, which included brainwashing, breaking up families and the supposed exploitation of its members, were found to be groundless. The Attorney General announced to the House of Commons that he was dropping the case and said that, had he known from the outset all that came to light during the proceedings, the case would probably never have been brought. So the Unification Church was reinstated on the Register of Charities as being a bona fide religion for the public benefit and charitable in law."

"Well at least that was a good outcome," said Edwin.

"Yes, but the main problem is that that nobody bothered to let the media know."

Edwin realised that as long as he was in England, if he wanted to do something that might help the Unification Movement, he should perhaps adopt a behind the scenes media role.

Edwin began by writing a letter to the Head of Religious Broadcasting at the BBC. In it he had outlined the outcome of the government's investigation as well as Reverend Moon's meeting with President Gorbachev and pointed out that the movement had evolved and withstood the test of time. He suggested that from a theological point of view its unique take on history lent itself towards an in-depth TV programme being made.

A few days later a reply came back from someone with the title of Chief Assistant to the Head of Religious Broadcasting saying that as he was sure Edwin would appreciate a programme about the Unification Church was rather too controversial a suggestion in the context of main stream religious broadcasting but that if at some stage in the future they wished to do something on the subject they would be sure to contact him as the first port of call.

No change there then, thought Edwin who had heard much the same sort of thing before. Oh well, let the BBC stick to its tried and tested religious programmes if that was as adventurous as it wanted to be.

His train of thought was momentarily distracted when he received a telephone call from Lou Jones in Gibraltar who had apparently landed a lucrative deal to put together a video compilation promoting Gibraltar as a finance centre and he wondered if Edwin might be sufficiently to free to be able to fly out and do it. Edwin asked a bit more about the proposed content, the budget and the time scale and said he would get back to him the following day.

Edwin was already working on a project with the TV production company in Bath that was nearing completion and there were more on their way. However, he might be able to juggle the dates around a bit so as to weave the work in Gibraltar into it. When he had come up with what he considered to be a workable timetable he phoned Lou back to let him know that he would be pleased to meet him in Gibraltar the following Monday.

An early morning flight from Bristol Airport to Malaga was followed by a coach journey down the length of the Costa del Sol to San Roque where Edwin was booked into the Hostal Hidalgo for the week. It felt strange walking past the block of apartment that just a year ago had been home and it felt even stranger to be having an evening meal in Bar España instead of something prepared in his former kitchen.

Gibraltar felt like an old friend. There was a kind of nostalgia about the place. As he walked up Main Street to meet Lou for coffee at the Montarik Hotel he ran into many familiar faces.

"Hallo Edwin, welcome back to the Rock," said one particular gentleman who just happened to the leader of Gibraltar's main opposition political party. It was a close-knit community.

The production brief was straightforward enough. Various financial companies in Gibraltar had agreed to participate in a promotional video compilation and all of them would be chipping in to the budget thanks to the salesmanship of Lou Jones, who would be taking his customary ten per cent. The schedule was likely to be a bit erratic because not all of the companies involved would be ready within the same timeframe. Coverage would include interviews with their spokespersons and an intrusion of a camera crew on their premises for shots of people going about their day-to-day activities. Arrangements were made for everything to be filmed in phases. That fitted in well will Edwin's other workload and allowed him to commute back and forth from the United Kingdom, which he did over the next few months. By mid-June the production was completed to everybody's satisfaction.

Working freelance was unpredictable in terms of income. A one-off production might be very well paid but it could then be offset by a period in which there was nothing coming in. Ironically, now that he was back in the UK, Edwin seemed to be picking up more work in Gibraltar. He continued to return there whenever there was something worth pursuing. Interestingly, he never saw anything more of Felipe Humphries, who had apparently relocated to somewhere in Spain.

THE UNIFICATION CHURCH IN Britain had announced that it would be holding an event in the grounds of its Wiltshire farm to celebrate twenty-five years of the movement's presence in Britain. It was an upbeat reunion and one of those occasions in which most of the day was spent bumping into people not seen for many years and realising the abundance of young families that had since sprung up. There were plenty of handshakes, recollections and introductions to new-born babies. A large marquee had been set up at one end of the field in which a morning service was held and a booklet was distributed that outlined the early pioneering days of the Unification Church in Britain from twenty-five years ago.

A barbeque lunch was available, although most families had opted to bring a picnic lunch with them. Sports activities had been arranged for the afternoon for those who wished, whilst others preferred to sit and chat with each other or to watch various musical performances taking place back in the marquee.

EDWIN WAS DUE BACK in Gibraltar the following week in order to put the finishing touches to an updated promotional video production about newly-built property on reclaimed land. Coincidentally, a few days before his departure, he was contacted by someone from the World Mission Department to ask if it would be possible for him to find suitable accommodation in Gibraltar for five Japanese sisters who were going to spend some time there. They were representatives of a recently-formed Women's Federation for World Peace that had been set up by Reverend Moon's wife. Apparently Japanese ladies were being assigned to numerous parts of the world. Ten would be in Gibraltar for several months but they planned to be there on a rotation basis, with just five of them there at any one time. In Gibraltar Edwin dropped in on one of the estate agents and secured them an apartment in one of the prestigious blocks called the Watergardens.

Their impact was enormous. Dressed in kimonos they began by holding a public Japanese Tea Ceremony in the centre of town, which won the hearts of many Gibraltarians. But they also got up very early in the mornings and, armed with bin bags, gathered up rubbish that had been strewn along the streets. They were very well-organised and soon gained a network of local contacts. Their positive presence on the Rock earned them front page coverage in the Gibraltar Chronicle and feature articles written by Edwin's local journalist and photographer friends.

CHAPTER FORTY-FOUR

ON ONE OF HIS return journeys from Gibraltar Edwin arrived at Gatwick Airport and decided to drop in on his Unification Church friend Bob Jamieson whom he knew felt similar frustration with no advances being made in the UK media.

Details of a further large wedding in South Korea had started to emerge and Bob Jamieson was under the usual instructions to keep it quiet from the media. The reason given was that it was a special occasion for those couples getting married and nobody wanted to spoil it by unwelcome media intrusion.

"It's actually going to be a massive event taking place in Seoul's Olympic Stadium and linked by satellite to local marriage ceremonies taking place simultaneously throughout the world," he said. "Not only that but there'll be several high level conferences running alongside the main event in Korea and numerous dignitaries will be flying in to attend."

"Well if it's going to be that large news of it is bound to get out sooner or later," said Edwin. "Surely it would be far more preferable for the movement to be supplying the information to the media first rather that leaving things wide open for critics with distorted viewpoints to get in on the act."

"I know. All this hush-hush policy is ridiculous." he agreed. "If I'd wanted to join a secret society I'd have joined the Freemasons. I mean, quite apart from the wedding event there's going to be an international professors' conference, a science conference, a student conference and a women's conference all happening there in that same week and yet we are supposed to keep quiet about it."

Edwin gathered as much information about such events as possible. Back in Glastonbury he put together a comprehensive package of material about everything that would be taking place and sent it off to selected journalists at major news desks a full month before the date of the events. He hoped it would work.

A couple of weeks later Edwin received a phone call from Bob Jamieson who was pleasantly surprised that the media had already got wind of the event.

"I've had phone calls from The Times, The Daily Telegraph, The Guardian and the BBC," he said, "and for some reason they seemed to be better informed about things than on previous occasions."

That summer Edwin and Helga went over to Germany with the children. From there Edwin viewed live coverage of the massive wedding event taking place in South Korea displayed on a large screen in a hired hall in the unlikely venue of Frankfurt Zoo. The place was packed full of friends from the German Unification Church. Some were in wedding dress and getting married simultaneously, others were there simply to observe the spectacular event. Because of the time difference, it went on throughout most of the night.

The German press didn't give it a mention. That was in contrast to media coverage in Britain. On returning to England Edwin visited the Lancaster Gate headquarters where there was an air of jubilation. They had never had such good press coverage before. Bob Jamieson was busily making photocopies of each press article and assembling them into packs for people to take away for reference. There had been good coverage on radio, television and in most major daily newspapers, most notably an excellent write up in the Guardian and also in the women's magazine, *Marie Claire*.

It demonstrated that not only was press coverage possible but that good press coverage was possible.

"Wow, spirit world must have worked really hard to bring this about!" commented one of the church members from Cornwall as he looked through the newspaper reports.

Such a welcome breakthrough in the British media led some of the members to realise the need to start building a healthy working relationship with the press.

It was then announced that the Unification Church was being replaced by a new organisation called the Family Federation for World Peace and Unification. It was more than just a new name. The Family Federation would be a broader-based group that created an alliance of people of all faiths who shared a vision of family values as the basis for healthy communities, harmonious societies and a peaceful world. It also meant that the infamous mass weddings would now be open to people of other faiths too. That was a news story in itself.

EDWIN WAS DUE TO go Cyprus for a meeting with the national television broadcaster CyBC regarding a possible co-production. There were no direct flights to Nicosia from Bristol Airport and so he intended going via Larnaca.

On learning that a former church member lived there Edwin decided to phone him to ask about onward public transport possibilities from there to Nicosia.

"Well blow me down, you're the first person from the Unification Movement to have contacted me since I parted company with it seventeen years ago," said the person in Cyprus, "and if you're going to be passing through here I'd be interested in meeting up with you. When do you get here?"

"I'll be arriving in Larnaca next Tuesday evening but I need to be in Nicosia on Friday morning," replied Edwin.

"Well, there is a regular coach service to Nicosia as well as a door-to-door shared minibus arrangement which would probably be your best bet. The journey takes about an hour.

"Oh, that sounds OK," replied Edwin.

"I'll tell you what. My wife and I own two houses next door to each other here in Larnaca. We don't use the second house and you're more than welcome to come and stay there for a few days for free," he said.

"That would certainly be an interesting possibility," replied Edwin. "Are you centrally located?"

"Yes, we're slap bang in the middle of everything here with easy access to the town and the beach which are walking distance," he said, "although it's unbearably hot out here at the moment.

"That's OK. I'm used to Gibraltar down at the western end of the Mediterranean," said Edwin.

"Well then, it's high time for you to come and meet the Eastenders!" he said, "What time does your flight get in?"

"10:20 next Tuesday evening," replied Edwin.

"I'll see you in the arrivals hall," he said, "and who knows, I might even have time on the Friday to run you into Nicosia myself."

"Brilliant," replied Edwin and they hung up.

Wearing an Australian bush hat and resembling Crocodile Dundee, Eric Buchanan was waiting for Edwin. It was the first time they had met each other even though they knew so many people in common.

"How come you live here in Cyprus?" asked Edwin as they drank late night coffee in Eric's kitchen.

"I was originally sent here by the Unification Church as a missionary," he replied. Back then in 1974 Turkey had invaded the north of the island in response to a military coup backed by the Greeks and that led to the island being partitioned. In Nicosia I became friends with a Greek Cypriot family who had been expelled from the north and had lost their entire haulage business in the process. Having driven large trucks myself I offered to go into the north and bring back their fleet of vehicles one by one for which they were extremely grateful. I was then asked by the Unification Church to go to Paris to study a jewellery business which was quite enjoyable but when I returned to London all geared up to set up a branch of it there they said that they were offering the position to somebody else. I was pissed off and so I walked out and left. I decided to come back out to Cyprus and when I did so that same family were pleased to give me a full-time job as one of their truck drivers which I've been doing ever since. I then met a young Greek Cypriot lady, got married and we now have two children.

It soon became apparent that since his departure from the Unification Church Eric had lived in something of a time warp. He was surprised to learn that communal living was a thing of the past and that members now had their own homes and went out to work for a living. However the thing that intrigued him the most was that the Marriage Blessing was now available to the wider world and not only to Unificationists.

"Does that mean that my Cypriot wife Phoebe and I could even participate?" he asked.

"Yes, the Marriage Blessing is open to all people," replied Edwin.

"That is very interesting indeed," he said. "At the end of the day I still have tremendous respect for Reverend Moon and I haven't come across a more logical theological teaching than the Principle. The problem for me was the way that the movement was organised. They had even that policy of buying up properties all over the United Kingdom but then when some members were called to work in America selling off all those houses again on the direction of some idiot who was completely clueless about the property market. If they'd hung onto them and let them out it would have provided a tidy income.

"I guess a lot of contradictory things took place in that era," said Edwin.

"Well I hope things have changed," he said. "I still hold many things close to my heart. Even though I left I didn't race off to join some other faith group because I know that the content of the Principle is true and that it is perfectly compatible with all major religions.

Edwin spent a pleasant few days in Cyprus in the company of Eric and his family. The meeting at CyBC in Nicosia went well. Arrangements were then made for Eric and his wife to take part in a Marriage Blessing ceremony.

BACK IN GLASTONBURY EDWIN and Helga were tuned in to a news programme on BBC Radio 5 Live. It was the eve of yet another mass wedding which this time was being held in Washington DC. A studio discussion took place in which the presenter tried to get a heated debate going but then found out that all of the contributors were more or less on the same side. The programme had sought to pitch the combined views of an Anglican Pastor and the Provost of Southwark Cathedral against a spokesperson for the Family Federation. If it was hoping for confrontation it backfired.

The provost said that in his view the Unification Movement had "evolved, grown and matured." Its second generation were brought up in its tradition but rather than being isolated from the real world most of them went to university, got degrees and landed professional jobs. They nevertheless tended to marry within the movement.

The Anglican pastor then said that members of the Family Federation for World Peace and Unification were "Pillars of society, preaching good things and that the movement pointed people towards traditional morality and traditional loyalty – which was all to the good."

It was then left to the spokesperson for the Family Federation simply to say, "I want to thank you for these comments. I agree with very much of what was said."

The BBC presenter didn't seem to know what to make of it.

THE SOMERSET TOWN OF Glastonbury where Edwin and Helga lived was steeped in legend and as one local historian put it, "A rumour on Monday becomes a legend on Wednesday and it becomes history by Friday."

A popular story was that as a boy Jesus came to Glastonbury with his relative Joseph of Arimathea who had been a tin merchant. The rousing song 'Jerusalem' makes reference to such the possibility of such a visit.

And did those feet in ancient time
Walk upon England's mountains green:
And was the holy Lamb of God,
On England's pleasant pastures seen!

Joseph of Arimathea was supposed to have dug his wooden staff into a nearby hillside which then took root and grew into the so-called Glastonbury Holy Thorn Tree which blossoms at Christmas and at Easter. In recent years a sprig was sent to the Queen at Christmas and the eldest pupil at the local infants' school had the privilege of cutting it from the tree. That December the particular duty fell to Edwin and Helga's seven-year-old son. Normally the sprig would then be sent to Buckingham Palace by post but this time the Queen asked for it to be delivered by the schoolchild in person. One parent was invited to attend.

"There comes a time for every Englishman to go before his queen!" said Helga.

Accompanied by the local vicar, the mayor and a town councillor, the occasion provided Edwin and son with a sense of history, a sense of continuity, a sense of loyalty and a renewed faith in the monarchy all in the space of a single day. The presentation took place in the Queen's parlour and was witnessed by several corgi dogs.

THE TV PRODUCTION COMPANY in Bath then received an unusual request. It was for a member of staff to direct a pilot programme for a new drama series set in Botswana. Edwin was assigned to the project and it meant being away for six weeks. The plane touched down at Gaborone Airport one Saturday morning but despite it having been a long haul flight at least the country was in the same time zone so it hadn't thrown his body clock completely out of sync.

At the airport he was given a warm welcome by Steve Ardley the manager of Kalahari Productions with whom he would be working. Edwin had spoken with him on the phone a couple of weeks ago.

"It's the oldest democracy in Africa and a very stable country at that with no racism at all," he explained. "And now that they've discovered diamonds here it's become a wealthy place too and they are frantically trying to modernise. I think you'll enjoy your stay. The drama project is going to break new ground too."

Edwin had been booked in at the President Hotel in the centre of town from where the production company was a five minute walk. They drank a cup of tea together after which Steve left Edwin to his own devices for the remainder of the weekend. They would meet again at the office on Monday morning.

Edwin went out to take his first look around Gaborone. A pedestrian precinct of small shops led to a neat layout of well-kept avenues with names such as Nelson Mandela Drive, Independence Avenue and Kaunda Road. Edwin looped around and came to the National Museum and Art Gallery. The door was open and so he went in and spent nearly an hour absorbing as much information as he could about Botswana. He remembered that his childhood stamp album had contained postage stamps from Bechuanaland as the country had then been called.

On Monday Edwin spent the first part of the morning reading through the English version of the script which had been written by two local authors. The production was a reflection of day to day occurrences in a Gaborone suburb and was perhaps Botswana's answer to Coronation Street. Edwin noted that instead of being centred on three or four main characters it had a tendency to keep introducing more and more characters into the plot which had resulted in a cast of thirty-five in that first episode.

The storyline involved fourteen different locations and Edwin asked Steve about them.

"Yes, that's right. We have got use of most of them for the next four weeks with the exception of scenes taking place at the African Mall which will need to be shot outside of normal working hours," he replied.

"Would it be possible for me to take a look at each of the places," asked Edwin. "In that way I can get them in my mind's eye."

"Sure," he replied. "We could even do that now if you like."

They spent the next few hours visiting each location which included a suburban house, a cafeteria some public gardens, a book shop, a street market and a car park. It turned out that the pilot programme would need to be shot using just one camera. That would mean a fair bit of repositioning to get different angles and a considerable amount of repetition on the part of the actors to allow for complete flexibility when editing the scenes together.

"How good is your cameraman?" asked Edwin.

"Well, to be quite honest it's going to be me," replied Steve, "I've got quite a bit of camera experience albeit for documentaries and before you ask who will be doing the editing that's going to be me too.

"I'm beginning to get the picture," replied Edwin.

"Good. Even though the pilot programme is being done on a shoestring budget we still want it to be as well made as possible," he said.

"Dumila-ra" greeted a young lady when they got back to the office.

"Dumila-ma" responded Steve. "Hey, let me introduce you to Edwin who has come all the way from England to help us out with this production. Edwin, meet Beauty who is going to play the part of Margaret.

She gave him a broad smile of dazzling white teeth. "Welcome," she said as they shook hands.

That evening whilst seated at the desk in his hotel room Edwin divided various parts of script into the locations at which they would be shot and began to devise a schedule for each of them. He calculated that, allowing for camera repositioning and any minor delays, it would take ten full days to film the programme in its entirety. That would then be followed by a massive editing session of a fortnight or so. Fortunately most of the actors belonged to an amateur dramatic society and between them had a lot of talent. Although used to projecting their voices from a stage Edwin encouraged them to speak at a normal conversational level that a microphone would be perfectly capable of picking up.

Edwin revisited each of the locations once again. This time, armed with the script, he made notes as to where the action would be taking place and where best to position the camera to capture it. To gather the desired variety of shots he had to work out at least three different camera positions at each place.

Edwin and Steve worked well together. By now each individual camera angle was shown on the script for ease of reference. Apart from actors fluffing their lines or occasions when a microphone appeared in shot, each scene was captured and then re-captured from a different camera angle before being captured yet again from yet another angle. The process wasn't as painstaking at it had initially sounded and the cast soon got used to their performance being gathered by such repetitive means.

All of the filming was successfully completed by the end of the tenth day exactly on schedule. They then spent the next couple of weeks in compiling the production to their satisfaction.

A viewing session was organised for everybody who had been involved and there was considerable enthusiasm for the completed programme. Steve was very pleased with the finished production and felt confident that it would lead to an entire series being commissioned.

Edwin still had a couple of days to spare before his flight back to Britain. He used the time to pay a courtesy visit to the branch of the Family Federation in Gaborone and met with some of its local members. They had been experiencing difficulty in being registered as a legitimate organisation. The reason was because of a knock-on effect from bad rumour that had recycled in the press over the years.

On the plane journey back to London Edwin stumbled upon an in-flight magazine article which reported that the Vatican had recently been rocked when it became known that Roman Catholic Archbishop Emmanuel Milingo from Zambia had taken part in a mass wedding officiated by Reverend and Mrs Moon. The Archbishop had been matched and married to a Korean acupuncturist. He was ordered by the Catholic Church to separate but he protested and said, *"How can I now leave my wife? ... For forty-three years as a celibate priest ... I only knew God as a male. Now, through my union with Maria, I have come to see the other side of God's heart, which is female."*

CHAPTER FORTY-FIVE

"G'DAY EDWIN! This is a blast from the past. It's Henry in Brisbane," said a familiar sounding voice on the phone.

"Henry! Good to hear you. How are you doing?" said Edwin to his old friend.

"Fine thanks. I just wanted to get in touch with you to let you know that Janet and I will be making a short visit to the UK and that we'll be arriving in London in a couple of days' time," he said.

"Well, that's great news!" said Edwin, "How long are you going to be over for?"

"Only a fortnight I'm afraid," replied Henry, "We're actually coming over for my mother's funeral next Wednesday but once that is out of the way, and if you and your wife are free, I'm hoping that we could arrange to meet up during the second week."

"Yes, of course – oh, and I'm sorry to hear about your mum," replied Edwin.

"Well, she was ninety-three," said Henry, "and I mean everybody's got to go sooner or later."

"True," said Edwin. "Where will you be staying?"

"Initially with my brother's family in Caterham in Surrey," he said, "but we'll also be hiring a car."

"Well, you're very welcome to come on down to us in rural Somerset." said Edwin, "What about your children? Are they coming over too?"

"No, they're all too tied up with their work here in Australia," said Henry, "It'll just be Janet and me."

"Well, give us a shout when you get here and we'll see what we can arrange," said Edwin.

HENRY AND JANET ARRIVED in Glastonbury on a Monday afternoon. Although there had been letters and the occasional phone call it was the first time Edwin had seen them for thirty-five years. They both looked well. Introductions were made to Helga and the children and in the evening the four adults went out for dinner at an inn in the nearby village of Kingsdon. Crab risotto and forest mushrooms were ordered as was stuffed veal and chicken with dauphinoise potato, purple sprouting broccoli, caramelised baby onions and sautéed spinach.

"Cheers!" said Henry as he raised a large glass of red Chilean Merlot, "It really is great to see you again, Edwin me old mate, and, of course, to meet you, Helga."

"This is just like old times," said Edwin, "Did someone turn the clock back?"

"I'm afraid the gap has been far too long," said Henry, "When are you going to come down under to visit us in Australia?"

"Oh, one of these days we will," replied Edwin, "and I still want to show Helga something of New Zealand."

"We sometimes pop back to New Zealand to see my mother in Palmerston North," said Janet, "but I guess you would be more interested in revisiting Christchurch and Dunedin. Mind you where you are now living in Glastonbury looks a quaint olde worlde town."

"It's got its history but it's a bit of a weird place," explained Helga. It tends to cater for an alternative community. As we'll show you tomorrow the High Street shops all specialise in things like tarot cards, crystals and psychedelic trousers for hippies. Whenever we want to buy something normal such as a pair of pillow cases, we have to drive to a different town altogether such as Taunton or Yeovil."

"But Glastonbury is also well known for its world famous rock concert, isn't it? I bet you don't get much sleep when that's going on," said Henry.

"Actually it doesn't affect us that much because the music festival is held on farmland in the village of Pilton which is about six miles outside of Glastonbury," said Edwin. "What normally happens is that the town fills up with the weird and the wonderful a few days beforehand but once the event gets underway it completely empties and becomes very quiet. And then when it's over everybody comes traipsing back through the town centre – invariably caked in mud."

"It can normally be guaranteed to bucket down with rain for the occasion," added Helga.

"Last summer a car pulled up on Glastonbury High Street and the driver asked me how to get to Glastonbury," recalled Edwin. "I told him that he was already in Glastonbury but he persisted in saying that he meant 'Glastonbury' and then I clicked what he was trying to say!"

"Incidentally, how is that religious group of yours doing?" asked Henry, "We don't seem to hear so much about it these days."

"It's still alive and well," replied Edwin, "It's evolved into something called the Family Federation for World Peace and Unification."

"What is it that distinguishes it from other religious organisations?" asked Henry.

"Well, most major faith groups claim that they are right and that everyone else is wrong. Ours says, look, you're all kind of right – but you just need the finishing touches," said Edwin.

"That sounds reasonable enough," said Janet, "and if your delightful family is an example of what it seeks to be doing then all I can say is that it must have got something good going for it."

A dessert of sticky toffee pudding and ginger ice cream was served.

THE FOLLOWING MORNING EDWIN and Helga took Henry and Janet on a local sightseeing tour. As they walked towards the famous landmark of Glastonbury Tor an American tourist approached them.

"Is the Abbey located somewhere around here?" he asked.

"The main entrance to the Abbey Ruins is on Magdalene Street which is just around the corner from the bottom of the High Street," replied Edwin

"You mean to say Glastonbury Abbey is in ruins?" asked the tourist.

"Yes, very much so," said Edwin.

"That damned Hitler again!" muttered the American as he continued on his way.

An essential part of anyone's visit to Glastonbury is to climb the conical shape of the Tor by means of a zigzag path of several flights of steps. Today was no exception and the physical exertion left all four of them completely out of breath. A lone and roofless church tower stood on the top of the hill as did a group of French tourists. The view of English countryside for miles around was marred only by the silhouetted shape on the horizon of Hinkley Point Nuclear Power Station.

"What's that place over there?" asked Henry, pointing to a township at the foot of the Mendip Hills.

"It's the city of Wells," replied Edwin, "and if you look carefully you can just about make out the cathedral."

"Oh yes, I see where you mean," he said.

"And that way you can see the Black Mountains of Wales in the far distance," said Helga.

"I can understand this Glastonbury Tor being described as magical and mystical," said Janet, "It's got a certain something about it."

Yes. It's generally acknowledged that there's a bit more to it than just a geographical feature. People have been coming here for a very long time. There's evidence of a pagan settlement as well as an early Christian settlement and Glastonbury itself is supposed to be a converging place for invisible energy lines," replied Edwin.

"But there's the dark side too," said Helga, "At the time of King Henry the Eighth's dissolution of the monasteries the last Abbot of Glastonbury was hanged on this hill."

"What? Right here where we're standing now?" asked Henry.

"Well somewhere up here, yes," said Edwin. "He was hung drawn and quartered and his body parts were then put on public display so as to put the fear of the king into as many hearts as possible."

"That's kind of creepy," said Janet, "Shall we go back down?"

They descended the Tor by the pathway that ran along its front spine. At the bottom they paused for a quick drink of the waters flowing from two different springs on opposite sides of a lane. The first was white and contained calcium and by comparison the second was reddish due to its iron content.

"The Chalice Well is supposed to have healing powers for any number of different ailments," said Helga, "There had once been a stampede to Glastonbury when the waters were publicised as being a cure for asthma."

They turned into the top of the High Street where in addition to the shops selling new age accessories there were advertisements for spiritual healing, astrological readings, a Goddess Conference and a sign pointing to something called the Miracle Rooms.

"You can imagine what it's like when someone asks for directions around here," said Edwin, "Just carry on past the lucky charm shop and crystal magic store on your left then cross the road at the Yin Yang Centre and, when you come to Harmonious Herbal Healing, turn right and go up past the Archangel Michael Soul Therapy Centre as far as Cosmic Image on the next corner."

"Is there some kind of pageant taking place?" asked Henry, "Almost everybody seems to be dressed in colourful costume."

"Actually that's just normal Glastonbury," replied Helga.

They rounded a corner and passed through a massive wooden gateway that led to a small building where Edwin purchased tickets for entry to the grounds of the abbey ruins. Once inside they walked across a long stretch of neatly cut grass that had once been the nave and transepts of the great church of Glastonbury Abbey and where some massive slabs of masonry still stood.

"If they are only a third of its original height it must have been some church," said Janet, looking upwards at the remains of the columns.

"In its day it was the largest church in England," replied Helga.

"But doesn't its destruction reflect the state of the established church today? Basically conked out?" asked Henry. "Maybe your Unification lot are in with a chance after all!"

"Oh, I wouldn't put it quite like that," said Edwin, "Historically it was a struggle for power between the crown and the papacy of which Glastonbury was very much a flashpoint."

"Every summer there's still an annual pilgrimage," said Helga. "The Church of England parades down the High Street and into the Abbey grounds on a Saturday and the Catholic Church has a similar procession on the Sunday."

"Almost as an advertisement for Christian disunity," added Edwin.

They walked around the perimeter of the 36 acres of parkland, stopping off at the Abbot's Kitchen, a surviving example of his power and wealth, before taking a look at the rest of the monastic remains and the herb garden. They then sat at a table at the outdoor snack bar alongside the Lady Chapel and Helga ordered coffees. Henry had picked up a leaflet.

"It says here that there is a prophecy that some bloke had in which the abbey will one day be rebuilt and only then will peace and prosperity return," he said.

"Yes but I don't think that means rebuilding it physically," replied Edwin. "It's more to do with building upon Glastonbury's role as the spiritual centre of Britain which is what some people tend to regard the place as – and perhaps some kind of a new revelation to go with it."

"You're a producer," said Henry, "What about making TV programmes about your religious group if its message is supposed to be so ground-breaking?"

"It would be interesting to make a television programme series about the Unification Movement's unique take on history and its understanding of the manner of the Second Coming," said Edwin, "although it would be far more effective for one of the main stream broadcasters to pick up on the untold story if they could be gently pointed in the right direction."

"They might make a complete hash of it," said Henry.

"Perhaps it could be done as a co-production," replied Edwin.

The remaining two days of Henry and Janet's stay in Somerset included a visit to a cider farm, a cheese factory, a clotted cream tea and a long hike around Cheddar Gorge before they had to return to London for their flight back to Australia.

IN ADDITION TO WORKING with the production company in Bath, Edwin continued to be offered one-off projects in Gibraltar courtesy of Lou Jones. Whilst much of Europe was experiencing economic recession Gibraltar was fast becoming a prosperous place. In a profound shift in its identity the tiny British overseas territory had established itself as the unofficial capital of the online gaming industry. Many of the new buildings on reclaimed land had become the offices of the likes of Ladbrokes and William Hill which had moved their online operations to the Rock for its tax advantages. Sixty percent of all global online casino and online gambling business was now based in Gibraltar. The sector employed three thousand people with many of its international workers commuting in from neighbouring Spanish towns. Luxury homes and entire new marinas had been built in Gibraltar. Construction work was taking place throughout the town centre as enhancement took place and there was now a brand new airport terminal building which looked far too large for the few daily flights that it handled.

Whenever time permitted Edwin attended regional meetings of the Royal Television Society in Bristol which tended to alternate between ITV West and the studios of BBC West. He also went to a Media Society event at the London Evening Standard which was housed in the former Barker's departmental store building on Kensington High Street. A guided tour of the premises revealed it to be something of a reassembled Fleet Street in which not only the Evening Standard but also the Daily Mail, The Mail On Sunday, the 'I' newspaper, The Independent, London Lite, Metro and the London Live TV studios were all present all under the same roof and all with different editorial teams that worked independently of each other. Whilst at the gathering held in the atrium on the third floor, Edwin couldn't help but cast his mind back to the days when once upon a time he had been reduced to working in the basement of that very same building packing Christmas hampers. The ups and downs of life were not without their coincidences. It all seemed such a reversal of fortune. Having started out well enough in New Zealand and Hong Kong he had hit rock bottom at that time when he had returned to the UK and yet somehow he had climbed up out of it again. By comparison he was now very content to lead an interesting lifestyle and to have a lovely wife and family.

A couple of months later Edwin was shocked to hear news of the massive earthquake that hit the city of Christchurch in New Zealand. Nearly two hundred people died and many of them had been inside the six storey television building which had collapsed in the tremor leaving just the lift shaft standing and the studios wrecked. The centre of Christchurch lay in ruins and thousands of homes had been destroyed.

Edwin spoke on the phone to one of his former workmates there who, like himself, was now an independent producer.

"The centre of the city is completely trashed," said Gilbert, "It's going to take years to fix it up. Buildings have been reduced to rubble and even the Cathedral is so severely damaged it'll probably need to be demolished – and in the meantime I'm just left with the heart-breaking task of going round filming it all."

IT WAS ALMOST A foregone conclusion that once the children had left home Edwin and Helga would move back to Spain. They had realised that if ever they were going to relocate it was perhaps the best time to do so.

"Let's face it, I don't want to hang around England forever," said Edwin, "and, realistically, I can work out of Spain just as easily as from the UK."

"I wouldn't mind living out there again," said Helga, "although I can't easily imagine us going back to San Roque."

"No, that era has passed. It would need to be a different part," said Edwin.

"Good," replied Helga, "Perhaps somewhere a bit higher up the Mediterranean although preferably not a holiday resort."

A fact-finding trip led them to buy a pleasant town house in a suburb of Valencia called San Miguel de los Reyes. They liked it there because it was essentially Spanish rather that being a tourist destination. Public transport was good and inexpensive and the airport was directly connected to the city's Metro and tram network.

Meanwhile their elder son, Leon, finished his studies at King's College and now worked at the Department of the Environment. He was engaged to a young lady from New Zealand called Susan Greenwood who was on a gap year from Victoria University of Wellington where she studied Psychology. She was also a second-generation member of the Unification Movement and they planned to marry the following year.

"You know what," said Leon to his father Edwin, "When Susan first mentioned our surname of Ravensdale to her parents her mother seemed to think that she might have met you during your time spent out in New Zealand."

"Well, I suppose that might just be possible," replied Edwin, "After all, New Zealand is a comparatively small place. What is her name?"

"Caroline Greenwood," he replied.

"Caroline Greenwood? No, I can't recall anyone by that name – unless – no, surely not? What was her maiden name?" he asked.

"No idea," said Leon, "but I can find out if you like."

That triggered off a two month holiday in New Zealand the following year. Together with Helga, Edwin was able to meet up with several of his former colleagues and friends. It felt particularly good to be back on New Zealand soil once again after such a prolonged absence.

Edwin's news editor friend Pete Cornwall was there to meet them at Auckland airport. "G'day you old bastard!" he said under his breath with a grin as they shook hands. As well as having held senior management roles throughout the remainder of his broadcasting career he was now a Justice of the Peace. He drove them around the sights of Auckland Harbour and they went out for a meal together.

Two days later Edwin and Helga flew down to Dunedin where Sara Jordan and her partner had invited them to stay for a few days in their home in the suburb of St Kilda. Sara had risen from being a current affairs researcher to TV station Manager but nowadays all of New Zealand's national television originated from Auckland and the former regional station in Dunedin had become a production company that specialised in natural history programmes. She now taught film and media studies at the University of Otago.

Edwin and Helga then hired a car and as they made their way up the South Island they stopped off to spend several nights staying in a motel in Christchurch near to where the city centre was still being reconstructed following the earthquake. Edwin's friend Gilbert arranged a get-together with a circle of familiar faces from the days of the NZBC. It was party time all over again.

And finally it was on to Wellington to meet up with Susan's parents.

They had already spoken on the phone on several occasions and everybody continued to be intrigued by the coincidence of Susan's mother and Edwin having been friends many years ago. Susan's father, James Greenwood, was a pleasant man of a similar age to Edwin and was a doctor by profession. Edwin glanced at Mrs Caroline Greenwood. He was pleased that she too had a good and stable marriage.

Both sets of parents were very happy that their children were to be married to each other.

Everything seemed to have gone full circle.

~ *END* ~